THE JAMES LOVEGROVE COLLECTION

ALSO BY JAMES LOVEGROVE

NOVELS
The Hope • *Days*
The Foreigners • *Untied Kingdom*
Worldstorm • *Provender Gleed*

Co-writing with Peter Crowther
Escardy Gap

The *Pantheon* series
The Age Of Ra • *The Age Of Zeus*
The Age Of Odin • *Age Of Aztec*
Age of Voodoo • *Age of Godpunk*
Age of Shiva

The *Redlaw* series
Redlaw • *Redlaw: Red Eye*

NOVELLAS
How The Other Half Lives • *Gig*
Age Of Anansi • *Age of Satan* • *Age of Gaia*

SHERLOCK HOLMES
The Stuff of Nightmares

COLLECTIONS OF SHORT FICTION
Imagined Slights • *Diversifications*

FOR YOUNGER READERS
The Web: Computopia • *Warsuit 1.0*
The Black Phone

FOR RELUCTANT READERS
Wings • *The House of Lazarus*
Ant God • *Cold Keep* • *Dead Brigade*
Kill Swap • *Free Runner*

The *5 Lords Of Pain* series
The Lord Of The Mountain • *The Lord Of The Void*
The Lord Of Tears • *The Lord Of The Typhoon*
The Lord Of Fire

WRITING AS JAY AMORY
The *Clouded World* series
The Fledging Of Az Gabrielson • *Pirates Of The Relentless Desert*
Darkening For A Fall • *Empire Of Chaos*

THE JAMES LOVEGROVE COLLECTION

VOLUME ONE

DAYS

UNTIED KINGDOM

SOLARIS

First published 2014 by Solaris
an imprint of Rebellion Publishing Ltd,
Riverside House, Osney Mead,
Oxford, OX2 0ES, UK

www.solarisbooks.com

UK ISBN: 978 1 78108 266 9
US ISBN: 978 1 78108 267 6

10 9 8 7 6 5 4 3 2 1

A CIP catalogue record for this book is available
from the British Library.

Designed & typeset by Rebellion Publishing

REBELLION

Printed in the US

DAYS

What are days for?
Days are where we live.

—Philip Larkin, “Days”

Prologue

The Seven Cities: According to Brewer's *Reader's Handbook*, seven cities are regarded as the great cities of all time, namely Alexandria, Jerusalem, Babylon, Athens, Rome, Constantinople, and either London (for commerce) or Paris (for beauty).

5.30 a.m.

IT IS THAT time of morning, not quite night, not quite day, when the sky is a field of smudged grey, like a page of erased pencil marks, and in the empty city streets a hushing sound can be heard—an ever-present background sigh, audible only when all else is silent. It is that hour of dawn when the streetlamps flicker out one by one like heads being emptied of dreams, and pigeons with fraying, fume-coloured plumage open an eye. It is that moment when the sun, emerging, casts silvery rays and long shadows, and every building grows a black fan-shaped tail which it drapes across its westward neighbours.

One building casts a broader shadow, darkens more with its penumbra, than any other. It rises at the city's heart, immense and squat and square. Visible for miles around, it would seem to be the sole reason for which the houses and tower blocks and factories and warehouses around it exist. Hard rains and hot summers have turned its brickwork the colour of dried blood, and its roof is capped with a vast hemispherical glass dome that glints and glimmers as it rotates ponderously, with almost imperceptible slowness. Hidden gearings drive the dome through one full revolution every twenty-four hours. Half of it is crystal clear, the other half smoked black.

The building has seven floors, and each floor is fourteen metres high. Its sides are just over two and a half kilometres long, so that it sits on seven million hectares of land. With its bare brick flanks it looks like something that weighs heavy on the planet, like something that has been pounded in with God's own sledgehammer.

This is Days, the world's first and (some still say) foremost gigastore.

Inside, Days is brackishly lit with half-powered bulbs. Night watchmen are making their final rounds through the store's six hundred and sixty-six departments, the beams of their torches poking this way and that through the crepuscular stillness, sweeping focal haloes across the shelves and the displays, the cabinets and the countertops, the unimaginably vast array of merchandise that Days has to offer. The night watchmen's movements are followed automatically by closed-circuit cameras mounted on whispering armatures. The cameras' green LEDs are not yet lit.

Across the dollar-green marble floors of the store's four main entrance halls janitors drive throbbing cleaning-machines the size of tractors, with spinning felt discs for wheels. The vehicles whirr and veer, reviving the marble's oceanic sheen. At the centre of each entrance hall, embedded in the floor, is a mosaic, a circle seven metres in diameter divided into halves, one white, one black. The tesserae of the white half are bevelled opals, those of the black half slivers of onyx, some as large as saucers, some as small as pennies, all fitted intricately together. The janitors are careful to drive over the mosaics several times, to buff up the precious stones' lustre.

At the centre of the gigastore, tiered circular openings in each floor form an atrium that rises all the way up to the great glass dome. The tiers are painted in the colours of the spectrum, red rising to violet. Shafts of light steal in through the dome's clear half, reaching down to a fine monofilament mesh level with the Red Floor. The mesh, half a kilometre in diameter, is stretched tight as a drum-skin above a canopy of palms and ferns, and between it and the canopy lies a gridwork of copper pipes.

With a sudden hiss, a warm steamy mist purls out from holes in the pipes, and the tree canopy ripples appreciatively. The water vapour drifts down, growing thinner, fainter, sieved by layers of leaves and branches, to the ground, a loamy landscape of moss, rock, leaf mould and grass.

Here, at basement level, lies the Menagerie. Its insects are already busy. Its animals are stirring. Snarls and soft howls can be heard, and paws pad and undergrowth rustles as creatures great and small begin their daily prowling.

Outside Days, armed guards yawn and loll blearily at their posts. All around the building people lie huddled against the plate-glass windows that occupy the lower storey, the only windows in the building. Most of them sleep, but some hover fitfully in that lucid state between waking and dreaming where their dreams are as uncomfortable as their reality. The lucky ones have sleeping bags, gloves on their fingers, and shawls and scarves wrapped around their heads. The rest make do with blankets, fingerless gloves, hats, and thicknesses of begged, borrowed or stolen clothing.

And now, at last, as six o'clock approaches, over at the airport to the west of town a jet breaks the city's silence. Its wingtips flaring like burnished silver in the low sunlight, it leaps along a runway, rears into the air and roars steeply skyward: the dawn shuttle, carrying yet another fuselage-full of émigrés westward, yet another few hundred healthy cells leaving the cancerous host-body of the motherland.

The echo of the plane's launch rumbles across the rooftops, reaching into every corner of the city, into the deeps of every citizen's mind, so that collectively, at four minutes to six, as is the case every morning, the entire population is thinking the same thing: *We are a little bit more alone than yesterday.* And those who continue to sleep are troubled in their dreams, and those who come awake and stay awake find themselves gnawed by dissatisfaction and doubt.

And still the day remorselessly brightens like a weed that, no matter what, will grow.

1

The Seven Sleepers: Seven noble youths of Ephesus who martyred themselves under the emperor Decius in 250 A.D. by fleeing to a cave in Mount Celion, where, having fallen asleep, they were found by Decius, who had them sealed up.

6.00 a.m.

THE BRASS HANDS on the alarm clock on Frank Hubble's bedside table divide its face in two. The perfect vertical diameter they form separates the pattern on the clockface into its component halves, on the left a black semicircle, on the right a white. A trip-switch clicks in the workings and the clock starts to ring.

Frank's hand descends onto the clock, silencing the reveille almost before it has begun. He settles back, head sighing into duck-down pillows. The roar of the departing shuttle is now a distant lingering murmur, more remembered than heard. He tries to piece together the fragments of the dream from which he was summoned up by the knowledge that the alarm was about to go off, but the images spin elusively out of his grasp. The harder he reaches for them, the faster they hurtle away. Soon they are lost, leaving him with just the memory of having dreamed, which, he supposes, is better than not dreaming at all.

The street below his bedroom window is startled by the sound of a car's ignition. The window's russet curtains are inflated by a breeze then sucked flat again. Frank hears the timer-controlled coffee machine in the kitchen gurgle into life, and moving his tongue thirstily he pictures fat brown droplets of a harsh arabica blend dripping into the pot. He waits for the sharp odour of brewing coffee to creep under the bedroom door and tweak his nose, then, with a grunt, unpeels the bedcovers and swings his legs out.

He sits for a while on the side of the bed gazing down at his knees. He is a medium-sized man, well-proportioned and trim, although the years have worn away at his shoulders and put a curve in his upper vertebrae so that he suffers from a permanent hunch, as though he is saddled with a heavy, invisible yoke. His face is as rumpled as his pyjamas, and his hair is a grey that isn't simply a dark white or a light black but an utter absence of tone. His eyes, too, are grey, the grey of gravestones.

In a bathroom whose midnight blue walls are flecked with stencilled gold stars, Frank urinates copiously into the lavatory bowl. Having pushed the flush and lowered the lavatory lid, he fills the basin with steaming-hot water, soaks a flannel and presses it hard against his face. Though his skin stings in protest, he holds the flannel in place until it cools. Then he lathers on shaving foam from a canister marked prominently with the same back-to-back semicircles of black and white as on the face of the alarm clock, and with a few deft strokes of a nickel-plated razor he is unbristled. He has his shaving down to such a fine art that he can leave his face smooth and nick-free without once consulting the mirror in front of him.

Frank fears mirrors. Not because they tell him he is old (he knows that), nor because they tell him how worn and weary he looks (he has resigned himself to that), but because, of late, mirrors have begun to tell him another truth, one he would rather not acknowledge.

Still, it has become part of his pre-breakfast ablutions to confront this truth, and so, resting his hands on the sides of the basin, he raises his head and looks at his reflection.

Or rather, looks *for* his reflection, because in the mirror he sees nothing except the star-flecked, midnight blue bathroom wall behind him.

Fighting down a familiar upsurge of panic, Frank concentrates. He is there. He knows he is there. The mirror is lying. He can feel his body, the organic life-support machine that keeps his mind going. He knows there is cool floor beneath his bare feet and porcelain basin in his hands because nerve-endings in his skin are reporting these facts to his brain, and fitted tightly and intricately into that skin is the configuration of flesh and bone and vein and sinew that is uniquely Frank Hubble. The air that slides over his lips as he breathes in and out tells him that he exists. He feels, therefore he is.

But the mirror continues to insist that he is not.

He fixes his gaze on the point in space where his eyes should be. His mind is descending in an express lift, swooping vertiginously down towards a dark well of insanity where writhe not gibbering demons but wraiths, a blizzard of wraiths who float soundlessly, mouth hopelessly, twisting around each other, oblivious to each other, invisible to each other. Neither guilt nor shame, the common demons, terrify Frank. What he fears most is anonymity. The nameless wraiths flutter like intangible moths. Nothing is appearing in the mirror. Today, of all days, may be the day that he is finally swallowed up by the emptiness inside him. Unless he can visualise himself, he will be gone. Lost. Forgotten.

He has to remember his eyes. If the eyes fall into place, he will be able to piece together the rest.

Gradually, with considerable effort, he makes two eyes emerge from the reflected wall, first the grave-grey irises, then their frames of white.

He makes the eyes blink, to prove they are really his.

Now the lids appear, purple and puffy with sleep and age.

Now he shades in two eyebrows of the same smudgy, forgettable grey as his hair.

His forehead follows, and quickly the rest of his face falls into place—fisted nose, fettered jaw, furrowed cheeks, foetal ears.

Below his chin he has a neck, below his neck a collarbone that reaches to both shoulders from which drop arms that end in basin-bracing hands. The stripes of his pyjama jacket are sketched out in jagged parallel lines. On the breast pocket a stitched monogram of the divided black-and-white circle manifests itself.

He can see everything of himself that is visible in the mirror. The struggle is over again for another day.

But it is not with relief that Frank turns away from the basin. Who knows—the moment he takes his eyes off his reflection, perhaps it vanishes again. Behind our backs, who knows what mirrors do?

It is a question Frank prefers not to ponder. Leaning over the bath, he levers up the mixer tap, and a fizzing cone of water spurts from the head of the shower. The mixer tap is marked with a black C on a white semicircle next to a black semicircle with a white H. Frank adjusts the water to a medium temperature, divests himself of his pyjamas, and steps into the bath, ringing the shower curtain across.

The shower curtain, the flannel Frank uses to scrub himself, the bottle from which he squeezes out a palmful of medicated shampoo, his unscented soap, all sport the divided-circle logo, as do the bathmat he steps out onto when he has finished showering, the towel with which he dries his body off, and the robe he drapes around himself. The logo, in various guises and sizes, appears on no fewer than forty-seven different fixtures, fittings, and items of toiletry in the bathroom. Even the treacherous mirror has a coin-sized one etched into its corner.

Warm-skinned and tinglingly clean, Frank shuffles into the kitchen, using his fingers to comb his hair into a lank approximation of how it will look when dry. The timing of the ritual of his mornings is so ingrained that as he enters the kitchen, the last few drips of coffee are spitting into the pot; he can pick up the pot and pour out a mugful straight away.

Blowing steam from the rim of the mug, he opens the blinds. Staring out at the hazy silver city, he takes his first sip of coffee.

Usually Frank admires the view for all of three seconds, but this morning he takes his time. Even though the present position of every building, thoroughfare and empty rectangle of demolished rubble is familiar to him and forms part of a detailed and constantly updated mental map, he feels that, for posterity's sake, he ought to make a ceremony out of this act of observation, so that in years to come he will remember how every morning at 6.17, for thirty-three years, he used to stand here and stare.

He suspects that all day long he will be highlighting mundane little moments like this, tagging the regular features of his daily routine which under normal circumstances he would perform on autopilot but which today he will fetishise as a long-term convict whose sentence is coming to an end must fetishise his last tin-tray meal, his last slopping-out, his last roll-call. Though it will be sweet never to have to do these things again, it will also be strange. After thirty-three years, routine has become the calipers of Frank's life. He hates it, but he isn't sure that he's going to be able to manage without it.

So, consciously and conscientiously he gazes out at a view that he has seen thousands of times before, either in the dark or in the false dawn or in broad daylight. He observes the thick-legged flyover, the spindly section of elevated railway along which a commuter train crawls like a steel caterpillar, the whole treeless, joyless expanse of flat-roofed concrete estates and crumpled, clustered houses. As with all employee apartments, the windows also offer him a view of Days, the distant store's upper storeys lying like a lid over the city, but by lowering his head just a little, he can block it out of sight behind the rooftops.

Now he feels he has gazed enough. Into his otherwise tightly timetabled rising ritual he has factored two minutes of slack so that, unless there is a major hold-up, he is never late leaving the building. He has used up one of those minutes, and it is wise to keep the other in hand in case of emergency.

It vaguely amuses him that he should be worrying about arriving late for work on what he fully expects to be his last day at Days, but a habit of thirty-three years' standing is hard to break. How long will it take, he wonders, for the robot in him to adjust to life after Days. Will he wake up punctually at six every morning until he dies, even if there is nothing to get up for? Will he continue to take his coffee-break at 10.30, his lunch-break at 12.45, his tea-break at 4.30 in the afternoon? The patterns stamped into his brain by years of repetition will be difficult to reconfigure into something more suited to a leisurely lifestyle. For more than half his life he has been locked into a groove like a toy car, travelling the same circuit six days a week. Sundays have been days of disjointed lethargy: waking at six as usual, he passes the hours snoozing, reading the newspapers, watching television and generally feeling sleepy and out of sorts, his body unable to assimilate the hiccup in its circadian rhythm. Is that what his life will be like after he resigns? One long chain of Sundays?

Well, he will have to deal with that when it happens. For now, he has today—a Thursday—to contend with.

He inserts a slice of bread into a chrome pop-up toaster which, with its vents and lines, calls to mind a vintage automobile. On the counter beside it sits a portable television set, which he switches on. Both toaster and television, needless to say, have the back-to-back Ds of the Days logo stamped on their housings.

The television is programmed so that whenever it comes on it automatically tunes in to the Days home-shopping channel. A pair of wax-faced women of indeterminable age are rhapsodising over a three-string cultured-pearl choker from the Jewellery Department, while a computer-generated simulation of the interior of the world's first and (possibly) foremost gigastore planes sea-sickeningly to and fro behind them.

With a click of the remote control, Frank cuts to a news channel, and watches a report on the construction of the world's first terastore in Australia—official title: the Bloody Big Shop. Intended to serve not just Australia and New Zealand but the Pacific Rim countries and South-East Asia as well, the Bloody Big Shop is an estimated eighteen months from completion but still, in its skeletal state, challenges its immediate neighbour, Ayers Rock, for size.

The toaster jettisons its load of browned bread. In one corner of the slice a small semicircle of charring backs against an uncooked counterpart. This is the corner Frank butters and bites first.

Frank does not eat much. He doesn't even finish the toast. He pours himself another coffee, turns off the television and heads for his dressing room.

Down a high-ceilinged hallway he passes doors to rooms he seldom uses, rooms whose immaculate and expensive furnishings would be under several inches of dust were it not for the ministrations of a cleaning lady Frank has never met. Shelves of books he hasn't read line one side of the hallway, while on the other side paintings he barely notices any more cover the wall. A fussy-fingered interior decorator from Days chose the books and the paintings and the furnishings on Frank's behalf, making free with Frank's Iridium card. Frank has not yet paid off the sum outstanding on the card, so when he resigns he will have to surrender almost everything he owns back to the store. This will be no hardship.

His Thursday outfit is waiting for him in the dressing room, each individual item hung or laid out. Frank put the trousers of his Thursday suit in the press the night before, last thing before he went to bed. The creases are pleasingly sharp.

He dresses in an orderly and methodical manner, pausing after each step of the process to take a sip of coffee. He puts on a cool cotton shirt with a blue pinstripe and plain white buttons, and knots a maroon silk tie around his neck. He dons a charcoal-grey jacket to match the trousers, and slips a pair of black, cushion-soled brogues built more for comfort than elegance over the navy socks on his feet. Then he addresses himself to the full-length mirror that stands, canted in its frame, in one corner.

Patiently he pieces himself in.

The clothes help. The clothes, as they say, make the man, and decked out in the very best that the Gentlemen's Outfitters Department at Days has to offer, Frank feels very much made. The crisp outlines of the suit fall readily into place. The tie and shirt and shoes fill out the gaps. Frank's head, neck and hands are the last to appear, the hardest to visualise. God help him, sometimes he can't even remember what his face looks like. Once it manifests in the mirror, its familiarity mocks his faulty memory, but in the moments while he struggles to recall just one feature, Frank honestly fears that he has finally winked out of existence altogether, slipped sideways into limbo, become a genuine ghost as well as a professional one.

He makes a point of fixing the time—6.34—in his mental souvenir album. At 6.34 every workday morning, give or take a minute, he has stood here newly dressed in an outfit every piece of which carries a label into which is woven a matched pair of semicircles, one black, one white, above the washing and ironing instructions. Tomorrow morning he will not be standing here. In one of the dressing-room wardrobes a packed suitcase waits. The fluorescent pink tag attached to its handle bears a flight number and the three-letter code for an airport in the United States. A first-class plane ticket sits on top of the suitcase. Tomorrow at 6.34 a.m. Frank will be aboard a silver-tinged shuttle jet, soaring above the clotted clouds, following the sun. One way, no return.

He pauses, still unable to conceive how it will feel to be hurtling away from the city, all connections with the only place he has ever called home severed, no certainties ahead of him. A tiny voice inside his head asks him if he is crazy, and a larger, louder voice replies, with calm conviction, *No*.

No. Leaving is probably the sanest thing he has ever done. The scariest, too.

Returning to the kitchen, Frank pours himself his third coffee, filling the mug to the brim as he empties the pot of its last drops.

Halfway through drinking the final instalment of his breakfast-time caffeine infusion he feels a twinge deep in his belly, and happily he heads for the bathroom, there to succumb to the seated pleasure of relieving his bowels of their contents, which are meagre, hard and dry, but nonetheless good to be rid of. Each sheet of the super-soft three-ply lavatory paper he uses is imprinted with ghostly-faint pairs of semicircles. When he was much younger, Frank used to treat the Days logo with almost religious reverence. As an icon, its ubiquitousness indicated to him its power. He was proud to be associated with the symbol. Where before he might have balked at such an act of desecration, now he thinks nothing of wiping his arse on it.

In the bedroom again, he straps on his sole sartorial accessory, a Days wristwatch—gold casing, patent-leather strap, Swiss movement. Before he slips his wallet into his inside jacket pocket, he checks that his Iridium card is still there, not because he expects it to have been stolen but because that is what he has done every morning at 6.41 for thirty-three years.

He slides the Iridium from its velvet sheath. The card gleams iridescently like a rectangular wafer of mother-of-pearl. Holding it up to the light and gently flexing it, Frank watches rainbows chase one another across its surface, rippling around the raised characters of his name and the card number and the grainily engraved Days logo. Hard to believe something so light and thin could be a millstone. Hard to believe something so beautiful could be the source of so much misery.

He returns the card to its sheath, the sheath to his wallet. Now he is ready to leave. There is nothing keeping him here.

Except...

He spends his second "spare" minute wandering around the flat, touching the things that belong to him, that tomorrow will not belong to him. His fingertips drift over fabrics and varnishes and glass as he glides from room to room, through a living space that, for all the emotional attachment he has to it, might as well be a museum.

How he has managed to accumulate so many possessions, so many pieces of furniture and *objets d'art*, is something of a mystery to Frank. He can vaguely recall over the past thirty-three years handing over his Iridium to pay for purchases which took him all of a few seconds to pick out, but he is hard pressed to remember actually buying the individual items—this Art Deco vase, say, or that Turkish kilim—let alone how much they cost. No doubt the Days interior decorator was responsible for obtaining and installing many of the pieces Frank has no memory of acquiring, but not all. That's how little the transactions have meant to him, how unreal they have seemed. He has bought things reflexively, not because he wants to but because his Iridium has meant he can, and now he is mired in a debt that will take at least another decade of employment to work off.

But as he cannot bear the thought of another day at Days, and as what he owns has no value to him, not even of the sentimental kind, he feels no qualms about his decision to tender his resignation today. To quit, as the Americans would say. (So direct, Americans. They always find a succinct way of putting things, which is why Frank is looking forward to living among them, because he admires those qualities in others he finds lacking in himself.) He has calculated that by repossessing the flat and all that is in it, his employers ought to consider the debt squared. And if they don't, then they will just have to come looking for him in America. And America is a very big place, and Frank can be a very hard man to find.

His tour of the flat is complete. It is 6.43, and he has pushed his timetable to its limit. There can be no more procrastinating. He takes a black cashmere overcoat from the coat rack by the flat door and flings it on. The door clicks softly open, snicks snugly shut. Frank steps out onto the landing, part of a central stairwell that winds around a lift shaft enclosed in a wrought-iron cage. He keys the Down button by the lift gate, and there is a whine and a churning of cogs from deep down in the shaft. The cables start to ribbon.

2

The Corporal Works of Mercy: In some Christian denominations, seven specific acts of charity that render physical aid.

6.52 a.m.

IT TAKES FRANK five and a half minutes to walk from his building to the train station. In his first few years at Days it used to take him four. Age hasn't slowed him. He still has the legs of a twenty-year-old. But his stride has lost its spring.

At the station's automated newsstand he inserts his Iridium into the slot and makes his selection. The newspaper flops into the chute and he extracts it. His Iridium is debited and ejected. A similar procedure buys him a return ticket and a styrofoam cup of coffee.

Through the turnstile he goes, and up the stairs to the platform, where a dozen commuters are standing and every so often casting hopeful glances along the tracks. Like Frank, they all have newspapers and hot beverages and invisible yokes. Their faces he knows well, and he has learned names to go with some of the faces by eavesdropping on their desultory conversations. He and they are old warriors, brothers and sisters in arms who have fought this daily battle for more years than they would care to think. To his surprise, Frank is saddened to think that this will be the last time he will be sharing their company. He moves along the platform, murmuring an inaudible goodbye to each person under his breath. One or two of them glance up from their newspapers as he passes, but the majority do not.

He takes his place by a wooden shelter whose burnt-ivory paintwork has been almost entirely obliterated with graffiti. A chilly breeze stirs the grit on the platform's asphalt surface and sends discarded sweet-wrappers and crisp-packets scuttering. Weeds shiver fitfully between the rust-encrusted iron sleepers. Finally an incomprehensible announcement burbles from loudspeakers that sound as if they are made of soggy cardboard, and, to everyone's relief, the tracks begin to sing.

The train comes rollicking in, grinds to a halt, and gapes its doors. Frank finds himself a seat. The doors close, and the train hunks and clanks away from the platform, cumbersomely gathering speed. The rolling stock is so old it could probably qualify as vintage. The carriages squeal and sway, their wheels shimmying on the rails; the seat fabric smells of burnt oranges, and the windows are a smeary yellow.

Frank knows he has thirty-one minutes, barring hold-ups, to read his paper and drink his coffee, but today he delays doing either in order to cast his eye around the carriage and fasten details in his memory. The tattered corner of a poster advertising a Days sale long since finished. The empty beer can rattling to and fro across the dun linoleum flooring. The slogan scrawled in blue marker pen, "fuk da gigastor"—a sentiment Frank has some sympathy with. The synchronised jerk of the passengers' heads, mirrored by the twitch of the handstraps that hang from the ceiling. The sulphurous glide of the city.

He will not miss this. He will not miss any of this.

The daily paper no longer contains much to interest him, if it ever did. He buys and reads it out of sheer habit. Nothing that happens in this country concerns him any more. All the news seems old. The unrest, the disputes, the crime, the prevaricating of the politicians, the pontificating of the clergy, the intriguing of the royals... it has always been this way for as long as he can remember, and longer. Nothing in the news changes except the names.

But America—something is always happening in America. A hurricane that leaves thousands homeless, a serial killer who leaves dozens dead. A trial that spectacularly acquits the defendant, a civic official who spectacularly turns down a bribe. Huge salaries, huge tragedies. Everything on a larger scale. *Two* gigastores, for heaven's sake! Not that a gigastore is necessarily a mark of greatness, but as the only continent to sport two of the things, North America has to be marvelled at.

Frank expects that he will visit both Blumberg's, N.Y. and Blumberg's, L.A., if for no other reason than professional curiosity. He intends to traverse the entire country coast to coast in trains and cars and buses, secretly observing the nation and its people. In a land that size, losing himself will not be difficult; nor will it be unprecedented. America teems with lost souls who rove its emptiness, who love its emptiness. Perhaps among them, among a secret sub-nation of nobodies, he will find fellowship and a home.

As for so many other people, *this* country is used up for him. Dried out. Husked. As for so many other people, there is nothing here for him any more except years of work, a brief retirement, and an unremarked death. This country has grown mean in spirit. This country has lost nearly everything it used to have and has become fiercely, greedily protective of the little it has left. This country, fearing the future, has turned its eyes firmly on the past. This country is no longer a home to its inhabitants but a museum of better days.

A voice that manages to sound bored even though it is only a recording announces the name of the approaching station twice. The train slows and comes to a halt, carriage banging into carriage like a queue of cartoon elephants butting up against one another's behinds. A scrawny girl in torn jeans and an engulfing anorak enters the carriage. She ambles along the aisle and plumps herself down in the seat next to a matronly woman. By means of a snort and a peremptory flap of her gossip magazine, the woman conveys to the girl that there are plenty of other perfectly good seats available, but the girl is not intimidated. She does not move, merely looks sullen and cunning.

Frank, feeling a familiar prickling at the nape of his neck, watches.

Sure enough, the train has hardly begun to move again when the girl's hand sneaks across the chair arm towards the clasp of the matronly woman's handbag. The girl's face remains a slack mask of indifference, her bored gaze elsewhere. She is good, Frank will grant her that. She has learned her job well, and probably the hard way, from beatings she has received when her fingers have not been nimble enough or her feet fleet enough. He knows what she is after, too. Sell a Days card on the black market and you will be eating well for a couple of weeks. (Sell one to an undercover police officer and you will be eating prison food for a couple of years.)

Peeking surreptitiously over the top edge of his newspaper, he follows the progress of the theft. The girl's hand, as it stealthily undoes the handbag clasp and delves in, seems not to belong to her. It seems to be operating of its own accord, an independent, spider-like entity. The matronly woman remains unaware that her handbag is being rifled, its contents being blind-assessed by expert fingertips. She is completely absorbed in the article she is reading and in the hangnail she is doggedly chewing.

Frank waits until the girl's hand emerges. There! A glimmer of silvery-grey plastic flashing across the chair-arm, vanishing almost the instant it appears.

Frank stands up, sets his newspaper down in his seat, strides across the aisle, grasps a handstrap, and bends down over the girl, fixing her with his grey gaze.

"Put it back," he says.

She looks at him blankly; in that blankness, defiance.

"I'm giving you one chance to put it back. Otherwise I pull the communication cord and summon the transport police, and you can explain to them what this woman's Days card is doing in your pocket."

At that, the matronly woman frowns. "Are you talking about *my* Days card?"

"Well?" says Frank to the girl, not breaking eye-contact.

She continues to glare back at him, then slowly lowers her head and sighs. Reaching into her pocket, she produces the card.

"S'only a crappy old Aluminium anyway."

The woman gasps, although it is unclear whether this is in surprise at the sight of her card in the girl's hand or in mortification at the broadcasting of her status as the holder of the lowest denomination of Days account. She snatches the card off the girl and hastily thrusts it back into her handbag.

The train is slowing. The name of the next station is announced twice.

"Get off here," says Frank, stepping back.

The girl gets up and hipsways along the aisle towards the nearest door, tossing her hair.

"And you're just going to let her walk away like that?" the woman demands of Frank. "She stole my card. She should be arrested. Stop her!" She addresses herself to the whole carriage. "Somebody stop her!"

No one makes a move.

"You got your card back," Frank says. "If you want her arrested so badly, stop her yourself."

The doors open, and, insolent to the last, the girl gives Frank and the woman a cocky little wave before alighting.

"Well!" the woman exclaims.

Frank heads back to his seat. The doors close and the train begins to pick up speed. A sudden lurch catches him off-balance and he sits down heavily, crushing his newspaper. He slides the paper out from under his backside and smoothes it flat on his lap. Before he resumes reading, he glances back at the matronly woman.

She is staring at him, shaking her head. Only after she feels he has been exposed to enough of her scorn does she turn back to her magazine and her hangnail.

No, there really is nothing for him here.

3

Pride: One of the Seven Deadly Sins.

7.24 a.m.

LINDA TRIVETT HAS been lying awake since shortly after five, watching the glow that frames the bedroom curtains brighten. It is too late now to pretend that she is going to go back to sleep. She is far too excited for that, anyway. In fact, she didn't think she was going to get off to sleep at all last night, and took a couple of pills to help her, little expecting them to work, but they did. Gordon, not surprisingly, needed no pharmaceutical assistance. As if it were just any other evening, he closed the book Linda had borrowed for him from the library (a self-help manual on assertiveness) after, as usual, managing less than a page of it, then set the book down on the bedside table, placed his spectacles on top, turned out the bedside light, rolled over, and started snoring almost straight away.

He is still snoring now, a grating suck-and-snort rhythm that Linda has almost, but not quite, trained herself to ignore. Lying there with a pillow bunched up under his head, a lock of his thin, sandy hair snagged on one eyebrow and a line of drool leaking from his slack mouth onto the pillowcase, he looks like a child. Sleep has eased years from his face.

Linda, experiencing a twinge of tenderness—but not love; she knows Gordon too well to feel love for him—reaches over and gently brushes the lock of hair back into place.

She climbs out of bed carefully so as not to disturb him, even though it would take a near-miss with a Howitzer to wake Gordon once he slips into REM. Putting on a velour dressing gown over her nightdress, she goes down to the kitchen and makes herself a cup of tea.

She can scarcely believe that today has finally arrived. She has been looking forward to this morning ever since, just over a week ago, she and Gordon learned by post that their application for a Days account had been accepted and that their Silver card would be arriving later that same day. Linda cancelled her hairdressing appointments and stayed home just so that she could be there to greet the courier when he came. *That* was an event to set the neighbours' tongues wagging: a Days courier pulling up in front of their house, resting his motorbike on its kickstand, unbuttoning the holster on his sidearm, and with wary glances to the left and right walking up the garden path to knock on the front door and hand over the bulky, securely wrapped parcel he was carrying in the pouch slung over his shoulder. Linda saw net curtains twitch all along the street as she signed for the package and the courier strode back to his bike, doing up the chin-strap of his half-white, half-black helmet.

How she managed to hold off opening the parcel until Gordon came home from work Linda has no idea. Her self-control astounded her, and disappointed Margie and Pat and Bella, all of whom dropped by that day on various pretexts, hoping to catch a glimpse of an honest-to-goodness Days Silver. Margie and her husband had applied for an Aluminium and were still waiting to hear if they had been accepted, so she was the one who stared at the package with the greatest envy.

"A Silver," she sighed. "We'll never manage Silver on Tim's salary."

It occurred to Linda that on the amount the packing plant paid Tim they would be lucky if they could manage Aluminium. It was a touch smug of her to think that, perhaps, but if she couldn't be smug then, when could she?

She said, "Well, the bank did give Gordon a small pay-rise recently, and add to that what I get from my hairdressing..." She shrugged, as if that was all there was to obtaining a Days Silver.

It wasn't. Her shrug belied five years of struggle, of hard graft, of sacrifice and self-denial and self-discipline, of pennies pinched and corners cut and weekends worked. Five years of clothes mended to last beyond their natural lifespan, of evenings spent in instead of being enjoyed out, of winters endured with the thermostat turned down low, of Christmases without a tree or decorations and with only the most modest of gifts exchanged. Five years of repeatedly postponing the decision to have children, children being such a financial liability. Five years, until she and Gordon had at last scraped together the minimum collateral required to qualify for a Silver. (They could, of course, have opened an Aluminium account as soon as the new grade was introduced, but Linda decided they should continue saving up for the Silver because a Silver was what they had set their hearts on and, more to the point, an Aluminium was common, in both senses of the word.)

And was it worth it? Of course it was! Anything was worth the moment she and Gordon sat down together, tore away the parcel's plain brown wrapping, and took out a Days catalogue and a slim envelope.

The catalogue was vast, as thick as three telephone directories, with the edges of its onionskin-thin pages colour-coded in six rainbow bands, one for each of the six shop floors still in service, Red to Indigo.

Gordon straight away began leafing through it. Linda, meanwhile, carefully slit open the envelope with a kitchen knife, delved in, and extracted a Days Silver.

A Days Silver with their names on it in embossed capitals.

The ecstasy she felt then as she held the card in her hands, angling it from side to side and watching the light flash across its surface and across the ridges of the letters that spelled out GORDON & LINDA TRIVETT—oh yes, any amount of hardship was worth *that*.

She proposed that they visit the gigastore the very next day, but Gordon pointed out that until they had signed and returned the disclaimer form enclosed with the card and had received acknowledgement of its receipt from the store, they were still not permitted to pass through the doors of Days.

He read out the form aloud, mumbling as he skated over paragraphs of dense legal jargon, which he promised to look at more closely later. Basically the form seemed to be saying that Days could not and would not accept liability for anything that might happen to the Trivetts while they were on the premises, and that should the Trivetts break any of the rules mentioned "heretofore and herein" they would not be in a position to seek indemnity or reimbursement from the store.

Linda listened patiently but none too attentively, and as soon as Gordon finished reading, signed her name next to his on the dotted line at the bottom of the form with a thrilled, quivering hand.

The next morning she posted off the form, along with the passport-sized photographs of herself and Gordon required for security purposes. The acknowledgement slip came back two days later.

That was last Saturday morning, and the moment the acknowledgement slip arrived, Linda suggested to Gordon that they visit the store right then. If they left immediately, they could be there by opening time. Gordon said he wasn't ready. He complained of a headache. He had, he said, had a hard week. And besides, he had heard stories about Days on a Saturday. Stories about packed floors and wrestling crowds, scuffles and riots and even deaths.

Linda replied that she had heard stories like that about Days on *every* day of the week, and had chosen to discount them as rumours, or at any rate exaggerations of the truth spread by people without Days accounts who are all too ready to condemn what they cannot have. But she had to admit that Gordon *did* look a little haggard, so she gave him the benefit of the doubt and proposed that they go to Days on Monday instead. Gordon pointed out that he couldn't afford to take a day off work, not if they were to maintain the level of income necessary to keep the use of the card, so therefore if they went, it would have to be on a Saturday or not at all. Linda replied that Saturdays were her busiest—and therefore most lucrative—hairdressing days, and that if *he* took a day off sick he got paid, whereas she did not. And anyway, had he not just objected to visiting Days on a Saturday on the grounds that it would be too dangerous? He couldn't have it both ways. Either they risked the Saturday crowds or they went on a weekday.

It occurred to her then, although she did not comment on it, that Gordon seemed to be making up excuses not to go at all. Surely he wasn't getting cold feet? After all this time and effort?

So she suggested Tuesday. She could, she thought, just about hold out till Tuesday.

Gordon, predictably, repeated his claim that he couldn't under any circumstances take a weekday off, to which Linda, her patience wearing thin, retorted that in that case she was going to go on her own. Much as she wanted Gordon to come with her on her first trip to Days, she simply could not wait until next Saturday.

That did the trick, as she had known it would. No way was Gordon going to let her loose in Days on her own with their card. He sighed and suggested a compromise: this coming Thursday.

And so Thursday it was, and Linda, magnanimous in victory, took her husband by the hand and, giving her best approximation of a knowing, lascivious grin, led him upstairs to the bedroom and there bestowed on him the Special Treat usually reserved for his birthday and Christmas Eve. And though the deed, as always, left a bad taste in her mouth (both figuratively and literally), it was worthwhile. When she returned from having rinsed out with mouthwash in the bathroom, Gordon was looking less defeated, more contented, as he lay flat out and naked on the bed.

And now, as she sits in the kitchen sipping her tea on this Thursday morning which she thought would never arrive, Linda feels like a child on

Christmas Day. In about an hour she is going to call her scheduled two blue rinses and a demi-perm and tell them that Gordon has a virulent 'flu and that she feels she ought to stay home and look after him. Then she is going to call the bank and tell the manager the same story: Gordon will not be coming in today, the 'flu, probably that twenty-four-hour strain that has been doing the rounds, he should be fine by tomorrow if he stays home today and gets some rest. She would ask Gordon to make the call himself, but he is the world's worst liar and would only make a hash of it, umming and ahhing and interspersing his sentences with feeble, unconvincing coughs. Besides, coming from the concerned wife, the lie will possibly sound more authentic.

Gordon hasn't taken a day off sick in as long as Linda can remember, not even when he has genuinely been feeling under the weather. These days no job is safe, and even if, like Gordon, you work as a loan adviser at a small local branch of a large national bank—money-lending being one of the few growth industries left in these days of high unemployment and low income—missing a day can still mean the difference between employment and the dole queue. Not only that, but for the past few weeks Gordon has quietly been trying to curry the manager's favour. The assistant manager is leaving soon to take over the running of another branch, and Linda has her eyes firmly set on the vacated post for her husband. He, however, instead of simply going up to the manager and demanding the promotion (which he fully deserves), has adopted the tactic of working hard and waiting and hoping. No matter how many times Linda has told him that nothing comes to those who wait and hope, that at the very least he should be dropping hints, but that preferably he should just come right out with it and *ask*, he has so far failed to pluck up the courage to do anything so forceful and positive. He would much rather believe that his diligence will be noted and duly rewarded. The poor, deluded innocent.

The Days catalogue is lying opposite Linda on the kitchen table. She heaves it towards her, marvelling yet again at the size of it. It needs to be this large, since it purports to list, and in many instances depict, every single item available at Days.

Every single item? Linda, in spite of herself, finds the claim hard to swallow. Days is supposed to be able to sell you anything you can possibly want, anything in the entire world. That is the store's motto, which can be found on the cover of the catalogue beneath the name of the store and its famous logo, in small type: "If it can be sold, it will be bought, and if it can be bought, it will be sold." That is the principle on which Septimus Day founded the store all those years ago, and the pledge which Days upholds to this day. (Linda has read the potted history of the store on the inside front cover.) But how can a catalogue, even one as immense as this, contain *everything*, every piece of merchandise in existence? It just isn't possible. Is it?

In the week that she has had the catalogue Linda has been able to peruse less than a quarter of it, but she has managed to pick out a number of items she would like to buy. She hoists the huge tome open and flips through to a section she has bookmarked with a slip of paper. Ties. Dozens of men's ties blaze up at her from a photo spread that illustrates just some of the thousands of items of men's neck apparel listed on adjacent pages. Linda has circled a dark green silk kipper with a repeating pattern of coins and made a note of its serial number. Gordon needs to jazz up his image. When it comes to clothing, his penchant for the plain and the simple is all very well, but a bit of excitement, a dash of colour to offset his sartorial conservatism, would not go amiss. She may never be able to persuade him to wear, say, a bright shirt, but she might just manage to get him to try out an interesting tie, particularly if, like the one she has chosen, it has a thematic connection to his job. And who knows, perhaps the tie will alert the branch manager to a facet of Gordon's character that Linda has for a long time known exists, or at any rate believed exists, or in fact (let's be honest here) *hoped* exists. She is sure Gordon used to be an exciting person once. When they were courting, and in the early days of their marriage, he was bold, spontaneous, impulsive, even dashing... wasn't he? Surely he was. And still is. It is simply that over the years this side of him has become buried beneath an accretion of responsibilities and concerns, like a ship's hull becoming encrusted and weighed down with barnacles. Now that they have their Days card, that is about to change. Everything is about to change.

She flips on through the catalogue to the Clocks section, where she finds another item which she is fully intent on buying today.

In itself the carriage clock is nothing special. A reproduction of an antique, its brass casing boasts sections of Gothic filigree laced over panels of dark blue glass, and instead of feet the clock rests on the backs of four winged cherubs, whose stubby arms hold trumpets to their lips and whose cheeks bulge with the effort of blowing. These are nice enough features, but there are many other more ornate and more beautiful examples of horology on display. However, the clock happens to be an exact copy of one that Linda's parents once owned, an heirloom that had been passed down the distaff side of the family, from Linda's great-grandmother to her grandmother to her mother. It used to sit in pride of place on the mantelshelf in the living room, and her mother devotedly used to keep it wound up and, twice a year, give it a thorough polish to bring up the gleam of the brass. It was, perhaps, the most elegant thing the family owned, certainly the object with the most sentimental value... until the day Linda's father saw to it that Linda never got to inherit it.

The moment she came across the picture of the reproduction clock in the Days catalogue, Linda understood that she had been offered a second chance to possess something which she had been deprived of by an act of cheap, casual malice while she was still a child. It was almost as if the clock had been waiting in the catalogue's pages for her to discover it, and as soon as she laid eyes on it, she knew it had to be hers. She had no choice in the matter. And though she has earmarked several other items for purchase today, even if she buys nothing else, she is determined that she will not leave Days without the clock, for her, and the tie, for Gordon.

It is 7.37 according to the digital timer on the oven. In a few minutes she will go back upstairs and wake Gordon, but for now she is going to enjoy her tea, the peace and quiet, and the sweet tingle of anticipation in her belly.

Today, she is confident, is going to be the greatest day of her life.

4

The Seven Wonders of the Ancient World: The Egyptian pyramids, the Hanging Gardens of Babylon, the Temple of Artemis at Ephesus, the statue of Zeus by Phidias at Olympia, the Mausoleum at Halicarnassus, the Colossus of Rhodes, and the lighthouse on the island of Pharos at Alexandria.

7.37 a.m.

"DAYS PLAZA NORTH-WEST. Days Plaza North-West."

Frank clambers to his feet, folds and pockets his newspaper, and makes his way down the carriage with his empty coffee cup in one hand, his body angled against the train's deceleration.

Out on the platform he meticulously disposes of the cup in a litter bin. No one else has disembarked except him. It is too early for shoppers and too early for most employees. On the other side of the platform a pair of janitors are waiting for the train going the opposite way. The backs of their green overalls are emblazoned with Days logos the size of dinner plates. They talk quietly and sombrely together. As Frank trots down the stairs to the ticket hall he recognises a Days night watchman slogging up the other way. If the night watchman is as tired as he looks, it has been a long night indeed.

Exiting the station onto Days Plaza, Frank is hit full in the face by a powerful gust of wind that momentarily staggers him. The store generates its own microclimate, its two-and-a-half-kilometre flanks funnelling the air currents that swirl around it into long sheeting vortices that collide at each corner and explode outwards, spiralling across the plaza in all directions, making the ornamental shrubberies shudder and the fountains' plumes bend sideways and overshoot their bowls.

Frank squares his jaw, lowers his head like a bull, and sets off across the plaza. His coat tails whip and flap about his legs and his hair is threshed this way and that. The gusts may not be cold but they are insistent and mean. The plaza's trees have grown up sickly and stunted as a result of their constant bullying.

There are train stations at all four corners of Days Plaza and a bus route runs around its circumference, with a single stop midway along each edge. This means that the shopper arriving by public transport has to walk at least half a kilometre to reach the store. The shopper travelling by taxi or private car is better served. Taxi-only approach roads lead up to turning circles outside the store's four entrances, while beneath the plaza lie seven storeys of subterranean car park with lifts that emerge in the entrance halls. The logic behind such an arrangement is faultless, if you have the mind of a retailer. Shoppers who know they are going to have to carry their goods home by hand will ration their purchases, concentrating on smaller, lighter and generally less expensive goods. The inconvenient location of the train stations and bus stops encourages them to use cars and taxis instead. Cars and taxis have plenty of room inside to store purchases. And car parks are, of course, an additional source of revenue.

Frank walks alongside the approach road to Days with his eyes averted, not just to shield them from the stinging particles of grit that are being tossed about by the wind but so that he won't have to look at the building. Even so, he can sense it looming ahead of him, a mountain made of brick. The plaza seems to slope down towards it, as though the weight of the world's first and (reputedly) foremost gigastore has warped the surrounding surface of the planet, although it is possible that this is simply some architectural conceit intended to make your footsteps quicken the closer you come to the store.

As Frank nears the north-western corner of Days, he at last dares to look up at the building that has dominated his life for thirty-three years. Its perspectives are dizzying, but what always strikes him is not so much the gigastore's size as the quantity of bricks used in its construction. There must be billions of them, and each was laid by hand, each individually trowelled with mortar and positioned by a workman who patiently pieced together his segment of the puzzle, making his unacknowledged contribution to the enormity of the whole. Time, wind and weather have pitted and pocked the bricks' surfaces, and the mortar that binds them is crumbling, but Days still stands, the dream of one man, the handiwork of thousands.

Window-shoppers are huddled, as always, one deep, occasionally two deep, beneath the huge display windows, long straggling lines of them running unbroken except at the loading bays, which are located midway along each edge of the building. Most of them are awake now. Some are picking at pieces of sandwich and morsels of pie that they have hoarded overnight. (Each evening, charity workers come and distribute food, water, and soup among the window-shoppers, a practice the Days administration tolerates without condoning.) Others are going through their personal exercise routines, flexing the night's stiffness out of their joints. A few have taken to the shrubberies to relieve themselves, and the rest are staking out their patches, unfurling moth-eaten blankets in front of their favourite windows and weighing down the corners with bulging, tattered Days carrier bags. Nearer to nine o'clock, unless the sky clouds over and it looks like rain, more window-shoppers—ones who have homes—will arrive, but by then the best places will have been taken. These other window-shoppers bring picnics, chairs, tables, families, friends with them to watch the displays, but they are not hardcore, all-weather devotees like those who spend their entire lives in the vicinity of Days, who eat and sleep in the gigastore's shadow. Tradition has it that window-shoppers are former customers who for one reason or other have been banned from the store, but this has never conclusively been proved.

At present, each window is draped inside with a pair of heavy green velvet curtains which sport the black and white halves of the Days logo on either side of their adjoining hems.

As Frank arrives at the corner of the building, a few of the window-shoppers look up, nod to him, and look away again. They recognise him not by his face—few people remember Frank's face—but by his demeanour. They recognise him as one of their own, one of the overlooked, the disregarded, the discounted.

He closes his nose to the smell the wind wafts his way, the reek of unwashed clothing and bodies.

A pair of guards wearing quilted jackets and fur-lined caps with Days logos on the ear-flaps are stationed at the top of the shallow flight of steps that leads up to the North-West Entrance. Hopping up the steps, Frank greets them both, showing them his Iridium. One of the guards takes the card and peers at it, at the same time adjusting the weight of the rifle strapped to his shoulder. There is no need for a visual check on the card, but he examines both sides of it just the same, several times, until, satisfied that it doesn't *look* like a fake (as if a skilful forgery would be detectable to the human eye), he turns and swipes it through the slot of the lock unit set into the frame of the pair of doors behind him. He punches in a seven-digit code on the lock unit keypad, and seven bolts within the doors shoot back in quick succession from bottom to top, their ascending clanks like notes in a rising scale. The handle on the left-hand door is a black semicircle, on the right-hand door a white semicircle. Their verticals meet flush when the doors are closed. Grasping the left-hand handle, the guard hauls back on it.

Frank nods his thanks, takes back his card, and steps through the open doorway. The door is closed behind him, and the bolts slide to in reverse order, descending the scale.

5

Seven Names of God: The seven Judaic names for the Divinity—El, Elohim, Adonai, YHWH, Ehyeh-Asher-Ehyeh, Shaddai, and Zeba'ot.

8.00 a.m.

IMMEDIATELY NORTH OF the glass dome on top of Days lies a flat-roofed, one-storey penthouse complex. At the southern end is a heptagonal room joined to the rest of the complex by one of its seven points. Within the heptagonal room resides the store's brain: the Boardroom.

Inside the Boardroom, a circular table seven metres in diameter sits at the centre of a spread of lush dollar-green carpet. One half of the table is ash, the other half ebony, and situated at one end of the join between the two halves, recessed snugly into the wood, are a computer terminal and a telephone.

Seven chairs are positioned equidistantly around the table. Each is different and reflects the character and disposition of the person who regularly occupies it. One is an ornate gilded throne; another is a wing-backed armchair comfortably upholstered with padded vermilion leather; a third is designed along Art Nouveau lines with a narrow seat and a straight back composed of staggered rectangles in the manner of a Frank Lloyd Wright window; and so on.

At eight o'clock, the venetian blinds that cover the triptych of windows at the Boardroom's southern end rise automatically, furling upwards to reveal an unhindered view of the base of the rotating dome. Currently the dome's clear half fills the windows, although a crescent-shaped sliver of its dark half is visible in one corner and will encroach more and more on the clear portion as the day wears on.

Opposite lie four oak-panelled walls, completing the heptagon. On one there hangs a gilt-framed, lifesize portrait of none other than the founder of Days, Septimus Day himself. Septimus long ago passed through life's great checkout, but still he glares imperiously down on the Boardroom and all that takes place within it with his good right eye glittering, its patched partner menacing. Anyone who knew Old Man Day thinks the artist has captured his likeness very well indeed. Chillingly well.

Set into the adjacent wall at chest height is a brass panel sporting a hinged knife switch of the kind Victor Frankenstein throws in old horror movies in order to animate his Creature, except that this one is seven times as large and requires a ceramic handle the size of a baseball bat to operate it. At present the switch stands upright in the Off position with the detached handle clipped next to it on the panel.

Each of the two remaining oak-panelled walls carries a bank of sixteen monitors arranged in a four-by-four grid. Their screens show computer-generated composites of the Days logo set against a dollar-green background.

A balding, prim-looking man in a butler's livery of shirtsleeves and a horizontally pinstriped waistcoat opens the pair of large doors that bridge the apex of the angle formed by the two monitor-bearing walls. Turning around, he grasps the handle of a serving trolley the size of a hospital gurney and hauls it backwards into the Boardroom. Seven heavy silver salvers press the trolley's wheels deep into the carpet, making it an effort to pull.

Reaching the centre of the room, the manservant leaves the trolley and goes round the table moving each chair one place clockwise, setting its feet in the indentations left by the previous chair. Then he returns to the trolley and repeats the journey, depositing a salver on the table in front of each seat. This second circuit of the table completed, he guides the trolley out of the room. He returns a minute later with another trolley, this one bearing a silver teapot, a bone-china teapot, three stainless steel coffee pots (one of which contains hot chocolate), a tall glass jug of orange juice, a bottle of gin, a bottle of tonic water, lemon slices on a dish, and an ice-bucket carved from a solid chunk of malachite, plus assorted cups, saucers, and tumblers. Once again he circumnavigates the table, placing the appropriate beverages in front of the appropriate chairs. If he experiences a twinge of disapproval as he sets the gin, tonic, lemon, and ice before the gilded throne, he hides it well behind the pinched, impassive mask of a family retainer of long standing who has learned over the years not to betray a hint of emotion either in or out of the presence of his employers.

The manservant, whose name is Perch, pauses to take out a gold fob watch. He flips up the lid, nods approvingly at the time, returns the watch to his waistcoat pocket, and wheels the second trolley out of the Boardroom.

A short corridor takes him past the head of a spiral staircase and along to the kitchen. He parks the trolley, goes over a couple of the finer points of the lunchtime menu with the chef, then makes his way on long, soft-stalking legs into an adjoining chamber which he has come to consider as his office, although it is also a repository for all the silverware—the cutlery, snuff boxes, cuspidors and humidors—which it is his duty to polish to brilliance once a month. He seats himself at a small oaken desk on the blotter of which rests an intercom fashioned as a replica of an antique black Bakelite telephone, complete with rotary dial, plaited brown flex and clawed brass cradle. He lifts the receiver and dials 1.

The line chirrups a few times, then there is a click of connection.

"Master Mungo," says the old retainer.

"Morning, Perch," comes the reply. There is the sound of wind and lapping water. Mungo is out by the rooftop pool.

"Good morning to you, sir. Breakfast is served."

"Another couple of lengths and I'll be along."

"Very good, sir."

Perch taps the cradle and dials 2.

"Master Charles."

A young woman answers. "Chas is in the shower."

"Who is this?"

"This is Bliss. Who are *you*?"

"Madam, you should not be using Master Charles's intercom."

"Chas told me to pick it up," the girl replies tartly.

"Then would you kindly inform Master Charles, madam, that breakfast is served."

"Okey-dokey. Will do."

"Thank you."

"No trouble. 'Bye."

Perch taps the cradle again and dials 3.

"Master Wensley."

A sleep-furred voice responds. "God, is that the time already, Perch? I'll be up there quick as I can. Keep my devilled kidneys warm, will you? There's a good fellow."

Perch dials 4.

"Master Thurston."

"Already here, Perch."

"My apologies. I didn't hear you come up the stairs."

"That's all right. These eggs are tasty."

"I'm most gratified, sir."

"Pass my compliments on to the catering staff."

"That I will, sir. I'm sure they will be most gratified, too."

Perch dials 5.

"Master Frederick."

"How's it going, Perch?"

"Well, sir."

"Papers arrived yet?"

"I shall check, sir. If they have come, I shall have them waiting for you at your position."

"Great stuff. See you in a mo."

Perch dials 6.

"Master Sato."

"Perch."

"Breakfast is served."

"Of course. Thank you."

"Thank *you*, sir."

Perch taps the cradle, hesitates, then, drawing on all his reserves of self-control (and they are deep), dials 7.

The line chirrups for the best part of two minutes and no one picks up. Master Sonny is either deliberately ignoring the ringing of his portable intercom or incapable of hearing it. Perch confidently suspects the latter. In fact, he would not be surprised if Master Sonny were presently lying on the floor of his bathroom, curled around the pedestal of a vomit-spattered lavatory, comatose. It would not be the first time Perch has gone downstairs to wake him and found him in such a position.

Replacing the receiver, Perch permits himself the merest twitch of a smile. The prospect of rousing Master Sonny from his alcohol-induced stupor fills him with no small pleasure.

Perhaps the glass-of-cold-water-in-the-face method again...

6

Seventh Heaven: A state of serene, transcendent bliss.

8.01 a.m.

THE QUIET HALF-HOUR.

Over the dollar-green marble floor of the entrance hall Frank goes, over the smooth opal-and-onyx cobbles of the Days logo mosaic, past banks of lifts waiting with their doors open, past conga-lines of wire shopping trolleys, past parked rows of motorised shopping carts, beneath an unlit chandelier like a waterfall captured in glass, towards the parade of arches that afford access to the store proper.

He is trying to work out how many times he has crossed this hall and at the same time trying to remember when he started trampling the jewelled logo beneath his feet instead of skirting it respectfully as most people do. The answer to the first question runs into so many thousands that he swiftly and incredulously abandons the calculation. The answer to the second is easier: he started walking over the logo instead of around it the day he realised that he could, that there was no specific rule against doing so, that all that kept people off the circle of precious stones was their belief in the sanctity of wealth—a belief he had ceased to share, or, more accurately, realised had never been part of his personal credo.

This was around the time when he first started to notice that he had lost his reflection. The loss was so gradual, in fact, it was only in retrospect that he realised that it had occurred at all. Every day he would look in the mirror and a little bit more of himself would be absent, and every day he would dismiss this as a trick of the light or the mind—to acknowledge it as an empirical fact would have been to entertain madness. Eventually, however, the truth was impossible to deny. He was forgetting what he looked like and who he was. He was slipping away, slowly, in increments.

The day that he became aware of this was the same day that he dared to set foot on the jewelled mosaic, and also the same day that the idea of leaving Days first stirred in the furthest reaches of his mind. He can almost pin down the genesis of his decision to quit to the moment he first rested his right foot on the tip of the opal semicircle and was not fried to a crisp by a lightning bolt from Mammon's fingertip.

Arriving at the arches, Frank halts, takes out his wallet, and yet again unsheathes his Iridium. Each arch is fitted with a set of vertical stainless steel bars two centimetres thick that slot snugly into the lintel. The uprights between the arches have terminals mounted on them at waist-level. The terminals are conical, with oval screens and chrome shells. Each invites Frank in large green letters to insert his card into its slot. He does so with the one nearest to him, and the screen swiftly bitmaps a Days logo, then runs a green message across it:

CARD INCORRECTLY INSERTED
PLEASE TRY AGAIN

Frank removes the ejected card, flips it over so that its logo is facing up, and reinserts it, tutting at his own carelessness.

A new message appears:

HUBBLE, FRANCIS J.
EMPLOYEE #1807-93N
ACCOUNT STATUS: IRIDIUM
CARD NO.: 579 216 347 1592

This is erased and replaced with:

LOG-ON TIME: 8.03 A.M.
HAVE A GOOD DAY'S WORK, MR HUBBLE

The card is ejected again, and the stainless steel bars of the arch to the left of the terminal retract upwards with a sharp pneumatic burp. He passes through, returning the card to his wallet. He knows metal detectors are scanning him, but as he has nothing metallic on him larger than his house keys and his fillings, alarms do not whoop. The bars descend again smoothly and swiftly like mercury rushing down transparent pipes.

The quiet half-hour.

As far as Frank is concerned the time between now and 8.30 is sacred. The store is still, its overhead lights at half-power. The night watchmen have gone off duty and the shop assistants have not yet arrived. Days is neither closed nor open but somewhere in between, in a semi-lit limbo of transition. Neither one thing nor the other, neither darkened and empty nor bright and bustling, the place is perhaps at its most honest. Everything it has to offer is laid bare beneath the dimmed bulbs. Nothing is hidden.

If you enter Days by the North-West Entrance, the first department you find yourself in is Cosmetics. As Frank begins to cross the department, he is aware of making a mental note of his impressions, recording what he is seeing as though he is a human video-camera. Frank the man is at one remove from Frank the creature of habit, who would normally stroll through the quiet half-hour in a meditative state, letting his thoughts flow and free-associate. He is observing himself like an anthropologist studying a primitive tribesman. What is he doing now? He is passing between a display of skin-care products in pastel-coloured packaging and a range of lipstick testers racked in individual cubbyholes like miniature missiles in silos. What is he thinking? He is thinking how large this room is—like all the departments in Days, a little over two hundred metres long on each side—and yet how cramped it feels, and how the counters, laden to above eye-level, form a honeycomb maze in which it only takes a moment to lose all sense of direction. How does he feel? He is remembering his first day at Days and the awe that filled him as he stepped through one of the arches with his card still in his hand—back then it was a Platinum—to find himself actually on the floor of the world's first and (he was thrilled to think) foremost gigastore. He still feels a trace of that awe now but it is no more than a sedimentary deposit, like limescale, that would be more trouble than it's worth to scrub away. Mostly he just feels a kind of silent emptiness.

All of which he dutifully files away for the benefit of the Frank Hubble of the future, for the man he is going to be as of tomorrow, the secret wanderer adrift in the immensity of America.

From Cosmetics, he has the choice of going either south through the Perfumery or east through Leather Goods. A pungent miasma of ten thousand different musks hangs perpetually over the Perfumery, strong enough to make your eyes water. The combined stench of hectares of cured cowhide in Leather Goods is marginally less stomach-turning, so Frank goes east, then jinks south into the Bakery. Deliveries of fresh bread have not yet arrived but the yeasty aroma of yesterday's batch still lingers in the air. Chilled cabinets loaded with pastries, pies, croissants, and bagels hum with full-bellied delight.

The next department is the Global Delicatessen. The Global Delicatessen is divided into subsections, each of which sells the specialities of a different country's cuisine from a counter decked out in stereotypically traditional style. For example, chapatis, samosas and bhajis can be found within a scale-model Taj Mahal made of painted chipboard, while pastas of every imaginable shape and colour are stored in jars in a mock-up of a room from a Florentine palazzo, complete with peeling stucco walls and exposed brickwork. An ersatz Bavarian market square offers sauerkraut and dozens of varieties of bratwurst, a *faux* French village square with boxed orange-trees and a *bar-tabac* backdrop has stalls where browsers may sample escargots, bouillabaisse and onion soup before buying, and trestle tables in a pseudo Greek fishing village groan with hummus, baklava, cabanos sausage and a wide assortment of olives—black, green, stuffed, dried. And so on. At opening time, each subsection will be staffed by shop assistants decked out in the appropriate national costume.

To the east lies the malodorous hell that is the Fromagerie, but Frank steers well clear of the connecting passageway and continues south through the Global Delicatessen to the Ice Cream Parlour. The air in the Ice Cream Parlour is chilled by over three hundred glass-lidded freezer cabinets. They contain tubs of ice cream that run the gamut of flavours from the traditional (vanilla, chocolate, strawberry) to the unlikely (rhubarb crumble with custard, spearmint'n'saveloy, lox and cream cheese, tapioca with a hint of violet), most of which are also available as frozen yoghurts, sorbets, and granitas. Frank draws his overcoat tightly about himself and bustles through, his exhalations wisping behind him like a gossamer scarf.

One more department lies between him and the building's heart. The Confectionery Department is a sweet-toothed child's vision of heaven and an honest dentist's vision of hell. Candy canes reach to the ceiling, jar upon jar of foil-wrapped toffees and fudges line the walls, and pyramids of handmade truffles wait on refrigerated shelves to be selected, boxed and weighed. Fistfuls of lollipops sit on countertops like gaudy bunches of flowers, plaited lengths of liquorice wind around the cash registers like electrical cables, and sticks of Days-brand rock—half white, half black, with the name of the store running all the way through in lime green—glisten in their cellophane wrappers. Pear drops, acid drops, and cough drops are available by the half-kilo. The polychromatic kaleidoscope of allsorts, jelly beans, and dolly mixtures on display would give a chameleon a heart attack. There are butterscotch rectangles, nougat triangles, and lumps of marzipan in every shape under the sun. There are gobstoppers, chews, and mints from mild to infernal. And there is chocolate—chocolate of every shade from pitch black to milk white, with a hundred grades of brown in between. Bitter, sweet, bittersweet, studded with nuts, raisins, nuts *and* raisins, from cubes as small as dice to slabs as large as tombstones... There is so much sugar in the air, just inhaling could send you into a diabetic coma.

Beyond Confectionery, Frank arrives at his destination, the goal of his south-eastward trek through the store. It is the hoop that encircles the Menagerie. Each floor has one, a broad, annular esplanade that offers shoppers somewhere to sit and rest between purchases, and also provides a shortcut from one corner of the store to the other. Furnished with pine benches and potted plants, mainly philodendra and succulents, and floored with white marble, the hoops would appear to be oases of calm and repose amid the relentless, hectic sell-sell-sell of the departments. Restaurants and cafeterias reinforce this impression. It should be noted, however, that the benches are few and far between, that the service in the restaurants is swift and perfunctory, and that the snacks served in the cafeterias are, to put it mildly, inedible.

The Red Floor hoop is deserted. The entire atrium, all the way up to the great glass dome, is silent except for the rustle of foliage, a faint trickle of running water, and the occasional animal-cry, all from the Menagerie.

Frank crosses over to the parapet that runs around the hoop's inner edge, rests his forearms on the guardrail, and leans out. Craning his neck until his windpipe stands proud like a bent arm, his Adam's apple its elbow, he peers up at the dome some hundred and twenty metres above him.

The dome's gyration, like the wheeling of the stars across the sky, is too slow for the human eye to detect. Frank knows that its revolutions are cunningly geared so that, whatever the season, the unsmoked half is always aligned with the sun, but he has never been able to fathom why Old Man Day opted for this arrangement when a static and completely clear dome would have been far cheaper to construct and would do the job of illuminating the atrium just as well, if not better. Yes, the bicoloured dome acts like a giant logo, stamping the imprimature of Days on the entire building, and yes, as a technological achievement it is deserving of admiration, but as far as Frank is concerned all the dome's twenty-four-hour rotation does is serve as an unwelcome reminder of the incremental, inexorable passing of each day. And according to the dome, every day is divided perfectly into equinoctial halves, twelve hours of light, twelve hours of darkness. According to the dome, every day is the same.

Frank lowers his head and looks across to the rising tiers of floor half a kilometre away, then down through the gauze of monofilament mesh and the gridwork of irrigation pipes to the Menagerie.

The Menagerie's canopy, which begins about five metres below where Frank is standing, is an undulating vista of palms with here and there a fern pushing up sharply between the fringed fronds. Bushy epiphytes cling to the trees' trunks, and in clearings Frank can make out orchids and bamboos clustering around their roots. The manmade tropical forest gives off a humid, steamy aroma, its jungle jade flecked with flickering leaf-shadows.

Over to the west, a macaque shrieks in the treetops. Something else closer to Frank replies with a series of stuttering laughs—*yak-yak-yak*—that develops into a full-throated whooping. The macaque offers its territorial argument again, and the whooping creature falls into submissive silence. There is a flash of whirring scarlet between the leaves: a parrot darting from one branch to another. Something small like a rabbit skitters through the undergrowth. A big electric-blue butterfly comes bumbling up to the net, flaps stupidly against it for a while, then swirls back down into the green. A thousand other insects softly sing and trill, a high-pitched glee club that will, once the store opens, be swamped by the din of voices and footsteps. Frank half-closes his eyes and lets the Menagerie's soothing susurration fill his ears. This he *will* miss, no doubt about it. On many a morning, the prospect of these few brief ruminative moments spent gazing down on the Menagerie's canopy before the madness of the day begins has been the only reason he has been able to find to drag himself out of bed.

The Menagerie is neither zoo nor conservation project. It is, quite simply, an elaborate cage. Animals are shipped in from around the world on demand and stored in the Menagerie temporarily until their purchasers can make arrangements to have them picked up. The store's policy on selling wildlife displays a refreshing lack of zoological prejudice. It doesn't matter if an animal is on the endangered species list or as common as dandruff, if a customer desires it and has the wherewithal to pay for it, it can be his.

Nothing stays in the Menagerie for long. The macaque, for instance, will be gone by tomorrow. Later today, trained sales assistants will venture into the manmade jungle clad in protective gear and toting tranquilliser-dart rifles, close in on the little monkey, put it to sleep, and present it in a cage to its new owner, an industrialist who wants to give his daughter an unusual pet as a gift for her thirteenth birthday. The Menagerie's only permanent residents are the insects, who form an integral part of its ecosystem. But since they breed quickly and are cheap to replace, they too are for sale.

In short, the Menagerie is just another department, like any in the store. Yet to Frank, who has spent his entire life as a city dweller, the Menagerie's lush green abundance is intoxicatingly alien, an exotic symphony of sight and sound and scent. Charged with secret life, the Menagerie is a city of Nature, where the bustle of industry goes on invisibly, and territory is claimed, and transients come and go, a daily round of business that carries on seemingly regardless of the store that encloses it.

Of course this autonomy is an illusion. The Menagerie is as dependent on Days to support it as Days is on the world outside. Without regular irrigation and climate control, the vegetation would die. Without the vegetation, the insects would die. Without the insects and vegetation, the smaller mammals would die. Without the smaller mammals, the reptiles and larger mammals would have nothing to hunt and eat while they wait to be recaptured and sent to their new homes; they would have to be fed directly by the sales assistants, and that would contradict the ethic behind the Menagerie. Old Man Day planted a jungle at the heart of his store for a reason: to symbolise the commerce of Nature, to show that preying and feeding on others is an accepted part of the natural order, perhaps even to justify the very foundation of Days. The Menagerie is a manifesto on a grand scale, a point lavishly made—and Frank knows this, and yet still it is more than metaphor to him. Somehow, with a gorgeous green eloquence, it speaks of truths that are not so easily interpreted. With the sighs of its flora and cries of its fauna it addresses a part of the soul not concerned with gaining and acquiring. After all these years, Frank still does not understand what the Menagerie is trying to say, but like a nursing infant who responds to the tone of his mother's voice, if not the sense of her words, he loves to listen all the same.

Through his serenely half-closed eyes Frank glimpses a white shape moving amid the blur of green. He inclines his head and focuses.

A white tiger has come stalking into a clearing fifteen metres below him and twenty metres away. A white tig*ress*, to be exact. She was captured in the dwindling Rewa forest of India only last week and is soon to be transferred to the private collection of a French rock star at a cost somewhere in the region of a million album sales.

A beautiful creature—her pelt spectrally pale between its black flashes, her eyes a light, lambent blue, her tail gently curved, uptilted and coat-hanger stiff—she walks with an unhurried grace on sinewy legs across the clearing to one of the several streams that meander through the Menagerie, pumped directly from the city's ring main. At its edge she stops, bends her head, and begins lapping languorously at the water with her thick pink tongue, pausing every so often to lick stray droplets from her whiskers and chin.

Frank watches her, transfixed. With her markings and colouring she is like some beast out of mythology, a ghost tiger whose ancestors doubtless inspired many a tall tale around the jungle campfire. Even the sight of her mundanely drinking water, her eyes slitted in contentment, sends chills up his spine. He wonders what it would be like to be standing down there beside her, to inhale her tiger smell and run his fingers over her glossy fur and feel the warmth and muscle of the living animal beneath.

Abruptly, the tigress breaks off from her drinking, lifts her head, and sniffs the air. Her pink nostrils gape and contract rapidly, opening and closing like a pair of tiny mouths, as her head bobs higher and higher, tracing the path of the scent, until, finally, she fixes her gaze on its source: Frank.

She stares at him without blinking. He stares back. She looks puzzled, and takes a few more deep, flaring sniffs. Her eyes narrow to azure almonds. Frank does not move.

The moment of contact stretches on, and on, and on.

8.16 a.m.

MEANWHILE, UP IN the Boardroom, Thurston Day greets his older brother Mungo and his younger brother Sato as they enter the room together. Neither is surprised to see Thurston already in his seat (a typist's chair with smooth-running castors and a fully adjustable, spine-sparing backrest). Thurston is usually first into the Boardroom even when it isn't his day of chairmanship, punctuality and punctiliousness being the principle character traits of Septimus Day's fourth son.

Thurston asks Mungo how his swim was, and the oldest Day brother runs a hand through his still-damp hair and replies that it was very pleasant indeed. A crisp morning, steam rising from the surface of the pool, twenty lengths instead of the usual fifteen. Thurston then asks Sato if he slept well, and Sato, folding his body like a praying mantis's forelegs into the tall, slender, Frank Lloyd Wright chair, thanks his brother for his kind enquiry and is delighted to be able to inform today's chairman that he enjoyed a very restful night's sleep indeed.

Satisfied, Thurston turns his attention back to the terminal at his elbow, which is displaying today's sales figures at the Unified Ginza Consortium in Tokyo, correct as of U.G.C. closing time, eight o'clock this morning.

Sato's movements are nimble and delicate as he pours himself a cup of jasmine tea from the bone china pot in front of him then removes the lid of the salver beside it to reveal a peeled hardboiled egg, a bowl of coleslaw, a plain roll, and a bowl of bean curd and fried seaweed. Of all the brothers, he is the one who has embraced the eastern side of their mixed Caucasian/Asiatic heritage. Mungo's breakfast is considerably heartier and more occidental. Along with a litre of orange juice in the glass jug, Perch has served him a rare rump steak, scrambled eggs, hash browns, four rashers of bacon, a pile of granary toast ten centimetres high (each slice lathered in crunchy peanut butter), a vanilla-flavoured protein shake, and, if Mungo is still hungry after all that, a bowl of muesli. Not surprisingly, Mungo is a robust figure. Swimming has broadened his shoulders to the width of the average doorway and lunchtime games of tennis and evening workouts in the brothers' private gym have toned his waist and legs. He exudes health from every pore of his taut, unpimpled skin.

Thurston, by comparison with his fitness-fanatic sibling, looks hunched, meek, and anaemic. While he sports the brown eyes, glossy dark hair and olive-tinged complexion common to all the sons of Septimus Day, his jaw is narrow and his cheeks are hollow and his wrists are so thin that Mungo could encircle them both at once with his thumb and forefinger. Thurston wears small round spectacles and favours high collars and thin, plain ties. But he is not as timid as he appears. When it comes to business matters, none of the Day brothers can match Thurston for aggression or ruthlessness. Thurston closing a deal is like a hawk swooping on its prey. Equally, if the wholesale cost of coffee beans, say, rises a couple of per cent, Thurston will be the first to suggest that Days hikes up the retail price twice that amount. Conscience is a weakness in any businessman, and Thurston cannot abide weakness.

Sato, though ascetic in his tastes, favouring that which is elegant yet simple, shares his brothers' passion for increased profits and their love of the wealth generated by the massive store beneath them. For Sato, however, it is not what money can buy that attracts him. Someone with his income could own anything they wanted, but Sato prefers his life to be as uncluttered with possessions as possible. Rather, it is money in the abstract that he finds enthralling. The principle of money. The theory of it. Sato lives for the accumulated sales total at the end of the week, which is also, by happy coincidence, his day of chairmanship. Come Saturday evening, as he sits in front of the terminal watching takings from every department float up on the screen, Sato is in his personal nirvana. Even if he cross-references the weekly total against those of the other gigastores and finds that once again the store's figures have fallen well short of those achieved by its international rivals, a league table habitually headed by the Great Souq in Abu Dhabi and Blumberg's, N.Y., he is never annoyed or envious, merely fascinated by the divergent differences. Money is merely numbers to Sato, and numbers obey the laws of mathematics, and the laws of mathematics constitute a system as elegant and as simple as you could wish for.

As Sato takes the first few nibbles of his seaweed and bean curd, using the chopsticks provided by Perch, and Mungo launches ferociously into his feast with fork and serrated knife, Fred arrives, clutching an armful of newspapers taken from Perch, whom he happened to intercept at the top of the spiral staircase. There is nothing Fred likes more than his morning papers (three tabloids, two broadsheets, and a couple of internationals). Like his brothers, he seldom leaves the premises. The Boardroom, the roof with its amenities—swimming pool, tennis court, jogging track, paved garden—and the Violet Floor where each brother has a private apartment, constitute the limits of their existence, and while they do venture down onto the shop floor occasionally and off the premises *very* occasionally, they prefer to stay within those limits. It is safer that way.

Fred's morning papers are his lifeline to the outside world, a tube through which he can breathe air from outside and so avoid being suffocated by his circumstances. Undoubtedly he is happy with his life and would not swap being a co-owner of Days for anything, but without his newspapers and, in the evenings, his cable television, the cloistered existence he and his brothers lead would surely drive him nuts.

Fred bids his three siblings good morning and takes his seat between Thurston and Sato, dumping the pile of newspapers on the table in front of him. His chair suggests a perhaps unconscious desire for freedom. It is a folding canvas chair of the type traditionally used by explorers and movie directors. Fred's longish hair, stubbled chin, and gaudy Aztec-patterned shirt reflect the same desire. His breakfast, however, is pure childhood comfort food: pre-sugared corn flakes, hot chocolate, and toast with butter and strawberry jam.

Fred opens one of his tabloids and is just starting to peruse the gossip columns when Wensley waddles in. Wensley has dressed hastily in his anxiety to reach his breakfast before it goes cold. One shirt-flap dangles beneath his voluminous belly, and he is walking on stockinged feet, clasping his shoes to his chest. He is breathing hard from mounting the spiral staircase.

Barely acknowledging his brothers' greetings, Wensley crosses to the table and plumps himself down in the wing-backed chair. Its vermilion-upholstered padding sighs beneath his weight. He plucks the lid off his salver, snatches up his knife and fork, and starts urgently scooping mouthfuls of devilled kidney between his pillowy, liver-coloured lips, losing several morsels to the bushy goatee that surrounds them. In addition to the kidneys, Wensley's meal consists of four soft-boiled eggs, kedgeree, a mound of fried potatoes drenched in ketchup and brown sauce, a pile of pancakes with maple syrup, and two hunks of white bread smeared with dripping, plus a jug of cream and twenty grammes of refined sugar for his coffee.

Mungo can seldom resist ribbing his less health-conscious younger brother. "Enough cholesterol there for you, Wensley?"

Wensley barely pauses from his eating to reply, "I'll work it off."

"Work it off? How? You've never taken a stroke of exercise in your life."

"Nervous energy," says Wensley, patting his mouth with a linen napkin.

"No one's *that* nervous," says Mungo with a grin.

"Are you genuinely worried about my well-being," retorts Wensley, "or is the source of your concern the fact that, were I no longer here, we would no longer be Seven?"

"A bit of both, to be honest."

"Ah, fraternal love and self-interest. For a son of Septimus Day the two are one and the same." Wensley pops one of the soft-boiled eggs into his mouth whole, shell and all. His cheeks bulge, there is a muffled crunch, and then he swallows the egg in one go with a huge, unhealthy-sounding gulp. "Am I not correct?"

Mungo has to laugh. "Point well made, Wensley. Point well made."

Sixth to arrive for breakfast is Chas, the second eldest and by far the best-looking of the brothers. In Chas the genes of Septimus Day and his wife, Hiroko, commingled to create the most aesthetically pleasing product they could, endowing him with lustrous eyes, a cleft chin, a square jaw, hair that no matter how it is brushed always seems to fall the right way, cheekbones a male model would kill for, an excellent physique that unlike Mungo's does not require intensive maintenance, sharp dress sense, and a firm grasp of the social graces. Chas is generally thought of as the "face" of the Days administration. He it is who goes to meet wholesalers personally when meeting wholesalers personally is absolutely unavoidable, and he it is who is most often called upon to mollify a disgruntled distributor via video conference or telephone and head down to the shop floor when a problem needs sorting out. What Chas lacks in business acumen he more than makes up for in charm. When the facts won't swing an argument the Day brothers' way, Chas's silver tongue usually will.

Chas offers his brothers a smile that displays twin rows of mint-white teeth so perfectly shaped and arranged they seem to have been plotted with a ruler and set square. He pats Mungo affectionately on the shoulder as he moves around the table to his place. He sits down in an antique desk-chair that looks like one half of a love-seat, its curved back fitted with hand-tooled spokes. His firm, shapely buttocks come to rest on a maroon velvet cushion trimmed with gold braid and gold corner tassels. His breakfast is half a cantaloupe melon, french toast with bacon, and tea.

Fred slyly comments that Chas is looking a little peaky this morning. He is not. As usual, Chas is looking magnificent. But he fakes a yawn and remarks that he did have a somewhat "interrupted" night.

"I'll bet," leers Fred. "And is this 'interruption' still with us?"

"I sent her downstairs with a spree card."

Thurston is quick to enquire whether Chas put a spending cap on the spree card.

"A grand," is the nonchalant reply.

"And I trust, Chas," Thurston continues, "that that was not the only precaution you took."

"Give me some credit, Thurston," says Chas, with a calculated measure of irritation.

"Forgive my concern, but you know as well as I do that our rivals would not hesitate to cast aspersions on our reputation if the opportunity—in the form of a paternity suit, for example—presented itself."

"You think I want that any more than you?"

"I'm merely saying that your behaviour does expose us to a certain level of risk. Honest competition we can contend with, rumour we can ignore, but the whiff of scandal tends to cling."

Mungo, seeing Chas bristle, intervenes. "Your women come from the Pleasure Department, don't they, Chas?"

Chas nods.

"Well, there you are then. They're under contract to us. If one of them were to get pregnant—and this is just a general statement, I'm not saying Chas would be responsible—but if she did get pregnant and she decided to sue us, she wouldn't have a legal leg to stand on. She'd be in breach of Clause 6 of her contract, the one about 'fitness to work'. We, in fact, could sue *her*, if we felt like it."

"See?" says Chas to Thurston.

Thurston concedes gracefully. "My sincerest apologies."

"Accepted."

It's a small squall, and the climate in the Boardroom quickly calms again. Fred helps lighten the atmosphere by reading aloud a gossip-column snippet about an opposition-party spokesman who was spotted yesterday shopping at Days with a woman who is neither his wife nor his secretary nor his official mistress. They were spied in the Lingerie Department making free with the politician's Iridium card.

"I *said* it was him, didn't I?" Fred crows, gesturing in the direction of the monitors. "Didn't I? I *told* you."

"Perhaps we should elevate him to Palladium," says Sato. "He seems to be a very good customer."

"The more Palladium politicians we have in both camps, the better," Wensley remarks through a mouthful of fried potato. "From a tax-break point of view."

"I'll make a note of it," says Thurston, and turns to tap a short reminder into the terminal. "Although we really ought not to be discussing business outside opening hours."

"Well, excuse *me*," says Fred, and immerses himself again in his newspaper, wiggling his eyebrows humorously for the benefit of anyone caring to look.

The breakfast-time conversation continues in fits and starts, counterpointed by the click of cutlery on crockery and the tap of keyboard keys and the peel of newsprint pages. Meanwhile, Old Man Day glares balefully down at his sons from the portrait, his good eye glittering. All six brothers studiously avoid looking at or mentioning the empty seventh chair, the mock throne, in front of which sit an untouched salver and all the ingredients for a good gin and tonic.

The ice cubes in the malachite bucket have started to melt.

8.28 a.m.

For five minutes Frank has been watching the clearing which the white tigress has now vacated, hoping she will re-emerge from the trees to look at him again, but at last he accepts that she has gone. And it is time he should be going, too. The quiet half-hour is almost over. Distant voices are coming faintly from all floors, drifting across the cathedral vastness of the atrium. Sales assistants are arriving, filtering in through the four main entrances and spreading out through the store to take up their posts by the counters and displays. He ought to be heading downstairs.

But still he keeps gazing down into the clearing, a gibbous striped afterimage of the tigress hovering before his eyes. Not that he believes in such things, but he can't help thinking she may have been an omen of some sort. An omen of his new life, perhaps. The tigress is soon going to be elsewhere, out of Days, as is he. Freed from captivity. But no. She is simply being transferred from one kind of captivity to another. He is not. So, not such a good omen after all. But then, since he doesn't believe in such things, what does it matter?

He stays by the parapet until the last possible moment. When a yawning restaurant chef saunters into the hoop, Frank silently turns and makes his way to the nearest staff lift.

7

Chapter 7: A provision of the U.S. federal Bankruptcy Act for the relief of insolvent debtors and their creditors.

8.30 a.m.

"Taxi's here, Gordon!"

Gordon Trivett comes trotting down the stairs, buttoning one shirt-cuff, and muttering, "Why'd it have to be on time?"

Linda is holding his coat for him in the hallway. She herself is all set to go. She has on her best blouse and skirt, over which she is wearing a cheap plastic mackintosh which has been taped up in several places where the seams have split. These homespun repairs are symptomatic of the make-do-and-mend ethic that the Trivetts adhered to during the time they spent saving up for their Days Silver. Today, that long, arduous, and sometimes seemingly endless period of belt-tightening is over, and Gordon and Linda can at last reap the rewards of their patience and self-denial.

Gordon, typically, has failed to grasp the wonder of the moment.

"Where are my keys?" he says, fishing frantically around in his pockets.

"Gordon, don't worry, I have mine," Linda says, holding up her set to prove it. "Now, are you ready?"

"I'd be readier if the taxi hadn't turned up on time. Whoever heard of a taxi turning up when it's supposed to?"

"The taxi turned up on time because the driver knows where we're going and wants to impress us by being punctual. No doubt he thinks we're big tippers."

"Now, have we got everything?" Gordon grabs his coat from his wife and whisks open the front door.

"I have my keys, my handbag..."

"What about the card? Where's the card?"

She blinks at him. "What card?"

Gordon's eyes bulge behind his spectacles. "The *card*, Linda! The Days card!"

"I'm just winding you up, Gordon. Here it is." Linda produces their

Silver from her handbag and shows it to him. Satisfied, Gordon turns and sets off down the garden path to the street.

"*Someone's* Mr Grumpy this morning," Linda says to herself under her breath, and she thinks she knows the reason. Gordon is anxious about taking the day off, scared that the branch manager will somehow, against all the odds, find out that he isn't suffering from the 'flu, and consequently not just deny him the promotion he is hoping for but fire him. She understands his fear, although she has no sympathy with it. She knows that if it weren't for his anxiety, he would never have dreamed of speaking to her the way he just did.

He really should have more faith, though. Her performance on the phone to the branch manager's secretary just now was a superb piece of dissembling. She played the concerned wife to the hilt, assuring the secretary that Gordon was mad keen to go to work but that she was refusing to let him leave the bedroom. She described his symptoms—the racking coughs, the streaming eyes, the dribbling nose—in avid detail. She even pretended to copy down some homespun cold remedy the secretary gave her involving whisky, honey, and fresh lemons. For that, Gordon shouldn't be snapping at her; he should be grateful to her. But she forgives him anyway. Today being the day it is, the greatest day of her life, she cannot bring herself to hold a grudge.

She closes the front door behind her, making sure the latch clicks to, then locks the two mortices and sets off after her husband down the straight strip of concrete that bisects the front lawn. She notes that the roses beside the path are withering and will have to be deadheaded soon, and that the privet hedge which separates their property from that of the Winslows, the family occupying the other half of the semi-detached, needs trimming again. It still hasn't quite been established whether the hedge is the Winslows' responsibility or hers and Gordon's, but she has taken its upkeep upon herself because the Winslows, frankly, don't have the first clue how to look after a home. Their half of the semi is a mess. They have let the garden grow wild and weed-strewn, the hulk of a broken-down car is rusting by the kerbside out front, and the house itself is a shambles: the brickwork needs repointing, the roof retiling, the curtains washing.

The Winslows have been dogged by a run of bad luck recently. Mr Winslow lost his job on the assembly line at the washing machine factory, his daughter's application to work in the Leisurewear Department at Days was rejected, and his wife has been forced to swap her full-time position at the local supermarket for a part-time one in order to care for her old and ailing mother. But Linda has only to look at *her* half of the house, with its neat front garden and sparkling white paintwork, and remember how little money she and Gordon have had to spare these past few years, to know that she is correct in her opinion that poverty is no excuse for untidiness. She feels sorry for the Winslows, but these are tough times and the only way to survive them is by being ruthless, both with yourself and with others. Often during her and Gordon's five-year struggle to earn their Silver Linda came close to calling the whole scheme off, unable to foresee a time when their deprivations would be at an end, but since despair was just another luxury they couldn't afford, she never succumbed to it. It was important, too, for her not to let her standards slip, so she taught herself the basics of home decoration, both internal and external, in order that the house would never *look* as though its occupants were in straitened circumstances. She also picked up the rudiments of plumbing and electrical wiring from books in the library, and thus saved on several hefty repair bills.

As for her sideline in hairdressing, after leaving school Linda spent a year as a trainee at a beauty salon, working at slave wages in the anticipation of a full-time job that, in the event, never materialised. Realising that Gordon's salary alone would not be enough to secure them a Silver, she put the skills she acquired at the salon to use, first on friends and then on friends' friends, building a client base by word of mouth. Right from the start she was undercutting the prices of any professional coiffeur by at least a quarter, which certainly contributed to her success, and that and the fact that she could do housecalls made her particularly popular among shut-ins and the elderly. It wasn't long before she had established a thriving, though not especially remunerative, little business that helped tide her and Gordon over through the five lean years and added to their growing Days nest-egg.

All in all, Linda feels she has every right to be proud of herself and disappointed in her next-door neighbours, who have allowed life to get the better of them. If only they would try a little harder, if only they wouldn't wear their defeat so openly, a Days card could be theirs as well—though not, she suspects, a Silver.

Gordon is ensconced in the back seat of the idling taxi, drumming his fingers on his knee. Linda deliberately takes her time over swinging the garden gate shut and ambling across the pavement to climb in beside him.

Not only does she not like to be hurried, but she wants as many of the neighbours as possible to see her leave. She knows for a fact that Bella, three houses away, is peering out from her kitchen window. Although Linda can't actually see Bella pinching apart two slats of the venetian blind, she has an instinct for these things. Likewise, five doors down on the opposite side of the street, Margie is watching from behind the net curtains in her living room. Linda has glimpsed her silhouette through the curtains' lacy folds. Others, she is convinced, have their eyes on her. Everyone in the street must know where she and Gordon are going today.

The taxi's interior reeks of an awful air-freshener, a pine scent so noxious that the first thing Linda does after closing the door is wind the window all the way down. The driver is a gaunt man with lank hair, sunken eyes, and a shaggy moustache. He glances at Linda in the rearview mirror, gives a tiny nod as if he has come to some sort of conclusion about her (although the gesture could simply be a hello), and indicates to pull out.

The taxi grumbles down the street. Linda puts her face to the open window not only so that she can breathe air which hasn't been "freshened" but so that people will be able to see her more clearly. She is so thrilled she can barely think straight. Days! They are on their way to Days! In all her thirty-one years Linda can't recall feeling this excited before. Even on her wedding day, although she is sure she was happy, she was too nervous and plagued by doubts to enjoy the occasion to its fullest. Now, unlike then, she is filled with the blissful certainty that this is what she really wants.

Of course it's what she wants! Ever since Linda was small, her ambition has been to have an account at Days. Her mother used to laugh at her when she would state, with absolute, unshakeable conviction, that one day she would walk through the doors of the world's first and (unquestionably) foremost gigastore with a card with her name on it in her hand. "Unless you win the lottery or marry a millionaire," her mother would reply with a laugh, "the only way *you'll* ever see the inside of Days is wearing a sales assistant's uniform." But then that was the kind of woman her mother was. Linda's father was a cold, distant brute of a man who kept his wife in her place with constant venomous criticism, and her mother meekly accepted being treated that way because she was scared to believe that life could offer her more, since that would mean admitting she had settled for less. Linda grew up determined that she would not end up like her mother, and glory be and halleluiah, she hasn't. Today is the proof of that.

As the taxi reaches the end of the street, Linda catches sight of Pat coming out of the tobacconist's on the corner. Pat has a Days lottery ticket in her hand and is stalwartly filling in her "lucky" numbers once again. Linda calls to her, and Pat glances up and waves. Her smile is uncertain. It seems she needs a moment to recall where Linda and Gordon might be heading in a taxi on a Thursday morning, despite the fact that for the past week Linda has talked about little other than their trip to Days. Linda returns the wave, turning the back of her hand towards Pat and languidly rotating it from the wrist in what she thinks is a funny imitation of royalty. Pat appears not to get the joke, because her smile disappears and is replaced by a frown. Linda will have to explain to her later the satirical intention behind the wave. She doesn't want Pat getting the wrong idea and spreading it about that Linda Trivett has become all la-di-dah since getting her Silver.

The driver turns right, giving a wide berth to a sack of rubbish that has rolled off the pavement into the road and split open like a dead man's belly, and aims the taxi for the heart of the city. The meter mounted on the dashboard busily clocks up the tariff. Gordon starts to fidget. He takes off his spectacles, polishes the lenses with a handkerchief and puts them on again. He fondles his lower lip. He traces abstract designs on his trouser leg with one fingernail. He plays with the card, slipping it in and out of its velvet sheath, in and out. Linda, meanwhile, watches the city pass by. The boarded-up shops. The pubs, doing a brisk trade even at this early hour. The cafés haunted by aimless souls trying to make one cup of tea last the whole morning. The beggars waiting at traffic lights, holding cardboard signs that say things like "Homeless—Will Work For Food" and "Mother Of Six, No Welfare". The school-age kids congregating around benches in threadbare parks to drink and smoke. A man who clearly ought to be in an institution shouting at himself as he stalks the gutters. People who, unlike Linda, have given up hope, who lack the energy and the resolve—the dynamism, that's a good word for it—the *dynamism* to improve their lot. The sight of them both angers and saddens her.

The taxi driver breaks into her reverie. "So, Days then, is it, missus?" he says, eyeing her in the rearview mirror. When he knows that he has got her attention, he twists around in his seat to look at her directly. "Don't tell me. I can guess just by looking at people." He turns back to watch the road. "Silver, right?"

Linda suspects that the driver has seen the card in Gordon's hands but gives him the benefit of the doubt. "Absolutely right. Well done."

"I can always tell. Got a knack for it. I bet this is your first time, too."

"How did you know?"

The driver snaps a quick grin round at her. "I'm right about that too?" He shakes his head. "I *am* on form today."

"We must look eager to get there."

"It's not that, missus. It's more that you both look... well, 'innocent' is the word that springs to mind. Fresh-faced. Like troops who haven't gone into combat yet."

"What an extraordinary thing to say."

"But it's true. You can always tell regular Days customers. They have this look about them, sort of wary and jaded."

"I'm sure we won't end up looking like that. Don't you agree, Gordon?"

Gordon grunts in the affirmative.

"Oh, you say that now," says the taxi driver, "but people have had some pretty nasty experiences at Days. Experiences that have, you might say, dampened their enthusiasm for shopping there."

"I've heard rumours."

"Oh, they're not—"

The taxi driver breaks off because a dust-caked van has pulled out from a parking space about thirty metres ahead. Spluttering with outrage, the taxi driver accelerates until his front bumper is less than a metre behind the van's tail-lights, then hammers repeatedly on the horn, cursing.

Linda notices that in the skin of dust which coats the van's rear doors someone has drawn a Days logo, etched a large X over it, and written beneath, in finger-thick capitals:

DAYS
DIES!

Just jealous, she thinks.

The van turns off at the next junction, its driver taking one hand off the steering wheel to stroke the air in a slow, masturbatory salute. The taxi driver growls, "Arsehole," then says to the Trivetts, "Did you see that? Did you see the way he pulled out *right* in front of me? I nearly went *straight* into him."

Gordon declines to comment, and Linda imperturbably resumes the conversation she and the driver were having before this incident. "You were saying they're not rumours."

"What aren't rumours?"

"The rumours about Days."

"The rumours about people getting killed?"

"Those rumours."

"Oh, they're not rumours. They're the truth."

"I know they're supposed to have some basis in the truth, but don't you think that these things have been blown up out of all proportion by the media? It can't possibly be as bad as people say."

"You obviously haven't been reading the papers lately, have you, love? Seventeen shoppers crushed to death in the run-up to last Christmas, another eight during the January sales—that seems pretty bad to me. And those are just the *accidental* deaths."

"But people still go there to shop."

"Course they do. It's Days, isn't it? And then there are the lightning sales..."

"Gordon and I are going to steer well clear of the lightning sales," says Linda. "Aren't we, Gordon?"

"Seems like a good idea," murmurs Gordon.

"A very good idea," says the taxi driver. "If you can."

"We will."

"And then, of course, there are the people who run foul of in-store security."

"You mean shoplifters."

"Exactly. Did you know, last year a total of thirteen shoplifters were shot dead by Days Security?"

"Because they ran."

"Wouldn't you? If you were faced with a choice between losing your account for ever and trying to get away, wouldn't you run?"

"I wouldn't shoplift in the first place," Linda states frostily.

"OK. All right. The point I'm trying to make here is that, even for honest customers like yourselves, Days is a dangerous place."

"We've signed the disclaimer form," says Linda. "We're aware of the risks." There, that neatly and tidily sums up her case. The taxi driver is referring to all the things that can happen to Days customers who are not careful or do not follow the rules. (Typically, like anyone who hasn't earned an account there, he can see only the store's bad side.) Days isn't to blame for the deaths that occur on the premises; it's the shoppers who are at fault. If you don't know how to behave while you're there, and if you lack the self-control not to take anything you can't pay for, then you thoroughly deserve the consequences.

This Linda thinks but does not say, believing it to be self-evident. Instead, she leans back, folds her arms across her chest, and scans the skyline ahead for a glimpse of the gigastore.

The taxi driver mulls some thoughts over for a while before opening his mouth again. "It's still a dangerous place. If I were you, I'd be taking some kind of protection in with me."

"What are you talking about, protection?" The taxi driver seems to be determined to ruin Linda's rosy mood, so the snappish edge in her voice can be forgiven.

"Protection," he says. "Self-defence. In case you run into a lunatic."

"Lunatics don't shop at Days."

"You'd be surprised."

"But that's the whole point of the place. Only a certain, for want of a better word, *class* of person can shop there."

"I wouldn't say class, missus. I'd say type. The type that loves to buy things. The type that *lives* to buy things. The type that goes bananas the moment a lightning sale is announced over the tannoy. The type that'll fly right off the handle if you happen to pick up the last item in stock of something they want. The type that'll bite your fingers off if you refuse to let go of it. *That's* the type of person that shops at Days, and that's the type you've got to watch out for."

"I've never heard such nonsense," says Linda. She looks at her husband. "Have you?"

Gordon shrugs. "I've heard that people can get a little strange in there."

"Too right," says the taxi driver.

"Well, we'll simply avoid anyone we don't like the look of."

"Right. See, love, I'm not trying to put you off going or anything. I'm just offering some friendly advice."

"Thank you," Linda replies curtly. Still, the taxi driver has piqued her curiosity. "Out of interest, when you said 'protection', what exactly did you mean? If you mean a gun, then that's absurd. Out of the question."

"Couldn't agree with you more, missus. You'd never get it past the metal detectors, for one thing. No, I'm referring to something that isn't going to kill anyone, right, but'll see off whoever's hassling you, should that happen, God forbid."

"And what would that be?"

Breaking into a broad grin, the taxi driver reaches across the passenger seat and opens the glove compartment. Inside are several small, shiny cylinders that resemble lipstick cases, black with gold caps, bound together with an elastic band.

"Got these off a mate of mine who used to be in the police force. Undercover policewomen carry them in their handbags. Pepper spray. Derived from those, what are they called? Jallypeeno peppers. Did I say that right?"

"Jalapeño," says Linda, stressing the aspirate "j".

"Yeah, that's the one. You know how nasty it is when you're cutting one of *them* up and you make the mistake of rubbing your eyes? Well, this is ten times worse. One squirt in the face and—voom!—your potential rapist, mugger, bargain-hunter, whatever, isn't bothering you any more." He closes the glove compartment and returns his attention to the road. "They're made of plastic, so you'll get them through security no problem."

"Are they legal?" asks Linda.

"Well, if the police can carry them, I reckon technically they must be. You interested?"

"You're asking me if I want one?"

"I'm suggesting you might need one."

Linda turns to her husband.

"Don't look at me," says Gordon, waving her away. "If you think you ought to get one, then get one."

"I don't think I *ought* to get one, but I think it might be wise to have one handy."

"It's up to you."

"Just in case."

"It's up to you."

"I'll probably never use it, but I'd feel safer if I was carrying it."

"You do what you have to, Linda."

"Can I use our Days Silver?" Linda asks the taxi driver.

"I'll add it to the fare," the driver says, reaching for the glove compartment again. "And look." He points ahead with one finger of the hand still on the steering wheel. "We're almost there."

And so they are. Above the rooftops, gliding towards them like a vast, strange galleon under full sail, there it is—a block of dried-blood brick whose dimensions would humble even the most arrogant of men. Linda has seen it before, of course, many times, but until now it has always been closed to her, an impenetrable gulag, a great blank space she has filled in with dreams and imaginings and expectations and longings. Until now, it has been Wonderland. Today, Linda is going to slip down the rabbit-hole.

Days!

8

Ancient Rome: Built on seven hills—the Aventine, the Caelian, the Capitoline, the Esquiline, the Palatine, the Quirinal, and the Viminal.

8.32 a.m.

THE BASEMENT IS a network of tunnels—broad corridors branching off into narrower corridors which in turn branch off into even narrower corridors, lit at infrequent intervals by ceiling-mounted striplights of low wattage. Ducts and pipes, the building's veins, run parallel overhead, and at each intersection the walls are marked with a colour-coded system of arrows, because it is all too easy to get lost down here, where every surface is painted battleship grey, except the floors, which are carpeted in a worn green cord with a repeating pattern of Days logos. When one stretch of corridor looks much like another, even employees of long standing sometimes have to consult the arrows to find their bearings.

Frank, though, is so familiar with the layout of every floor of Days that he doesn't even glance around as he steps out of the lift, simply turns and heads unerringly in the right direction.

On the way, he falls in beside a pair of Eye screen-jockeys, one skinny, one blimp-big, both with blue-tinged cathode tans. Matching his pace to theirs, he eavesdrops on their conversation. They are discussing the football match last night. Apparently the national side lost at home to a scratch team from a remote Micronesian atoll, but the screen-jockeys console themselves with the fact that at least it was only a five-nil defeat. Given the national side's current form, it could have been a lot worse.

Not being a follower of football or any other sport, Frank rapidly loses any interest he might have had in the screen-jockeys' conversation, and drops back a few paces, only to find that he is walking alongside a fellow Ghost. He recognises the other man as a Ghost not so much by his face as by the way he sidles down the corridor, hunch-shouldered and close to the wall.

As is always the case when two Ghosts unexpectedly cross paths, there is a *frisson* of distant familiarity between them, as though they are a pair of violin strings tuned to the exact same pitch: when one is plucked, the other vibrates in sympathy. For each, it is like meeting an identical twin he didn't know he had. In this instance, as is customary, neither offers the other the slightest acknowledgement, and Frank slows to an amble, allowing his co-worker to get ahead.

Reaching a door marked "Tactical Security", Frank stops and waits until the other man has gone through before stepping forward to do the same. He detects the presence of another Ghost behind him, a woman this time, and does her the courtesy of not holding the door open for her, so that she won't feel obliged to make eye-contact and thank him.

Tactical Security is one of several self-contained facilities within the Basement labyrinth, with its own cafeteria, cloakrooms, and locker rooms. Frank shares a locker room with twenty other Ghosts, most of whom are present when he enters. They are men and women of nondescript appearance, indeterminate age, dressed smartly but far from showily. The women wear the minimum of make-up and all the men look as if, like Frank, they trim their hair themselves. Few of the women wear any jewellery, and those that do restrict themselves to plain gold ear-studs and simple finger-rings. There isn't a wedding band in sight. The Ghosts avoid looking at each other, exchange no conversation, just quietly, imperturbably get ready for work. Frank, too.

He springs his locker open with a swipe of his Iridium, removes his overcoat and drapes it over the hanger inside, then shrugs off his jacket and hooks it over the corner of the door. Taking out his shoulder-holster, an infinity symbol of canvas webbing and soft leather, he puts it on and adjusts the buckles until the straps sit comfortably around his chest and the sagging planes of his shoulderblades.

He reaches into the locker again and removes a gleaming stainless steel .45-calibre automatic pistol from a velvet-lined case. He prefers the lightweight version of the regulation store-issue handgun because it doesn't drag down on the holster like the heavier guns do. A lighter gun means a harder recoil, but that seems a fair price to pay in exchange for greater ease of carrying, given that he seldom actually fires the thing.

Drawing back the slide, he checks that the chamber is empty, even though he never leaves a round in the chamber unless he is about to fire the gun—the habit of checking is as much an act of ceremony as it is a safety procedure. Then he lets the slide snap back into place. He cleans the gun religiously once a month, so the slide action is oil-smooth.

On a shelf at eye-level inside the locker there is a rack holding three clips of thirteen bullets, each with its black teflon tip grooved as though a tiny cog-wheel has been removed, and each with the Days logo stamped into its brass shell casing. Two of the clips Frank slots into the holster's double off-side ammo pouch under his right armpit; the third he thrusts into the grip of the gun, ramming it home with the heel of his palm. He uses his Iridium to take off the gun's safety, running the card's magnetic strip through a centimetre-deep groove in the underside of the barrel. A green LED next to the trigger guard winks alight as the decocking lever disengages. He runs the card through the groove again, the light goes out, and the decocking lever snicks back into place. He holsters the gun beneath his left armpit and puts his card away.

Next, he takes out his Eye-link, and having unravelled the fragile-looking tangle of surgical-pink wires and components, slots the fitted audio pick-up into his right ear then leads the attached wire back over the ear and down behind the lobe. At the other end of the wire is a wafer-thin short-wave receiver/transmitter which he pins inside his shirt collar. Running from this is another wire that ends in a tiny microphone, slender and curved like a fingernail, which he clips into place behind the top button of his shirt, tightening the knot of his tie so that the microphone presses snugly against his throat.

The only piece of equipment left in the locker is his Sphinx. He unplugs the slim black box from its recharging unit, switches it on, and as soon as the Days logo scrolls up on the screen, flicks the power button back to Off and slides the Sphinx into his trouser pocket.

Ready. Another ritual over and done with for the last time.

It is 8.43, and the morning briefing is imminent. Frank accompanies the other Ghosts as they drift out of the locker room, joining the rustling flow of bodies moving down the passageway which leads past the self-service cafeteria to the briefing room. One by one, without a word, eyes averted, the Ghosts glide through the briefing-room doors to take their places on the plastic chairs which are arranged in ten rows of ten, facing the podium at the far end. Sensibly they fill up the rows from the middle outwards, so that no one will have to step over another person's legs, thus minimising the risk of accidental physical contact. They aren't bothered whom they sit next to. Among Ghosts there are no friends, no favourites. All are equal in their lack of individuality.

Seated, the Ghosts adopt postures of nonchalance or self-absorption.

Some gaze in fascination at the ceiling, as though they see the work of Michaelangelo up there rather than grey-painted plaster, while others gnaw at their cuticles or scratch repeatedly at nonexistent itches.

The last Ghosts enter, filling up all but a few of the chairs, and the briefing room whispers with the sifting-sand hiss that is the sound of almost a hundred pairs of lungs softly filling and emptying.

At 8.45 precisely Donald Bloom, the Head of Tactical Security, appears. He eases the doors shut behind him and strolls the length of the room to the podium. He is a short man, amiably portly, with close-cropped hair that, apart from a tuft that clings indomitably to the top of the forehead, is confined to the sides and back of his scalp. He sports a white carnation in his buttonhole which he buys fresh every morning from a flower stall on his way to work, and he is carrying a clipboard with a sheet of computer printout attached to it. A folded handkerchief pokes out from the breast pocket of his houndstooth-pattern tweed jacket.

The Ghosts focus their attention on Mr Bloom as he climbs onto the podium. Those at the rear lean forward in their seats in order to hear him better.

Mr Bloom begins the briefing with the traditional *bon mot.*

"Another day, another debt."

There are smiles, smirks. Some shoulders twitch in amusement. Traditions, no matter how time-worn, how trite, are respected here.

Mr Bloom consults his clipboard.

"Right. Nothing much out of the ordinary going on today. Expect lightning sales at 10.00 in Dolls, 10.45 in Travel Goods, 11.30 in Farm Machinery, 12.00 in Ties, 2.00 in Third World Musical Instruments, 3.00 in Religious Paraphernalia, 4.00 in the Funeral Parlour—I can't see that one being particularly popular, but you never know—4.15 in Perennial Christmas, and 4.45 in Trusses And Supports.

"Next, those bogus spree cards we saw so many of last year are back. Technically this is Strategic Security's problem, not ours, but if you see a customer using a spree card you might want to run a check on it. All spree cards issued since Monday have been tagged with new security codes which your Sphinxes have been reformatted to recognise, and everyone who has bought a spree card or won one in the lottery in the past six months has been contacted and asked to return it to us to be replaced, so anyone who isn't using an up-to-date card probably isn't on the level. Use your judgement, and don't be afraid to err on the side of caution.

"Same goes for bogus ID badges. The police tell me they've just busted a forgery ring, but they haven't yet established how long the forgers have been operating and how many of the fake badges, if any, have been sold. So keep an eye out for any employees who don't look like employees. I'm aware that in some cases the badge is the only thing that tells you that an employee works here. You're going to have to trust your instincts on this one.

"The good news is: arrests were up last month. Well done. The bad news is: shrinkage also went up. One's immediate instinct, of course, is to blame shop-floor employees, and I fear a certain amount of pilfering does go on under the counter, despite the fact that we're all account-holders here. I know it's a cliché, but some people don't seem to appreciate that stealing from the store is stealing from themselves.

"However, I have another theory about the shrinkage problem, and like it or not I'm going to share it with you. My theory is that bargain-hunters have learned to take advantage of the confusion of a lightning sale to slip items into their pockets or bags, which is why it's all the more important that Ghosts be on hand during a sale to monitor the crowd. Remember, no matter how hard we try to make it for people to boost from us, they'll always find a way. We are up against mankind's greatest virtue and greatest vice: ingenuity.

"Lastly, I have it on good authority that the Books/Computers dispute is finally, *finally* coming up before the brothers today for arbitration. I know. Sighs of relief all round. It's dragged on for, what, getting on for a year now?"

"A year and a half," someone says.

"A year and a half, thank you. Well, the wheels of administration may turn slowly around here, but turn they do, so with any luck we can look forward to a swift resolution to that disagreeable little contretemps."

Mr Bloom glances down the list on his clipboard, making sure he hasn't missed anything. "Oh yes, Mr Greenaway's greatly-deserved holiday began this morning, so I'm going to be minding the Strategic side of things until he comes back. Lucky me. I feel like I've been put in charge of the gorilla cage at the zoo."

A ripple of laughter.

Mr Bloom consults his clipboard one last time. "And that really *is* it, ladies and gentlemen. Have a good day out there." He concludes with the Ghosts' motto: "Be Silent, Vigilant, Persistent, Intransigent. The Customer Is Not Always Right."

The Ghosts intone the words along with him, a sibilant echo. Then they rise from their seats and begin filing out, shuffling in lines towards the exit, taking care not to touch one another. Mr Bloom steps down from the podium and makes for the doors too, moving slowly so that the Ghosts can assimilate him into their flow.

He is halfway to his office when he senses someone walking behind him at the very limit of his peripheral vision, in what the driver of a car would call the blind-spot. Knowing better than to stop and address the Ghost, Mr Bloom keeps going. It isn't until he is actually sitting down behind the functional, Formica-topped desk in his cramped, windowless office that he looks up to see who has followed him in.

"Frank," says Mr Bloom, both pleased and puzzled, and indicates that Frank should take a seat in the chair on the opposite side of the desk.

"No," says Frank. "Thank you, I'm fine. I can't stop for long. I'm here because I wanted to say—"

But Frank isn't sure how to put it. He scratches the crown of his head and hums to himself.

"Go on, sit down," Mr Bloom insists, but Frank shakes his head emphatically.

"I have to be out on the floor in a moment."

Mr Bloom glances at his watch. "It's 8.49, Frank. It surely can't take more than eleven minutes to talk about whatever you want to talk about, and even if it does, I feel certain that the store will be able to manage without you for a brief while at the beginning of the least busy hour of the day."

"Yes, well, it might, Donald." Frank thinks of his superior as "Mr Bloom" and refers to him as such behind his back, but to his face it is always "Donald". "Look, I'll tell you what, can we do this a bit later? I mean, you're busy right now."

"Well, Greenaway's lot *are* due for their pep-talk in a moment, then I've got to oversee a practice at the firing range, then I've got to brief a new bunch of sales assistants on the basics of security. But I'm never too busy to talk to you, Frank. What is it?"

Frank wants to tell him, but something prevents him, and he thinks it might be fear but he also thinks it might be guilt. He has known Donald Bloom for all of his thirty-three years at Days. There is a bond between them—he wouldn't call it friendship, because the concept has as much meaning for him as the concept of air does for a goldfish in a bowl, but certainly they have developed a mutual respect over thirty-three years, and sometimes Frank has found himself thinking about Mr Bloom when Mr Bloom isn't present, thinking it would be nice if they could perhaps go to a pub together after work and sit and have a drink and a chat, talk about things that have nothing to do with Days or shoplifters or Ghosts, the sort of things people normally talk about, whatever *they* are. He has never plucked up the courage to suggest the idea to Mr Bloom, and anyway, by closing time he is usually too exhausted to want to do anything except head straight home and go to bed, but the fact remains that he and Mr Bloom have a long history of acquaintance, and for some reason Frank feels sure that Mr Bloom is going to be upset by his decision to resign, and he is reluctant to deliver the blow.

The surge of bravado that carried him all the way into Mr Bloom's office has lost momentum, receded, leaving him high and dry—hesitant, confused, embarrassed.

Mr Bloom, with a patient smile, is still waiting for him to say something.

His nerve cracking completely, Frank gets up to leave.

Mr Bloom sighs. "All right then, Frank. Have it your way. The door's always open. OK?"

He gives one last enquiring look at the doorway through which Frank has just exited hastily.

Strange behaviour, he thinks. Frank has always been one of the more level-headed Tactical Security operatives, not to mention one of the best. The constant lurking, the constant suspicion of others—has it finally got to him?

No, Mr Bloom tells himself. He might expect that of any other Ghost, but not Frank. Never Frank.

9

The Seventh Son of a Seventh Son: Traditionally regarded as gifted or lucky.

8.51 a.m.

SONNY'S BED HAS not been slept in. Perch would have been surprised if it had, but hope springs eternal. He tries the bathroom, and there he finds Septimus Day's youngest son not, as expected, curled around the lavatory pedestal but stretched out in the bath, one leg hooked over the side, his head resting awkwardly against the taps. Dried vomit stains encrust the lavatory ring, but Sonny appears to have had the presence of mind to flush his spewings away before crawling, fully dressed, into the tub and passing out. Perch mentally applauds the young master's self-control.

He bends down and rifles Sonny's pockets until he finds his portable intercom. Flipping it open, he keys 4.

"Master Thurston?"

"Perch."

"I rather fear that Master Sonny is not in a fit state to participate in the opening ceremony this morning."

A short silence. Then a sigh. "All right, Perch. Try and get him up and presentable as soon as you can."

"I shall endeavour to do my best, sir."

Perch breaks the connection and sets the intercom down on the lid of the cistern. A trace—just the faintest, remotest scintilla—of contempt can be discerned in his voice as he says, "Very well, Master Sonny. Let's be having you."

He reaches up and makes minute adjustments to the angle of the shower head like an artilleryman sighting his target, until at last he is satisfied that the rosette is aiming directly down at Sonny's face. Then he grasps the handle of the cold tap beside Sonny's cheek, pauses a moment, savouring the sweet anticipation... and turns the water full on.

* * *

8.54 a.m.

"The Afterthought isn't going to be able to make it," Thurston informs his brothers.

"Now there's a surprise," says Wensley.

"Maybe we should have a blow-up Sonny doll made," says Fred. "It could sit there in his chair and say nothing, and that way everybody would be happy."

"Sonny is blood," Mungo admonishes Fred. "Never forget that."

"What Sonny is, is a pain in the arse," Fred replies, unabashed. "He needed what the rest of us got from Dad when we were growing up." He aims a respectful if wary nod towards the portrait of Old Man Day. "Discipline. If Sonny had been indulged a little less when he was a boy and beaten a little more, he might not have turned into the unspeakable über-brat he is now."

"I did the best I could with him," says Mungo. "If anyone is to take the blame for the way he in today, it's me."

"Don't be too hard on yourself," says Thurston. "We all had to be a father to Sonny in one way or another."

"For all Sonny's flaws," says Chas diplomatically, "we must accept him and love him for who he is. He is a son of Septimus Day. He is our brother."

"Don't keep reminding us," says Fred, rolling his eyes.

"I think I could tolerate his behaviour," says Sato, "if only he pulled his weight around here."

"That he is one of the Seven is enough," says Chas.

"I'm with Chas there," says Wensley. "Sonny's an obnoxious so-and-so, but we can't do without him."

"In every rose-bed a nettle grows," Sato murmurs with a hint of genuine bitterness. "In every Eden a serpent hisses."

"It's five to," says Thurston, rapping the table with his knuckles. "We should get started."

The brothers set down their cutlery and push aside their breakfast plates. Wensley wolfs down one last bite of bread and dripping, chewing furiously and swallowing hard. Fred closes the tabloid he is reading and lays it tidily on top of the pile of newspapers. Chas, on instinct, runs his fingers through his hair and discreetly huffs into a cupped hand to check that his breath passes muster.

Silence descends on the Boardroom.

Thurston speaks. "Welcome, my brothers, to another day of custom and commerce, of margins and mark-ups, of retail and revenue, of sales and success, of profit and plenty."

He makes a fist of his left hand, then extends the thumb and forefinger to form a stooping L, across which he places his right index and middle fingers. His brothers, with ostentatious and not entirely convincing solemnity, copy the gesture.

"We are the sons of Septimus Day," Thurston continues. "We are the Seven whose duty it is to manage the store founded by our father and to uphold his philosophy, that if it can be sold, it will be bought, and if it can be bought, it will be sold. That is our task, and we are glad of it."

Now he locks his right forefinger around his left thumb to form an S, bringing his right thumb up and his left middle finger down until they overlap, bisecting the S vertically. His brothers, as before, emulate him. Chas yawns.

"Each of us was born, or induced to be born, on the day whose name he bears, and each raised in the knowledge that an equal seventh share of the responsibility of running the store and the rewards resulting thereof would be his. Each of us is a seventh part of a greater whole, and Mammon willing, long may it remain so."

Fred rolls his eyes at Wensley. Wensley responds with a broad smirk. Mungo glares at them both, but it is clear that he, too, finds this opening ritual, which their father instituted and insisted be maintained after his death, somewhat absurd.

Thurston's hands move again. He points the thumb and forefinger of his left hand upwards at an angle to each other, so that they make a Y-shape with his wrist, and just beneath the webbed stretch of skin where they join he lays his right index and middle fingers horizontally. His brothers follow suit.

"We make the symbols of Sterling and Dollar and Yen," intones Thurston, "three ordinary letters ennobled, raised to a state of grace by that which they represent, to remind us that money transfigures all."

He forms an O with his left thumb and forefinger, and lays his right index and middle fingers vertically over it. His brothers do the same.

"We make the symbol of Days to remind us of the source of our wealth."

As one, the brothers lift away their two right fingers, leaving just the O's.

"And we make an empty circle to remind us that without Days we are nothing."

There follows a moment of silence which is intended for sober contemplation but which, in the event, most of the brothers use to scratch an itch or grab another bite of breakfast.

"Now," says Thurston, "the clock ticks towards opening time once again, and as chairman for the day, the day that bears my name, I would ask you, my brothers, to join me at the switch."

All six brothers rise to their feet and walk with measured tread to the brass panel mounted on the Boardroom wall. Septimus's good eye seems to follow them as they cross the room. The white dot of reflected light the artist put in his cruel black pupil glistens as though the eye is alive.

Thurston unclips the ceramic handle from its rest and, lifting it up with some effort, screws it into the fitting on the crossbar of the knife switch. Each brother then reaches out with his right hand to grasp the handle, which is exactly long enough to accommodate seven male fists. Mungo fills the space for the seventh with his left hand.

"I will pull for two," he says.

Thurston extends his left wrist from his sleeve to consult his watch. Less than a minute to go till nine. The second hand sweeps inexorably round. The brothers stand there patiently, clustered together, their arms radiating from the switch like ribbons from a maypole.

"Fifteen seconds," says Thurston.

Beneath their feet the store waits, like a dead thing about to be reanimated.

"Ten seconds," says Thurston.

And it seems that the knife switch's contacts, through which all the power in the store flows, are crackling in their eagerness to be connected.

"Five," says Thurston. "On my mark. Four."

And the brothers can feel a vibration through the soles of their shoes, a low bass drone like the humming of a million bees.

"Three."

And each fancies he can hear a stunned hush as of a thousand breaths being held.

"Two. One. And *pull!*"

It takes the combined strength of all six of them, with Mungo performing the work of two, to haul the switch down from its upright position. The brothers grunt and gasp as they lever it through horizontal on its squealing hinges, and push and keep pushing until its two brass prongs are nearly touching the contact clips. One more shove, with all the effort they can muster, and the switch slides home.

They let go at once. The lights in the Boardroom dim, then brighten again.

"My brothers," says Thurston, shaking out his aching right arm, "we are open for business."

10

Hebdomad: In some Gnostic systems, a group of seven "divine emanations", each personifying one of the seven then-known planets of the Solar System; collectively, the whole sublunary sphere.

9.00 a.m.

IN ALL SIX hundred and sixty-six departments, the lights go from half strength to full, bathing the counters and displays of merchandise in brilliance.

At each of the four corner entrances the bolts in the doors shoot back and a handful of waiting shoppers swarm forward. The guards, for whom opening time means night shift's end, hold the doors open for them and usher them through, a courtesy that largely goes unremarked. The guards then head indoors themselves.

In the hallways, the lifts to the car parks are summoned down.

Escalators on every floor, frozen in place, start to crawl.

Outside, the window-shoppers, who have been growing increasingly agitated and excited as nine o'clock has neared, sigh with one voice as the curtains in the windows part.

The green LEDs on the closed-circuit cameras that scan every square centimetre of the shop floor come alight. Signals flash along the cables threaded through the spaces between the walls, a fibre-optic web whose thousands of strands radiate throughout the store. All the cables originate in the Eye, a long, low bunker in the Basement where several dozen half-shell clusters of black-and-white monitors occupy all the available wallspace, each cluster attended by a screen-jockey in a wheeled chair. The only light in the chamber comes from the monitors and the screens of the terminals affixed to the chairs' arms: flickering, sickly, blue-grey. The screen-jockeys begin speaking into their headset microphones, at the same time unwrapping Days-brand chocolate bars and popping the ringpulls on cans of Days-brand soft drink.

The two banks of monitors in the Boardroom also come on. Fuzzy bands of static jump down their screens simultaneously, then stabilise and resolve to show different corners of different departments. The images start to change, switching at random between feeds, one after another at seven-second intervals, a hypnotically shifting televisual collage.

Sales assistants take their places, adopting practised expressions of mild, polite interest. Floor-walkers stand ready to greet the first influx of customers. Promotional reps tense, poised to pounce with their samples and testers.

Oblivious to all this activity, the creatures in the Menagerie continue to go about their business, secretly beneath the jungle's green canopy.

11

The Seven Joys of Mary: Namely the Annunciation, the Visitation, the Nativity, the adoration of the Magi, the presentation in the temple, the finding of the lost child, and the Assumption.

9.03 a.m.

THE TAXI PULLS up to the turning circle outside the South-East Entrance, and Linda, imagining a carriage arriving at a stately home, hears the crackle of gravel beneath iron-banded wheels rather than the thrum of tyre-tread on tarmac. As the taxi comes to a halt at the foot of the steps, she extends the Silver to the driver between two fingers, flourishing it beside his left ear. He takes the card and stuffs it into the meter with the air of one who has handled Palladiums and even Rhodiums in his time and for whom a mere Silver holds no mystique. Gordon butts open the door and swings his legs out. Standing up, he straightens a crick out of his spine and turns to look at the window-shoppers, who are already in thrall to the displays.

The taxi driver, tapping keys on the meter, tots up the cost of the fare, plus the pepper spray, plus tax, plus tip, and announces the total, the steepness of which surprises Linda. Reminding herself, however, that she is the co-holder of a Days Silver account, she adopts a serene smile and signs the authorisation slip without a murmur. The taxi driver hands her back the card and wishes her a safe day's shopping, laying emphasis on the word "safe". She thanks him and climbs out into a gust of wind that sways her with its unexpected force. The taxi pulls away.

Bowing her head, Linda mounts the steps, clutching the Silver in both hands. At the top, she divests herself of her taped-up plastic mackintosh and folds it into a neat square package which she stuffs into her handbag. The wind knifes through her blouse, stippling her skin with gooseflesh and making her shiver. Looking round to see what has happened to Gordon, she finds him still staring at the window-shoppers. She trots back down, calling his name.

Gordon does not respond.

"Gor*don*," she urges. "Come *on*."

But Gordon is mesmerised. Whether by the sight of clumps of ragged, hunched, wind-blown human beings sitting or squatting or reclining before the one-storey-high windows along the edge of the building, or by the displays themselves, Linda cannot tell, but as she reaches his side, she finds her eye drawn to the window immediately to the left of the South-East Entrance, and all at once her eagerness to enter the store melts away, to be replaced by rapt, acquiescent fascination.

A window display can attract a crowd anything up to a hundred strong. Some are more popular than others, but even the least well attended regularly draw audiences of two or three dozen. The window-shoppers have a tendency to drift from one to the next as the whim takes them, but certain displays have devoted followers who stay with them from opening time to closing time. There is no rhyme or reason why one display should command greater loyalty than another, since they are all essentially alike. But then, popularity is as much a product of the herd instinct as it is of superior quality.

The display Linda is watching isn't among the best attended but boasts a respectable number of fans. The window-frame forms the proscenium arch to a set dressed to look like the interior of a typical suburban home, comprising a well-appointed living-room-cum-dining-room and, at the top of a flight of stairs, a recessed upper-level master bedroom with bathroom en suite. Through the ground-floor windows can be seen a backdrop diorama of a garden with a neatly-mown lawn ending in flower beds and a fence. The interior of the house is decorated in no particular style, unless an abundant, disorganised profusion of furnishings, ornaments, and gadgets can be called a style. The rooms are crammed with knickknacks, bric-a-brac, baubles, trinkets, and high-tech appliances, in the midst of which a family of four—father, mother, teenage daughter, young son—are eating breakfast.

The four living mannequins, who bear scant familial resemblance to one another, are talking animatedly over their meal. Their conversation is relayed to the window-shoppers through loudspeakers mounted on either side of the window and angled toward the audience. Every utensil they use and every item of clothing they wear has a price tag dangling from it, and the family are careful to refer to the cost and the quality of any product they come into contact with. As Linda watches, the actress playing the mother gets up and goes to the sideboard. There, she slices some oranges in half, first holding up the cutting board so that everyone can have a good look at it (and its price tag), then making a great show of the sharpness of the knife, running the ball of her thumb along the blade and pretending to give herself an accidental nick. Laughing, she sucks at the imaginary wound. Her stage family laugh along with her.

When she finishes cutting the oranges, which she assures her family are the freshest and finest on offer anywhere, she holds up a Days-brand electric orange squeezer, showing off its attractive, ergonomic styling and its easy-to-disassemble, easy-to-clean components. In fact, she liked the squeezer so much she bought two, one in white, one in beige. Her family are equally admiring of both. Son demands to be allowed to squeeze the oranges, and excitedly scampers up to the sideboard and starts turning the orange halves to juice. Mother looks on proudly, saying, "See, it's so straightforward and safe, even a child can use it!"

Meanwhile, Father is complimenting Daughter on her hairdo. She shows him how easy it is to put your hair up in a chignon with a loop device which she just happens to have with her at the breakfast table and which is available exclusively from the Styling Salon Department at Days. Father is fascinated by the simple yet cunning implement. He strokes his thinning crown and says that he would do something similar with *his* hair, if only he had enough. Daughter finds the joke unbelievably hilarious, giggling and slapping her father's forearm in an oh-you! way.

Linda wonders if she might not buy that loop device. She will, if nothing else, visit the Styling Salon Department and bring herself up to date on the latest tools of the trade.

Mother and Son, returning to the table with a jug of delicious, freshly squeezed orange juice, give the other two members of the family looks of amused confusion, which sends Father and Daughter into paroxysms of conspiratorial glee.

Then an elderly neighbour comes in by the front door, stage right, clutching a bottle of pills which she simply *has* to tell the family about. She reminds them of her *terrible* back pains, bending double, clapping a hand to her lower lumbar region and wincing. It used to feel as though someone was stabbing knitting needles into her spine. Mother shakes her head compassionately as she recalls what miseries the poor dear suffered. But then Elderly Neighbour's face brightens. She taps the lid of the bottle of pills and says that after just five days on these, she noticed a significant improvement. Mother can scarcely believe it. "Just five days and you noticed a significant improvement?" Elderly Neighbour nods enthusiastically. She straightens her back. "See? The pain is all gone."

The family—and the window-shoppers—gaze at the bottle of pills as though it contains water from Lourdes. Elderly Neighbour holds it up with the label and Days logo showing, so that no one watching can be under any misapprehension as to where these miracle-working analgaesics can be purchased.

Linda finally manages to tear her gaze away from the scene, only to find her attention roving to the other displays, each of which is equally absorbing in its own way. Families, couples, flat-sharing friends, holidaymakers at a tropical resort, women at a beauty parlour, workers in an office, fitness enthusiasts in a gym, schoolchildren in a classroom, swimsuit-clad sunbathers basking on a narrow strip of sand and bronzed by a battery of arc-lights, thespians all, theatrically sing the praises of the items of merchandise that surround them in a cornucopic clutter.

Up until at least the age of eight, Linda used to think that the people in the displays lived there all the time. Never mind that her mother insisted that they were just actors and actresses, Linda remained firmly convinced that when the people inside the windows walked off-stage they carried on being who they were on another hidden part of the set—a belief which survived long after the truth about Santa Claus and the Tooth Fairy was out.

Remembering this childhood misapprehension now, she feels both affection for the naive creature she was and amazement that, given her upbringing, she had any illusions left at all by the time she was eight. But then Days has always been a magical place for Linda. Every Advent, she and her mother would make the pilgrimage here to see the Christmas displays. On cold December afternoons, wrapped up in so many layers of clothing that she could hardly move her limbs, she would hold her mother's hand tight as they strolled from one window to the next. It was impossible for them to circumnavigate the building completely, ten kilometres being much too far for a child to walk in a single afternoon, but every year, as Linda grew taller and stronger, they would cover a little more of the distance than previously, and as they walked they would stop at any window that caught their eye and gaze in at a wintry outdoors set with leafless trees and drifts of fake snow or a cosy, firelit interior scene where the living mannequins would be busy decorating the hearth or wrapping gifts or singing carols, scenes of domestic harmony utterly unlike the sullen Christmases at Linda's house, with her father stomping and grumbling like Ebeneezer Scrooge for the entire festive season and moaning at Linda's mother whenever she tentatively broached the subject of having relatives over for lunch on Christmas Day or getting Linda the bicycle they had been promising her year after year, calling her a sentimental old cow or a swindling bitch.

Those trips to Days are among the few happy memories Linda has of her childhood. Her mother, no doubt because she was free of her husband's debilitating influence, would talk and laugh with a brightness and lightness in her voice Linda never heard at any other time of the year, and as the two of them rode the bus home afterwards through the deep-blue dark, they would discuss which window was the best and how this year's displays compared with last year's and what might have been in the windows they were unable to reach and what novelties they might look forward to seeing next year. And those were the only times that Linda could reassert her claim that one day she would have an account at Days and receive nothing from her mother in reply but a slow, sweet, and, in retrospect, sad smile.

"Gordon," Linda says softly, and her husband starts and blinks, unaccustomed to hearing his name spoken with such tenderness. "Let's go in, shall we?"

She slips her hand into his and tugs him toward the steps. She wishes her mother was alive to see her now, her mother who never had faith in anyone because she was never allowed to have faith in herself. She wishes her mother could see how believing in yourself makes anything possible.

They mount the steps and pass through the entrance doors. The hallway makes Linda gasp. Photographs she has seen have not prepared her for the real thing. Bustling with customers. The lifts disgorging new arrivals. The lofty ceiling. The sea-green marble floor. The chandelier. The mosaic of precious stones, too beautiful to pass by. The Trivetts pause at its perimeter, and Linda gazes down in awe at the twin semicircles of opal and onyx.

"Wish I'd brought a hammer and chisel with me," says Gordon.

Linda tells her husband not to be vulgar. That's precisely the sort of thing a Days customer *doesn't* say.

A woman approaches them. Her jacket and skirt are a matching dollar green, and around her neck she wears a silk scarf with tiny Days logos printed on it, pinned at her throat with a cloisonné Days-logo brooch.

Her hair, Linda notes, is hennaed. It doesn't match her dark eyebrows, and anyway, no one's hair is naturally that red. A skilful job, nonetheless, and the way the woman wears it scraped back offsets the roundness of her face, giving her the appropriate air of authority and efficiency. The ID badge attached to her breast pocket says that her name is Kimberly-Anne. Below her name is her employee barcode.

"Lovely, isn't it?" says Kimberly-Anne, gesturing at the jewel mosaic. If her smile were any brighter you would need sunglasses to look at it.

Linda nods.

"Is this your first visit to Days?"

"It is," says Linda. She is too entranced by the floor mosaic to be annoyed that her and Gordon's inexperience is apparently so obvious to everyone.

"Then let me tell you a little bit about finding your way around the store. First of all, you'll need this." Kimberly-Anne hands them a booklet from the small stack in her hand. "It contains maps to all six floors, showing every department and indicating where the cloakrooms, lifts, escalators, and restaurants are. Usually we advise newcomers to plan out a route beforehand so that they can visit all the departments they need to with less risk of getting lost, but you look like intelligent people, you probably won't have to do that."

Linda graciously thanks her for the compliment.

"The next thing you have to consider is something to put your purchases in. We have a range of options available. Would you care to accompany me?"

Before either of the Trivetts can answer, Kimberly-Anne is striding off in the direction of the motorised carts and shopping trolleys. Linda turns to Gordon, he shrugs, and they follow her.

Kimberly-Anne leads them to one of the motorised carts, an electric buggy that seats two, with a large cubic volume of open boot space at the rear. She waves her hands over it like a conjuror's assistant demonstrating the apparatus for the next trick.

"A cart is the most comfortable and convenient way of getting around Days," she says, "and is complimentary to all Osmium and Rhodium customers."

"That's not us," says Linda, flattered by the implicit assumption that she and Gordon look like the sort of people who could hold one of the two highest accounts.

"Then for a small hire-charge—"

"We don't need one," says Gordon. He looks at his wife. "Well, we don't."

Kimberly-Anne indicates the phalanxes of gleaming wire trolleys. "Then how about a trolley instead? Every wheel guaranteed to turn without wobbling or sticking, and complimentary to all Palladium and Iridium customers."

"That's not us either," Linda admits, a touch ruefully. "But it might be a good idea to hire one."

"Linda," says Gordon under his breath, "we haven't been here five minutes, you've already made a large dent in our account, and now you want to make a larger one. I thought you said we were going to be careful."

Linda vaguely recalls saying something to that effect, once, before their application was accepted. "Fair enough, the taxi was an extravagance," she replies, "but a shopping trolley is a necessity."

"It'll only encourage us to buy more than we can afford."

To appease her husband, Linda relents. "How about one of those?" she asks Kimberly-Anne, pointing to some tall stacks of wire handbaskets.

"Of course," says Kimberly-Anne. "Free to anyone with a Platinum or Gold account."

"Platinum or Gold."

"That's right."

"Not Silver."

Kimberly-Anne's smile loses a degree of candlepower. "Not Silver, no. Silver account-holders may hire a handbasket for—"

"You mean we have to pay to use a basket?" exclaims Gordon.

Kimberly-Anne flinches but quickly recovers her composure and her smile, although the latter is perceptibly dimmer now.

"Silver and Aluminium account-holders *are* expected to pay a nominal charge in return for the use of any of the available carrying devices," she says.

"It won't kill us to hire a basket, Gordon," Linda insists. "We can afford it."

"That's not the point. They shouldn't be charging us for something that should by rights be free. That's extortion. Daylight robbery."

"Gordon, the Day brothers don't run Days for the fun of it. This isn't a charitable concern. This is a business, and the purpose of a business is to turn a profit. Isn't that so, Kimberly-Anne?"

Kimberly-Anne nods warily, not certain if it is wise to agree with one customer at the expense of another, even when the other customer is obviously in the wrong.

"There's a difference between turning a profit and ripping people off," grumbles Gordon. "Come on. We'll do without."

He is heading for the arches before Linda can stop him. She apologises to Kimberly-Anne, whose smile has by now been reduced to a feeble one-amp flicker, and hurries after her husband.

Catching up with him, she hisses, "You embarrassed me awfully back there, Gordon."

Gordon does not reply, merely strides purposefully up to an arch and waits for her to join him there with their card.

An obliging guard shows Linda how to insert the Silver into the wall-mounted terminal and gain admittance. Linda is so annoyed with Gordon that neither the sight of their names appearing on the terminal screen (confirmation that they belong here) nor the sight of the bars retracting to let them through thrills her. Luckily, her anger also means that she forgets about the pepper spray in her handbag and is thus spared the anxiety she would otherwise have felt over smuggling it through the metal detectors.

Then they are on the shop floor.

12

Covetousness: Another of the Seven Deadly Sins.

9.05 a.m.

STILL SMARTING OVER his cowardly behaviour in Mr Bloom's office, Frank takes a lift from the Basement to the Red Floor, then rides a double-helix strand of escalators, zigzagging up through the levels. As one escalator after another lifts him higher and higher, a vague, dismal dread settles in his stomach. The prospect of the day ahead, with its tedium, its irritations and its unpredictable dangers, is a gloomy one, scarcely alleviated by the knowledge that for him it is going to be the last of its kind. His thoughts start to clot like bad milk, and he literally has to shake his head to disperse them. Eight hours, he tells himself. Less, counting breaks. Less than eight hours of this life to go, and then he is a free man. He can grit his teeth and endure the job for another eight hours, can't he?

On a whim he gets off at the Blue Floor. There is never any pattern to Frank's working day once the store opens except the timing of his breaks, which are staggered with those of his fellow Ghosts so that at least eighty per cent of the Tactical Security workforce is out on the shop floor at any given moment. He travels at random, letting impulse and the ebb and flow of events direct him. The difference between the hours leading up to opening time and the hours after is the same as the difference between waking thought and dreaming—a matter of control. Frank surrenders himself to the random.

Finding himself in Taxidermy, he wanders through to Dolls, from there to Classic Toys, and from there to Collectable Miniatures, staying with a knot of customers, then latching on to a lone browser, then hovering for a while beside an open cabinet of temptingly pocketable hand-painted thimbles.

He keeps an eye on customers carrying large shoulder-bags, customers with rolled-up newspapers clutched under their arms, customers with long coats on, customer pushing prams with blanket-swaddled toddlers on board. They could all be perfectly innocent. They could all be as guilty as sin. His job is to hope for the former but always suspect the latter.

He watches a customer engage a sales assistant in conversation, and immediately he starts looking around for an accomplice. It is an old pro trick. While one shoplifter diverts the sales assistant's attention, his partner makes the boost. In this instance, however, it seems that the customer is on his own, and is genuinely interested in some Meissen figurines.

Then a pair of Burlingtons swan past, and Frank moves off silently in their wake.

The Burlingtons are a cult of spoilt teenage boys who parade their parents' wealth like a badge of honour, wearing the glaringly expensive designer trainers, the crisp white socks, the tight black trousers, and the gold-moiré blouson jackets that are the unofficial uniform of their rich-kid tribe. These two, it transpires, are on the hunt for rare baseball cards, and Frank dogs them so closely that he could, if he wanted to, raise his hand and stroke the fuzz of their close-shaved hair, half of which has been dyed black, half bleached blond.

The Burlingtons lead him into Showbusiness Souvenirs, where he detaches himself from them in order to circulate among the displays of stage costumes, old props, production stills, foyer cards, autographed publicity shots of long-faded stars, and crumbling movie and concert posters preserved behind clear perspex.

The centrepiece of Showbusiness Souvenirs is a locked, reinforced-glass case that holds, among other things, a pair of incontinence pants soiled by an internationally renowned rock'n'roll star during his drug-sodden twilight years; the polyp removed from a former US president's lower intestine; the skull of a universally despised yet unfathomably successful blue-collar comedian; the steering wheel from the car fatally crashed by a screen legend; a blunted bullet retrieved from a dictator's shattered head by a souvenir-seeking soldier at the climax of a successful *coup d'etat*; the stub of the last cigar ever smoked by an unusually long-lived revolutionary leader; a specimen of blood extracted post mortem from the body of a notoriously bibulous politician and decanted into a phial disrespectfully labelled "100% Proof"; a preserving jar containing the aborted foetus of the love-child begotten by an actress and a prominent member of the clergy; a razor-thin cross-section of a famous theoretical physicist's brain sandwiched between two plates of glass; and a framed arrangement of pubic-hair clippings from various porn-film artistes. All of the above items are accompanied by certificates testifying to their authenticity.

A ponytailed man in a navy blue suit is loitering beside this cabinet of curiosities, and at the sight of him Frank's nape hairs start to prickle, as they did at the sight of the girl on the train.

There is nothing intrinsically suspicious about what the ponytailed man is doing. Plenty of people linger over the collection, gazing at the rare and expensive mortal mementoes with disgust or fascination or a ghoulish combination of the two. And he isn't exhibiting any of the tics and mannerisms that usually prefigure an act of store-theft. His casual air seems genuine. He isn't aiming surreptitious glances at the sales assistants or other customers, one of the "flagging" signs Frank was trained to recognise. His breathing is controlled and steady. But Frank doesn't always go by visual clues alone.

Frank would be surprised if over the course of his thirty-three-year career he *hadn't* developed an instinct about shoplifters. In the same way that older deep-sea fishermen can somehow sense where the big shoals are going to be and experienced palaeontolgists sometimes seem to know that a patch of ground will yield fossils even before the first spade has struck soil, Frank can identify a potential shoplifter almost without looking. It is as if thieving thoughts send out ripples in the air like a stone cast into a pond, subtle fluctuations which he has become attuned to and which set alarm bells ringing in his subconscious. It is not the most reliable of talents, and has been known to mislead him, but as a rough guide it is right far more frequently than it is wrong.

The closer he gets to the ponytailed man, the deeper his conviction grows that the man is planning to steal something. Possibly not from this department, and certainly not from the case in front of him, not unless he is carrying a sledgehammer or a set of skeleton keys, but soon, very soon. The man is pausing here to prepare himself mentally, turning his intentions over and over in his head. Outwardly he betrays not the slightest sign of anxiety or anticipation. A professional.

When the ponytailed man finally moves away from the glass case, Frank falls in behind him and follows him like a silent second shadow.

They proceed out of Showbusiness Souvenirs in tandem, the suspect unsuspecting of his pursuer. Their course takes them away from the centre of the building, and the further from the atrium they go, the less frequented, less splendid, and less brightly illuminated the departments become. Soon they arrive at the dim and dusty perimeter departments known as the Peripheries.

A kind of commercial vortex holds sway on the floors of Days: the closer you get to the centre of the building, the more popular the departments become. The most heavily in-demand departments with the fattest profit margins are clustered around the tiered hoops overlooking the Menagerie, while, at the opposite end of the retail scale, the departments that constitute the Peripheries are consigned to the far-flung edges by the slightness of their sales figures. The only exception to this rule is the Red Floor, which, being the one floor every customer has no choice but to visit, consists of nothing but in-demand departments.

Conditions in the Peripheries are commensurate with their lowly status. You might expect them to enjoy windows and a view to compensate for their remoteness and for the fact that they are accessible from only three adjacent departments—in the case of those at the corners of the building, only two—instead of the usual four, but though the Peripheries possess exterior walls, the exterior walls are solid. No windows on the shop floor of Days means no outside world to distract the customers within from their shopping. The only natural light to be found anywhere in the store enters via the clear half of the dome, a semicircular gift of sunshine to nourish the chlorophyll of the Menagerie.

The Peripheries specialise in commodities that are obscure, exotic, inessential, or just plain arcane. Some of the items on offer are of great value, but buyers are few and far between, hence trade is always slow and sales figures always low.

Quiet, intense, obsessive men and women, all experts in their particular fields, staff the counters here, and so absorbed are they in their daily round of cataloguing recondite items of stock and rearranging merchandise according to abstruse personal systems that they barely notice when the ponytailed man passes. When Frank ghosts by a few paces behind, his rubber-soled shoes padding softly on the carpeted floor, they fail to notice at all.

Through Used Cardboard, through Occult Paraphernalia, through Vinyl & 8-Track, through Beer Bottles, the quiet, leisurely chase continues. If the ponytailed man pauses for a moment to inspect some piece of merchandise, Frank pauses to inspect a piece of merchandise, too. If the ponytailed man slackens or quickens his pace, Frank slackens or quickens his. If the ponytailed man scratches his earlobe or purses his lips, Frank finds himself reflexively copying the action. He becomes the ponytailed man's doppelgänger, matching him move for move, gesture for gesture, in split-second-delayed symmetry.

At one point, in Nazi Memorabilia, the ponytailed man glances behind him, and catches sight of a man dressed as smartly as you would expect a Days customer to be dressed, a man intently inspecting a display of Luftwaffe uniform insignia, a man in every respect unremarkable, unmemorable. A second after he has glimpsed Frank's face, the ponytailed man has forgotten it. When, a department later, he happens to look over his shoulder and catch sight of Frank again, he doesn't even register that this is the very same person he saw before.

On they go, shadower and shadowee, possible perpetrator and Ghost, until they reach Cigars & Matchbooks.

As the ponytailed man passes through the connecting passageway to this particular department, there is an all but imperceptible stiffening of his spine, and Frank knows in his gut that this is where the suspect is going to make his play.

He utters a subvocal cough to activate his Eye-link.

Eye, says a male screen-jockey.

Hubble.

Mr Hubble! What can I do for you?

The connection is so clear that Frank can hear other voices in the background, keyboards rattling, the trundle of chair-wheels across linoleum, a muted but urgent warble of activity underpinned by the cicada whine emitted by hundreds of heated cathode-ray tubes—the ambient hubbub of the Eye leaking through into his ear.

I'm on Blue, trailing a possible into Cigars & Matchbooks.

Cigars & Matchbooks? Cor, strike a light, guv! The screen-jockey giggles at his own joke. Eye employees and their tiresome sense of humour are aspects of the job Frank will definitely feel no nostalgia for in his retirement.

He's a white male. About a metre eighty. Medium build, I'd say seventy-five to eighty kilos. Early thirties. Suit, tie. Ponytail. Two small hoops in right earlobe.

Hang on. A ferocious tapping of keys. Cigars & Matchbooks, Cigars & Matchbooks... OK, got him. Corporate non-conformist type.

If you say so. I think he's a professional. I don't recognise the face, but that doesn't mean a thing.

Early bird, isn't he?

The early bird catches the worm unawares. Or so he hopes.

Nice one, Mr Hubble. That was almost funny.

Eye, please just get on with what you're supposed to be doing.

Actually, says the screen-jockey with a school-playground inflection, I've already triangulated him.

A quick upward glance confirms this. The security camera above Frank's head is locked on to the ponytailed man, following his every movement. In another corner of the ceiling a second camera also has a fix on him. Swivelling on their armatures, the two cameras track his progress like a pair of accusing fingers.

I can't see you yet, Mr Hubble, the screen-jockey adds.

I'm about ten metres behind.

Oh yes. It's so easy to miss you lot. Want me to start recording?

Yes, I do.

Okey-doo. Smile and say cheese.

Please, says Frank, striving to inject a note of impatience into his ventriloqual drone.

Sor-ree, says the screen-jockey, and mutters to a colleague, off-mic but loud enough for Frank to hear, I've got old Hubble Bubble, Toil and Trouble.

His colleague offers a sympathetic groan.

Frank says nothing, and two seconds later the short-wave automatically cuts the connection in order to conserve its tiny lithium cell.

The Cigars portion of Cigars & Matchbooks resembles the smoking room of a gentlemen's club, with magazine-strewn coffee tables and green-shaded lamps, dark-framed etchings on the oak-panelled walls and bookcases lined with old volumes of the kind bought by the metre. Lounging on the buttoned-leather furniture, their feet resting on footstools, customers—predominantly male—make their selections from humidors held open for them by liveried sales assistants. Some, unable to wait until they get home to sample their purchases, have lit up and are sitting back contentedly puffing out plumes of smoke, idly leafing through a periodical or admiring the shine on their toecaps.

The Matchbooks portion, which once boasted the floorspace of an entire Violet Periphery department to itself, now occupies a partitioned-off area roughly a tenth of the size it used to enjoy. When the Day brothers took over the Violet Floor for themselves, Matchbooks was merged with—though perhaps the correct phrase should be absorbed by—Cigars, and in order to adapt to its reduced circumstances, most of its existing stock was sold off and its staff whittled down to one. It could have been worse. Those displaced Violet departments that could not be found a natural lodging on a lower floor, which constituted the majority, were simply closed down and deleted from existence.

The smells of cigar smoke, cardboard, and sulphur mingle and tingle in Frank's nostrils as he trails the ponytailed man towards the burnished mahogany rolltop desk that serves as Matchbooks' sales counter. Along the way the ponytailed man pauses to admire several of the matchbooks mounted in clear vinyl wallets on the partition walls. He's a cool one all right; so relaxed and confident Frank could almost believe that this is one of the occasions when his instinct has let him down.

Except the man's eyes are unfocused. He doesn't look at the matchbooks he is supposed to be examining, only goes through the motions of looking, his thoughts elsewhere. Another giveaway sign, obvious if you have been trained to recognise it.

At last he approaches the mahogany desk. The sole remaining Matchbooks sales assistant is a man whose white hair and sallow, wrinkled features put him somewhere in the same age bracket as Frank. The name on his ID badge is Moyle, and at present his attention is absorbed by the matchbook he is examining through the jeweller's loupe screwed into his right eye-socket. The ponytailed man ahems to attract his attention. He ahems again, and this time Moyle notices. He looks up, the loupe dropping expertly into a waiting cupped hand.

"Sir," he says. "How may I help you?"

"I'm looking for a birthday present for a friend of mine. He's into matchbooks."

"Well, you've certainly come to the right place. What did you have in mind?"

"I'm entirely in your hands."

"Avid collector is he, this friend of yours?"

"Oh yes, very."

"Then I suggest the easiest thing to do would be for you to name a price range, and I can tell you what we have that fits the bill."

The ponytailed man mentions a figure that causes Moyle to raise his chin and purse his lips in a silent whistle.

"A most generous birthday present, sir. A close friend of yours, I take it?"

"Very close."

"Well then, let's see what we've got, shall we?" Moyle turns to the baize-covered board behind him to which are pinned several dozen more of those vinyl wallets containing matchbooks of various colours and sizes—prime specimens all. He plucks three down.

"This is no less than a Purple Pineapple Club matchbook," he begins, holding the first wallet up delicately by the corner for the ponytailed man to view its contents at close quarters. "As your friend will no doubt be able to tell you, the Purple Pineapple Club was shut down three days before it was due to open when the principal member of the backing consortium filed for bankruptcy and took his own life. Fifty specimen promotional matchbooks were printed up, but only about half that number are believed to be currently in circulation. Note the use of purple metallic ink for the logo and the cheerful cartoon illustration."

"All of your matchbooks have had the matches removed."

"Oh, sir, one never leaves the matches attached. Oh no."

"Why not?"

"For one thing, the phosphorus discolours the card. Mainly, though, it's because matchbooks are better stored and displayed flat."

"I didn't know that. All right, how much?"

Moyle picks up a scanning wand from the desk and runs its winking red tip over the barcode sticker attached to the back of the vinyl wallet. The price appears on the readout of the credit register linked to the scanning wand by a coil of flex. He draws the ponytailed man's attention to the figure.

"I see," says the ponytailed man. "Anything slightly more expensive?"

"More expensive," says Moyle, with poorly disguised eagerness. "Well, there's this one." He picks up another of the wallets. "A special edition released to coincide with the official coming-out of a member of the royal family. Note the coat-of-arms motif featuring a pink crown and an entwined pair of human bodies. Rampant, as a heraldry expert might say. The story behind this one goes that the royal in question got cold feet at the last minute, hence the public proclamation of his sexual proclivities was never made, but a small number of the special edition matchbooks were pocketed by an equerry and thence made their way into the hands of private collectors. Naturally the palace press office denied there ever was going to be a coming-out announcement of any description and implied that the matchbooks must have been issued by an anti-royalist faction in order to discredit the royal family."

"Like they need discrediting."

"As you say, sir. Regardless, palace-authorised or not, a tiny quantity of these matchbooks exist, and the story attached lends them a certain novelty, don't you think?"

"I don't suppose there's any way of guaranteeing its provenance?"

"None at all, I'm afraid, sir. That's the trouble with what we call curio matchbooks."

"Pity. My friend's a stickler for provenance."

"All the best phillumenists are."

Frank, hovering close by, observing all this unnoticed, makes a quick check of the security cameras. Every one he can see is trained on the ponytailed man. Good.

Eye?

Still here, Mr Hubble.

Is there a guard on standby?

I've alerted one. He's two departments away. Name of Miller.

Well done.

You see? We're not all incompetent idiots down here.

I wish I could believe that.

There is a spurt of sarcastic laughter. You're on form this morning, Mr Hubble!

Thinking thunderclouds, Frank returns his attention to the scene being played out at the counter.

"What about that one?" says the ponytailed man, pointing to the third matchbook Moyle has selected.

"Ah, this one. The Raj Tandoori, an upscale Indian restaurant. First printing. Lovely design but, as you can see, there was a typographical error. 'The Rat Tandoori.' Unfortunate oversight or malicious printer's prank? Who can say? Either way, the restaurateur felt, understandably, that the association of rodent and food might not encourage repeat custom and ordered a new batch printed up and the originals pulped. A few, however, survived. Much sought-after. Almost unique. But there is some slight damage to the striking pad, as you may have noticed, and the cover hinge has a tiny split in it."

"May I take it out and have a look anyway?"

"Certainly. Just be careful with it, I beg of you."

"Of course."

The ponytailed man slips the matchbook out of its wallet and looks it over. Moyle watches with a concern that is not wholly proprietorial, which is almost that of a parent for a child, his hands poised to catch the matchbook should it happen to drop, but the customer seems to know how to handle precious artifacts such as this, holding it by the corners only, touching it with his fingertips alone, treating it with the kind of awed respect usually accorded a venerable, crumbling religious relic.

Satisfied that the man isn't about to damage the matchbook, Moyle turns back to the baize-covered board. Tapping a thumb against his lips and humming, he casts an eye over the stock, then reaches up decisively and unpins two more wallets, which he lays in front of his customer just as the ponytailed man is resealing the "Rat Tandoori" matchbook into its wallet.

"Interested?" Moyle enquires.

"Not in that one, no."

"Any particular reason why, might I ask?"

"My friend has a penchant for the immaculate."

"For a mint-condition 'Rat Tandoori' original you're looking at a price considerably higher than the admittedly handsome sum you mentioned, sir, but I could try to track down one in slightly better health if you like. One's bound to turn up at an auction sooner or later."

"Bound to," agrees the ponytailed man. "But in that case, I'd rather buy it myself and avoid your outrageous mark-up."

"Then I'm afraid neither of these will suit you," says Moyle, puzzled by his customer's sudden bluntness.

"They both look a bit tatty," the ponytailed man agrees, glancing briefly at the new offerings.

"Remember, we're dealing with ephemera here," Moyle points out. "The appeal of matchbooks as collector's items is their very lack of durability. I'm sure that's the way your friend feels about them."

"I'm beginning to think I'd be better off spending my money on something else for my friend," the ponytailed man says. "Thanks for your time anyway, but no sale." He turns to go.

Moyle's shrug doesn't adequately hide his obvious dismay.

Eye?

Yup.

Get Miller to intercept. He's heading back out of the Peripheries into Oriental Weaponry.

He boosted? I didn't see a thing.

Let's hope one of the cameras did.

Cunning devil, thinks Frank as he dogs the ponytailed man out of the department.

9.19 a.m.

The ponytailed man has stopped to admire a pair of *katana* in beautiful black-lacquered scabbards when a hand grabs his upper arm, fingers digging into his biceps with a polite but insistent pressure.

"Excuse me, sir."

The ponytailed man looks round into a crinkled, saturnine face into which are embedded a pair of eyes the colour of rainy twilight. He fails to recognise a man he has seen at least twice already in the last quarter of an hour.

"Tactical Security," says Frank. "Would you mind if I had a word?"

The ponytailed man immediately starts looking for an exit, and in doing so catches sight of a security guard ambling towards them. The guard is over two metres tall and as broad at the waist as he is at the shoulders, packed densely into his nylon dollar-green uniform like minced meat into a sausage skin.

The ponytailed man tenses. With a weary inward sigh Frank realises he is going to make a run for it.

"Please, sir. It'll be so much better for everyone if you stay put."

Miller, the guard, is still ten metres away when the ponytailed man wrenches his arm out of Frank's grasp and makes his bid for freedom. Miller moves to intercept him, and the man blindly dashes right, running headlong into a rice-paper screen on which has been mounted an array of *shuriken*. The screen folds around him and collapses, and the ponytailed man collapses with it. Throwing stars fly off in all directions, spinning like large steel snowflakes.

Miller rushes forward, but the ponytailed man scrambles to his feet, snarling and brandishing one of the *shuriken* like a knife.

"Get away! Get away from me!"

Shrugging, Miller raises his hands and backs off a few paces.

"False arrest!" the ponytailed man shouts. "I haven't done anything! False arrest!"

A small crowd of spectators swiftly gathers.

"I haven't stolen anything!" The man gesticulates frantically with the throwing star.

Frank is by Miller's side. "Can you take him?" he asks.

"Course I can," Miller growls. "When I was inside, I used to kick seven shades of shit out of blokes like him all the time. Just for fun."

"What about the throwing star?"

"He doesn't know what he's doing with it. You get 'im on disc?"

Eye?

I'm searching, I'm searching. Hang on. Yeah, there it is. Shit. That was fast.

Frank nods to Miller, and the guard breaks into a huge, humourless grin.

He moves swiftly for a man of his bulk. Three brisk strides, and he is inside the arc of the ponytailed man's arm. Before the man can bring his weapon around, Miller's hand flashes out, encloses the fist holding the *shuriken*, and squeezes. The ponytailed man shrieks as the star's points pierce his palm. He falls to his knees, and Miller twists his arm behind his back, still squeezing. Blood streaks the ponytailed man's wrist and smears the back of his jacket. He tries to writhe his way out of the hold Miller has him in, but the guard only tightens his grip on the *shuriken*-wielding hand, forcing the throwing star's points further into the flesh of the ponytailed man's palm until they grind bone. The man bends double, snivelling with the pain, unable to think about anything except the pain, the riveting, sickening pain.

Frank has his Sphinx out. He hunkers down beside the agonised shoplifter and recites the Booster's Blessing.

"For the record, sir," he says, "at 9.18 a.m. you were spotted removing an item from the Cigars & Matchbooks Department without having purchased it and with no obvious intent to purchase it. For this offence, the penalty is immediate expulsion from the premises and the irrevocable cancellation of all account facilities. If you wish to take the matter to court, you may do so. Bear in mind, however, that we have the following evidence on disk."

Frank holds the Sphinx's screen up before the man's face and the Eye duly transmits a recording of the theft.

It was a skilful piece of sleight of hand, one no doubt practised countless times until it was honed to perfection. While Moyle's back was turned, the ponytailed man whipped out a duplicate of the "Rat Tandoori" matchbook from his pocket, simultaneously palming the original into a slit cut in the lining of his jacket. It was the duplicate he was reinserting into the vinyl wallet when Moyle turned back to the counter, and were it not for Frank the substitution would most likely have gone unnoticed until the day a genuine matchbook aficionado with money to burn chose to add that particular rarity to his collection.

The crime is replayed on the Sphinx's screen in two short clips from two different angles. The first clip shows the fake matchbook coming out but not the real one going in. The second leaves little room for doubt, although, even when slowed to half-speed, the exchange seems to take place in the blink of an eye. Much as he hates to, Frank has to admire the shoplifter's dexterity. Just as he thought: a professional.

"Do you understand what I'm showing you?"

Frank isn't certain the ponytailed man was looking, but when he repeats the question, the man nods and says yes.

"Good. Now, I need to see your card."

"Come on, you, on your feet," says Miller, hoisting the ponytailed man upright. "Get your card out. Slowly. No tricks."

His face is livid and streaked with tears but the ponytailed man's eyes are still defiant as he reaches into his inside pocket with his uninjured hand and produces a Silver.

"Cheap sod," mutters Miller. "Couldn't score better than that?"

"Fuck off," says the ponytailed man, without too much enthusiasm.

Having extracted the *shuriken* from the ponytailed man's palm, the guard proceeds to handcuff him. Frank, meanwhile, runs the card through his Sphinx. Central Accounts has no record of the card being reported as stolen, but when the account-holder's picture appears on the Sphinx's screen it doesn't take Frank long to deduce that the man standing in front of him is not Alphonse Ng, aged 62, a balding, jowly, pugnacious-looking Korean.

"How much did you pay this man Ng?" he asks the shoplifter.

"I don't know what you're talking about."

"And how long did he agree to wait before reporting it missing? A week? Two weeks?"

The man does not answer.

"OK, fine. We'll have a word with Mr Ng, see what he says."

But Frank and the shoplifter both know what Mr Ng is going to say. He is going to say either that he lost the card or that it was stolen from him, and he will express delight at having it back, and he will swear to look after it more carefully in the future, and nothing further will be done about the matter. The store's policy is always to reunite cards with their owners, whatever the circumstances, no questions asked. To do otherwise would not make commercial sense.

"Now," Frank tells the ponytailed man, "the guard is going to take you downstairs for processing and eviction. If at any time you attempt to resist him or to escape, he is within his rights to subdue you using any means necessary, up to and including lethal force. Do you understand this, sir?"

The shoplifter gives a short, weary nod.

"Very good. Don't come back."

Yet even as he utters those last three words, Frank knows it is useless. The shoplifter will be back just as soon as his hand heals, if not sooner. The ponytail will be gone, as will the earrings and the blue suit, and he will be disguised—as a Burlington, perhaps, or a foreign diplomat, or a priest (it has happened)—with yet another black-market card in his pocket and yet another legerdemain tactic for obtaining goods without payment. If only the Days administration didn't cling to their belief that permanent banishment from the store is suitable punishment for any crime committed on the premises and didn't refuse to prosecute shoplifters through the courts, professionals like this one wouldn't exist and Frank wouldn't feel as if he is trying to bale out a leaky boat with a sieve. As it is, all he can do is make the arrests, have the thieves thrown out, and catch them at it again the next time. The most he can hope for is that one person in the now-dispersing crowd of onlookers, just one, having seen how shoplifters are treated when they are caught, will think twice before succumbing to the temptation in the future. It's a slim hope, but what is the alternative?

None of this, of course, will matter after today, and that is why Frank is calmer than he might have been as he pulls back the flap of the shoplifter's jacket and fishes out the purloined matchbook from the slit in the lining. It gladdens him to think that tomorrow he will no longer have to be stoically playing his part in this cyclical exercise in futility; that tomorrow he will be free.

9.25 a.m.

"Oh my," says Moyle. "Oh dear." He holds up the two matchbooks side by side for comparison, switching them over, switching them over again. "That's a skilful piece of forgery, that is, and no mistake. He must have had it made up from the picture in the catalogue. A perfect copy right down to the split in the cover hinge. You can see why I was fooled, can't you?"

"Yes, I can," says Frank, "but what I can't see is why you turned your back on him. That was negligent in the extreme."

"He seemed legitimate."

"They *all* seem legitimate, Mr Moyle."

"True. And you know, now that I think about it, the way he suddenly changed his mind about buying a matchbook *was* rather odd, wasn't it? It was as if he couldn't wait to get out of here."

"He couldn't."

"Well, you've caught him, that's the main thing," Moyle says. "You've caught him and I get my Raj Tandoori original back. All's well that ends well, eh?" He raises his eyebrows hopefully.

"It'll have to go down in my report that you turned your back on him."

Moyle nods slowly to himself, digesting this information. "Yes, I thought as much. That's the sort of mistake that can cost a chap his job, isn't it?"

"I'm sure it won't come to that. A few retirement credits docked. A slap on the wrist."

Moyle gives a resigned laugh. "That I can live with, I suppose. The main thing is that you recovered the matchbook, for which I and all other *genuine* phillumenists thank you, Mr Hubble, from the bottom of our hearts."

"Just doing my job."

Moyle carefully slots the genuine matchbook into its wallet and tosses the replica contemptuously into the waste-paper basket.

"It must seem rather odd to you, my interest in these little cardboard trifles," he says with a self-deprecating smile. "Most people find it incomprehensible. My former wife, for one. Though that surely says more about her than it does me."

"I must admit the fascination is rather lost on me."

"You obviously don't have the soul of a collector."

"I do accumulate objects. Possessions. By accident, mostly."

"And then, without realising it, you find your possessions have come to possess you?" It is more of a statement than a query.

"I try to keep things in perspective."

"Then you aren't a collector," says Moyle. "A collector's perspective is entirely skewed. He sees only that which obsesses him. Everything else is relegated to the background. I speak from experience." He sighs the resigned sigh of a man too set in his ways to change. "But I mustn't keep you. I know your job prohibits you from fraternising at length with other employees. Thank you again, Mr Hubble. I am in your debt, and if there is any way I can repay the favour, I will. I mean it. If I ever have the chance to do something for you, I'll do it. Anything you need, anything at all."

"Just keep a closer watch on your stock," says Frank.

13

Seven: In the Bible, indicative of "many sons", for instance in *I Samuel*, ii, 5—"The barren has borne seven, but she who has many children is forlorn."

9.26 a.m.

Up in the Boardroom, Thurston has been rattling through the day's admin with characteristic efficiency, typing notes and e-memos into the terminal at the same time as he talks.

Currently he and his brothers are discussing a fire which broke out at one of the Days depositories the previous week. Thurston can reveal that an exhaustive internal investigation has traced the culprit: a sacked forklift operator nursing a grudge. However, since the fire was discovered and extinguished by a night watchman before it could do much damage, and the destroyed stock was insured anyway, the brothers vote as one not to prosecute the arsonist—a decision which has nothing to do with magnanimity and everything to do with the brothers' aversion to dealing with the courts of the land. Days, they like to think, is a nation within a nation, a law unto itself, and resorting to common legal procedures would tarnish, and perhaps diminish, the store's scrupulously cultivated aura of sovereignty.

Next on the agenda is the possibility of a new and even lower grade of account. This idea has been put forward by Fred, who, as he is only too keen to remind everyone, was responsible for initiating the Aluminium scheme that rescued them during that bad spell a couple of years back when the monthly figures dropped into the red for the first time ever. Now, with sales falling again—though still healthy enough, Fred hastens to add—it might be a good idea to allow another stratum of the population in through the doors of Days.

Wensley wants to know what Fred would call the new grade. Tin? Lead? Rusty Iron?

Fred thinks Copper has a nice ring to it.

Thurston wonders whether an account which will be available to just about anybody might not fatally compromise the exclusivity that Days relies upon to attract and keep its clientele. Why not, he says, if the store is going to go *that* downmarket, simply throw the doors wide open and let the whole world in?

Mungo concurs. For all the extra income that another grade of account will bring in, wealthier customers and regulars of some years' standing might decide that the world's first and (naturally) foremost gigastore has let its standards slip a shade too far and transfer their custom to another gigastore in protest—the EuroMart in Brussels springs to mind as a likely candidate, confusingly laid-out and ill-organised though it is. Besides, the effort it takes to become an account-holder is precisely what makes Days so alluring to so many. You don't value highly what you haven't had to struggle for.

Fred concedes the point, and in the ensuing show of hands votes against his own proposal, which is defeated six to none.

Thurston then lists the latest appeals that have been made to the brothers for charitable donations. Each is voted on in turn. Human rights campaigns are summarily dismissed. The countries that supply the store with the cheapest raw materials and manufactured goods tend, by uncanny coincidence, to be those whose governments most loosely interpret the meaning of the term "democracy", and the brothers are reluctant to be seen to be censuring the dictatorships and military juntas that help fatten their profit margins. Animal rights groups, conservationists, and disarmament lobbyists are also deemed too politically sensitive. Which leaves societies for the disabled, arts funding, and a scheme for providing inner-city children with two-week holidays in the countryside as the least controversial recipients of tax-deductible gifts from Days, and at the same time the most likely to enhance the store's prestige.

Thurston mentions in passing that the cost of maintaining Days Scholarships in Retail Studies at the nation's two oldest universities is due to increase as a consequence of fresh government education cuts, and that they should give serious consideration to scrapping at least one of the endowments. Since all of the brothers attended one of the universities and not the other, their natural inclination is to favour their alma mater at the expense of its rival. However, as Sato slyly points out, since the other university can't boast the Day brothers among its distinguished alumni, it, surely, is more deserving of their beneficence. The vote is split, three to three, and since Sonny is not on hand to cast a deciding vote, Thurston resolves that both scholarships will remain in place for the time being.

Then there are the numerous requests for television and newspaper interviews to be dealt with. These the reclusive brothers turn down without exception, but it is always a pleasure to read the letters from editors and producers forwarded to them by the Public Relations people in the Basement. They find the tone of the letters—a syrupy cocktail of flattery and extreme unctuousness—amusing.

Likewise, it is customary for invitations to attend this or that prestigious dinner or art gallery opening or film première to be read out by the day's chairman, and then equally customary for them to be consigned with lofty disdain to the rejection pile. The brothers take great pleasure in confounding all efforts to popularise and demystify them. There is always speculation, of course. Almost daily the electronic and print media run stories attributing bizarre illnesses, manias, and eccentricities to the sons of Septimus Day, and at Thurston's request Fred, the brothers' self-elected media monitor, reads aloud a list of the latest, gleaned from the tabloids and the TV gossip shows.

> 1) Sato has taken to walking naked around the Violet Floor all day long;
> 2) Wensley's weight has ballooned to two hundred kilos;
> 3) Thurston has contracted a wasting disease;
> 4) Thurston is going blind in his left eye (a story headlined, "Their Father's Disfigurement Is A Curse!");
> 5) Fred is dependent on barbiturates and can't sleep at night unless he is sharing a bed with Mungo;
> 6) Mungo has so overdeveloped the muscles in his arms and thighs that he can no longer straighten his limbs fully;
> 7) Chas has had plastic surgery to correct a minor defect in the cleft in his chin; and
> 8) Sonny has cleaned up his act and has subscribed to a phone-in alcoholics support group—anonymously, of course.

If only (the brothers wish) that last story had any basis in the truth. As for the other fictions, they laugh them off. Let the world believe what it wants to believe about them. Let it ridicule them, turn them into cartoon figures. Nothing anyone can say can affect them. Almost a hundred metres above the ground in their self-contained Violet Floor eyrie, insulated from the sweat, fuss and filth of the city, why should they care what people think of them? As long as customers keep coming to Days, what difference can a few tall tales make?

Further points of business are raised and tackled, and then Thurston comes to the matter of a territorial dispute between two departments.

"This one's been pending for quite a while," he says. "I came across it yesterday evening while going through the files in preparation for this morning. Something we've all been overlooking."

"Probably with good reason," mutters Fred.

"The e-memo comes from both sections of Security," Thurston continues. "E-memos plural, actually. The first reads, 'The Heads of Strategic and Tactical Security would be grateful if the administration would investigate the present hostilities between the Books Department and the Computers Department and deliver a binding judgement to resolve the situation.'" He taps keys, reading selections from the texts of the subsequent e-memos. "'The ongoing "state of siege" that exists between Books and Computers shows no signs of improving and every indication of impending deterioration.' 'Numerous customers have been caught in the "crossfire" of acts of aggression and intimidation...' 'Possibility of fatalities arising as a consequence of the state of mutual intimidation...' 'Violence and sabotage...'" He looks around at his brothers. "Has anyone heard anything about this before?"

Heads are shaken.

"Apparently it's been going on for well over a year, ever since we authorised Computers to expand into floorspace occupied by Books."

"A sensible decision," says Sato. "Computers has a larger turnover of product and therefore demands a greater amount of display area. Books has been consistently running at a loss, so it seemed logical that it should surrender floorspace to its immediate neighbour. We told Computers to annex a strip of floorspace one metre wide and ten long. Ten square metres of Books."

"And the Bookworms don't like it," says Wensley. "Well, we made our decision. They're just going to have to learn to live with it."

"The trouble is," says Thurston, "they haven't. In a series of what the memos call 'guerrilla raids', the Bookworms have systematically been throwing out whatever merchandise the Computers Department employees set out in this ten-metre strip and replacing it with their own merchandise. And the Computers employees—"

"Technoids, I believe they call themselves," Chas offers helpfully, keen to show off his knowledge of shop-floor jargon.

"The Technoids," says Thurston, using the nickname with some distaste, "haven't been taking it lying down. Fights have been breaking out and sales assistants on both sides have been getting hurt." He pulls up another e-memo on the terminal: "'Three sales assistants had to be hospitalised today as a result of a skirmish on the strip of floorspace between Books and Computers, the latest and bloodiest episode in this rapidly escalating conflict. This matter now demands the administration's most urgent attention.'"

Sato winces. "Sick-leave. Sick-pay."

"Worse," says Mungo, "stock has been damaged. Why didn't anyone draw our attention to this sooner?"

"As I said, it was on the files," says Thurston. "Security has put in a total of seventeen e-memos, but the first was filed under Employee Disputes and all the subsequent memos were automatically routed the same way."

That explains it. Every once in a while a head of department will single out one of his subordinates for a hard time or a floor-walker will be accused of claiming others' commissions as his own, but the arguments almost always resolve themselves by the time the reports reach the Boardroom, and so the brothers have taken to ignoring Employee Dispute e-memos. Why bother?

"But still we should have noticed," says Chas, "because Employee Dispute e-memos usually come from Personnel and these ones came from Security."

There are murmurs of agreement.

"So it's an oversight," says Wensley, shrugging. "It's not too late to rectify it."

"Quite," says Sato. "But in the light of our apparent inefficiency, instead of issuing our decision electronically it would be more politic if one of us actually went down there and dealt with the matter in person. The personal touch may make all the difference."

"And we all know who that someone's going to be," says Chas, with feigned rancour. As though he never has any choice in the matter.

"Oh, Chas," says Fred, clasping his hands together beseechingly. "Please. None of us wants to go down there, and you're the best at dealing with, you know, *ordinary* people. Oh, please say you'll do it for us. Please.

I'll get down on my hands and knees and kiss your patent leather brogues if I have to. Anything. Just say you'll go."

"Chas, would you mind?" says Thurston. "It's simply a question of getting the heads of both departments together and giving them a good talking-to."

"Threaten them with their jobs if you have to," says Mungo. "That's what I'd do."

"Just get them to stop damaging our property," says Wensley.

Chas is about to raise his hands in surrender and agree to do as his brothers ask, at the same time declining Fred's generous offer for fear that his brother's lips will ruin the shine on his shoes, when one of the Boardroom doors is flung open.

A moment later a head appears round the other door, followed by a body. The hair on the head shows signs of having recently been towelled dry, while the body is clad in wrinkled jeans and a checked shirt that has been buttoned incorrectly.

The new arrival comes tottering into the Boardroom, a hand clamped to one side of his forehead as though to keep his brains from spilling out through a fissure in his cranium. He shuffles across the floor, each step seeming to cost him a world of effort, until he reaches the table. There he stops, steadying himself against its edge, and, swaying slightly, stares around at the faces of the six brothers, who look back at him with expressions ranging from mild concern to thinly-veiled contempt. He takes his hand from his forehead and examines the palm as though genuinely expecting to find it smeared with grey matter. Then he returns his gaze to the brothers.

His brothers.

"Morning, all," he says, then lets out a short, abrupt laugh, as though he has cracked the funniest joke of all time.

"Good morning, Sonny," says Thurston, icily. "We were wondering where you'd got to."

14

Benten: One of the Shichi Fukijin, the seven Japanese gods of luck, and the only female among them, she brings good fortune in matters pertaining to wealth, feminine beauty, and the fine arts.

9.58 a.m.

A GLANCE AT a wall clock reminds Frank that a lightning sale is about to take place.

Having memorised the order of the day's sales while Mr Bloom was running through them during the morning briefing, he doesn't have to check his Sphinx for the location. First on the list is Dolls. Four departments away, and therefore close enough for him to feel obliged to attend.

Since collaring the shoplifter, Frank has been wandering the Blue Floor, mulling over his conversation with Moyle. Moyle is right about him not having the soul of a collector. But how to account for the objects and gadgets that cram his apartment? All the artworks and items of furniture he has accumulated over the years almost without being aware of it, all the possessions purchased on a whim, all the *things* he has surrounded himself with and barely notices—what absence in him do these fill?

The root of the problem lies, he thinks, in his time at the Academy. In his Ghost Training.

Frank was eighteen and fresh out of school, a young man with high hopes and low self-esteem, when he applied for a job at Days. He had no idea what aptitude he might have for working at the store. His exam results had been good, but they alone would not guarantee him employment even as a sales assistant, and anything higher than a sales assistant—anything at the administrative level, for instance—was barred to all but university graduates with good degrees. He filled in the relevant forms and sent them off simply because that was what everyone else was doing, and while he waited for the response to his application to come through, he found work as a night porter in a medium-grade hotel, a nice, unobtrusive job that gave him plenty of time to read, think, and generally be by himself.

Months went by, and every once in a while he would ring Days Personnel to enquire whether his application had even been received. More often than not he listened to a recorded message informing him that all the lines were busy. On those rare occasions when he got through to a human being, he was assured that job applications were being processed as fast as humanly possible and that his would doubtless be got round to eventually.

He was beginning to lose hope, and considering reapplying, when the reply came. Inside a fat brown envelope watermarked with Days logos was a vast questionnaire dozens of pages long that covered over a thousand topics, some as innocuous as Frank's favourite foodstuffs, television programmes, and newspapers, others as prurient as his religious inclinations, his sexual feelings (if any) for children under the age of consent, and his relationship with his parents (which was almost nonexistent, seeing as his father had passed away several years ago and his mother was surviving on state benefit and a diet of prescription tranquillisers). The questionnaire took hours to fill in, but he persevered, suspecting that it was intended as a kind of first hurdle for prospective employees, there to winnow out the half-hearted.

He sent it back, and expected to have to wait several months more before learning if he had earned an interview or not. The form letter accompanying the questionnaire had warned him that interviews were being booked as far as two years in advance. He resigned himself to a long wait, and continued working nights at the hotel.

But the response from Days was surprisingly swift. Barely weeks passed before a letter arrived asking him if he could come in for an interview that autumn.

The interview, in a chamber in Personnel in the Basement, lasted three hours. Senior Personnel administrators went over many of the same topics that had been covered by the questionnare, interrogating Frank closely in order to ascertain whether he had been telling the truth or not.

He was an only child?

That was correct, he told them.

Good. And his father?

Died when Frank was eleven.

He rated family and friends low on a scale of "things important to him". Why was that?

Because he found people in general troubling and intrusive.

Good, good. And did he have trouble getting served in shops?

Sometimes, yes.

Did people sometimes barge in front of him in queues without apologising?

That had happened, yes.

Did he often find himself standing alone in the corner at parties?

He didn't get invited to too many parties.

And so it went for three long, gruelling hours, and at the end of it Frank was sent to sit out in the hallway while the Personnel administrators conferred. He slumped on a chair, feeling like a wrung-out dishrag. Some time later, he wasn't sure how long, he was invited to come back in, and was told that his personality profile was ideally suited to Tactical Security.

Embarrassed by his ignorance, he asked what Tactical Security meant, exactly, please.

Store detection, he was told. Would he consider training to become a Ghost?

Not entirely sure that he wanted to spend the rest of his life as a store detective, and a little hazy about what the job entailed, Frank was nevertheless not so stupid as to turn the opportunity down, reasoning that if things didn't work out he could always go back to night portering or, since it appeared that he had a bent for law enforcement, apply to join the police force. He told the administrators yes, went home and told his mother what had happened (she, predictably, was underwhelmed), went to the hotel and handed in his notice (the manager there was considerably more impressed and encouraging), and almost immediately embarked on the year-long course of Ghost Training.

The first six months of Ghost Training took place at the Academy, a fenced-in compound on the outskirts of the city, situated in one corner of the spacious grounds of the mansion owned by Septimus Day. There, at the hands of a team of instructors made up of former Ghosts, Frank was taught the basics of self-defence, use of sidearms, and the technique of guttural ventriloquism known as subvocalisation. He learned how to recognise the flagging signs that identify a shoplifter and was instructed in the methods the more inventive professional boosters employ, such as carrying a box with a false side for slipping stolen goods into, or pushing a hand through a slit in a coat pocket in order to pillage shelves under cover of the coat flap.

Once he had mastered those skills, he was initiated into the mysteries of congruity—the art of blending into the background, of appearing just like anyone else and therefore like no one. In this his natural drabness helped him greatly. Since childhood Frank had always been one of those people who are overlooked, whose face no one remembers, whose name slips out of people's memories and lodges on the tip of their tongue where they can't find it. He was, not to put too fine a point on it, a nobody, and naturally this was an attribute he had always considered a drawback, but his Ghost Training showed him that it could also be a virtue. He was taught to cultivate a bland, abstracted air and never let his face show what he was thinking; to avoid making sudden, erratic gestures which might mark him out as an individual; in short, to damp down what little spark of personality he possessed until it was no more than an infinitesimal wink of light, dimmer than the farthest star. By the end of the six months he had refined his innate innocuousness to such a degree that he could, if he wanted to, walk through a crowded room and pass entirely unnoticed.

Halfway through his training his mother died. He was given time off to organise the funeral, which he did in an efficient but perfunctory manner. At the ceremony itself, in the company of a handful of estranged relatives and his mother's semi-estranged friends, he felt some sadness, but not much. Perhaps this was a by-product of his training, perhaps not. For a long time there had been a distance between him and his mother, a drug-chilled void. Death only made that distance slightly more remote. In many ways losing her came as a relief. It shaved further complications from his personality, helping to strip away the emotional ties that stood between him and full Ghosthood.

On average, only a tenth of the trainees at the Academy develop congruity sufficiently to go on to become fully-fledged Ghosts. The rest are advised to seek an alternative career. Frank was singled out by his instructors as being an exceptionally apt pupil. Without much difficulty he graduated to the second part of the course: six months of practical experience on the shop floor.

Donald Bloom, who himself had been a Ghost for only a little over a year, showed Frank the ropes. Under Mr Bloom's affable tutelage he learned the ins and outs of the store, tramping the floors (all seven of them, because this was back in the days before the brothers commandeered the Violet Floor for themselves), going over and over the same ground until he had the location of all seven hundred and seventy-seven departments securely locked away in his memory. At the same time he further refined the skills he had acquired at the Academy. Side by side with Mr Bloom he drifted behind customers and lurked where he was least likely to be seen but where *he* could see as much as he needed. The two of them loitered without intent, lingered with languor. It was Mr Bloom who helped Frank make his first official collar, and that was a moment of achievement whose sweetness Frank will never forget.

By the time the year of Ghost Training was up, the metamorphosis was complete. Frank had become a living cypher. A professional nonentity. Congruous. A Ghost.

And in return for effecting that transformation, Days offered him a gun, a Platinum account with the performance-related possibility of promotion to Iridium, and a job for life.

It is hard to believe now that he could have thought this a fair trade, but then how many sane twenty-year-olds would turn down the offer of a generous salary linked to a secure career?

In short, Days made him who and what he is today. Days took a shy, introverted young man and stripped him of any last vestige of personality he might have had. His Ghost Training hollowed him out like a rotten tooth, and since then the only means he has found of filling the emptiness inside him is by buying expensive things that he has little time or desire to enjoy.

And the worst of it is, all this was done with his consent. He has no one to blame for how he is but himself. Days merely capitalised on a natural asset, and he willingly allowed the exploitation.

At least the imminent sale gives him something to think about other than himself. With his intimate knowledge of the store it doesn't take him long to work out the quickest route to Dolls, and off he goes. East through Private Surveillance, filled with all manner of bugs, phone taps, body wires, and miniaturised recording devices—a therapeutic playpen for paranoiacs. North through Oriental Weaponry, where sales assistants dressed in black ninja garb have almost finished resurrecting the folding screen of *shuriken*. North again through Military Surplus, the department for the professional mercenary and for anyone who can't get through the night without a camouflage hot-water bottle cover. And once more north, this time through Classic Toys.

He arrives at the passageway connecting Classic Toys to Dolls just as a phrase of seven notes chimes out over the store's PA system, followed by a female voice announcing the lightning sale in the stern yet seductive tones of a dominatrix.

"Attention, customers. For the next five minutes there will be a fifteen per cent reduction on all items in Dolls. I repeat, for the next five minutes only, all items in Dolls will be marked down by fifteen per cent. Dolls is located in the north-eastern quadrant of the Blue Floor and may be reached using the banks of lifts designated B and C. This offer will be extended to you for five minutes only. Any purchases made after that period will retail at full price. Thank you for your attention."

The hush that descends on the store for the duration of the announcement is absolute. Then, as the seven-note phrase is repeated, shoppers begin to move. They drop whatever they are doing, and hoisting up their handbaskets or swinging their trolleys around or stamping down on the Go pedals of their motorised carts and spinning the steering wheels, they make for Dolls. Never mind that few of these people, if any, had the urge to buy a doll until now, and never mind that a fifteen per cent discount hardly amounts to the offer of a lifetime, a lightning sale is a lightning sale, and it summons bargain-hungry customers like an aid convoy summons the starving.

To those awaiting them in Dolls, the sound of their approach starts out as a distant whisper that shivers through the air like the wind before a storm. The expressions on the faces of the thousands of pieces of merchandise in Dolls remain unchanged but the expressions on the faces of the sales assistants and guards become apprehensive as the whisper increases in volume, deepening to a rumble like far-off thunder in the hills, the noise of wheels on carpet and of hundreds of pairs of feet beating the floor.

The sound grows and grows, exploding to a crescendo as the first customers spill into the department. They rush in by all four entrances and swiftly fan out among the displays, plucking items off the shelves and scrutinising price-tags, their mouths wide open in avaricious rictus grins.

Frank has to leap smartly aside as a motorised cart comes hurtling past him through the passageway, missing him by a whisker. The driver is a hunched, withered old woman, ninety if she's a day, with brown, broken teeth, a jet-black pompadour wig perched on her head, crimson lipstick smeared roughly in the vicinity of her mouth, and a manic gleam in her eye that would perturb a psychopath. Frank recognises Clothilda Westheimer, the multimillionaire heiress.

Waving a walking stick in the air like a cavalryman's sabre and tooting on the cart's horn at anyone careless enough to get in her way, Clothilda

Westheimer careers around the aisles until she almost collides with a florid-faced, heavy-set man who is examining a box containing a lifelike plastic replica of a six-month-old baby. Brakes whine, the cart grinds to a halt, and Clothilda Westheimer screams at the man to move, using language that would make a sailor blush. The man's startled response is to hold up the baby in front of him as if its production-line innocence will somehow ward off this cursing, haranguing crone, but Clothilda Westheimer merely snatches the box out of his grasp and aims her cart for the nearest cash register.

A regular customer since the day the store opened, Clothilda Westheimer buys all her groceries at Days, and also buys extravagant gifts which, having no one else to lavish them on—she has disowned her relatives and has remained unmarried, despite the attentions of a stream of suitors—she lavishes on herself. She has an unmatched eye for a bargain and, as she has just proved, an unequalled skill at getting what she wants.

And on they come, flooding in by the dozen, more customers and yet more, barging, shouldering, elbowing one another out of the way, seizing merchandise off the shelves like a rabble of looters. All pretence of civility disappears, the rules of etiquette are abandoned, as they battle for bargains, dive into the displays, emerge with their prizes, and then join the crowd around the cash registers, there to brandish cards of all hues from dull grey Aluminium to pink-tinged Rhodium. Knowing they only have a limited time in which to secure a purchase and grimly determined not to leave the department without the doll they didn't know they wanted so desperately until now, the customers clamour for the sales assistants' attention and squeal like frustrated infants when other, less deserving individuals are given precedence.

Keeping to the shifting perimeter of the crowd, careful to stay out of reach of jabbing elbows and butting shoulders, Frank watches for suspicious behaviour, but all he sees is a collection of well-dressed, well-heeled men and women behaving like ravening animals. He sees two middle-aged men in lounge suits tussling over a purple-haired troll, each insisting, with mounting indignation, that *he* saw it first. He sees a rosy-cheeked porcelain Bo Peep, one of a collector's series based on characters from nursery rhymes, being used as a club by its prospective owner to batter a path through the heaving throng. He sees a small boy clasping a khaki-clad action figure to his chest and bawling raucously while his mother tries to force both him and herself through the crush of bodies to the cash registers. At one point the top half of the largest of a nest of Russian dolls pops clear of the mêlée and goes rolling across the carpet to fetch up at Frank's feet, its painted babushka face gazing up at him plaintively, as if begging him to intercede in the madness.

Disagreements degenerate into arguments. Queue-jumpers are dragged back by the scruff of the neck. A rough kind of frontier justice holds sway.

And all the while the harassed, wand-wielding sales assistants process the purchases as fast as is humanly possible (but nowhere near fast enough to satisfy the baying, demanding mob), and the overhead cameras, under manual control from the Eye, wheel and nod, viewing the activity below with a lofty, lazy curiosity.

A glance at his watch tells Frank that the sale has less than a minute to run, but the frenzy shows no sign of abating. If anything, the customers become more agitated as they sense the seconds slipping away. Pushy latecomers are given short shrift. Competitive jostling gives way to blatant shoving.

Then, at last, the seven-note sequence chimes out again and the female voice, with incisive calmness, pronounces the sale at an end. There is a collective sigh of disappointment from unsuccessful customers as they turn away from the cash registers, disgustedly discarding the dolls that only seconds ago they were frantic to buy. Those who were lucky enough to make a purchase leave the department hugging their booty, boasting to anyone who will listen how much money they saved. Arguments peter out, the antagonists coming to their senses as though awakening from a trance. They blink at one another in confusion, suddenly no longer sure what all the fuss was about. Some even exchange apologies (they don't know what came over them).

Slowly, in dribs and drabs, the crowd departs, leaving behind a litter of débris, dolls of all shapes and sizes lying everywhere, limbs twisted, like corpses in the aftermath of a nerve-gas attack.

The sales assistants, glad it's over, set about tidying up. The guards, shaking their heads in weary disbelief, stroll away.

Frank is just turning to go when a voice buzzes in his ear.

Mr Hubble?

Hubble here.

A guard's made an arrest in Optical Supplies. You're in the vicinity. Can you get over there?

No problem.

Cool. The screen-jockey breaks the connection.

Optical Supplies: two departments west, one south. Frank sets off, wondering if the rest of the day is going to be this busy and rather hoping it will. At least that way the hours will pass quickly.

10.07 a.m.

THE GUARD IS a young, petite, wiry-looking woman with dark eyes offset in a slight cast. Her black hair is pinned up at the back of her head in a tight bun. Frank knows her face, and her ID badge reminds him that her name is Gould.

He introduces himself—"Hubble, Tactical"—and casts a cursory glance over at the arrestee, who is sitting in a chair with her back to the wall, slumped and gazing abjectly at her hands in her lap as if they are the ones who have committed the crime, independently of her. She is—to judge by the fine striations that star her mouth and radiate like lines of magnetic polarity from the outer corners of her eyes to her temples—in her early fifties, and she is dressed in a pair of dark slacks and a maroon mohair jersey with a gold-and-diamanté brooch fastened at her collarbone. Her hair is a rich, dark-chocolate brown shot through with streaks of silver. Although some effort has been made to organise it, it looks matted and unkempt. Her slacks are rumpled and in need of pressing. In fact, the overall image she presents is a curious blend of customer and baglady, but despite this it occurs to Frank—a thought beamed down from an alien planet—that she is far from unattractive. In the right clothes, the right situation (which this abundantly is not), she could be quite striking. There is no ring on the fourth finger of her left hand, an absence Frank notes because it is a store detective's task to be alert to such details and not for any other reason.

"What did she take?" he asks Gould, drawing out his Sphinx.

"Just this." Gould holds up a bottle of contact lens solution. "Between you and me..." She moves closer to Frank for a confidential whisper. Frank recoils a fraction, but Gould does not appear to notice. "She's one of the clumsiest shoplifters I've ever seen. I mean, she might as well have walked in carrying a placard saying, 'I Am Here To Steal Something.' Even without my training I would have known she wasn't kosher the moment I clapped eyes on her. She was trembling so badly I thought she had some kind of condition, you know, Parkinson's or something, but then when she spotted me, she jumped like a scalded cat, turned away, you know, like this." Gould ducks her head to one side, hunching her shoulders and raising a hand to shield her face. An exaggeration, surely, and looking over at the arrestee again, Frank is pleased to see that the woman is still contemplating her hands and has not witnessed Gould's tactless impersonation.

"So I kept an eye on her," Gould continues, "and sure enough, not two minutes later she boosted. Her hands were shaking so much she could hardly get the thing into her pocket. It'd be laughable if it wasn't so pathetic," she concludes with a grim twist of her mouth.

"Did you get her card off her?"

"She says she doesn't have one. Says she lost it."

"Then how did she get in?"

"I have no idea. We'll find out downstairs, but I need you to make the arrest formal before I can take her down."

"Of course."

Frank goes over to the shoplifter. As he draws near he catches a strong scent of perfume emanating from her. Several different perfumes, in fact, a mingling of musks intended to disguise the smell of bodily secretions but, like a white sheet draped over a patch of wet mud, not wholly effective.

His nose and forehead wrinkle simultaneously.

At his approach the woman raises her head, and he sees that her eyes are inflamed, their whites crazed with capillaries, their lashes slick with moisture, all of which adds to her general look of haggardness and disarray. The rest of her well-shaped face, though, is serene, resigned, perhaps even hopeful.

"Do I know you?" she asks, blinking rapidly and rubbing one eye.

"I don't think so."

"I'm sure I recognise your face."

It is possible she may have glimpsed him before somewhere on the shop floor, but she won't have remembered his face. No one does. That's the whole point.

He shakes his head. "Not likely."

"Oh. And I'm usually so good with faces. Have you come to throw me out?"

"That's not my job." For some reason Frank finds himself unable to resist the inclination to speak gently to this woman. "I'm here to arrest you."

"I thought I'd already been arrested."

"Procedure."

"What about her?" She points to Gould.

"As soon as I'm done with you, the guard will assume responsibility for your processing and eviction."

"I know what you are," the woman says slowly. "You're a Ghost."

"I'm with Tactical Security, yes."

"Does anybody call you a store detective these days?"

"Sometimes. That, at any rate, is how I prefer to think of myself."

"You prefer 'store detective' to 'Ghost'."

"Most definitely."

"How interesting," the woman says, nodding to herself. Frank has the impression that she thinks she is at a cocktail party, making small talk. Consequently her next question catches him off-guard. "Have you ever shot a shoplifter?"

He hesitates before deciding that he has nothing to lose by telling her the truth. "A few times."

"How many times?"

Frank frowns. "Five, perhaps six. Back when I was starting out."

"And did you kill any of them?"

"I shoot to wound."

"But it's not always possible to aim accurately, not in the heat of the moment."

"No, it isn't."

"So have you killed anyone by accident?"

"Not me," he says. "But it has happened."

"And would you shoot me?" The woman fixes her bloodshot gaze on Frank, giving him such a searching look that for a worrying moment he fears she can actually see into him, see into his soul.

"If you resisted arrest or ran," he answers eventually, "it would be my duty to bring you down using any means at my disposal."

"Would the fact that I'm a woman make any difference?"

Thinking of Clothilda Westheimer at the sale, Frank replies, "None at all."

"How interesting," she says again.

Frank holds up a hand, pausing the conversation to subvocalise to the Eye. Did you get a clip of the woman in Optical Supplies?

Certainly did. I was following her all the way. Subtle she was not.

All right. He clears his throat and addresses the shoplifter formally. The Booster's Blessing. "Madam, I regret that it is my duty to inform you that at 10.03 a.m.—10.03?" He looks to Gould for confirmation.

The guard nods. "Thereabouts."

"Well, is it or isn't it 10.03?"

"Precisely?" Gould retorts coolly. "I don't know. I was looking at *her*, not my watch."

"We'll say 10.03 for now, but the time is subject to amendment." Testily, Frank returns his attention to the shoplifter. "At 10.03 a.m. you were spotted removing an item from the Optical Supplies Department without having purchased it and with no obvious intent to purchase it. For this offence—"

"I needed it."

"I'm sure you did, madam."

"My contact lenses were hurting, and I'd lost my card. I'd never have taken it otherwise."

"For this offence, the penalty is immediate expulsion from the premises and the irrevocable cancellation of all account facilities. If you wish to take the matter to court, you may do so."

"I don't."

"Bear in mind, however, that we have the following evidence on disk."

He presses the Play key on his Sphinx, and he and the woman watch the clip of the theft on the screen. Gould was right: the woman is no natural born shoplifter. Trying to act casually while at the same time trembling like a palsy victim, she spends far too long inspecting the plastic bottles on the revolving rack in front of her before reaching out to take one, and as she does so she makes the elementary mistake of darting a glance over each shoulder—the quintessential flagging sign. She tries three times to slip the bottle into the pocket of her slacks, becoming visibly more flustered with each attempt, until in the end she actually looks down in order to guide the stolen article into its hiding place. By this time Gould has appeared on-camera, coming up behind her. The clip ends with Gould taking hold of her arm.

"Do you understand what I'm showing you, madam?"

"Yes. Yes, I do." The woman peers up at the ceiling. "You know, I've often watched those little cameras following people around. I suppose I should have realised that they've also been following *me*. Perhaps I did realise but preferred not to think about it. It's quite disconcerting to think that someone is watching us all the time, seeing everything we do, don't you agree? I'm not a religious person, but that's how I'd feel if I were. That God has His eyes on me every second of the day, like those cameras, and that He's just waiting for me to slip up." She returns her gaze to Frank. "And what does that make you, I wonder, Mr Store Detective, if those cameras are God's eyes? You whose job it is to hover at our shoulders and not be seen? You who force us by the threat of your presence to listen to our consciences?" Her tone shifts from ruminative to sly. "An angel, perhaps?"

"Hardly." Frank allows a small measure of irony to lift the word. "I'm nowhere near pure enough."

"Oh, angels don't need to be pure. They just need to be there."

"Then that's us," he says, humouring her. "That's store detectives. Always there, always at your shoulder."

"But not mine," the shoplifter points out with a sorrowful little smile. "Not any more. I broke the rules, didn't I? I'm not coming back."

Neither am I, thinks Frank. Which makes them a pair, of sorts. The sinner and the disaffected angel, both denied a place in Mammon's heaven, one because she has strayed from the straight and narrow, the other because he can no longer bear the notion of staying.

"Well, let's get it over with, then," says the shoplifter, rising stiffly to her feet. "Mr Store Detective? You've been polite and considerate. Thank you." The woman extends a hand. "My name is Mrs Shukhov. Carmen Shukhov."

The gesture utterly flummoxes Frank, who only touches people when he has to, when he has no choice, for instance when collaring a shoplifter. This woman, this Mrs Shukhov, wants him to take her hand in his? Their bodies to make contact, skin against skin? Absurd. It's bad enough that she has got him conjuring up abstract similarities between them. Now he has to form a physical bridge with her? Out of the question.

He bows instead, just a tiny forward tip of the head.

Realising she has stumbled over an unseen boundary, Mrs Shukhov embarrassedly withdraws the proffered hand. She tries to apologise, and is almost relieved when Gould takes her by the elbow and leads her away from Frank and her *faux pas*.

As the guard and the shoplifter leave the department, Mrs Shukhov makes a doomed attempt to pat her unruly hair into shape, and again Frank is puzzled by her air of neglected elegance. It looks as if she has been wearing the same clothes for at least a couple of days, and in that time hasn't been near a make-up case or a bath. None of which would mean anything if she didn't come across as the kind of woman for whom appearance and personal hygiene matter. And then there is the question of how she got in without a card, unless she is lying about losing it. And why risk your Days account over a bottle of contact lens solution, for heaven's sake?

All very perplexing, but let them sort it out in Processing. Ultimately, it's not Frank's problem.

15

Heptarchy: Government by seven persons.

10.07 a.m.

BY NOW THE rightmost of the Boardroom's triptych of south-facing windows is almost entirely taken up by the dome's dark side. A dazzling reflection of the cloudless sky whitens the surface area of clear glass that still predominates, a convex mirror of the convex heavens, while scratches and flaws in the ever-encroaching segment of smoked glass refract the light into needle-thin rainbows.

Inside the Boardroom there is a strained silence as six of Septimus Day's sons look on while the seventh painstakingly mixes himself a gin and tonic.

Sonny, the tip of his tongue lodged in one corner of his mouth, is concentrating as hard on the task at hand as if he were constructing a scale model of a Gothic cathedral out of matchsticks. He has succeeded in pouring a generous measure of gin and a top-up of tonic into the glass without spilling too much of either, but now he finds himself having to grapple with the slippery problem of how to get half-melted cubes of ice out of the malachite bucket with only a pair of silver ice tongs to help him.

The way Sonny handles the tongs, you could be forgiven for thinking that they were not a tool designed expressly for the purpose of retrieving ice cubes from an open container. He operates them as though hampered by an invisible pair of gardening gloves, and whenever he does manage to secure one of the deliquescing lozenges of frozen water between the tongs' clawed tips, it invariably escapes and goes skidding across the tabletop (and more often than not over the edge of the table and onto the carpet) before he can transfer it to the glass.

For his audience it is the worst kind of slapstick, teeth-grindingly aggravating to watch. Each brother has the urge to go over, snatch the tongs out of Sonny's hands and, as if he were an invalid, do the job for him. Anything to bring the whole pitiful performance to an end.

Sonny saves them the trouble. Losing patience, he abandons the tongs, reaches into the bucket, and plucks out a fistful of ice to toss into his drink. A slice of lemon follows. Then, carefully sliding the brim-full glass towards him, he brings his nose to the surface and inhales, revelling in the tangle of tangy aromas—juniper, quinine, lemon. Puckering his lips into a funnel, he sucks up a mouthful.

"Fabulous!" he croaks, slapping the arm of his throne, and takes another long, noisy slurp, and another.

Having drained two centimetres of liquid by this means, he feels he can safely pick up the glass. He polishes the drink off in two swift swallows.

His hands are steadier, his movements more fluent and less grimly precise, as he pours himself a follow-up. Gulping it down, he feels the pulsing, nauseating rage of his hangover begin to dim as the alcohol spreads its glacial tendrils through his bloodstream. The hot iron bands cinching his eyeballs slacken their pressure, and his brain begins to feel less like a dozen kilogrammes of molten magma and more like an organ capable of reason and deduction. To his observers, the outward signs of this inward regeneration are the pinkish glow that dawns in his pallid cheeks and the substantial improvement in his physical co-ordination.

Confidently Sonny reaches out to pour himself a third drink. This one winds up being nine parts gin to one part tonic, a tongue-blistering ratio that, when swallowed, sends a wave of regurgitative heat burning back up his throat. He sucks in air. "Whoa! Ooh! Ah!"

Eventually the inside of his mouth cools, and a big fat grin butters itself across his face.

"Well," he says, beaming blearily around the table, "here we all are again. Another day of custom and commerce and profit and plenty and all that shit. What have I missed?"

"Only everything," says Sato tonelessly.

"Perhaps a quick recap of the morning's admin would refresh all of our memories," says Mungo to Thurston.

Thurston sighs, twists his lips into a Möbius strip, then punches his minutes of the day's meeting back up onto the screen and scrolls quickly through them, reading each heading aloud. He concludes by saying, "We've voted decisions on all of those," and sits back in his typist's chair, folding his arms.

"Actually, not all," says Mungo. "That interdepartmental dispute..."

"We came to a decision on that." Thurston eyes his eldest brother cautiously.

"But we didn't actually vote on it, and now that Sonny's here, it's only right that his opinion be sought and his vote counted. So, Thurston, run through the details of the dispute again, and if Sonny or anyone else feels like adding any comments, fine. If not, let's just vote on it and call the meeting to an end."

"Thanks, Mungo," says Sonny. "I knew I could count on you."

Thurston, with a surly grimace, leans over his terminal again, calls up the history of the disagreement between Books and Computers, and summarises it in a few terse sentences. Sonny, meanwhile, takes the opportunity to mix himself a fourth drink. The food on the silver salver in front of him—grilled bacon, eggs and tomatoes, a round of toast with butter and marmalade—goes untouched. Sonny rarely feels up to eating anything until after midday, by which time he has relaxed his stomach with a soothing lining of liquor. Nevertheless, at Mungo's insistence Perch serves Sonny a solid breakfast every morning as well as a liquid one, in the hope that one day the former will suggest itself as an appetising alternative to the latter.

"And so," Thurston concludes, "we decided that Chas should go down and sort it out."

"Good idea," says Sonny, without looking up. "A few silken words from the Sultan of Smooth and they'll be rolling over onto their backs, begging to have their bellies tickled."

"You have a better suggestion?" says Chas, a crease of annoyance unbalancing the enviable symmetry of his features.

"I do, but what chance does it have of getting a fair hearing?"

"Not much," Chas admits.

"There you go. No point opening my mouth. But then *that's* hardly news, is it? For all the influence I have around here, I might as well be a janitor."

"It's not our fault you don't get a day of chairmanship," says Wensley in what he hopes is a placatory tone. "It's just how Dad arranged it. We may think that his obsession with the number seven was perhaps a little misguided, a little *anal*, but there's nothing we can do about it. What's ordained cannot be unordained."

"Yes, it can," says Sonny. "We could open on Sundays, for one thing. That would put me on an equal footing with the rest of you."

The response is as immediate as it is inevitable. Sonny would have expected little else of his brothers. He knows what each is going to say almost before he has said it.

"Out of the question," Thurston snaps.

"Think of the expense," says Sato. "We'd have to put employees on shifts and we'd have to pay them overtime rates. That would never do."

"And we wouldn't want to offend our Christian customers," adds Chas.

"And what about the living mannequins?" says Fred. "They deserve a day of rest as much as anyone."

"*We* need a day of rest," says Wensley.

"Besides," says Chas, "Dad specifically decreed that the store would never open on a Sunday. 'Sunday,' he said, 'is the keystone of the week.' Remember? 'Its purpose is to hold the other six in place, and for that reason it must be kept distinct from the rest.'"

"How predictable, how absolutely fucking predictable." Sonny looks imperiously from his gilded throne at each of his brothers in turn. "And how absolutely fucking hypocritical, too. I can think of at least two conditions Dad laid down when he handed the store over to us that you've overridden since he died."

"Introducing the Aluminium was a sound commercial move," Fred asserts. "And a necessary one. Dad would have approved."

"But he said there should never be more than seven grades of account."

"And as for taking over this floor for ourselves, we needed to," Wensley says. "We couldn't go on living out *there*." The sweep of his arm indicates the unseen city beyond the Boardroom's walls. "Out among the *customers*, for heaven's sake."

"But he said the store should always occupy all seven floors of the building."

"If you count the Basement as part of the shop floor, then it still does," says Sato.

"I see," says Sonny. "So it's all right to bend Dad's rules when it suits us but not when it doesn't. Not, for instance, if it means that *Sonny* might actually have some responsibility."

The hush that falls around the table—each brother expecting another to respond—implicitly acknowledges the truth of what Sonny has just said.

"We realise that Dad's conditions were unfair," says Mungo, aware that he is arriving a little too late with this piece of conciliation, "and we fully intend to give you some responsibility, Sonny, but only when you prove you're worthy of it."

"I *am* worthy of it."

"Maybe, but you haven't yet *shown* us that you are."

"It's a vicious circle. How can I show you if you won't give me the opportunity?"

"If you turned up for work in the mornings on time, smartly dressed and sober," says Thurston, "that would be a start."

"What difference would it make?" The words are prettified with a laugh, but not enough to disguise the despair in them. "You'd still ignore anything I had to say."

"We might not," says Mungo. "Didn't you say you had a suggestion about the dispute?"

"You'll only laugh when you hear it," says Sonny sullenly.

"We won't."

"You will."

"We won't. I swear. We all swear." Spoken so solemnly by Mungo that no one else at the table dares demur.

"All right then. You asked for it. Hang on a second." Sonny takes a courage-instilling sip of gin and tonic, gulps it down, and says, "Send me instead of Chas."

His brothers break out into hoots of derision.

"I knew it!" Sonny's face sags with dismay. "I knew you wouldn't take the idea seriously. You're nothing but a bunch of bare-faced fucking liars, the lot of you."

"I'm sorry," says Mungo, shaking his head, grinning. "If I'd known you were about to crack a joke, I wouldn't have promised not to laugh."

"It *wasn't* a joke. I mean it. Let me go down and talk to the heads of the departments. All I have to do is let them know that we stand by our decision about the area of floorspace and that if they don't like it, they can bugger off."

"I doubt an approach like that would do much to resolve the situation," says Chas. "The job calls for tact, diplomacy, subtlety, empathy, a certain delicacy of touch. Hardly your strong suits, Sonny."

"Yeah," says Fred, "sending *you* would be like sending an axe-murderer to perform brain surgery."

But Sonny is determined to be heard out. "Look, how can I possibly screw up? They'll listen to whatever I have to say to them, and they'll do whatever I tell them to do. I'm a Day brother. I'm their boss."

"Yeah, right," snorts Fred.

"He does have a point there," Mungo admits, nodding slowly.

"He does?"

"One of us going down to visit them in person will make it clear we're serious. What difference will it make which one of us it is? As far as they're concerned each of us carries the authority of all seven, and they'll be too awed to do anything but go along with whatever Sonny says."

"Don't do this, Mungo."

"Don't do what, Thurston?"

"Don't take his side. It's not profitable."

Mungo turns to face his youngest sibling, commanding his full attention. "Sonny, if we do confer this responsibility on you, and I'm not saying we're going to, but if we do, you have to be prepared to give us something in return."

"What sort of something?"

"An assurance."

"I'm not sure I follow you."

"If, perhaps," Mungo says, "you were to leave that drink in front of you unfinished, and we had Perch come in and take away the gin bottle..."

"You mean jump on the wagon?" Sonny says, in the same stilled, chilled tone of voice he might use to say, "You mean jump off a cliff?"

"For this morning, to begin with. At least until after you've been downstairs. I think the employees will respond more favourably if you're not falling-down drunk when you address them, and more to the point your head will be clearer and so will your judgement."

"Wouldn't you say I was drunk now?" Sonny gestures at the level of gin in the bottle, which is several centimetres lower than it was when he arrived.

"For someone with your capacity, Sonny, it takes three and a half G and T's just to reach minimum operating efficiency."

Sonny nods. "True. That's true."

"And if you prove that you can stay sober, or as sober as you need to be, when we ask you to, then maybe we'll give you other things to do," says Thurston, tumbling to Mungo's scheme and quietly impressed. "Work will be your incentive to clean up your act."

"I see," says Sonny. "You're offering me a deal."

"Correct," says Mungo. "Which indicates that I respect you as a son of Septimus Day."

"So let me get this straight. If I don't drink the rest of this bottle, you'll let me go down and deliver an arbitration."

"That's about the size of it."

"I can't believe this. This is a practical joke, isn't it? I'm going to go downstairs and find you've made this whole Books/Computers thing up."

"I wish we had."

"So you'll really let me do it?"

"As long as you keep your side of the bargain."

"No problem."

"So that's a promise?"

"It is."

"Then you can go."

Sonny lets out a whoop. "Wow! This is great! This is fantastic! What can I say? Thanks, brothers. Thanks a lot."

"You're welcome," says Chas.

"If," Mungo adds, "no one has any objections."

He sees Sato bite his lip.

"Well?"

"I think we're making a mistake," says Sato after a moment.

"That's a reservation, not an objection."

"I'm aware of that, but given the mood currently prevailing around this table, to make any sort of protest will seem churlish and lacking in public spirit, so it'll be better for all of us if I hold my peace."

"And does anyone else have anything further to add on the subject?"

No one does.

"We have to vote on it," says Thurston.

Sonny's hand shoots up to the full extent of his arm. "And the rest of you," he cajoles. "Come on."

Five other hands are raised one after another. Sato's comes last, slowly and reluctantly joining its fellows in the air.

"Carried unanimously," says Mungo.

"Who'd have thought it?" says Fred with a whistle. "We just agreed to let Sonny do some work."

"Wonders will never cease," says Wensley.

"Right, I'm off down to my apartment to get ready," says Sonny, excitedly shunting back his throne and rising to his feet. "Have to look my best for the staff, eh?"

Chas offers to come down with him and give him a few fashion pointers, but Sonny replies that he will be fine. "I can still remember a thing or two about turning myself out well, from back in the dim and distant past."

"Thurston," says Mungo, "send an e-memo down to both departments warning them Sonny's coming."

"Tell them to roll out the red carpet," says Sonny as he skips away from the table.

"And contact Strategic Security and have four guards waiting for Sonny on the Yellow Floor at, oh, let's say eleven thirty."

"Very well."

"Got that, Sonny? Eleven thirty."

Sonny is at the door. "Yup, half eleven, no problem."

A moment after he leaves the Boardroom, Sonny pops his head back through the doorway. The look of earnest gratitude on his face is touching to behold.

"You won't regret this," he tells his brothers, brow knotted in sincerity. "I swear you won't."

"You'd damn well better hope we don't," says Thurston, under his breath.

16

House of Marriage: In astrology, the seventh house.

10.16 a.m.

Oh Mum, I wish you could be here to see this with me. It's so much more wonderful than either of us could ever have imagined.

That was Linda's first thought as she passed through the arch and emerged into Silks. The shiny drapes and swathes of material swooping down in all directions and hollowing into aisles brought to mind a vast, labyrinthine sheik's tent, and as she stared around, Linda's irritation with Gordon instantly abated, to be replaced by a serene, almost hypnotic sense of contentment.

An hour and eight departments later, she still feels as if she is floating rather than walking. Nothing is entirely real, everything brighter and more colourful than usual, yet at the same time vague and somehow insubstantial. Half convinced that the entire store and all the merchandise and people in it are concocted from smoke, she is scared to touch anything in case it shimmers and vanishes and the illusion is spoiled, and so she touches nothing, merely looks. And what her vision reports, her memory hoards.

Persian and Armenian rugs hanging in leaved rows like the pages of a gigantic illuminated manuscript. Bolts of curtain material and upholstery fabric stacked in ziggurats whose peaks brush the seven-metre-high ceiling. A seemingly unending chain of kitchen showrooms, each opening onto the next like the different-coloured chambers in the Edgar Allen Poe story. Wallpapers—chintz, flock, screenprinted, anaglypta, plain. And the constant, courteous attention of the sales assistants and floor-walkers. "May I help you, madam?" "See something you like, madam?" "Would madam like to look at...?" "Would madam care to try...?"

Madam! In all her life Linda can't recall being referred to as madam before, except by her father when he was in one of his moods and everything he said was laced with snarling sarcasm. *These* madams are sincere and deferential; likewise the sirs that come Gordon's way. It seems that Days staff genuinely find it a pleasure to serve customers, and it doesn't matter that she graciously turns down their offers of help, because they sound not one jot less polite as they apologise for troubling her and wish her a very pleasant day's shopping.

She could spend the rest of her life here. The sheer abundance of worldly goods on display, the respect she is automatically accorded, and the sense of being on an (almost) equal footing with the wealthiest and most powerful people in the land, make the world outside the store seem cheap and hard and coarse by comparison. There is a refinement to Days and a feeling of order that is not to be found elsewhere in the city. Some part of Linda has understood all along that she belongs in here rather than out there, and she feels she has found her haven, and knows the exhilaration of a bird when it finally alights at the end of a long, arduous migration.

Even when the lightning sale was announced at ten, Linda was pleasantly surprised to discover that there was nothing mindless or aggressive about the way several of the shoppers in the immediate vicinity turned and bolted for the nearest lift or escalator. They didn't, as she had been conditioned by rumour and hearsay to expect, behave like a rabble. Rather, they mobilised themselves with military efficiency, as if they existed in a state of perpetual readiness for moments like these. That impressed her, and she looked forward to a time when she, too, would be familiar enough with the layout of the store and confident enough of her place here to make such well-judged and well-informed decisions. That, surely, would be soon.

She is beginning to think that she was a fool to listen to the taxi driver and buy his pepper spray. Judging from her experiences so far, Days isn't a dangerous place at all. She has seldom felt safer or more at home.

If there is a fly in the ointment, it is a small one, but an irksome one nonetheless: her husband.

It is nothing Gordon has said over the past hour that has annoyed her. Rather, it is the fact that he hasn't said *anything*, in spite of her best attempts to engage him in conversation. She has asked for his opinion on various kinds of shelving, on a spice rack, on a tortoiseshell photograph frame, all things to do with the house, the living space he shares with her, all things he ought to be interested in, and what has she received in return? At best, monosyllables; at worst, grunts. He has been traipsing after her from department to department like an old, footsore dog on a leash. Any enthusiasm he might have had an hour ago has definitely waned, while she is as brisk and as eager as ever. Proof (as if she needed it) that men do not have the stamina for serious shopping.

Finally, when she can bear Gordon's sullen, uncommunicative presence no longer, Linda comes to a halt at the entrance to the Lighting Department. Squinting against the blaze from several thousand lamps and lanterns, she can just make out sales assistants equipped with tinted goggles drifting to and fro within, ministering to the merchandise, replacing expended bulbs with spares from bandoliers strapped across their chests. Haloed by brightness, the sales assistants are etiolated, angelic figures.

She turns to her husband. "Gordon, what would you say to going our separate ways for a while?"

The question takes him aback.

"It only makes sense," she goes on. "After all, you don't want to be tagging along behind me all day. There must be departments you want to explore by yourself."

"No, this is fine."

"Your voice rises an octave when you lie, Gordon, did you know that?"

"It does not," Gordon protests squeakily.

"Go on, I know you're dying to head off on your own. It's ten twenty now. Let's meet up again at a quarter to one, here." That should give her enough time to buy the tie she picked out for him from the catalogue, and then she can present it to him over lunch.

Gordon, with a great and not wholly convincing show of reluctance, gives in. "So which one of us gets to hang on to the card?"

"I do, of course."

"Is that wise?"

Linda thinks he might be teasing her, but he isn't teasing her. His eyes are narrow and serious behind his spectacles.

"Gordon, I'd hate to think that you don't trust me with our Days Silver."

"I do trust you," he says, too quickly.

"But still you think it'll be safer if you hold on to it instead of me."

"That's not what I said."

"That's what you implied."

"I'm sorry if that's how it sounded. What I meant was, since the account is held jointly in both our names, every purchase made with the card ought to be agreed on by both of us. Don't you think?"

"Whatever happened to man and wife being one body, one flesh?"

"Come on, that's just a metaphor."

"I don't know about you, Gordon, but when I took my marriage vows, I meant every word of them sincerely."

"You're not being rational, Linda."

"And you're not being fair. This is just as much my card as yours." She waves the Silver in front of his nose. "Either one of us on our own couldn't have earned it. Together, we did. This card represents the fact that we are greater than the sum of our individual parts. It shows what two people can achieve if they pool their resources and work as one."

"The majority of those resources coming from my salary."

"I'm not just talking about the money, I'm talking about the sacrifices we made *together*, the hardships we endured *together*. And anyway, I've done my bit. What with the upkeep of the house and shopping thriftily and coming up with money-saving scheme after money-saving scheme, not to mention my hairdressing, I'm at least an equal partner in our Days account."

"Well, let's not get into that now," says Gordon. "What concerns me, Linda, is that we don't run up a debt we can't pay off. I see people at the bank every day who've got themselves into all sorts of difficulties over credit cards or Days accounts."

"And they've come to you for help, which you give them in the form of a loan, on which, of course, the bank charges interest." Linda grins venomously. "Or have I got it wrong, Gordon? Have banks started giving money away free?"

"Better to owe money to a reputable bank than to some dodgy character who'll break your legs if you don't pay up," Gordon replies, unflustered. "But that has no bearing on the point I'm making. The point I'm making is, people wouldn't be tempted to borrow money if borrowing wasn't looked on as an acceptable alternative—no, as *preferable*—to doing without what you can't afford. It takes strength of character to say no and wait rather than say yes and have immediately, and it's that lack of strength of character in all of us that gets exploited time and time again."

"We did without for five years," Linda asserts firmly. "We've earned the right to our Silver."

"But let's be careful with it, eh? That's all I'm getting at. Let's not go mad."

"Have I gone mad yet, Gordon? Have I? So far I haven't bought one item from this store. I've looked around, I've seen dozens of things I'd like to own, things that would look nice in our home, but what have I bought? Nothing. Not a thing."

"And I admire your restraint. For most people the limit on a credit account is a goal rather than a boundary, something to race for rather than keep as far away as possible from."

"You of all people, Gordon, should know that I have more self-control than 'most people'."

"Linda, please. I'm not criticising you. I'm just sounding a note of caution."

"But don't you see, that's all I've heard all morning!" She clutches the air in exasperation. "People warning me, people trying to sow doubts. It seems like no one except me believes I know what I'm doing. This is *my* day, Gordon. This is the day I've been dreaming about all my life. All my life!" She can feel her face growing hot as her voice rises, but she is unable to do anything about either. Shoppers are turning and looking in her direction. She strives to ignore their scrutiny. "I've suffered and struggled and compromised just to get to the place I'm in now, and I won't have you, I won't have *anyone*, ruining this for me. This is *my* moment of glory. Please have the good grace to let me savour it. You can caution me all you want when we get back home tonight."

Gordon has more to say on this subject but deems it wise to save it for later. He simply nods. "All right, Linda. All right. Let's have it your way. We'll split up, and you can hang on to the card. I trust you."

"Do you? Do you really?"

"Do I have a choice?"

Linda beams at him in vindication. "*That's* more like it, Gordon."

17

Seventh-Inning Stretch: A traditional pause during a baseball game, after the first half of the seventh inning.

10.30 a.m.

IT IS TIME for Frank's mid-morning break and, on cue, his bladder starts to exert a mild, insistent pressure against his lower abdominal wall. Not painful, but not to be ignored either.

From years of repetition, Frank's body has synchronised its urges with the dictates of his daily timetable. He wakes moments before his alarm clock tells him to wake, he starts to feel hungry just when his schedule permits him to eat, and his bladder has learned to regulate the incoming flow of liquid so that it reaches capacity just when it is convenient for him to drain it. Indeed, his physiological functions dovetail so immaculately with the pattern of his working days that on Sundays, when in theory he ought to be free to do as he pleases, he ingests and eliminates at the exact same times as during the rest of the week. Some might cite this as a demonstration of mankind's evolutionary talent for adapting to circumstances, but Frank knows better. To him it implies that inside every human brain sits a mainspring regulating the turn of the cogs that govern the body's rhythms. People run on clockwork, and if they are forced to go through the same routine day after day, their rhythms become rigidly attuned to the work-metronome—so much so that, sometimes, they find they literally cannot live without it. Frank knows of numerous retired or sacked employees who have gone mad or dropped dead shortly after their last day at Days, unable to cope with being liberated from the strict tick-tocking of a timetable. Time suddenly slackens its grip on them, and their mainsprings whirl and spool out.

By leaving today he may be able to prevent suffering the same fate himself. If he stays any longer, it may be too late.

This is Frank Hubble, he subvocalises to the Eye. I'm clocking off for half an hour.

OK, Mr Hubble, says a screen-jockey, a girl this time. Frank hears the rattle of a keyboard. Enjoy your coffee break.

Polite, cheerful—she can't have been on the job more than a week. It won't be long before poor diet, stress, and overexposure to the ion-charged atmosphere generated by myriad TV screens have turned her into a short-tempered, facetious pest like her colleagues.

Finding a staff lift, Frank summons it with a swipe of his Iridium, and on his way down studies his smeary reflection in the steel doors. This blurred other Frank appears and disappears and reappears over and over as his concentration waxes and wanes, until finally he stops bothering to look for it, and it vanishes altogether.

I am there, he tells himself, *I am there, I am there, I am.* But the words ring hollow when the evidence of his eyes tells him the truth.

He longs for the day when he will once more be able to glance into a reflecting surface and see himself there without having to make a conscious effort, and suddenly his resolve to seek out Mr Bloom and tender his resignation burgeons again.

But first, having arrived in the Basement, he heads for Tactical Security, and there, in the Gents cloakroom, he assumes the position at a urinal and braces himself for his regularly-scheduled relief.

10.33 a.m.

YEARS AGO, THE Tactical Security cafeteria had a buffet counter manned by serving staff, but they found it a disagreeable place to work. The Ghosts—as cold a bunch of fish as you could ever hope to meet—treated them as though they were beings from another dimension, barely talking to them beyond the basic courtesies of "Please" and "Thank you" and never able to look them in the eye, until after a while some of the staff actually started to believe that the Ghosts' behaviour was normal and that it was they themselves, with their friendly, outgoing attitude, who had something wrong with them.

Automation was infinitely preferable for all concerned, and was introduced shortly after Frank started at Days. The food is of an inferior quality, tending towards the prepackaged and the microwaveable, the preservative-laced and the just-add-water instant, but the Ghosts find the dispensing machines a great deal more amenable than real people. The machines do not try to strike up a rapport, do not jabber pointlessly about the weather or politics, and do not take umbrage when their conversational overtures are rejected. The machines dole out food and drink at the touch of a button, without fuss, with comforting predictability, and thanks to them and to plastic cutlery, paper napkins, and cardboard plates and cups, the need for human staff in the Tactical Security cafeteria has been all but done away with. There remains a skeleton staff of two: the janitor who comes in after closing time to empty the bins and mop up, and the technician who comes in once a week to restock and service the machines.

Withdrawing a near-scalding cup of coffee from the delivery chute of the hot-beverage dispenser, Frank scans the cafeteria for an unoccupied table. He manages to reach one and set the coffee down before its heat, efficiently conducted by the polystyrene cup, starts to blister his fingertips.

He will go and see Mr Bloom once he has finished the coffee. The coffee is a delaying tactic, he knows that, but a few moments to clear his head before tendering his resignation won't go amiss.

He has barely had a chance to take more than a few sips when Mr Bloom strolls into the cafeteria.

Nonchalantly the Head of Tactical Security fetches himself a cup of milky tea and a jam doughnut, and chooses an empty table. Mr Bloom seldom eats in the cafeteria, and it can't be coincidence that he has chosen to be here at a time when Frank is likely to be here too.

Frank contemplates slipping quietly out of the room, but he realises that would be childish. Besides, Mr Bloom's attempt to pin him down—if that is what it is—may be an abuse of their thirty-three years of acquaintance, but it is a miscalculation rather than an act of malice.

With a sigh, Frank takes a last swig of the by now merely piping-hot coffee, gets up, and strides heavily over to Mr Bloom's table. A part of him cannot believe what he is about to do, and begs him not to put himself through this ordeal. Why this compulsion to make his resignation official? Why not just slip away without telling a soul?

Because that would not be proper. Because he owes Mr Bloom, if no one else, an explanation. And because to sneak away furtively is the action of a thief, and thieves are a breed Frank has dedicated half a lifetime to thwarting.

"Donald?"

"Frank." There is little surprise in Mr Bloom's eyes.

Frank can almost hear the grinding of neck bones as the Ghosts around him surreptitiously strain to listen.

"Could we have that chat now?"

"Of course. My office?"

"Of course."

10.39 a.m.

FOR THE FIRST time Frank notices the homely touches in the office as he sits facing Mr Bloom across his desk. The small framed photograph of a young girl (Mr Bloom has mentioned a niece in the past). The paperback novels sandwiched on a shelf between bulky file boxes—Joyce, Solzhenitsyn, Woolf. The yellowed, frail clipping from a financial newspaper tacked to one corner of the year planner on the wall, an amusing ambiguity in its headline: "Spring Figures Prove That Days Has Not Lost Its Bloom." The yellow smiley-face sticker pasted over the Days logo on the desktop terminal. Tiny, personal additions it would never occur to Frank to make were this bland subterranean cell his own.

Mr Bloom is waiting for him to speak. He has been waiting a full three minutes, patiently eating the jam doughnut and licking the sugar granules off his fingers, sipping the tea. Frank's silence is about to cross the line dividing hesitation from rudeness.

He admits defeat. "I don't know where to begin."

"Begin at the beginning," says Mr Bloom.

"That's the trouble. I'm not sure where the beginning is. Things just seem to have... *accumulated*. I thought I was happy in my job, now it seems I'm not."

"Ah." Mr Bloom's eyebrows lift, parallel wavy furrows bunching across his brow all the way up to his tenacious foretuft. "And is there any particular aspect of the job that you're not happy with, or is it nothing you can put a finger on?"

"It's... me, I suppose. The job is the job. It doesn't change, so I must have changed." Why is he making this so difficult for himself? He should just come right out with it, American-style. *I quit.* That's all he needs to say, those two little words. Why this pussyfooting about? Why the absurd desire to break it gently? What difference will it make to Mr Bloom, one less Ghost, one less responsibility?

"Changed in what way?"

"It's hard to say."

"Frank, I appreciate that this can't be much fun for you, so take your time, and when you're feel ready, tell me what's on your mind. I don't need to remind you that nothing you say will go beyond these four walls, so feel free to have a go at the customers, the brothers, a co-worker, a sales assistant with offensive halitosis, me, anyone you want."

"This has nothing to do with anyone else. This is just *me*."

Mr Bloom regards Frank placidly. "Yes, I know. I was just trying to get you to crack a smile. Silly me."

"Donald, why did *you* leave the job?"

"I thought we were here to talk about you."

"It might help."

"Really? Well, if you say so. Why did I give up the Ghost? Mainly because I couldn't hack it any more. I wasn't making as many collars as I used to. Customers were noticing me. I was losing my touch."

"Losing touch?" Frank asks carefully, pretending to have misheard.

"No, losing *my* touch," says Mr Bloom, flashing a look of curiosity across the desk. "I was offered the promotion at just the right time. I didn't accept it because I wanted to, I accepted it because I had to. I had no choice. There was no way they could keep me on as a Ghost, so it was either this or retirement, and I wasn't ready for the pipe and slippers just then. I'm still not. And the Academy wasn't an option. How could I be expected to train people to become Ghosts if I didn't have the talent for it myself any more? Is any of this relevant to your problem?"

"Not really."

"I didn't think so. *You* still have the knack for it, Frank. Your arrest record is as high as ever. You're one of the best, I might even say *the* best, and Lord, I'd give my eye-teeth to be out on the shop floor like you, still plugging away, still getting the old tingle when you spot a likely one. Granted, it can be godawful at times, it can get as boring as hell, and there are days when your feet feel like two lumps of lead and your legs have knives in place of bones, and there are departments you hate going into but feel obliged to go into anyway, and you get sick of looking at customers' faces day in, day out, those empty, eager faces—you'd think they'd have enough of what they wanted, but it's never enough, and even the fat ones look hungry, don't they? And the screen-jockeys, God, the screen-jockeys! Imps of the perverse, sent to torment us. But Frank—isn't it all worth it the moment you make a good, clean collar? When you catch a real smooth operator red-handed, and you know the sticky-fingered bastard is *yours*, he's not getting away from you, he's a done deal? Isn't any amount of crap worth the wonderful feeling of utter conviction you get as you lay your hand on his shoulder and show him what he did on your Sphinx and recite the Booster's Blessing? Those few minutes of pure, sweet clarity of purpose are a Ghost's reward for all the hours of fuss and tedium and aggravation. Don't you agree?"

Frank is about to reply when two things happen. First, seven notes ring out over the loudspeaker mounted outside the door, the echoes bouncing down the corridor, and the announcement of a lightning sale in Travel Goods commences.

"Attention, customers."

Almost simultaneously, the Eye whispers in Frank's ear.

Mr Hubble? It is the same girl he spoke to quarter of an hour ago. I'm sorry to interrupt you on your break, but they want you over in Processing.

What?

It's a shoplifter you collared. Wants to talk to you. Insists on it.

I have something else on at the moment.

"Frank?"

"Travel Goods is located in the south-eastern quadrant of the Orange Floor and may be reached using the banks of lifts designated I, J and K."

Processing think it'll help if you go over there.

"Frank?"

Excuse me, Dona— "Excuse me, Donald. I'm talking to the Eye." Eye, this is highly irregular.

I know, Mr Hubble, and I wouldn't have dreamed of bothering you, but Processing says the shoplifter won't talk to anyone until you get there.

Talk? What about?

I'm sorry, they didn't tell me.

Well, the timing stinks. *But actually*, Frank thinks, *it could have been a lot worse.*

What can I say? I'm sorry.

Hubble out. "Donald, I have to go."

"What's up?"

"I'm not sure."

"Well, can't it wait? Can't someone else deal with it?"

"Apparently not."

Mr Bloom keeps his suspicions to himself. It wouldn't be out of character for a Ghost to fake an emergency appointment in order to get out of a situation that was in danger of becoming uncomfortably personal. "All right. Look, we obviously have a lot more to talk about. Let's meet for lunch."

"Donald, I don't—"

"One o'clock, at the Italian restaurant on the Green Floor hoop."

"I don't think that's such a good place for a talk."

"Frank, no one'll pay any attention to you. Or to me, if I really don't want them to."

"Well..." Frank is at the door.

"It's a date, then. One sharp. Promise me you'll be there."

Embarrassed at the eagerness with which he has seized his chance to escape, Frank can hardly refuse.

"I usually eat lunch at quarter to one," he says.

"Quarter to it is, then."

18

Sze: The seventh hexagram of the *I-Ching*, usually interpreted as meaning the need for discipline and for the leadership of a superior general with age and experience on his side.

10.32 a.m.

Over dinner, Septimus Day was fond of lecturing his sons in the art of retailing, which was also, as far as he was concerned, the art of life. In lieu of proper conversation, the founder of the world's first and (for the best part of his lifetime) foremost gigastore would spend the duration of the meal holding forth on any topic that entered his head and contriving to draw from it lessons that applied to the store, in much the same way that a priest in his sermon draws lessons from everyday events and applies them to his religion. Always Septimus's homilies ended in epigrammatic maxims, of which he had dozens, his equivalent of Biblical quotations.

In Septimus's later years, the audience for these lectures consisted for the most part of just Sonny and Mungo. With the other five brothers away at boarding school or university, Mungo having graduated *summa cum laude* in the same year that Sonny graduated from nappies to a potty, the three of them would eat their evening meals in the sepulchral, candlelit cavernousness of the family mansion's dining room, scrupulously waited on by Perch. Regardless of the empty places at table, the old man would pontificate as usual, bestowing only the occasional glance on his oldest and youngest sons, as though Mungo and Sonny were just two of many present.

Sonny grew up watching his father physically and mentally decline. He never knew a time when Septimus was not in poor health, and as he saw the shine in his father's remaining eye grow daily duller and observed the increasing fragility of the old man's hands and thought processes, he wished in his child's heart that there was something he could do, some gesture he could make to reassure Septimus that all was well, that there was no need for this quiet sadness that seemed to be eating him from the inside out. A simple hug might have helped, but displays of affection, especially those of the spontaneous variety, were out of the question in the Day household. Septimus Day was training the men who would assume control of his business after he died, not raising a family.

As Sonny turned five, six, seven, the dinnertime lectures grew ever more discursive and rambling. Sometimes, in the depths of a long and convoluted sentence, the old man would give a start, as though he had been asleep and someone had just shouted in his ear. He would stop talking, blink around, then resume the lecture on a completely different tack. Other times, he would get himself stuck in a loop, repeating a sentence over and over as though unable to stress its meaning enough or with a sufficient variety of emphases. And even the prepubescent Sonny could tell that it was a good thing that Mungo had assumed the burden of running the store. Their father was clearly no longer up to it.

If the lectures taught Sonny nothing else, they taught him patience. He learned how to sit through them in respectful silence, and he learned how to tune out the sound of his father's voice until almost nothing the old man said penetrated. Still, many of Septimus's maxims did somehow—perhaps through sheer repetition—lodge in his brain, and there have stuck fast.

For example: "Other people exist to be subjugated to your will. Will is all. With will, anything can be achieved. Dreams can be forced into existence, a vast building can be raised out of a wasteland, wealth can be generated. Lack of experience and lack of expertise are no obstacle as long as you have will."

And: "Numbers have power. Numbers are the engines with which one can assault the stronghold of Fate, scale its ramparts and loot its treasures. And there is no number quite as significant as the number seven. I myself am the youngest of seven brothers, and I have sired seven sons for the express purpose of ensuring the continuation of my success. The number seven is a charm that has many meanings, great power, and should never be broken."

And: "Customers are sheep and expect to be treated like sheep. Treat them like royalty, and though they will remain sheep, they'll be less likely to complain when you fleece them."

And: "A contract improperly worded deserves to be broken. If one party fails to specify down to the finest detail what is required, the other party has the right, if not the duty, to take advantage of such carelessness. *Caveat emptor!*"

The lectures were frequently punctuated with that phrase, "*Caveat emptor!*", usually accompanied by a loud, cutlery-rattling thump on the tabletop. It was Septimus's amen.

Other than watching his father totter off into the grounds of the estate for long walks, his white head bowed in melancholy contemplation, Sonny's memories of the old man consist almost entirely of those dinnertime discourses. This is hardly surprising since, evening meals apart, there was little contact between Septimus Day and any of his sons.

Sonny was eight years old when the old man succumbed to an inoperable liver cancer.

At the funeral, in front of a battery of news cameras from around the world, he surprised himself by crying.

As he stands in his walk-in wardrobe now, gazing at a long row of suits on hangers, he is thinking not how sorry he is that he hardly knew his father but how proud the old man would be of him today, were he alive. Sonny has taken the first step on the road to acceptance by his brothers. Until today they have merely tolerated his presence in the Boardroom, making it clear that they consider him superfluous to requirements and that he is there only to make up numbers. His exclusion from their six-man enclave has been a source of some bitterness and not a little misery. Many a night Sonny has lain awake in bed seething at the unfairness of it all. To be born a son of Septimus Day, to inherit a seventh part of total control of the world's first and (sinking sales be damned) foremost gigastore, and yet never to be fully his brothers' equal, has seemed the cruellest and most unjust punishment ever visited on a human being. But today—by the electric tingle all over his skin Sonny knows this to be true—today a corner has been turned. Today everything has begun to change. And the catalyst for that change was none other than Sonny himself. Certainly Mungo did his bit, but reviewing what occurred in the Boardroom a few minutes ago, Sonny is convinced that he himself was at least ninety-nine per cent responsible for the shift in his brothers' previously intransigent stance. He coaxed them. He persuaded them. He subjugated them to his will.

As Sonny examines the dozens of tailor-made suits in front of him, each ordered from the Gentlemen's Outfitters Department on a whim, few ever worn, he feels a tune well up in his chest. He starts to hum as he lifts suit after suit off the rail, holding each up by the hook of its hanger and rating its suitability for the job ahead.

A three-piece in mustard-yellow flannel? Too garish.

A chessboard-chequered two-piece with lapels whose pointed tips rise clear of the shoulderpads? Too gangsterish.

A double-breasted jacket and a pair of pleated trousers stitched together from blackcurrant-purple cotton? Not bad, except for the embroidered gold Days logos adorning the cuffs and pockets, which make the suit look like some sort of bizarre military dress-uniform.

This one in silver lamé? Sonny can't bring himself to look twice at that particular monstrosity, and tosses it aside. What on earth could have been going through his mind when he ordered it? He must have been drunk. But then it's pretty safe to say that anything Sonny has done since achieving his majority has been done drunk.

His humming evolves into a warbling whistle.

What he is looking for is an outfit that will combine seriousness with approachability. A look that will say, "Here I am. Respect me but don't fear me." Surprisingly, given the range of suits available, finding one that fits those criteria is proving quite a challenge. Still he rummages on, content that the right suit will present itself soon enough.

Downstairs. Sonny hasn't been downstairs, on the shop floor itself, in quite a while. A couple of years, at least. Two years spent living cloistered above the store, confined to one floor and the roof, cut off from human contact, his only company his brothers, Perch, and the flitting, furtive menials who are under permanent instruction to vacate a room immediately should he or his brothers enter. It's a peculiar way to live, if you think about it, but it seems to agree with him, with all of them. When you consider the alternative, a home somewhere out there in the teeming city, rubbing shoulders with the rest of the world, it actually seems quite a desirable lifestyle, if somewhat monastic.

He wonders if the store will look and feel any different from the way he remembers, and suspects that things will have stayed pretty much the same. Days is like a granite mountain, through sheer size resisting everything but the most incremental changes. The departments will be the same, the sales assistants will be the same, the customers will be the same...

Abruptly, the whistled tune dies on Sonny's lips. He remembers only too clearly the last time he was downstairs. It was the day he returned from his final term at university, and instead of using the private lift from the car park to the Violet Floor he decided to ride the escalators up to the

Indigo and take the lift from there. It was meant to be a kind of triumphal homecoming procession, and with his entourage of security guards Sonny certainly felt the part of the heroic soldier returning from some distant conflict, until he became conscious of the stares of the customers he passed. Dozens of pairs of strangers' eyes turning, being brought to bear on him.

He dismisses the memory with a shudder. He is older now, wiser, and anyway, it's only to be expected that a son of Septimus Day should be an object of curiosity.

Except there seemed to be more than curiosity in the customers' stares. They were looking at him as if they knew everything there was to know about him and hated what they saw.

He would say that his imagination was conspiring to play tricks on him had he not also seen that same look in his brothers' eyes from time to time. Occasionally, he would see it in his father's eye, too. Every now and then at the dinner table he would catch the old man watching him very carefully. His schoolmates, too, had it in certain lights. And his fellow undergraduates. A look with actual weight, exerting a tangible pressure on the object of scrutiny.

A look of accusation. A look of resentment.

At that, a subtle scratching begins in Sonny's head.

The scratching sound is made by a creature which Sonny imagines has claws like a rat's, claws that carry all kinds of festering infections beneath their white crescent sharpness. He knows that it does not pay to listen to that creature's soft, insinuating scurry, or to let it come too near with its talons. He refocuses his attention on the task at hand.

A fiery ginger camel-hair number? Uh-uh. Nope.

A baggy green-and-orange woollen tartan jacket with matching trousers? Only if he has a pair of clown shoes and a squirting buttonhole flower to go with it.

He delves on through the racks, trying not to think about the purpose for which he is searching out a suit, trying to think only of the positive aspects of the responsibility that has been thrust upon him, the fact that it shows that his brothers are prepared to take him seriously at last.

But the creature, having emerged from its lair, will not be sent back there so easily. In wainscot whispers it reminds Sonny of the mother's love he never knew, and of the envy he used to feel when other boys at school were picked up for exeats by their parents—both parents, both smiling, a hand-shaking father, an embracing mother—while he had to make do with a hired chauffeur-cum-bodyguard, grim and vigilant. It speaks to him of the basic right granted to almost every other living thing but denied him, and it hisses the sibilant name of the one to blame for his deprivation.

"No." Sonny has to dredge the word up out of himself. The sky-blue nylon suit he is holding trembles. He clenches his eyelids shut and presses his forehead against the edge of a shelf bearing folded pullovers, a narrow line of pain. His upper teeth slide out to gnaw his lower lip.

Everything that moments ago was rosy and delightful crumbles away. His enthusiasm for the task ahead is gone with a pop, like a floating soap bubble jabbed by a killjoy's fingertip. He attempts to recover the mood of optimism—the feeling of near-invulnerability—that had him waltzing out of the Boardroom and down the spiral staircase and along the corridors of the Violet Floor to his apartment, but it is ruined beyond repair, and the act of trying to recapture it only damages it further.

And now the creature—an emotion Sonny cannot give a name, a patchwork beast of doubt and guilt and paranoia—is scuttling and snuffling around yet more busily.

What if the task his brothers have set him is a hopeless one? What if the dispute proves impossible to arbitrate? What if they *intend* for him to fail? After all, if he fails, that will justify once and for all their lack of faith in him. No longer will they have to hunt around for excuses to deny him equal status. A disaster downstairs will give them all the proof they need that he is unreliable. It will be an example they can trot out whenever he campaigns for a fair crack of the whip in the future. "But Sonny," they will say, "look what happened the last time we gave you something to do. Look what a mess you made of *that*."

The suit slips from Sonny's fingers, billowing to the floor, forming a rumpled silky puddle of sky blue.

There is a way to get rid of the nagging creature, banish it back to its lair. A guaranteed method. Tried and tested.

But he made a deal with his brothers.

He imagines them laughing at him right now, their faces around the table: Sato tittering, Fred chortling, Thurston chuckling almost soundlessly, Wensley hurrh-hurrhing throatily, Chas gently snickering, Mungo guffawing with authoritative gusto. Laughing at him because they never really expected him to keep his half of the bargain. Laughing because he was a fool to try.

And he pictures customers and employees staring at him as if he is half god, half madman. Whispers passing behind cupped hands: "Do you see that? That's Sonny Day. The Afterthought. If it hadn't been for *him...*"

He must have been mad to agree to go downstairs sober, with all his nerve endings exposed, raw to the world, without the extra lucidity and calmness that a drink or two brings.

No, the conditions Mungo laid down were completely unreasonable, and Mungo knew it. His brothers want him to screw up the arbitration, that's all there is to it. They have deliberately put him in an impossible situation. If he isn't drunk, he won't have the courage to go downstairs, and if he goes downstairs drunk, he will have reneged on the deal. Damned if he does, damned if he doesn't.

The creature in his head is hopping from foot to foot with all the glee of a crow that has alighted on fresh carrion. Its talons tick-tack on the inside of Sonny's skull, a sound like sinuses cracking.

He could silence it in seconds. All he has to do is go to the bar in the living room, pour himself a measure of something (anything), pour himself another, and keep on pouring. In no time the creature will be gone.

Which is exactly what the creature wants. It crawls out from its lair with the sole purpose of tormenting him into drinking it back into submission. Allowing the creature into his head means it has one kind of weakness to feast on, exorcising it with booze offers it another kind. The creature doesn't care. Either way, it gets its fill of frailty. *His* frailty.

But he made a deal, and what kind of Day brother is he if he can't make a deal and stick to it? What kind of son of Septimus Day?

At that precise moment, the old man's opinion on the subject of deals comes zinging to the forefront of Sonny's thoughts.

"A contract improperly worded deserves to be broken."

And he can see again, as if it were only yesterday, his father seated at the head of the dining table, bent nearly double over his plate with didactic fervour, spearing his point home with a thrust of his fork in the air.

"If one party fails to specify down to the finest detail what is required, the other party has the right, if not the duty, to take advantage of such carelessness."

And then the thump of fist on rosewood, making everything on the table jump, and the familiar oath:

"*Caveat emptor!*"

All very well and fine, sound advice, but with his brothers there was no written contract, just a simple verbal agreement.

"If, perhaps, you leave that drink in front of you unfinished," Mungo said, "and we had Perch come in and take away the gin bottle..."

Even when Sonny clarified the conditions, the deal sounded no less watertight. "All I have to do is not drink the rest of this bottle." No room for manouevring there.

Or is there?

"All I have to do is not drink the rest of this bottle."

Of *this* bottle.

No one said anything about any other bottle.

"Sonny," Sonny Day says to himself, "you are a genius." He raises his forehead from the shelf and opens his eyes. "A grade-A, certified genius."

The creature is rubbing its grubby paws together, obscenely gratified.

Sonny turns and stumbles out of the wardrobe, out of the bedroom. Down a broad corridor wanly illuminated by skylights he hurries, until he reaches a large chamber that used to be the Wickerwork Department before it was absorbed into Handicrafts on the Blue Floor, and which now serves as his living room. The decor is entirely of Sonny's choosing. Cream-coloured shagpile carpet covers the floor like an ankle-deep layer of milk froth. Chairs and sofas upholstered in white suede, marshmallow-plump, are arranged around a sheared slab of basalt a metre thick and three metres square that serves as a coffee table, its polished surface strewn with magazines, handheld electronic puzzles, and gimmicky executive toys. A state-of-the-art home entertainment system takes up virtually one entire wall, stacks of matt-black units clustered around a television set the size of a chest of drawers. A parade of picture windows offers a widescreen view of the city most ordinary citizens would give all they owned to have—roads busy with twinkling traffic, sun-warmed buildings basking shoulder to shoulder. Kept at bay by Days Plaza, at this remove the city actually looks like a pleasant place to live.

One corner of the living room is taken up by the bar, a dipsomaniac's dream built of glass bricks and mirrors, with stainless steel stools and rack upon rack of bottles inverted over optics. Sonny heads for it like a homing missile. Grabbing a tumbler, he hesitates, momentarily bewildered by the choice before him. Every type of spirit is represented by several brands. Which should he have? He selects one at random, thinking, *What difference does it make? Booze is booze.* A shot of cinnamon-spiced vodka glugs into the glass. The optic bubbles greasily. What the hell, make it a double. He chugs it down at a swallow.

The rest of this bottle.

Idiots. They thought they had him on a hook, but he has outsmarted them, has found a way to wriggle off. He tosses another six measures of the vodka down his gullet in quick succession, toasting his brothers one after another with furious sarcasm. The result is as swift as it is magnificent. A warm, rising tide of confidence engulfs him from belly to brow.

Oh yes, this is better. Much, much better.

The old man would definitely be proud of him, there's no doubt about it.

There's no doubt about anything at all.

19

Commit the Seventh: Break the Seventh Commandment, i.e. commit adultery.

10.51 a.m.

FRANK HAS SENT innumerable shoplifters down to Processing, but he has never actually had cause to go there himself. There's a first time for everything, he supposes. Even on your last day at work.

As he makes his way through the Byzantine twists and turns of the Basement corridors, it strikes him as fitting that a shoplifter's last few minutes on the premises should be spent down here. How better to drive home to the criminal the full consequences of his crime than by leading him out of the bright, bustling departments, filled with people and opulence, down to a functional, stuffy layer of grey duct-lined corridors and confined spaces sandwiched between the seven storeys of the store and the seven levels of underground car park? For in this drab limbo, this dimly-lit interzone, the shoplifter is granted a foretaste of what he can expect from the life that awaits him, a life without Days: a monotonous tangle of dead ends and drudgery.

Processing turns out to be a plain, rectangular chamber, one side of which is partitioned off into a row of glass-fronted, soundproofed interview booths. Three shoplifters waiting their turn to be processed sit on wooden benches facing away from the booths—their fates, so to speak, behind them, sealed. They are paired off with the security guards who escorted them down and who will remain with them, a constant hip-joined presence, right up until the moment of eviction. They make for ludicrously mismatched couples—stiff-spined guards, slumped shoplifters. One of the shoplifters is quietly sobbing. Another, clearly a troublemaker, sits hunched forward with his hands manacled behind his back. There is a bruise below his right eye, swollen and puffy, pale yellow turning to black. "I was going to pay for it," he keeps telling the guard, over and over, as if honesty can be earned by insistence. "I was going to pay for it. I was going to pay for it."

Obtrusive to no one, Frank glides past the booth windows. Through one of the large double-glazed panes he spies a familiar profile, but he continues to the end of the row before turning back, mildly vexed. For some reason he was expecting it to be the arrogant ponytailed professional who summoned him here, not sore-eyed, dishevelled Mrs Shukhov.

He taps on the door to the booth in which Mrs Shukhov is sitting. Also inside are the guard Gould and a short, trim, sandy-haired man in a Days dollar-green suit, the employee in charge of Mrs Shukhov's processing. All three look up. Mrs Shukhov smiles, but Frank ignores her. The processor rises from his desk and steps out of the booth for a quiet word.

"You're Frank Hubble?" he asks in frowsty Celtic tones. The name on his ID is Morrison, and if his tie were any more tightly knotted, it would be strangling him.

Frank says, "I hope you appreciate what an imposition this is."

"I do, but she was being difficult. She *had* to have you here."

"Any idea why?"

"If I didn't know better"—Morrison flashes a narrow-toothed grin—"I'd say the lady's taken a shine to you."

"Ridiculous," Frank snorts, and bats open the door and strides into the booth, Morrison in his wake.

"Mr Hubble." Mrs Shukhov half rises from her seat to greet him.

Frank scowls at her, and she hunches contritely, crumpling in on herself like a withering flower. "I've put you out, haven't I? How rude of me. Please, go back to whatever it was you were doing. I've obviously dragged you away from something important. Go on. I apologise for having disturbed you."

"I'm here now," he says, and shrinks back to allow Morrison to squeeze past him to reach the desk, making himself small so that there is no danger of even their clothes touching. There isn't room for a fourth chair in the booth, so Frank does what he can with the meagre area of floorspace available to him between the edge of the desk and Gould's knees. He sets his shoulderblades against the wall, squares his feet on the carpet, and folds his arms across his chest, feeling the butt of his gun pressing into his left triceps, and he tries not to think how close he is to three other human beings, close enough to be breathing in their exhalations, claustrophobically close. Four people crammed into a few cubic metres of air, a miasma of scents, personal spaces overlapping. Stifling.

"I feel such a fool," Mrs Shukhov confides to Gould.

"All right then," says Morrison, seating himself at his desk. He brisks his palms together. "No more time-wasting, Mrs Shukhov, eh?"

"Yes, of course," says Mrs Shukhov. "I really am very sorry. About everything."

"Fine. Now, for Mr Hubble's benefit, I'm going to recap what little information I've managed to glean so far. The lady here, Mrs Carmen Andrea Shukhov, née Jenkins, is, or I should say was, the proud holder of a Platinum account. On Tuesday last, she happened to mislay her card, and for reasons she is just about to reveal to us did not report it missing and request a replacement, as you or I might have done, but chose instead to embark—with, I might add, a singular lack of success—on a career of five-fingered discounting. A decision made all the more curious by the fact that her account is in an acceptably healthy condition. No outstanding debts, and still some way below its limit." Morrison gestures at the lists of dates and figures scrolling up the screen of his terminal, a record of every transaction carried out with Mrs Shukhov's Platinum since its issue. With a single keystroke, he pulls up a second list. "Same goes for her bank account, which receives a handsome credit on the first of each month from an offshore account held in the name of a Mr G. Shukhov. Housekeeping, I take it, Mrs Shukhov?"

"Actually, maintenance."

"You and Mr Shukhov are no longer together."

"Not for over a decade. After the divorce, Grigor remained in Moscow, I came back home. We met and married while I was working out there. We had a few good years together. We lived in a gorgeous apartment in a converted mansion on Tverskaya, and Grigor looked after me well, and promised to continue to look after me even after the marriage fell apart. He was always generous with his money. The problem was, I wasn't the only woman who benefited from his generosity." The bitterness is buried so deeply in her voice as to be almost undetectable.

Mrs Shukhov goes on to explain that a condition of the divorce settlement was that her entitlement to the money depended on her not holding down a paying job of any description. The result was that she came to rely on the monthly payments, a decision she regrets now but which at the time seemed eminently sensible. If the alternative to living on a nice monthly stipend for no effort is working full-time for less money, probably a great deal less, who but a lunatic would opt for the latter?

"Then last month the payments suddenly stopped, and that, basically, left me up the creek without the proverbial paddle. No source of income and no prospect of being able to find a source of income in the immediate future."

"Ah," says Morrison, referring again to the screen. "Yes, they did stop, didn't they? Why was that, Mrs Shukhov?"

"Because Grigor himself stopped."

There is a moment of uncertain silence.

"Dead," she clarifies. "A heart attack. Sudden, massive, instantly fatal. Brought on, no doubt, by one of those gymnastic floozies he was so fond of, or by a glass too many of vodka, most likely a combination of the two."

"My condolences," says Gould sincerely.

Mrs Shukhov waves the sympathy away with a flap of her hand. "No need. Grigor and I hadn't had any contact, apart from through our lawyers, for years. I mourned his loss long before he died. To me he was already a memory."

"Even so."

"An old wound. Besides, I'm currently too busy being angry with him to be sad. Leaving me high and dry like that, without a penny to my name! Silly, I know, but that's how I feel about it. How *dare* he not make provision for me in case of his death. Although, if I'm to be honest with myself, it's as much my fault as his. I ought to have known he'd leave no assets, no capital, nothing. That's the kind of man Grigor was. His philosophy was live for today and let tomorrow take care of itself. That's what charmed me so much when I first met him—his lack of worry, his pleasure in whatever was in front of him wherever he might be, his delight in the moment. I was working at Novi GUM at the time, taking groups of foreign customers around, mainly tourists from Western Europe. It was a stressful job, and Grigor was so carefree. The perfect antidote."

Morrison can't resist an opportunity to trot out the old joke about Russia's only gigastore. "Novi GUM—they changed the name, they rebuilt the store, but there still isn't anything on the shelves."

"Not true, Mr Morrison, not true," says Mrs Shukhov. "Yes, the place was hopelessly disorganised when I was there, definitely. A shambles compared to most other gigastores, and you couldn't buy anything you wanted, not like here. But that was part of its attraction, that uniquely Russian atmosphere of amiable chaos. Like the country itself, a huge old bumbling institution that somehow, almost in spite of itself, muddles through. At the very least Novi GUM, in my day, was full of surprises. How many gigastores can you say that about?"

Certainly not this one, thinks Frank, a man neck-deep in the mire of routine.

"Every day there was a chance you could round a corner and come across something that wasn't there the night before," Mrs Shukhov goes on. "Sometimes, without warning, whole departments would swap around. Whichever department needed extra floorspace got extra floorspace, that was how it worked. A strangely democratic game of musical chairs, which made my job more difficult but also kept me from getting bored and falling into a rut. What was available depended on what the management could get hold of, you see. One day the store might take delivery of ten thousand pairs of chopsticks, the next it might be a hundred gross of ping-pong balls, the next several tonnes of tinned baby food. There was never any rhyme or reason to it, but people bought the stuff because the feeling was, 'Well, you never know when chopsticks or ping-pong balls or baby food might come in handy.' Which, I suppose, only goes to prove old Septimus Day's point about whatever can be sold will be bought and vice versa. One morning, I remember, they cleared out the Hall of Samovars and wheeled in this huge woolly mammoth which someone had chiselled out of the Siberian ice. It had been stuffed and mounted on a car chassis. On a car chassis, can you believe it!" She chuckles at the recollection, shaking her head. "A day later it was gone and the samovars were back. Somebody bought it, some museum I expect. I don't know who but museum curators would have a use for a stuffed woolly mammoth on wheels, do you?"

"I've heard Novi GUM is run much more efficiently these days," says Gould.

"Since the mafia took it over? Probably. Grigor always used to say that the whole of Russia would move over to a black market economy eventually, and he was right. He used that to his advantage, naturally. He was in the fur trade, and there fur isn't a luxury, it's a necessity, so he did well for himself. And for me. This is all somewhat off the point, isn't it?"

Morrison has to agree. "Somewhat."

"What you really want to know is why I didn't report the loss of my card."

"Well, I think you've explained that already, in so many words. You didn't report it because you were concerned that, since your ex-husband's alimony payments had ceased, Days wouldn't issue you with a replacement."

"Concerned? Terrified, more like. And without my Platinum, how would I live? More to the point, who would I be?"

"And you were right. Not only would the store have refused to replace the card until a suitable level of income had been re-established, but even if you hadn't lost it, your account would automatically have been suspended as soon as its limit was reached. But there's still one thing that puzzles me." Morrison glances at his terminal. "The last transaction carried out on the card took place the day before yesterday, the day you say you lost it, Tuesday. You bought, let me see, a Russian phrasebook."

"And I was going to buy a one-way plane ticket to Moscow next. I still have friends back there, and under the circumstances it seemed like the best place for me to be."

"You weren't by any chance planning on doing a bunk?" Gould asks, raising an eyebrow.

Mrs Shukhov confesses that she was.

"You'd never have got away with it," Morrison states with authority. "Days would have caught up with you. In fact, there's every chance you would have been stopped at the airport before you could leave the country. Nothing, Mrs Shukhov, but nothing, comes between Days and a debt."

Frank knows the truth of this. There is a clause in the disclaimer form which states that should a customer die owing more on his account than can be recovered from immediately accessible funds, the store is entitled to scoop the remainder from his estate, plus any legal expenses incurred during this process, the store's needs taking precedence over those of the relicts named in the deceased customer's will. Not even death is an escape from Days.

"Well," says Mrs Shukhov with a light shrug, "you can't blame a girl for trying."

"But back to the point," says Morrison. "You say you lost the card two days ago."

"And rotten luck it was too. I can't for the life of me think what happened to it."

"So tell me—how did you get in this morning?"

And at that Mrs Shukhov gives a broad, clever grin, and suddenly Frank thinks he has the answer. It is an unlikely answer, to be sure, but one that fits all the facts.

"She's been hiding out inside Days," he says.

Mrs Shukhov blesses him with a gracious, approving nod. "How astute of you, Mr Hubble."

"But surely..." Morrison grapples with the concept and comes off worst. "No, there has to be some other explanation."

"That's why she needed the contact lens solution," says Frank, "and why she looks and smells the way she does."

"Blunt," Gould mutters to Mrs Shukhov.

"Let's be kind and call it pointed," Mrs Shukhov mutters back.

"No, it's ridiculous," Morrison insists. "How could she? The night watchmen... The Eye..." He swings his head from side to side as though trying to evade a persistent fly.

"Believe me, Mr Morrison, it wasn't easy," says Mrs Shukhov, "but you'd be surprised what you can do when you have no fear of the consequences."

And she explains.

As soon as she noticed her card was missing, she realised that whether it had been handed in by some honest person or pocketed by some unscrupulous person, it didn't matter; either way, she wasn't going to see it again. She retraced her steps anyway, hoping against hope that she would come across it lying on the floor somewhere, peeking out from under a counter perhaps. She spent the whole afternoon looking for it, in a state of silent, panicked disbelief.

Then suddenly it was closing time, and she knew that if she walked out of the store that evening she was never going to be allowed back in again. And at that moment she stopped and said to herself, "So why not stay?"

At first she found it hard to believe that she could have come up with such an idea, but the more she thought about it, the more deliciously audacious, and at the same thoroughly sensible, it seemed. After all, if she got caught, what was the worst that could happen to her? She would be thrown out and forbidden to return. So what had she got to lose?

She didn't know whether she would have the courage to pull it off, but she decided it would be a shame not to try, so she asked herself where would be the best place to spend a night in Days, and the answer that came to her was both logical and childlike in its simplicity. Where would anyone spent a night in Days but in the Beds Department on the Orange Floor?

So, while other customers were making their way to the exits, Mrs

Shukhov made her way to Beds. There, she loitered in one of the show bedrooms, waited until she was sure that all the sales assistants were looking in the other direction, then knelt down and crawled beneath a four-poster with a long counterpane that went all the way down to the floor. Huddled beneath the bedsprings, curled up on the carpeted floor, she heard everyone leave, the store close, silence fall. Soon, in spite of everything, she was asleep.

At this point Gould cannot help breaking into a smile, although she does her best to hide it by lowering her head and putting her hand to her mouth. Morrison, meanwhile, scratches one cheek sceptically. Frank just says one word: "Uncomfortable."

"You don't know the half of it, Mr Hubble," says Mrs Shukhov. "From about four in the morning onwards I was bursting for a pee, but I didn't dare creep out and go and look for a Ladies, not with all those guards with torches roving around, and I'm too well brought up to go on the spot, so for five long hours I had to lie there with my legs crossed and my teeth gritted. Nine o'clock couldn't come soon enough, let me tell you. Even then, I decided to put off emerging for another quarter of an hour, because I'm sure it would have raised a few eyebrows among the sales assistants in Beds if someone were to miraculously appear in their department only seconds after opening time."

"No one saw you crawl out?" says Gould.

"I was very cautious. Also very lucky."

"*Very* lucky," says Morrison. "What happened then?"

Then Mrs Shukhov beat a path to the nearest Ladies, did her business, washed as best she could in the basin, smartened herself up, and went out and spent the whole day wandering around the store.

Once she had settled into the idea of being a stowaway of sorts, it was fun. She tested out various perfumes, partly to cover up the fact that she had slept in her clothes and hadn't had a bath, but also because it amused her. A nice salesgirl in Cosmetics did her make-up for free, and shortly after that, while looking at casserole dishes in Kitchenware, she was propositioned by a young female customer—the first time something like *that* has happened to her, and very flattering, although not her thing at all. She browsed, she meandered, she tried on shoes and hats, and when she got hungry she headed for the food departments and filled up on free samples, picking and moving on, a little bit of this, a little bit of that, until her stomach stopped growling. In short, she did everything that she could have done as a legitimate account-holder except make a purchase, and no one was the least suspicious because as long as she looked and behaved like a customer, as far as everyone was concerned she *was* a customer.

Mrs Shukhov pauses a moment to collect her thoughts, and in that moment Frank notices how self-possessed she has become during the telling of her tale. Something radiates out from her towards her audience of three, in particular (Frank feels) towards him. He can only suppose it is her confidence, drawn to his lack of that same quality like a current sucked along a wire from the positive to the negative terminal of a battery. It gives her a regal air, lending her attractive looks a deeper, truer beauty. He listens with a more attentive ear.

It was an exciting day (Mrs Shukhov continues), though tiring, too. At one point in the afternoon she sat down in a plush leather recliner to rest her feet for a moment, and the next thing she knew a sales assistant was shaking her and telling her to wake up. She had been out for half an hour, but the fellow was very kind about it and told her that people were dropping off in his chairs all the time.

"Do you know, I think on my travels I took in every single department there is," Mrs Shukhov proudly tells them, "including the Peripheries, and I've never dreamed of visiting the Peripheries before. For me there's never been much call for departments like Single Socks or Buttons & Shoelaces or Used Cardboard. All that walking! My legs are *still* stiff." She rubs her calves emphatically. "Although Mr Hubble here probably thinks nothing of covering such distances."

Frank, not knowing how to respond, inspects the uppers of his shoes and says nothing.

"Shall we hurry this along?" says Morrison. "I think Mr Hubble wants to get back to work."

"There isn't much more to add," says Mrs Shukhov, with just a hint of a pout. "When closing time came round again, I went back to Beds, making sure I'd emptied my bladder thoroughly first, and I did the same as the night before, crawled under that four-poster while no one was looking. After the sales assistants had gone home I raised the counterpane a chink to let in some light and brushed up on my Russian with the help of my new phrasebook—I used to be fluent, you know—till I fell asleep. I slept pretty well, except that I was woken up at about two in the morning by somebody with a vacuum cleaner. Fortunately for me, whoever it was didn't do their job properly and vacuum under the beds, otherwise I might have been in trouble. I went back to sleep again, woke about six, and as I was lying there waiting for opening time, it occurred to me that if I had a mind to it and was careful, I might be able to keep it up indefinitely, this game of living secretly inside Days. There was nothing to stop me, or so I thought.

"It turned out that there was one thing. I hadn't taken my contact lenses out in almost forty-eight hours, and they were starting to dry out and become painful. I'm blind as a bat without them, so I knew that if I was going to continue as a stowaway I had to get hold of some contact lens solution. I mulled the problem over while eating breakfast on the hoof in the Bakery and the Global Delicatessen—how to get hold of a bottle of contact lens solution without my Days card—and in the end I came to the conclusion that there was only one way. You know the outcome of that, and, well, here I am. A convicted shoplifter. My little escapade at an end.

"To be honest with you," she adds, "I'm relieved. Despite what I said just now, even if I had got away with my crime, realistically I doubt the game of stowaway could have gone on for longer than about a week. Sooner or later one of the sales assistants in the food departments was bound to think it strange, the same woman coming along and stuffing her face with samples day after day, and there's only so much a lady of a certain age can do with one set of clothes and a cloakroom basin before her appearance degenerates to a level unbecoming of a Days customer. But you know, apart from the shoplifting bit, which I hated, I enjoyed it. It was a thrill. For a decade my life has been too easy. I needed a challenge, and the past couple of days have been, if nothing else, certainly that. And if the chance ever arose, I'd do it again, like a shot."

She stops talking, clears her throat, smiles.

"Well, that's a pretty tale you've spun for us, Mrs Shukhov," says Morrison. His face hardens. "Now how about the truth?"

"That *is* the truth," says Mrs Shukhov firmly, with just a hint of a pout. "Why would I make something like that up?"

"Oh, you'd be surprised the nonsense some shoplifters come up with in the hope that I'll be lenient with them and let them off with a warning," says Morrison. "Yours, I admit, is definitely not the run-of-the-mill hard-luck yarn I'm used to hearing. Starving children, dying grandmothers, sisters with leukaemia, that's the usual standard of sob-story I get. Yours at least has the virtue of originality. Not that that makes it any more credible."

"But—"

"Now look, Mrs Shukhov, I've been fair with you. I've played along. I dragged Mr Hubble away from his break because you asked me to. I've been as co-operative as can be. The least you can do is co-operate back."

"I *am* co-operating! I haven't denied that I shoplifted, have I? In fact, I admitted it, and I'll admit it again if you want me to. I shoplifted! There you have it. A confession. Throw me out and banish me for ever." A fuschia spot of indignation blooms on each of Mrs Shukhov's cheeks. "For God's sake, what could I possibly hope to gain by lying? I only told you what I told you just now because... well, partly because I'm quite pleased with myself, I'm not ashamed to admit it, but also because I thought you and a senior member of the security staff might be interested to hear about certain loopholes in your apparently not-so-infallible security system. But honestly, if I'd known you were going to react like such a pompous ass, I'd have kept my mouth shut."

"If you want my opinion," Frank says, pointedly glancing at his watch (the time is three minutes past eleven, and his break is very definitely over), "her story sounds plausible enough."

"*Thank* you, Mr Hubble." Mrs Shukhov lets her hands fall into her lap and fixes Morrison with a defiant glare.

"And I think you, Morrison," Frank continues, "ought to make out a detailed report concerning Mrs Shukhov's activities, with her help, and then file it to the heads of both divisions of security. That's what I think."

His soft tones carry a deceptive weight, like a feather landing with the force of a cannonball. Morrison blusters, because he has to in order to save face, but inevitably relents. "Well, if you really think it's necessary..."

"I do. I also want you to get Accounts to flag her card, in case someone tries to use it."

"Of course." Morrison recovers some of his composure. "I was going to do that anyway."

And then Frank does a strange thing. An impulsive thing. The words are out of his mouth before he can stop them. "And have the Eye contact me if the card is used."

Morrison eyes him curiously. "What for?"

"If someone has appropriated Mrs Shukhov's card, I want to personally supervise their apprehension."

That sounds good, but it isn't standard operating procedure, and Morrison's doubtful look says he knows it. There is no reason why Frank has to be present for that particular arrest. Any other Security operative could do the job just as well.

So why did he just say what he said? Even Frank isn't quite sure, and he is alarmed by the rashness of the action, quite out of character. He supposes he did it because, regardless that Mrs Shukhov is a shoplifter, he admires her. He admires her nerve, stowing away in the store like that. Desperate she might have been, but it was still a plucky thing to do. He feels sorry for her, too, and who can begrudge him a small act of decency towards a woman who has earned both his admiration and his compassion? Besides, given that he has just half a day left at Days, chances are he will not be here when the card is used, if it is used.

Realising this considerably reduces his alarm.

"Well, I'll do as you request," says Morrison, making a note on his computer, "although I'd like to go on record here as saying that it is somewhat irregular."

"I think it's a very nice gesture," says Gould.

"So do I," says Mrs Shukhov. "It's reassuring to know that Mr Hubble himself will be personally responsible for recovering my card."

Frank pretends to ignore the meaningful look that passes between the two women.

"Am I needed for anything further?" he says to Morrison.

"Not that I can think of."

"Then if you'll all of you excuse me, I should have been back at work well over five minutes ago."

He bolts for the door, but cannot avoid taking one last glance at Mrs Shukhov. Her bloodshot gaze, strangely serene, holds his.

"Grigor would have liked you, Mr Hubble," she tells him quietly. "He liked everybody, but you he would have singled out for special attention. He called people like you 'compass needles wavering from north.'"

"And that means...?" says Frank, poised in the doorway.

"You think about it," says Mrs Shukhov.

On the way back upstairs he does think about it.

A compass needle has no choice but to point to magnetic north. It may waver on its axis as if attempting to point elsewhere, but in the end it will always fix itself in that direction. Was Mrs Shukhov implying that his fight against the path his life has taken is in vain?

He doesn't know. He wishes he knew. Maybe she is wrong. He hopes so.

20

The Seven Sacred Books: The seven major works of religion—the Christian Bible, the Scandinavian Eddas, the Chinese *Five Kings*, the Muhammadan Koran, the Hindu Three Vedas, the Buddhist *Tri Pitikes*, and the Persian *Zendavesta*.

11.06 a.m.

Miss Dalloway sneers at the boxes of software that have been placed just inside one of the entrances to her department.

It is a familiar tactic. First, a few innocuous items of computer paraphernalia appear—an exploratory foray. Then, if the incursion is not swiftly nipped in the bud, a display stand follows. Then, suddenly, as if by magic, there is a computer there too, gleaming with keyboard and monitor and hard drive. Sometimes, if the Technoids are feeling especially bold, a complete workstation—desk, chair, computer, printer with stand—is wheeled covertly into her department, to occupy space which rightly belongs to hardbacks and paperbacks, novels and works of reference, coffee-table books and discounted titles.

A familiar tactic indeed, wearying in its predictability, and ordinarily Miss Dalloway would go up to the group of Technoids who are slouching and grinning in the connecting passageway between her department and theirs, no-man's land, and she would shout at them, perhaps pick up their merchandise and hurl it at them, send them running. Ordinarily that is what she would do, but this morning she is content just to sneer, refusing to be provoked. For the moment at least, she is going to turn a blind eye to their deeds.

The Technoids, crackling in their tight white polyester shirts, their breast pockets bristling with ballpoint pens, jeer at her anyway.

"What's wrong, Miss Dalloway? Aren't you going to swear and throw stuff?"

"Maybe she's finally getting the message. That's *our* floorspace."

"Careful, lads. She may set one of her darling Bookworm boys on us."

"Ooh, a Bookworm! I'm scared!"

"Why, what'll he do? Read us some poetry and *bore* us to death?"

Their goading, however, is confounded by her apparent indifference, and lacks conviction. If nothing else Miss Dalloway is usually good for a tirade of baroque threats, but today she just isn't rising to the bait, and that confuses and disappoints the Technoids. Consequently they resort to a time-honoured ritual for baiting Books Department employees: chanting the words, "Dead wood," over and over.

"Dead wood. Dead wood. Dead wood. Dead wood." The chant gathering speed. "Dead wood, dead wood, dead wood, dead wood." Growing in volume, until soon it resembles the rhythmic whoop of apes. "Dead wood dead wood dead wood dead wood!"

But today not even this elicits a response from Miss Dalloway. Instead, the Head of Books merely turns on her heel and strides away, and as she disappears from view between two tall bookcases, the Technoids fall silent and look at one another as if to say, "What do you suppose has got into *her* then?"

As the bookcases rise around her, enfolding her like a pair of embracing arms, Miss Dalloway feels shoulders that she didn't realise were taut slacken and hands that she didn't realise were fists unclench. The bookcases, old guardians, are a comforting presence—bulwarks, fortifications. A huge weight of wood (no plastic here, nothing so ephemeral), they bear the eternal verities of the printed page ranked cover to cover, forming dense walls of words, and around their bases books litter the floor in unruly stacks; on their shelves, books hide behind books; on the steps of their wheeled ladders, books balance precariously. The sweet clove smell of ageing paper wafts over Miss Dalloway as she moves through her realm, and gradually the Technoids' insults are soothed away, though not forgotten. Nothing the Technoids do is ever forgotten.

She threads her way among the bookcases, a tall woman, narrow and bony. She walks with a birdlike precision, picking her way around piles of merchandise and browsing customers with long ostrich unfoldings of her tweed-trouser-clad legs. Everything about her, from her flat chest to her tight mouth, says iron and impenetrability; her flinty eyes and bunned black hair, iron and impenetrability. She is forty-five years old, looks fifty-five, feels sixty-five. She is not a woman you would want to have as an enemy, nor one you would much like to have as a friend—her passions are too intense, too internalised, too focused, to make her easy company. But she is, for all that, a worthy Head of Books.

She reaches the heart of the department, the information counter, where a dozen young men are waiting for her. Her faithful subordinates. Her darlings. As one they raise their faces towards her, like chicks in the nest when the mother bird returns with a worm. Glad as the sight of them makes her, Miss Dalloway purses her lips tighter still, crushing any possibility of a smile.

"What do you want us to do, Miss Dalloway?" one of the young men asks, a gloomy-looking lad with a bulging forehead like a cumulonimbus cloud. "Do you want us to go and sort them out?" It is evident from the way he poses the question that he doesn't relish the prospect of a physical altercation but is nonetheless ready to carry out whatever orders his head of department gives.

"That won't be necessary, Edgar. Not yet."

"I could set up a dumpbin there," offers another—poor, plump Oscar, who, as a result of a run-in with the Technoids a couple of weeks ago, is wearing a cast on his forearm. It started out as name-calling across the connecting passageway, escalated to pushing and shoving, and climaxed in a brawl, with Oscar in the thick of it. Poor, brave boy.

"Thank you, Oscar," says Miss Dalloway, "but for now we're going to sit tight and wait. Master Sonny will be down within the hour, and whichever way he resolves the matter will govern our next move. 'Our patience will achieve more than our force'—for now."

"What chance do you think we have of getting that floorspace back, I mean legitimately?" asks another of the Bookworms.

"I can't say, Mervyn. The best we can hope for is that Master Sonny hears the strength of our argument and judges fairly."

It isn't much comfort to her dear worried darlings, but Miss Dalloway herself isn't convinced that the arbitration will go their way and, much as she would like to, she cannot project an optimism she doesn't feel. Her misgivings are many, but principal among them is the concern that although she has right on her side (about that she *is* convinced), she isn't going to put her case across as charismatically as Mr Armitage, Head of Computers, will put his. She has never had much skill as a diplomat, largely because she has never had to be much of a saleswoman. She is firmly of the belief that books should be bought on their own merits, without hype or pressure tactics, and so hard sell is anathema to her and her department, whereas in Computers hard sell is all customers get from the moment they cross the threshold. And so Miss Dalloway fears that, the rightness of her cause notwithstanding, Mr Armitage's polished, coaxing, genial style will prove more appealing to Master Sonny than any fervent, impassioned pleading on her part.

She wishes her uncertainty and anxiety were not so transparent to her darlings, she wishes she could spare them worry, but she can't, so instead she orders them back to work. Work is the eternal balm for the troubled mind.

"Mervyn, some of the titles in the Mystery section have got out of alphabetical order. Salman, the Bargains table needs tidying up. Oscar, there's a customer over there who looks like he needs serving. Colin, you and Edgar set out that delivery of atlases in the Travel section. The rest of you all have things to do. Off you go and do them. Come on, chop-chop!"

She claps her hands, and they scatter obediently. They would die for her. They would.

Miss Dalloway retires to her desk, which is tucked away in a corner of the department more book-strewn than most, and which is sheltered on one side by piles of hardbacks which rise to form a teetering, haphazardly stacked crescent three metres high. The desk is an antique cherrywood monster with scroll feet and deep drawers. On it sits the only computer Miss Dalloway will permit in her department. If it was up to her she would do without the machine—nothing wrong with pen, paper, and typewriter, in her view—but she is obliged to use the computer in order to submit inventories and accounts, carry out stock-taking, and send and receive internal memoranda. It's a handy enough tool in its way, but Miss Dalloway cannot for the life of her understand the mystique, the hysteria, that seems to surround anything even remotely computer-related. All this talk of cutting-edge technology when there exists already a piece of technology so honed, so refined over the ages, so wholly suited to its task, that it can only be described as perfect.

A book.

As a source of easily retrievable information, portable, needing no peripheral support systems, instantly accessible to anyone on the planet old enough to read and turn a page, a book is without peer. A book does not come with an instruction manual. A book is not subject to constant software upgrades. A book is not technologically outmoded after five years. A book will never "go wrong" and have to be repaired by a trained (and expensive) technician. A book cannot be accidentally erased at the touch of a button or have its contents corrupted by magnetic fields. Is it possible to think of any object on this earth more—horrible term—*user-friendly* than a book?

Dead wood. The Technoids' chant echoes dully, hurtfully through her head.

That, alas, is how the majority of people, not just Technoids, regard books: not simply as artifacts made of pulped tree but as obsolete things, redundant, in need of paring away. Dead wood. It's cruel, and no less so for being true. More and more these days people are deriving their entertainment and education from electronic media, the theatre of the screen replacing the theatre of the mind as the principal arena of the imagination. That is understandable, in that it requires less effort to look passively at visual images than to synthesise one's own mental images from the printed word. Yet how much more intense and indelible in the memory than a computer graphic is the mental picture evoked by a skilled writer's prose! Take the pleasure of being led through a good story well told and compare it with the multiple choices and countless frustrating U-turns, reiterations, and dead ends of the average computer game or "interactive" (whatever *that's* supposed to mean) CD-Rom—no contest. By simple virtue of the fact that it takes place on a machine, digital entertainment is cold and clinical, lacking tactility, lacking *humanity*, whereas a book is a warm, vibrant thing that shows its age in the wear and tear of usage and bears the stamp of its reader in fingerprints and spine creases and dog-ears. On a winter's night, beside a blazing log fire, with a glass of wine or a mug of hot chocolate to hand, which would you rather snuggle up with—a computer or a book? A construct of plastic and silicon and wires that displays committee-assembled collages of text and image premasticated into easy-to-swallow chunks, or the carefully crafted thoughts of a single author beamed almost directly from mind to mind through the medium of words?

Oh, Miss Dalloway knows in her heart of hearts that it is wrong to single out computers (and Computers) as the source of her department's woes when there are dozens of other factors contributing to the decline in popularity of the printed word, but it is better to have an enemy that is concrete, visible, and conveniently close-to-hand than to rail vainly against the growing indifference of the entire world. And so, for better or worse, she has chosen Computers (and computers) as her enemy. Or rather, her enemy was chosen for her by a callous, thoughtless decision made eighteen months ago in the Boardroom of Days.

And that is another reason why she does not feel confident that the imminent arbitration will go her way. The Day brothers run their store electronically, dispensing their edicts and e-memos from on high, and none of them has, to her knowledge, ever expressed a particular fondness for the literary arts, unless you count Master Fred's love of newspapers, which Miss Dalloway does not. (Newspapers, in her view, can barely be described as *literate*, let alone literary.) The Day brothers were the ones who handed over part of her department to Mr Armitage and his Technoids. How can she expect them to be on her side?

With a weary sigh, Miss Dalloway switches her computer on and waits for it to boot up. (You don't have to wait for a book to boot up.) She has achieved the minimum level of computer-literacy necessary to operate the machine, no more, so her fingers are not confident on the keyboard as she calls up the e-memo that arrived half an hour ago from the Boardroom.

From: The Boardroom
Time: 10.28
To: Rebecca Dalloway, Books

The MANAGEMENT's attention has been drawn to various uncontractual deeds perpetrated by members of your department, arising as a result of strained relations with an adjacent department.

The MANAGEMENT is keen to resolve the situation as quickly as possible, and to this end will be sending down a representative to hear the grievances of both department heads and deliver a binding judgement.

Once MASTER SONNY's judgement has been delivered, both departments are to abide by his decision. Any further violations of employee behaviour protocols as stipulated in Clause 17 sections a) to f) of the employer/employee contract will result in the immediate dismissal of the staff members involved and their head of department.

MASTER SONNY will arrive between 11.30 and 11.40 this morning.

cc. Roland Armitage, Computers

She studies the e-memo carefully in the hope of finding something new in its wording, some hitherto unnoticed hint of bias that will reassure her that everything is not as dark as it looks. Nothing about it offers a clue to the mood prevailing in the Boardroom, although, given that Security has been advising the brothers about the dispute since it began, the phrase "keen to resolve the situation as quickly as possible" wins a small, mirthless smile from her each time her eyes pass over it. Having shown absolutely no interest in the acts of vandalism and violence going on in their store for so many months, for the brothers suddenly to send down one of their number at such short notice smacks of irritation. It is as though they have been hoping the problem would go away of its own accord but, as it hasn't, have finally decided that enough is enough. That, again, does not bode well. Exasperation and clear-eyed impartiality seldom go hand in hand.

The fact that it is Master Sonny and not Master Chas who is coming down gives Miss Dalloway further cause to frown. A visit from Master Chas to the shop floor is a rarity, from Master Sonny unheard of. Everyone knows about Master Sonny's drinking habit, his dissolute lifestyle. Is this a mark of how seriously the brothers are taking the dispute, that they are sending down the youngest, least experienced, and least reliable of them? But then why should that be a surprise? It has often occurred to Miss Dalloway that the sons of Septimus Day don't have the faintest idea what they are doing, and that it is in spite of them, and not thanks to them, that the store continues to turn over a profit at all.

Things were not like this in Mr Septimus's day, an era Miss Dalloway is not alone in recalling with fondness. The founder of Days might have been a hard, fearful man, but at least you knew where you were with him. *He* was not prone to issuing decrees wilfully. *He* did not go around allocating portions of one department to another for no worthwhile reason. He was a man whose very ruthlessness meant he could be trusted.

Miss Dalloway well recalls how every day Mr Septimus would tour the premises, striding through departments with perhaps a valued customer or a cherished supplier in tow but more often than not on his own, unafraid, wearing his aura of authority like an invisible suit of armour, pausing now and then to chide a sales assistant for sloppy dressing, or listen to a query from a head of department, or receive the compliments of a passing (and patently awestruck) shopper.

Was that when things began to go wrong for Days, when Mr Septimus, in the wake of his wife's death, gave up his public appearances in the store, withdrew to his mansion, and handed over the reins of management to his sons? Was that when the rot set in, when the proprietor no longer appeared accessible, and therefore accountable, to staff or customers? Or is it simply that Mr Septimus's seven sons cannot hope to maintain the high standard he set? It would seem inevitable that the clarity of one man's unique vision should be diffused when his sons try to take his place, as when a single beam of white light, refracted, breaks up into a blurred spectrum of colours, losing its sharpness and its power to illuminate.

Miss Dalloway switches off the computer and reaches for the well-thumbed paperback edition of Sun Tzu's *The Art of War* which is lying on the desktop. The book has become her Bible since the dispute began. Opening it, she extracts a Days card she has been both concealing inside it and using as a bookmark.

The card is a Platinum, and the name on it reads MRS C A SHUKHOV.

Malcolm—like all her darlings, a good, honest boy—handed the card in to her on Tuesday afternoon, saying it had been left behind on the counter accidentally by its owner, a rather distracted-looking woman who had used it to buy a Russian phrasebook. Miss Dalloway's first instinct was that of any honourable employee: she would contact Accounts and inform them about the lost card.

Then it occurred to her that a God-given opportunity had just fallen into her lap.

She glances over her shoulder. The haphazard stack of books which seems to have accumulated arbitrarily over the past few weeks around her desk is tall enough to hide her from the security camera that is positioned to include her desk in its viewing sweep. It is unlikely that her department is scanned very thoroughly anyway, since shrinkage has never been much of a problem in Books. Nevertheless, the privacy afforded by this screen of hardbacks (which her Bookworms built to her specifications, carefully and conscientiously adding to it day after day over the course of a couple of months) has been useful in masking from the Eye some industrious activity of the kind that the Day brothers, were they to learn of it, would doubtless consider extremely "uncontractual".

Within the books, in a small, hollowed-out cavity specially created for its concealment, lies the fruit of her industry.

Waiting.

Almost complete.

Whatever happens this morning, whether Master Sonny decides in favour of her department or Computers, Miss Dalloway has an appropriate response. Should things go her way, she will organise a celebration for herself and her Bookworms, and for that the purloined card will not be necessary, since she will use her own card to buy wine and paper hats. Should things not go her way, however, then she will put her primary plan into effect, and for that plan to succeed Mrs Shukhov's Platinum account is going to be vital.

Flexibility, adaptability, readiness. As Sun Tzu says:

> As water varies its flow according to the fall of the land, so an army varies its method of gaining victory according to the enemy.
>
> Thus an army does not have fixed strategic advantages or an invariable position.

Miss Dalloway is prepared for every contingency, and while she prays that she will not have to resort to her primary plan, she knows that if it comes to it, she will not hesitate, not for an instant.

If justice does not prevail, there will come a reckoning.

Oh, such a reckoning.

21

Seven Senses: According to *Ecclesiasticus* there are two further senses in addition to the standard five: understanding and speech.

11.25 a.m.

A FUNGUS HAS formed over his senses, furring his vision and hearing and touch, a fog of fine penicillin strands spun between him and reality. His brain twirls like a coracle loose of its moorings. Trying to stand, he sits back heavily.

The sofa beneath him is a cloud. The world spins erratically, stopping and starting, a broken centrifuge. The weight of gravity shifts and shifts: one moment he feels light as anything, the next a bowling ball rolls down the alley of his spine and rams into his pelvis. Trying to stand, he sits back heavily.

There is dampness in his lap as though he has pissed himself. His glass is empty, the crotch of his jeans cold and clinging. How *did* that happen? Ah yes. He recalls. A momentary lapse of concentration. His fingers fumbled. A waste, such a waste of good alcohol. But it doesn't matter, there is plenty more where that came from. Over there at the bar, a plethora of bottles. Over there. If only he could stand up, he could go and fetch himself a refill. If only he could stand up...

He tries, and sits back heavily.

He giggles, loud and hard. If his brothers could see him now, how they would despise him, how high-and-mightily disapproving they would be.

"Well, fuck 'em," Sonny snarls, his eyebrows knotting. Then he giggles, louder and harder.

Raising his head, he peers around his apartment, dislocated, not belonging. The planet's spin is still juddering and irregular. He has to steady himself with his hands on the sofa cushions in order to stay sitting upright. The building is at sea, a gigantic oceangoing galleon tossed on a mountainous swell, with Sonny in its crow's nest, grogged to the gills, the ship's sway even worse for him than for those down below. Pitch and yaw, pitch and yaw.

He really ought to be standing up. Isn't there something he has to be doing?

There *is* something, although what precisely it is has escaped him for the moment. He is sure it will come back if he doesn't rack his brains for it. A thought on the cusp of memory should not be chased down. Like a sheep on a clifftop, it will panic and run over the edge if you try. Leave it alone and it'll come home.

Chirrup-chirrup.

What was that? He must be hallucinating. He could have sworn he heard a cricket.

Chirrup-chirrup.

The sound is coming from beneath his right buttock. He's sitting on the little bugger! Not that the cricket seems to mind, chirruping away merrily like that.

Chirrup-chirrup.

Sonny lolls over to his left, raising his backside like a rugby player about to unleash a fart. He peers underneath. Nothing there.

Chirrup-chirrup.

It's coming from his back pocket of his jeans.

Where he keeps his portable intercom.

Ah, of course. He knew what was really making the noise all along. A cricket? Just his little joke with himself. Ha ha ha.

He attempts to insert his fingers into the pocket in order to extract the slim intercom unit, but his fingers exhibit all the dexterity of uncooked sausages. Prodding rubberily, torso half twisted over, he grunts in frustration and gives up. Trying another tactic, he presses down on the base of the pocket and succeeds in squirting the intercom out of its denim pouch like some hard fruit from its skin.

Chirrup-chirrup.

He unfolds the mouthpiece, and after a few misses manages to hit the Receive button.

"Sonny?"

Thurston.

Instinctively Sonny knows he has to sound sober. It's important.

His tongue feels as though it is swathed in peanut butter, but he manages to curl it around a single word: "Yes?"

Was that the right answer?

"Sonny, is everything all right?" Suspicious.

"Of course. Why shouldn't it be?"

"It's just that you took so long picking up."

A ripple of panic. He remembers now why he has to appear sober. Because he is meant to *be* sober. Because he has to go down to the shop floor soon. Because he promised his brothers he wouldn't drink beforehand. Oh shit. Shit shit shit. What if Thurston guesses? If Thurston guesses he has been drinking, that'll be it, his chance blown.

It is an effort to force out one innocent little lie.

"My intercom was in my other trousers."

And then there is a long whisper of white noise, static fluttering in the connection, the aural equivalent of a piece of lint caught in the lens of a movie projector.

And then Thurston says, "No. Never mind. Not even you would be that stupid."

Relief flows out through, it seems, Sonny's every orifice, his every pore, lightening him by evaporation.

"The security guards are waiting for you down on the Yellow. You're ready, aren't you?"

"Yes," Sonny replies, glancing down at his shirt and damp-crotched jeans. "Absolutely."

"Now, if there are any problems, if you run into any difficulties at all, for God's sake call me. Remember, all you're down there to do is deliver a message."

"Deliver a message, yes."

"Chas wants to say something. Hold on."

"Sonny? Listen. If the heads of department start to get shirty, back out and leave. Don't stand there arguing with them. It's unseemly. I doubt they're going to give you any grief, you being who you are, but you never know. When feelings are running high, people sometimes forget their place. Just don't let them rattle you. Be calm, unflappable. You're right, they're wrong. Got that?"

"I'm right, they're wrong."

"OK, I'm handing you back to Thurston. Oh no, hang on. Mungo wants a word."

"Sonny?" Mungo's deep, resonant voice, the bass pipes of a church organ. "We're counting on you. I have faith in you. You're going to do fine."

Sonny is filled with so much love for his eldest brother that he almost bursts into tears.

"I'll do my best, Mungo."

"That's all we ask."

Distantly, from across the Boardroom table, Fred can be heard. "Give 'em hell, Sonny-boy!"

"Off you go then. The guards are waiting."

"'Bye, Mungo. 'Bye."

Sonny clasps the intercom shut and presses it to his chest. He must get moving. Urgency injects adrenalin into his bloodstream, bringing a surge of clear-headedness, brief but sufficient to enable him to resist the plush seducing suck of the sofa and the wobble of the world's wild whirling. He clambers triumphantly to his feet.

Upright, he staggers, his brain flushing empty of blood. The apartment rises to a tremendous peak then swoops down, down, down into a trough. For an instant Sonny thinks he is about to faint. Then everything calms, settles, evens, levels out.

Half walking, half lurching, Sonny sets off for his bedroom.

11.28 a.m.

"I HATE TO say this," says Thurston, taking his intercom from Mungo and laying it in front of him on the table, "but I can't help feeling we've made a terrible mistake."

"You worry too much," says Fred.

"Why don't we follow him with the Eye?" says Sato. "At least that way we'll have some idea what he gets up to."

"I'll get them to patch the feed through," says Thurston. "Good idea, Sato."

If the portrait of Old Man Day on the wall could speak, it would probably say that nothing that has happened in the Boardroom today has been a good idea.

11.29 a.m.

SUITS HURTLE OUT of the walk-in wardrobe one after another like canaries from a cage.

Inside, Sonny is frantically rifling through his extensive collection of formal wear, hauling each outfit off the racks in turn and giving it a cursory once-over before flinging it over his shoulder to join the other rejects in a lavish, polychromatic jumble on the floor.

What to wear? What to wear?

Earlier, when it seemed he had all the time in the world, he couldn't make up his mind which of his suits was suitable. Now that he is in a hurry, not to mention drunk, it's as hard, if not harder, to decide. He knows he ought just to grab a suit, any suit, it doesn't matter which one, and throw it on, but this is his one-time-only chance to make an impression and he wants to look absolutely right. If only there wasn't such a wide range, if only so many of the damned things weren't so garish and unwearable...

The tangled heap in the wardrobe doorway continues to grow layer by layer, discard by discard, and then, abruptly, is no longer added to.

Sonny has made his choice.

11.41. a.m.

Between them, Jorgenson, Kofi, Goring, and Wallace, the four security guards waiting in the Yellow Floor hoop outside the doors to the brothers' private lift, have a combined previous work experience of fifteen years in the armed services, six years in the police force, and eight and a half years in a variety of correctional centres, either as warders or inmates. They are four stone giants, weathered but not worn, seemingly impervious to pain and emotion, and so it is impossible to tell if they are at all excited to have been detailed as escorts to one of the seven human beings in whose hands rests control of the world's first and (oh, what the hell, give it the benefit of the doubt) foremost gigastore. In fact, to look at them, you might think that accompanying a Day brother around the store was an everyday occurrence on a par with picking a shred of meat from between two back teeth.

Prepared for anything, the guards stand with their arms wrapped across their chests, their legs spread slightly apart, and their heads cocked to one side, the classic pose of paid thugs the world over. Not a word is exchanged between Jorgenson and Kofi and Goring and Wallace as they wait for Master Sonny to descend. His lateness is not commented on, not even by a covert glance at wristwatch or wall clock. The guards merely stand and wait as they have been told to do, just as mountains were told to stand and wait by God.

Shoppers mill past, some wondering why these four guards are stationed before a set of lift doors marked "PRIVATE—NOT FOR CUSTOMER USE," but none so bold as to approach and ask. Even the most geographically bewildered customer in the store would take one look at these four and go and find someone else to ask for directions.

When they hear the lift finally begin to descend from the Violet Floor, the four, as one, unfold their arms and unbutton their hip-belt holsters. Ready for anything.

There is no floor indicator above the doors to the brothers' private lift, and so the guards have no idea that Master Sonny has arrived until the lift-car heaves to a halt and the doors roll open.

Jorgenson, on whom was conferred the task of rounding up the three of his colleagues for this detail, and who therefore considers himself in charge, swivels on his heels, puffs out his chest, and snaps a salute at his employer.

Sonny, after a moment's swaying hesitation, raggedly returns the salute.

"Good morning, sir," Jorgenson says without so much as a flicker of his unsurprisable eyes.

"Good morning," Sonny replies brightly, like a child. He slaps his fingers to his forehead again, then, taking a liking to this saluting lark, turns and repeats the action three more times to Kofi, Goring and Wallace in turn. He bids them all good morning, and they wish him the same back.

Sonny is wearing the blackcurrant-purple suit he previously rejected, the one with the embroidered gold Days logos at the shoulders, cuffs, and pockets. Second thoughts, and a large quantity of cinnamon-spiced vodka, have convinced him that the hue and the logos work in the suit's favour rather than against it. The jolliness of the one and the vaguely military aspect of the other together create the desired balance between approachability and authority. He has put on a saffron shirt and a lilac tie, and his feet are the meat filling to a pair of pie-like light-brown cross-stitched loafers. His flushed, perspiration-sheened face rounds out the ensemble perfectly.

"Shall we be on our way then?" he enquires, and the guards fall quickly into position, Jorgenson and Kofi in the lead, Goring and Wallace behind, four corners of a square of which Sonny is the central point.

There isn't a smirk to be seen on the guards' faces as they march towards Books and Computers.

22

The Seven Years' War: The war in which England and Prussia defeated Austria, Russia, Sweden, Saxony, and France (1756-63).

11.46 a.m.

ON ONE SIDE of the connecting passageway between Books and Computers, Miss Dalloway waits, along with three of her Bookworms, Oscar, Salman and Kurt. Opposite them, a couple of metres and an ideological gulf away, stand Mr Armitage and three Technoids. Originally Mr Armitage brought along more of his staff to accompany him, but seeing that Miss Dalloway had confined herself to a retinue of just three, he dismissed the rest. The courtesy has not been remarked upon, has in fact been studiously ignored.

The air between the two four-person factions is cat's-cradled with antagonistic stares. Silence holds sway.

11.48 a.m.

EVERYBODY IS LOOKING at him. Of course. Who wouldn't stop and look at a man being escorted by four security guards? A few of the shoppers recognise him, most don't. Recent photographs of the Day brothers are hard to come by, but the family features are definitely there for all to see. The nose, the Oriental colouring—unmistakable.

But the stares have no weight. That is what's important to Sonny as the guards steer him anticlockwise around the Yellow Floor hoop towards the entrance to Computers. No one is peering at him with that intense light of knowledge in their eyes that says that they are privy to his secrets. None of them are using that look that seems to claim ownership of his soul, as if the public have some kind of proprietorial right over public figures. Perhaps it is because they can't see into him properly through his gauze of inebriation, or perhaps it is because *he* can't make *them* out properly. Either way, it makes no difference. The effect is the same. He is protected. So let them look.

* * *

11.49 a.m.

THERE IS A shimmer of commotion from the opposite entrance of Computers. A whisper races across the department like an electric current. *He is coming. Master Sonny is coming.*

And Miss Dalloway thinks, *How typical that he should choose a path that takes him through Computers.* She is aware that Computers, being one of those sales-favoured departments that abuts onto a hoop, lies directly between her department and the brothers' private lift; it would be absurd for him to come any other way, and yet... *How typical.*

There is a bustle of noise between the high-stacked racks of computer paraphernalia and peripherals, the mouse mats and manuals, the dust-covers and disk drives. Master Sonny is not yet in view but the hissed news of his approach breaks before him like a bow wave. Mr Armitage switches on a smile in readiness. That is the first thing Master Sonny will see as he reaches the connecting passageway: Mr Armitage's studied smile. Miss Dalloway grits her teeth and puts it out of her mind. Nothing matters except stating her case. The truth. Justice.

And here he is. Not as tall as she expected, although the four guards surrounding him would make a dwarf of anyone. Not as assured in his bearing as his father. An incipient puffiness around the jawline which, given time and no change in his habits, will develop into jowls. Eyes averted, watching the floor, or perhaps the boots of the guards in front. And that outfit! The outfit has to be some kind of joke, doesn't it? It chills Miss Dalloway to think that Master Sonny might consider what he is wearing appropriate attire for a serious businessman. A catwalk model at one of the more eccentric fashion shows might be able to pull off a get-up like that, but one of the joint owners of the world's first and (formerly) foremost gigastore? No. Never.

Here he is, and Mr Armitage is stepping forward, hand outstretched, seizing the initiative.

"Sir, a great honour. Roland Armitage, Computers. A great honour indeed. We're so grateful you could make it down here. It'll be good to have this misunderstanding straightened out for once and for all."

The leading pair of guards move apart, leaving Sonny standing, perplexed, staring at Mr Armitage's proffered hand. Then, as if suddenly remembering what to do in such circumstances, he reaches out and clasps it.

After a few forthright pumps of Sonny's arm, Mr Armitage disengages, turns, and begins introducing the Technoids present by name. Greeting their employer, they writhe humbly.

As for Miss Dalloway, she is so furious over Mr Armitage's remark about a "misunderstanding" she can barely think straight. Was he simply trying to annoy her or does he sincerely believe that her committed resistance to eighteen months of attempted annexation has stemmed from nothing more than a *misunderstanding*? But it quickly dawns on her that standing there seething will get her nowhere, and so, with a resolute snort and a shake of her head, she steps forward into the connecting passageway.

Technically nowhere on the shop floor is out of bounds to Miss Dalloway, but since the dispute began she has struck the Computers Department off her personal map, refusing to acknowledge its existence, even if that has meant having to make time-consuming detours to avoid it. Now, crossing the threshold to that department, she feels like a soldier venturing behind enemy lines.

Behind her, the three Bookworms hesitate. Miss Dalloway has forbidden them to enter Computers territory. Should they continue to obey that order, or does showing support for their head of department take precedence? They decide to follow her, and cross no-man's land in a nervous gaggle.

Pushing her way past the trio of Technoids, Miss Dalloway thrusts herself between Mr Armitage and Sonny. Mr Armitage has been telling Sonny how useful the extra display space has proved in enticing shoppers into Computers. He is halfway through suggesting that the department's other entrances might benefit from a similar arrangement when she interrupts him.

"Rebecca Dalloway."

Sonny's head snaps round. His eyes and his attention seem to follow a couple of seconds behind.

"And you are?"

"Rebecca Dalloway," she repeats patiently.

"No, I mean, what do you do?"

"Head of Books."

"Oh. OK. Right."

"I'd like you to know, Master Sonny, before anything else is said, that as a loyal employee of some twenty-five years' standing I have nothing but the utmost respect for the way you and your brothers manage Days, and I would never dream of calling your undoubted competence into question."

"Easy does it with the flattery, Miss Dalloway," Mr Armitage mutters, too low for Sonny to hear. "A paintbrush rather than a trowel."

That's rich coming from the arch sycophant himself, but Miss Dalloway refuses to be waylaid. "Nor is it for me to argue with any decision made on economic grounds. After all, we're all working together for the common good of the store, aren't we?" Here she attempts an ingratiating smile. It is not a pretty sight, as she would be the first to admit, but desperate times call for desperate measures. "However, I think you'll agree, when you see for yourself the size of the area of floorspace involved, that the negligible increase it brings to the Computers Department's sales figures scarcely warrants the time and effort Mr Armitage and his staff spend setting out their stock there."

That's good, she thinks. *Appeal to his need for cost-effectiveness. There, surely, lies the Day brothers' Achilles heel.*

"But, Miss Dalloway," says Mr Armitage, butting in before Sonny has been able to stir himself to reply, "by the same token, if the area of floorspace is so small, it scarcely warrants the time and effort *your* department devotes to trying to keep *my* department out. Perhaps you'd be better off channelling the energy you put into thwarting us into drumming up custom and improving your department's dismal sales figures."

"My sales figures might not be so 'dismal', Mr Armitage, were I allowed to keep all the floorspace I'm entitled to."

"Hear, hear," says Oscar, and he is echoed by Salman and Kurt.

The encouragement stiffens Miss Dalloway from head to toe like a leather scabbard when the sword is sheathed. "And as my staff will testify," she continues, "our attention to our duties as Days employees has inevitably been compromised by the Computers Department's repeated acts of aggression and intimidation. How can we be expected to concentrate on our customers and merchandise under a constant barrage of threats and harassment?"

"If by threats and harassment you mean laying claim to what is rightfully ours, then my staff and I stand guilty as charged," says Mr Armitage. "We have threatened, we have harassed. But we wouldn't have had to resort to such drastic action if you and your Bookworms, Miss Dalloway, hadn't been so obstinate from the start. Not just obstinate, downright rebellious."

"Rebellious!"

"The e-memo granting my department the extra floorspace came, did it not, from the Boardroom. Is that not so, Master Sonny? From the very highest authority in Days. And so resisting the order contained in that e-memo would seem to me an act of insubordination at the very least, if not open rebellion."

"Don't exaggerate." Miss Dalloway can feel her cheeks reddening. She knew this would happen. Mr Armitage is twisting her argument around, trying to make it look like *she* is the one in the wrong. She turns to Sonny. "He's exaggerating, sir. He wants you to believe that by opposing him I have somehow been opposing *you*. That certainly is not the case. As I told you just now, I am a loyal employee of some twenty-five years' standing. It's hardly likely that I'm going to turn against the people who have employed me for a quarter of a century, now, am I?"

"Aren't you?" Mr Armitage gives a tiny, knowing tweak of his eyebrows.

"Of course not."

"But if I'm carrying out the brothers' orders and you oppose me, by definition that means you must be opposing the brothers."

"A equals B and B equals C, therefore A must equal C. If only the world ran according to your simple, logical patterns, Mr Armitage." Miss Dalloway moves a step closer to Master Sonny, narrowing, she hopes, not just the physical distance between them. She catches a whiff of his breath, and suddenly the reason for his bleary indifference becomes clear. She is appalled, but she knows she mustn't allow anything to deter her. "If you could only have seen, sir, how eagerly Computers leapt on the new floorspace, without so much as a syllable of apology in my direction, not one gramme of remorse, only the arrogant, gloating assumption that I was going to let them have whatever they wanted. If you could only have seen that, I think you would have agreed with me that they didn't deserve it."

"Ah, so now it's down to what we deserve as opposed to what we've been granted," says Mr Armitage. "It's about our *attitude*, which you, in your infinite wisdom, have judged inappropriate."

"Inappropriate, insensitive, insulting ..."

"Would it have made a difference if we'd approached you with a bunch of flowers and a box of chocolates and asked, pretty please, Miss Dalloway, would you let us have the ten square metres of your department the Day brothers have already said are ours? Would you have given them up without a murmur then? I doubt it."

"I might at least have thought about it."

"Thought about it and then gone ahead and done exactly the same." Mr Armitage shrugs extravagantly at Master Sonny. "It's no use, sir. There's no point discussing this. We aren't going to get anywhere until Miss Dalloway realises that an order from you and your brothers isn't just something she can ignore if she doesn't like it. We all understand about wounded pride, but there are times when you have to admit defeat and accept the inevitable. Take it—if I can use the phrase with reference to a lady—like a man."

"A man wouldn't take the way I've been treated half as well as I have," says Miss Dalloway. "My sex has a long history of bearing up nobly in the face of injustice and oppression. It's about time they changed the phrase to 'take it like a woman'."

"However you wish to put it, then. Bite the bullet. Concede gracefully. Bow under pressure. Go with the flow."

"This particular flow I would rather resist."

"The willow that bends with the breeze survives."

Miss Dalloway cannot suppress a burst of contemptuous laughter. "Where did you dig up that fatuous little epigram, Mr Armitage? From some self-improvement manual for ambitious executives?"

There. Is that a twitch she sees? A tiny wrinkling in Mr Armitage's oh-so-smooth-and-placid surface? Has she finally succeeded in getting to him?

If so, he recovers his composure swiftly and with consummate skill. "It's a wise person, Miss Dalloway, who knows how to handle change."

"It's a wiser person who knows how to distinguish good change from bad. Not everything new is improved, Mr Armitage. That may be the reigning philosophy in the world of computers where a piece of equipment is obsolete almost from the moment it hits the shelves, but in most other walks of life the new does not automatically oust the old, at least not without a Stalin or a Mao or a Pol Pot in charge. In most walks of life change is an extension of tradition. It happens naturally. It isn't forced on you like a software upgrade or a faster processing chip; you don't *have* to have it if you don't want it."

"When you talk about tradition, Miss Dalloway, the image that comes into my head is of a bunch of cobwebby old books mouldering in a pile on a table, unbought and unread."

"But some traditions survive because they *work*. For example, when Mr Septimus divided Days into seven hundred and seventy-seven departments and allotted each department exactly the same amount of floorspace irrespective of its profit potential or the dimensions of the merchandise it would stock or the number of staff members required to sell that merchandise, he did so for a purpose, to show, in effect, that he regarded every department as the equal of its neighbour, no one department less worthy of his attention than any other."

"But you can't compare one of the Indigo Floor Peripheries, where they're lucky if they make a sale a day, with, say, Jewellery. That's preposterous."

"Let me finish, Mr Armitage. To Mr Septimus—to your father, Master Sonny—each department was as important as the next. Obviously in financial terms you can't compare Jewellery with Single Socks, only a fool would, but the fact that there *is* a Jewellery Department ensures that a department like Single Socks—which is a godsend to anyone who has ever lost a sock in the laundry and doesn't want to spring for a brand new pair—can continue to exist. Days was designed to be in equilibrium, every part in harmony with every other part."

"If that's so, then how come all those departments disappeared or got merged when the brothers took over Violet for themselves?" says Mr Armitage. "Why would the brothers disturb this precious equilibrium of yours if it was one of the main reasons the store was raking in money?"

Miss Dalloway chooses her words carefully. "Perhaps the brothers were not entirely aware of the significance of what they were doing." She watches Sonny for an adverse reaction, but nothing in his glazed demeanour suggests that she has offended him or, indeed, that he has taken on board anything she has been saying for the past few minutes.

"There she goes again!" Mr Armitage throws his hands in the air despairingly. "Questioning your decisions, Master Sonny, casting doubt on your managerial wisdom. How can you let her get away with this?"

"You make it sound as if disputing store policy is a form of heresy."

"Isn't it?"

"Only an idiot or a fanatic goes along with everything his superiors say and do." Miss Dalloway knows she isn't helping her argument any by saying this, but nevertheless she feels it has to be said.

"Really, Miss Dalloway," Mr Armitage replies, "I think you must be confusing me with someone you've invented. You want to paint me as some sort of grasping, rapacious ogre because that's how you need to think of me, whereas all I am—and you know this in your heart of hearts—is a head of department who follows instructions."

"Master Sonny, sir," says Miss Dalloway, "you've heard from Mr Armitage's own lips that he and his staff have harassed and threatened my staff and me. You've seen how contemptuous he is of my department. It's clear that he's simply using a Boardroom edict as an excuse to further his own ends and expand his little empire. Natural justice would demand that you rescind your original decision. It wouldn't be admitting a mistake, it would merely be making a *better* decision."

"Sir, there's a principle at stake here. If you let her get her way, you'll be sending a message to every head of department, every member of staff, that they can do however they feel, and to hell with discipline or the corporate structure."

"Sir, the principle at stake here is the right of every department to manage itself as best it can, according to its needs."

"Sir, that's of no benefit to the store."

"Sir, on the contrary, it is."

"Sir? Hello?"

"Sir?"

"Sir?"

11.56 a.m.

THROUGHOUT THE FOREGOING exchange, Sonny's head has been bobbing to and fro, now to listen to Mr Armitage, now Miss Dalloway. The alternating currents of their dialogue have switched him this way and that until he is no longer sure what has been said by whom. Here and there a random phrase has snagged in his brain, but for the most part it has all been so much gibberish, a melange of words thrown together for no obvious reason except perhaps to confuse him, somehow made all the more incomprehensible by the occasional flashes of sense. He feels like a radio tuned between two stations, receiving intermittent bursts of signal from one or the other amid a surf of white noise.

The faces of the two people talking are no help. The man looks honest enough, the kind of chap you can trust, but the woman—all those forward jabs of her sharp nose—has the air of someone who has never been wrong about anything in her life. Is it possible they can both be right? Is this a problem without a solution, like one of those Zen thingies about trees falling in forests and one hand clapping?

Thurston's words flit into his head: "All you're down there to do is deliver a message." The trouble is, Sonny has only the dimmest recollection now of what that message is. But unless he wants to stand here all day listening to these two yammer at him, he is going to have to say something to keep them happy.

They're saying, "Sir?" to him. "Sir? Sir?" They want him to speak.

Very well.

11.57 a.m.

"ONE OF YOU'S right, one of you's wrong."

"True."

"Yes, sir."

"Well, at least both of you agree on that. I don't suppose there's any chance you'll agree on anything else, is there?"

Miss Dalloway and Mr Armitage exchange glances.

"No, sir," they say in unison.

"Thought not. Well..." Sonny delves into a pocket of his blackcurrant-purple jacket. "What we used to do at university when we'd lost track of whose round it was..." The pocket is empty. He tries another. "Is we'd flip a card." That pocket, too, is empty, as is the next he tries. "Usually it was my card we'd flip." He digs into both trouser pockets. "Everyone liked it when I brought out my card." Finally he tries his breast pocket. "It gave them a thrill. Ah, here it is."

He produces his Osmium. Tar-black and gleaming, it is an object so rarely glimpsed on the shop floor, so mythical, that even those lucky enough to have seen one before cannot take their eyes off it and follow its every movement mesmerically as Sonny waves it for emphasis.

"So I'm going to do the same now. I'm going to flip this, and if it lands with the logo side facing up then *you*"—he points the card at Mr Armitage—"get to keep the floorspace, and if it lands with the side with the magnetic strip and my signature on it facing up then *you*"—now he aims the card at Miss Dalloway—"get to keep the floorspace. OK? Got that? Logo, you. Magnetic strip, you. Couldn't be simpler, could it? Or fairer. All right. Ready, everyone? Here goes."

Sonny makes a fist of his right hand, cocks the thumb, and balances the Osmium carefully across the middle joint. Mr Armitage calmly folds his arms, letting it be known that he isn't too much bothered which way the card falls or, for that matter, that the dispute is being resolved by the flip of a card. Clearly, if this method of arbitration is good enough for a Day brother, it's good enough for him.

Miss Dalloway, on the other hand, can scarcely believe what she is seeing. She would like to think that Master Sonny is simply teasing them, and that in a moment he is going to wink and put the card away and say, "Just kidding," and then deliver a reasoned and well-considered assessment of the situation... but no, it seems that he means it, he is really going to go through with this, her fate really does rest on the spiralling trajectory of a piece of plastic.

And what can she do about it? Can she snatch the card off him and tell him not to be so ridiculous? Can she grab him by the scruff of the neck and shake him until he sobers up and starts behaving like an intelligent adult and not like an inebriate lout in a college bar? Of course she can't. All she can do is reach behind and grope for the hands of her darling boys, and from the three sweaty palms that grip her thin dry fingers draw strength and succour.

The Osmium topples from Sonny's none-too-steady fist and tumbles to the floor.

It lands with its logo downwards, the brown magnetic strip and the white oblong containing Sonny's scrawled signature facing up, plain as day.

Miss Dalloway's heart gives a little leap. She has won!

"That doesn't count." Sonny stoops and retrieves the card from the carpet. "That was an accident. Doesn't count."

Hope crouches down again in Miss Dalloway's breast, swaying back and forth on its hunkers.

"All right." Sonny perches the card on the two knuckles of his thumb once more. It seems that not only has the Computers Department gone quiet but that a hush has descended over the entire store. It is as if the outcome of more than a mere dispute over a strip of floorspace depends on which way up Sonny Day's Osmium lands, as if the very future of Days revolves around this moment, this cocked thumb, this poised wafer of black plastic.

Everyone is concentrating on the card: Miss Dalloway, Mr Armitage, the Bookworms, the Technoids, the small crowd of intrigued customers that has gathered over the past few minutes. Even the guards—who are meant to be looking elsewhere, scanning for potential threats to their employer—are squinting sidelong at the Osmium and at the man holding the Osmium.

And Miss Dalloway, no great believer in God, nonetheless prays. She prays that, though the rest of the world seems to have lost its head, there still exists a pocket of sanity wherein things turn out as they are meant to. She prays that, though justice has been reduced to a fifty/fifty lottery, there is still some hope that right will prevail. She prays that Samuel Butler was not mistaken when he wrote that "Justice, though she's painted blind,/Is to the weaker side inclin'd." But above all she prays that, when Master Sonny flicks the Osmium into the air, it will exactly reproduce the pirouette it performed just now, executing the exact same number of turns, and landing the same way up.

Sonny locks his thumbnail beneath the pad at the tip of his forefinger. Flexing tendons dimple the heel of his thumb.

Nothing happens, and for one awful instant Miss Dalloway believes that time has ground to a halt. Master Sonny will never flip the card. She will remain trapped in this ecstasy of fear and trepidation for ever.

Then the sprung thumb is released and the card is launched, an oblong black projectile spinning upwards from Sonny's fist on the rising curve of a parabola, end over end over end over end, light planing across its two rectangular faces in turn, end over end, reaching its zenith in front of Sonny's nose, then beginning its descent, describing an arc that mirrors the curve of its ascent, still gracefully whirling around its own axis like a drum majorette's baton, with Miss Dalloway willing it to fall logo side down, willing the very air molecules through which it is passing to strike it leniently as it begins the long drop to the logo-patterned carpet of the Computers Department, willing it to land favourably on enemy ground. And down it goes, this thin, fragile thing that, were the wealth it represents realised as a block of precious metal, would need a dozen strong men to lift it—down it goes, turning and turning, down and down and down, until one rounded corner strikes the carpet's green furze and it bounces, comes down on another corner, twirls like a ballerina, slumps onto one edge, then flops flat.

Miss Dalloway can't bring herself to look.

"Oscar? Which way up is it, Oscar?"

Oscar's silence is all the answer she needs.

She lowers her gaze to the Osmium, and there they are—the grainy and smooth semicircles of the card's Days logo, the right half sanded to a pale grey sheen, the left as shiny as fresh creosote on a roadway.

11.58 a.m.

"WHAT'S HE DOING?" says Wensley. "I can't make out what he's doing."

"It's clearer on the other camera," says Mungo. "Slightly." He points across the table to the second four-by-four bank of monitors, which shows the same scene at a different angle: Sonny addressing the heads of Books and Computers, flashing his Osmium at them. Both images, expanded to fit sixteen screens, are blurry and ill-defined. The card is a vaguely rectangular black blob, Sonny's suit a man-shaped mass of dark grey, and the employees' faces ovals of white, their features dark smudges.

"What's he got his card out for?" Fred asks.

"A badge of authority," Thurston suggests.

"You can't argue with an Osmium," says Chas, nodding.

"Especially one which has the surname Day on it," Sato adds.

"Whoops! Dropped it!" says Fred, chuckling. "You're going to have to learn to keep a tighter grip on your money, Sonny. There, pick it up, that's a good boy. No! Fumbled again!"

"Was that a fumble?" says Thurston with a frown. "Looked to me more like he flipped it."

"It was a fumble," says Mungo with a confidence he does not entirely feel. "See, he's picking it up again and putting it away. He just wanted them to see that he means business."

"I wish the angle were better," says Sato. Sonny has his back to both cameras.

"These are the best feeds the Eye could give us," says Thurston. "We'd have a better view if he wasn't so close to the entrance. The deeper you go into a department, the more cameras there are."

"This is good enough," says Mungo. "We can tell he isn't doing anything stupid. He's listened to the heads of department, and now he's telling them what we think."

The dark side of the great dome now occupies fully half of the Boardroom's triptych of windows. Septimus Day continues to glower impotently down from his portrait. The brothers begin to relax. It seems that Sonny has pulled it off, that their fears were unfounded. Perhaps, after all, they can work together, all seven of them, as their father wanted them to.

Mungo reminds Chas that they are due for their daily tennis game, and as the two of them leave the Boardroom to go down to their apartments to get changed, Mungo feels that the respect his brothers hold him in has been immeasurably enhanced by the bravery of his decisions this morning.

It is a good feeling.

11.59 a.m.

"WELL," SAYS SONNY, stowing away his Osmium, "I have to go now. I'm sure my brothers must have other work for me to do. Congratulations to the winners, commiserations to the losers. Goodbye to you all."

The guards fall in place around Sonny, and off they go, a phalanx of five.

"Wisely made?" splutters Miss Dalloway, finally finding her voice after a full minute of stunned inarticulacy. "It wasn't even a *decision*. It was the absolute antithesis of a decision. It was a travesty. 'Judgement drunk, and brib'd to lose his way,/Winks hard, and talks of darkness at noon-day.' Sir? Master Sonny, sir?"

She makes to pursue her employer, but Mr Armitage restrains her with a firm hand.

"Miss Dalloway," he says, "accept it, you've lost. Deal with it."

The Head of Books has never been so tempted to punch someone. Instead, she growls and brushes Mr Armitage's hand away as though it is a tarantula that has dropped onto her shoulder.

"This isn't over," she tells him. "This is far from over." And with an imperious toss of her head, she strides off into the connecting passageway.

Her darlings cluster around her as she storms back into Books.

"What now, Miss Dalloway?" asks Kurt.

"We have to let them have the floorspace, don't we?" says Oscar.

"We don't have a choice," says Salman. "Master Sonny—"

"Damn Master Sonny!" Miss Dalloway snaps. "Damn him, damn his brothers, damn the whole sorry lot of them! If they think they can get away with treating a loyal employee like this, they've got another think coming."

"But we've lost."

"Lost, Oscar? *Lost*? On the contrary. In the words of John Paul Jones"—Miss Dalloway is incandescent with righteous rage; her fury is awesome in its purity—"'I have not yet begun to fight.'"

It is midday.

23

Seventh Avenue: A street in New York City, part of which is nicknamed "Fashion Avenue"—also known as the "garment centre."

12.00 p.m.

MIDDAY FINDS LINDA Trivett in Ties on the Blue Floor, rummaging through her handbag for her shopping list. She needs to find the catalogue serial number of the tie she wants to buy for Gordon, because the department has turned out to be too full of merchandise for her to track it down unaided. There are ties everywhere. Ties dangling like jungle lianas from wires suspended across the ceiling. Ties hanging on rotating stands. Ties knotted around the necks of torso mannequins. Ties snugly rolled in presentation boxes. Ties interleaved on the walls head to tail, like long, thin segments of a huge silky quilt. Ties snaking around pillars in candystripe swirls. A wilderness of ties, in which Linda has about as much chance of locating the one she wants as she does of locating a specific grain of sand in a desert.

Still, it is fun to look, and she has been looking for over quarter of an hour, roaming the aisles, running her fingers over the merchandise, admiring. Yes, letting Gordon go off on his own is the best thing she could have done. She would never have had this luxury to browse (and, of course, the tie would not be a surprise) were he still tagging along behind her. Without him she can wander where she wants and linger as long as she likes over any items that happen to catch her eye, free from the insistent, nagging pressure of his impatience. She misses him, really she does. She would love to be able to spend the entire day with him, because the taste of triumph is that much sweeter when shared with another, but she acknowledges that the temporary separation is for the best, and she suspects that, in the future, marital harmony will be best maintained if she and Gordon visit Days apart rather than together.

Wherever he is, she hopes he is safe and enjoying himself.

At last she unearths the slip of paper containing the serial numbers of the tie, the cherub carriage clock, and the other items on her shopping list. She approaches a nearby sales assistant.

"Excuse me, please. I'm looking for a particular—" She stops mid-sentence.

"A particular what, Madam?"

Linda smiles. "Never mind. I've just found it."

"Isn't that always the way, madam?" says the sales assistant. "The moment the plumber arrives, the tap stops dripping."

Linda laughs, thanks him, and goes over to the rack she spotted where, among others, hangs the coin-motif tie.

"Attention, customers."

She glances up. How exciting. Another lightning sale. There was one only half an hour ago in Farm Machinery, and although a swift examination of the leaflet map showed Linda that she was four floors up and on the opposite side of the building from that department, she was tempted to make a dash for it all the same. Seeing other shoppers spin on their heels and head off, she felt a tug, an instinctive pull. *I could go too,* she thought. *I am part of the pack, I could run with them.* Fortunately she retained sufficient presence of mind to realise that her small, well-tended plot of garden at home was unlikely to be improved by the deployment of heavyweight agricultural equipment. Had the sale been in another department—any other department—she might well have gone.

She listens attentively.

"For the next five minutes there will be a twenty per cent reduction on all items in Ties. I repeat, for the next five minutes only, all items in Ties will be marked down by twenty per cent. Ties is located in the south-eastern quadrant of the Blue Floor and may be reached using the banks of lifts designated G, H and I. This offer will be extended to you for five minutes only. Any purchases made after that period will retail at full price. Thank you for your attention."

Linda looks around to see which way other shoppers are going to move. She will join them this time. Race with them, hunt down that bargain. Yes.

The faces she sees are taut and anxious.

Then she hears the sales assistant she just talked to whisper under his breath, "Oh shit."

Then it dawns on her.

The announcement said Ties.

Here. The sale is *here*.

The emotion that wells up in Linda Trivett then is too pure and blinding to sully with a name. It surges through her in a great white wave, clarifying her thoughts, sharpening her senses, purging her of uncertainty. She knows what she has to do, but more than that, she knows that this is what she was *born* to do. Never has she felt such an undiluted sense of purpose before. It races through her veins, as cold and clear as a subterranean stream. Deep in her being she is suddenly connected with all that is and all that was and all that is meant to be.

Trembling in the throes of epiphany, she snatches the coin-motif tie from the track and casts about for the nearest sales counter. The announcement said twenty per cent off. A whole fifth. Other shoppers are grabbing merchandise, seizing ties by the handful. She can hear a faint rumbling from afar. Twenty per cent. Quickly, thoughtlessly, she turns and plucks another three ties from the rack. One has a squadron of blue pigs with wings embroidered on it, another is printed with close-typed rows of random binary-code sequences that form a sort of variegated polka-dot pattern, while the third is a duplicate of the tie with the coin motif already in her hands. Well, after all, Gordon always wears a tie to work. He can never have too many. She looks around again for a sales counter, and in doing so catches sight of the first bargain-hunters as they come stampeding in through the nearest connecting passageway.

In they charge, like the Mongol Horde sweeping across a plain, wielding Days cards instead of scimitars and their gaping mouths silent where the troops of Genghis Khan would be screaming battle-cries, but their eyes just as wild, their intent just as clear. And Linda with her fistful of ties doesn't step cowering out of their way but holds herself steady, erect, ready to meet them. These are *her* ties, and no one shall have them except her.

The customers in the vanguard of the charge reach her, and unresisting she lets their impetus carry her along. She has glimpses of teeth and well-coiffed hair, whites of the eye and flashing jewellery, clutching fingers and bulky shoulderpads, and suddenly a fist flails out of nowhere and catches her a glancing blow to the cheekbone, and someone stamps with elephant force on her foot, but still she rides along with the mob, struggling to keep herself upright and planting an elbow in someone's ribs and a knee in someone else's thigh, while the air around her head resounds with the whipcrack of ties being snatched from stands.

A shove from behind sends her stumbling forwards, her teeth clacking painfully on her tongue, the ties nearly spilling from her grasp. She wheels around to find a woman with a shoddily home-bleached frizz of hair waving a chrome-coloured card at her and yelling, "Those are mine! I have a Palladium! You have a Silver! My Palladium trumps your Silver! Those are *my* ties!"

"No, they're not, they're mine," Linda replies calmly, "and the last person I'd to give them up to is a stingy little bitch with an inch of root showing and abominable split ends."

The bottle-blonde roars like a lioness and makes a grab for the ties. Linda's response is as swift as it is savage. Stepping back, she swipes the woman's legs out from under her with a scything kick—a physical feat which she would never have been able to pull off under normal circumstances but which, in the heat of the moment, she executes with perfect and ferocious accuracy.

As the bottle-blonde goes down she makes an ineffectual grab for Linda's blouse, but Linda leaps nimbly aside, batting her hands away.

"Bitch!" the bottle-blonde wails, prone on the floor.

"Slut!" Linda yells back, as the flow of bargain-hunters sweeps her away once more.

Like a swimmer in a crowd-torrent Linda is borne thunderously along, until suddenly, dead ahead, through a gap in the seethe of customers, she sees a sales counter, and she heaves herself toward it, at the same time groping for the clasp of her handbag with her free hand. How long has it been since the sale was announced? How many minutes? One? A thousand? Buffeted left and right, Linda propels herself up to the sales counter, at the same time fumbling her card out. She squeezes in sideways between two other customers and thrusts the ties into the face of the sales assistant, a young man barely out of his teens who, according to his ID badge, is a first-year trainee.

"These!" she cries. "Now!"

"He was about to serve *me*," one of her neighbours asserts crossly. "Isn't that right?"

The sales assistant blinks in uncertainty. He is terrified, close to tears. Who can blame him, all these red, raging faces surrounding him, bellowing at him?

"*I* was next," someone else insists.

The sales assistant gyrates plaintively from one customer to another.

Whom should he serve? Whom?

Linda stretches her free hand across the counter, grabs him by the lapel, and yanks him close.

"Serve me or it's your job."

That galvanises him. He takes the ties and the card off her, which causes the customers on either side to gasp and gripe and grumble and glare their resentment. Linda responds with a serene sneer.

If only they knew this was her first ever lightning sale. Then they would *really* have something to complain about.

And as the sales assistant runs his scanning wand over the four ties one after another and swipes Linda's Silver through the credit register, Linda nurses a warm, spreading glow of contentment.

She beat the other customers fair and square. She has a real talent for this.

24

Dance of the Seven Veils: The erotic dance performed by the title character in Wilde's play *Salome* to entertain Herod before the beheading of John the Baptist.

12.00 p.m.

MIDDAY FINDS GORDON crouched with his back to a mirror. A pair of Iridium cards are being waved to and fro mere millimetres from his face. The rainbow coruscations at play across the cards' surfaces are hypnotically beautiful. Not so beautiful is the smear of blood staining one edge of one of the cards. *His* blood.

The blood comes from a throbbing, burning wound in the palm of Gordon's right hand, and there is more of it, warm and sticky, trickling down his fingers and dripping off the tips. It feels as though his hand has been slashed to the bone, but, much as he would like to, Gordon doesn't dare examine the cut.

The pair of Burlingtons who have cornered him in this dead-end aisle in Mirrors move in closer, snickering. Their Iridiums fan a breeze across Gordon's cheeks as they weave their hypnotic cobra dance around his face. He can see how sharp their edges have been filed, razor-sharp, and thinking of the damage edges so sharp could do to him, a dull little whimper escapes his throat.

He didn't even mean to be in this department, that's the awful irony of it. If it hadn't been for the woman in Pleasure. If it hadn't been for Rose...

And despite the pain and the paralysing fear of the moment, Gordon feels a faint, residual flush of lust as he recalls his first glimpse of Rose—Rose in the clinging pink nylon gown that sinuously emphasised her curves and contours, flowing over her naked body like cloudy pink water over a riverbed of worn-smooth rocks. He remembers how the dark ovals of her nipples loomed alluringly through the gauzy material, and he remembers the intoxicating perfume of her smile, and the way she boldly took his hand and said, like a teacher to a little boy, "Come on then, let's see what we can do with you." Words that sent a shockwave of images—

possibilities—through his brain. He remembers it all clearly, even though it seemed to take place a lifetime, and not just a few minutes, ago.

He hadn't meant to set foot in the Pleasure Department either, but the muted red glow emanating from its entrance caught his eye as he was wandering by, and a waft of sweet incense drew him inquisitively in, past an at-attention security guard whose expression, he thinks now, did have something of a knowing smirk about it.

Having no sense of where he was in the store, and without the map to guide him, Gordon was at first unable to fathom what could possibly be sold in this department. In front of him a pair of long bare partition walls reached all the way to the opposite entrance, with bead-curtained doorways set into them on either side at regular intervals. Cubicles of some sort. Two similar rows ran off to the right and the left. There seemed to be no sales assistants about, and if it hadn't been for the pungent, aromatic smoke purling from ornate silver censers that hung from the ceiling on silver chains, Gordon might have thought the department had been abandoned or was in the process of being refurbished.

He was about to turn and ask the guard where this was when he became aware of muffled sounds issuing from several of the cubicles. His initial thought was that these were the grunts and gasps of people trying on outfits several sizes too small. It seems ridiculous now, but that is honestly what he first took the sounds to signify—that the cubicles were fitting rooms, and that in each there was a fat person struggling to get into clothing intended for someone thinner. It made a kind of sense. It was only after listening more closely for several moments that Gordon realised that the sounds were coming in pairs, each grunt matched to a reciprocal grunt, each gasp to an answering gasp, a rhythmic, guttural strophe and antistrophe interspersed with random sighs, squeals, and moaned obscenities.

When the penny finally dropped, the quietly rational part of his mind which usually assesses loan risks and calculates interest percentages simply said, *Well, it's a business deal like any other, isn't it? A straightforward exchange of commodities,* even as something unruly and libidinous stirred within him.

He didn't realise the woman was standing by his side until she addressed him, saying, "Welcome to the Pleasure Department, sir." The woman in her diaphanous rose-pink gown. The woman who then took his hand and said the words that unleashed a torrent of pent-up fantasies—all the positions he had never attempted with Linda, all the acts he had never dared ask her to perform, all the deeds he had pored sweatily over in novels and magazines but never, in his very limited sexual experience, actually tried. Dazed by the enormity of the horizons suddenly opening up before him, and giddy with the reek of incense, he meekly let the woman lead him down the left-hand row of cubicles and usher him into one. There, as the bead curtain rattled back into place behind him, he took stock of the narrow single bed, the table groaning with all manner of lubricants, prophylactics, and alarmingly-shaped rubber devices, and the credit register mounted on the wall adjoining the next cubicle, which was shuddering with the exertions of the transaction taking place on the other side.

The woman asked him his name, and he told her, and he asked her hers, and she said he could call her whatever he liked, and looking at the colour of her gown he said, "Rose," and she said, "Then Rose I am."

And then she said, "Gordon, what kind of account you have?"

And he said, "Silver."

And trying to disguise her pity, Rose said, "I'll be honest with you, Gordon, there's not a lot I'll do for a Silver." And he must have looked crestfallen because she then said, "But we can still have some fun, can't we? If we're imaginative."

And he said, "Yes."

And with that, she removed her gown, just like that, slipping the shoulder-straps off with a shrug, letting it slither down and crumple around her feet, and there she stood, naked and pink in the low red light, her arms outstretched, completely open about her nudity, unlike Linda, who clutches an arm across her breasts whenever Gordon walks in on her while she is taking a bath, and who will only make love with the lights out. And she was trim and firm where a woman should be, voluptuous where a woman should be, majestically so. Quite unlike Linda.

And she said, "Out with it, then," and Gordon blindly and obediently began fumbling with his fly, and she said, "No, not *that*," and laughed. "Your card."

And he said, "My wife..."

And she said, "Ah, your wife. Seven-year itch, is it?"

And he said, "No. My, um, my wife has our card."

And Rose laughed again, coldly this time, and said, "Then, Gordon, you had better leave, because without your card you don't get anything.

And I should warn you that if you try to take something that you can't pay for, I can have a guard here in three seconds flat to arrest you." She indicated a red emergency button fixed to the wall above the bedhead.

"Arrest me?"

"For taking goods without payment. Shoplifting, Gordon."

And Gordon nodded numbly, and Rose said, "Off you go then. Another time, perhaps."

And she bent to put her gown back on, and Gordon turned and fled. Bursting through the bead curtain and sprinting down the row of cubicles, ashamed and embarrassed and guilty and desperate to get out of the department as quickly as possible, he ran, and for a while it seemed that the row of cubicles would never end and that he would have to keep running for ever, and then suddenly he was in Mirrors, and blushing madly—because everyone must have known where he had just been and what had happened to him there, it must have been written all over his face—he foundered deeper into the department, losing himself amid a dizzying myriad of reflected Gordons, furtive, manic Gordons, flustered, panicked Gordons, until he found himself running towards himself and he realised he had stumbled into a dead end, and skidding to a halt before his likeness he turned, only to be confronted by a pair of gormlessly grinning Burlingtons, and before he could say anything something blurred through the air towards him, and not knowing what it was he instinctively raised a hand to protect himself, and felt his palm scorch...

And now he tries to speak again, to ask the Burlingtons what they want with him, why are they doing this to him, why him, but again all that comes out of his mouth is another fear-filled, knock-kneed little whimper, which the taller of the two Burlingtons is quick to mimic, compounding the humiliation. This Burlington, the one who cut Gordon, has a long horselike face and long horselike teeth exaggerated by the tapering inadequacy of his lower jaw. The other has been even less well served by the limited genetic scope of upper-class in-breeding. His forehead is low and his eyes close-set, his protruding lips are rippled like the mouth of a clam, and his skin is so wattled with acne scabs and scars that it looks like burgundy leather. Where his comrade is gangly and tall, this one is short and squat, but their half-black, half-bleached buzzcuts and their matching uniform of gold moiré jacket, black drainpipe trousers, and designer trainers lessen the physical differences between them, making them look, in a strange, scary way, almost like twins.

Gordon scans around desperately for help, but this section of the department is deserted and all he can see is his predicament reflected back at him from a dozen different angles, each image a variation on the same theme: that of two Burlingtons cornering a hunched, white-faced figure whose spectacles are askew and whose breathing is coming in heaving, irregular shudders and the fingers of whose right hand are barber's poles of blood. And it almost seems possible to Gordon that if, in the mirrors, one of the two razor-sharp Iridiums were to suddenly whir through the air and carve a gash in his reflection's throat, it wouldn't be him that would gargle to death on his own blood but an inverted Gordon safely tucked away in looking-glass land. It is a crazy thought, but no crazier than the grotesque insanity of his present situation.

The first Burlington sneers down at Gordon speculatively, saying, "This is the kind of riffraff they're letting in these days? This is the sort of jumped-up nobody we have to share our store with?" He snorts. "Pathetic."

"Pathetic," his comrade agrees.

"Please," Gordon says, risking another whimper but managing, at last, to find his voice, or at any rate a pale imitation of same. "Let me go. I promise I won't report you to anyone, I'll just be quietly on my way. Please."

"Bit of a nasal twang there," the taller Burlington remarks, leaning back. "What do you think, Algy? Something in the service industries? Middle management?"

Algy, clearly selected as a friend and sidekick because he possesses no opinions of his own, merely chuckles and nods.

"Please," says Gordon. "I'm just a customer like yourself."

"Got it now. Banking or insurance. Possibly accountancy, but I'm betting on banking or insurance. That servile note in the voice, that horrible job's-worth whine."

"I'm the loans manager for a branch of a major national clearing bank," Gordon intones, neither defiantly nor defensively but because it is the truth.

"And you've saved up all your hard-earned pennies to become a Days account-holder, and—don't tell me—wifey's chipped in by taking on extra work, because it's all about bettering yourselves, isn't it? It's all about clawing your way up the ladder."

"It was Linda's idea," Gordon whispers.

"But don't you see, you four-eyed nonentity?" The Burlington clamps a hand around Gordon's throat and shoves his head back against the mirror with a surprisingly resonant clack of skull against glass. He inserts the bloody Iridium beneath the left-hand lens of Gordon's spectacles and skewers the corner into Gordon's eyelid, pricking out a droplet of blood. "There *is* no ladder. That's just a lie dreamed up to give your insignificant little lives hope and meaning, to make you work your fingers to the bone for your precious Aluminiums and Silvers, but it doesn't make any difference. *It doesn't make any difference.* You're born boring, lower-middle-class drones, and that's all you'll ever be."

"Er, Rupert?"

"Not now, Algy," says the taller Burlington, still staring fixedly into Gordon's face. "I'm busy."

"Um... Rupert, I really think you should let him go."

Rupert sighs testily. "What *is* it, Algy? What could be more important than a demonstration of the class system in action?"

He glances up into the mirror behind Gordon's head and his undersized chin plummets.

There is a guard. He is holding Algy by the collar of his jacket. His other hand is resting on the grip of his hip-holstered pistol.

Instantly Rupert lets go of Gordon and steps smartly back, the sharpened card vanishing from view. Gordon staggers and wheezes, one hand flying to his neck to palpate his tender throat.

"Morning," says Rupert to the guard, from sneering snob to guilty schoolboy in no time flat.

"Afternoon, actually," says the guard.

"Sorry. Afternoon. My friend and I were just, er... just helping this fellow with directions. Appears he's lost. Took a wrong turn somewhere."

"Is that so? How thoughtful of you."

"We thought so too."

Gordon tries to force words out through his traumatised trachea but it isn't possible to make sense of the hoarse, moist clucks his throat produces. Luckily, the guard has seen all he needs to see.

"Perhaps it would be better if you left us now, sir," he tells Gordon, politeness itself. "The boys and I have some private matters to discuss. I have to demonstrate to them how the class system really works."

Gordon needs no further prompting.

As he scurries away, he hears Rupert the Burlington say, "Look, can't we sort this out like rational human beeeEEEYARRGHHH!"

Then there is only the sound of fists smacking flesh, and awful cries.

25

Seven-League Boots: Ogre's boots donned by the fairy-tale hero Hop-o'-my-Thumb, enabling him to walk seven leagues (approximately 34 kilometres) at a stride.

12.00 p.m.

AT THE TURNING point of the day, high noon, after an hour of fruitless wandering without so much as a sniff of a possible perpetrator to break the monotony of department after department after department, Frank has walked himself into a state of dulled lethargy.

Nothing is happening. Around him customers are ambling, browsing, pausing, lingering, staring, discussing, comparing, matching, calculating, considering and acquiring, while sales assistants are smiling, bobbing, bowing, suggesting, hinting, agreeing, detagging, scanning, checking, bagging and returning. Nothing is happening but the give-and-take of commerce, as elemental and eternal as the ebb and neap of the tide, and Frank has nothing to do except plod from one department to another, through the various vectors of Days, his legs carrying him along in a mindless, relentless forward-urge. Every so often he checks in with the Eye. Anything nearby? Anything that requires his presence? Each time the answer comes back the same: nothing. The Eye sounds quieter than usual, its background hubbub subdued, as though down there in that screen-lit Basement chamber they are experiencing their own doldrums.

Frank's trail crosses and recrosses itself as he proceeds through the immensity of Days, covering ground purely for the sake of covering ground, because that is what he is paid to do. He walks neither towards any particular goal nor to put distance between him and anything but simply to rack up the kilometres. There is no finishing line ahead, no Sodom behind, just the journey itself, the act of going. He travels hopefully, never to arrive.

Riding a lift, he is still moving.

Idling by a display, he is still moving.

Standing on an escalator, he is still moving.

Waiting until a traffic jam of shoppers clears so that he can continue down an aisle, he is still moving.

Hovering at the entrance to a fitting room to make sure that customers come out wearing the same clothes they had on going in, he is still moving.

Still moving, moving and still, as though his thirty-three years as a store detective have built up an inner inertia that pushes him on even when stationary. If his legs suddenly stopped working, perhaps deciding that they had had enough, that they had covered several lifetimes' worth of distance, far more than their fair share, and they refused point-blank to go another step—if that happened, he feels that somehow his body would be unable to remain at rest. The accumulated momentum of thirty-three years of day-long walking would propel him onwards for ever, like a space probe sailing effortlessly through the void, endlessly, without entropy, into infinity.

Time slows when nothing is happening, and thoughts spit in all directions from Frank's becalmed brain like sap-sparks from a smouldering log. His head fills with a babble of his own creation, a stream-of-consciousness monologue so loud and inane that he has, in the past, wanted to put his hands over his ears and yell at himself to shut up.

Simply talking to someone else might help relieve the mental pressure, but Ghosts are discouraged from unnecessary communication with other employees while on duty. Ghost Training, in fact, teaches you to have as little contact as possible with your co-workers, for to open your mouth is to draw attention to yourself. As for customers, in the unlikely event that one should mistake you for a fellow shopper and attempt to strike up a conversation, the terser your replies are, the better. The four main attributes of a good Ghost are, as the Ghost's Motto says, silence, vigilance, persistence, and intransigence. The greatest of these is silence. Silence at any price, even at the cost of being driven insane by your brain's unconscious blather.

Sometimes when he passes a fellow Ghost, Frank thinks he can see in the other's face a reflection of the look that must be on his own. Beneath the Ghost's affected impassiveness, in the eyes, he thinks he can discern a barely-restrained yearning to uncork a head-full of bottled-up thoughts, preferably in banter, failing that as a scream.

But perhaps he only imagines this. Perhaps it is just something his brain, in its skull-bound isolation, invents while his legs drive him aimlessly through the over-familiar, never-changing storescape. Perhaps, after thirty-three years of pounding the same floors, going over and over the imprints of his own footsteps, wearing the Days-logo carpets thin with his soles, he is simply displacing his pent-up frustrations on to others.

And as he keeps on walking and nothing keeps on happening, Frank feels himself veering down once again into the pit of wraiths inside him, into that well of milling, voiceless creatures who writhe heedlessly around one another like a knot of mating snakes. Loud and clear he hears the unspoken summons as they call to him with goldfish-gaping lips and begging eyes, saying in their inarticulacy that this is the place to be, down here in anonymity, down here where there are no individuals, where your name will be Legion, where you can be just one of many, where the configuration of meat and bone that is Frank Hubble will cease to have significance. Withdraw, withdraw. Pull yourself in like a snail into its shell and never come out again.

How easy it would be to answer that call. He knows of other Ghosts who did succumb. There was Falconer a few years back, who came to believe that he was genuinely invisible and arrived for work one morning stark naked, thinking that no one would notice. (He was pensioned off quickly, quietly, without fuss.) There was Eames, who failed to come in two days running, and was found at his apartment, sitting in a corner of his bedroom, dressed in his pyjamas and hugging his knees and rocking to and fro, staring vacantly into space, drooling. And then there was Burgess, who went on a killing-spree through the store, shooting four customers dead and wounding another six before security guards brought him down. No one could have predicted that any of these loyal, hard-working Tactical Security employees would all of a sudden, and for no apparent reason, snap the way they did, but they did, and another few months at Days and that is probably what will happen to Frank, too. One morning he will wake up and won't feel the urge to get out of bed or feed himself or clothe himself or go anywhere. It will all be too much effort. They will find him like Eames, lying in bed, catatonic. Down among the wraiths. Down among the wraiths for ever.

That would be his future for sure, were he not going to do something about it today; were he not going to tender his resignation to Mr Bloom in—a discreet glance at his watch—three quarters of an hour's time.

Three quarters of an hour of slow time. Forty-five oozing minutes. Two thousand seven hundred syrup-seconds measured out in steady footfalls in the protracted somnambulistic dream-random of Nothing Happening at Days.

26

Heptathlon: A seven-event Olympic contest consisting of 100 metres hurdles, shot put, javelin, high jump, long jump, 200 metres sprint, and 800 metres race.

12.15 p.m.

A COLD, BRISK wind snaps across the rooftop, whipping between the huge vents that rise like ships' funnels and warp the air with their hot exhalations, whistling around the blockish lift-heads that poke up at regular intervals, tousling the pollarded trees and potted shrubs of the sunken garden, wrinkling the surface of the swimming pool, and rattling the chainlink fence that encloses the tennis court.

Mungo, on the tennis court, extends his arms upwards, grunting pleasurably at the fluent meshing of his biceps, triceps, and laterals. Linking his fingers, he swivels his torso from the waist. The wind pricks gooseflesh from his bare legs. It feels good to be out of the Boardroom. Not that Mungo dislikes immersing himself in the day-to-day concerns of running the store, far from it. He relishes the daily mental challenge. But out here or down in the gym, where the only exertions he has to make are physical—that is when he is at his happiest.

Chas, at the other end of the court, is leaning louchely on the end of his racquet, one leg crossed over the other. He is dressed in crisp white shorts and a pale-pink polo shirt, with a cream woollen jumper slung around his neck, the sleeves knotted. His long fringe is flapping this way and that in the wind. He yawns provocatively, but Mungo, ignoring him, continues with his warm-up routine, crouching down for a hamstring stretch.

The yawn having failed, Chas continues to feign boredom by gazing around, first at the sky, then at the city that crowds beyond the lip of the roof, huddled and brown and inferior all the way to the sun-hazed horizon. After a while he returns his gaze to his eldest brother, to find that he has completed his limbering up and has begun jogging on the spot.

"Ready at last?"

"Ready."

"About time too. I was beginning to lose all feeling in my toes."

"Ten a point?" says Mungo, picking up his racquet and unloading a ball from his pocket. Mungo, on account of his seniority, always serves first.

"Let's make it twenty. I'm feeling confident today."

"Confident or extravagant?"

"I'm a Day. Extravagance is my middle name."

Mungo steps back to the baseline, bounces the ball a couple of times on the smooth green clay of the court, and winds himself up to unleash a devastating serve. The balls skims the corner of the service box and rockets into the chainlink fence, ricocheting with a loud clattering shimmer.

"Nice one," says Chas, having made no move to intercept the serve. He crosses to the other side of his baseline. "Fifteen-love."

"And twenty down."

"It's only money."

Of Mungo's next three serves Chas makes the effort to return only the one that is delivered virtually to the head of his racquet. Mungo counters the half-hearted return easily, volleying the ball into the opposite corner from where Chas is standing.

As they change ends, Mungo remarks, "I see you've decided to take it easy today."

"Lulling you into a false sense of security, big bro."

Chas's serves are deceptively languid, the ball leaving his slow-rising racquet at lightning speed even though its only propulsion is a tiny, last-minute flick of the wrist. Mungo lunges to make the returns, pounding across the clay. The rallies are lengthy, the ball traversing the net seven, eight, and on one occasion eleven times. Chas wins. Mungo aces the next game, but by now he is huffing heavily and his heart is beating hard, while Chas hasn't even begun to perspire.

They meet at the net.

"Do you know what I think about sometimes when I'm up here?" says Chas. Chas has a tendency to draw out the intervals between games so as to spread out the minimum amount of physical effort over the maximum period of time. It is a habit Mungo tolerates only because none of his other brothers will play tennis with him.

"I've no idea," Mungo replies, thumbing sweat from his eyebrows. "I only know that the way you play leaves you a great deal of time for thinking."

"I think of a castle and the village that lies beyond its ramparts. I think of the seven of us as feudal barons taking our tithes from the peasants around us."

"I knew you should never have read PPE at university."

"Oh, don't get me wrong, I'm not saying that the arrangement is a bad one. I'm just saying that it's been going on for centuries. We're all of us hostages to history, conforming unconsciously to social archetypes laid down long ago."

"Whatever gets you through the night, Chas. Your serve."

The next game goes to deuce. Chas wins the advantage point, and with a backhand of elegant insouciance clinches the game.

"Don't start celebrating yet," says Mungo. "You still owe me nearly a hundred."

Chas puts up a fight for the next game, but Mungo's mighty serve wins through.

As they meet again at the net, Chas says, "It's a crazy person who would resist you, Mungo."

Mungo looks at his brother askance. "I take it you're not just referring to my game."

Chas nods, pleased that his subtext has been noted. "You did a brave thing this morning. I mean, you always stand up for Sonny, we've accepted that, and in a perverse way it's quite admirable. But this morning you really stuck your neck out for him. For a while there Thurston and Sato looked fit to shit."

"It was a gamble, I admit."

"I'll say. If it had backfired..."

"The rest of you would have locked Sonny up in his apartment and thrown away the key."

"Something like that."

"It's what Dad would have wanted."

"Sonny locked up?"

"The integrity of the Seven preserved."

"At all costs?"

"At all costs. Why else would he have gone to the effort of having seven of us?"

"As I recall, it was our mother who went to the effort. All Dad did was calculate due dates and bribe doctors to make sure that each of us arrived on the correct day of the week. He was an odd sort, Dad, really, when you think about it."

"He was a visionary," says Mungo, as if this excuses everything.

"A visionary with only one eye. What do you call that? A semi-visionary? A monovisionary?"

"That was all part of his vision," says Mungo. "Now, are we going to stand here flapping our lips all day or are we going to play tennis?"

"Are you offering me a choice?"

"No."

"Attaboy. That's the Septimus Day in you talking."

Mungo breaks Chas's serve and holds his own. Chas, for all that he exploits the vagaries of the wind to make his shots unpredictable, cannot compete with Mungo's dogged determination to reach the ball no matter where it bounces.

"Four-two, two-four," says Mungo, hurdling the net. "I hope you've got your card to hand, because by my reckoning you're over a hundred and fifty in the hole."

"All according to plan, Mungo. I keep this up, and you'll become overconfident and start making mistakes."

"As if."

Chas laughs, holding the net down to step over it. "God, you really are a chip off the old block. The same unswerving conviction in yourself, the same absolute refusal to contemplate the possibility of failure."

"To contemplate failure is to court failure."

"Well said, 'Septimus'. But would you, I wonder, gouge your own eye out in order to prove a point?"

Mungo considers this. "Probably not, no. I need depth of field so that I can keep trouncing you at tennis."

"Seriously. Would you ever go that far?"

"Our father was an exceptional human being," Mungo replies. "He did what he felt he had to do. He made what he considered the appropriate sacrifice to ensure the success of his venture. If I was in his shoes, gambling millions of other people's money on a project as insanely ambitious as Days, and I thought—no, I firmly believed—that removing my left eye with a pen-knife was going to make the difference between triumph and disaster, who knows, perhaps under those circumstances I'd do it. An offering to Mammon, a few moments of agony in return for a lifetime of success—I don't know. A fair deal? I don't know."

"But he also did it to prove that it could be done, as a test of will."

"It was both a test of will *and* a propitiatory offering to the gods of commerce. In Dad's eyes—eye—will and fate were inextricably linked. 'Fate isn't what happens to you, it's what you make happen.' Isn't that what he used to say? And let's face it, he certainly made this place happen. When he first dreamed up Days, investors were hardly beating a path to his door waving blank cheques at him. He had to browbeat people for every single penny, he had to *force* them into believing in him. And the same goes for fate, or the gods of commerce, or Mammon, or whatever you want to call it. The divine order of things. Dad had to show the universe how determined he was, how far he was prepared to go in order to get his way, and he did, and it worked. Whether I'd be able to convince myself that it would work for me, I'm not sure."

"Oh, I can picture you doing the same," says Chas blithely, knowing that there is nothing his older brother likes more than to be compared favourably with their father. "I can picture you kneeling in the middle of an empty tract of wasteland you've just purchased, looking around at the land that your building is going to occupy, knowing as you do so that this is the very last time you are going to have the use of both eyes. The boarded-up shopping arcade on one side, the row of short-lease charity shops and thrift shops on the other, all to be demolished soon to make way for your dream—the dream set out on the blueprints flapping in the mud around your feet. I can imagine you digging the small, shallow hole that is shortly going to contain a part of you, and then taking the pen-knife out of your pocket, unclipping the largest blade, and bracing yourself as you bring it up to your left eye..."

Chas seems to take a gleeful delight in rehearsing the details of their father's act of self-mutilation. Mungo, however, only shudders. "You may be able to imagine it," he says. "I can't. Which suggests that I lack our father's capacity for making sacrifices, and therefore that I'm nothing like him."

"Sacrifices? What do you call the way you stick up for Sonny if it isn't a sacrifice?"

"Losing the esteem of one's brothers is hardly as painful as losing an eye, Chas, and esteem can always be recovered, whereas an eye can't. Enough of this. We have to be back in the Boardroom for lunch soon. You to serve, again."

During the next game, perhaps spurred on by the memory of their father, Chas evinces an increased enthusiasm for victory. He uses every trick he knows to make Mungo's life difficult, from high lobs to low backspin grounders. He feints powerful shots that barely trickle over the net and launches volleys across the court masterfully, but somehow Mungo manages to reach every ball, however unreturnable it seems, and snatch it across the net, always recovering in time to respond to the next of Chas's challenges. Throughout the game he grins and pants like a happy dog.

Deuce is reached, and continues interminably. Mungo enters a delicious delirium of effort, grunting explosively with each swing of his racquet, and Chas in his own way becomes engrossed in the game too, frowning like a chess grandmaster as if each exchange of shots is a conundrum he has to solve. Neither of them is aware that they have been joined on the rooftop by a spectator who, slumped against the chainlink fence with his face pressed into the diamond-shaped holes, is following the back-and-forth of the game with a glassy, ill-focused interest.

Mungo finally capitalises on an advantage point and batters the ball home to win the game. Exhausted, he drops his racquet and bends double, bracing his hands on his knees. It is then, looking up from under a red, dripping brow, that he notices the new arrival watching from the sidelines.

Chas spots the spectator at the same time, and says, drolly, "Ah, the conquering hero returns. Nice outfit, Sonny. I assume you didn't go out on the shop floor dressed like that."

Sonny doesn't reply. His fingers are clawed into the fence; this appears to be all that is holding him upright. His eyes moon from one brother to the other as though, as far as he is concerned, the game hasn't come to an end.

Mungo straightens up warily. "Sonny? Is everything all right? How did it go downstairs?"

There is a pause. Then, slowly, Sonny turns his face in Mungo's direction. "Hm?"

"I said—"

"What's the score, Mungo? Who's winning?"

"Oh Christ," whispers Chas.

Mungo reaches the fence in a few brisk strides. He lowers his face to Sonny's and inhales once, hard, then leans back, nodding sombrely. Sonny grins sloppily up at him. One of his hands loses its grip and he slips and almost collapses, but manages to secure himself a fresh handhold just in time.

Mungo's words begin as a moan but rise steadily to a roar. "Oh, you little bastard, you little fucking bastard, you idiot, you fucking idiot, what have you done, what have you done, what in Christ's name have you done? Couldn't even abstain for a couple of hours, could you? A couple of hours, you mindless fuckwit, you stupid little turd! You couldn't even do that one thing, that one tiny thing you were asked to do, without screwing it up! You useless piece of shit, you useless, traitorous piece of shit! Do you know what I'm going to do to you? Do you? I'm going to *kill* you! I'm going to rip your heart out of your chest and fucking *feed* it to you, that's what I'm going to do!"

"Mungo, cool it."

"No, Chas, I will not 'cool it'. I will *not* fucking 'cool it'! I bend over backwards to help this fly-covered heap of dogshit, I give him another chance, a chance he does *not* deserve, and what do I get? How does he reward me? By spitting in my fucking face!"

Regardless of the fence between them, Mungo makes a furious lunge for Sonny. Likewise regardless of the fence between them, Sonny backpedals hurriedly. Stumbling, he falls squarely on his behind, scraping his hands on the gravel.

"What happened downstairs, Sonny?" says Mungo, shaking the chainlink. "What did you do? What did you say to the heads of Books and Computers? Did you tell them what we told you to tell them? Or did you just manage to make *us* look ridiculous? What did you do, Sonny? What did you *say*?"

For the first time Sonny is fearful. Mungo's bulging scarlet face looms in his vision like a medieval gargoyle. It would seem to be well within Mungo's power to tear a hole in the fence and reach through the gap to do the same to Sonny.

Chas lays a tentative hand on Mungo's shoulder. "Mungo, listen."

Mungo twitches his head, not taking his eyes off Sonny. "What, Chas?"

"We don't know what went on down there."

"We don't have to know. Look at him. Pissed out of his skull. And don't tell me he got that way since coming back upstairs. I know Sonny's drinking habits, and these are the results of a good hour's worth we're seeing here. He *must* have gone down there drunk and he *must* have screwed things up."

"But we don't know that for sure, not yet. And until we do, our best course is to get him stowed away safely out of sight. Take him down to his apartment and make sure he stays there."

"Why?"

"Because if the others find out that he went downstairs in this state, there's no telling what'll happen. I mean, look how well *you* reacted, and you're supposed to be his ally."

Mungo peers down at Sonny, who has by this time lost interest in his brothers and is distractedly picking pieces of grit from his palms. "Wouldn't it be better just to drag him straight to the Boardroom and show them? Show them what a worthless little prick he is?"

"Possibly, but like I said, I doubt they'll take it well."

"So what? Why do you all of a sudden care what happens to Sonny?"

Chas hesitates, then says, "Let's put it this way. I may not completely believe in this Seven business, but that's no reason to put it in jeopardy."

Mungo lets the implication of his brother's statement sink in. "Yes. I see. So we keep Sonny's condition hidden from the others, and hope and pray that he did what he was supposed to downstairs."

"That's about the size of it."

"All in the name of preserving the integrity of the Seven."

"Correct."

Mungo draws in a deep, controlling breath and lets it out again, his shoulders slumping, his anger unbinding. "You're right, of course. The Seven comes before everything else." He lets go of the fence and turns in the direction of the tennis court gate. "But I swear to God, Chas," he growls, "if he's done any damage down there, any damage at all, I'll murder him with my bare hands."

"If it turns out he did, Mungo, you'll have to take a number and join the queue."

Neither of these statements is an idle boast. Mungo and Chas are the sons of a man who gouged out his own eye with a pen-knife in order to get his own way. That streak of determination, that desire to succeed whatever the cost, is in their genes. Just as Septimus committed violence against himself, so his offspring have the potential to commit violence against *them*selves. It is, you might say, a sin of the father that is ready to be visited upon the sons.

27

7th December, 1941: The day the Japanese launched their surprise air attack on the U.S. Naval base at Pearl Harbor, Hawaii, precipitating active U.S. participation in World War II.

12.35 p.m.

In her office cubicle Miss Dalloway sits with a Brie-and-cucumber sandwich in one hand and *The Art of War* open on her knee. The book's spine is so well broken that she does not have to hold the pages down with her hand.

She eats the sandwich mechanically and methodically, and when she has finished she licks the tips of her fingers clean one by one. Then she drinks a small bottle of mineral water, and fastidiously disposes of the empty bottle and the sandwich wrapper in the waste-paper basket. Silly, she knows, to be so concerned about tidiness when, if all goes according to plan this afternoon, a litter-free office will be the least of her worries. But old habits, of course, die hard.

She closes *The Art of War* and places it on top of the desk. She has read the book so many times by now that she knows it by heart, but she finds the familiar cadences of the sentences reassuring, the logical precision of Sun Tzu's words comforting and calming.

Taking a key from her trouser pocket, she unlocks one of the desk's drawers and takes out another book, this one a more recent addition to her personal library.

It is a cheaply-produced trade paperback printed on thick, coarse paper and published by a small press whose list otherwise consists of conspiracy-theory tracts, UFO-spotting manuals, and how-to guides on the subject of growing and smoking marijuana. The book's front cover mimics a manila dossier, with the title "rubber-stamped" across it at an angle in blockish, rough-textured characters, as though this is in fact some top-secret goverment file. No author is credited anywhere, not even in the publisher's indicia.

The book is called *Kitchen-Sink Arsenal*, and like *The Art of War*, it shows the signs of having been well-read and well-used.

Miss Dalloway sets *Kitchen-Sink Arsenal* down beside *The Art of War* on her desktop and smooths it open, ready, at a certain page. Then, stiffly, she stands up, pressing her knuckles into the small of her back, all of a sudden conscious of a dozen skeletal aches and pains that she could have sworn weren't there before. She feels old. Not just in years. Spiritually. Her soul sick and weary—the legacy of a life of devotion to the ailing and ungenerous master that is literature.

Picking up the Platinum card belonging to Mrs C A Shukhov, she heads out to the information desk.

Oscar and Edgar are on duty. The rest of her darlings are either at lunch or busy elsewhere in the department.

"My boys," she says.

The two Bookworms melt with delight at the tenderness with which she has addressed them.

"My boys, I have need of you."

"What can we do for you, Miss Dalloway?" says Oscar. "Anything you want. Name it."

Before she can tell them, a customer approaches the desk, wanting to know where he can find books on cassette.

"We don't stock books on cassette here, sir," Miss Dalloway informs the man. "You'll find those in the Visual Impairment Department on the Indigo Floor. The only kind of books we stock in this department are the kind you read."

"Books on cassette!" Oscar exclaims before the customer is quite out of earshot. "What a joke!"

"Pretty soon you won't have to bother reading any more," says Edgar. "All you'll do is attach an electrode to your head and download a book directly into your brain in a couple of seconds."

"Edgar, we don't use words like 'download' in this department."

"Sorry, Miss Dalloway."

"But the sentiment is a noble one, and appreciated. Thank you. Now, as I was saying. The mission. As you will no doubt recall, last Tuesday afternoon I sent a number of you out into the store to buy me certain items. You, Oscar, I asked to get me a can of fuel oil."

"And you asked *me* to buy you a nine-volt battery," says Edgar.

"And didn't Malcolm have to get you a camera flashbulb?" says Oscar.

"And it was Colin, I think, you sent for a bag of garden fertiliser."

"And Mervyn got you a beer keg."

"Quite," says Miss Dalloway. "And I'm sure you all thought it was an eccentric shopping list, but you went out and brought back every item on it all the same, without question, because you're good boys, all of you."

At the compliment the two Bookworms preen and quiver like stroked cats.

"And now I need one of you to go and buy two more items in order to complete the list."

"Say no more, Miss Dalloway," says Oscar. "Just tell me what they are, and I'll go and get them."

"Thank you, Oscar," says Miss Dalloway, "but, as you will see in a moment, this task is going to require someone who is quick on his feet." She gently pats the roll of fat that bulges between the base of Oscar's skull and his collar. "No offence, my darling, but you're hardly built for speed. Not to mention the fact that you have a broken arm..."

Oscar puts on a not wholly convincing show of dismay.

"Besides, I have need of you here," Miss Dalloway adds. "For moral support."

"But—"

"'They also serve who only stand and wait,' Oscar."

"Which therefore, by a process of elimination, leaves me," says the habitually gloomy Edgar, managing to look both pleased and put-upon at once. "What is it you want me to buy, Miss Dalloway?"

"Before I tell you that, Edgar, I feel it is only fair to warn you that there is going to be an element of risk involved. If, once you learn what I want from you, you change your mind, I will understand perfectly, and I won't think any less of you."

Edgar reassures his head of department that nothing can be too much trouble, that she can never ask too much of him, that she is in fact doing *him* a favour by sending him out on this mission, risky though it may be. And even though Miss Dalloway knew that that was what his response would be, she is still touched.

"Then listen carefully. I need a roll of insulated copper wire and an alarm clock—the old-fashioned kind, nothing digital, one with a wind-up mechanism and bells on top."

"I thought you said the mission was going to be dangerous," says

Edgar with a snort. "I think I can manage to get you some wire and an alarm clock without too much difficulty."

"Perhaps. However, unlike last time, this time you won't be using your own card. You'll be using this." And she holds up the purloined Platinum.

"Isn't that the one Malcolm handed in the other day?" says Oscar, squinting.

"That's correct."

"So shouldn't you have—?" Oscar catches himself before he can finish a question that might be construed as casting aspersions on his beloved head of department's judgement.

Miss Dalloway finishes the question for him anyway. "Yes, Oscar, you're right, I should have passed it on to Accounts, and I didn't. A breach of regulations, but then posterity will show that, on balance, I have been a woman more sinned against than sinning."

"But surely it'll have been reported lost," says Edgar. "If I try to use it, Security will come down on me like a tonne of bricks."

"Which is what lends the mission its element of risk. Knowing that, are you still willing to go?"

"May I enquire why you want me to use that particular card, Miss Dalloway?" says Edgar. "You must have a reason. You always have a reason for everything you do."

"True, Edgar, and yes, you may enquire. The answer is simple. I want Days to know what I am up to. I want everyone to know."

"Um, Miss Dalloway," says Oscar hesitantly. "Sorry for asking this, but what *is* it, exactly, that you're up to?"

Miss Dalloway shakes her head. It will be better if she doesn't tell them yet. That way Edgar's pleas of ignorance, should Security catch up with him, will have the added virtue of authenticity. "When the time comes, all will be revealed. Until then, I must ask you to trust me, and for you, Edgar, to demonstrate that trust by buying the wire and the clock and bringing them safely back here."

"Does it have something to do with what you were up to yesterday behind the books, at your desk?" says Oscar. "You know, when you told us not to disturb you for a couple of hours?"

"Oscar!" Miss Dalloway holds up a hand. "'How poor are they that have not patience.' All will be revealed soon enough."

"Yes, Miss Dalloway. Sorry, Miss Dalloway."

"I also have need of a trolley," she tells Edgar, handing Mrs Shukhov's

Platinum to him. "That should be the first thing you obtain, and I suggest you use your own card to hire it. For the wire and the clock, however, you must use the Platinum."

"And then run like hell," says Edgar.

"Precisely. Your employee ID badge should give you a certain immunity from suspicion, but still your principal concern is going to be staying ahead of Security. Now that you're aware of the possible consequences of this mission, are you still prepared to go? Speak now or for ever hold your peace."

Edgar swallows hard and says, "I'm prepared to go."

"Then bless you." She strokes his head. "I have every confidence in you to succeed."

"I won't let you down, Miss Dalloway."

"Well? What are you waiting for?"

"You want me to leave right away?"

"Stand not upon the order of your going, my darling, but go!"

28

The Seven Golden Cities of Cibola: A collection of seven towns, a pueblo of the Zuñi Indians in what is now Zuñi, New Mexico, fabled by Fray Marcos de Niza to be the source of great riches, which prompted Francisco Vásquez de Coronado in 1540 to head an expedition of 1,300 men to conquer them—no riches were found.

12.45 p.m.

"Frank," says Mr Bloom, smiling and gesturing to the chair on the opposite side of the small table. "I took the liberty of ordering wine."

"I don't drink during the daytime," says Frank, sitting down.

"Go on, give the cat a goldfish." Mr Bloom makes to fill Frank's glass from a wicker-bound bottle of Chianti. "It's not bad. Not as raw as some of these Italian wines can get."

Frank clamps a hand over firmly the rim of the glass. "No. Please."

"Suit yourself."

The restaurant is a mock trattoria on the Green Floor hoop, white-painted wrought-iron tables and matching chairs clustered beneath a wooden pergola densely interlaced with vine leaves. Mr Bloom's rank has secured them a table directly next to the parapet. Some twenty metres below their elbows lies the Menagerie, one half of its canopy illuminated by a vast shaft of sunlight that descends almost vertically from the great dome, the rest in smoky shadow. The brightness in the atrium is so intense that several of the diners have resorted to wearing sunglasses.

The atrium resounds to the sound of six floors' worth of activity. Around lunchtime, shoppers gravitate toward the hoops. Many of them have come to Days for the sole purpose of meeting for lunch, since the store provides a dining venue of unparalleled social cachet. Indeed, the first thing Mr Bloom does after refreshing his own glass is draw Frank's attention to the celebrities at neighbouring tables. He indicates the famous model alone at a table, studiously not eating the Caesar salad in front of her; the pair of well-respected actors colluding conspiratorially over some project; and the *enfant terrible* fashion designer in the company of the movie director and the head of the huge PR company (the smell of a major deal being struck at the latter table is pungent even at a distance). Frank obligingly steals a sidelong glance as Mr Bloom points out each famous person, but he only vaguely recognises their faces and, frankly, doesn't care who they are. To him they are merely customers.

"So," says Mr Bloom, hoisting a menu aloft and flapping it open. As if to compensate for a lifetime of reticence, he has taken to making his post-Ghosthood gestures as grandiose as possible. "Let's have a look what's on offer today."

Frank picks up his own menu and runs his eye down the handwritten list of available dishes, but his mind is not on food. "You order for both of us," he says, setting the menu aside. He rests an elbow on the table, slots his chin into his cupped hand, and stares across the atrium to the parapet opposite, drumming his fingers against his lower lip.

Mr Bloom catches a waiter's eye—something Frank cannot easily do—and summons him over. He orders minestrone soup, followed by fettuccine puttanesca.

"You don't have a problem with peppers, do you?" he asks Frank.

Frank shakes his head.

The waiter departs.

A silence falls over the table.

"Well," says Mr Bloom, "seeing as you're not going to come straight to the point, I will. From our earlier, abortive conversations, I think I can pretty much guess what you have to say to me."

Frank continues to stare across the atrium. Mr Bloom pauses, then goes on. "I'm sure this isn't a decision you've reached lightly, Frank, and I'm sure you're quite determined that nothing I can say is going to make you change your mind. So you'll no doubt be relieved to hear that I'm not going to try. All I'm going to say is that Days will miss you. No emotional blackmail here, the honest-to-goodness truth. You are an excellent store detective. It'll be a shame to see you go."

Again, no reaction from Frank, but Mr Bloom is used to the ways of Ghosts. He knows he is not wasting his breath.

"Is it the use of guns that bothers you?"

A shake of the head so infinitesimal that only another Ghost would spot it.

"Ah. Usually it's the use of guns. It gets to some Ghosts after a while.

Got to me. The idea of causing pain and injury to others, and worse than pain and injury. Mostly I could justify it to myself. Shoplifters know the risks they're taking, and if they don't then they deserve what comes to them. But every once in a while..." Mr Bloom scratches his foretuft with his little finger. "When I told you earlier about losing my touch, Frank, I didn't tell you why it happened. I'm not sure if this is the reason, but... well, it *seemed* to be the reason at the time. You remember when I shot that kid?"

"I'm sorry, no."

"No reason why you should. We don't go around boasting about these things, do we? He couldn't have been more than fifteen or sixteen. Skinny as a lizard. He stole a comic, and I nabbed him, but he was a slippery devil, twisted right out of my grasp, leaving me holding the big baggy coat he was wearing. A guard hadn't yet arrived, and I knew the kid would have no trouble outrunning me, so, of course, out came the gun. I shouted a warning. He didn't react. I fired. I was aiming to wing him, but he was so thin, not an ounce of meat on him... He was just a kid, but I shot him all the same, without hesitation, because that's what I was trained to do. The bullet tore out half his ribcage. I still have nightmares about it. I've killed five shoplifters, wounded half a dozen others, and every time I've told myself I was just doing my job. Just doing my job. But when I think about that kid's face and the horrible wheezy gargling he made as he bled to death right there on the carpet, right there at my feet... Well, 'just doing my job' doesn't begin to cover it, does it?"

For a moment Mr Bloom looks older than he is, the pain of the memory casting a haggard, spectral shadow over his face. His private remorse has been dredged up, at great personal cost, as a bargaining chip—*I've given you this much, now you give me something in return*—but Frank, unskilled in the wheeling and dealing of human relationships, isn't clear how to respond.

"I've never killed anyone," he says, without turning his head.

Mr Bloom nods slowly. "I know. In fact, you've hardly ever drawn your gun. The mark of a good Ghost."

"Usually it takes nothing more than tact and firmness to deal with a shoplifter."

"There you go. That's what I'm getting at. You were *born* for the job, Frank."

"That's a good thing?"

"It's not a bad thing for a man to be doing the work that best suits him."

"To be born to do a job that requires you to have no personality, to blend into the background and be ignored—that's a good thing?"

The bitter edge in Frank's normally mild voice is not lost on Mr Bloom. "Congruity," Mr Bloom says carefully, "need only be an art. It doesn't have to become a personality trait."

"But what if that's unavoidable?" Frank at long last looks directly at Mr Bloom, bringing the full sad weight of his gravestone-grey gaze to bear on his superior. "What if it's impossible to prevent the one leaking across into the other, the art becoming the personality trait, the job becoming the man? Remember Falconer? And Eames?"

"They were exceptional cases, Frank."

"But what does it take to become an exceptional case? How much or how little of a push do you need to go over the edge?"

Just then the minestrone soup arrives, vegetable-packed and steaming, in earthenware bowls with Days logos hand-painted around the inside of the rim. The waiter also brings them foccaccia bread in a napkin-lined basket. Mr Bloom tucks in immediately. Frank leans back in his chair and resumes his finger-drumming, this time on the lip of the table.

"So what do you intend to do with yourself?" Mr Bloom asks between slurps of soup. "If you resign?"

"Travel."

"Where to?"

"America."

Mr Bloom splutters into his spoon. "America, Frank? Why in God's name America?"

"Because it's big. You can get lost in it."

"So is Days big, and people are getting lost in here all the time. Honestly, Frank—America? I know it's supposed to be a wonderful place, the land of opportunity and all that, but if it's really so great, how come everyone who lives there is seeing a psychiatrist?"

"That's an exaggeration, Donald."

Mr Bloom dismisses the objection with a wave of his spoon. "Whichever way you look at it, Frank, Americans are a strange lot."

That annoys Frank. What does Mr Bloom know about America? What does he know about anywhere that isn't Days?

"America is just a starting point," he says, working hard to restrain his irritation. "Ultimately it doesn't bother me where I go, as long as it's somewhere that isn't here. I'm in my early fifties, and I haven't once travelled beyond the outskirts of this city. Isn't that pathetic? I've covered thousands of kilometres in my career, maybe millions, I've walked around the world several times over, and yet all I've seen is this city and the interior of this store."

"It's not pathetic, Frank. You're a dedicated employee. We all know how hard it is to tear ourselves away from Days. Take me, for instance. I've been meaning to visit my sister and her family in Vancouver for years. I haven't seen my niece since they emigrated. She was fourteen then, she'll be a grown woman now. I'd love to pop over and see them, but I can never seem to find the time. The job always gets in the way. There's always too much unfinished business, too much to be done."

"But that's precisely what keeps us here, Donald. We keep convincing ourselves that the job needs us and that we need the job and that our loyalty and dedication will eventually be rewarded somehow, I don't know how. But it's an excuse; it's pure cowardice and nothing more. Believe me, I know. For years I thought there was nothing on this earth worth having more than a job at Days, but lately I've come to realise that it can't compensate for what I've lost by working here. I've lost things that normal people take for granted—friends, a social life, a family. I want to start clawing back everything this store has taken from me before it's too late, and I want to start as soon as possible."

Should he tell Mr Bloom that he has also lost the ability to see his own reflection? Probably not a good idea. He wants to be seen to be leaving for rational, considered reasons. The same goes for the imaginary wraiths who long to claim him as their own. These things must remain his secret.

"Well, fine," says Mr Bloom. "Far be it from me to stop you. I assume you have a ticket already booked. Take a holiday then. Jet off to the States. Have a rest. Relax. You deserve the time off. Come to think of it, that's probably the best thing you can do. A change of scenery, a chance to breathe some different air..." Mr Bloom nods to himself and spoons more soup into his mouth. He seems to have convinced himself that all Frank wants is to take a break, although he could be hoping that if he believes this misconception to be the truth hard enough, then, by a kind of emotional osmosis, Frank will come to believe it too.

"Going away and coming back won't change anything, Donald. I have to leave, full stop. I have to resign. To quit."

There. He has finally said the word. Finally it has come tripping from his lips. *Quit*. Oddly, though, he feels none of the exhilaration he was expecting to feel. He had hopes that that one small word would carry on its narrow shoulders the whole burden of his concerns, and that in sallying forth from his mouth it would leave him lighter and freer, a purged man. But the anticipated relief is not there; just a permanent residual clutter, the dusty, cobwebbed accumulation of a career's worth of unspoken frustrations.

Mr Bloom says nothing, merely goes on drinking his minestrone, while around their table other conversations rattle back and forth, their echoes rolling across the atrium. When his bowl is empty, he grabs a hunk of focaccia bread and uses it to mop up the remnants of soup. "So what are you going to do for money? Have you thought about that?"

"Transient jobs. Find work for a little while, save up, move on."

"Easier said than done."

"I'll manage."

"A man your age should be looking forward to a comfortable retirement, Frank, not a life of dishwashing and floor-cleaning and fast-food serving. You really haven't thought this through properly, have you? How about Ghost Training? Did you consider that possibility? You could become a teacher. That wouldn't be so bad, would it?"

"I want to have a life beyond Days."

"Don't we all, Frank, don't we all?" Mr Bloom's smile is, Frank feels, a touch patronising. "But like you say, this place owns us. Everything we have, everything we are, belongs to the store. We may not like it, but that's what we signed on for. And if you want to abandon all that, that's your prerogative, but bear in mind that without Days you'll be nobody."

"Then what have I got to lose? I already *am* nobody."

"And you think that leaving will make you somebody?"

"It can't hurt to try."

"I admire your courage, Frank, but in case you haven't noticed, it's a grim old world out there. It's fine if you're rich—it's always been fine if you're rich—but if you're not, it's a struggle from start to finish, with no guarantee that the struggling is going to get you anywhere. That's why gigastores have become so important to people. With their rigid rules and their strict hierarchies, they're symbols of permanence. People look on them as refuges from the chaos and undependability of life, and whether, in practice, that's true or not, that's what Days and Blumberg's and the

Unified Ginza Consortium and the EuroMart and all of them represent. The rest of the world may be going to hell in a handcart, but the gigastores will always be there."

"Why would I forsake the life of luxury and the security that Days has brought me and throw myself out into a harsh and uncertain world? That's what you find so hard to understand, isn't it? Why fly the gilded cage, unless I've gone mad?"

"Whatever hardships you have to endure in here, Frank, they can't be any worse than what you'll find out there."

"I'll take my chances."

The waiter brings the main course and clears away the two bowls of soup, one wiped clean, the other untouched. He returns a moment later with a cheese-grater and some parmesan. Mr Bloom requests that his pasta be sprinkled liberally. The waiter obliges, and then leaves without thinking to offer Frank the same service. Frank is so used to this kind of accidental oversight that he doesn't even notice.

Mr Bloom gets straight to work with a fork. After a few mouthfuls he gestures at Frank's plate and says, "Aren't you going to eat anything? It's very good."

"I'm not that hungry."

Sensing that his eagerness for his food might be considered insensitive, Mr Bloom reluctantly sets down his fork, a bandage of fettuccine wrapped loosely around its tines.

"Listen, Frank. I want you to think this over a bit more. Compare how much you stand to lose with how little you can hope to gain. You spend the rest of the afternoon weighing up what I've said, and then come and see me at closing time. If by then you haven't changed your mind, I'll accept your decision and see if I can't try to negotiate some kind of severance settlement with Accounts. Not a likely prospect, I grant you, Accounts being the tight-fisted bastards they are, but I may be able to swing something. If, however, you *have* changed your mind, then it'll be as if this conversation never happened. Fair enough?"

"I don't see what difference a couple of hours will make."

"Probably none at all," Mr Bloom admits, picking up his fork again. "But you never know. Now, you may have got away with ignoring your minestrone but I will not tolerate a plate of excellent fettuccine puttanesca going to waste. Eat!"

Frank heaves his sagging shoulders and complies. And anyone looking at the two of them, Frank and Mr Bloom, as they sit facing one another, quietly forking pasta into their mouths, would take them for a pair of old friends who have run out of things to say but who still find pleasure in each other's company. But then, no one is looking at two drab, ordinary, middle-aged men in a restaurant that is patronised by the famous and the beautiful and the notorious.

29

Seven Years' Bad Luck: According to superstition, the penalty for breaking a mirror, seven years being the length of time the Romans believed it took for life—and thus the ruined image of life—to renew itself.

12.48 p.m.

Gordon finds the way to his and Linda's prearranged meeting point more by luck than judgement. Wandering from department to department in a state of shock, his sense of direction, fortunately, does not desert him.

Linda is waiting outside the entrance to the Lighting Department, clutching a small Days bag in one hand. Gordon is three and a half minutes late, and the fact that she refrains from commenting on this would, under any other circumstances, be cause for alarm. When Linda fails to pick up on a fault, it usually means she is already brooding on another pre-existing fault, one far more serious, which she will let him know about only after making him sweat a while wondering what else he has done wrong. At that precise moment, however, Gordon's main concern isn't Linda's scorn; his main concern is getting out of Days as quickly as possible.

"Let's go home, shall we?" are the first words out of his mouth as he draws up to her, shielding his eyes against the golden glare radiating from the connecting passageway.

The same light seems to lend Linda's face a balmy, seraphic glow. "What happened to your hand, Gordon?"

"It's nothing. So? Home, eh?"

"Let me take a look."

Reluctantly, Gordon lets her examine his wounded hand.

As soon as he regained his composure after his hasty exit from the Mirrors Department, he found a cloakroom and cleaned up his wounds at the basin. Once he washed the caked blood off his hand under the cold tap, he was surprised to find the cut in his palm both shorter and shallower than it felt. What he imagined to be a deep gash turned out to have barely broken the skin. A lot of blood for very little actual damage.

It still hurt like buggery, but not as badly as when he had assumed that the hand was lacerated to the bone.

And it was while he was in the cloakroom bandaging the hand with his handkerchief and inspecting the nick in his eyelid in the mirror above the basin that he asked himself whether or not he should tell Linda the truth about his injuries. He had a pretty good idea what she would say if he informed her that he had been assaulted and insulted by a pair of teenagers. "You mean you just stood there and let them threaten you? Two boys? You didn't fight back? You let them say those things to you and you didn't give back as good as you got?" That is what *she* would have done in his shoes. Nobody, not even a Burlington brandishing a sharpened Days card, abuses Linda Trivett and gets away with it—as many an uncivil shopkeeper and talkative cinemagoer has discovered to their cost. No doubt about it, Linda would have stood her ground, head held high, and given the Burlingtons the tongue-lashing of their lives. She might even have seen them off, browbeating them into retreat. That fierce indomitability of hers is what Gordon loves about her the most, and envies about her the most, and fears about her the most.

And (he decided in the cloakroom) there was another reason why lying would be a good idea. Confessing his cowardly behaviour in Mirrors would be one thing. He could probably live with the shame. But if, even jokingly, he were to mention to Linda about his close encounter in the Pleasure Department, his life would not be worth living. Even though nothing actually happened in that red-lit cubicle, it so nearly did, and Linda would hear the guilt in his voice. She would smell it on him, the way a lioness can smell fear.

So, all things considered, it would be better to forget both those unfortunate episodes, and the easiest way to do that would be to act as if they had never happened, and the easiest way to do *that*, he concluded, was to lie. Drawing a veil over his cowardice in Mirrors would mean he could also draw a veil over his close shave in Pleasure, the lesser omission legitimising the greater. If he could come up with a cover story clever enough, both events would remain secrets he could carry with him to the grave.

So he racked his brain, and came up with a cover story, and it went like this. He was in Mirrors, looking for something to go above the mantelshelf over the fireplace in the lounge. (Yes, that was good. It would show he did care after all about the living space they shared.) And he had a little accident. He tripped on the join between two sections of carpet, stumbled, and put out a hand to break his fall. The hand landed on a small shaving mirror, and the mirror snapped. Hence the cut in his palm. (It would be a good idea to laugh here. Laughing at his own clumsiness would appeal to Linda. Self-deprecation always goes down well with her.) At the same time, extraordinarily enough, a tiny fragment of glass flew up as the mirror broke and hit him in the eye. His glasses would have protected him but—would you believe it?—they had slipped down his nose as he tripped. Luckily for him, the fragment only nicked his eyelid. A few millimetres higher and he might have been left like Septimus Day. Ha ha ha ha ha!

Not the most plausible of explanations, perhaps, but it was the best he could come up with in the time available, and the only way he could think of to account for both wounds. And as he made his way to the rendezvous, he rehearsed the story over and over in his head until he was halfway to believing that it was the truth.

Now, as he nervously allows Linda to untie the handkerchief bandage, he regales her with his fabrication, cunningly placed laughter and all, interrupting himself only once in order to let out an involuntary hiss of pain as her fingers probe the edges of the cut a little too firmly.

She lets go of his hand just as he reaches his conclusion: "... A few millimetres higher and I'd have been left like Septimus Day. Ha ha ha ha ha!"

For an agonising moment Linda makes no reply. It would not surprise Gordon to find out that his wife possesses the forensic skills to distinguish between a cut caused by a shaving mirror and any other kind. Then she says, "You'll live," and starts refastening the makeshift bandage. "But we should maybe think about getting hold of some sticking plaster and antiseptic ointment from the Medical Supplies Department."

"It can wait till we get home."

She peers at his eyelid. "And also have a doctor look at your eyelid, just in case."

"Right." Finding it hard to believe that Linda has swallowed the story whole, because she is normally a sensitive lie detector, Gordon decides to risk sounding out a further reaction. "It was incredible bad luck."

"Broken mirrors usually are," she replies vaguely. "Now, shall we go and find ourselves some lunch? According to the map, there are places to eat in the hoops."

No courtroom-style cross-examination? Not even a quizzically raised eyebrow? Is it possible that he can have got away with it?

No, there is something not right—something decidedly un-Linda—about her lack of suspicion. And as Gordon trots alongside his wife in the direction of the Red Floor hoop, he notices that the lambent serenity in her face, which he assumed to be a reflection of the glow of the Lighting Department, is not fading as they leave that department behind. It is her own expression. The glow is coming from within her. And her gestures aren't as abrupt as usual. She no longer walks in a series of tight, quick steps—her strides are long and graceful. And her voice seems to have lost much of its customary brittleness.

He can't for the life of him fathom what can have brought about this change in her. The Days bag means she has made a purchase, but a mere purchase alone can't explain it. Perhaps the store has a tranquilising effect on certain customers.

They emerge onto the hoop, into the flare of sunlight glancing off white marble flooring. The air, cleaned by the green lungs of the Menagerie, is appreciably fresher and sharper than the dead conditioned air in the departments, and is laced with food smells from the kiosks and cafés.

After they have dutifully spent a few minutes admiring the Menagerie, Gordon asks Linda what she would like to eat, and she surprises him by letting him decide.

The cheapest foodstuff on offer seems to be Chinese noodles, so Gordon tentatively suggests those. Linda says Chinese noodles will be fine, and hands Gordon their card. And so Gordon Trivett makes his first purchase at Days: two helpings of chicken chow mein, plastic chopsticks an optional extra.

They take the cartons of chow mein to the nearest unoccupied bench, and eat sitting side by side, gazing up at the rainbow tiers of the atrium.

"It's like being inside some great big hollow cake," Gordon murmurs.

He is resigned to Linda telling him what a crass remark he has just made, but she merely nods.

Very strange.

"So what did you get?" he asks, gesturing at the Days bag.

"See for yourself. A present for you."

"A present?" Gordon puts his chopsticks down, wipes his fingers on a paper napkin (another optional extra), opens the bag, and peers in.

"There was a lightning sale," Linda says. "I was right in the middle of it."

Gordon reaches into the bag and takes out the four ties, arranging them in a row along his thigh. "All for me? Why so many?"

"Don't you like them?"

"I like the coin ones."

"Really?"

"Really." And he means it, he genuinely does like them, and he is touched that she went to the trouble of buying the ties for him, all of them, even though he, in effect, is the one who is going to be paying for them. "But did you really need to buy four? And why two with the same pattern?"

"It was a lightning sale, Gordon. You grab what you can get. And they were at twenty per cent off. That means the fourth one was almost free."

"Almost."

"I don't think you quite realise what I went through to get those for you. I *fought* for those ties."

"Fought for them?"

Linda shakes her head sadly. "I wouldn't expect you to understand. If you haven't been in a lightning sale, you won't know what I'm talking about." She says this with grave authority, like a hoary, battle-scarred war veteran reminiscing about his time in the trenches.

"From what I've heard about lightning sales, I'm not sure I *want* be in one."

"It was an incredible experience, Gordon. I can't really put it into words. It was as though I'd been asleep for years and suddenly an alarm bell rang in my soul and I was awake, I mean truly *awake*." She becomes animated at the memory. Sparks scintillate in her eyes. "I'm tingling all over just thinking about it. Look at my arm." Gordon does. The hairs on her arm are standing on end. "It was quite scary, actually," she goes on, "but thrilling too. There was a lot of noise and confusion. I think I might have hit someone... Some of what happened is a bit hazy... But I got what I went in there for, that's the main thing."

"Hit someone? Linda, what *has* come over you?"

"Nothing bad, Gordon, so don't give me that disapproving frown. I just think I've learned, at last, how much I'm capable of. What's the phrase? My full potential. I've discovered my full potential."

"By hitting someone?"

"Like I said, I wouldn't expect you to understand. You came here with negative expectations. Don't try to deny it, Gordon, you did. You came here convinced you were going to have a rotten time. That's why you were so bad-tempered in the taxi. And what happens? You break a mirror and cut yourself. Whereas I came here firmly convinced that today was going to be the greatest day of my life. And guess what? It is. What does that tell you, Gordon? It tells *me* that we make our own luck in this life. It tells me that attitude governs outcome. And that's such a simple lesson, and yet so many people could do with learning it."

The glow is gone from her face. A hard, imperious expression has taken its place, her facial muscles becoming taut again, as if not designed to stay relaxed for long. The old Linda is back, and Gordon is strangely relieved to see her return. He was finding the somewhat slightly dazed Linda who was letting him make the decisions for both of them not a little unnerving.

"These noodles are horrible," she says, setting the carton of chow mein aside. "Why did you make us eat noodles?"

That's more like it. Gordon feels like leaning over and kissing the woman he knows and loves, and envies, and fears. Instead he merely copies her, setting his chow mein aside.

"You're right. The chicken is rubbery."

Equilibrium restored, order returned to his world, Gordon resolves to keep a very close eye on his wife for the rest of the afternoon. Since it seems that he has no choice but to remain in Days, he would rather spend the time with her than off on his own.

It will be safer that way.

For both of them.

30

Hell: According to Islamic belief, Hell is divided into seven distinct regions, for Muslims, Jews, Christians, Sabaeans (a pagan cult who worshipped Orpheus as a god), Zoroastrians, idolaters, and hypocrites.

12.51 p.m.

MUNGO AND CHAS escort Sonny down the flight of access stairs that connects Sonny's apartment to the roof (each brother's apartment has one). At the foot of the stairwell, Mungo uses his knee to nudge open the door to the hallway, and they manhandle Sonny through.

Their entrance startles a cleaning woman. Hurriedly stowing away her spray-polish and dustcloth, she slips past the three of them with a bob of her head and exits by the apartment's main door.

Sonny is slung between his brothers, his arms looped around their necks. He didn't actually need their support for the journey down from the roof, but since they were kind enough to offer it, it would have been rude to refuse. Besides, Mungo was quite insistent that he accompany them in this manner, almost as if he didn't trust Sonny to make it down the stairs unaided. And Mungo is angry with him, and when Mungo is angry with you, it is best just to do as he says.

Recognising his own apartment, Sonny chants, "Home again, home again, jiggedy-jig," then adds, "Drink, anyone?"

"This way," Mungo says to Chas grimly.

They march Sonny into the living room and dunk him down on one of the marshmallow sofas.

"Bar's over there, help yourselves," says Sonny, waving in the wrong direction. He slumps over onto his side.

Mungo grabs a fistful of blackcurrant-purple lapel and yanks him upright, splitting seams.

"Hey, careful of the suit," says Sonny, inspecting a tear in the underside of his jacket sleeve. With ruffled dignity, he smooths out the creases Mungo has put in his lapels.

Mungo, meanwhile, lowers himself down onto the edge of the basalt-slab coffee table so that he is sitting directly opposite Sonny. Splaying his hands on the hillocks of his bare thighs, he hunkers forward, arms akimbo.

"Look at me."

Sonny attempts to bring Mungo's face into focus, but it is difficult. Mungo's face is a moving target swaying in every direction, up, down, left, right, back, forth. Hard to get a fix on.

A firework ignites in the left half of Sonny's field of vision, the force of the detonation slamming his head sideways. The pain arrives a second later, swelling the left side of his face like acid seeping into a sponge.

"Ow," he says, gingerly touching his cheek. "What did you do that for?"

The pain subsides, to be replaced by tingling numbness. The numbness takes the shape of Mungo's open hand, so clearly defined Sonny thinks he can feel the imprints of individual fingers.

"Now look at me."

This time Sonny has more success in focusing on his eldest brother's features.

"If you drop your gaze for a moment, I will hit you again. Understood?"

Sonny nods.

"Good. Now tell me a couple of things. First, did you go downstairs dressed the way you are for any other reason than to look an absolute prize idiot?"

Sonny launches into a spirited defence of his choice of outfit, but Mungo silences him by raising a hand, the same hand that slapped him.

"I don't want to listen to any long convoluted explanations. A simple answer: yes or no?"

"Yes. I mean, no. I don't know."

"The public sees so little of us," says Chas, "that we have to make the best impression we can each time. Therefore you looking like an idiot makes us look like idiots, too."

"Precisely," says Mungo. "Which leads me to my next question. We watched you via the Eye talking to the Heads of Books and Computers. What did you say to them? The abridged version, if you will."

"I adjucidated... I adjuti— I acudjidated..."

"Adjudicated."

"I adjudicated in favour of Computers."

"You did? You're quite sure about that?"

"Yes."

Mungo glances round at Chas. "Not a complete disaster, then."

"Did anyone give you any grief, Sonny?"

"Not as far as I recall. They did talk to me for a long time."

"Yes, we saw that."

"But I decided by ..." Sonny thinks it would be better not to mention the means by which he made his decision. "By how you told me to decide." Yes, the method is immaterial. The important thing is that, by luck, he arrived at the right result.

"I wouldn't advise lying to me, Sonny," says Mungo. "I'm going to check into this later and ask both heads of department for a report, so make sure of your story now. If it doesn't tally with what I find out later..."

A sudden dismal chill descends on Sonny, and he debates whether to own up about using his Osmium to settle the dispute. Perhaps if he dresses it up in heroic terms and says he used the card like Alexander the Great used his sword to cut through the... cut through the... the Something-or-Other Knot. What was it called? The Guardian Knot? That's not it. Something like that, but... No good, he can't remember. He doubts Mungo will go for it anyhow. It wasn't very professional of him, he has to admit, though he was under pressure and both heads of department did seem to have a point and he really couldn't think of any other way to choose between them and besides, it always used to work perfectly well in pubs...

He will just have to hope Mungo doesn't find out about it. The heads of department probably won't mention it. They wouldn't dare say anything that would show a Day brother in a bad light, would they? Not if they value their jobs.

"That's my story," says Sonny, "and I'm sticking to it."

"All right." Mungo draws a deep breath and lets it go as a long sigh. "Well, youngest brother. It seems you haven't disgraced yourself as badly as I thought. Don't get me wrong, you've let me down—let us all down—by going back on your word and drinking before you went downstairs."

Sonny feels this isn't the time to mention the loophole he found in their bargain. Mungo would not take it well.

"Moreover," Mungo continues, "you've abused the trust of your brothers and tarnished our reputation, and that's something I take a very dim view of. Were Thurston and the others to learn about your behaviour, I'm sure the view they would take would be even dimmer. But I'm going to do you this favour. I'm not going to tell them. Neither is Chas. This is going to remain our secret. And in order for it to remain our secret, I need you to stay down here for the rest of the afternoon. Drink, sleep, watch daytime fucking television, I don't care what you do, just as long as you stay out of the Boardroom. Chas and I are going to tell our brothers that we visited you here after our game and found you sober but in a celebratory mood. Got that? You were a good boy, you did as you were told, you didn't touch a drop before you went downstairs, but then afterwards, when you came back here, you decided you were free to indulge, so you did. Therefore, should anyone check up on you this afternoon and find you three sheets to the wind, you will have got that way *after* Chas and I left you. Is that clear?"

Sonny is confused by the tenses Mungo is using but thinks he has the gist of it. He nods.

Mungo says, "This is the last time I am ever going to do anything like this for you again. From now on you are on your own. You and you alone are going to have to take responsibility for your fuck-ups. I am washing my hands of you."

Sonny nods once more.

Mungo's tone and expression soften—a little. "Sonny, ever since Dad died, I've tried to raise you the way he would have wanted, but it hasn't been easy. For any of us. We're Day brothers, but that doesn't mean we're not human too. We do the best we can but sometimes our best isn't good enough." He lays his other hand—his non-hitting hand—on Sonny's knee. "So I'm begging you. For the last time. Clean up your act. Straighten yourself out. We want you to help us run the store. We need you. We need to be Seven."

The tears catch Sonny by surprise, springing from his eyes in a sharp, burning squirt. He asks himself why he is crying, and realises that he is crying because Mungo loves him and he is unworthy of that love. He is a cockroach, an amoeba, a speck, a useless piece of matter stuck to the bootheel of humanity, and yet his brother still loves him.

"I'm sorry, Mungo," he says. "I'm sorry, I'm sorry, I'm sorry. It's all my fault. Everything's my fault. Everything. If it wasn't for me, Dad would still be here, Mum would still be here..."

Mungo hears Chas tut softly. *Not this again.*

"Sonny," Mungo says, "you know as well as I do that you weren't to blame for that."

"But if she hadn't had me..."

"It was an accident. These things happen."

"But why did he choose me? Why not her? Why me over her?" These last sentences are hacked out of Sonny in a series of choking coughs. His cheeks are glazed with tears, and his fingers clutch convulsively at his trouser legs. His entire body is wracked with shudders, as though his despair is a physical thing, a parasite trying to squirm its way out.

"Dad believed he was doing the right thing," Mungo says, words of cold comfort he has uttered countless times before. "He never forgave himself."

"Or *me*," Sonny wails. A bulb of yellow mucus droops out of one nostril. He reels it back in with a sniff. The tears continue to pour. "He never forgave *me*. The way he used to look at me. The way you sometimes look at me. The way *everyone* looks at me."

"Sonny..."

Sonny slumps over onto his side again, bringing his knees up to his chest, burying his face in his hands. "Everyone knows what I did, and everyone hates me for it," he sobs through his fingers. "Why did he let me live, Mungo? Didn't he realise what he was doing? Didn't he realise what he was condemning me to?"

Mungo can't answer that. Truth to tell, he has never found it easy to accept the way their father acted over Sonny's birth.

He recalls taking tea one afternoon with their mother in the mansion drawing room, when she was six months pregnant with Sonny. She was lying propped up against a landslide of cushions on the oak sill of the drawing room's huge bay window, her upper body framed in profile against a diamond-paned vista of the mansion lawns in autumn. He remembers that she looked as regal as ever, for Hiroko Day had come from a Japanese family of good stock and had been brought up to hold herself well whatever the circumstances, but that she also looked tired, drawn, uncomfortable, mother-to-be heavy, and old, much too old. She had been in her late twenties when Mungo was born, and Mungo was now only a few weeks away from his twenty-first birthday.

No one else was around, and in response to a casual enquiry about her health, his mother stroked her swollen belly thoughtfully for a while before replying, "It would break your father's heart if I didn't have this child." It was not the answer to the question Mungo had asked but the answer to a question she had been asking herself.

"But why not adopt?"

"Not part of your father's plan, Mungo," said his mother. "Not part of the deal he struck with himself when he founded the store. For your father's filial cosmology to be complete all seven of his sons have to be his and my flesh and blood." She lowered her voice conspiratorially. "You know, I shouldn't tell you this, but I was secretly hoping for a daughter. Amniocentesis says it's going to be yet another boy, of course. As if I could bear the great Septimus Day anything but the boys he requires. But a daughter ..." A gentle smile played about her mouth. "That would have been my little act of rebellion."

"But it's dangerous, isn't it? I mean, the doctors recommended that you..." Mungo was not at ease discussing such matters with her. "You know."

"Terminate," said their mother. "Oh yes. And your father, grudgingly, accepted that recommendation as wise, and gave me permission to go ahead. But the way he looked at me when he said that, the pain in his eye..." She smiled ruefully at her firstborn, and shifted around on the cushions to get comfortable. "I know how much he wants this child. What else can I do except give him what he wants? Since when has anyone ever refused Septimus Day anything?"

"But the risk involved," said Mungo. "A woman your age..."

"No one's forcing me to go through with this pregnancy, Mungo," said their mother, not sternly. "No one except myself."

And Mungo remembers, even more vividly, the night Sonny was born—a Sunday night, of course. When the college porter conveyed to him the news that their mother had gone into labour, Mungo went straight round to Chas's digs, and together they drove the hundred kilometres home through driving rain in Chas's sports convertible, running red lights and breaking speed limits all the way. A police car pulled them over for doing a hundred and eighty k.p.h. on the motorway, but all it took was a flash of their Osmium cards and a promise to the officer that they would arrange a Days account for him, and they were on their way again. The promise was forgotten as soon as the police car's flashing blue lights were out of sight.

They arrived home to find the mansion a flurry of anxious doctors and midwives. It didn't take long to establish that there were complications with the birth. The baby was not coming out the right way. Their mother was haemorrhaging. Their mother was in danger, and the best medical help money could hire was helpless. Either the baby lived or she lived. It was one or the other. It could not be both. Their mother, drugged but lucid, had said she was prepared to sacrifice herself for the child. It was up to their father whether her wish should be granted.

They found the old man pacing the floor of his study. His eye-patch was lying on the desk. It was not the first time Mungo and Chas had seen him without it, but it was still hard to avoid staring at the sealed lids of his left eye, sunken and puckered like the mouth of someone who has resolved never to speak again.

"I don't know what to do," their father said in a hoarse, haggard whisper. "The doctor said even if she lives through this, she'll never be able to bear another child. This is my last chance."

The founder of the world's first and (as if it mattered at that moment) foremost gigastore was foundering, torn between the woman he loved and the child who would, he believed, ensure the future of his store. He looked desolately at his two eldest sons. "I don't know what to do!"

To this day Mungo still isn't certain which terrified the old man more—the mortal danger his wife was in, or the fact that, after a lifetime of confident, correct decisions, he was, for the first time, paralysed by uncertainty.

"Well, which is more important to you," he said to the old man, as angrily as he dared, "Mum or Days?"

Septimus Day could not answer that.

The decision was made eventually. A crisis point was reached, and the obstetrician in charge asked their father which it was to be, the mother or the child.

Gravely the old man told him.

He was never the same again. From that day on, he slipped into a long slow twilight of depression. He withdrew from the world, divested himself of responsibility for running the store, neglected all but the most fundamental of his personal needs (eating, bathing, sleeping), and restricted contact with his sons to those didactic dinnertime monologues in which he rambled through his obsessions as if trying to justify them to himself, reminding himself with his cries of "*Caveat emptor!*" of the price at which he had bought his dream. *He* was the buyer who should have been beware.

Gradually, one by one, the old man unpicked the threads that tethered him to life, until there was nothing left to hold him here, and when he reached that point, too proud to commit suicide by any of the grisly traditional methods, he waited instead for his own body to call it a day. It could have been a heart attack, it could have been a stroke, but in the event it was cancer, and when it came it was spectacularly devastating, spreading swiftly from his liver to other organs like dry rot, eating away at him from the inside out. And it is Mungo's belief that their father willed this death upon himself. He had, after all, brought a gigastore into existence by the power of will alone. He removed himself from existence the same way. A slow suicide.

None of the brothers has ever laid responsibility for either the old man's decline or their mother's death at Sonny's feet. Not overtly, at any rate. That would be like blaming the deer in the middle of the road for murdering the driver who kills himself swerving to avoid it. All the same, the link between Sonny's birth and their parents' deaths is undeniable, and sometimes it has been easy to make more of Sonny's indirect guilt than fairness might permit. Sometimes, indeed, the brothers have taken a vindictive pleasure in doing so. The contempt latent in their nickname for Sonny—the Afterthought—has never been that well disguised, and over the years, as Sonny has increasingly disgraced himself, it has become harder and harder for them to damp down their feelings of resentment.

Mungo knows this because he has had those feelings himself. He has, perhaps, kept them under better control than his brothers, but as he looks at the laughably dressed creature writhing on the sofa in front of him, the words of compassion he spoke just a moment ago ring hollow. What he really wants to say is, "You killed our parents, Sonny. You may not have meant to, but you did, as surely as if you put a gun to their heads and pulled the trigger. It might have been Dad's decision to let you live at our mother's expense, but if you had been an easy birth, if you hadn't—typically—insisted on making life awkward for everyone, she would have survived and the old man would not have hated himself to death..."

And if that's how *he* feels, he who has interceded on Sonny's behalf on more occasions than he can remember, and who has only now abandoned his efforts to get his brothers to accept their youngest sibling as an equal, if that is how he truly feels, then the loathing the others must harbour deep down for Sonny must be awesome indeed.

"Bear in mind what I've said, Sonny." Mungo pushes his hands down on his thighs to lever himself upright. "Stay put."

"I don't think he's going anywhere," says Chas.

They leave Sonny curled on the sofa in a foetal clench of sorrow and self-pity. And Mungo also leaves there, in Sonny's apartment, any last vestigial traces of compassion he might have had for his youngest brother.

Whatever torments Sonny faces now, he faces alone.

31

Septempartite: Divided or separated into seven parts.

1.21 p.m.

EDGAR GAZES MOROSELY up at the floor-indicator light as it flicks from red to orange, his chin resting on the push-bar of the trolley he has just hired.

He is not so blindly loyal to Miss Dalloway that he cannot see that what she has asked him to do may well end up costing him his job. His job and, if he is lucky, nothing more. And it seems a terrible shame to be jeopardising what he hoped would be a lifelong career in gigastore retail. It seems, in fact, insane. But to Edgar, as to his fellow Bookworms, Miss Dalloway is more than merely the Head of the Books Department of Days. She is an initiate into the Mysteries of the printed word, a Sibyl who speaks in the tongues of quotation, a warrior-priestess steeped in the lore of literature, and to serve her is to serve the ghosts of every man and woman who ever set pen to paper in the hopes of achieving immortality; to earn her approval is to earn the approval of all the poets and authors and essayists whose souls are embedded in the works they wrote.

The floor indicator winks from orange to yellow.

Edgar has no desire to return to the menial level of employment—petrol-station attendant, bar work, telesales—which he endured while waiting for his interview at Days, but there are, he realises, some things more important than a mere job. A tradition—a principle—is at stake. That, surely, is worth any sacrifice. Although he wonders if he will think so tomorrow, when he is signing on for the dole.

The floor indicator goes from yellow to green, there is a soft *ping*, and the same female voice that announces the lightning sales over the public address system informs Edgar—in less strident, more confidential tones—that he has reached the Green Floor. The lift doors slide apart, and Edgar manoeuvres the trolley out and sets off in the direction of Electrical Supplies.

* * *

1.29 p.m.

"Afternoon," says the sales assistant in Electrical Supplies, a well-bellied man whose girth strains the waistband of his dollar-green overalls. "Just that then, is it?"

Edgar lays the spool of rubber-insulated wire on the counter. His throat is suddenly terribly dry. He manages to wheeze out, "Just this, yes."

The sales assistant runs his scanning wand over the spool's barcode sticker. "Staff discount, of course." He has spotted Edgar's ID badge. "A handsome five per cent."

"Handsome," echoes Edgar. It's an employee in-joke.

"Card?"

Edgar takes out the Platinum and passes it over, deliberately (though, he hopes, not obviously) obscuring Mrs Shukhov's name with his thumb.

In the event, as Miss Dalloway predicted, the fact that Edgar is an employee means that the sales assistant does not scrutinise the card. Instead, scarcely glancing at it, he swipes it through the credit register and hands it back.

1.30 p.m.

The credit register flashes the information encoded in the card's magnetic strip down to the central database in Accounts, where Mrs Shukhov's account is checked, its validity assessed, its status confirmed, all in a fraction-of-a-second flutter of silicon synapses.

An anomaly is noted, and a message is sent back to the credit register, scrolling across its two-line readout:

CARD REPORTED LOST/STOLEN
SECURITY HAS BEEN ALERTED

Security has, in fact, not been alerted at the time the message is sent, but by the time it arrives at its destination in Electrical Supplies, a second message *has* reached the Security CPU, giving details of the card and the location of the department in which it has been improperly used.

Two seconds have elapsed since the card was swept through the reader. The sales assistant is still returning the card to Edgar. His eyes have registered the message on the credit register's readout but the information it contains has not yet percolated all the way along his optic nerves to his brain. Meanwhile, in the hyperaccelerated world of computer time, a third message is already winging its way from Security to the Eye, fizzing along the fibre-optic connection as a speeding pulse of light.

The message is routed to the first available on-line terminal in the Eye. By now, Mrs Shukhov's card has left the sales assistant's hand and is firmly lodged between Edgar's thumb and forefinger, and the sales assistant's brain has processed the series of hieroglyphs displayed on the credit register's readout and interpreted them as a set of formal symbols denoting concrete and abstract concepts—in other words, words.

A second later the same process takes place between the eyes and brain of a screen-jockey in the Eye. The message from Security, which is important enough to have been highlighted in red and enclosed in a blinking box, is transmuted in the screen-jockey's cerebral cortex into an instruction. His response, when compared with the speed of information technology, is slow.

Standard operating procedure in a situation such as this is for the screen-jockey to locate and alert a guard in the vicinity of Electrical Supplies, which he would do by tapping a command into the terminal mounted on his chair arm and calling up the position of every guard within a three-department radius of that department, as provided by the transponders in their Sphinxes. From the section of floorplan that would instantly map itself out on his screen, he would select the guard closest by, contact him, and inform him of the probable felony in progress.

However, before the instruction to begin typing can begin its journey from the screen-jockey's brain to his hands, it is belayed by the appearance on his screen of a subsidiary message, a corollary to the first from Security.

This one says:

CARD FLAGGED
SPECIAL ATTENTION:
TACTICAL SECURITY OPERATIVE HUBBLE, FRANCIS J.
EMPLOYEE #1807-93N

The screen-jockey, rereading the message, sucks on his teeth, then calls up Link Dial mode and enters the Ghost's employee number—also the call-number of his Eye-link—in the prompt box.

The screen-jockey then leans back in his wheeled chair, bends the mic arm of his headset so that the pick-up is to one side of his mouth, and gropes behind him for the cooler box on the floor that holds several cans of his favourite carbonated drink, a sugar-saturated, highly-caffeinated Days-brand concoction rumoured to pack a greater stimulant punch than a fistful of amphetamine.

"Old Hubble Bubble, Toil and Trouble again," he murmurs to himself as he pops the ringpull on a cold-sweat can. "Just my luck."

1.30 p.m.

EDGAR IS PLACING the spool of wire in the trolley when the sales assistant says, softly, "Hold on a minute."

"What's up?" says Edgar, aiming for innocence but achieving only a querulous falsetto.

"Let's have a look at that card again. I think there's been a mistake."

Edgar swings the trolley around.

"Wait," says the sales assistant, baffled. "I *said*, I think there's been a mistake. Where do you think you're going?"

His first attempt to grab Edgar is foiled by his voluminous belly, which butts up against the edge of the counter, so that even at full reach there is still a gap of several centimetres between his fingertips and Edgar's sleeve. With some discomfort he leans further over, but his miss has given Edgar the opportunity to start pushing.

By the time the sales assistant has made it round to the front of the counter, Edgar is well away, haring down an aisle of fuses, the spool of wire bouncing and rattling around inside the trolley basket.

1.30 p.m.

ACROSS THE TABLE from Frank, Mr Bloom is savouring a portion of tiramisu which, if his frequent sighs of pleasure are anything to go by, tastes ambrosial. A Days logo has been stencilled in icing sugar and chocolate powder on top of the portion, and this Mr Bloom has, with childlike precision, eaten around, so that all that remains on his plate is a sagging cylinder of layered pudding topped by twin semicircles, one white, the other light brown. Frank, meanwhile, is midway through a cup of espresso.

The two of them have been sharing a long silence which has been interrupted only by the arrival of the waiter to remove their main-course plates and take their orders for dessert. During that long silence Frank has considered, and rejected, dozens of potential topics of conversation. With the awkward business of his resignation out of the way, he has not wanted to waste this opportunity to sit and converse casually with Mr Bloom—an opportunity snatched from his dream of an ordinary life—but it seems that that faculty, which others take for granted, has atrophied in him. He envies the diners around him the ease with which they fill the air with talk.

He has thought about dredging up some incident from the recent past to twist into an anecdote for Mr Bloom's entertainment, but it is hard to single out an individual event from his life that might remotely be considered amusing. His life seem to have telescoped into one long procession of indistinguishably dull nights and days, sleeping giving way to working, working to sleeping, so that reminiscing is like looking back at an empty road which traverses a succession of low rolling hills of uniform size, a narrowing grey ribbon whose peaks and troughs diminish endlessly into the distance.

He can at least remember the events of this morning clearly enough, and has contemplated giving Mr Bloom a description of his encounters with the ponytailed shoplifter, with Moyle in Matchbooks, and with Clothilda Westheimer at the lightning sale in Dolls. But where is the novelty there? Especially for Mr Bloom, who has been walking these floors for longer than he has.

It has even occurred to him to tell Mr Bloom about Mrs Shukhov's impromptu two-night stay at the Hotel Days, but he has decided that that would be unwise. He has a duty to let his superior know about the breach in security, but frankly his feelings about the woman and about his inexplicable, spontaneous gesture in the booth in Processing—what *was* he thinking?—have confused him, and Mr Bloom would detect that confusion in his voice the moment he mentioned her name, and would read more into it than is there. Would jump to conclusions. Ridiculous conclusions. Would say that Frank is exhibiting all the symptoms of infatuation. Which is of course absurd. Frank doesn't even know the meaning of the word infatuation. An infatuated Ghost? Ghosts are men and women with hermetically-sealed hearts. Ghosts keep a lid on their feelings as tight as the drum-skin monofilament net strung over the Menagerie. You may catch a glimpse of an emotion every once in a while, something as frivolous as a blue butterfly or as nobly graceful as a white tigress, but nothing gets in and nothing gets out. The area is cordoned off, secure.

Besides, Processing will file a report. Mr Bloom doesn't have to learn about it from *his* lips.

In the end, saying nothing at all has seemed the course least likely to bore or embarrass either of them. The silence, because it is mutual, is acceptable. But of all the things Frank expected to come away with after this meeting with Mr Bloom, a feeling of chagrin was not one of them. Some kind of catharsis, yes; the lightening of the soul that traditionally comes with confession. Instead, all he has been left with is the lingering, frustrating impression that, although Mr Bloom may have successfully clambered his way up out of Ghosthood, he is still walled in by his work, trapped in a trench too deep to see out of. For Mr Bloom there is still only, and ever shall be, the job. His world is Days.

Which disappoints Frank because he expected more from Mr Bloom, and, perhaps more importantly, because it doesn't bode well for his own future.

Mr Hubble?

Frank sets down his coffee cup. Hubble here.

Mr Hubble, we have an improper usage of a lost or stolen card. Green Floor, Electrical Supplies.

Well, I happen to be on Green, but I'm off-duty. Why did you contact me?

The card was flagged. Special attention you.

Who is the rightful owner of the card?

C A... Some kind of Russian name. Shuckoff?

Shukhov. Frank's throat mic transmits to the screen-jockey a grunt that was not intentionally subvocalised. All right. Have you alerted a guard?

Not yet.

Don't until I tell you to.

Okey-doo.

Eye?

Yes?

I'm speaking to you as an individual operative. Have you and I been in contact already today?

Yep, we have.

Matchbooks?

Yes.

I feared as much. Hubble out.

That grunt—a cross between a ruminative hum and an expulsion of breath, Frank's way of saying to himself that he should have known that his moment of recklessness down in Processing would not be without its consequences—alerts Mr Bloom to the bobbing of his Adam's apple. He waits until Frank has finished talking to the Eye, then says, "Duty calls again?"

"Something like that." Frank stands up, laying his napkin on the table. "Do you mind?"

"Not at all. Always the job, eh? Always the job."

"Let me pay." Frank reaches for his wallet.

Mr Bloom flaps a hand. "Won't hear of it. What's the point in having a Palladium if I can't use it to buy someone a meal every once in a while?"

"If you're sure."

"Go, Frank. Go and do what you do so well. And don't forget to think over what I've said."

"Donald..." Suddenly Frank wants to say a dozen things. Now, at last, when there is no time, he realises how much he has to communicate to Mr Bloom. In the end all he says is, "Thanks."

Then he is hurrying out of the restaurant.

1.32 p.m.

ONLY WHEN EDGAR has passed through Horticultural Hardware and is halfway across the Gardening Department does he risk a glance over his shoulder. He is surprised to find that the sales assistant from Electrical Supplies is not hard on his heels. Still he does not slacken his pace. On he goes, the trolley's hard rubber wheels trundling over Gardening's synthetic lawn, which carpets a smoothly-contoured fibreglass framework of hillocks, berms and dells. Dwarf cypresses in urns dot the billowing, bright-green landscape, and *trompe l'oeil* murals on the walls and ceiling continue the pastoral idyll, adding details that cannot be reproduced indoors by practical means, such as hedgerow mazes, lily ponds, gambolling nymphs and satyrs, and an electric-blue sky wisped with strands of white cloud and flecked with the tiny black }-shapes of high-flying birds. The illusion has been well crafted. If you squint, the department's physical boundaries seem to disappear, and the parklike vista stretches limitlessly into infinity, the painted perfection betrayed only by the connecting passageways hollowing through to neighbouring departments.

Grecian-style follies—plaster Doric columns supporting plywood porticos—serve as sales counters, and the sales assistants are costumed like characters from a Miltonian masque, the men in shepherds' smocks and broad-brimmed felt hats, the women wearing simple gowns with wreaths of silk flowers garlanded in their hair. Littered about in large, incongruous piles are the items actually for sale: sacks of compost and packets of seeds and net-bags of bulbs and stacks of clay pots; tools and trugs and stakes and canes and gloves and strap-on knee-pads; secateurs and grass-clippers and branch-loppers and apple-pickers. It is in the adjoining Horticultural Hardware Department that automated gardening implements such as lawnmowers, as well as less nature-friendly items such as pesticides and weed-killer, can be found. The Gardening Department is for the hands-on enthusiast who lives for the feel of earth beneath his fingernails and for the Arcadian dream of Nature shaped and tamed by the sweat of Man's brow.

The trolley, having not been designed to perform well at anything more than a gentle walking pace, is difficult to control, exhibiting a definite leftward bias. It requires all the strength in Edgar's forearms to keep it running straight and true. His breath is starting to come in hard, short gasps, and his face is bathed in a gloss of perspiration. He runs on through the bucolic tranquillity of Gardening, oblivious to the eyebrows and remonstrations raised by his noisy progress.

For the first time since setting out on this mission, he thinks he is in with a chance of pulling it off successfully.

1.35 p.m.

ENTERING ELECTRICAL SUPPLIES, Frank makes for the main sales counter where Mrs Shukhov's Platinum was used. He introduces himself to the sales assistant and, looking significantly around, asks where the perpetrator is.

The sales assistant shakes his head contritely. "Ah, well, you see..."

"Don't tell me you let him get away."

"It was just a spool of wire." The sales assistant is aware that retirement credits are at stake here. "Hardly the sort of thing to arouse suspicion, you know what I'm saying? And I tried to stop him, but"—he pats the solid swell of his belly resoundingly—"I'm not exactly built like a cheetah, am I?"

"So he was male, and yet the fact that the card had 'MRS' printed on it didn't make you just the slightest bit suspicious?"

The sales assistant gives a hapless shrug. "He was an employee. He had an ID badge."

"ID badges can be faked."

"Like I said, as soon as I realised something wasn't kosher, I tried to stop him. And it was just a spool of wire, remember."

"Theft is theft," says Frank. "Can you at least describe him?"

"Young. Twenty-two, twenty-three—thereabouts. Had a trolley. And a huge forehead. You know, as though his skull has sort of expanded forwards, pushing back his hair."

"All right." Turning away from the counter, Frank coughs discreetly into his throat mic. Eye? Hubble. We're looking at a male perpetrator, early twenties, with a trolley. Distinguishing feature: big forehead. Possibly an employee, more likely a pro with a bogus ID.

Gotcha. Any idea where he is?

Somewhere west of Electrical Supplies. Begin a sweep of the area now.

On it. Could he be making for the exits?

I don't think so. It's unlikely anyone would go to the trouble of obtaining a forged ID and a Days card just to get hold of some wire. Frank frowns. There's something odd going on here, but I'm damned if I know what it is.

32

Heptane: A paraffin containing seven atoms of carbon.

1.41 p.m.

CROUCHING BEHIND THE crescent of hardbacks that screens her desk from the prying Eye, Miss Dalloway locates a section marked by such apt titles as *The Winds of War*, *The War of the Worlds*, *War and Peace*, *The Stand* and *Mein Kampf*. Book by book she clears away this literary seal, like an archaeologist excavating a tomb, stacking the hardbacks behind her, until she has exposed the cavity within. Oscar stands by, ready to offer whatever assistance he can.

Reaching both arms into the cavity, Miss Dalloway carefully—oh so carefully—eases out a ten-litre steel beer keg. The keg is full and heavy, and she moves it a centimetre at a time, wincing grimly at every slop and lap of its contents. When the keg is clear of the cavity, she squats down, embraces it, and lifts. Carrying it to the desk, she sets it gently down beside the open copy of *Kitchen-Sink Arsenal*, then steps back, letting out a long-held breath. Oscar is curious to know what a beer keg might contain that merits such respectful caution, but decides not to enquire. He has a feeling he may not like the answer.

Miss Dalloway returns to the cavity and extracts a sealed sandwich bag, which she also places on the desk. Inside the bag are a Roman candle, a box of matches, a camera flashbulb, a nine-volt battery and a roll of parcel tape. Oscar recognises items his fellow Bookworms were instructed to buy for their head of department the day before yesterday. But where is the can of paraffin he himself purchased for her? And the fertiliser Colin obtained from Gardening?

He watches Miss Dalloway unscrew the cap of the keg, her movements precise and delicate. As she uncovers the circular aperture in the top of the keg, a sharp, ammoniac smell steals out, stinging his nostrils. Through the aperture he glimpses the surface of some kind of thick brown liquid that reminds him of a chocolate-cake mix.

He can contain his curiosity no longer.

"Miss Dalloway...?"

"Not now, Oscar. No distractions."

The formidable Head of Books scans the desktop. Her gaze alights on a perspex thirty-centimetre ruler, which she picks up and inserts into the keg. She stirs the thick brown liquid with the ruler slowly, peering into the aperture every so often. When she is satisfied that the liquid has achieved the desired consistency, she withdraws the ruler and hands it, dripping, to Oscar for disposal. Holding it gingerly by its dry end, he drops it into the waste-paper basket.

Now Miss Dalloway unseals the sandwich bag and lays its contents out in a row on the desk. She tears off a few strips of parcel tape with her teeth and tamps them loosely to the edge of the desk, then uses one of them to attach half a dozen of the matches to the Roman candle so that the matches' heads are in contact with the firework's blue touchpaper. She picks up the camera flashbulb and whacks it against the desk repeatedly until its glass shatters, then tapes the broken flashbulb to the firework and adds more matches to bridge the gap between the touchpaper and the exposed bulb filaments. Finally she tapes the battery securely to the side of the keg. She compares her finished handiwork with the illustration on the open page of *Kitchen-Sink Arsenal* and seems satisfied.

"You may ask your question now," she tells Oscar.

"It isn't a question, really," Oscar replies. "It's more of a..." He scratches his plaster cast distractedly. "Are you making what I think you're making?"

"That, Oscar, depends on what you think I'm making."

"Well, in the keg—that's fertiliser and paraffin, right?"

"Correct. High-nitrate fertiliser and paraffin, with some salt added to stabilise the mixture. Although it remains, of course, highly volatile. Hence my care in handling it."

"Yes," says Oscar, thinking that this has got to be a practical joke, but then remembering to whom he is talking. Whatever Miss Dalloway does, she does in earnest. "Then that..." He gestures at the makeshift-looking contraption she has just assembled from the Roman candle, matches and flashbulb.

"Is the detonator," the Head of Books confirms. "Like the deflagrating device itself, concocted from common-or-garden household items, all of which, as you are aware, were purchased on the premises. A neat irony, don't you agree? Days harbouring all the elements necessary for me to inflict my revenge upon it."

"Neat, yes," says Oscar, numbly. "So the clock and the wire that Edgar's getting...?"

"Will form the timer with which I will be able to trigger the explosion."

Oscar barely manages to choke out his next question. "Miss Dalloway, you're not going to blow up the whole store, are you?"

"Oh no, Oscar," says Miss Dalloway. She gives a light, dreamy little laugh—a strange sound coming from this particular woman. "Don't be silly. What I've made here isn't nearly powerful enough for that. No, not the whole store. Just a portion of it. One department. One particular department."

"Computers," Oscar whispers.

"My little genius," says Miss Dalloway fondly.

33

The Chicago Seven: Seven defendants who were convicted of conspiracy to incite a riot at the U.S. Democratic Party's National Convention in Chicago in 1968.

2.00 p.m.

"ATTENTION, CUSTOMERS. FOR the next five minutes there will be a twenty-five per cent reduction on all items in Third World Musical Instruments. I repeat, for the next five minutes..."

Linda was reaching into her handbag even before the echo of the announcement's seven-note overture had begun to fade. Now she pulls out the map booklet, flourishes it open, flicks through to the department index at the back, and on hearing the words "Third World Musical Instruments" finds T and runs her finger down the column:

Tableware
Red
Tanning Equipment
Blue
Tapestries
Orange
Tea
Orange
Teddy Bears
Green
Telecommunications
Yellow
Theatrical Supplies (see also Costumes)
Indigo
Third World Musical Instruments
Yellow

"Yellow," she says with hushed excitement. "It's on this floor, Gordon."

"Oh?" replies her husband cautiously.

"... Instruments is located in the south-east quadrant of the Yellow Floor..."

Linda flicks to the double-page floorplan for the Yellow Floor, excited to think that she is already a step ahead of everyone else. "And I have a feeling we're *in* the south-east quadrant."

"Oh?" says Gordon again, more cautiously.

"This offer will be extended to you for five minutes only."

"Yes, here we are. Look." She jabs a finger at the map. "Next to Clocks. And Third World Musical Instruments is in the Peripheries. It's three departments away. Three departments, Gordon!" She orients the map and points. "That way. No, wait a moment." She turns the booklet around. "*That* way."

"Thank you for your attention."

"We can make it!" She pulls on her husband's forearm. "Gordon, it's a *sale*. Come on! You'll love it!"

Around them other shoppers are also consulting their maps and starting to move, gravitating in the direction Linda indicated, breaking from a walk into a run. It is as though a wind is sweeping through the Candles Department, one that only affects people and doesn't disturb the flames that flicker in votive ranks all around, on chandeliers, candelabra, and seven-stemmed menorahs. Gordon plants his feet firmly on the floor, determined to resist, to be like those flames, unmoved.

"Linda, neither of us knows how to play any kind of musical instrument, let alone one from the Third World."

"That's not the point, Gordon. A quarter off—*that's* the point."

"But if we don't buy anything, we'll save a whole lot more."

"Please, Gordon." There is nothing endearing or enticing about that "please". Gordon has heard swear words phrased more sweetly. "I want you to come with me. I want you to see for yourself."

"And I don't want you to go."

Linda does a double-take. "What did you just say?"

That's the question Gordon is asking himself too: *What did I just say?* But he can't pretend nothing came out of his mouth. He spoke clearly enough. "I don't want you going there to buy something we don't need."

Linda gives an unpleasant bark of a laugh. "Very funny, Gordon. All right, I'll see you back here in, what, ten minutes?"

She turns to leave, and Gordon, as if a passenger in his own body, sees his hand reach out and grab hold of the strap of her handbag, and hears himself say, "I mean it."

Linda halts and looks slowly round, first at his hand, then at his face, puzzled.

"Listen, Linda. You can't keep doing this. You can't keep buying things just because everyone else is buying them."

A growing rumble of voices and footsteps reverberates through the departments surrounding Third World Musical Instruments.

"You can't because we can't afford it. If you carry on the way you're going, we'll be paying off our debt to the store for the rest of our lives."

Linda continues to glare at him, but he has the tiger by the tail. He can't let go.

"We have to keep things in perspective. We don't belong here. We're not a part of this place like everyone else is. Remember what the taxi-driver said this morning? He said we looked fresh-faced, innocent. He said regular Days customers have permanently wary and jaded expressions. That's not us. I don't want that to be us."

Linda's upper lip draws back from her teeth in a sneer. No one, but no one, tells her what she can or cannot do.

"If you go to this sale, Linda, that's it. I'm taking my name off the account. I can do it. You know I can. Quite frankly, I'm beginning to wish we never applied for the card in the first place. It was a mistake. We can be just as happy without it. Being a Days customer isn't the be-all and end-all. Think: we'll be able to buy all those things we've had to do without for five years. We'll be able to live like ordinary people. How about it, Linda? Eh? How about we give it up as a bad idea?"

The blackmail threat clinches it. Linda realises that her husband has gone quite mad.

"Gordon," she says with acid politeness, "take your hand off me."

Gordon does as he is told.

"And wait here. I won't be long."

She goes a few steps, then stops and turns.

"Oh, and Gordon? You wouldn't dare take your name off the account. You don't have the guts."

"I do," Gordon says under his breath, but what is the use in talking to yourself if you know you are lying?

* * *

2.01 p.m.

THIRD WORLD MUSICAL Instruments used to deal, as its name suggests, exclusively in tools of Euterpean expression from the poorer regions of the globe, but, when the Folk Music Department was displaced from the Violet Floor, evolved into a repository for all musical instruments not served by the standard classical repertoire.

Since the department is on one of the lower floors and the discount on offer is larger than usual, the lightning sale is better attended than most. By the end of its first minute a hundred-odd bargain-hunting customers have arrived, and as the second minute ticks to a close another hundred or so find their way in via the department's three entrances. There is jostling and shoving in the aisles, and the occasional strum or hollow bonk can be heard as a Senegalese kora bumps against a Chinese flowerpot drum or a pair of Moroccan clay bongos accidentally strike the strings of an Indian israj, but by and large tempers remain in check, the bargain-hunters perhaps inspired by the beauty and fragility of the merchandise to treat it, and each other, with respect.

By the end of the third minute, however, customers are finding themselves crammed around the sales counters with little room to move or breathe, and with the pressure mounting as more and yet more bargain-hunters enter the department it isn't long before the relative orderliness of the crowd disintegrates, to be replaced by animosity, which rapidly gives way to naked aggression. Without warning, several dozen fights break out at once, a spontaneous upwelling of violence. At the majority of lightning sales altercations between individuals are given a wide berth, a pocket of non-interference in which the antagonists can settle their differences, but in this instance there isn't space for the skirmishes to remain isolated. Hence it isn't surprising that some angry blows should miss their intended targets and land on unwitting third parties. Nor is it surprising that these third parties, understandably aggrieved, and feeling that such unprovoked aggression should not go unpunished, but not always able to locate their assailants in the throng, should decide that visiting retribution upon another innocent is better than not visiting retribution upon anyone at all.

And so, like the confusion of ripples caused by a handful of stones being cast into a pond, the violence spreads out through the crowd, strike demanding counterstrike, retaliation triggering further retaliation, one confrontation sparking off another, chain reactions of violence overlapping and cross-colliding, until in almost no time at all every customer in the department is grappling with another customer, as in a bar-room brawl in a movie Western, although instead of a tune plinked on a honky-tonk piano (inevitably truncated when the piano-player, too, is dragged into the mêlée), this fight boasts the rather more exotic accompaniment of drums, xylophones, didgeridoos, maracas, castanets, timbales, flutes, pipes, gongs, and miscellaneous other stringed, woodwind and percussion instruments colliding haphazardly with one another and with various portions of the human anatomy, an improvised soundtrack of arrhythmically and sometimes insistently generated notes which no critic would describe as great music but which, as a background score to widespread score-settling, could hardly be bettered.

The Eye, per standard operating procedure, is observing the sale, and a couple of Ghosts and a handful of guards are in attendance, but the violence erupts so swiftly that there is little anyone can do to halt it. One of the Ghosts, in fact, is caught up in the free-for-all almost before she is aware that it has begun. When all is frenzy, when everyone to everyone is a faceless, anonymous enemy, congruity is no camouflage, and the Ghost finds herself besieged on several sides at once. Her principal assailant is a customer brandishing a Jew's harp like a stubby dagger, and although his first stab succeeds only in tearing a slash in the Ghost's jacket, that is enough to convince her to draw her gun. In the madness of the moment, however, the customer, not recognising the sidearm for what it is, thinking it just another unusual item of merchandise, fearlessly swats it out of her hand. The gun hits the floor, is accidentally kicked by a passing foot, and goes skidding under a podium, and the customer resumes his attack. Unarmed, the Ghost is far from defenceless, but in the heave and buffet of bodies it takes her longer than it otherwise might to subdue the customer, and by the time she finally manages to bring him howling to his knees, her face and wrists are bleeding from a number of shallow cuts and scrapes.

The guards, meanwhile, do their best to stem the influx of customers into the department, but they have their work cut out for them. More and more shoppers are arriving at the sale, and for every one the guards prevent from entering another three slip past unhindered. The violence, far from deterring the bargain-hunters, has the opposite effect. If people are fighting, goes the thinking, then the bargains on offer must be worth fighting over, ergo they must be great bargains. And so the demented atonal sonata of strums and bongs and plucks mounts in a crescendo, counterpointed by sporadic splintering cracks of breaking wood and snaps of sundered catgut and human yelps and howls in every register.

One might regard it as a clash of cultures, iktara meeting bodhran, moszmar being deployed against oud, ocarina warding off blows from djembe. One might equally regard it with an ironically zoological eye, as lion drums and monkey drums and guiro frog boxes and cow bells and water bird whistles are used to give vent to bestial urges. And then again, one might simply view the proceedings with world-weary dismay, as instruments crafted to inspire finer feelings—lutes, dulcimers, panpipes, Tibetan meditation bells, Chinese harps and the like—are pressed into service for untranquil, belligerent ends.

Down in the Eye, however, the only emotion evoked by the fighting is glee, as the traditional cry of "Shopping maul!" goes up and every screen-jockey not otherwise engaged tunes in to watch. The security cameras in Third World Musical Instruments were switched from automatic to manual just before the sale began so that they wouldn't fuse a servomotor trying to keep track of every source of activity in the department, and the scenes they now show—a sea of battling bargain-hunters seething to and fro, display stands being flattened, sales assistants cowering behind their counters while stock scatters and shatters around them—give rise to whoops and cheers. The screen-jockeys start laying odds: how many casualties; how long before the mayhem dies down; whether Strategic Security will resort to a baton charge or gunfire; estimates as to the total cost of the damage. Chairs shuttle back and forth across the Basement chamber as bets are agreed on with a handshake.

Such is the mood, gloating and festive, when Mr Bloom enters, having been alerted as soon as the maul broke out. His arrival brings an immediate calm, like the entrance of a teacher into an unruly classroom. The screen-jockeys scurry back to their posts and adopt attitudes of concentration. Some start muttering into their headset mics as though in the middle of conversation with security operatives on the shop floor.

Mr Bloom glances up at the nearest screen showing the fracas, then looks around the room. "I trust reinforcements have been called in."

Straight away half a dozen of the screen-jockeys are contacting guards on the Yellow Floor and on the floors directly above and below.

Mr Bloom turns back to the screens. Reduced to a series of fuzzy black-and-white images, the hand-to-hand combat looks like something out of an old Buster Keaton movie. But there is real pain up there, real anger and suffering, and Mr Bloom wonders briefly—but only briefly—if Frank, in his determination to leave Days, might not have the right idea after all.

2.03 p.m.

LINDA WILL PROBABLY never realise it, and if she does she would never admit it, but had Gordon not delayed her in Candles she would probably right now be in the thick of the fighting. Instead, the precious seconds he cost her with his sudden, inexplicable lapse into Neanderthal-husband behaviour mean that she reaches the lightning sale after the violence has already taken hold. What confronts her as she rushes in through the connecting passageway from the next-door Periphery, Ethnic Arts & Crafts, is not the rowdy rough-and-tumble she remembers, with such delight, from Ties. What confronts her is naked savagery: men and women with their faces contorted in vicious scowls, beautiful artefacts of teak and bamboo and reed and clay and steel being swung and broken, and blood—blood pouring from cuts, blood spattering the dollar-green carpet—and the injured staggering and rolling, clutching their wounds. Here, two customers are going at each other with Chilean rainsticks, parrying and thrusting with the rattling lengths of dried cactus like two fencers. Here, a woman is trying to force a nose flute up another woman's nasal passage. And over here, a pair of maracas are being rammed violently up between a man's legs, causing him to sag to his knees in wordless, white-faced agony. This is not healthy, aggressive competition for bargains but nothing less than communal insanity, a rhymeless, reasonless free-for-all. And something inside Linda, something sufficiently uncorrupted by Days, recoils at the sight. While other shoppers push by, eagerly throwing themselves headlong into the throng, she hesitates. She knows that a once-in-a-lifetime bargain is waiting for her somewhere in the midst of the bellicose mob in front of her. She can all but hear it crying out to her above the clang-twang-bang of musical weaponry. Desire sways her forward; caution sways her back.

Then a woman running past grabs the sleeve of Linda's blouse, and, in a spirit of kamikaze comradeship, hauls her into the department. Perhaps Linda is not as unwilling to become involved as she thought, because she allows herself to be dragged several metres before it occurs to her that she might like to make this decision for herself. She digs her heels in and the sleeve tears, but the woman is swallowed up by the crowd before Linda can remonstrate. Her best blouse!

At the edge of the tumult Linda loses the sense of perspective she had in the connecting passageway. At close quarters, all she can see are raking fingernails and flying fists, gouging thumbs and snarling grins. Then something small and wet slaps against her cheek, sticking there. She picks the object off. It is a tooth, still with a shred of gum attached.

That's it. Tossing the tooth aside with a disgusted shudder, Linda begins to pace backward, away from the chaos, moving slowly so as to be unobtrusive, not wanting to catch anyone's eye. As far as she can tell, you don't have to attack anyone in order to be attacked yourself. People already embroiled in the fighting are rounding on newcomers and laying into them as if they are old antagonists in a long-running feud. Still she hears the siren-song of her bargain urging her to dive in and battle her way through to it, but the sound is faint now, and becoming fainter, disappearing beneath the rising cacophony of pain and abused musical instruments.

Suddenly, as though an invisible membrane enclosing the crowd has burst, the fighting spills towards her. A man charges at her with a zither, fully intending to drive one blood-smeared corner of it into her skull. Stumbling backward, Linda catches his wrists and twists his arms aside, so that the zither glances off her temple. There is a hot gush of breath on her cheek. The man is screaming at her, spouting an incoherent stream of obscenities. He brings the zither back up. The trapezoid instrument wavers centimetres from Linda's face. The man's wrists are sinewy, slippery in her grasp, but she doesn't let go. He is bigger than her, stronger, but she is damned if she is going to let him hurt her.

In a vivid flash, she recalls seeing her parents in a very similar pose. She had been lying in bed listening to the argument downstairs rage for the best part of an hour until finally, unable to sleep, she had sneaked out of her bedroom and gone and sat on the staircase. Peering timorously through the banisters, she had seen her father, scarlet-faced, pacing about the living room, snorting and cursing and, between snorts and curses, accusing her mother of all sorts of things: of never listening to him, of failing to understand his needs, of not showing him sufficient respect as her husband and as the breadwinner of the family. Her mother was saying nothing in her own defence, no doubt because she thought the accusations too absurd to merit a response; instead, she simply sat there while her husband worked himself up into a frenzy, until at last, unable to bear her silence any more, he lunged at her as if to strangle her. Reacting with a quickness that suggested she had been expecting something like this to happen, Linda's mother caught his wrists before his hands could connect with her throat and, bracing them away from her, trembling, arms rigid, she began talking softly, soothingly, to him, the way you do to a fierce dog.

The two of them remained locked together like that, a frozen tableau depicting anger versus reason, until, slowly, as Linda's mother's words penetrated her father's haze of rage, he began to back off. She did not let go of his wrists until she felt sure he had calmed down. She (and Linda) then watched him cross the room to the fireplace, both of them expecting him to say he was sorry, as he usually did at this point, for he was not wholly without a conscience, not entirely a hostage to his own desires. The apologies he tendered after any kind of dispute might have been mumbled and grudging, but at least served as an admission that he had been out of line.

On this occasion, however, he had not yet calmed down and was not about to apologise. His anger had temporarily subsided, but it was seeking a new outlet, and quickly found one.

He snatched down the carriage clock with the cherub feet and weighed it speculatively in his hand. Linda and her mother both realised what was about to happen but both were powerless to do anything about it. They could only look on in appalled disbelief as he drew back his arm and hurled the clock against the nearest wall.

He bent to pick up the clock and inspected it. Even from the staircase Linda could see that the glass covering its face had a crack in it, a clean, jagged line coming down from one corner like a lightning bolt. Once again her father drew back his arm and dashed the clock against the wall. This time, something inside the clock came unsprung with an audible twang, and one of the cherub feet snapped off. Once more he picked up the clock and, shaking it beside his ear, grinned as its innards rattled. Then he raised it up above his head and threw it to the floor. Glass sprayed out in slivers. Another of the cherubs went flying.

The clock lay on its side on the carpet, a sad, dented, disfigured thing. Linda had to resist the urge to cry out, "Leave it alone!" Couldn't he see that it (and she and her mother) had had enough? Clearly not, because the next thing he did was raise his foot and stamp on the clock, once, twice, and then again and again, repeatedly.

The clock had been well made, but it could only take so much punishment. It wasn't long before, beneath the pounding of her father's foot, its casing gave way and gleaming metal movement parts spilled out—cogs, flywheels, escapement, a coil of spring.

Linda's father looked down at what he had done, then up at his wife, his smug, self-satisfied expression that of an infant that has got out of eating an unwanted meal by tipping the bowl onto the floor.

"One day," he said, "I'm going to do the same to you, you bitch."

With a quiet, mournful dignity, Linda's mother set to picking up the pieces of the clock, and Linda, tears in her eyes, padded back to her room, and there, in bed, cried herself to sleep.

In the event, her father never made good on his threat. In fact, not once during the course of their marriage did he actually land a blow on his wife, though this was perhaps as much due to her quick reactions as to his reluctance. Nevertheless, the possibility was always there that one day his rage would grow too great to be vented in insults or placated by carefully chosen words, and this meant that Linda's mother had to tread cautiously around the house at all times, a habit Linda herself learned to emulate, even though it was her mother who always took the brunt of her father's temper. He was the sullen, angry planet around which they, two moons, a larger and a lesser, silently circled, and when he finally walked out on them and went to live in another city with another, younger woman, it was as though they had been freed from his gravitational pull. They felt lighter for his absence.

Understandably, Linda grew up fearing men, believing that they were all like her father, liable to turn on you at the slightest excuse. This led to a series of awkward, superficial, unconsummated affairs which earned her a reputation in her social circle as a frigid man-hater. It wasn't until she met Gordon that she at last understood that not all men were made the way her father had been; that some of them could be meek and mild and—yes, no harm in admitting it—malleable.

The memory of the destruction of the cherub clock gives Linda the boost she needs. In the man with the zither's distended, filth-spewing face she sees an echo of her father's, and resentment and revulsion well up inside her, lending her strength. With a grunting shriek, she thrusts him away. He totters back, arms windmilling, and his zither strikes a nearby customer in the neck. This other customer wheels around. He has a balalaika in his hands. He swings it like a club. It smashes the man with the zither square in the face, strings first. A spiky open chord sings out, and parallel slashes across the man with the zither's nose and cheekbones bead crimson and start to run.

Linda starts to run, too.

Her sense of direction has been thrown and she has no clear idea which way the connecting passageway to Ethnic Arts & Crafts lies. She can see nothing except people, but she can detect a current to their movement, a flow. Bargain-hunters are still pouring into the department; therefore, if she heads the opposite way, counter to them, like a salmon swimming upstream, she will get to where she wants to go.

A fine plan in theory, but the inrush of shoppers is an almost solid wall of bodies, pushing her back. She has to force her way through them, wedging a shoulder or a leg into every gap she sees. Several times her feet are swept out from under her and she nearly goes down, saving herself by clinging onto someone's arm or clothing, desperately recovering her footing before the owner of the arm or clothing shakes her off. She knows that if she falls she will most likely be trampled.

At some point during her struggle to reach the exit she hears, dimly, the end of the sale being called out over the PA system, and she entertains the vain, vague hope that, as it did in Ties, the announcement will bring a halt to the proceedings. But no one else seems to hear or, more to the point, to care. The fighting continues unabated, the bargain-hunters keep on coming, and Linda has to carry on pushing against the tide, enduring the knocks and thumps that come her way, gritting her teeth and not retaliating because her goal is getting out in one piece. Everything else is secondary to that.

It begins to seem hopeless. Wave upon wave of bargain-hunters crashes against her. The undertow of their single-mindedness tugs at her. The effort it takes to resist is draining. Linda feels as though she has jumped off the rail of a foundering ocean liner and is trying to swim away against the pull of the vortex created by the sinking ship. For all her striving she doesn't appear to be making any progress. Her reserves of energy are ebbing. It would be easier, her tiring limbs tell her, just to give in and let herself be sucked back into the maelstrom. She has failed to obtain her bargain, whatever it was. Someone who deliberately passes up an opportunity like that (a quarter off!) doesn't deserve to get anything else she wants.

She decides to abandon the attempt to escape from the department and let the flood of bargain-hunters take her where it will.

And in that moment of letting go she thinks of Gordon, who all his life has allowed events to happen to him, who has never once tried to improve his circumstances of his own accord but has invariably adapted, complied and compromised. And for the first time in their marriage she understands why. To choose the path of least resistance has always seemed to her a sign of weakness. The root of her strength has been her willingness to stand firm no matter how overwhelming the odds. But sometimes there is a strength in admitting defeat. Rigid defiance is admirable but not necessarily, in every situation, wise.

She thinks of Gordon, and there in front of her, as if somehow conjured into being by the power of her imagination, *is* Gordon. Gordon extending a hand to her. Gordon shouting, "Grab a hold, Linda!"

She takes his hand, and he hauls her toward him, and together they form a small island around which the torrent of bodies breaks and diverges. Standing, embracing, husband and wife ride out the onslaught.

34

Fortitude: One of the Seven Cardinal Virtues.

2.05 p.m.

Miss Dalloway consults her watch. By her estimate Edgar should have secured the insulated wire by now and be on his way to getting the clock—assuming he hasn't run into difficulties.

Events are for the moment out of her control, and that is an uncomfortable feeling, but Edgar, she reminds herself, is a bright boy. Devoted, diligent. She couldn't have chosen better. Still, the possibility that he might fail is a real one, and she would be a fool not to acknowledge it.

Oscar, standing a few wary yards away from the incomplete bomb, has been busy thinking.

"Miss Dalloway? Forgive me if this sounds impertinent, but you've obviously had this planned for a while, so why leave getting the timer to the last minute?"

"I told you earlier, Oscar," Miss Dalloway replies. "I want the store to know what I am up to. I want the powers-that-be watching when I get my own back for the shabby, shameful way in which I and my department have been treated."

"You mean the brothers."

"The brothers, Security, the Eye. I want everyone to be looking on when it happens."

"You want them to see that you're not just some ordinary terrorist."

"Precisely, my love."

Yes, that is right. She is not some terrorist. Certainly she has a cause she feels passionately about, as most terrorists claim they do, but her goal today is not to force people into seeing things her way through the indiscriminate use of suffering and fear. Her goal today is to teach the management of Days a lesson it will never forget. She is going to show the Day brothers that they cannot treat their employees like ants; they cannot push them around and step on them with impunity. She is going to demonstrate to them, in spectacular fashion, that running the world's first and (in their father's day) foremost gigastore is a serious responsibility and not, as they seem to think, a boardgame with human beings—human lives—for counters.

That and the prospect of getting her own back on the Computers Department for eighteen months of persecution furnish Miss Dalloway with all the armour of resolve she needs.

Edgar *will* succeed.

He has to.

2.07 p.m.

The lift arrives at the Yellow Floor and Edgar manouevres the trolley out. He hasn't gone more than a couple of metres when he spots a guard lumbering towards him. He halts, seized by panic, unable to think about anything but the size of the man. The guard is one of those human beings who seem to have been designed for no other purpose than inflicting physical injury on other human beings. His fists are like hammers, his eyes close-set and compassionless.

Edgar resolves then and there to come quietly. Meek as a lamb. He no longer cares about losing his job; getting through the next few moments with the minimum amount of suffering is all that matters. It isn't that he is a coward. It's just that pain *hurts*.

He stands there as the guard homes in...

... and rushes past without so much as a second glance.

It is then that Edgar hears the faint, far-off thundering—a sound he has no difficulty recognising. But according to his watch it is seven minutes past two. An on-the-hour lightning sale should be over by now.

Which means that this one must have developed into a maul.

Another guard comes his way, hurrying after the first, and this one Edgar watches go by with considerably less anxiety. There is a perceptible lightening of his habitually gloomy expression as he resumes pushing the trolley in the direction of the Clocks Department, comforted by the knowledge that for as long as the maul lasts Security is going to have more important things to think about than a Bookworm using a stolen card.

* * *

2.08 p.m.

THE SCREEN-JOCKEY LETS out a hiss of triumph and slaps the arm of his chair. He brings his mic round to his mouth.

Mr Hubble?

Hubble here.

I got 'im.

Where?

Down on Yellow. Man with a trolley. Big fucking forehead. Got to be him. Lift-bank K. Moving west now.

Good work, Eye. Keep him in sight. Hubble out.

"All right, all right, my big-browed friend," the screen-jockey murmurs as he calls up a map of the departments around lift-bank K on Yellow. The position of each security camera is marked by a red dot which is tagged with a reference number and surrounded by a circle denoting the camera's arc of coverage. "I have you locked and loaded and I'm not going to lose you." A quick glance shows the screen-jockey the location of the next camera that will be able to pick up a visual of the man with the trolley. A few taps of the keys, a toggle of the joystick, and he has the perpetrator in view again, from a new angle.

God, he loves this job! Never mind that the average length of a screen-jockey's career, from training to burnout, is ten years. And never mind that there is a higher-than-average of incidence of cancer and heart disease among Eye retirees. All that is for the future. What matters is moments like this. Pursuit. Hopping from camera to camera. Quick, nervy decisions. Fingers flying over the keyboard. Like a computer game but with real people. All the thrill of the chase but conducted at a safe remove. It makes him feel alive.

"Oh, I'm good at this," the screen-jockey tells himself. "I'm so fucking good at this. I'm the best..."

"I'm glad to hear it," says a voice at his right shoulder.

The screen-jockey looks sharply round.

Mr Bloom is standing behind him, one hand resting on the back of his chair.

"S-sir," stammers the screen-jockey. "I didn't, um, didn't realise you were..."

"Did I just hear you mention the name Hubble?"

"That's right, sir, yes. We're following a perpetrator using a stolen card.

Mr Hubble says he thinks he's a pro using a fake employee ID."

"Mind if I watch?"

"Not at all, sir. But what about the maul?"

"The department entrances have been sealed off. It'll burn itself out soon enough." Mr Bloom draws up an unoccupied chair. "Forgive me, I don't know your name."

"Hunt, sir."

"All right, Hunt," says Mr Bloom. "Where is Mr Hubble right now?"

2.09 p.m.

FRANK IS ON an escalator descending from Green to Yellow. In front of him stands a customer with several bulky carrier bags in each hand, blocking the way. Twice Frank has said, "Excuse me." Twice he has been ignored. Aggravating though this hindrance is, he can't quite bring himself to tap the customer on the shoulder, so instead he agitatedly drums his fingers on the rubber handrail and stares daggers at the customer's back.

Mr Hubble?

Go ahead.

The perpetrator's reached Jokes & Novelties. Looks like he's going south now into Boardgames.

OK, fine. If I cut through Fishing and Photography, I can intercept him in Clocks.

That's the good news. The bad news is, there's a maul over in Third World Musical Instruments, so we're going to be a bit short on guards at the moment.

That shouldn't be a problem, says Frank.

The escalator flattens out, the bag-toting customer steps off, and Frank skirts around him and sets off at a lope in the direction of Clocks.

35

The Seven Benedictions of the Jewish Marriage Ceremony: The traditional recital of seven blessings which align the state of matrimony with the history and hopes of the state of Israel.

2.09 p.m.

SENSING AN EASING in the flow of bargain-hunters, the Trivetts start to move towards the exit. Their progress is slow, awkward, and shuffling. Neither is willing to relinquish their grip on the other, not just yet.

The fighting rages on behind them as they reach the connecting passageway to Ethnic Arts & Crafts, where they discover that the flood of shoppers coming into Third World Musical Instruments has been pinched off by a dam of human flesh and dollar-green uniforms which plugs the passageway from wall to wall: guards, standing shoulder to shoulder and hip to hip, three deep, impenetrable.

"And where do you think you're going?" asks one of the guards in the front row, as Gordon attempts to steer Linda through.

"Out," Gordon replies simply, but the guard shakes his head and says, "No, you're not."

Gordon has to ask, "Why not?" several times before he is granted the privilege of an answer.

Until the fighting dies down, the guard explains, no one is allowed to leave the department. "We have to take names when it's over, see."

"Names?"

"Everyone involved in a shopping maul has to pay for their share of the damage," the guard says, spelling it out in terms so simple even an idiot can understand. "It's in the disclaimer form, under 'Reparations for Damaged Merchandise.' Just stay where you are. You'll be all right."

"Here, don't I know you?"

This from a guard in the second rank of the blockade. Gordon fails to recognise the man at first, but after a few seconds of scrutiny the penny drops with an awful, chilling clunk.

"No, I don't think so," he says, unconvincingly.

"Yeah. In Mirrors."

"No, I really don't think so," Gordon insists, even less convincingly.

"Yeah, you're the one who was being hassled by a couple of Burlingtons."

Gordon darts a glance at Linda, but she is busy inspecting the rip in her sleeve and doesn't appear to be paying attention.

"Go on, take their card details and let them go," this other guard says to his colleague in the front row. "The poor bastard's not been having a good day."

Gordon asks Linda for their Silver, and passes it over resentfully for the guard to scan with his Sphinx. The blockade then parts to allow them through.

Emerging on the other side, the Trivetts find a milling congregation of frustrated bargain-hunters, who throw them envious looks, then resume craning their necks to catch a glimpse of the action over the guards' shoulders.

Gordon and Linda keep walking, still holding on to one another, through the masks, totems, and clay statuettes of Ethnic Arts & Crafts. Soon they have left the Peripheries behind and are retracing their steps towards Candles, returning to the spot where Linda told Gordon to wait for her because neither is able to think of anywhere else to go.

Gordon decides it would be best to make a clean breast of his encounter with the Burlingtons now, while Linda is in a subdued mood, and he begins to recount what really happened to him in Mirrors, but Linda silences him with a raised hand. "It's all right," she says. "You can tell me about it another time."

"I only lied a little bit."

"It doesn't matter. I'd prefer it if you explained something else to me."

"What?"

"Don't sound so anxious. I simply want to know what you were doing at the sale back there."

"Oh, that. Well, I changed my mind."

"Why?"

"I hated being... *separate* from you, is the only word I can think of for it."

"Separate?"

"Because of what you'd gone through at that previous sale. It was like you knew a secret I didn't. So I said to myself, 'I'll just go and have a peek in through the entrance and see what goes on,' and when I got there, there was all that fighting, and then I spotted you trying to make your way out, and..." The words trail off into a shrug.

"And in you went to rescue me."

"And in I went to rescue you. Your knight in shining spectacles."

Linda disengages from him so that she can take a step back and appraise him fully, from head to toe.

"So how are you?" he asks, self-conscious under her scrutiny.

"Oh, bruised, battered, annoyed that my best blouse has been torn... but happy."

"Happy?"

"I wouldn't expect you to understand." But she says it in such a way that Gordon thinks he does understand.

"Ah," he says, with a slow smile.

They walk on a few metres in companionable silence, and then Gordon hazards the suggestion that they go home.

Linda surprises him by agreeing, and surprises him even more by adding, "And when we get there, we'll discuss whether we're going to keep our account or just pay it off and close it."

A knock on the head, Gordon thinks. *By the time we get home, she'll have forgotten what she just said.*

She reads his thoughts. "I can change my mind, too, Gordon."

"Yes, but—"

"Did I look like I was having a good time back there?"

"Well, no, but—"

"There you are, then."

"But—"

"Gordon, most people don't even get one day at Days. We've had that. We'll always have that."

"Well," says Gordon, "if you're sure."

"I just want to visit one last department, and then we can be on our way. I made myself a promise to buy two things today. A tie for you was one. The other is that carriage clock I showed you. In the catalogue. Remember?"

Gordon does remember. "The reproduction of the one your mother used to have."

"Call it a memento, if you like. A souvenir of our day at Days."

She smiles at him, and despite her mussed hair, despite the tear in her sleeve, despite the raw-looking lump at her temple that is beginning to blossom into a large, prune-coloured bruise, or perhaps because of these imperfections, these chinks in the armour of her appearance, Gordon is won over.

"All right," he says.

"My knight in shining spectacles." Linda raises herself up on her toes to give him a brief but warm peck on the cheek, the ghost of which clings long after she has set off in the direction of the Clocks Department.

36

Seven Dials: A conjunction of seven streets in Holborn, London, named after the Doric pillar with (actually) six sundials that used to stand at its centre.

2.17 p.m.

IN CLOCKS, TIME is divided into infinitesimally small increments, split into thousands of pieces by thousands of timepieces. In Clocks, time does not pass second by discrete second but cascades in a massed cricket-chorus of busy movements, a great fibrillating fusillade of ticks and tocks delivered by everything from slender ladies' wristwatches to stately grandfather clocks, from sleek bedside radio-alarms to curlicued, pendulum-driven ormolus. In Clocks, the arrival of each quarter-hour is attended by a carillon of bells, chimes, cuckoos, and digital bleeps, each half-hour by a slightly longer and louder version of the same, and each hour by an even longer and louder outburst. The deafening peals that announce noon and midnight go on for almost a minute.

In addition to the regulation quota of sales assistants, Clocks employs three people full-time just to keep mainsprings wound, replace batteries and make sure every single face and readout in the department is in agreement, the which task they perform diligently, meeting up at regular intervals to check that their personal chronometers have not deviated one iota from complete accord. Even so, it is impossible for so many thousands of clocks and watches to be synchronised precisely. The edges of minutes overlap, and time becomes so blurred and fragmentary that it returns to its true state: a nebulous, unquantifiable abstract. Every-time and no-time.

If you wish to buy a device for monitoring or detecting the passage of time, the Clocks Department is the place to go, but while you are there, be prepared for your temporal perception to be thrown off by the staggered succession of thousands of seconds happening almost, but not quite, at once. Be prepared, for an immeasurable period of time, to see time from a number of different angles at once.

* * *

2.17 p.m.

LINDA FINDS THE cherub carriage clock more easily than she expected, almost as if led to it by an instinct. It is beautiful. Its brass casing has been burnished to a golden shine, and the cherubs that serve as its feet are exquisitely detailed. You can see the strain on their faces as they blow into their trumpets. You can make out every feather in their stubby little wings. It is her mother's clock, reproduced in every detail, perfect in every part. The past resurrected. A memory made real.

She motions to Gordon to come over and have a look.

2.17 p.m.

GORDON COMES OVER and has a look.

"Well?" his wife asks him. "What do you think?"

He wants to say that the cherubs appear ridiculously uncomfortable, as if they are being squashed by the clock, the breath whistling out of them in trumpet-shaped puffs. He wants to say that he doesn't think it will look good in their house. But he knows how much the clock means to her.

"If you like it, I like it," he tells her.

Linda removes the clock reverently from the shelf.

2.17 p.m.

"ALARM CLOCK, ALARM clock," Edgar mutters as he cruises an aisle specialising in bedside horology, searching for the second and final item on Miss Dalloway's list. The end of the mission is in sight, and its successful completion seems likely—no, not just likely, inevitable. He is very much looking forward to returning to Books a hero and receiving his head of department's praise, which, other than the chance to serve her well, is all he could ever ask for from her. Once he has made this purchase, all he has to do is go north through two departments, and it will be over.

There. A straightforward wind-up alarm clock. Brass bells. Narrow Roman numerals on a white face. That should do the trick.

Edgar pops the clock into the trolley and sets a course for the sales counter at the end of the aisle.

There is a soft thudding of rubber-soled footsteps behind him, slowing to a halt. Someone speaks to him.

2.17 p.m.

"TACTICAL SECURITY. STOP where you are and turn around."

That the perpetrator hesitates suggests to Frank that he is someone who, by nature, abides by the rules. That he then starts to run suggests that he is determined, not to mention desperate.

"I said stop."

But the perpetrator does not stop, and Frank's Ghost Training takes over.

In a single fluid motion he draws his gun with one hand while his other hand slips into his wallet, slides out his velvet card sheath and extracts his Iridium. He inserts the card into the slot beneath the barrel and zips it through. The green LED winks alight, and the gun ceases to be an inert configuration of metal parts and becomes a coiled steel trap waiting to be sprung. He can sense the bullets within the clip within the grip within his fist, all thirteen of them impatient to be chambered and released. Suddenly he is holding death in his hand. Suddenly he has power over the perpetrator, the ability to change him at a distance at the touch of a trigger, to transform him from intact human to bleeding, anonymous meat. It is frightening and thrilling. Thrilling because it is frightening, and frightening because it is thrilling.

He draws back the slide, lets it go—*ker-chunk*—and extends his arm. Arm and gun must become one. That is what he was taught. The gun must be an extension of himself, another body part. It comes back to him now even after all this time when the gun has just been a weight he has worn, an object that has hung beneath his left armpit and every so often butted against the Sphinx in his pocket as if to remind him it is still there. It comes back to him like a forgotten name to go with a remembered face. This is what he must be prepared to do if he is to retain his Iridium lifestyle. This is the ultimate price of his employment. This, a few kilograms of oiled steel, is duty.

His left hand rises to cup the bottom of the grip.

Barrel-tip sight covering target. Legs apart in a shooting stance. Aim to wound. Shoulder or thigh.

He calls out the statutory warning: "Halt, or I am contractually obliged to shoot."

The perpetrator slips around the corner.

Damn!

2.18 p.m.

Fuck! Fuck! Fuck! Fuck! Fuck!

The word chimes through Edgar's brain, a tocsin of terror.

Gun. Security. Security man with gun.

Fuck! Fuck! Fuck! Fuck! Fuck!

2.18 p.m.

Linda gives Gordon the carriage clock to hold while she delves into her handbag for their card. She hears someone nearby shout something, and a few seconds later sees a man with a trolley hurtling full tilt towards her and Gordon.

The trolley whisks past them with millimetres to spare, and Linda, on Gordon's behalf as much as her own, says very loudly and pointedly, "Well, excuse *me*."

2.18 p.m.

Gordon is about to chip in with a wry comment to the effect that *someone* seems to be in a hurry, but then he catches sight of a second man coming towards them, a man brandishing a gun, and the words die on his lips.

2.18 p.m.

Frank thinks the bespectacled customer with the bandaged hand is going to step out of the way. He is running too fast to avoid him if he doesn't.

He doesn't. They collide. Frank's finger accidentally clenches around the trigger. The world is filled with the roar of the gun.

2.18 p.m.

A KNITTING NEEDLE punches a hole in Gordon's left eardrum. Burning pinpricks sparkle across the left side of his face.

His first thought is: *I've been shot in the head.*

His next thought is a logical extrapolation of the first: *I'm dead.*

2.18 p.m.

AT THE SOUND of the gunshot, everyone in the department flinches and ducks, except Edgar, who is too busy running for his life to hear.

Which is why, when he feels an impact in his back like a punch, just above his pelvis and to the side of his spine, he fails to realise what has hit him.

2.18 p.m.

IN SLOW MOTION, as though someone has cranked down the speed of her life, Linda watches her husband sag to the floor. She watches Gordon's glasses slither down his nose, over his chin, onto his neck. She watches the cherub carriage clock slip from his limp fingers and tumble face first to the carpet.

He isn't dead. She knows that. The gun was pointing past him when it went off. He has collapsed, that's all. Shock. He's fine.

But then the man with the gun bends down beside Gordon and places the barrel against the side of his head. At the same time, inside Linda's handbag, something small, smooth and cylindrical rolls against her fingers.

She acts without further thought. Her hand closes around the pepper spray, and she levers off the cap with her thumbnail.

* * *

2.18 p.m.

THE IDIOT! STANDING there like a mannequin!

Using his gun hand, Frank feels the customer's neck. A faint but steady pulse. He'll be OK. His left ear will probably ring for a day or two, and the powder burns on his cheek will be sore but won't leave any permanent scarring. Bloody fool. But it was his own fault. He should have moved.

Frank is about to resume his pursuit of the perpetrator when he registers movement at the periphery of his vision. He fleetingly recalls seeing a woman standing next to the man. Now she is lunging at him, her lips twisted in a snarl. He realises, too late, that there is something in her hand. A perfume atomiser? A can of deodorant?

A fine white mist hisses from the nozzle, and his eyes are bathed in liquid fire.

He recoils, bringing his knuckles up to wipe away the scalding, viscous stuff, but that only succeeds in pushing it deeper into his eyes. Tears spring, and they feel like acid. His sinuses squirt a choking mucus into the back of his throat. Coughing and retching, he staggers backward into a display of mantel clocks. One of them tumbles off, striking him on the shoulder and rolling off to land on the floor with a crunch of breaking glass and a tinkle of loosened cogs.

What did she spray him with? His eyelids are swelling, closing, reducing his vision to a narrow slit of swimming opalescence. What was in that can?

2.18 p.m.

"WHAT WAS IN that can?" says Mr Bloom. "And who is that woman?"

"No idea, sir," says Hunt. "Some customer."

"Quick. Zoom in."

"But the perpetrator..."

"Forget the perpetrator! Get a better visual on that woman *now*."

The screen-jockey obediently tweaks his joystick and the woman looms large on the screen. She is readying herself to attack Frank again.

"Tell him to move!" barks Mr Bloom.

* * *

2.19 p.m.

THE SCREEN-JOCKEY'S VOICE, inside Frank's head, in the blinded, burning dark with him, yells out a warning. Mr Hubble! She's coming at you again!

"Security!" Frank splutters out. "I'm with Tactical Security!"

2.19 p.m.

THE WORDS "TACTICAL Security" mean little to Linda, coming as they do from a man who appeared to be trying to kill her husband. All the same she hesitates, the pepper spray poised, her forefinger on the button. She knows she ought to give him another squirt for good measure. After all, he hasn't dropped his weapon. Something, though, prevents her. A thought. A suspicion.

The gun.

Who in Days carries a gun except...?

Oh good God.

Oh good heavens above, what has she done?

Slowly Linda lowers the canister. She knows she ought to say something, but what do you say to a Security operative you have just erroneously spritzed in the face with an anti-personnel spray? "Sorry" hardly begins to cover it.

The Ghost is seized by a bout of violent sneezing. When the wet nasal explosions have run their course, Linda takes an oft-darned cotton handkerchief from her handbag and holds it out to him. Realising he can't see it, she guides his hand to it. He hesitates, then accepts the handkerchief and blows his nose.

"Better?"

"Acid?" he says hoarsely, circling a finger around his face, which resembles that of a bawling infant's—squinched, scarlet, and soaking wet. His puffed-up eyes are like two split plums, glazed with their own juices.

"Um, no. Extract of jalapeño peppers."

"Small mercies." He sneezes again.

Gordon, prone on the floor, lets out a groan.

"That's my husband." Linda catches herself pointing at Gordon, realising the gesture is wasted. "I thought you were going to kill him. That's why I... you know." She coughs in embarrassment. "Perhaps I should see how he is."

"Good idea."

Some sort of apology, she feels, is in order. "I can't begin to—"

The Ghost isn't interested. "Stay put. Somebody will be along shortly to arrest you. Obstruction of a Security operative in the course of his duty."

Linda takes this information on board with a stoical nod and kneels to attend to her husband.

2.20 p.m.

FRANK EXPECTORATES A wad of fiery phlegm into the handkerchief. Clearing his throat to activate his Eye-link feels like gargling with broken glass.

Eye?

Mr Hubble, are you OK?

As well as anyone can be who's just had a face-full of pepper spray. Frank dabs at his eyes with a dry corner of the handkerchief.

She was carrying pepper spray on her?

I don't think she just found it lying around, Eye.

Well, don't you worry. We'll have another Ghost there in no time. Unless, of course, you feel up to collaring her yourself.

I've other fish to fry. Which way did the perpetrator go?

Um, afraid to say I lost him. Mr Bloom was more concerned about you.

Mr Bloom?

Yeah, he's right here. Want a word?

No time. Perhaps later. Right now I'm going after that perpetrator.

Leave him to us, Mr Hubble. We'll deal with him.

I'm not letting him get away. Which way did he go?

Well, last I saw, he was heading north. I'll get another Tactical operative onto it.

No, says Frank, holstering his gun. I can catch him. This fellow has put me to a lot of trouble. It's only fair that I should be the one who nails him.

But you can't see where you're going. That stuff that woman sprayed you with...

I know this store like the back of my hand. I could find my way around it blind. But I'm not going to be blind. You're going to be my eyes, Eye.

2.20 p.m.

LINDA PICKS UP Gordon's glasses, without which he always looks so puzzled and forlorn, so babyish, and gently settles them on the bridge of his nose, looping the arms around his ears. Then she inspects the cherub clock. Its glass cover is cracked in two, and its jolted movement has stopped, leaving its hands frozen at eighteen minutes past two. She heaves a sigh, for the clock and for herself.

The greatest day of her life.

Or it would have been, if...

If what? If Gordon had moved out of the Ghost's way? She can't blame him for that.

If she hadn't bought the pepper spray from the taxi driver? Possibly. But even without it, she would still have attacked the Ghost. She honestly thought the man was about to put a bullet in her husband's head. What wife, in those circumstances, wouldn't leap to her husband's defence?

That is what she will tell whoever comes to arrest her, although she doubts it will do much good. The fact remains that she attacked a Days employee, and for that she and Gordon are going to lose their account. They are going to be banned from the premises for life... and yet for some reason Linda doesn't care. She doesn't care that she is going to have to explain to Margie and Pat and Bella why she and Gordon are never going to visit Days again (perhaps she will think up a lie to tell them, perhaps not). She doesn't care that she and Gordon may have to move to another street, another suburb, even another city, to get away from the knowing looks and the sly, insinuating comments of acquaintances and neighbours. None of that matters. All that matters is the man lying on the floor in front of her, the sandy-haired, baby-faced, bespectacled man who came to her rescue in Third World Musical Instruments, who appeared just when she needed him, and who, in turn, needed her protection and was given it.

Gordon groans again, stirring. His eyes flutter open. He blinks up at her. Focusing on her face, he braves a smile.

"Not dead then?" he croaks.

"Not yet," Linda says. "But when we get back home, I'm going to kill you."

It takes him a moment or two to realise that she is joking.

37

Christ on the Cross: During the Crucifixion, Christ spoke seven times.

2.24 p.m.

THERE IS NO pain.

At first, it is a simple statement of fact. Despite the tennis-ball-sized exit cavity in his abdomen, all Edgar can feel down there is an awful, unnatural coldness, a freezing/burning sensation like ice. His breathing is constricted, but miracle of miracles, there is no pain.

There is no pain. And as he pushes the trolley from Clocks into Stationery, and from Stationery into Newspapers & Periodicals, and as the pins-and-needles coldness creeps upwards into his chest, Edgar tries not to think about the damage inside him, how much of him may have been ruined beyond repair. He tries to ignore the dark stain slicking over the waistband of his trousers down towards his crotch. Above all, he tries to ignore the hole, with its fringe of gore and shredded shirt, but it is hard to resist looking at it. That is *him*. That is *his* torn flesh. That bulge of something yellow-pink and glistening peeking out of the wound is one of *his* internal organs, which he was never supposed to see.

He is faintly aware of people ahead of him stepping aside, looking perplexed then horrified. He is faintly aware of gasps and little screams arising around him as he goes. But the main thing is that there is no pain.

And then suddenly there *is* pain, and Edgar staggers under the sheer stupefying *wrongness* of it. It feels as though someone has reached inside him and twisted his guts around their fist. His feet become tangled. He nearly falls, but recovers, saved by his grip on the trolley push-bar. Just one department to cross. One department between him and Books. A couple of hundred metres. He can make it.

There is no pain. Now it becomes a silent incantation, to be repeated by the mouth of the mind through gritted mental teeth. *There is no pain, there is no pain.* And although there *is* pain—fearsome pain, sheets and sheets of it sweeping through him like wind-gusted rain—the chant sees to it that there is no pain where it counts: in his head, in the brain that drives the body. For as long as his brain insists that there is no pain, his body will not succumb.

And there, up ahead, framed in the connecting passageway to Books—there she is. Waiting for him, her arms folded across her chest. Scanning this way, scanning that. Kurt and Oscar beside her. She knew which direction he could be coming from. Of course she did. She is Miss Dalloway.

Oscar spots him first, and points him out to the others.

there is no pain there is no pain there is no pain

And Edgar can already hear the compliments that Miss Dalloway is going to pour over him like honey.

there is no pain

And then he sees Oscar's jowls sag and his double chin become quadruple, and Oscar says something to Miss Dalloway, and Miss Dalloway's bony hands fly to her mouth.

thereisnopain

And Edgar is no longer breathing. He is hiccuping air in, in, in, but none of it seems to be reaching his lungs. He covers the last dozen metres through a vacuum, through silence, through weightlessness, his legs spasming in an autonomous approximation of running.

There is pain. There is all the agony in the world, and it is concentrated inside him, a vast, white-hot furnace in his belly.

"I made it," he wants to tell Miss Dalloway, but there is too much pain.

His hands slip from the push-bar. His legs cycle through empty space. The carpet looms like a wall. Newspapers & Periodicals revolves around him, as though he has become the still centre of the turning universe. He is lying on the floor, staring up into striplights. Miss Dalloway is near. She takes hold of his hand, and her face appears above him haloed with light. She is by far the most beautiful thing he has ever seen. Her usually stern expression has melted into one of such sublime, supreme tenderness that he is convinced that she has been transfigured, that she has become a saint. No, not a saint. An angel. She looks how an angel must look to a soul in hell.

He hears the sound of every book he has ever read closing.

And then there really is no pain.

* * *

2.25 p.m.

Miss Dalloway lets Edgar's limp hand fall gently to the floor. With the tips of her thumb and index finger, she draws his eyelids down over his empty eyes. With the same index finger she touches his lips, as though to stop any recriminations he might have for her, even in death. Softly shaking her head, she gets to her feet, standing upright but a few sorrow-stooped centimetres short of her full height.

"Who did this?" Kurt spits out angrily. "Was it the Technoids? Say the word and we'll get them, Miss Dalloway. We'll make them pay."

"Have no fear, Kurt, the hour of vengeance *is* at hand," Miss Dalloway replies, her voice as controlled as a laser beam. "Now, quickly. Go and round up the others. Divide yourselves up into four teams and post one team at each entrance. No one is to enter the department, under any circumstances. Is that clear? No one."

"Clear," says Kurt. "But what—"

"Just do as I tell you."

Kurt turns and hurries back into the department.

"What *is* going on, Miss Dalloway?" Oscar asks, looking down in trembling-lipped disbelief at Edgar's body.

"The end, Oscar. The bitter end."

Miss Dalloway strides over to where the trolley coasted to a halt, propelled by Edgar's dying fall, a metre inside the connecting passageway. She inventories the contents quickly. Wire and clock, present and correct. Thou good and faithful servant.

A sob clutches her throat. She forces it down with a hard swallow, takes hold of the trolley push-bar, and orders Oscar to follow her.

2.25 p.m.

Hands held out in front of him at chest height to fend off against obstacles, Frank lurches through Stationery, looking like a mime pretending to be drunk, or a drunkard attempting mime.

The department, to his inflamed, streaming eyes, is a kaleidoscope of distorted shapes and smeary colours. It is hard to tell what is near and what is far, what is sharp-edged and what is soft, what is living and what is inanimate. The Eye helps out with a constant running commentary, alternately coaxing and warning—"A row of filing cabinets to your left, that's it, a customer a few metres ahead, there, that's good, a ninety-degree turn to the right coming up, you're doing good, Mr Hubble, you're doing fine..."—but nonetheless the pursuit of the perpetrator has become a tortuous succession of stops and starts, bumps and knocks, angles and trajectories, corners and rebounds. At one point the screen-jockey refers to Frank as a human pinball in the world's largest pinball machine, and even Frank cannot be annoyed by the flippancy, because that is exactly how it feels.

Still he perseveres, still he staggers on, with every banged elbow, every barked shin, his determination to catch his quarry increasing.

2.28 p.m.

Her movements urgent yet precise, hurried yet efficient, Miss Dalloway finishes assembling the bomb. Cutting off four lengths of wire from the spool, she strips a centimetre of the insulating rubber from the end of each with her teeth, then uses two of the lengths to join the contacts of the flashbulb to the stem of one of the alarm clock's bells and to the striking hammer. Holding the detonator by these wires, she lowers it into the mouth of the keg until the Roman candle is just above the fertiliser-and-paraffin mixture, firing end pointing downwards. Then she screws the cap of the keg back on so that the wires secure the detonator in place.

The alarm clock is fully wound up and telling the correct time. Miss Dalloway is pleased to note that the Clocks Department's dedication to temporal accuracy remains undiminished. It is nearly half-past two now. A quarter of an hour should do it. She rotates the alarm-setting control until the alarm hand is pointing to the third of the three increments between II and III. Then she tapes the clock tightly to the top of the keg, on its back so that the alarm-setting control cannot be readjusted. The clock ticks softly and steadily.

Now she takes the remaining two lengths of wire and uses them to link the battery to the striking hammer and the bell stem.

The bomb is primed. The final minutes of her life are numbered.

"Oscar?"

Oscar comes to attention. "Miss Dalloway?"

Unable to resist the urge to hug him, she wraps her arms around his shoulders. Startled at first, Oscar quickly succumbs to the unwarranted gesture of affection, and reciprocates, slipping his good arm around his head of department's narrow waist. She presses his fleshy cheek to the sharp ridge of her collarbone. Oscar breathes in the cool, fresh-laundered smell of her jumper.

"Oh, Oscar," Miss Dalloway says. "You've always been my favourite. You know that, don't you?"

Oscar shudders with delight from head to toe.

"And I've always hoped it'll be you who takes over the reins when the time comes for me to step down."

Oscar thinks he is about to faint with joy.

"Will you do that for me, Oscar? Will you look after my department? Make sure the brothers never try to close it down? Resist them to your last breath?"

Oscar can barely choke out his assent. "Of course, Miss Dalloway. Of course."

"I knew I could count on you."

He tries to raise his head to ask a question, but she simply presses him harder to her chest and starts stroking his hair. If he looks into her eyes, he may realise what her real intentions are. He may try to stop her, talk her out of it.

"I've put in a memo to the brothers exonerating you from all involvement in what I'm about to do, and recommending you as my replacement," shc says. "Whether those philistines pay attention is anyone's guess, but hope springs eternal."

"I'll do the very best I can, Miss Dalloway. I'll do you proud. But of course, you'll always be just a phone-call away, should I need advice. I mean, I can never hope to manage everything by myself, not without your help. I won't know where to start."

Miss Dalloway closes her eyes. No tears. She vowed to herself. No tears.

"You will, Oscar," she says. "You will."

2.31 p.m.

OK, YOU'RE NEARLY there. It's, I'd say twenty metres ahead. You should be able to see it.

Peering out through his swollen eyelids, Frank can just about make out the rectangular opening of the connecting passageway that joins Newspapers & Periodicals to Books, and through it, rows of bookcases. He can also see, in front of the connecting passageway, a small crowd—bloblike bodies on spindly legs, human-shaped silhouettes merging and overlapping. They are gathered around what seems to be a pile of rags, but as Frank comes closer the pile of rags glimmers into focus and he sees that it is a supine body, and as he comes closer still he recognises, by the clothing more than anything, the perpetrator. He can discern a wound in the young man's stomach, a dark comet whose tail streaks the front of his shirt and trousers. Frank knows a bullet wound when sees one.

That's him, isn't it? says the screen-jockey. That's the one we've been chasing.

That's him, Frank confirms.

Then you must have...

Yes.

It was, Frank supposes, inevitable, although he had hoped that his policy of using his gun only as a last resort would permanently postpone the day. The irony is, another couple of hours and he would have got through a thirty-three-year career without taking a life. Obviously it was not to be, and there is nothing to be gained by dwelling on might-haves and if-onlys.

More to the point, the gun fired when Frank collided with the customer in Clocks, so the perpetrator's death can hardly be considered his fault. He is sorry that the young man is dead. He is sorry that anyone has to die violently. But there you go. Perhaps he ought to feel more than a mild sense of regret, and perhaps he will, later, but right now he is simply relieved that the chase is over.

Mr Hubble? says the Eye. Mr Bloom says to tell you, "Well done."

Tell Mr Bloom that I still haven't changed my mind.

About what?

He'll know what I mean.

The screen-jockey relays the comment. He says there's still two and a half hours to go till closing time.

Frank had a feeling the answer would be something like that. Well, we'll see. He takes out the handkerchief the woman gave him and has another dab at his face. The excruciating burn of the pepper spray is beginning to subside, to be replaced by an unpleasant but more tolerable itching. He blinks around. The world is foggy and speckled, but getting clearer. Eye,

I'm going to check the fellow's ID. In the meantime, you have a look for that trolley.

Frank approaches the body, slipping through a gap in the crowd of onlookers. Kneeling down, he takes out his Sphinx and scans its infra-red eye over the perpetrator's ID-badge barcode. Barely noticing him, the crowd continue to whisper and coo over the corpse.

A message appears on the Sphinx's screen:

WORKING ...

Then a picture appears of a young man with a huge forehead that bulges beneath a crop of wavy black hair and overshadows a pair of sunken, mournful eyes—eyes that seem to have known long in advance of the brutal, miserable fate awaiting their owner.

Even with his vision blurred, Frank can tell that the living face on the screen matches the dead face in front of him. He hits a key, and the Sphinx lists the employee's name (Edgar Davenport, as on the badge), number, account status (Silver, and in good order), and the name of the department in which he works.

Frank frowns at the screen, then glances up at the connecting passageway leading to Books, his frown deepening. Eye? Do you happen to know if one of the brothers came down to sort out the Books/Computers dispute this morning?

I've no idea. I'll ask Mr Bloom.

A brief conversation ensues off-mic with Mr Bloom, and then the screen-jockey comes back with the reply. He says the arbitration went ahead. One of the guards detailed to escort Master Sonny told him that Master Sonny said that the Computers Department should keep the extra floorspace. And he says why do you ask?

The perpetrator's a Bookworm.

You think there's a connection?

I'm not sure, says Frank, switching off and pocketing his Sphinx.

Frank knows how notoriously militant the Head of Books, Rebecca Dalloway, is, and he knows, too, that it is almost entirely her fault that the territorial dispute between her department and Computers has dragged on so long and been so acrimonious. Surely, then, it is more than a coincidence that, on the same day that the dispute is resolved (and not in the Books Department's favour), a Bookworm goes shopping with someone else's card. And it is hard to believe that a Bookworm would do something like that if his head of department had not instructed him to. A Bookworm doesn't sneeze without seeking Miss Dalloway's permission first.

She is up to something. But what?

Eye? Run a sweep of Books. I'm betting that the trolley's in there somewhere.

2.35 p.m.

HUNT CALLS UP feeds from the security cameras in the Books Department. One by one the images appear on successive screens: unfrequented alleyways of bookshelves, large tables slabbed with books, the sales counters.

Mr Bloom peers at the screens. Everything appears to be normal, except... "The sales counters. No one's staffing the sales counters. Where are they all?"

"There. Look." Hunt points to a screen showing one of the entrances to the department, just inside which a group of Bookworms are loitering. "And there." Another entrance, and another group of Bookworms, all of them carrying thick hardbacks.

"What are they all standing there for?"

"Beats me. They look like they're waiting for someone."

As Hunt and Mr Bloom watch, a customer arrives. The Bookworms gather round him, words are exchanged, and the customer, with a puzzled and somewhat irritable gesture, about-faces and walks out again.

"They're turning people away," says Mr Bloom, running a hand over the top of his scalp as though temporarily forgetting that, apart from his foretuft, there is no hair up there. "Why the hell are they turning people away?"

"Sir?" Hunt points at the screen showing the huge, crescent-shaped stack of books around Miss Dalloway's desk. "Activity."

From behind the stack of books a figure has emerged. The long, bony physique is unmistakably that of Miss Dalloway, and in front of her she is pushing a trolley in which sits a squat grey cylindrical object.

"What's that?" says Mr Bloom. "Get a close-up of that."

Hunt's fingers are already at work. The image on the screen expands, blurs, comes into focus again. He toggles the trolley into shot, keeping it there by means of delicate taps on the joystick.

"Some kind of barrel?" he suggests.

"Yes, but what's that on top of it?"

"Looks to me like a clock."

"Coming out of it—are those wires?"

"Maybe strings."

"No, see the way they hang? Definitely wires."

Hunt looks at Mr Bloom, Mr Bloom looks at Hunt, each seeing on the other's face the same expression of disbelief that he knows must be on his own.

"It can't be," says Hunt, in stilled, chilled tones. "It just fucking can't be."

"Guards," says Mr Bloom urgently. "Get guards there, *now*."

"But all the guards in the vicinity are at the maul."

"Then call them up from Orange and down from Green. Do it! And tell Mr Hubble to stay out of Books."

2.36 p.m.

MR HUBBLE. THE screen-jockey sounds anxious, agitated. Mr Hubble, listen. She's built a bomb.

What? Who's built a bomb?

What's-her-name. The Head of Books. I'm not shitting you. Mr Bloom says you've got to stay out of there.

You're absolutely certain it's a bomb?

Well, it sure as hell looks how a bomb ought to look.

And where is she?

Heading due east.

Of course, thinks Frank. *Computers.*

Mr Hubble? Guards are on their way.

They won't get here in time.

Frank sets off for the connecting passageway to Books.

2.36 p.m.

"HE WOULDN'T LISTEN, sir," says Hunt. "He's going in."

"Tell him not to. Tell him I order him not to."

"He has a point, though, sir. Guards aren't going to get there for at least another five minutes. If anyone's in a position to stop her, it's him."

Mr Bloom can see the sense in that. He sighs a sigh of resignation and slaps his hands against his thighs. "Yes, all right."

"Sir, something else. Shouldn't we let the brothers know what's going on?"

"Yes," says Mr Bloom. "Yes, you're right, we should. Send them a priority e-memo." He looks up again at the screens and murmurs softly to himself, "Frank, you bloody idiot. Be careful."

2.37 p.m.

THE FIRST BOOK comes hurtling past Frank's left ear, flapping like a panicked duck. Another follows almost immediately, and also misses him, but a third hits him squarely just below his breast pocket. He hears a glassy crunch, and guesses that his Sphinx, which took the brunt of the impact, has been broken.

He reaches into his jacket and draws his gun. The green LED is still alight, the safety still off.

"Tactical Security. I don't want to have to hurt anyone."

There is a pause. Then someone shouts, "She said everyone, lads, so she meant *everyone*," and books start flying at Frank from all sides.

Shielding his face, he wades into the barrage. He glimpses, through the hail of printed matter, Bookworms ducking behind shelves and darting between bookcases. No clear shot. Salvoes of books—novels and memoirs, collections of essays and short stories, biographies and autobiographies, self-help manuals and scientific treatises—rain down on him, their pages riffling and clattering. A spiral-bound children's puzzle compendium glances off his hand. All three parts of a grandiose sword and sorcery trilogy smite his body, one after another in quick succession, like blows from a dull axe. An epic family saga spanning several generations strikes him in the thigh, just missing a more vulnerable region. Slim volumes of verse buzz through the air at him, their narrow edges packing a fierce sting.

Mr Hubble! Behind you!

Frank whirls around to find a figure lunging at him, swinging the L-M volume of an encyclopaedia. He fires reflexively, without aiming. The shot punches the book out of the Bookworm's grasp and sends it sailing away, trailing flecks of charred paper from a singed bullet-hole, to land on the floor with a loud clop. The shocked Bookworm stares at his empty hands. Frank's eyesight still hasn't cleared enough for him to be sure of a wounding shot, so he simply lowers his head and charges the Bookworm. Shoulder butts chin, and the Bookworm goes down.

Left, Mr Hubble! To your left!

The warning from the Eye comes a fraction too late this time. As Frank turns, a *Complete Works of Shakespeare* crunches into his arm, filling it with numbing, vibrating pain from biceps to fingertip. He fires at the Bookworm, aiming deliberately high. The Bookworm drops the Shakespeare and scurries for cover.

A dictionary spirals out of nowhere to slam into the back of Frank's skull. His teeth clack down on his tongue, and he tastes blood.

That's it. The next Bookworm who attacks him can expect a bullet wherever it goes. If shooting these buggers is the only way to get them off his back, so be it.

He doesn't see the bookcase behind him swaying and tottering until it is too late. Spilling the contents of its shelves in a great regurgitative rush, the bookcase falls, knocking him flat and burying him beneath several hundred kilograms of wood and woodpulp.

The toppled bookcase settles, a last few loose books slip and slither to the floor, and all is still.

38

The Case of the Seven Bishops: Seven bishops who protested against King James II's Declaration of Indulgence.

2.39 p.m.

PERCH LEAVES HIS pantry office and heads through the clatter of the kitchen, out and along the corridor to the Boardroom.

He judges his arrival perfectly, with an instinct born of decades of service. Just as he enters by the Boardroom's double doors, the last morsels of a long lunch are being scraped up, knives are being set down on empty plates, glasses and coffee cups drained.

Throughout the meal much laughter has been issuing from the Boardroom, echoing down the corridor to the kitchen, and the atmosphere as Perch comes in is markedly relaxed and convivial. The brothers have treated themselves to a couple of bottles of fine wine to accompany their veal escalope with potatoes au gratin and steamed mange touts followed by champagne mousse and a selection of cheeses and biscuits, but wine alone cannot account for the merriment. Perch suspects that the real reason is the absence of Master Sonny. There is always less tension in the Boardroom when he is not around.

As Perch covers the distance between the doors and the table, another peal of laughter springs from six sibling throats. Perch is neither so self-conscious nor so naïve as to think that he is the object of the brothers' amusement.

"I trust the meal was acceptable?" he enquires as he gathers up the first of the empty cheese plates, Mungo's.

"More than acceptable, Perch," says Chas.

"I don't suppose there's any more of that champagne mousse, is there?" asks Wensley.

The enquiry is greeted by barracking hoots and pig-like grunts from his brothers.

"My blood-sugar level's low," Wensley protests.

"Alas, Master Wensley, your third helping entirely depleted our stocks," says Perch with an exaggerated archness which is calculated to evoke further chortles and jeers from Wensley's brothers, and which succeeds.

"Hey, Perch," says Fred. "We were just discussing something. Perhaps you could help us."

"I shall endeavour to assist in any way I can," replies Perch, adding Thurston's empty plate to the stack balanced expertly on the spread fingertips of his left hand.

"Do you think it's true what they say about absolute power?"

"Corrupting absolutely?"

"That's it."

"I cannot for the life of me imagine what could have precipitated such a discussion among the sons of Septimus Day."

"Let's just say it's an occupational hazard. Here you go." Fred sets his plate on top of the stack. "Well? Do you have an opinion?"

"It isn't really my place to have opinions, sir, and those I do hold it is not my place to air."

Genial cries of "Come off it!" and "Nonsense!" are showered down on him.

"Very well then," says Perch, coming to a halt between Fred and Sato. "I shall offer my opinion, but *only* because it was solicited. Power, sirs, is open to abuse if it is not subject to a system of checks and balances, as when, for instance, it is wielded by a dictator who can use oppression to silence those who raise their voices against him and force to eliminate those who would attempt to overthrow him. But does this mean that power *per se* is a corrupting influence? Surely the corruption exists already within the dictator; the flaw is already there, and power merely exacerbates it. Power of one person over another is created out of mankind's willing need for guidance and rule. It would not exist were there not a demand for it, therefore we must assume that it is a good thing, a necessary thing, beneficial to all as long as those in authority remain answerable to those they have authority over. To draw an example from my immediate experience: you, sirs, might be said to have absolute power over this store and every customer and employee in it—and that is some considerable responsibility, given a gigastore's importance to the economy and prestige of the nation it serves. But in order for your decisions to be beneficial to yourselves, they must also be beneficial to everyone under you. To put it at its crudest, any unwise policy you implement will lose you custom, therefore it is in your best interests to ensure that your policies are wise. Which, I hasten to add, they invariably are. In this sense, the absolute power you wield, far from corrupting you, encourages you to aspire to the highest nobility in thought and deed. In short, absolute power makes absolute sense." He gives a small bow to indicate that he is done.

"Bravo!" exclaims Fred. "Good man!" He leads a warm round of applause, which lasts for as long as it takes Perch to gather up Sato's plate and proceed, solemnly and unsmilingly, around the table to Sonny's place, where an untouched main course sits, cooled and congealed.

"Am I to take it that Master Sonny will not be joining us?"

A furtive look passes between Mungo and Chas, which Perch pretends not to have noticed. The other brothers appear oblivious, perhaps busy mulling over his sagacious and not uncomplimentary words.

"It's still possible," says Mungo. "When Chas and I left him downstairs, he seemed open to the idea of some kind of solid sustenance for lunch."

"No doubt he was referring to ice cubes," quips Fred.

"I could have his meal reheated and take it down to him," Perch offers.

Another brief meeting of Mungo's and Chas's gazes. Perch is quick to perceive that some kind of deception is going on.

"He seemed quite set on having lunch with us," says Chas. "Something's delayed him, obviously."

"Best leave it here," Mungo tells Perch.

"Very good, sir."

Perch has no sooner left the Boardroom than the terminal by Thurston's elbow gives a long, loud beep.

"Priority e-memo," says Thurston. He removes his spectacles, huffs on the lenses, polishes them with his jacket sleeve, and returns them to the bridge of his nose, then hits a couple of keys.

"Who's it from?" Sato asks.

"The Eye." Thurston starts to read the message appearing on his screen.

His brothers look on, silent and curious. Chas catches Mungo's eye and mouths the word "Sonny?" Mungo shakes his head fractionally: the e-memo can't possibly have anything to do with Sonny's trip downstairs.

"Shit," says Thurston. He rests his thin wrists against the sides of the keyboard.

"Is that a good news 'shit' or a bad news 'shit'?" Fred asks. "They sound pretty much alike."

Thurston does not answer or take his gaze off the monitor. His eyes flick from left to right, rereading.

"It's a bad news 'shit'," Fred confirms. "Shit."

39

Leases: In Britain, leases used to run for seven years or multiples thereof, a tradition said to hark back to the notion of "climacteric years", those years in which life was supposed to be in particular peril.

2.41 p.m.

Miss Dalloway, with her trolley, pulls up beside the central sales counter in Computers, a huge square slab of black plastic perched on dozens of spidery steel legs in imitation of a microchip.

"Well, look who we have here," says Mr Armitage. If he is at all surprised to see Miss Dalloway in his department, he doesn't show it. "Come to apologise, have we? Declare a truce?"

"I come not to send peace, but a sword."

"Is that not a keg of beer I see?" Mr Armitage leans over the edge of the sales counter to peer into the trolley. "A keg of beer would seem to me to be a peace offering."

The word "beer" gets the attention of every Technoid within earshot. They cluster around the trolley, rubbing their polyester sleeves gleefully until they crackle with static.

"Not beer," says Miss Dalloway, as, with some difficulty, she clambers into the trolley and squats down facing the push-bar, with her legs straddling the keg. "Rather, I have here journey's end. The poor man's nearest friend. This fell sergeant. The cure of all diseases."

"I'm sorry?" Something about the gleam in her eye puts Mr Armitage on his guard.

"Death, Mr Armitage. Pale Death, the grand physician. 'Pontifical Death, that doth the crevasse bridge/To the steep and trifid God.' Death, a necessary end."

Miss Dalloway slips her arms around the keg, hugging it tight—a mother bird incubating a lethal metal egg.

* * *

2.41 p.m.

"Mr Hubble? Mr Hubble? *Mr Hubble?*" Hunt turns to Mr Bloom, batting aside his headset mic. "It's no use, sir. Either his Eye-link's busted, or he's out cold, or—"

"There is no third option," Mr Bloom states firmly. "Where are those guards?"

Hunt checks his chair-arm monitor. "On their way. The first of them should be arriving in Computers in a couple of minutes, lifts permitting." He catches a neighbouring screen-jockey peeking over his shoulder, and sees him off with a snarled, "Nothing better to do, dickwit?"

The other screen-jockey hurriedly returns his attention to his own screens, but the tension in Hunt's corner has radiated out into the rest of the chamber. Something serious is going on upstairs, and everyone in the room is keeping a watchful eye on their colleague and the Head of Tactical Security.

"Come on, Frank," Mr Bloom mutters. "Be all right. Please be all right."

2.42 p.m.

The rubble of books stirs. An arm appears.

Bracing his elbow against the canted bookcase, Frank wriggles out from underneath. He hauls himself up onto all fours. He stands unsteadily, his legs sluggishly remembering how they work. He swivels his head from side to side in order to uncrick his neck, then tenderly rubs his chin, which, when the bookcase fell on him, struck the floor, temporarily stunning him. He clears his throat to activate his Eye-link, but does not hear the click of connection in his ear. He tries again, but it is obvious that the Eye-link's delicate circuitry has been knocked out of commission.

A quick glance in front and behind shows Bookworms at either end of the aisle. They are surprised to find him standing, but overcome their confusion quickly enough, and arm themselves for a new assault by plucking books from shelves.

Wearily Frank reaches for his gun, only to find his holster empty. Of course. He was holding the gun when the Bookworms tipped the bookcase over onto him. It is buried somewhere beneath the pile of books, but there is no time to go rooting around for it. The fallen bookcase has left a gap leading through to the next aisle. The Bookworms are closing in on him, thumping books into their open palms menacingly. Frank takes a step to the side, and leaps over the bookcase and through the gap. He sprints along the parallel aisle towards the connecting passageway that joins Books to Computers, hearing footfalls and shouts behind him as the Bookworms give chase.

There are Bookworms clustered around the exit, but they are all peering intently into Computers and don't hear him approach until he is almost upon them. He pushes past them easily, and is soon deep into Computers, heading for the main sales counter, the heart of the department.

And there, sure enough, he finds the trolley, and sitting in it a figure he recognises, even through the haze that veils his vision, as Rebecca Dalloway.

Miss Dalloway is addressing Roland Armitage and the assembled Technoids, delivering some kind of speech. It appears from the casual postures of those around her that no one else knows what the keg contains. Then she finishes speaking and hunches over the keg, and suddenly everyone is backing away.

2.43 p.m.

"THOSE WHO HAVE ears to hear, let them hear," Miss Dalloway intones. "I am become death, the destroyer of worlds. I am the enemy you killed. The foe of tyrants. Look on my works, ye Mighty, and despair!"

There might be more to her speech, but at that moment Frank shoulders past two desperately backpedalling Technoids, seizes the trolley push-bar, and starts to shove.

"No!" shrieks Miss Dalloway.

Frank scarcely hears her. He is scarcely aware of anything except the pounding of his heartbeat in his ears. He is not thinking. Were he thinking, he would not be doing what he is doing. His head, as he steers the trolley in the direction of the Yellow Floor hoop, is not filled with notions of heroism or sacrifice, only with the urge to get the bomb as far away from people as possible. This, to him, seems an objective necessity rather than an act of suicidal bravery.

Spitting and screeching in fury, Miss Dalloway hauls herself over the keg and launches herself at Frank, fingers outstretched, clawed for throttling. Frank jerks his head back. Her nails scrape his neck, her left hand catching the wire of his Eye-link. The Eye-link pops out of his ear and detaches itself from his collar, and Miss Dalloway collapses back into the trolley, clutching a coiling tangle of surgical pink wire and electronic hardware.

The sound of the trolley's wheels changes from a clatter to a clack, marking the transition from carpet to marble. They are out of Computers, out on the hoop. Frank avoids a pot plant and skirts around a group of startled customers. Miss Dalloway tosses the Eye-link aside and stretches over the keg again, groping for the push-bar. Her face is contorted, riven with vertical lines. She rakes her nails across the backs of Frank's hands, ploughing ragged furrows in his skin. When Frank fails to let go as expected, she resorts to trying to pry his fingers free from the push-bar, but his fingers seem glued in place.

The rim of the hoop hoves into view. Frank slews the trolley around, slamming it sideways against the parapet. Miss Dalloway is thrown onto one hip, off-balance. Frank takes advantage of her momentary incapacity and leans over the push-bar, intending to pick up the keg and toss it over the parapet into the Menagerie. It is then that he catches sight of the clock with its straggling wires.

He makes a grab for one of the wires in order to wrench it loose, but Miss Dalloway anticipates the move and, seizing the keg, stands up, hoisting the bomb aloft out of Frank's reach. However, as she does so, the trolley skids sideways and overbalances, and she is tipped backside-first onto the parapet.

Teetering there with her face stretched in an almost comical look of alarm, she clutches the bomb with one arm while her other arm flails out for something to hold on to. Frank's lapel is the first thing that comes to hand, and she seizes it just as she topples and begins to fall.

Unable to brace himself in time, Frank is yanked head-first over the parapet after her.

The Menagerie yawns below him, a lake of lush green. Though he feels a sudden wrench of pain in his elbow and shoulder, it takes him a moment to realise why he and Miss Dalloway are not falling. His arm has hooked itself over the guardrail. Ape-reflex. But the purchase is far from secure, and Miss Dalloway is still clinging to him, and still hugging the bomb.

Seams pop in his jacket. He lashes out at the keg with his foot, hoping either to kick it out of Miss Dalloway's grasp or, failing that, at least dislodge one of the wires. He has no idea how many seconds the clock has left to run.

Then Miss Dalloway's grip on his lapel starts to slip, and for a brief instant her eyes meet his, and he sees in their iron depths how profoundly she feels she has been betrayed, by Days and by life. And then, dimly through his misted vision, he watches her slip away from him and fall.

Still cradling the bomb, she hits the monofilament net, and the net rips like silk to let her through.

She hits the gridwork of pipes, and they buckle and snap beneath her, spurting tropical-warm water.

She hits the jungle canopy, and the leaves seem to absorb her into their moist green intricacy, sucking her out of view.

Frank dangles there for several seconds, staring at the rift in the Menagerie's seal, half expecting plants and animals to come surging out like the contents of a pressurised canister when its casing is cracked. Then, suddenly remembering where he is and what is about to happen, he frantically twists around, bringing his other hand up to grab the guardrail.

His hand never makes it. There is a faint trilling sound from far below, and then his body is borne up on a cushion of air. For a moment the laws of gravity are rescinded. He floats suspended in space, the great dome of Days filling his fogged vision. He thinks he could sail up towards that gleaming hemisphere of black and clear glass, rising like a saved soul towards its eternal, time-telling sameness, for ever.

Then he begins to descend, plunging backwards into heat and flame.

40

The Book of Revelation: The *Apocalypse* of St John the Divine offers a plethora of sevens—seven churches of Asia, seven golden candlesticks, seven stars, seven trumpets, seven spirits before the throne of God (one of them holding a scroll with seven seals), seven vials, seven plagues, a seven-headed monster, and a Lamb with seven horns and seven eyes.

2.45 p.m.

DEEP IN ITS joists, deep in the lath and plaster of its walls, deep in its very foundations, Days groans.

The basso-profundo *whump* of the blast travels through the store, the shockwave rippling out around the hoops and through every department to the farthest-flung Peripheries. As it reaches the edges of the building it sends a shiver of particles puffing out from the pitted surface of the dried-blood brickwork and sets the window displays' huge panes shaking in their frames, alarming the window-shoppers and the living mannequins. For one brief instant, the living mannequins look directly at their audience, acknowledging their existence for perhaps the first time ever, sharing their fright. For one brief instant, performers and spectators are made equal.

On every floor, display cabinets rattle, merchandise shudders on shelves and in several instances topples over or off, and people let out involuntary gasps and cries.

In the Eye, static zigzags across screens, and a fall of fine grey powder sifts down from the ceiling. In the Boardroom screens also flicker, the ash and ebony table jumps on the spot, and Old Man Day's portrait skews a couple of degrees from true.

The echoes of the explosion reverberate boomingly along aisles and passageways and lift shafts, through all the hollow spaces of Days, like a disturbance in the bowels of some ailing leviathan.

Even Gordon, despite the ringing in his left ear, hears it. He and Linda look at each other, and then at the Ghost who has been assigned to take them down to Processing. She is as startled as they are, and can offer them no explanation.

And Sonny, on his marshmallow sofa, is rudely awakened by what he thinks is a clap of thunder. He hauls himself upright on the sofa with an irritable sigh and focuses his bloodshot gaze on the bright, clear, anything-but-stormy skies beyond the windows.

Slowly the anomaly sinks in.

2.46 p.m.

Up in the Boardroom, Thurston and Mungo stand facing each other, their bodies angled like opposing beams in a vaulted ceiling, their chins jutting, their teeth clenched, their knuckles pressed to the surface of the table, their noses less than a centimetre apart. The slightest of the sons of Septimus Day is dwarfed by the well-developed physique of the largest, but Thurston is far from cowed. His limbs are rigid with rage, the tendons in his neck strain, and his nostrils flare and contract with his rapid breathing. Mungo looks down at him, calm, fiercely intractable, like a stern god confronted by a rebellious worshipper.

"Accuse me all you like," he says to his younger brother, "but I have no idea what he did downstairs."

"What he did downstairs doesn't matter," Thurston replies, each word like a hand-grenade going off inside a reinforced-steel safe. "What matters is that *you* talked us into sending him down there."

"You do yourself and our brothers a disservice. Each of us has the intelligence to make up his own mind. I talked no one into anything. Besides, there's no proof that anything Sonny said or did downstairs led directly to this." He gestures to the two sets of screens by the Boardroom door, which show two different views of the Menagerie. In both, smoke is filtering up from a section of the tree canopy, filtering through the net and twisting and turning lazily into the atrium.

"Oh, it's a little bit too much of a coincidence, isn't it? Sonny goes down to arbitrate between Books and Computers, and next thing we know the Head of Books tries to blow up Computers, and very nearly succeeds. Call me unimaginative, but I can't help but think the two events are connected. Or perhaps you can come up with a better explanation."

"It would seem to me—and would to you, were you thinking clearly—that the Dalloway woman has had this act of terrorism planned this for a long time, and was simply waiting for an excuse to put her scheme into action."

"An excuse Sonny provided."

"We don't know that yet."

"I don't *need* to know that. I can feel it. I can feel it in my bones. In my blood. Only Sonny could screw things up on such a monumental scale."

"I agree. But the benefit of the doubt—"

"Fuck the benefit of the doubt!" Thurston cries, flecking Mungo's face with stray spittle.

Mungo wipes the spittle off with the back of his hand. He would be angry with Thurston if Thurston were not right. What makes it worse is that Thurston knows he is right, and knows that Mungo knows it, too. Neither of them, though is willing to be the first to back down.

"Come on," says Wensley. "Look on the positive side. According to the Eye, nothing's been damaged except the Menagerie, and no one's been hurt except a couple of employees. We're safe, we're alive—"

"As usual, Wensley, you're missing the point," Thurston snaps, not taking his eyes off Mungo. "I don't care about the Menagerie and I don't care about the employees. Those are problems money can fix. Money cannot fix our imbecile of a brother."

"I trust that that isn't a reference to me."

In through the Boardroom doors comes Sonny, hands filling out the pockets of his trousers.

He saunters across to the table, offering his brothers a bleary but affectionate grin. For the first time in as long as he can remember, he doesn't feel as though he is walking into enemy territory. He is one of them now. He is their equal.

Which is why he fails to understand the looks that greet his arrival. He has become used to a certain amount of resentment whenever he enters the Boardroom. Outright hostility—much of it originating from Thurston—he is not familiar with.

"Sonny," says Mungo.

"Mungo?"

"I wasn't expecting to see you here." Mungo's tone is wary and significant.

"Well, here I am," says Sonny. His recollection of events between coming up from the shop floor and falling asleep on the sofa is hazy. He vaguely recalls being shouted at by Mungo and then bursting into tears, but the reason for either event is lost in alcoholic amnesia. Mungo's warning to stay clear of the Boardroom for the rest of the day he has entirely forgotten. "Did anybody else hear that noise just now? Like thunder or something?"

One by one his brothers nod.

"Any ideas what it was?"

"That's an interesting outfit you're wearing, Sonny," Thurston says.

"This?" Sonny glances down at his suit, which is rumpled from having been slept in. "Smart, huh?" He pats the golden Days logo embroidered on the breast pocket. "I thought it would impress them downstairs."

"Jesus..." says Fred, half to himself.

"And the arbitration, Sonny?" says Thurston. "How did that go? I must admit, I was surprised you didn't come back up here straight away to report."

"It went fine."

"You told the heads of department what you were supposed to tell them?"

"Yes. I mean, I think so. Sort of. No, I did. Yes."

"You don't sound very certain." Thurston's spectacles glint dully in the dimmed light. The dark side of the dome now nearly fills all three of the Boardroom windows.

"Well, there was a lot going on. They were both talking so much, I..." It was a neat idea. Why be ashamed of it? "I flipped my card to decide. You know, like at university."

There is a sixfold intake of breath.

"You flipped your card," Thurston repeats coldly.

Sonny, all of a sudden feeling like a suspect on trial, fixes his gaze straight ahead. "I wanted to be fair."

"And don't tell me—your card fell in favour of the Computers Department."

"That was the result you wanted, wasn't it?"

"My God," says Wensley, "what was he thinking?"

"What was he *drinking*?" says Fred.

"I don't understand." Sonny's new-found confidence is starting to crumble, and his voice along with it. "What did I do wrong? All right, so I didn't follow your instructions to the letter, but you sent me down to sort out the dispute, and I sorted it out."

"And if the card had fallen the other way?" says Thurston.

"But it didn't."

"But if it had?"

Sonny looks for Mungo, knowing his big brother will back him up, but while Thurston has been interrogating him, Mungo has moved out of his eyeline. He turns around to find that Mungo has gone stealthily over to the knife switch, has quietly plucked the ceramic handle of the knife switch from its clips, and is now standing with the handle in his hands, brandishing it like a huge cosh.

All of a sudden Sonny is very afraid.

Mungo wouldn't. Not his own brother. Not his own flesh-and-blood.

So Sonny tells himself, but in the deepening gloom of the Boardroom it is difficult to make out what Mungo's intentions are, what is in his eyes.

"Sonny, it was so simple," says Mungo huskily, apologetically. "All you had to do was stay in your apartment."

Sonny shakes his head, wanting to beg Mungo to put the handle back on the wall, but unable to find the words.

"This way is better for all of us," says Mungo. "I can't go on protecting you any more. I can't go on helping you if you won't help yourself."

Tears spill from Sonny's eyes, bright in the unnatural twilight, but he makes no move to defend himself or get out of the way when Mungo comes at him, swinging the handle like a baseball bat.

The handle connects with Sonny's cranium with a crack like a log splitting in two. He reels backwards, blood blurting from his nose. Staggering into the table, he just manages to prevent himself collapsing to the floor.

Mungo draws back the handle and swings it again, this time striking Sonny on the jaw.

Sonny slams back flat onto the tabletop, moaning and clasping his chin. His eyes seek out Mungo, staring, blank with incomprehension. Mungo stares back, panting hard.

Chas appears by Mungo's side, holding out his hands. Mungo hesitates, then meekly surrenders the handle to him, expecting that to be the end of it.

But something has been unleashed in the Boardroom, something that has been bubbling beneath their lives of polite formality, homegrown ritual and quiet paranoia for far too long. Something wild. Something dangerous.

"Hold him down, somebody," says Chas, and Fred and Sato take up position either side of Sonny and, with the grim efficiency of old-time doctors in the days before the invention of anaesthesia, grab his wrists and pin them to the tabletop with their knees. Sonny searches Fred's and Sato's faces frantically, twisting his head from side to side in the hopes of finding pity or mercy, but there is none. His brothers have come to the conclusion that payment for the trials and tribulations he has brought upon them is finally due, in full. Sonny protests, but his words fall on deaf ears. Chas raises the handle and brings it whistling down onto his sternum.

Although the impact is a savage one, Sonny's ribcage holds. At the next blow, however, a rib gives, snapping like dry bamboo. He bucks and writhes, howling in grinding agony too immense for words.

Chas passes the handle to Wensley.

With three swift strikes, Wensley shatters Sonny's jaw, smashes his nose into a lump of crushed cartilage, and ruptures several internal organs with a blow to the abdomen. Then he passes the handle to Thurston.

By the time Thurston has finished with it, the handle's thick end is coated with blood, hair, and fragments of teeth, bone, and skin.

Then it is Fred's turn. Then it is Sato's. Sonny no longer has to be held down. The switch handle rises and falls, rises and falls, becoming bloodier and yet bloodier with each blow.

The brothers go about the slaughter with precise, businesslike detachment, handing over the murder weapon in strict rotation after each has taken a few swings with it. Soon they have reduced their flesh-and-blood to flesh and blood.

The Boardroom resounds to the thudding wet impacts of the handle against Sonny's body, and for once the old man's good eye appears to be glittering with something other than disdain.

41

7.0: The pH value of a neutral solution, one which is neither acidic nor alkaline, i.e. pure water.

2.51 p.m.

LIQUID SOUNDS: THE babble of distant voices, the trickle of running water.

Liquid warmth: sweat-pricking heat, the slow drift of humid air.

Chilly dampness down his back and down the backs of his legs.

Softness clenched between his fingers—spongy, fibrous, and cool.

Water spattering intermittently into his face.

The faint smell of smoke.

And then—eyelids prised apart—vision. The undersides of palm fronds. Varying thicknesses of green shadow. A tunnel hollowing down through the leaves directly above him, ragged-edged, lit with shafts of hazy yellow light and draped with lianas and dazzling chains of water drops. His path of descent. The net, then the irrigation pipes, and finally the trees broke his fall. Branch by branch the trees delivered him to the ground, slapping his back lustily like midwives.

Myriad aches and sore spots all over him, too many to distinguish one from another. His body one huge dull throb of pain. Whether to get up or not isn't so much a question of being unable to as being scared to. What if he tries to move and can't? The loamy floor of the Menagerie is snug and comfortable. He feels welded to the spot. He could happily lie here all day, half buried in the soil, hidden amongst the undergrowth.

Could. Won't. The Menagerie is not the safest of places. *Here there be tygers*. And God knows what other items of livestock waiting to be collected by their purchasers.

Frank steels himself. Courage. Courage.

He tries to raise his right arm.

It won't budge.

Christ. Paralysed. Christ, no.

Then, with a mighty sucking squelch, the arm springs free of the ground.

He brings his hand up to his face and rotates it on its wrist, articulating the individual fingers. His palm and the underside of his sleeve are caked in moss, soil and dead-leaf mulch.

He levers up his head.

At low level, he can see ferns, grasses, and bamboos, their intricate linkings weaving a dense wall of green. Higher up, epiphyte-studded trunks. Higher still, mingling foliage.

Again he smells burning, but around him he can see nothing black or charred or dead. Everything is green and lush and living. He must have fallen some way from the explosion, carried out from the edge of the hoop by its updraught.

It is an effort to stand. The ground does not want to let go. It clings to him like a mother to her child, and even when he has discharged himself from its embrace, still lays claim to him with the weight of earth, plant matter and moisture coating his back.

Frank looks himself over. He has been divided into two halves, one clean, the other filthy. Viewed from the front, he would appear normal; from behind, a muck-encrusted mess. Where he landed there is a body-shaped impression in the ground, lined with flattened plants. Pour in plaster of Paris, let it set, and you would prise out a rough half-statue of a spreadeagled man.

He checks his limbs. All working, some with more complaint than others. He checks his eyes. Everything is haloed with a pale, peach-skin furriness, but his focus sharpens if he moistens his corneas with a few blinks.

He glances around. Which way is out?

If he was on the shop floor proper, he would know without hesitation, but the Menagerie is unknown turf. (*Here there be tygers.*) This is the one part of the store he hasn't tramped through thousands upon thousands of times. Every footprint he leaves here will be a first.

Think.

There are two gates allowing access into the Menagerie from the Basement, one to the north, the other to the south. All he has to do is head for the perimeter wall, follow it around, and he will reach one or the other eventually. Of course, he could simply stay put until a team of Menagerie staff locate him. He has no doubt that they are coming. Mr Bloom will have alerted them. But with nearly two square kilometres of jungle for them to search, that may take some time. Getting out will be safer if he waits for them, but making for one of the entrances by himself will be quicker.

Walking, the skill which has been so indispensible to his career, has to be learned all over again. He is hampered by snaking ground vines and ankle-snaring weeds; the slippery underlayer of moss and the unevenness of the ground. Each step has to be planned, carefully considered, before it can be executed.

The smell of burning grows stronger, and he discerns wisps of smoke trailing through the air towards him. From somewhere ahead comes the crackle of flames. From overhead, the jabber of customers on all six hoops massing their voices in a chorus of opinions and concerns, and a distant wail of fire alarms. What he cannot hear are birdsong and the rustling of hidden creatures. The bomb has shocked all of the Menagerie's denizens, even the insects, into silence.

As the smoke thickens, tingeing the air grey, Frank comes across trees that are seared on one side. The ground turns ashy. Flecks of soot swarm around him like gnats. Soon he is walking among charred and tattered foliage which hangs from singed branches like torn black lace, although, higher up, the trees are intact and the canopy is still green and tightly intertwined. Feeble flames lick along ground-shoots, shrub-tendrils and the leaves and petals of orchids, flickering fitfully before petering out—everything here too wet, too full of juices, to burn well. His footsteps crackle as his soles tramp down singed-brittle stems. He accidentally kicks over the furless, flash-fried body of a small mammal. Its blistered flesh gives off a not unappetising aroma of cooked meat.

The smoke becomes chokingly thick, and he decides to turn back, but not before glimpsing the epicentre of the detonation. The trees there are blasted but still standing. The crevices in their scorched bark glow orange, and their passenger epiphytes have been reduced to shrivelled black lumps. But they are still standing. The Menagerie was big enough to absorb the fury of the explosion, and damp enough to snuff out its fire.

Frank retreats from the ghostly, fuming ground zero, heading back into the emerald depths of the unharmed jungle.

Unaware that he has been spotted and is being followed.

2.54 p.m.

It could hardly be called walking. It is more like a cross between a stagger and a lurch—in terms of effort to result, disproportionately strenuous. But still she drives herself on. One foot drags, one arm dangles uselessly by her side. Her body is partially encased in a carapace of melted clothing, burnt hair clings to her scalp in gobbets like tar, and her skin hangs in crisp strips that loop her limbs and sometimes snag and tear and fall away when she bumps against something. Slivers of steel from the beer keg protrude from her flesh. Bone can be seen where bone should not be visible. One eye—her right eye, the one that was not baked to a cinder in its socket by the blast—shines balefully. She hurts beyond hurting. She should not be alive. But she is.

And as she shambles after the Security operative who thwarted her plans, Miss Dalloway stoops and, with the blackened claw that is her functioning hand, picks up a rock.

She knows she is dying. Dashing his brains out will be her final gesture of vengeance and defiance.

2.55 p.m.

Frank loosens his tie. Its silk has begun to wrinkle in the humidity. He undoes the top button of his shirt. Then he undoes the next one down. What the hell. Go crazy. There isn't much point in trying to pass himself off as a smart, well-heeled Days customer in the heart of a replica jungle.

He tries to put out of his mind all thoughts of large, untamed creatures roaming noiselessly among the trees or lurking in the undergrowth, observing him, but with so many shadows around it is hard not to imagine predatory eyes peering out, tracking his movements with calm animal intelligence. There is no way he can blend in here or belong. Even half covered in organic muck, he sticks out like the proverbial sore thumb.

He wishes he hadn't lost his gun. Whether or not he would be quick enough with it to kill an attacking animal, simply having it in his hand would make him feel safer.

Chances are he will make it to one of the gates unscathed. Chances are the animals are more scared of him than he is of them.

An inhuman screech directly behind him halts him in his tracks.

2.56 p.m.

Miss Dalloway understands, at some primal, lightless level far below the surface of conscious thought, that she cannot hope to creep up on her target by stealth. Her only chance is speed and the element of surprise.

Summoning up every last erg of energy left in her body, she makes her final charge. Sheer stubborn perversity coaxes her dragging leg to function properly and lends her the strength to lift the rock above her head. The very air itself seems to be trying to hold her back, like an invisible hand, but she wills herself on, accelerating from a stumble to a run.

Even if her eardrums had not been blown by the explosion, she would not recognise the warcry that issues from her throat as a sound created by her own vocal cords.

2.56 p.m.

Some kind of ape? A bear on its hind legs?

That is all Frank can think as the scarecrow-like, tatterdemalion creature comes rushing at him through the trees, howling, its one eye shining with a terrible inner illumination. It does not occur to him that this shaggy, screeching, upright beast could possibly be human.

The rock in its paw begins its arc of descent. There is no time for defensive or evasive action.

Then something slams into the ape-bear creature, knocking it sideways, sending the rock flying out of its grasp. Frank has an impression of muscularity, pale fur, vertical black stripes...

The tigress.

The ape-bear is pushed to the ground, supine. It flails madly at the tigress as she sets her forepaws on its chest to hold it down. It gropes frantically at her pelt for some kind of purchase as she lowers her head and clamps her jaws around its neck, and it continues to resist even after she has torn out its throat with a single sideways toss of her huge white head. Gargling horribly, the ape-bear fights on like a machine that has been shut down but continues to run on momentum alone, its stuttering, spastic efforts growing feebler as the tigress chews further chunks out of it.

It is only when the ape-bear ceases struggling that Frank spots, affixed to its chest, a warped, blistered rectangle of plastic still just about recognisable as an ID badge, and realises what (or rather who) the ape-bear is (or rather was).

That is when he turns away. However, though he can avert his eyes to shut out the sight of the tigress savaging Miss Dalloway, he cannot shut out the sounds of human flesh being consumed. They are sounds that will haunt him for ever.

They cease, eventually. Sated, the tigress turns away from her eviscerated kill.

Frank hears the sound of her paws delicately crushing the undergrowth, coming closer, and he holds himself perfectly still, closes his eyes and longs for congruity. If only he knew how to camouflage himself among trees and vines as well as he does among displays and merchandise. If only he could somehow tune himself out of the tigress's perceptions by immersing himself in the jungle equivalent of the everyman ordinariness which makes shoplifters overlook him so easily. But he cannot. Here, he is the suspicious character, the tigress the Ghost.

The tigress halts in front of him, and extends her blood-pinkened muzzle forwards to sniff. She runs her nose over his right hand, up his sleeve to the elbow and down again, down one leg of his trousers and up again to his crotch. The air moves in and out of her nostrils with an audible hiss. Her musk is earthy, urinary, potent.

Frank wants nothing in the world so much as to run, but he orders himself to stay still, not to move.

The tigress peers up at his face with her azure eyes and makes a noise deep in her throat, like a growl, only softer.

So faint is this noise that Frank will never be sure if he imagined it or not. However, just as he will always remember the sounds of the tigress eating Miss Dalloway, so he will always remember that low, subtle rumble. And he will always wonder if it really was, as he thinks at the time, a purr.

Fur brushes briefly, lightly against the fingertips of his right hand—a brittle tickling—and he parts his eyelids a crack, and there the tigress is, loping away from him with her tail slung low, past the mauled corpse of the Head of the Books Department, heading deep into the viridian gloom of the Menagerie, gradually merging her paleness into its darkness, slipping her stripes in among its fretted shadows, becoming a spectral grey tiger-shape, and then becoming a part of the jungle and no shape at all.

3.12 p.m.

Some time later, Frank finds himself sitting on a rock by a stream in a clearing, very possibly the same clearing in which he caught sight of the tigress this morning. Above the membrane of the net, the tiers of the atrium rise, narrowing, to the dome. Faces fringe the parapets, many of them peering down at him.

A squad of Menagerie staff are crashing through the jungle towards him. He can hear them shouting to one another. Clad in their chain-mesh suits and armed with their tranquilliser rifles, they will escort him out to safety.

The stream burbles over its bed of pebbles in a long, shallow, sinuous curve, here and there bubbles beading and breaking spontaneously on its smooth surface. The irrigation pipes hiss a mist that drizzles down onto Frank's head, plastering his hair into flat, matted rat-tails. Nature has tapped her baton, and the Menagerie's birds have tentatively begun to sing again; the insects have picked up their instruments once more and are starting to play.

In his hand he is holding his broken Sphinx, angled towards his face. He is gazing hard into the cracked glass of its screen. Gazing in delight and mild wonderment.

The Menagerie staff are coming.

He will be out of here soon.

42

Seven-Day Fever: An acute infectious disease caused by a spirochaete transmitted by ticks or lice, and characterised by recurrent attacks separated by periods of remission lasting approximately seven days; also known as relapsing fever.

4.30 p.m.

THE PROCESSING ITSELF was not so bad. The dour little Scotsman who officiated was terse but not rude. Unlike many whose jobs bring them into close contact with human failings on a daily basis, he had not entirely lost his respect for his fellow men. He remained essentially civil, and for that Linda was grateful. It was a small shred of comfort; she had not entirely been stripped of her dignity.

In the cramped booth, with the Trivetts seated opposite him and an accompanying guard to one side of his desk, the processor listened as Linda recounted her version of the incident with the Ghost in Clocks. She put as sympathetic a slant as possible on what she had done, but under questioning could not deny either that she had smuggled the pepper spray onto the premises or that she had assaulted an employee. Not knowing at the time that he was an employee was no excuse. Nor did it help that her offence had been observed and recorded by the Eye. The Eye did not lie. Morrison (for that was the processor's name) showed Linda the clip of her squirting the Ghost in the face. There it was in smudgy black and white. Incontrovertible.

Spinning the monitor back round, Morrison then told Linda that, in the light of the evidence against her, he had no alternative but to suspend the Trivetts' account permanently and banish them from Days for life. Both of them. Linda because of her misdemeanour, and Gordon because he was co-signatory of their account, and so guilty by association.

Even though she had been expecting this, the words fell on Linda's ears like a funeral knell. Gordon's left ear was still ringing so sonorously that he had to ask the processor to repeat himself several times to him until he got the gist. He seemed none too upset.

Morrison asked Linda to hand over their card, and used it to call up their account details. With a few brief keystrokes he transferred sufficient funds from their joint bank account to pay off the debt they had run up. There would, he said, be an additional sum to be paid once the cost of the damage done in Third World Musical Instruments had been established. Since the total was going to be divided equally among the four hundred or so participants in the shopping maul, the Trivetts' portion would be well within their financial limitations, although still not inconsiderable.

The unkindest cut came when Morrison gave Linda back their Silver, along with a pair of blunt-nosed safety scissors.

"We prefer our customers to perform this task themselves," he said.

She almost burst into tears while cutting the card in half. Almost, but not quite.

After that, there was nothing for her and Gordon to do but go out and sit on one of the benches in the main room and wait to be escorted off the premises, and here they have remained for the past hour. This is the really humiliating part, sitting here among the criminals and the opportunist fools, although of course Linda does not think that she and Gordon belong in either of those categories. Linda would like to believe that she and Gordon belong to a third distinct group, that of hapless unfortunates.

At last a guard calls their names. He takes them out of Processing and down a narrow corridor, at the end of which lies a short flight of concrete steps. At the top of the steps there is an unprepossessing metal door, secured by a number of locks and bolts. Unlocked, unbolted, the door scrapes inwards to reveal another short flight of steps heading off at right angles.

"Out you go," says the guard, holding the door open, and out Linda and Gordon go. The door clangs shut behind them.

They are outside. The steps lead up to Days Plaza. Wind buffets them as they ascend to street level, in full view of dozens of window-shoppers. Linda braces herself for jeers and catcalls, but the window-shoppers obviously do not consider the sight of exiled customers coming up nervously into the daylight either a particularly novel one or, indeed, more interesting than the events going on inside their favourite window, although one man, noticing them, is prompted to smile and say, "Welcome to the club."

Linda's cheeks flush furiously. She strides off, Gordon in tow.

Taxis are parked in the turning circle outside the nearest entrance, waiting for the closing-time crowd. Linda approaches the first in line, checking before she climbs in that the driver is not the same one who ferried her and Gordon here. That would be too much. The final straw. An embarrassment too far. Although, thinking about it, she wouldn't mind having a few words with that particular taxi driver about the pepper spray he conned her into buying...

The driver of this taxi reluctantly agrees to accept cash. "Reached your limit, have you?" he says.

Linda, ignoring the remark completely, gives him their address, then slides the privacy window between the front and rear seats shut.

"So that's that then," says Gordon loudly, as the taxi pulls away from the world's first and (emphatically, resoundingly, deafeningly *not*) foremost gigastore.

"It was fun," Linda replies, nodding. "For a while." She longs to take a backward glance but she can't. She mustn't.

"Pardon?"

"I said, it was... Oh, never mind. How's your poor ear?"

"Pardon?"

"I said—"

"I heard you that time. I was just joking."

She punches gently him in the ribs.

"So we've learned our lesson, have we?" he says, reaching along the back of the seat and tentatively placing a hand on Linda's shoulder. When she doesn't shrug it off, as she has been known to in the past, he slowly begins to massage the shoulder, proceeding to the back of her neck. She submits gratefully. "Never again, eh?"

"Never again," she says. "Although," she adds, "there is always the EuroMart."

Gordon stops massaging. "Linda ..."

She talks quickly. Best plant the seed as early as possible. "Once we've paid off what we owe Days, it won't take long to build up enough credit again to apply for an account there. Think about it. We could go on day-trips to Brussels. They do discount fares. Package holidays. We could stay in a cheap hotel ..."

"*Linda* ..."

She smiles at him, a little sadly. "Just a dream, Gordon. Just a dream."

"Well, as long as that's all it remains." He resumes massaging.

But as the plan slowly evolves in her mind, Linda thinks that yes, it will be possible. It will take time, but eventually she should be able to talk Gordon round. Patience and perseverance are her strong suits. She will win him over. It may take another five years, it may take even longer, but so what? In the end it will be worth it.

And this time she isn't going to settle for a Silver. When they qualify for an account at the EuroMart, Linda Trivett is going to accept nothing less than a Gold.

43

Libra: The seventh sign of the Zodiac, represented by a pair of scales.

5.00 p.m.

CLOSING TIME WAS announced a quarter of an hour ago, and again five minutes ago, and with the third and final announcement, at five o'clock exactly, those customers who haven't yet started making for the exits begin to do so. They descend in the hallway lifts to the seven levels of car park and disperse to their vehicles, or file peaceably out of the four entrances with their ballast of carrier bags, emerging into a world tinted saffron by the setting sun. Stragglers, hoping to make one last purchase before they leave, are hustled out of the departments and shepherded towards the exits by guards.

Sales assistants reckon up the day's sales and transmit the totals up to the Boardroom. In the produce departments food is covered or, if likely to rot or go stale overnight, binned.

The heavy velvet curtains close inside the window displays, bringing to a close the real-time soap operas. The window-shoppers, glutted on vicarious consumerism, sigh and smile in mild dismay, and gather up their belongings. Those who have homes to go to, go, while those who have made the base of the building their home settle down for the night.

Staff put on their overcoats and make their way down to their cars or out to the train stations and the bus stops. It would, in every respect, have been a typical day, but for the explosion mid-afternoon, which set off a wave of excitement that has yet to die down completely. Employees, like customers, are still exchanging stories about their experiences—where they were, what they were doing, when the bomb went off. Rumours, naturally, abound. The one that holds most currency is that terrorists were responsible. Certain other rumours concerning the Books Department have been widely discounted. Several people know someone who knows someone in Computers who swears that Security has rounded up all the Bookworms and arrested them—but that sounds like just the sort of thing a Technoid would say. And it has been mentioned by more than one source that the Head of the Books Department was the one who detonated the bomb, and that she was killed in the explosion. But a Days employee trying to blow up the store? Surely not!

All the rumours, factual and fanciful, are duly passed on by the employees coming off-shift to the night watchmen and janitorial staff coming on-shift. The consternation felt in the immediate aftermath of the bomb has, through the mysterious alchemical processes of time, been transmuted into exhilaration. In retrospect, it was quite exciting, really, to have been inside the store during a real live terrorist attack. The night-shift employees are left in no doubt that they have missed out on something thrilling and rare.

A repair crew is brought in, on overtime rates, to mend the Menagerie net. Butterflies and birds are escaping through the rifts caused by the two falling employees, and though the repair crew set to work quickly, Menagerie staff will be busy tracking down and recapturing rogue merchandise for the next week or so.

The lights dim all over the empty store.

5.22 p.m.

FRANK CLOSES THE door to his locker and picks up the carrier bag containing his mud-caked clothes and shoes. He is dressed in an exact replica of his original outfit, correct down to the rubber-soled brogues and the maroon silk tie. With his hair dried and combed, he looks freshly pressed, new-minted.

He casts his eye around the locker room, not expecting to feel nostalgia, and, as expected, not feeling any. But then this isn't necessarily going to be the last time he stands here, gazing on these two rows of unremarkable steel doors with their padlocks and vents.

He turns and walks out into the corridor, where Mr Bloom is waiting for him.

"Everything OK?" Mr Bloom asks. "The clothes, I mean. They fit all right?"

"They're fine. Thank you for getting them. You will, of course, transfer the cost to my account."

"I will do no such thing."

"I insist."

"Frank, after what you've been through today—"

"Please, Donald." There is an edge of resentment in Frank's voice. "I don't want to owe anyone anything."

"You'll always owe Days." Mr Bloom sugars the remark with a laugh.

"I think I've paid off that debt," Frank replies, absentmindedly itching at the parallel rows of fish-scale scratches on the backs of his hands, left there by Miss Dalloway's fingernails.

They walk side by side towards the staff lift, Mr Bloom slowing his pace to match Frank's stiff, awkward gait. Several times Mr Bloom looks as if he is on the point of asking something.

Frank finally saves him the trouble. "No, I don't know yet about leaving. I'm still thinking about it."

"That's an improvement, at least. At lunchtime, you were dead set."

"Don't go looking for significance in my words that isn't there, Donald. All I'm saying is that something has happened, something that... Well, I can't really explain it."

They reach the lift.

"For what it's worth, Frank," says Mr Bloom, pressing the Up button, "I've put in a recommendation to the brothers to allow you to retire on full pension, no penalties, if you so desire. In fact, I was hoping to have received an answer from them before you left, but obviously they've a lot else to deal with. The insurance company, for one. Still, after what you did for them today, they can hardly refuse. That's how things stand, at any rate. You can stay on, or, if the brothers agree, you can retire with all debts discharged and no strings attached."

The lift arrives.

"So, what's it going to be?"

Frank steps through the open doors, and turns around, setting the bag of soiled clothing at his feet.

He looks at the only man in the world he might possibly consider a friend.

"Donald," he says, "I don't know. I honestly don't know."

The doors shut.

5.31 p.m.

He steps out into the evening. The darkening air smells sweet, which is surprising considering he is downwind from several hundred unwashed window-shoppers. The sweetness, perhaps, is not in his nose but in his mind, the air smelling that way simply because it is not the air inside Days. It is air that belongs to the whole of the rest of the planet, and the sweet smell is freedom and limitless possibility.

There are reporters at the foot of the steps, and they are interviewing employees as they leave. Some outside broadcast vans are parked in the turning circle; more are arriving. Arc lights probe, cameras jut, boom microphones intrude, as the bombing incident yields to the surgery of telejournalism.

Bidding goodnight to the guards, Frank sets off down the steps. He notes the woman standing at the foot of the steps, but taking her to be one of the reporters, walks straight past her.

"Deliberately ignoring me, Mr Hubble?" says a polite, familiar voice.

Frank stops. Turns.

Mrs Shukhov takes two tentative steps towards him.

"The guard told me you're a creature of habit," she continues, smiling. "Always arrives and leaves by the north-western entrance, she said."

"You," Frank says slowly, "have put me to a great deal of trouble."

She can't interpret his tone. Anger? Or sly mockery? His face offers no clues. "Well, I apologise if—"

"No. It wasn't your fault. You couldn't have known." The corners of Frank's mouth give an almost imperceptible twitch.

"Are you teasing me, Mr Hubble?"

"I have no idea. Am I?"

Mrs Shukhov sighs. "Why do men always have to make things so awkward?"

A thought occurs to Frank. "Mrs Shukhov, you weren't by any chance waiting for me, were you?"

"A glimmer of intelligence! There's hope for you yet, Mr Hubble." She takes another two steps towards him. He remains where he is, a stranger to the patterns of this verbal and physical dance. "I was wondering if you might like to go for a cup of coffee with me," she says. He frowns. "If that's all right," she adds hastily. "I mean, if I've overstepped the mark, say so. If there's some rule you people have about fraternising with disgraced customers, or if you just don't want to, I'll understand."

"Let me get this straight. You'd like me to go for a cup of coffee with you?"

"Or something stronger, if you'd prefer."

"No, coffee would be... would be all right."

"Is that a yes?"

"It isn't a no."

Mrs Shukhov rolls her eyes. "Honestly! I'm sure if I looked 'obtuse' up in a dictionary, the definition would be just one word: men."

5.53 p.m.

AT THE EDGE of Days Plaza, Frank and Mrs Shukhov cross the road, which is clogged with commuter traffic. The dusk has reached that stage when half the vehicles have their headlights on and half do not. The moon, in half-phase, glimmers in the purple sky, its left side dark, its right mottled ivory. Looking up at it, Frank thinks, *No, Days does not own the night. At least, not yet.*

Up a narrow street on the opposite side of the road he and Mrs Shukhov find a café, with plastic tables and chairs in front taking up most of its allotment of pavement, overlooking a litter-choked gutter. Inside, the café is about quarter full, and a pleasant but not especially enthusiastic waitress invites the two new patrons to choose where they want to sit. Mrs Shukhov selects a booth, and she and Frank slide in on opposite sides of the formica-topped table and make themselves comfortable on the padded bench-seats.

Frank looks around him at the framed, faded posters of continental beach resorts and foreign landmarks, at the potted plant straggling up a fan-shaped trellis by the door to the kitchen, at the other diners chatting or solitarily inspecting evening newspapers. It would be a lie to say he is not nervous. He hasn't been inside a public café since his early twenties.

"So," says Mrs Shukhov, resting her elbows on the table.

"So," says Frank, his mind turning over. Conversation. "So," he says again. Then: "Your eyes. Your eyes aren't as red as when I last saw them. Saw *you*."

Mrs Shukhov feels encouraged that he is at least looking in the right region. "That guard—Gould was her name?—Gould went up and bought me a contact lens case, some cleaning solution, and even a bottle of eye drops. At her own expense. What with that and you standing up for me in Processing... well, I'm wondering what I could have done to deserve such kindness."

"So you can see all right?"

"Can't see a thing," she replies, laughing. "My lenses are in my handbag. I'm surprised you didn't notice me squinting and peering all the way over here."

"I'm having a little eye trouble myself at the moment." The pepper spray's residual itch is still unpleasant. His eyeballs feel sandpapery in their sockets.

"They do look somewhat pink. Perhaps you'd like to use my eye drops."

"Perhaps."

"Did you know that, except for our eyes, everything we show to the world is dead?" says Mrs Shukhov. "Our skin, hair, nails, even the insides of our mouths—we sheathe ourselves in a casing of dead tissue in order to protect our flesh and inner organs from the ravages of oxygen, and the only living parts of ourselves we show one another are the irises of our eyes, seen through our corneas. That's why eye-contact is important, both between strangers and between friends, because that way we can demonstrate to each other the truth of ourselves, the life rather than the death."

"Interesting."

"Isn't it? I read that in some scientific journal in Newspapers & Periodicals yesterday."

"It's good to know you didn't completely waste your time."

"Mr Hubble," says Mrs Shukhov, shaking her head, "I wish you'd hold up a flag or wink or *something* when you're being ironic. Humour as dry as yours is hard to detect."

"I'm sorry."

"No, don't be. I like it. I was simply remarking."

"Actually," Frank says, rising, "if you don't mind, Mrs Shukhov, I *would* like to take you up on that offer of eye drops."

"Of course." Mrs Shukhov roots around in her handbag and produces a small, conical plastic bottle with the Days logo prominent on its label. "And please—call me Carmen."

Frank takes the bottle and heads for the cloakrooms.

The gents cloakroom smells strongly of industrial bleach and pine air freshener, and less strongly of urine. Frank bolts the door and approaches the basin warily. He lowers his head as if in supplication, and leaning on the basin, peers slowly up into the speckled, tarnished mirror.

There is his reflection, just as it was in the cracked glass of his Sphinx's screen. Immediately appearing, without having to be willed into existence. Solid, stable, and staring back at him—a reversed Frank in a reversed café cloakroom, large as life, there, inarguably, indubitably *there*.

He looks at himself from the side. He looks at himself down his nose. He looks at himself from up under his eyebrows.

He doesn't want to ask how this miracle has happened, because to question it would risk destroying it, like a boy bursting a soap bubble in his eagerness to capture it. But he knows it has something to do with the white tigress.

The white tigress neither overlooked him nor spurned him. With her sniffing inspection and the elusive purr that followed, she *accepted* him.

She accepted him into the restless green commerce of the Menagerie. She said, in effect, "Here, and in the forests where I came from, things come and go. Predator preys on prey. Herbivore feeds on plant, carnivore feeds on herbivore. That is how it is. Everything is useful to something else. Dead plant matter, living creatures—everything has its purpose and its place. Everything grows to be destroyed so that something else may grow again. The natural order is an eternal to and fro, a give and take, a buy and sell. And you have known this. All along, though you may not have realised it, you have known this."

Miss Dalloway tried to kill him. The tigress killed Miss Dalloway.

Give and take. To and fro.

And the tigress accepted him. Understood him. Comprehended him.

And he realises that congruity is not, as he has believed, a curse. He remembers the tigress's camouflage, how she blended into her surroundings, but still remained powerful, potent, lethally efficient. Congruity is a question of fitting in to exactly the right degree, not too much, just enough. Being a part but also apart. There is a balance to be struck, a line to be walked between two extremes, a thin grey area, a narrow shadow of overlap. Over thirty-three years he forgot where it is and how to find it, that's all.

He squeezes a couple of the drops into each eye, and the lingering irritation of the pepper spray is relieved.

With one last glance at himself in the mirror, Frank leaves the cloakroom.

Mrs Shukhov has taken the liberty of ordering coffee for both of them. Two full cups sit steaming on the table. Frank finds himself searching for something that isn't there. He quickly realises what it is. A Days logo. There are no Days logos on the cups and saucers.

He sits and takes a grateful sip. It may not have been made using the finest beans money can buy, but it is still the best coffee he has ever tasted.

Conversations ripple around the café. The street outside is growing dusky. The streetlamps come on, shedding a hard orange light. You can feel it: the city drawing in on itself like a closing flower.

Opposite him Mrs Shukhov—Carmen, her name is Carmen—holds herself erect. Good posture. Handsome features. She is waiting for him to speak. Wanting him to speak.

He thinks he will tell her about his day. It has, even by Days standards, been a hellish one. He thinks he will tell her about the lengths he had to go to in order to keep his promise to recover her Platinum, about his pursuit of the Bookworm, and the bomb. Who knows? Somewhere along the way, using his dry humour, he may even be able to amuse her.

Tomorrow, things may change or things may stay the same. Tomorrow, he may fly off to America or he may simply turn up for work as usual. For now, there is this evening, and a woman who is intrigued by him, who wants to fathom him. Tomorrow, when it comes, will take care of itself.

And Days will always be there.

The thought is strangely comforting.

Days—constant, immutable, enduring, too huge and solid to change—will always be there.

44

Shiva: In orthodox Judaism, the period of seven days of mourning for a parent, spouse, brother or sister.

6.00 p.m.

SIX O'CLOCK!

Perch leaps to his feet. He was so busy preparing tomorrow's menu and compiling a list of groceries to be bought that he completely lost track of time.

He hastens out of his office. The kitchen is empty and clean. The brothers prefer to cook their evening meals for themselves in their apartments and eat them on their own, a necessary antidote of solitude after spending the entire day in one another's company. Thus the catering staff have, as usual, tidied up and gone home.

Normally by six the only brother left in the Boardroom is he whose day of chairmanship it is, working late to fulfil his duty of collating the sales figures and passing on the total to a press agency which will then disseminate it to the media. Perch intends to ask Master Thurston for the full story about the explosion earlier. A news item on the radio an hour ago mentioned that reports were coming in about an incident at Days. No details had been confirmed as yet, the newscaster said, but she promised to keep the public informed as the story developed. Rather than wait for the media to grope their way slowly to the truth, Perch will get it straight from a Day brother himself—one of the small perks of being intimate with the owners of the first and (what else would he say?) foremost gigastore.

Perch is surprised to find all of the brothers present in the Boardroom when he enters, but, of course, he hides his surprise masterfully.

The brothers are seated around the table in their respective chairs. The dark side of the dome fills the three windows from corner to corner, from edge to edge, a solid wall of blackness, and the brothers have not switched on the ceiling lights. Perch can barely make out their faces. He can see their eyes, though. All of them turn to stare at him as he comes in, except Master Sonny, who is slumped in his mock throne and seems to be asleep.

Master Sonny still here, too? Extraordinary.

None of the brothers speaks as Perch approaches the table. Their eyes follow him, glimmering in the gloom, but none of them addresses him, which is strange. Strange, too, is the smell that grows in Perch's nostrils as he nears the table, a tangy, clean, metallic odour that is desperately familiar, although he cannot quite place it.

He notes some dark stains on the tabletop, like spattered oil. He noticed similar stains on the switch handle as he came in, but dismissed this as an illusion caused by his eyes not being accustomed to the gloom. The stains on the table are definitely there, though, and there are further stains on the carpet nearby. Perch tuts mentally. He will be on his hands and knees till midnight scrubbing *those* out.

He halts a metre away from the edge of the table, Mungo to his left, Sonny to his right.

"I came to see if that will be all, sirs."

The silence holds for a while, until finally Mungo says, "Since you ask, Perch, I think we would all like something to eat. Nothing fancy. Could you possibly rustle us up a snack?" His voice seems to be coming from somewhere deep down inside him, faint and hollow as though issuing from the bottom of a well.

"A snack? Certainly, sir. I think there is some cold roast beef in the refrigerator. Will roast beef sandwiches do?"

"Roast beef sandwiches will do fine."

"Seven rounds?" says Perch, with a brief glance at the sleeping Sonny. There is something odd about the way he is sitting, the way his arms are hanging down, the way his chin is resting on his breastbone...

"Absolutely," says Thurston. "Seven. One for each of us."

"Because all seven of us are here, are we not, Perch?" says Sato.

"Of that there can be no dispute, Master Sato," says the brothers' indefatigably phlegmatic manservant.

"Because the charm of Seven is vital to the continued success of the store," says Wensley. "That's what our father used to say."

"Those were his words, sir."

"And it mustn't be broken," adds Fred.

"No, it must not, Master Fred."

The brothers are talking in the dull, numbed tones of survivors of a train crash, and Perch wonders if they might not be suffering from some kind of delayed shock as a consequence of the explosion.

"If nothing else is required, then?" he says.

His eyes have by this stage adapted to the dim light, and as turns to leave he takes a good look at the figure of the youngest son of Septimus Day.

Sonny hardly resembles Sonny at all. Sonny is a twisted, mangled, lumpen approximation of Sonny, like a wax effigy left out too long in the sun. His skin is webbed with patterns of blood, the same blood that besmirches the table and the carpet. His dangling hands are horribly misshapen, and the angle at which his jawbone is lodged against his clavicle would, for a living person, soon become unbearably uncomfortable. One eye is lost beneath puffy black lids, while the other bulges alarmingly, veiny and gelatinous. His lips have bloomed like a pair of purple fungi, and his nose lies almost flat against his face, as though it is made of putty and someone has squelched it down with their fist. His hair is clotted with indefinable matter and splinters of bone.

This time, keeping his features calm and inexpressive, the habit that has come to Perch naturally throughout all his years of service to the Day family, is the hardest thing he has ever had to do.

He looks round at the six still-living sons of Septimus Day, and in their widened, white eyes sees fear, and something else besides, something he is reluctant to name.

"Sonny is going to be with us every day from now on," Mungo tells Perch. "He's turned over a new leaf."

"I... I see, sir. Yes."

"I personally will make sure that he gets up in good time and is prompt for breakfast. Do you understand?"

"Yes, sir, I do."

"Very good. Well, Perch?" Mungo attempts to instil the words with his usual authority, but it sounds like a child's gruff imitation of a grown-up. "Our snack?"

Perch takes one last look around the table, then closes his eyes very slowly and, equally slowly, nods.

"Of course, sir," he says. "Sandwiches for seven, coming up."

Acknowledgements

Adam Brockbank was involved with *Days* since its inception, and helped shape a handful of amorphous concepts into a plot, suggested ideas, proposed different (and invariably better) ways of doing things, and throughout the writing of the novel offered accurate, insightful comments and criticisms.

On the technical side of things, Lieutenant Hugh Holton of the Chicago Police Department initiated me into the mysteries of handgun use and arranged a memorable and eye-opening tour of his precinct station. Ian Hillier, meanwhile, was kind enough to give me a few pointers on how to go about constructing a homemade deflagrating device. Viva the Kew Liberation Front!

Peter Crowther has been a constant source of support and reassurance, always ready to give me a metaphorical clip round the ear whenever I've started whingeing but also always ready to cheer me up whenever I've really needed it.

Simon Spanton found the book a good home at Orion, and his incisive editing, far from inflicting a death of a thousand cuts, proved to be fat-reducing surgery of the highest order.

John Kunzler and Lesley Plant I have to thank for countless Sunday suppers and Sega sessions. I am equally grateful to the boys at Flying Pig Systems Ltd. for many things, the least of which is calling their company Flying Pig Systems Ltd.

Finally, Susan Gleason took on the unenviable role of being the squeaky wheel that gets the oil, or, as it's technically known, "literary agent". It is a task she has performed with grace, dedication and a necessary measure of good humour.

These are the people without whom, etc. etc.

James Lovegrove

UNTIED
KINGDOM

This book is dedicated to my sisters
Philippa and Kate
(because they'll kill me if it isn't)

Contents

1.
Downbourne

"SIR? MR MORRIS?"

"Yes, Clive?"

"Sir, did you hear that?"

"Hear what?"

"I'm sure it was a motor."

Fen listened, and heard nothing but the arrhythmic tick and buzz of bluebottles throwing themselves against the classroom's only closed window. Six other windows wide open, liberty readily available, yet this particular batch of flies was too stupid, or too lazy, or too intent on suicide, to realise. He continued to listen, making a show of it now, head cocked, hand cupping ear. Nothing.

"Can't hear a thing, Clive," he said.

"But sir..."

"Get on with your reading, Clive."

The rest of the class, the brief distraction over, bent their heads again, returning their attention to the books in front of them. Clive looked as if he was about to insist that his teacher was wrong, then decided against it and bent his head, too. He was reading a hardback copy of *The Red Badge of Courage* which, as with every book from the school library, was battered and dog-eared and life-supported by a few brittle, browned snippets of scotch tape.

Reading hour. The final hour of the school day, when Fen's pupils, crammed to the brim with learning, could relax a little, and so could he. From his table at the head of the classroom he cast an eye over the boys and girls, each of whom was concentrating with an intensity of frown in inverse proportion to his or her age. The room was silent again, or at any rate there were just the background noises that signified all systems normal: the shuffles and snuffles, the dry turn of pages, a cough here, a scratch of an itch there, and of course the bluebottles, still battering their heads against the panes. They had been at it since morning, and had developed a kind of rota, so that whenever one knocked itself insensible and tumbled to the sill, another rose to take its place, attacking the window in a frenzy until it, too, was stunned—glazed!—and sank to the sill, unable to continue.

The hush was, to Fen, contented. It spoke to him of work done, another day finishing, a satisfying sense of things being rolled up and put away. He glanced at his watch. Ten minutes to go. Leaning back in his chair, he listened again for the motor Clive had thought he heard. From outside came the thrum of a blazing hot afternoon, insects and birds and the ruffle of a breeze through summer-cured leaves. The one remaining swing in the school playground (the other had had to be dismantled after its plastic seat developed a dangerous split) was swaying almost imperceptibly back and forth, its chains emitting tiny, mouse-like squeaks. A collared dove hooted the same three notes over and over and over. Far off, the lazy bleat of sheep.

No motor. Clive had been mistaken. But then the boy was only eleven. An eleven-year-old born and brought up in a town like Downbourne had probably heard a motor, what, a dozen times in his lifetime? If that.

It had just been the flies, that was all. The buzzing of the foolish kamikaze bluebottles, trapped behind the one window that was stuck fast in its frame, impossible to open.

The idiot flies.

CLASS WAS DISMISSED punctually at three-thirty. The books were piled up on Fen's table, and then his pupils were out, away, free, gone. Fen realigned desks and wiped the blackboard clean with a rag. Proper chalk was hard to come by, so he was obliged to use the raw stuff, rugged lumps of it harvested from the downland soil. The marks they made were greasy and indistinct, only just legible, but at least (a small compensation) they could be erased with minimal effort. A flip of the rag, and that morning's maths test—basic geometry questions for the younger portion of the class, trigonometry posers for the older—vanished.

When the classroom was tidy, Fen closed all the windows, then stooped to pick up the folded mouse mat that he used to wedge open the door and create a through-draught. He tossed the mouse mat over on to the pile of computer hardware which sat, haphazardly stacked, in one corner of the room. It amused Fen to think how all this equipment—costing several thousand pounds when new, monitors and hard drives and keyboards and peripherals—now lay in a heap, gathering dust, cream-coloured housing going yellow in the sun. It amused him, too, in a mildly astonished way, that his pupils could barely comprehend what these devices were for, what they used to be capable of. In a short space of time, a startlingly short space of time, computers had gone from technological be-all and end-all to hunks of redundant, inoperable junk. To a whole generation, the concept of deriving information and entertainment and a sense of connectedness from them now seemed bizarre, even implausible. Likewise television. Some of the kids, the older ones, thirteen and up, could remember watching broadcasts, back when the electricity worked, back when TV stations transmitted. Some of them could even remember watching programmes that weren't government public-information bulletins or street-riot reportage. For the younger ones, though, the big glass-fronted box that still occupied a corner in most living rooms and lounges was just an inert object, an item of furniture of considerably less practical significance than a table or a bookcase. They had never watched images dance across its screen, never been captivated by its firelight thrall; they had no idea of the reverence in which this defunct household god had once been held.

Fen strode along the corridor that led to the school's main entrance, his footsteps echoing through the empty building. The school was two storeys tall, blocky and utilitarian. Built in the early nineteen-sixties, its facilities were designed for a student body of about two hundred, a staff faculty of about twenty. A decent-sized local school, in other words. So it housed hollowly, like a dried kernel with a few seeds rattling inside it, its one class of seventeen and its solitary teacher.

Emerging into sunshine, Fen squinted, loosened his shirt collar, and set off for home.

Moira glances at the kitchen clock and thinks, He'll just be leaving now.

Within minutes, the walking had brought him out in a sweat. He had been perspiring throughout the day, stickiness accumulating at his armpits and crotch, but this was different; this was good sweat, the sweat of activity, a cooling release, profuse and welcome. Opting for one of the more circuitous routes home, Fen made his way down to the river and followed the towpath, passing first a meadowy football pitch where a few horses were contentedly browsing inside a hazel-fenced enclosure, then the backs of the units of the town's business estate, empty aluminium-sided shells where the only industry now was the web-spinning of spiders and the scavenging scurry of mice. Soon he arrived at a footbridge, a cantilevered arc of concrete and steel whose shadow lay pristine on the river's chocolate-milk surface.

Reginald Bailey was, as ever, stationed at the bridge's midpoint, a human keystone. Bent-backed, the old widower leaned on the railing, clutching his fishing rod and staring down at the float on the end of his line and the tiny ripples that trailed from it in a chevron pattern.

"Any luck?"

Reginald raised a hoary eyebrow. "Afternoon, schoolteacher. No, not yet."

"Oh well. Still worth a try, eh?"

Reginald nodded, and for the umpteenth time Fen wondered whether the old fellow knew, as everyone else did, that the river ran rich with heavy metals and other pollutants and had not played host to a living fish in years. He must do. Yet every day, without fail, Reginald trooped down to the footbridge, cast his line into the water and stood for hours, patiently waiting for a bite. Hope? Madness? Maybe a little of both.

Moira fills the kettle from the rainwater butt and lights the hob, thinking her husband ought to have a nice cup of tea waiting for him when he gets home.

Past the bridge lay a small public park that was kept in shape by a group of dedicated volunteers who regularly clipped and sickled its bushes and shrubbery, and also by a troupe of tethered goats which happily discharged the responsibility of keeping the grass trimmed, their work taking the form of overlapping circles that were nibbled to a neatness any bowling-green groundsman would have been proud of. Children often played a game here in which they would tiptoe through the unkempt passages between the circles, daring the goats to butt them. This was not happening today, however, and that was just as well, since the game was not approved of. Fen would have been obliged to tick the participants off, and he didn't like being the teacher outside as well as in the school.

Beyond the park was a patch of waste ground, through which ran a footpath worn by countless shoe soles, meandering among clumps of brambles taller than a man, clusters of stinging nettles that sprang even higher, great airy clouds of cow parsley, purple-taloned profusions of buddleia. Here and there, embedded amid the greenery, could be glimpsed items of domestic detritus: a porcelain lavatory minus its lid, a rusted bicycle wheel, a refrigerator, an anglepoise lamp, a stereo speaker, all so surrounded and interpenetrated by shoots and stems that to retrieve any of them, should anyone have been overcome by the inexplicable urge to do so, would have entailed a good half-hour's work with machete and sécateurs.

Undergrowth rustlings attended Fen's progress through the waste ground, for a colony of feral cats had made this spot their home. They skittered away as he approached. Now and then he glimpsed a pair of eyes glowing amid the plant shadows; more often, a flash of rear paws and tail as a cat darted for deeper cover.

The footpath eventually disgorged him onto Hill Street, which, true to its name, climbed a steep slope, with a staggered parade of terraced Victorian houses on either side. Several of the houses were empty, but it was difficult to tell from appearances alone those that were from those that were not. Front doors stood ajar, windowpanes were broken, roof-tiles had slipped, paintwork had peeled, guttering sagged on occupied and unoccupied premises alike. All along the kerbside, cars rested on prolapsed tyres, their bodywork rust-riddled, their chrome trim dulled, their windows opaque with dust. They looked as purposeless as people queuing for an event which no one had told them had been cancelled.

To escape the sun, most of the residents of Hill Street were indoors, but, outside one of the better-maintained houses, Fen came across little Holly-Anne Greeley. He said hello, and Holly-Anne solemnly enquired whether he would like to join in her game. She was sitting with dolls spread out in a circle on the pavement in front of her, an assortment of smooth pink plastic humanoids, all of them unclothed and many of them missing at least one limb, in a couple of cases their heads. Tiny twelve-inch amputee women in round-table conversation with decapitated monster babies. Fen shook his head and said no thanks, maybe another time. Holly-Anne sniffed and rubbed her dirt-smudged nose and said OK, never mind.

"Are you looking forward to coming to school?" Fen asked. "We're looking forward to having you join us."

Holly-Anne nodded vaguely. Just turned six, she was due to enrol as his pupil in the autumn. Her father, Alan Greeley, was a skilled handyman, able to mend almost anything around the home. He was also a Mr Fix-It when it came to obtaining hard-to-get supplies, and the promise of repairs whenever they were needed at the Morris household, plus a couple of butane cylinders for the stove, had seemed to both him and Fen a fair price in return for a year's worth of education for his daughter.

Inside the house, an infant began to cry.

"That's my little brother," Holly-Anne explained.

"I know," said Fen. "Nathan."

"He's noisy," Holly-Anne said, with a very adult sigh.

"Little brothers always are," said Fen.

Moira goes to the back door and calls into the garden: "Come on in and get washed. Your father'll be home any time soon."

At the summit of Hill Street, most of Downbourne came into view. Lichen-speckled roofs spread to the east, south and west, a mile in each direction, shelving away to the town's outskirts. From there the houses continued out along the approach roads, spaced further apart the further from town they were. Five miles away, blurred by the hazy air, lay a ridge of hills, a great rumpled chalk undulation running parallel to the one on which Downbourne rested. It was possible to make out what remained of a figure etched into the distant hillside, the nameless giant who had presided over the valley since pre-Norman times, calmly observing Downbourne's evolution from peasant collective to market town to Home Counties backwater to whatever it was these days—perhaps a large peasant collective again. All that was left of the figure's white outline were the stumps of its legs. The rest was a deep ragged gouge, courtesy of an

International Community fighter pilot who had taken it upon himself to obliterate the giant with an air-to-ground missile, either mistaking it for a legitimate target or, more likely, out of a savage (if strategically unsound) sense of fun.

Fen headed downhill on Monks Avenue, famed as Downbourne's most sought-after address, a sycamore-lined haven of detached des-res gentility. Or at least, it had been, before its residents abandoned it, moving abroad to live in holiday homes or with expat relatives, or else bribing their way to political asylum in Canada and New Zealand—part of the national exodus of the well-heeled who had used their money, what was left of it after the government had plundered their bank accounts, to escape when things started getting tough. The big houses were now in decay. Their front gardens had welled up, thick and rank, and brimmed over their boundary walls, intertangling, uniting. Driveways where people carriers and latest-model saloons had once proudly stood were scribbled over by ivy and bindweed. Where there had been spreads of striped lawn, daisies and summer celandine ran rampant. The sycamores themselves, untrimmed, had grown exultantly profuse, and formed a tunnel over the roadway. Pavements were verges.

The end of Monks Avenue intersected with Harvill Drive, which, if Fen had turned left, would have taken him to the town centre. As he neared the junction he heard the ringing clip-clop of horses' hooves on tarmac. Three horses, he guessed, judging by the pattern and cadence of iron-shod strikes; and sure enough, as he rounded the corner, turning right, he was confronted with a trio of riders coming towards him at a gentle amble.

Two of the three riders were dressed in ordinary outdoor gear—jeans, checked shirts, hiking boots—and looked less than comfortable on their mounts, clutching the reins too tightly and sitting tense, as if expecting to be unsaddled at any moment (though the horses beneath them seemed placid, nodding creatures, too docile even to think about bucking). They looked like people who would have much preferred to be at desks, signing documents and making phone calls, rather than patrolling through town on horseback. Their names were Henry Mullins and Susannah Vicks, and they were both prominent members of Downbourne's town council.

The third rider, who was perched astride a magnificent dappled-grey steed, cut an altogether more imposing figure. He had a vast, bushy growth of beard and deep-set, piercing blue eyes, and he sat tall in his saddle, head high, shoulders relaxed, arms exerting just enough pressure to keep the reins taut, no more. The most striking thing about him, however—striking even to someone like Fen who was well acquainted with the man—was that he was, from top to toe, green. Not only was his clothing green (green canvas gilet, green shirt, green corduroy trousers, green wellingtons) but his skin was green, too, and every visible strand of his hair, so that from the shoulders up he was more hedge than head. He was an emerald emir, a vision of virescence, startling and majestic, and as he drew alongside Fen he brought his horse to a halt and acknowledged Fen with a brief, stately nod.

"Mr Morris, good afternoon," he said, while his two colleagues pulled up, with some awkwardness, beside him.

"Afternoon, mayor," said Fen. "Lovely day."

"Mother Nature has once more blessed us," the Green Man pronounced, with a glance at the cloudless heavens. "And how are the flower of Downbourne's youth? I take it they have just benefited from another day of learning at the feet of our esteemed pedagogue."

Fen had become practised at the art of hiding smirks in the Green Man's presence. "One does what one can."

"No need to be so modest, Mr Morris. Everybody knows what a fine job you do, training and guiding our young saplings so that they may grow into mighty oaks."

"Perhaps I'd believe that if more people were prepared to send their children to me."

The Green Man nodded and sighed. "Alas, though I wish it were otherwise, not everyone has goods or a skill to offer in exchange for your services, and perhaps not everyone sees the need for a traditional education any more."

Fen gave a shrug, as if to say he was only too aware of this sad fact. In truth, he would not have been able to cope with more than perhaps a half-dozen extra pupils. A class size greater than twenty would be hard to handle, for above a certain number children achieve a sort of critical mass and become wilful and unruly, beyond the power of a single adult to control. Fen had raised the subject simply so as to demonstrate that he was a good and loyal member of the community, keen to do his bit. That sort of attitude pleased the Green Man, and there was something about the Green Man that made you want to see him pleased.

The Green Man pointed to his two-person entourage. "We're on our way to see how preparations for the festival are coming along," he said. "I expect we shall see you there this evening?" It was only partly a question.

"You shall."

"And your lovely wife, of course."

"If she can make it."

"Excellent." The Green Man lofted a hand in a farewell salute, then, with a cluck of his tongue, urged his horse into motion. His sidekicks followed suit, albeit with more trouble, yanking on their reins and digging their heels in several times before their horses at last—possibly just because they felt like it—got going.

Fen watched them trot away, this queer little procession of three, then turned and resumed his journey along Harvill Drive.

Water splashing in a bowl; a bit of rubbing to remove a patch of really engrained dirt; protests as a rogue lock of hair is wetted and smoothed into place; then everyone is clean and smart and ready, and the kettle is just starting to whistle.

Ducking down a narrow cut-through between two houses, Fen walked the length of their back gardens, towering leylandii on one side of him, a half-collapsed slat fence on the other. He crossed a back alley, passed between two more gardens, two more houses, and finally emerged onto Crane Street.

Seven doors down on his right lay his destination, number 12.

He did not deliberately slow his pace as he neared home. All the same he was conscious of his stride shortening, his legs seeming to grow heavier, every step becoming incrementally more difficult to take than its predecessor, until, for the final few yards to his front gate, he was all but trudging. A weary kind of anticipation balled in the pit of his stomach as he undid the latch and swung the gate open. He hated the feeling. More, he hated himself for feeling it.

He went up the path. He grasped the handle of the front door. He turned the handle and pushed the door inwards. He entered.

Silence in the house. A silence heightened by the ticking of the hallway clock, counting out the half-seconds like a time bomb.

He listened hard and discerned a soft snoring coming from upstairs. He crossed the hallway and entered the kitchen. The kettle sat on the hob, stone-cold. He took the plastic washing-up bowl from the sink and went out into the garden to fill it to the depth of an inch from the rainwater butt. Indoors again, he removed his shirt and washed himself, dousing his face and torso with the sun-warmed water, then using a sparing amount of soap—some strongly-scented French brand—to clean his armpits and neck. He rinsed himself off, went outside and poured the soapy water over his onions. He stood for a while in the garden, relishing the prickling sensation of coolness as his skin dried. Just a few feet away from him a fearless blue tit foraged in his herb bed for grubs. Next door, the neighbour's chickens clucked and flustered in their run.

Back in the house again, Fen heard movement upstairs, a crunch of bedsprings. The act of washing had been his way of informing Moira, quietly, that he was home. Turning over in bed was her way of letting him know she had heard and was awake.

Pulling his shirt back on, he went up to see her.

The bedroom was hot and stuffy, and filled with the rich stench of shit. Moira had used the chamberpot and not emptied it out.

She was lying beneath a single sheet, wearing just a grey T-shirt. Her long auburn hair was clumpy and dishevelled, stray tendrils of it adhering to her forehead. Her face was doughy from sleep. She peered up at Fen, blinking as though he were the source of a bright light. Her voice was a croak:

"What time is it?"

"Gone four."

"Fuck."

"How long have you been asleep?"

"How should I know?"

"I only asked."

"Since midday, maybe."

"Are you hungry?"

"I don't know."

"I could make us something to eat."

"I don't know if I want anything."

"We've still a couple of eggs left. We should use them. I think they're near their best-by."

"Don't feel like eggs."

"OK. Something else then."

"Look, if you want to eat, go right ahead. I can't be bothered."

"Well, all right. You have a think about it. I'll be back in a mo."

Fen picked up the chamberpot, which was draped with a tea towel, and carried it downstairs to the garden. There, carefully and at arm's length, he tipped the contents out over the roots of the runner beans that were growing along the rear wall, then folded the earth over with a trowel, soil over soil. He rinsed out the pot with a trickle of rainwater and took it back upstairs.

Moira was sitting on the edge of the bed, hands on knees, arms straight, collecting her thoughts. Her T-shirt had ridden up around her waist, exposing a delta-shape of ginger curls that bushed out over the cleft where her thighs joined. Fen's gaze was reflexively drawn to this, but his interest, once attracted, was more clinical than anything, as though he were a trichologist and the density and texture of Moira's pubic hair conveyed all manner of scientific information. If the sight stirred any sexual excitement in him, it was only the faintest of frissons, a vestigial response to a stimulus that had long since ceased to have any meaningful effect.

He checked himself, averting his eyes. If Moira caught him staring, it might be an excuse to have a go at him. Not that she always needed an excuse.

Setting the chamberpot down next to the bed, he went to open the window.

"Bumped into the Green Man just now," he said, wrestling with the window's stiff upper sash.

Moira gave a snort.

"What?" he asked, glancing round.

"'The Green Man'," she said. "His name is Michael Hollingbury. Why not call him that?"

"Because he wants to be known as the Green Man."

"Is that what you call him to his face?"

"I don't call him anything to his face. Except 'mayor'."

"But whenever you talk about him you refer to him as the Green Man."

"Because that's how he wants to be known."

The sash finally budged, and fresh air drifted into the room.

"But don't you see," Moira said, "it only encourages him."

"Encourages him?"

"To be a deluded prat. The man is a dairy farmer called Michael Hollingbury who dresses up in green and dyes his skin and hair green with vegetable dye and make-believes that he's some mythical figure from English folklore, just like all those idiots up in Nottingham who go around saying they're the reincarnations of Robin Hood, and that fellow who thinks he's King Arthur, the one down in Cornwall."

Nowadays it was known as St Piran's Peninsula, but Fen did not correct her. Moira was clearly not interested in accuracy just at this moment.

"And?" he said.

"Well, they're all just stupid sad-arses and they shouldn't be encouraged!"

He took a deep breath. As pretexts for an argument went, it was not one of Moira's better, or for that matter more original, efforts. He kept his voice even, remaining reasonable. "Say what you like, Moira, but they do a lot of good. King Arthur. The Robin Hoods, however many of them there are. That Lob fellow in Oxfordshire. Herne the Hunter over in Kent. Lady Godiva in Coventry. What's-her-name up near Leeds, Queen Mab. Them and all the others. They've kept communities together, given people something to gather around, a rallying point. I admit it's a bit hokey, what they do. The costumes, the folklore aspect of it. A bit daft."

"A *bit!*"

"But without them, certain areas of this country would be in a lot worse shape than they are. Including Downbourne, probably."

"Oh yes. Let's let a bunch of nutters lead us. Let's put the posturing loony show-offs in charge."

Fen gave vent to a rounded, cynical laugh. "Well, isn't that what we've always done? Anyhow, look—I'm really not in the mood for a fight."

"You never are," Moira muttered.

He ignored the comment. Adopting a tone of for-your-information formality, he said, "I'm going downstairs to make something to eat, then I'm going outside to do a spot of work in the garden, then I'm off to the festival, which you may recall is on this evening. If you wish to join me in any of these activities, you're welcome to do so. If not, that's fine too."

Judging this a neat line to exit on, he made for the door. But Moira, as was so often the case, had to have the last word.

"You just don't care any more, do you?" she said, not with rancour, but tiredly, dispiritedly.

Fen shrugged. He could have answered back, made some comment such as *Perhaps if you gave me a reason to care,* but in the event he merely held his tongue and left the room, easing the door shut behind him.

HAMMER IN HAND, a one-inch nail sticking out from the corner of his mouth, Fen stepped back to inspect the repair. The fruit cage looked secure again. Sometime during the day, birds—blackbirds most likely; they were devious buggers, blackbirds—had unpicked one corner of the nylon net curtain that served as a mesh, tugging it away from the frame to create an opening. He reckoned the gang of thieves could not have numbered more than three, because the blackcurrant and raspberry bushes inside the cage hadn't suffered too severely from their depredations. The raiders had eaten their fill, then flown the scene of the crime, and luckily no other members of their species had taken advantage of the opportunity that they had provided. The damage, he gratefully acknowledged, could have been much worse.

He was proud of the fruit cage. He was proud of all his horticultural structures: the fruit cage, the arrangement of canes that supported the runner beans, the cloches he had created out of old mullioned windows, the piano-wire trellises along which he had trained apple and pear trees, the tunnels he had fabricated from bin-liners and straightened coat-hangers to cover his rows of root vegetables. He had never thought of himself as an especially practical person, and so had been pleased and surprised to discover, when put to it, an aptitude for improvised garden engineering. That wasn't to say that the skills had come easily to him. Each project in the garden was the end-product of a lot of sweat and fuss, a significant amount of trial and error, and a great deal of swearing. Nevertheless he had put these contraptions together himself, with his own hands, with little advice or assistance from anyone else, and, rickety though some of them were, they worked. He had learned the basics of produce-growing, too—crop rotation, not putting onions close to peas, things like that—so that now, through knowledge and constant ministration, he and Moira had fresh food to eat and, in times of abundance, exchange for other goods at the weekly town market. By the standards of others this might be considered a minor achievement, but for Fen it was a triumph.

Satisfied with his repair work, he thrust his hammer handle-first into a loop of his belt, like a knight sheathing his sword after the battle is done, then spat the nail into his hand and pocketed it. As he glanced around the garden, wondering if there was anything else that needed to be fixed, he caught sight of Moira at the back door, watching him. She had pulled on a pair of shorts. Other than that, she was exactly as she had been in the bedroom: puffy-faced, somnolent, dishevelled. How long had she been standing there?

He waved to her jauntily, as though the sniping conversation of forty minutes ago had never taken place. "Did you see the bowl on the sideboard? Spanish omelette mix. I've used half for myself. You can use the rest, if you want it. Very tasty."

Moira nodded noncommittally.

"I'm pretty much done here," he continued. "I just need to change my shirt, then it's off down to the festival. Maybe you'll come along too? When you've eaten?"

She fixed him with a look of such spite then, such withering contempt, that had he felt more for her than he did—had there remained any love for her in him beyond a hard-baked residue, the indelible patina left behind by a dozen years of coexistence—he would have been crushed. As it was, the look inspired only weariness. Just for a change, it would be nice to receive a kind word from her, an expression of gratitude however token, a brief acknowledgement of the efforts he made on her behalf, the many things he did for her. Was that really too much to expect?

Probably, he thought. These days, probably.

He headed for the door, and Moira stepped back to allow him through.

"Thank you," he said.

Had Fen known that this was the last time he would see his wife for a long while, might he have said something different? Might he have tried to fix an image in his head of how she looked in the kitchen? Taken a mental snapshot of her, retouching it so that she was not so unsmiling, not so sullen-eyed? Might he have made more of this parting moment, ceremonialised it with all the paraphernalia of taking leave, the speeches, the promises, the drawn-out goodbyes?

Perhaps.

And perhaps, even gifted with foreknowledge of what was to come, Fen would have said and done nothing more than he said and did: "Thank you", and upstairs to find a fresh shirt, and downstairs again and out through the front door without another word, heading down the path and onto the street and, without a backward glance, starting to walk.

THE FRONT DOOR closes and he's gone. All that's left is a faint lingering whiff of his BO from when he washed here earlier.

Maybe you'll come along too? When you've eaten?

Damn him. Damn him and all that I'm-so-thoughtful, I'm-so-fucking-tolerant crap of his. Why can't he just be honest? Why can't he, just for once, come out and say what he really feels? Admit that he can't stand me? He won't even *argue* with me. If he had the guts to argue with me, stand up for himself, at least I'd feel an equal to him. I'd feel like a real person. But oh no, he can't do that. Instead, he's got to humour me. Treat me like a simpleton. A special case.

And it's not strength, being so patient and sensible and understanding. It's not strength, it's weakness. An aggressive type of weakness. Weakness being used as a weapon.

Hard to believe that I used to like that about him. That I used to find it charming that Fen was so agreeable, so compliant all the time. Always so concerned about me, wanting to be sure I was happy.

Why doesn't he just leave me? At least then he'd be showing some spine.

But of course he couldn't do that, could he? He couldn't let the whole town know that we're a failure. So he insists on keeping the illusion going, letting everyone think it's all fine and wonderful with the Morrises... when of course everyone knows the illusion is bogus, everyone knows he's faking, everyone knows we *are* a failure.

Idiot.

Let's have a look in this bowl, then.

Looks like someone's thrown up in it.

I'm not hungry anyway.

But I suppose I shouldn't let it go to waste...

And once I smell the omelette frying, I realise I *am* hungry after all, very hungry, and when the omelette's ready I wolf the whole thing down in about three bites and I actually feel a little grateful to Fen.

Maybe I *should* go along to the stupid festival.

No. I don't have the energy to wander around all evening being nice to people, or pretending to be nice, which is what it'll have to be, and which is much harder work.

Then again, it'll be good to get out of the house for a bit. I'm sick of this place. And Fen won't be expecting me to turn up.

Yes, maybe I'll go, just to spite him.

DOWNBOURNE, LIKE ALMOST every other small provincial town, hadn't been able to evade the hawk-eyed aim of modern commerce. Back in the early nineteen-eighties it had been winged and bulls-eyed by that traditional two-shot attack, the out-of-town supermarket and the pedestrianised shopping precinct, a both-barrels blasting that few of the local retail businesses had survived. Those which the supermarket, part of a massive conglomerate chain, had failed to annihilate, the shopping precinct had comfortably finished off. The precinct had also had the effect of effacing the centre of town. With its mix-and-match selection of established brand-name outlets, it had rendered a segment of Downbourne's High Street effectively anonymous. Standing in the middle of it, one could have been anywhere, in a shopping precinct in any one of countless towns.

That was then. Now was now. The supermarket had long ago closed its doors, rolled away its trolleys and decommissioned its petrol station with the enticing per-litre discount. A few cars, hollow wrecks, still occupied spaces in its car park, as though in anticipation of a grand reopening. Meanwhile, inside the building itself, rats roamed the aisles, hunting for morsels, while pigeons made their nests on the steel ceiling joists and Jackson Pollocked the empty refrigerators and bare shelves with their droppings.

The shopping precinct, likewise, lay abandoned. Gone were the travel bureau, the stationer-cum-newsagent, the fashion boutique, the off-licence, the chemist, the record shop, the electrical-goods store, the choose-from-catalogue emporium. Gone, leaving only empty premises and logo-flagged façades behind.

The precinct, however, had not fallen completely into disuse, since its brick-paved broadway was where Downbourne's residents gathered once a week for market, once a month for town meetings (weather permitting—in town hall if wet), and once a season for festival.

Of the four annual festivals, the summer one was always the best-attended, for the obvious reasons—longer evening, warmer weather. Not only townsfolk came but inhabitants of the outlying villages too, trooping in on foot, on horseback or by bicycle to join in the celebrations. What was actually being celebrated remained something of a mystery. Each of the other three festivals was more-or-less related to a specific calendar event: spring to the vernal equinox, autumn to the harvest, winter to Christmas. Summer was problematic, unless you considered the season itself a cause for rejoicing, as many did. Others regarded the lack of clear *raison d'être* for the summer festival as the best *raison d'être* possible, for what better excuse to be frivolous and have a good time than no excuse at all? For many, too, the absence of celestial, agricultural or religious significance was a kind of statement. It symbolised freedom from tradition, from convention, and therefore a rejection of the past and of a culture which, arguably, could be blamed for England's present parlous state.

Such were the rationalisations, but once the drink was flowing and the music was playing and the dancing got under way, people generally forgot why they were at the festival and simply enjoyed being there.

Approaching the precinct from the direction of the war memorial, Fen heard a drumbeat first, then tinkling music to accompany that drumbeat, then the sound of voices. He had joined a loose-knit, slow-going flow of people, all converging on the same destination. With nods and smiles and innocuous friendly comments, they acknowledged one another. Most were carrying bottles, some whole boxfuls of them, along with china mugs, tin cups, plastic beakers. The bottles contained home-brewed beers, wines and spirits—concoctions that Fen knew from experience could be potent in the extreme. There were seldom any identifying labels on them, so if you were not careful you could find yourself drinking a moonshine strong enough to power a moon-rocket, a gin that was a fatal trap to the unwary, a dandelion wine that could blow you away, a near-homicidal cider. More hazardous yet, you could find yourself mixing your drinks and turning your stomach into the vessel for an uncontrolled experiment in organic chemistry. Getting generously sozzled was all part of the fun of the festival, of course, but Fen had reached the age when the costs of inebriation now far outweighed the pleasures. A hangover was no longer something he could laugh off, the way he used to in his twenties. A hangover was a debilitating, head-clenching nightmare that could lay him out flat for an entire day, and consequently a thing to be avoided if at all possible. He promised himself there and then, as he turned a corner onto the High Street and the precinct came into view, that this evening he would exercise moderation. He knew, however, that it was a promise he might not necessarily be able to keep. Where alcohol was concerned, circumstances had a way of hijacking good intentions. And given the situation at home, if he *were* to get totally plastered—well, who could blame him?

There were perhaps a hundred and fifty people already in the precinct, milling about beneath the lines of tattered bunting strung between the eaves of the shop buildings. Torches—short shafts of wood with tar-soaked rags wrapped around one end—had been fixed to every lamp-post. Their illumination would not be required for another four hours at least. On a podium of trestle tables sat the band: flautist, trumpeter, violinist, accordionist, and drummer with three-piece kit. They were bashing out a jazzed-up version of "Widecombe Fair", each instrument taking it in turns to carry the melody while the others improvised.

Fen moved among the revellers. Since it was still early and there were children present, the mood was good-natured rather than, as it was bound to become later, boisterous. A man in a homemade jester's outfit was juggling three beanbags, now four, now five, for the entertainment of a gaggle of under-tens. Another group of children, teenagers, watched from several yards off, vaguely scornful of the junior group's rapt fascination but also not unimpressed by the juggler's feats. Someone was making bespoke origami animals out of old magazine pages, demonstrating each twist and fold to a mixed-age audience who did their best to follow suit, and in a corner well away from the band a husband-and-wife team of puppeteers had set up a stage and, masked by a screen of bedsheets, were manipulating papier-mâché marionettes to tell the story of *The Prime Minister and the Chancellor*. Meanwhile, the bottles and drinking vessels that people were bringing were being collected and stowed behind the counter of the erstwhile off-licence for later distribution.

At the far end of the precinct, a bonfire-to-be—a tall, teetering mound of wood, like the ruins of a collapsed cathedral—arose from an area of paving that bore the scorch-marks of numerous previous conflagrations. Good-quality firewood was a precious commodity, so for each festival the bonfire builders scavenged the area for the kinds of combustible material that would not fit or burn cleanly in a living-room hearth: big unwieldy chunks of plywood and chipboard, sections of painted timber, with the odd tractor tyre, chair cushion and foam mattress thrown in for good measure. This generated an impressive blaze but also, invariably, an acrid smoke which, if the wind was unfavourable, had been known to bring the festival to an abrupt, choking halt. Tonight, Fen reckoned, they would be spared that. Such breeze as there was, was blowing along the precinct towards the bonfire. The smoke would carry towards the river, most likely staying well above the rooftops.

"Fen!"

It was Alan Greeley, Holly-Anne's father. He and Fen shook hands, Greeley grinning. He was a short, thickset man with an almost cubic head and an air of unfettered geniality about him that made him impossible to dislike. He used this to his advantage when striking deals. Even though, as a customer of Greeley's, you always suspected he was getting the better end of the bargain, somehow you didn't mind. It seemed somehow right and proper that he should profit at your expense, as if there existed an unofficial surcharge for niceness.

"Holly-Anne says she talked to you today. 'The Lesson Man', as she calls you."

"That's me. She wanted me to play dollies with her."

"The dullest game on the planet. They just sit there and have long conversations about the most boring shite you can think of. It's an obligation for parents only. No one else should be expected to endure it."

"At least she's using her imagination. Mind you, kids don't really have a choice these days, do they? It's imagination or nothing. Anyway, I politely declined."

"Good on you. You should have called in, though."

"I was a bit tired. Wanted to get home. Andrea here?"

Greeley shook his head. "Nathan's teething and we thought it better not to bring him out."

"What about Holly-Anne?"

"Over there."

Holly-Anne was among the puppeteers' audience, sitting cross-legged and watching the show with open-mouthed concentration. On the stage, the Prime Minister was arguing with his Chancellor in the House of Commons. The two puppets were yelling the names of various international currencies at each other, their voices growing louder and squeakier by the second. Eventually, enraged beyond endurance, the Prime Minister snatched the Mace off the table in front of him and started bashing the Chancellor over the head with it. The Chancellor retaliated with his battered old red Budget Box. Behind them, rows of cardboard-cutout Members of Parliament jostled up and down. The puppeteers made rhubarby crowd noises to convey outrage. The children squealed with delight.

"A valuable cautionary fable," said Greeley. "Let's hope the younger generation learn from it." He cast a quick glance over Fen's shoulder. "Moira manage to make it?" He phrased the question airily—*just a casual enquiry, nothing meant by it.*

"I don't think she's up to it today."

"Not well?"

"A bit tired. You know."

"Ah. Shame." Greeley leaned closer. "Listen, Fen..."

Fen sensed a sales pitch coming.

"I've just been 'down to the coast', if you know what I mean. Took my cart, did my usual human dray-horse impression, picked up a few nice little items. Toiletry essentials, that sort of thing. I don't suppose you'd be interested in having a look? Priority customer. Ahead of the pack."

"I might. We are a little low on lavatory paper right now."

"Been a while since the last International Community leaflet drop, hasn't it?"

Fen laughed. "'Now is the time for a concerted effort to overthrow the government at Westminster.' It's hard to decide if they're really that ignorant about the situation here or they just have a finely developed sense of irony."

"Still, good absorbency, eh?"

"If only."

"Well, my cross-Channel chums have provided the answer to your prayers."

"*Vive* the Dunkirk spirit."

"Come round and see me tomorrow, and we'll see what we can do for you."

"Sure. OK."

"Oh, and I'd recommend the damson gin in the Perrier bottles."

"Yours, of course."

"Of course."

"Thanks."

"Really, it's very good, even if I do say so myself."

"I'll give it a try."

Greeley trotted off to accost someone else—another potential customer, most likely—and Fen wondered with what he could barter for the lavatory paper tomorrow. Garden produce? He knew Greeley was well catered for on that front. Candles? Greeley was not short of them either.

What about some AA-size batteries? Fen had been given a boxload of them as part-payment for teaching Bill and Janice Sayer's son Clive (he of this afternoon's imagined motor noise). He wasn't certain that all the batteries still worked—a couple of them had leaked their corrosive ichor—but those that did work were undoubtedly valuable. Many people used small portable radios to find out what was going on in the outside world, and also what was going on in their own country, by tuning into news broadcasts from Wales and Scotland. Those radios needed a power source. A couple of four-packs of batteries in exchange for a roll or two of lavatory paper—that would probably do it.

Now the band was performing some medieval-sounding piece, one of those plodding, repetitive hey-nonny-nonny numbers, which they were giving a reggae treatment, to surprisingly good effect. Parents and children were dancing in front of the podium, fathers jiggling toddlers on their shoulders, mothers and older offspring swaying from side to side, hand-in-hand, or clapping together. Watching this display of familial togetherness, Fen felt a sudden and unexpected pang. It was envy, but also it was an emotion far deeper, something closer to grief. He searched around, the emotion turning outwards, becoming resentful, demanding appeasement. He caught sight of Gilbert Cruikshank, sitting hunched on an upturned plastic milk crate, hands resting on the crook of his white-tipped walking stick, chin lodged on top of his hands.

Ah yes.

To look at him, you would have thought Cruikshank was soaking up the atmosphere, relishing the sounds of music and gaiety as they washed over him, deriving delight from the happiness of others. Anyone who knew him, however, would recognise the sneer in the old man's nutcracker smile, the irony with which he nodded along in time to the music. Misanthropic and all but blind, Cruikshank loathed this sort of occasion. He came, like a spectre at the feast, to jar with his presence. He came to silently mock.

"Mr Cruikshank?"

Cruikshank's head twitched. His cheeks and chin were a battlefield of shaving nicks and small patches of bristle his razor had missed. His nose was large and spongy, as only an old man's can be. "Who's that? I know you."

"It's—"

"Don't tell me who it is! It's Morris, isn't it? Our saintly Mr Chips."

"How are you this evening?"

"My hip aches like hell and I have clouds of grey blobs floating in front of my eyes. Like you give a damn."

"You seem to be having fun. It's a marvellous occasion, this, isn't it?"

"It's absolute sodding nonsense and you know it."

"I like to think it brings everyone together. Like that line from Larkin: 'something they share/That breaks ancestrally each year—'"

"Don't ruddy quote poetry at me!"

"'—into/Regenerate union.'"

"I said don't ruddy quote poetry at me!" Cruikshank stabbed the air with an open hand, the gesture aimed in the general direction of the off-licence. "Have they started dishing out the booze yet?"

"Not yet."

"Pity. Otherwise you could have made yourself useful and gone and got me some."

Now the resentment was riding high in Fen. He couldn't curb himself. His tone became breezier as he shifted up to a more piquant level of baiting.

"D'you know something, Mr Cruikshank?"

"What?"

"It puzzles me. Why you always come to the festivals when you so obviously dislike them."

"Why not?"

"In fact, it puzzles me why you live in Downbourne at all."

"What's got into you? What are you jabbering on about?"

"You with your London permit. If I had a London permit, I'd be off up there like a shot. Running water, cars, electricity—all mod cons."

Cruikshank, who had so far kept his focusless gaze fixed straight ahead, now turned his head in Fen's direction, zeroing in on the sound of his voice.

"London's not all it's cracked up to be, Morris, believe me. They're supposed to have things sorted out there, but that's not true. They don't, not really."

"Yes. And also, you wouldn't get the free handouts there that you get here."

"If people want to bring me food, who am I to refuse it? Anyway, who says I have a London permit?"

Fen just chuckled. Cruikshank had left London a little over six years ago when his eyesight began to fail, moving to Downbourne because he had a sister living there. Having had no communication with his sister in a long time, it was only on reaching the town that he learned that she had in fact been dead for a year. However, the difficulties he had experienced on his journey south, and the compassion shown him by the local community, convinced him that he had nothing to lose by staying, so he stayed, although for the first few months he made it clear to anyone who would listen that he could return to London any time he felt like it (perhaps believing that this made his presence in the town somehow the more cherishable). After a while he seemed to realise that this boast, while not hindering his cause, was not helping it either, and so he fell silent on the subject. It was nonetheless reasonable to assume that he was in possession of a London permit—how else could he have left the capital and retain the option of going back?—and it was an assumption Cruikshank had never explicitly refuted.

"Yes, well," Cruikshank said, "one could of course ask *you* a similar question, Morris. Why do *you* persist in living here? I mean, there's nothing to keep you in Downbourne, is there? You could leave any time you wanted."

"And go where?"

"Anywhere."

"But I like it here. I've lived here for fifteen years. And there are my pupils. And there's Moira to consider."

Cruikshank's lips pulled back, revealing an old broken boneyard of teeth. "Ah yes. Moira. Moira who sits around the house all day doing nothing. Darling Moira who hasn't had a civil word to say to you in ages."

"Now, hold on a second. I don't see that that's any of your—"

"I wonder when was the last time you and she actually, you know..." Cruikshank leered. "*Relations*. I wonder, Morris, when was the last time you actually felt like a properly married man."

"Mr Cruik—"

"She was *my* wife, I'd damn well assert my conjugal rights. Force her if I had to. Force her to do what a good wife should."

Fen spun on his heel and stormed off.

"What's the matter, Morris?" Cruikshank called out after him. "Can't handle a few home truths?"

Red-faced, fuming, Fen strode to the opposite side of the precinct, where he could no longer see Cruikshank.

Well, *that* had worked out nicely, hadn't it?

He had got no more than he deserved, of course. He had provoked Cruikshank, misjudging how far he could push him. And Cruikshank was notorious for his sharp tongue. But still...

Bastard.

As if Cruikshank knew anything of how it was with Moira. As if a lonely, crotchety old git like him understood anything about vows and loyalty and patience and hope. Life with Moira would get better, Fen was quite convinced of that. Had to. It was just a matter of time, that was all.

But how long has it been? How many months have you been putting up with her like this? Twelve? Eighteen? Nearly eighteen. For nearly a year and a half you've been making allowances for her. Pitying her. And it's not as if you too weren't affected by what happened eighteen months ago. You deserve pity too.

Fen made a beeline for the former off-licence.

Hazel Watson was laying out cups on the counter. A plumpish woman (she had, before the nation's current state of attrition, been downright fat), Hazel was just good-looking enough and just the right side of middle-aged to make flirting with her a credible proposition, absurd to neither her nor Fen. A few smiles, a couple of well-chosen compliments, and Fen had secured himself a decent-sized dose of Alan Greeley's damson gin. "Only because it's you, Fen," Hazel told him, with a conspiratorial, just-this-once wink.

The damson gin had the colour and consistency of blood, and tasted very little of fruit and very much like fire. Fen gulped it down. Heat seared his oesophagus. He visualised a thermal-imaging picture of himself, his body lit up in rainbow colours, with a sinuous, bright white band tracing the path of the gin from his mouth to his stomach.

That was better.

He was considering whether to go back for a second helping when he heard the band launch into "Greensleeves", the tune that traditionally accompanied the official arrival of the Green Man at the festivities. Craning his neck, he saw the Green Man enter the precinct and proceed towards the podium, greeting people as he went, bestowing nods and smiles on either side. Arriving at the podium, he exhorted everyone to carry on dancing, and joined in himself.

He was not what you might call a natural mover. It was clear from his rictus grin, the inhibitedness of his gesticulations, that he considered dancing to be a necessary indulgence, beneath his dignity. Yet he danced anyway, and the crowd danced with him, taking their cue from him, swaying as he swayed, falling in line like breeze-brushed corn. All at once, where the Green Man was had become the focus of things. All other activities ceased. The children in the precinct couldn't take their eyes off him. The same, Fen noted, was true of most of the adults. As if unable to help themselves, everybody moved towards him, summoned by some tug inside, needing, fascinated. The desire to be close to him and do as he did was all but overwhelming.

The music swelled and accelerated, the band progressing from "Greensleeves" to "Green Grow the Rushes" in a transition so smooth it seemed that even they themselves were not aware they had done it. The dancers picked up their pace, and then the Green Man, with his stern jollity, broke into song:

> "...What is your one-oh?
> One is one and all alone
> And ever more shall be so."

No further prompting was necessary. Dozens of voices joined in at the top of the next verse, and the precinct resounded to the chorusing of the song's countdown lyrics, words that over the course of centuries had lost their meaning but now, in this England, seemed to make an arcane kind of sense again:

> "...Three, three, the rivals,
> Two, two, the lily-white boys,
> Clothèd all in green-oh,
> One is one and all alone
> And ever more shall be so."

Fen was among the very few who did not take part, either as dancer or singer. He adopted, instead, a detached stance, happy to observe and ponder. He felt the same affinity for the Green Man as everyone else, the same attraction to him, and yet was distanced enough from the feeling to wonder at its nature. What was it about the Green Man that commanded this attention, this affection? Perhaps it was just that old indefinable, charisma. Michael Hollingbury certainly had it in spades.

But Fen wondered, too, whether the allure was not altogether more fundamental; whether, by adopting the guise of a mythic archetype, Hollingbury hadn't also adopted some of that archetype's power. The Green Man, as a concept, had survived for centuries, openly during pagan times, latent during more rational, orthodox eras. Perhaps a male incarnation of Nature was an iconic image preprogrammed into the human software, an evolutionary default setting. That was why people responded to Hollingbury so positively; why, for all his grandiloquence, his pomposity, he commanded loyalty and respect.

Or was that just a load of Jungian bollocks?

"Green Grow the Rushes" rolled to its conclusion, and the Green Man took this as a signal—possibly an excuse—to call a halt to the proceedings and beg in a loud voice for silence. As silence came, in dribs and drabs, he clambered up onto the podium where everyone could see him.

"Friends," he said, "fellow townspeople, neighbours, I shall keep this short."

Predictably, a couple of humourists yelled out, "Hear hear!"

"In these uneasy times," the Green Man continued, unabashed, "there are few certainties and even fewer causes for cheer. This, the Downbourne summer festival, is one. We come together here, as we have for several years now, to roister and revel, and defy misery with our laughter, just as summer, with its warmth, defies winter. The rest of the world has turned its back on this country and treats us with arrogance and contempt. It blockades our ports and punishes us randomly with missiles and bombs. Even our fellow Britons despair of us and despise us, erecting walls and defences to keep us out. Yet we are still England. England endures in us."

This time the "Hear hear!" was widespread and heartfelt.

"And here, tonight, in Downbourne, we commemorate that fact. With song and dance and merriment, we show the world that we are not bowed, that our spirits are not broken. We—"

The rest of the speech would forever go unheard, for at that moment a distant rumble echoed through the town, a deep mechanical drone, low at first but rapidly gaining in strength and volume, and a few perplexed murmurs drifted up from the crowd, coalescing into a nervous hubbub. Engines? Yes, engines. Lots of them.

Heads turned this way, that way. It was hard to tell where precisely the sound was coming from. It seemed to be coming from all directions at once.

Then the first of the vans appeared, rolling down the High Street towards the precinct.

THE VAN, A white Ford Transit with tinted windows, moved like a cruising predator, certain of itself, unnervingly unhurried. People coming to the festival along the High Street scuttled out of its way, seeking the sanctuary of the kerb, to stand and stare as it rumbled by. To them, and to those in the precinct, the van was an apparition of a kind they had not set eyes on in years, a ghost from the past, a once-familiar sight that had been made, by its abrupt recession from their lives, infinitely strange. Eyes were wide. Fingers pointed. Children pressed themselves against their parents.

Then a second van appeared, trailing in the wake of the first. A little Bedford, also white, also with tinted windows.

Simultaneously, at the other end of the precinct where the bonfire stood, a third white van, a lofty-sided Luton, drove up to the iron bollards that had been put there to enforce the distinction between pedestrian and non-pedestrian territory. A fourth pulled up in swift succession.

And now another white van hove into view on the High Street, and another, and yet another; an entire convoy of them, all makes and models, and more appeared beyond the bollards. In no time both ends of the precinct were blocked off, the vans parking at angles to one another, interleaving, forming an almost impenetrable cordon.

It was only then, as the festival-goers in the precinct realised that the vans had trapped them in a pincer movement, cutting them off from the rest of town, that their murmurs mounted to a clamour and a sense of panic began to swell. Fen saw Gilbert Cruikshank turning his head this way and that, demanding that someone, anyone, tell him what was going on. On the podium, the Green Man appealed for calm. He had to shout to make himself heard.

The white vans sat there, motors idling, windscreens menacingly blank, radiator grilles grinning. No one seemed in any hurry to disembark from them.

Gradually the Green Man's pleas began to take effect. It was either that or the puzzling reluctance of the vans' occupants to emerge that led to voices petering out among the crowd and an anxious quiet prevailing. The vans' engines growled on, the smell of diesel exhaust permeating the precinct, causing a number of people to cover their noses. The Green Man fixed his gaze on the vanguard van, the Transit. He waited. Everyone waited.

At last, the Transit's engine cut out, its driver-side door opened, and a man climbed out onto the road.

He was short and stockily built, and his hair had been shaved to a fine down, a transparent fur cap. He had a lumpen nose, evidently once broken, and eyes that were set deep in their sockets, as though pushed into place by force. He was dressed in a polo shirt, tracksuit bottoms and trainers, all of them adorned with trademark logos, and there were tattoos on his arms and neck, blurry blue statements of oath and fealty. One was a monochrome Union jack. Another, on his right biceps, was simply two words in Gothic script:

King Cunt

The man stared, hard and contemptuously, at the crowd. Dangling from his right hand, twitching like a pendulum, was a stubby length of two-by-four.

Then another van door opened and another man stepped out. He was almost the twin of the first—same close-cropped hair, similar clothing, tattoos. Slightly taller, slightly leaner, but from a distance the two of them could well have been brothers. From *his* hand hung a stainless steel baseball bat.

And then more such lookalikes were climbing out from all the vans, from their front-seat doors, from their rear doors, from their sliding side doors. The vans rocking and jolting, the men filed out like paratroopers, falling swiftly into position, forming a line across either end of the precinct, a dozen of them, two dozen, three, four. Sportswear was their uniform, close-cropped hair their chosen tonsorial style, tattoos their *de rigueur* body ornament, along with the occasional earstud or signet ring. Though of various sizes and shapes and complexions, they all conformed to a sartorial template, doing their best to resemble one another, or one particular exemplar, as closely as possible. And all of them toted hitting weapons of some kind—if not a length of two-by-four or a baseball bat, then a cricket bat, or a broom handle sawn in half and brandished like a truncheon.

Still more of these men appeared, and the Downbourne residents began drawing together, moving towards the middle of the precinct, putting distance between them and the strangers. It was the instinctive response of the gazelle herd when the lions appear, gathering into a tight knot so that no single individual stands out and makes itself a target. Fen happily became a part of the communal merge. By his estimate, the Downbournians outnumbered the new arrivals three to one, but that made no difference. There were old people and children here, and the new arrivals were true thugs. Professionals in violence. It was written in their physiques, their stares, the stance that each of them adopted: head slightly cocked, feet apart at shoulder-width, muscle-corded arms folded or hanging at their sides with cocky insouciance. Even unarmed, each would have been a match for any three Downbourne adults.

Only the Green Man was not cowed, or if he was, he gave no sign of it. Standing his ground on the podium, he eyed up the opposition, his gaze finally settling on the driver of the Transit, the first of the interlopers to have shown his face.

"You, sir," he said, pointing to him. "Whatever you may want here, we do not have it. Please leave."

The other man took the suggestion on board, seemed actually to consider it, and then smiled, displaying a glint of gold tooth. "You know what?" he said. "You don't half look a twat."

There was a churning sound, laughter, from his near-identical cohorts. Shoulders pumped up and down.

The man with the gold tooth, pleased that his witticism had been so well received, decided to expand it into a full-blown comedy routine: "In fact, you look like a fucking human cabbage. Don't he, lads? Was your mum fucked by a cucumber? Was your dad a fucking cucumber? Or was it the Jolly Green Giant? The Jolly Green Giant stuck his jolly green dick up your mum, and you were the result. And what's that lawn doing stuck to your head? Oh yeah, it's not a lawn, it's hair."

The Green Man bore the invective impassively, while Gold Tooth's colleagues chortled and guffawed their appreciation.

Then, when Gold Tooth had run out of permutations on the theme of greenness, the Green Man said, "I've asked you to leave. Please do so. We are a poor, peaceful town, holding a small celebration. We have nothing for you, and we don't want any trouble."

"Ah now, that's a shame, innit," said Gold Tooth. "'Cause *we* do, don't we, lads?"

There was a lowing cheer of assent.

"'Cause what are we?"

As one, the men from the white vans cried, "British Bulldogs!"

"And who's our boss?"

"King Cunt!"

"And what does he like?"

"Havoc!"

This finely-turned example of strophe and antistrophe was evidently a prearranged cue for the so-called British Bulldogs to attack, for no sooner had they uttered the word "Havoc!" than they launched themselves at the assembled Downbournians, laying into all and sundry with their weapons. People screamed and ran this way and that, trying to escape. Parents carried children, or crouched around them to protect them. The puppet-show stage was knocked over and collapsed with a splintering of wood and a billow of bedsheet. With practised efficiency the Bulldogs set about their victims, teeth bared in ravenous glee. All at once the world became a milling, buffeting, terrified confusion, and Fen was in the thick of it. He glimpsed a Bulldog coming straight for him and took evasive action, moving left, but this brought him into contact with another Bulldog, who was busy belabouring someone with a baseball bat (the victim was a neighbour of Fen's on Crane Street, Stephen Talbot, or so Fen thought, although he could not tell for sure on account of all the blood). The Bulldog broke off from his task to lash out sideways at Fen with the bat, catching him a glancing blow on the shoulder, and as Fen reeled away he collided with the man in the jester costume, the juggler, Saul Oliver was his name, and he clawed at Fen, trying to shove him out of the way, but then a Bulldog caught Oliver by the collar of his jester's tunic, yanked him backwards and set about him with his fists, punching him again and again in the face, while Fen stumbled off in another direction.

It wasn't all fear and fleeing on the part of the residents of Downbourne. There were small pockets of resistance as here, there, people stood up to the Bulldogs, attempting to fight them as equals. Fen glimpsed Alan Greeley trading punches with a fellow almost twice his size. He saw the flautist from the band, Colleen someone-or-other, pounding the back and shoulders of a Bulldog with her instrument while he, apparently oblivious to her blows, continued to stomp on the shin of one of her fellow band-members, the accordionist, who lay on the ground, writhing. Up on the podium, the Green Man was grappling with the Bulldog with the gold tooth, both men holding on to the length of two-by-four, each trying to wrest it from the other's grasp. While Fen looked on, one of the trestle tables beneath them overturned and they went crashing out of sight in a flail of limbs.

For all that, the outcome was inevitable. The British Bulldogs had chosen their moment well. An hour later, and there would have been too many locals present, more than even they would have dared to tackle. With that tactical genius common to all bullies, they had picked a fight they knew they couldn't lose.

Fen, to his astonishment still barely scathed, reeled through the mêlée, all around him blood and thumps and yelps of pain and the shrilling of frightened children. He hunched low, trying not to draw attention to himself. He was no fighter. He had never raised a hand in anger, not even as a kid. He saw fists and feet and weapons inflicting damage, and he cringed inwardly, praying it would not be his turn next.

Then, appearing almost magically in front of him through the throng: an open doorway. The off-licence. He stumbled towards it, obeying some animal imperative, the need for shelter when the storm comes down. There was a back room, he recalled. Somewhere in there he might be able to hide till all this was over.

He made it through the door and as far as the counter, and then heard footsteps behind him and a shout of "Oi!"

Instinctively, not fully comprehending what he was doing, Fen reached for one of the dozens of bottles stowed behind the counter. He snatched it up and hurled it desperately at the Bulldog behind him. The projectile found its mark, but Fen had made a poor choice of weapon. A glass bottle might have done some harm, might even have knocked the man unconscious, but the one that had come to hand was plastic. It struck the Bulldog on the shoulder, splitting on impact and showering him with a clear yellow liquid, then bouncing off onto the floor and rolling away, leaking.

The Bulldog wiped his face, snarled "Wanker!" and lunged at Fen.

WITHIN MINUTES, IT was over. Across the precinct the festival-goers sat in defeated clusters. Here and there a body lay sprawled on the brick paving—whether dead or out cold, it was impossible to say. The British Bulldogs, meanwhile, strutted around, clapping one another on the back, sharing jokes, and every so often breaking into a chant, gracing the tune of "Rule, Britannia" with lyrics of their own:

> "British Bulldogs!
> We're tough, we're brave, we're class
> And... if... you get in our way
> We'll kick your arse."

Fen was in one of the clusters. He hunkered miserably down, beset by injuries. His lower lip was a stinging bulge of flesh that tasted of blood when he probed it with his tongue. He could feel his left eye swelling, the lids thickening and tightening. A finger felt broken (although it was probably just badly bruised). The left side of his ribcage throbbed. Each source of pain had a cycle of intensity, increasing and then abating, and the cycles were out of phase, so that the pain became a kind of sonata, an interplay of crescendos and diminuendos that every so often coincided and massed to a gruelling peak. He could only be grateful, for what it was worth, that the Bulldog who had attacked him had elected not to use the cricket bat he was carrying, preferring instead the medium of feet and fists. In the Bulldog's own words, as he had set the bat aside: "You ain't worth the trouble."

Worse than the pain, though, and the vague humiliation of being deemed too unthreatening an opponent to merit assault by cricket bat, was the fact that someone whom Fen had never seen before in his life and with whom he had no quarrel had taken it upon himself to hurt him. That, somehow, was the truly awful part. Not the beating itself, but the injustice, the *affront* of it. What had he done to deserve such treatment? By the expressions on the bloodied, bowed faces around him, he could tell others were asking themselves the same question.

The children, thank God, had been spared. Though, like all the adults, they were shiveringly scared, none of them had been attacked, so far as Fen could determine. The British Bulldogs had left them alone. That was something.

Amid the turmoil of his thoughts, Fen remembered Moira. Earlier, on the way here, he had felt guiltily relieved that she wasn't with him. At the last festival she attended, winter the previous year, she had embarrassed him by moping around with a face like thunder, refusing to talk to anyone, then heading home after less than an hour, complaining she was cold. Now, he found he was still relieved that she wasn't with him, but, happily, for a far more charitable reason.

There, Cruikshank, he thought. Isn't that suitably husband-like behaviour, to be glad that your wife is safe and well, even while you yourself are suffering? Isn't that what one would expect of a "properly married man"?

Of course, that was not exactly the point that Cruikshank had been making. And Fen wasn't, he realised, that much more concerned about Moira's welfare than he was about the welfare of the children here. And it said a lot about the state of his marriage that he had to consider justifying himself, even in his thoughts, to someone like Gilbert Cruikshank.

His various bodily aches and pains came together in throbbing, sickening symphony, then receded again.

He wondered what was happening beyond the precinct. The rest of the town had to have heard the vans, and the people coming to the festival had seen the British Bulldogs close in on the precinct. They must have been able to deduce, from the rumpus, what had gone on subsequently. The question was, what were they going to do about it? Might they get together and launch an attack on the Bulldogs in an effort to liberate their fellow townspeople? Had the Green Man been out there to organise them, then yes, doubtless they might. As it was, Fen thought the likelihood of a rescue attempt a slim one, and even if such a thing did take place, he rated its chances of success as minimal. The Bulldogs had the precinct sealed off. They would be able to hold out with ease against any incursion. They were free to do whatever they liked with the people they were holding captive here.

All at once, through his misery and the ebb and flow of his pain, Fen became aware of a crackling sound, and then the peppery, pungent smell of woodsmoke. He looked up.

The British Bulldogs had pulled down the torches from the lamp-posts, ignited them using the cigarette lighters from their vans' dashboards, and thrown them onto the bonfire. Separate cores of flames were brightening and growing, gathering strength, slowly uniting.

Why had they lit the fire? What were they going to do with it?

An answer occurred to him.

He didn't like it.

As the flames took hold, reaching up into the guts of the bonfire, seething and raging, two of the British Bulldogs dragged the Green Man in front of their gold-toothed leader.

The outcome of the fight between Gold Tooth and the Green Man was abundantly clear. The Bulldog stood erect, chest out, hands clasped together behind his back sergeant-major style. One sleeve of his T-shirt was slightly torn, but that was it as far as damage went. The Green Man, by contrast, sagged, staring vacantly ahead, his eyes white moons amid the glistening, blood-marbled pulp that had been his face. The two Bulldogs gripped him firmly by the arms, but their task was more one of support than one of restraint. Without them, the Green Man would have been incapable of remaining upright.

Gold Tooth eyed his vanquished opponent for a moment, then reached for the Green Man's shirt collar and wrenched downwards. Buttons tore, and the Green Man's chest and navel were exposed. Below the level of his collarbone, his skin was pallidly, vulnerably white, his chest and belly wisped with unremarkable brown hair.

Gold Tooth nodded as if this was no more than he had expected. He jerked a thumb, and his two cohorts hauled the Green Man off to the bonfire.

The Downbournians, in their huddled groups, watched in dull horror as the two British Bulldogs, grimacing against the heat from the bonfire, held the Green Man out in front of them, offering him a foretaste of his fate. At first the Green Man was too dazed to react, but the heat soon stirred him to his senses. His eyes swirled and found a focus in the flames. His mouth began to move, but no words came out, only a long stringy gobbet of blood that unspooled to the ground. The Bulldogs pushed him closer to the bonfire and held him there for several seconds while patches of his facial hair crinkled and shrivelled. Then, laughing, they pulled him back.

"Want me to put that out?" one of them offered, gesturing at the Green Man's singed beard and eyebrows, and then at his own crotch. "Got my fire extinguisher right here."

There was, in the throat of every Downbournian looking on, a cry of protest, a great painful *NO!*, caught like a fishbone, impossible either to choke out or to swallow down.

The Bulldogs assembled around the bonfire to watch, and a debate sprang up among them as to whether the Green Man should be thrown into the flames head-first or feet-first. Then Gold Tooth said, "Hold up, fellas. I think he wants to say something."

A mockingly attentive silence fell.

"Come on, out with it, mate. Your famous last words."

The Green Man moaned a few mumbled phrases.

"Louder," said Gold Tooth, grinning. "Can't hear you."

The Green Man repeated himself. Fen caught only snatches of what he said. Something about immortality. Being impossible to kill. You could harm him but never destroy him.

Fen would never be able to decide if the Green Man genuinely believed this or if it was just bravado.

Either way, it didn't save him.

Gold Tooth started the countdown.

"Three!" he shouted, and the Green Man was swung backwards.

"Two!" the rest of the Bulldogs joined in, and parents covered their children's eyes, and some of the Downbournians looked away and others wished they could.

"One!" the Bulldogs all yelled together, and the Green Man, groaning, was launched forward and propelled headlong into the bonfire's heart.

He shrieked and writhed for a full minute. After that, he no longer shrieked, and his body continued to move only involuntarily, twisting and squirming as it cooked, contorting with heat and internal pressures, flesh bubbling greasily. The British Bulldogs cheered, faces aglow with the bonfire's radiance, while the air was filled with a horrid barbecue stench that set several Downbournians retching.

On a pyre of denatured wood and man-made products, the Green Man slowly roasted.

HAVING JUST SEEN their mayor burned to death, the captive Downbournians could do nothing other than meekly comply when the British Bulldogs ordered them to get to their feet. With Gold Tooth issuing instructions, the townspeople were separated into three groups, men, women and children. The men were then subdivided into smaller groups and herded off, limping and shuffling, into the surrounding buildings. Fen was pushed, along with five others, into a stockroom at the back of the one-time record shop, a musty, windowless space littered with broken shards of CD case and trodden scraps of old promotional poster.

"Stay in there and keep your traps shut," one of their escorts told them, and slammed the door, leaving them in total darkness.

For a while the six of them did as advised and kept quiet. There was a clenched, agonised knot in each man's belly. Each was certain that what had been done to the Green Man was going to be done to him too. This stockroom was merely a temporary holding pen, an antechamber to death.

Finally one of them, unable to contain his dread any longer, started whimpering. Somebody else told him to shut up, but this only succeeded in making the whimperer more vocal, not less. He began to babble, uttering imprecations to the Almighty, a patchwork of fragments of half-remembered prayers.

"Please, for heaven's sake, stop," said Fen, his voice tight and tremulous too. His fat lip had given him a slight lisp. "They'll come for us first if you don't stop."

That did succeed in silencing the whimperer, though had he, whoever he was, been thinking more clearly, he would perhaps have spotted the logic-flaw in what Fen had just said, namely that it made little difference whether the British Bulldogs came for them first or last, and indeed postponing the inevitable might well, under the circumstances, be a bad thing.

For the next few minutes the six men did nothing but listen. They heard one another's breathing and, dimly, like a portent of another, more lasting inferno, the crackle and roar of the bonfire.

Finally someone, in the faintest of whispers, said: "Why?"

"Why what?" said someone else, no more loudly. The second speaker was Henry Mullins, town councillor.

"Why are they here? Why are they doing this to us?"

"Because they can," said a third hushed voice, which Fen knew to be that of Donald Bailey, retired policeman and elder brother (by a year) of Reginald, the footbridge fisherman.

"Donald," Fen said, "it's me, Fen Morris."

"I know you're here, Fen. There's also Andrew Quinlan, right? And young Kenny Gibbs."

The latter mumbled an assent, and judging by the direction his voice came from Fen was pretty sure Kenny had been the one whimpering. He felt sorry for him. Kenny, not much older than twenty, had simply been articulating what everyone in the room was feeling.

"'Because they can'?" Fen prompted Donald.

"Because we can't stop them and they know it. Why else do you think they've come all the way down here? Fifty miles' worth of diesel. Hundred, if you bear in mind it's a round-trip. That's a hell of a lot of fuel. But they knew when they got here it'd be worthwhile, because there'd be no opposition to speak of. Up in London, they'd never get away with this sort of thing. The other gangs. There's a kind of truce on. A balance of power. Down here..." Fen didn't need to be able to see Bailey to know that he had just shrugged.

"You're sure they're from London?" asked Mullins.

"That accent? That tribal look? Of course they are."

"But the International Community..." This was Kenny talking now, offering up those two words—International Community—which had become, to the English, both a curse and another name for God. "I thought the whole point of the bombings and the blockades was to keep people like those lot in their place."

Someone laughed hollowly.

"Unfortunately, Kenny," Fen said, as kindly as he could in order to compensate for the laughter, "what the International Community claims it's trying to achieve and what it actually does achieve are two different things."

"*Very* different things," Mullins chipped in.

"Fact is," said Donald, "I reckon we should count ourselves lucky."

"Oh yeah? And just how do you come to *that* conclusion?" This comment, scornful and with an edge of hysteria, came from a new source in the room, its sixth occupant. Fen recalled glimpsing, just before the stockroom door was closed, an out-of-towner among them. The man's face was familiar but Fen had no idea of his name.

"Lucky it hasn't happened sooner," Donald elaborated, patiently. "We've all heard of London gangs straying beyond the M25, haven't we? It was only a matter of time before one of them got this far. Actually, I'm surprised it took this long."

"Oh well, that's great," said the out-of-towner. "That makes me feel a whole lot better."

"I'm not saying it to make anyone feel better. I'm saying it as a statement of fact."

"Perhaps we *should* have been prepared for it," said Andrew Quinlan.

"The Green Man mentioned something like that to me the other day," said Mullins. "He said Downbourne has had it peaceful for so long, there's been so little trouble in this area, that if trouble does come we won't be ready for it and we won't be able to defend ourselves against it."

"Well, great," said the out-of-towner. "That's great. So the Green Man knew this was going to happen."

"It was just a passing comment. He couldn't have predicted this."

"Yeah, well. Still. Serves him right what's happened to him, then."

"Hey!" said Mullins. "That man was a friend of mine, you know."

"All right, keep it down, everybody," urged Donald. Voices had risen somewhat. "Come on, let's be calm."

Mullins muttered some comment about respect for the dead, and an unhappy silence prevailed.

Then Fen said, "I heard a van engine this afternoon. Well, not me. A boy in my class did. It must have been them. The British Bulldogs. Reconnoitring. If they'd come in on the northern road, they could have stopped a mile outside town, on the rise there. Up there they'd have got a good view of everything. They'd have seen the festival preparations, the bonfire, all that."

"Your point being?" said the out-of-towner.

"Nothing, except..." Except he should have believed Clive Sayer. He should have informed the Green Man that a vehicle engine had been heard at the outskirts of town. Would it have made a difference? Perhaps. Then again, perhaps not. "Well, it might at least explain how they knew we'd be here, a whole lot of us together in one place at one time."

"But it still doesn't explain why they're doing this," said Quinlan, who was the one who had raised the question of the Bulldogs' motives in the first place. "Unless it's just to... you know, for kicks."

"Locusts," said Donald. "They're like locusts. Swarm all over a place, stripping it bare."

"Of what?"

"Food, supplies, things they can't get in London, or can't get easily."

"That might mean they aren't going to kill us," said Kenny.

"Possibly," agreed Donald.

It was only a small *possibly*, a thin fingernail of a likelihood, but all of them, even Kenny and the out-of-towner, drew succour from it. Suddenly the outlook no longer seemed bleak. Suddenly there was a chance, just a chance, that they might survive this after all.

As time passed, that chance appeared to improve. No one came to fetch them for the bonfire. Even more reassuringly, although they heard voices out in the precinct, sometimes shouting, there were no screams or entreaties or other sounds to indicate that a programme of systematic execution was under way. It still didn't seem safe to believe that everything was going to turn out all right, but as the minutes ticked by, the odds against their imminent immolation lengthened and more and more reasons suggested themselves as to why the British Bulldogs might spare everyone's lives. What, besides an arbitrary, bloodthirsty thrill, would the Bulldogs have to gain from slaughtering a couple of hundred people? They had killed the Green Man just to set an example, to demonstrate to the townspeople that they meant business, to intimidate them even further than they were already intimidated. Not only that but, without their leader, the captive Downbournians were less likely to mount a concerted resistance.

So the men's fears, which they could now perceive to have been exaggerated, began to subside. They weren't about to die. They felt this, they hoped it, but they were not sufficiently confident to put it to the test. None of them dared open the door and take a peek outside to see what was going on. The possibility was raised and rejected several times. What, and be spotted by a Bulldog standing guard outside? That, surely, would invite down on their heads the fate they were beginning to believe they were going to evade. And since the door was secured by a Yale catch, the option of peeping through a keyhole was out.

Gradually, one after another, the six men settled down on the floor, each finding an area for himself, fitting his legs in around the others' legs.

There wasn't a chink of light in the stockroom. The darkness was absolute. In the invisible proximity of five others, each of the men waited. Silent. Afraid. Hoping.

In all, the townspeople shut away by the British Bulldogs in the back rooms of the shops spent a little over half an hour as prisoners. To some of them it felt a great deal longer, to others barely a few minutes. Half an hour was what it was, however, and although they didn't realise it, throughout that time they were not, strictly speaking, prisoners at all. No one was standing guard outside their makeshift cells. The doors were not locked. They could have opened them and walked out any time, had they dared. Just as the Bulldogs had intended, fear was their jailer. Fear kept them subdued and in place, while the Bulldogs took what they had come for and departed.

No sooner had the last of the white vans vanished from view than the people who were left in the precinct hurried to liberate those who were interned in the shops, while the people who had been prevented from entering the precinct now came rushing in, demanding to know what had been going on. With the rumble of diesel engines still audible in the air, but dwindling fast, out came the prisoners, blinking in the early-evening light, shielding their eyes against the low sun and the flare of the bonfire. Children ran to fathers. Husbands and wives were reunited, often tearfully.

But some reunions did not take place. People were missing, and the ex-prisoners were soon enlightened as to what had gone on in the precinct during their incarceration.

Only the menfolk had been forced into the shops. The Bulldogs had then gone among the women and children like prospective buyers at a cattle market, grading and evaluating. Selections had been made, and those chosen—all females, all young, all classifiable as attractive—had been manhandled into the vans. Anyone who refused to go or who struggled had been threatened with the bonfire or a further beating. All told, some dozen women had been taken. The oldest was thirty-nine, the youngest fifteen.

The news was met with silence. Then rage.

But the rage was unfocused, diffuse. Mainly it was outrage, which is rage of the least productive kind. There were protests and expressions of indignation and half-formed plans of action and plenty of impassioned breast-beating. No one, however, had any clear suggestion to make, any clear idea what to do. Somebody proposed chasing after the Bulldogs on horseback. Somebody else pointed out that, even if a horse rider did manage to catch up with the vans, what then? He was just going to ask them to pull over? Another idea mooted was to send a delegation over to Wyndham Heath, the nearest large town, where there was a police station still open and still staffed. But the police station, everyone knew, was of chiefly symbolic significance. Run by volunteers, few of them trained law-enforcement professionals, it was, for the residents of Wyndham Heath and its immediate environs, a comforting reminder of past certainties, but its efficacy in pursuing wrongdoers and punishing their misdemeanours was negligible.

The dispiriting truth, which none of the Downbournians present wanted to acknowledge yet, was that they were helpless. A dozen women had been abducted—wives, mothers, daughters, girlfriends, friends—and, realistically, there was nothing anyone could do about it except wail and agonise and despair.

The bonfire burned on, sending gouts of black smoke up into the air, as a pall of gloom settled over the festival-goers. A few people, those not directly affected by the abductions, started to drift away, heading home to nurse wounds or put children to bed. Others knelt to tend to the victims whom the British Bulldogs had beaten senseless, checking to see how badly they were hurt and attempting to revive them. The rest congregated in knots of three or four and continued arguing, not only about the monstrous offences the Bulldogs had committed but also, now, about whether the whole terrible episode could somehow have been prevented. Here and there, people stood alone or in clutching couples, weeping, desolate.

Fen, surveying the scene, decided there was little to be gained by remaining. He was unable to open his left eye at all now, his bruised finger had swollen to sausage size, and his ribcage was so sore that it hurt to breathe. Time to go home.

He wondered how Moira would react when he showed up, battered and bruised, and told her what he had just been through. Probably with her usual indifference.

But maybe not.

"Oh God, Fen. Those poor women. Poor you*! Look at you. Thank heaven it's not worse, that's all I can say. I mean, those men, they could have... I don't even want to think about it."*

Yes. Maybe this was the catalyst he had been waiting for. The jump-start his marriage needed. Seeing him hurt, learning about the women being abducted—maybe it would startle Moira out of her Slough of Despond. Bring her round like a dash of icy water. It wasn't entirely inconceivable. Maybe that was the good that would come of this episode, the silver lining to this cloud.

As Fen was leaving the precinct, Donald Bailey fell in step beside him.

"See you've had the same idea," Donald commented. "Not much point in sticking around."

Fen nodded.

"How you doing?"

"Been better."

"Any aspirin at home? Paracetamol? Something like that?"

"I think so. Well out-of-date, but..."

"Better than nothing. Of course, an ice pack would do wonders for that eye."

"An ice pack frozen how?"

They turned off from the High Street, heading towards the war memorial. Fen observed that Donald was favouring one leg as he walked. He also saw dried blood, cracked and black, encrusting the rims of the old man's nostrils.

"How bad did they hurt you?"

"Could have been worse. Would have been, if I'd fought back. Maybe I should have, but sod it, I'm sixty-three. Thirty years ago—well, then it would have been a different story. Obviously *you* stood up for yourself."

"Um... yes," said Fen. Well, he *had* thrown that bottle. He moved swiftly on to another subject. "So, what do you think's going to happen to them? The women they took?"

"I really don't want to imagine. What really gets me is it's so damn barbarian. So damn Genghis Khan. They come, they kick us around, they steal our womenfolk. I mean, what century is this?"

"Think there's any chance we can get them back?"

"Doubt it. Look at it this way. London's a big place, and even if we did know where these British Bulldogs live, what part of the city they call home, how are we going to get there? No permits, and I don't know about you but I don't fancy my chances trying to get across the M25. You'd have to be mad even to think about it."

"Perhaps we *should* send someone over to Wyndham Heath."

"What for? You don't need to be an ex-copper to know there's no law there. There's no law anywhere, at least not 'law' in the sense that we used to understand it. There's just people agreeing to pull together and pool their resources and get on, and then there's people like the Bulldogs who come along and take advantage. And until things improve, if they ever do, that's just how it's going to be. I know how you're feeling, Fen. I'm the same. Sickened and angry. They took Frank Fothergill's kid. Did you know that? Zoë. Fifteen. Fifteen years old. That's plain evil. Don't think I wouldn't move heaven and earth to get that child out of their clutches, if I thought I had any chance of succeeding. But I can't. At least, I don't think I can." Donald sighed. "Sometimes, you know, I wonder if brother Reg isn't the only sensible one among us. He may be a bit simple, but... Go down to the river every day and fish. Don't think about any of it, just let it happen around you. Maybe that's the way to be. Anyhow..." He halted and gestured towards a side-street. "Here's where you and I go our separate ways. See you around."

Fen continued homewards alone. He was finding walking tricky with only one functioning eye. Distances were hard to judge and he had to concentrate on every step, making sure his feet came down where they were supposed to. Wherever he went, townspeople were out on the streets, gathered in groups. There was distress in their faces, disgust in their voices. Word of events at the precinct was spreading outward through town, like tremors from the epicentre of an earthquake. Beneath a dusk-tinged sky and an early, opalescent moon, Downbourne was assessing and assimilating its misfortune.

On the corner of King Alfred Street and Harvill Drive, Fen had to stop. All at once his legs felt rubbery, boneless, and he was cold all over, shaking uncontrollably. He grabbed a wall to steady himself while the shudders passed through him, beginning at his groin and running up through his chest. He saw the Bulldogs rushing through the precinct, hitting, kicking, beating, bludgeoning, hurting. He saw himself on the off-licence floor, curled up on his side, his ribs getting stamped on. He saw the Green Man being tossed into the bonfire like so much human lumber.

Nausea overcame him. His stomach heaved. He bit back bile. He told himself he would not vomit. It was just shock. Delayed reaction. He would not vomit.

Gradually the shaking subsided, and Fen took a few deep breaths, then looked up. There were people around him, some of them neighbours, faces he knew, faces showing concern. Concern and... something else? Something more?

One woman, Beth Allworthy, laid a hand on his shoulder. "Fen?"

He nodded weakly. "I'm fine," he said hoarsely. "Just need to..." He straightened up. "Need to get home."

"Fen, please understand," Beth said, "there was nothing we could do."

Fen frowned at her. "What do you mean?"

"They came this way," said someone else. "Those vans."

"They just climbed out and grabbed her," said a third person. "It happened like *that*." A snap of the fingers. "There was no time to react."

Now Fen began to look carefully at the people addressing him, and he recognised the expressions on their faces around him for what they were: not concerned but pitying.

Her.

Grabbed *her*.

"Moira?"

"One of the vans stopped and a couple of men jumped out, Fen," said Beth. Her hand was still on his shoulder. "Jumped out, grabbed her, pulled her into the van, drove away. I can still hardly believe it. It happened just a few minutes ago. She put up a fight, but..."

It was a joke. Fen swivelled his head, peering from one face to the next. They were having a joke on him, surely. Moira? It hadn't been Moira. Mistaken identity. Moira wouldn't have been here on King Alfred Street because Moira had not been going to the festival. She was at home. It was someone else who had been snatched by the Bulldogs, someone who looked like Moira. Not Moira. It wasn't possible.

Was it?

He pushed Beth aside. He shoved past another woman. Then he was staggering up the slope of Harvill Drive, gaining speed, breaking into a clumsy run.

He lurched along the cut-through.

He lumbered down Crane Street.

He stumbled up the front path.

He tumbled through the front door.

The house was empty. He checked every room. He even checked the back garden. No Moira.

And in the bedroom, the drawers of the chest of drawers were open, each protruding a little further out than the one above, like a staircase to nowhere. There were signs that Moira had put on clothes. A pair of her shoes were missing from the floor of the closet.

He slumped down on the unmade bed, breathing hard. The sheets smelled of her. Her body, her sweat. Ghosts of her secretions. The pillow still bore the dimpled imprint of her head.

Gone. Taken. Like the women at the precinct.

He couldn't believe it.

He didn't want to believe it.

And at the same time, in a small dark corner of his soul, he not only wanted to believe it but was eager to.

THEY MAKE ME lie down. Among their feet. Feet in trainers. Sweat-smell and perished rubber. White socks. All I see are logos. Logos, flashes, names, imprints, ticks, initials, numerals. The lumpy treads on soles.

They make jokes. They swear and they talk about "bitches". A bitch-hunt. That's what this has been, apparently. A bitch-hunt.

I'm too scared to move. There's an ache in my throat. My heart's going nine to the dozen. They're talking about me, but I don't want to hear what they're saying. It's my hair. Something about my hair. That's why they stopped for me. Red hair. "He" will like it. Whoever "he" is.

The van sways and bounces, and down here on the floor I feel every blemish in the road surface, every crack and bump and pothole, and there are plenty, and the driver swerves a lot, perhaps to avoid the worst of them, and the shock absorbers creak, and sometimes I hear the sound of other vans up ahead, the rest of our convoy. When was the last time I was in a motor vehicle of any kind?

My heart's hammering, I'm scared beyond belief, but I can still wonder about the fact that I'm travelling in a motor vehicle. Isn't the mind a strange thing?

After a while they let me know that I can sit up if I want to. I think they liked seeing me on the floor. It amused them. Then it got boring. So I sit up, because I'll be more comfortable that way. I press myself against the side of a seat, doing my best to make sure I'm not touching any of them and none of them's touching me. No physical contact. No eye contact either. I want to be small. I want to be insignificant. I stare at my feet. My shoes. Old shoes. Is there any other kind? Simple comfortable sandals. Stitching split on the right one. Upper and sole starting to part company. Dust engrained in the wrinkles in the leather, like pale capillaries.

It's dim in the van. The tinted windows don't let in much light. I'm aware of how we all move together, the men, me, synchronised. Jerking like puppets whenever the van jolts.

If only I hadn't...

No. Mustn't think like that. Too late to think like that.

Eight years ago. Early autumn.

That was the last time I was in a motor vehicle.

We had some petrol. We took Fen's battered old Renault down to the coast. Things were starting to get very bad then. The political situation. Deteriorating. I think, deep down, we knew we might not have another chance to do something like this. This might be the last opportunity we had. That sweetened it.

It was a bright, clear, warm day. The sea was every shade of blue imaginable. At least, that's how I remember it. Shades of blue you'd expect in the tropics, but not in the Channel. Cobalt. Turquoise. Peacock. Sapphire. Aquamarine. Purples, too. Lilac. Amethyst. We parked on a clifftop and looked down, and it was like looking down on the contents of a vast jewel-box. God's own treasure chest, opened for our benefit.

We had a picnic on the clifftop, on a blanket. Sandwiches, pie, soup from a thermos flask, cherry tomatoes. Halfway through the meal a magpie appeared and began strutting around us, flexing its wings, fluffing out its feathers, flicking its tail up and down, chattering. Fen waved it away, laughing, but it kept coming back. Then it started making aggressive feints towards us, and we realised it was after our food. We were, it seemed, being mugged by this avian hoodlum, and successfully, because in the end the only way to get the magpie to leave us alone was to throw it chunks of bread crust, which it snatched up and gulped down until eventually, glutted and appeased, it flew off.

"I suppose," Fen said, with a droll smile, "you could call that 'demanding manna with menaces'." Then, the smile fading, he said, "That bird is our future, you know."

"What, one for sorrow?" For a moment I thought he was referring to me and him, and could not see why. "Fen, is there something you need to tell me?" I added, only half joking.

"Something...? Oh no. No, nothing like that, Moira. I meant the nation's future." He pointed to the magpie, which had alighted on a clump of gorse a hundred yards away and was cawing and preening triumphantly. "If everything goes the way it seems to be going, if the government keeps on throwing good money after bad with such reckless abandon, then the country's going to belong to bullies like him. It'll be their time. They're the ones who'll thrive."

I felt a chill. A presentiment, on that magnificent autumn afternoon, of the depth of the downward spiral into which England was headed. Fen was right. But I didn't want him to be right. "You don't think that really. Do you? You don't. I mean, it'll all get sorted out, won't it? This is just a dip in our fortunes. We've weathered worse in the past."

Quickly he said, "Of course. Of course it is. Of course we have." Lying for my sake, as people often have to with their loved ones. "I just like to be the voice of doom. You know that. A professional Eeyore."

And he took my hand and we kissed.

We were happy then. Even then.

The van lunges into a deeper-than-usual pothole, twice, front left wheel, rear left wheel, and the men all jeer and hoot and call the driver names, and the driver calls them names back and says any of them is welcome to come and take over.

On we roll for a while, and the light inside the van gets dimmer and dimmer, until the men are all silhouettes. They go quiet. Some of them start to snooze, and I think about making a bid for the rear doors. I could scramble over, pull down the handle, hurl myself out... but I know someone would grab me before I got there, and even if I managed it I know they'd stop the van and come out after me.

Even more time later, I don't know how much, a long time, we slow down, and then we halt, and then we move forward in fits and starts, and one of the men says to me, "We've got this all covered, but just to be on the safe side you keep your head down and you *shut up*. Got that? Not a dicky-bird or I break your neck. Understand?"

I nod.

A minute or so later we halt and the driver pulls on the handbrake and winds down his window. A torch beam shines in.

"Permits."

The driver hands over a sheaf of documents, and something else. A bribe of some sort, I assume, because he says, "There you go," meaningfully, and the man with the torch, just as meaningfully, replies, "Right. Thanks. Well..."

The torch beam flashes briefly over the interior of the van.

This is the moment. If I'm going to scream, it should be now.

But a hand clamps on the back of my head, just where my skull meets my vertebrae. The man who told me to shut up or he would break my neck. His fingers exert pressure, enough to tell me that they can clench much harder. Much, much harder if necessary. It's as if he knew what I was thinking.

I'm not sure I want to live, not if my future is these men. But I realise I don't want to die either. Not yet. Not like this.

"That all seems to be in order," says the man with the torch. "On your way, then."

The van moves off, and the hand lets go and pats me on the head. Like I'm a pet. An obedient dog.

And I hear someone say, "Welcome to London."

TWO DAYS AFTER the raid by the British Bulldogs, a town meeting was convened.

Very few people turned up and not much was resolved. It was agreed that Henry Mullins should act as mayor *pro tem*, until such time as an election could be organised. It was also agreed that a funeral service should be held at St Stephen's Church for Michael Hollingbury (dead, destroyed, Hollingbury was no longer the Green Man, just a man). Other than that, nobody had much to suggest or much to say. The purpose of the meeting was to discuss the Bulldogs' actions and formulate some kind of response, but there was a general reluctance to address the subject. There was a general reluctance even to mention the word "Bulldogs", or, for that matter, the names of the women they had abducted.

The same was true all over town. While there were those who spoke loudly in favour of following the Bulldogs to London and getting into the capital somehow and locating the abductees somehow and rescuing them somehow, the great majority of Downbournians appeared to have come to the conclusion that it was best simply to forget the whole episode and act as if it had never occurred. The unfeasibility of any rescue attempt—all those *somehows*—was too daunting. Rather than openly admit defeat, however, people admitted nothing. A veil was drawn. The subject of the kidnapped women became taboo. When it cropped up in a conversation, the conversation faltered. If ever it was referred to, it was referred to by a stretch of silence. It was as though a huge alien spacecraft was hovering over town and everyone was acting as if it wasn't there, even though everyone felt its immane presence, the chill of its shadow.

England had suffered greatly since the government's Unlucky Gamble and the series of escalating crises that had followed as the country was first bankrupted by its leaders then pushed into a brief military expedition that was supposed to restore its fortunes and didn't, then finally abandoned by its elected representatives, who jumped ship before angry mobs of protestors could, as it were, shove them overboard. Stripped of any last illusions of faith in its leadership, England slid inexorably into anarchy. Even in a town like Downbourne, bypassed by the worst of the upheaval, significant adjustments in lifestyle had had to be made. Surrogates for central heating, electric lighting and running water had had to be found, as one by one these basic amenities ceased to function. Luxuries large and small had had to be forgone. Things once taken for granted had now to be treated, if they could be obtained, as treasures. Privation and frugality had become a way of life, and this had led to a sense of resignation which had in turn led, inevitably, to an outward and inner toughening—a thickening of skins, a hardening of hearts. People, sometimes surprising themselves with their own fortitude, had learned to do without; to settle for less; to endure. And the ability to endure often meant the ability to turn a blind eye to unpalatable truths and bear with a shrug situations they knew they could not change. Emotional sensitivity is not a survival trait, and over the past few years Englanders had become, if nothing else, survivors.

So the residents of Downbourne embraced a policy of mute denial, and tried to get on with life as before. It was as if the Bulldogs incident was a price that had to be paid for the comparative good fortune the town had up till now enjoyed, a sacrifice that had to be offered up to the gods of balance. The townsfolk, with a few murmurs of dissent, gave up their due.

Physical injuries inflicted by the British Bulldogs were seen to by Nurse Chase. Downbourne's last remaining GP, Dr Whittaker, had died of salmonella poisoning four years previously, after eating a bad tin of corned beef—a physician who had healed many but, when it came to the crunch, proved unable to heal himself. Anne Chase, his surgery nurse, had stepped into the breach to perform what curative works she could with her dwindling stocks of dressings and pharmaceuticals. As she tended to the Bulldogs' victims, she was relieved (and somewhat surprised) to find that nobody had been too severely hurt. The exception to this was Fen's neighbour Stephen Talbot, who had been beaten into a coma. For him, alas, Nurse Chase could do nothing other than advise his family to make him comfortable and pray he recovered consciousness soon. Otherwise, it was just contusions and abrasions and the odd broken bone, all things that were in her power to treat.

As for non-physical injuries, it was left to the individual to handle these as best he or she could. Psychiatry was one of the excrescences of the past which present national circumstances had ruthlessly pruned. There was no therapy any more, no counselling to featherbed the tortured soul, so people either coped with the traumas fate threw at them or caved in; and of course, among the residents of Downbourne—as among all Englanders—

coping rather than caving was the norm, so that even in households where a family member, a loved one, had been lost to the Bulldogs, the prevailing mood was one of stoic acceptance. There was anger, certainly. Frustration too. There was sorrow and mourning, for the loss was in many respects a bereavement. But after only two days there was also a sense that life must continue as usual, or at any rate be seen to do so.

12 Crane Street appeared to be a perfect example of this.

Here, one need look no further than the front garden, where, on the afternoon of the day of the town meeting, Fen was out trimming the hedge. There had been no school yesterday—there never was, the day after a festival—and it was the weekend now, so Fen was free to carry out domestic duties. Which he did, just as if nothing had happened. Stripped to the waist, he manoeuvred the shears along the hedge, vertically, horizontally, cutting the little privet leaves and twigs with aggressive precision, going over every patch several times, clipping nature to geometric perfection. The sound of the shear-blades' incisive applause echoed along the street.

It was hot yet again, and Fen's torso was bathed in sweat, which glazed and intensified the colours of the bruise that spread over several square inches of his left flank, making the browns chestnut, the purples aubergine, the yellows buttercup. That contusion was now the most evident, and the most painful, of Fen's injuries. His lip and finger had shrunk back almost to normal size, and his left eye was reddened and puffy but looked like it was afflicted with a bad stye rather than suffering from the after-effects of a right royal shiner.

Frowning with concentration, Fen ministered to the hedge until he was interrupted by the arrival of a visitor.

Alan Greeley, having dared to engage in fisticuffs with one of the British Bulldogs, had paid for his temerity with a broken wrist. His arm, splinted and bandaged by Nurse Chase, hung in a sling, and walking was exquisite torture for him. However carefully he trod, each step jarred the wrist and sent crackles of pain shooting along to the elbow. Nevertheless, having learned of Moira's abduction, he had decided to call on Fen as soon as he felt able to, in order to ascertain how Holly-Anne's "Lesson Man" was faring.

Greeley was, in his way, as altruistic as the expatriate smugglers who supplied him with the goods that he passed on to his fellow townspeople. What the smugglers brought over from the Continent they brought over at their own expense and, since they were braving the International Community naval blockades, at considerable personal risk. Greeley benefited greatly from these freely donated gifts, but anyone would agree that he earned whatever he gained. He went to a great deal of time, trouble and effort to retrieve the goods from various stashes all along the local coastline. He was, moreover, no stranger to acts of charity, always quick to offer a handout, slow to call in a debt.

So the fact that Fen was a valued customer, and it was therefore pragmatic to display concern for him, was neither here nor there. Greeley's solicitude was genuine enough. He liked Fen.

As Greeley approached, Fen laid aside the shears and ran a thumbnail along each of his eyebrows, scraping away the sweat.

"Nice job," Greeley commented.

"Hm? Oh, yes. Well. Needed doing."

"You all right?"

"Yeah. Sure. Yeah." Fen nodded at Greeley's arm. "You?"

"Bloody awful," Greeley replied, and smiled a smile that was half grimace. "Hey, look." He was carrying a bag, in which there were several small brown bottles. "French beer. Fancy some?"

Fen was on the point of refusing, then relented. "Why not?"

In the back garden, on a small square of patio, the only space that was not given over to produce-growing, Fen set out a pair of deckchairs. Their striped canvas had once been white and dark green. Now those colours were fish-flesh grey and a spearmint-toothpaste shade. The chairs' metal frames were oaty with rust.

The two men made themselves comfortable, and Fen uncapped two of the bottles and passed one to Greeley. Each took a sip and winced.

"Disgusting," said Greeley.

"Could do with being chilled," Fen agreed.

"You can just hear a Frenchman laughing somewhere, can't you? 'Ze Eenglish and zeir warm beer.'"

Fen half-smiled and took another sip. Disgusting or not, the beer was welcome. He and Greeley sat and drank in companionable silence for a while, and Fen could not help being struck by how ordinary it was, how classic: two Englishmen sitting in a garden in deckchairs, sharing a beer and a moment of quiet.

"I heard, of course," said Greeley, not knowing how else to start this conversation. "About Moira."

"Of course."

"I'm really sorry."

Fen rested the rim of his bottle against his lips. "Yes."

"I mean, I know things weren't... you know. Between the two of you."

"No. No, they weren't."

"And feel free to tell me if this isn't any of my business."

"It wasn't really a secret, I suppose."

"But if I've overstepped the mark..."

"No. No."

"But Christ, you must be... Well, shit, if it was Andrea they'd taken, I'd..." Greeley shook his head. "Frankly I don't know what I'd do."

"She wasn't meant to be at the festival," Fen said, after a moment's pause. "Well, she wasn't *at* it, was she? Wasn't meant to be heading there. I don't know why she went. She didn't seem to have any intention of going. She must have changed her mind."

"Or she heard the vans. Came out to investigate."

"Possibly. I've thought about it and thought about it. Why did she go out? But in the end it doesn't make much difference, does it? They got her, that's the thing. She was walking by, and they pulled over and climbed out and got her."

"And no one tried to stop them."

Fen shrugged. "Not that surprising, really. Is it?"

"Maybe not." Greeley gave his damaged arm a gingerly pat. "If they had, I doubt they'd have come off any better than I did."

"What are people saying?"

"About Moira?"

"Generally? About all this?"

"I've not been out and about much, but the feeling I get is no one really wants to talk about it."

"Yeah. Me too."

"The Green Man—Hollingbury—would have done something."

"You think so?"

"Don't you? Organised everyone. Had a plan. Told us what to do."

"Probably."

"Without him, we're a bit of a lame duck."

"I'd say a headless chicken."

Greeley laughed. "Damn schoolteachers. Always correcting you."

"It's my job."

"Yeah, it is," Greeley said. "Again, stop me if I'm overstepping the mark here, Fen, but does it bother you at all?"

"Bother me?"

"That they took her."

"Of course it does. Why? Does it look like it doesn't?"

Greeley studied him, and saw in his posture—hunched forwards in the deckchair, elbows on thighs, the stringy muscles of his arms taut, the joints of his spine standing out like the ridges of a rolltop desk—certainty. In his face, too: in his fixed-focus eyes, in the deep vertical crevices which, pilgrim-style, scored his cheeks. Unmistakable, unshakeable certainty.

"No," he concluded. "In fact, it looks to me like you've very definitely made up your mind about something."

Fen nodded. "At first I wondered if I had a choice. It seemed—I'll admit this to you, Alan—it seemed that perhaps, without realising it, the Bulldogs had done me a favour. Like you said: things between me and Moira haven't been right for a while. A long while. And ghastly as it sounds, once it sank in that they'd taken her, I was actually quite glad. Deep down, selfishly, I thought: well, here's the answer. Here's the way out for me. Handed to me on a plate. Nothing I can do. Not my fault. She's gone. Problem solved. It felt like I'd been presented with a clean slate, a chance to start afresh. If I had the guts to take it. No, not the guts. If I could be callous enough. Calculating enough. If I had the capacity to just shut Moira off in my head, close the door on her and pretend she didn't matter any more and had never mattered."

"But..."

"But I couldn't. I can't."

"So you're—"

"So I'm going after her." Fen took a long swig of his lager. The bubbles pricked and stung his tongue. "I've got a plan. Well, an outline of a plan. A sketch of an outline of a plan. And I'm going to do it because I don't have a choice. It's as simple as that. That's what it comes down to. I don't have a choice."

"But London..."

"Yeah, I know. London. And the M25."

"And getting there."

"I know."

"And I don't think the Bulldogs, if you find wherever they are, are just going to let you have her back."

"Me neither."

Greeley shook his head. "I don't know what to say. You're crazy."

"Certifiable."

"You'll never manage it."

"Absolutely not."

"It's the daftest thing I've ever heard."

"I don't doubt it."

"I should try and talk you out of it."

"Don't bother."

"Don't worry, I'm not going to. Because if it wasn't for this arm, and the fact that I have a family to consider, I'd be going with you. Really, I would."

"I believe you."

"I think someone else should."

"I think I'll manage better on my own."

"Well, I'll fix you up with some provisions. That's the least I can do."

"Thank you for saving me having to ask."

"I wish I could fix you up with a London permit, but you know... Gold dust. Hen's teeth."

"That's all right. I know where I can try and get hold of one."

"Cruikshank? You'll be lucky."

"Yeah, I know."

There was a pause, then Greeley reached out across the space between them, lager bottle extended. "Here."

Fen reciprocated, and the necks of their bottles clinked in mid-air.

"To noble but insane enterprises," Greeley said.

"To doing the right thing," Fen replied.

Later, after Greeley had gone, Fen resumed work on the hedge. Three bottles of lager had left him a little light-headed, but not so that his facility with the shears was impaired. Three bottles of lager had also encouraged him to drag up once again the doubts and questions that had been plaguing him since yesterday, when he had finally, firmly decided that he was going to go in search of Moira. These same doubts had plagued him all through last night, making him toss and turn, dog-restless in his bed. Had he developed amnesia all of a sudden? Had he completely forgotten what the past year and a half had been like? Moira wallowing in bed all day long. Her long sullen silences. Her surliness. Her petty complaints. Her pickiness. Her resentment. The different person she had become, and the compassion he had shown her, constantly, fruitlessly. Here was his chance to be shot of all that. No one would blame him. No one else in Downbourne was even thinking about doing what he intended to do.

And then there were the kids at school to think about. He would be abandoning them, for who knows how long. Maybe for good. He had undertaken a commitment to them, to their parents. Their parents, in good faith, had recompensed him in advance for his services. They wanted their children to be able to read, write, add, understand, *think*. How could he shirk that responsibility?

And even—for Christ's sake—his garden. Here he was, trimming the hedge, and a short while from now, a day, two at the most, he would be off. Even if he was only gone for a fortnight (and that was his lowest estimate, his lowest estimate by far, his if-fate-smiles-on-everything-I-do estimate), when he came back he would have lost produce to the birds and the slugs and the snails. The main picking season was at hand, that time of universal burgeoning and bearing. Without him here to harvest, so much would go to waste. He could always ask a neighbour to mind the garden for him, but could he really expect someone else to look after things as well as he could, and to take on the job without knowing when, if ever, he would return?

Such were the anchors, the gravity of obligation that held him here. Good, sound, logical, valid reasons not to leave, all of them. But at the same time, just excuses. No argument Fen could come up with against going after Moira could withstand the scorchingly irrefutable simplicity of his urge to find his wife, to get her back, to Do The Right Thing. Next to that imperative, all else fell away.

And so, even as he clipped and snipped with the shears, he knew that he wasn't going to be deflected. His doubts made him, if anything, all the more determined. They fired the clay of his resolve.

He wasn't happy about going after Moira.

He didn't believe his search for her was going to have a successful outcome.

There was, however, no other course of action that his conscience would abide. Anything else was unacceptable.

THAT EVENING, FEN presented himself at the door to Gilbert Cruikshank's house.

Ludicrously, he had smartened himself up, like someone going for a job interview. He had washed his hair. He had shaved. He had put on his cleanest, most ironed-looking shirt. He was even wearing a tie.

All to make a good impression on a blind man.

The door opened a full two minutes after he knocked, Cruikshank's appearance being preceded by mutters, grumbles and curses of mounting volubility that reached their climax with the pulling of the bolt and the parting of door from jamb to the maximum distance permitted by a security chain.

Out poked the spongy nose. Out peeped the sightless eyes.

"Yes?"

"Mr Cruikshank."

"Morris. What do you want?"

"A word. Please."

"How about 'piss off'? There's *two* words."

"First of all, I want to apologise."

"No, you want something from me. That's the only reason anyone ever calls on me. Even the ones who bring me food. They say they do it out of the goodness of their hearts, but they want something."

"I was out of line the other night. At the festival."

"So?"

"So I want to say I'm sorry."

"Do you honestly think that (a) I care, and (b) it makes any difference?"

"I hoped—"

"Morris, let's cut the crap, shall we? I know your wife has been taken, and I think I can guess what you've come here to ask for. What I don't understand is what on earth makes you think I would have any intention of parting with my London permit, for anyone and particularly for the likes of you?"

"If you'll invite me in and let me talk to you for just five minutes, Mr Cruikshank, I think I can convince you why you should lend it to me."

"Oh, *lend* it to you, eh? *Lend* you my permit when there's very little chance I'll get it back. Interesting use of the word 'lend' there, schoolteacher."

"Please. Just five minutes of your time."

Cruikshank's face—the slotted section of it visible to Fen—looked thoughtful. Then, abruptly, the door slammed shut. There was silence, followed by several seconds of clatter as the security chain was fumblingly disengaged. Then the door reopened, wide.

"Enter," said Cruikshank, dipping from the waist and uncurling his arm like an unctuous *maître d'* at a high-class restaurant.

Cruikshank lived in a cul-de-sac just off Clement Road. The street consisted of two rows of identical flint-and-brick artisans' cottages, each of them two storeys tall, with a short, steep staircase, low ceilings, and cramped rooms. Cruikshank's house—strictly speaking, his sister's house—differed from its neighbours only in the extent of its filthiness, both outside and, especially, inside. A certain amount of dirt and disarray was to be expected nowadays, but Cruikshank's home was, by any standards, squalid. Upon entering, Fen found himself in a narrow hallway where the carpet was rucked and wrinkled and the wallpaper was peeling away in curls. This, along with several shelfloads of damp-swollen paperbacks, served to give the impression that he was walking into some kind of diseased, foetid throat. A couple of yards along from the front door, next to the foot of the staircase, Fen paused at the entrance to the living room. The interior of the room looked as if a lunatic decorator had been let loose with a spray-gun and several gallons of matt-black paint. Everyone knew the story. One winter's evening Cruikshank was lighting a camping stove for warmth and managed to knock it over so that it fell against the side of an armchair. The chair cover, 100% pure polyester, ignited, and by the time Cruikshank managed to fetch a bucket of water, the flames had taken hold and the room was filled with acrid smoke. Neighbours risked their lives and used gallons of their own precious rainwater to douse the fire, in return for which Cruikshank, true to form, offered not a word of thanks, complaining instead about his soaked carpet and furnishings. Nothing had been done to the room since then. Either Cruikshank still used it as it was—every object and surface in it charred and soot-caked—or else he simply avoided it, confining his solitary life to the house's three other rooms.

Cruikshank struck Fen's ankle sharply with his stick. "Why have you stopped?" he snapped. "Keep going, keep going. The kitchen."

Fen moved on.

If the hallway and living room were bad, the kitchen was ten times worse. In the dim evening light, Fen saw precarious stacks of long-unwashed crockery on the sink's work-surface. There were rinds of mould in crannies and along edges, and all over the linoleum there were dried, spattered stains whose origin he did not want even to guess at. He was aware, too, of movement all around, a peripheral scuttling and hustling, tiny leggy things active among the remnants of meals, scavenging the scabs of food. The smell of rot and decay was strong but there was also a darker, mustier odour in the air which he could only assume was insect turds. Even blind, Cruikshank could not have been oblivious to the repellence of this room, so Fen had to conclude that, perversely, he relished it, and relished, too, ushering visitors into it.

"Sit down," Cruikshank said, rapping the top of the kitchen table with a loosely clenched fist.

Fen pulled out a chair circumspectly and, discovering nothing untoward on its seat, sat.

Cruikshank remained standing. "All right then," he said, "let's hear it. You want my permit? Go on. Beg for it."

A recalcitrant urge welled up in Fen. Beg for it? Why should he? Why should he have to grovel to, of all people, Gilbert Cruikshank?

But so long as there remained a chance, however remote, that Cruikshank might let him have the permit, he had no choice.

"Mr Cruikshank," he said, "I need it. I can't put it any more simply than that. I need your permit so that I can get into London and find my wife and bring her back."

"Go on."

"Ummm... OK. I realise that you probably don't like me very much."

"Not necessarily."

"But I have to say I admire you. The way you've carried on, in spite of your disability. The way you've—"

"Oh no no no, Morris!" Cruikshank stamped his stick on the floor, causing the haphazard stacks of crockery to jump and jingle. "No. You were doing fine up till then. Honest, straightforward, and then all of a sudden you veer off into flattery, and that won't do at all. I asked for begging, not arse-kissing."

Fen drew in a deep breath, expelling it slowly. "I suppose you want me to say something like 'I won't be able to succeed without your help'."

"I want you to say what *you* want to say."

Again Fen felt that recalcitrant urge. Again he damped it down. How was he meant to play this? What was Cruikshank after? Perhaps he should try an appeal to Cruikshank's better nature. Assuming Cruikshank had one, that is.

"Moira means a lot to me, Mr Cruikshank."

Cruikshank cocked his head to one side, like someone who has detected strains of fine music. "There, that's more like it."

"I love her."

"You do? Still? Despite her hating you?"

"She doesn't hate me," Fen countered. "She never has. It's just that things have been... difficult for her."

"Things such as?"

"You know what I'm talking about."

"Tell me about it."

"No. Why should I?"

"Because I'm nosy. Because I like to hear about other people's miseries. Because I have a London permit and you want it."

"So that's it, is it?" Fen said, bristling. "That's your price?"

"Look at it from my point of view, Morris," Cruikshank said. "That permit is important to me. It means I can go back to London any time I want. Whether in practical terms that's possible, I don't care. I'm blind and arthritic; I'm not likely to be making any fifty-mile journeys in the near future. But that's not the point. I have an official document that says I'm not stuck here in this piss-awful little hole for ever. It says I don't have to live here indefinitely, surrounded by backward provincials like you. Now, do you think I'm going to hand over something so precious to me to just any old person who comes along and asks for it? Give it away? I'm not doing that without getting *something* in return."

"Forget it." Fen stood up. "I'm not playing along."

"Oh come on. It won't hurt. You can start by telling me how it felt when Moira became pregnant. You'd been trying for a while, hadn't you? You must have been overjoyed."

"Cruikshank, I said forget it. I'm not doing this."

"But what about the permit?"

"I'll manage without."

"Oh, you will, will you?"

"I'll find a way."

"Brave talk. But the M25... Watchtowers, dogs, mines, barbed wire, and the rest. That's quite a gauntlet."

Fen weighed it up: satisfying Cruikshank's spiteful prurience against losing the one thing without which his chances of rescuing Moira went from marginally-better-than-nil to nil.

He sank back into the chair. "OK," he sighed. "All right."

"Good man. So: when you found out Moira was pregnant—was it overjoyed, or not overjoyed?"

Fen paused, casting his mind back. "Mixed feelings, I suppose."

"Only natural."

"After all, this isn't the best of worlds to bring a child into. The best of countries, I mean. Not with things the way they are. Then again, there are a lot worse places to be in England than Downbourne. And children do represent hope for the future."

"So everyone would have us believe. I can't understand it myself. Another squalling, foul-tempered little proto-adult—how is *that* in any way hopeful? Just one more human being, destined to make a mess of things and die, like the rest of us."

Fen almost laughed. "But you think you can do better with each child, don't you. It's part of an ongoing process. The refining and improving of the human race. Each generation learning from the mistakes of the previous one and passing on what it's learned to the next."

"A sentiment tidily disproved by our nation's current predicament."

"Perhaps. Still, you've got to try. That's how I saw it. Still see it. You can't give up on the future just because the present isn't so brilliant."

"And it was going to be twins, wasn't it? How did you feel about that? A brace of the little tykes. Was that twice as exciting?"

"We didn't know. Not at the time. It was only afterwards that..." Fen's voice faltered.

"That...?" Cruikshank prompted.

Fen stood up again, this time shunting the chair forcibly backwards so that its feet scraped judderingly across the crusted linoleum. "No. That's enough. I'm not going on with this. It's not worth it."

"But Morris, things were just starting to get interesting."

"Fuck you." Fen pushed past Cruikshank, deliberately banging shoulders with the old man, knocking him off balance. He headed into the hallway, hurrying past the flocculent wallpaper, the bloated books, the entrance to the ruined living room. He seized the front-door handle. He needed to be out. Out of this house, away from its occupant.

"Wait."

Cruikshank came hobbling after him, one hand spidering feelingly along the wall.

"Morris, wait."

Fen, still grasping the door handle, waited.

"Listen. All right. Maybe I went too far. I simply wanted to find out..."

"What?" Fen said tersely. "What did you want to find out?"

"How far you were prepared to go. What you'd be prepared to do."

"Well, now you know."

"The permit is yours, Morris. You can have it."

Fen didn't reply, unsure whether this was just another game, a blind man's bluff.

"You do need it," Cruikshank said. "You deserve it."

"Deserve it. Because my hard-luck story is sufficiently tragic."

"No, you idiot. Because, unlike the rest of the arseholes in this town, you've actually shown some spine."

Fen peered over his shoulder, looking into Cruikshank's eyes. The old man returned the gaze, blinkless as a lizard. Cruikshank wasn't totally blind, but sometimes it seemed his vision was better than he let on. Perhaps he exaggerated the extent of his disability, the better to earn himself charity. Alternatively, perhaps he was adept at hiding how blind he truly was. Either way, he was managing to give the impression now of scrutinising Fen's face, searching it for a response.

"Yes," Cruikshank said, "that caught you up short, didn't it? You weren't expecting *that*."

"I don't understand."

"I think you do. It's quite simple. You're the only one, Morris, the *only one* who's decided to act. Oh, certainly there's been talk of going after those Bulldog bastards. Not a lot of talk, but some. But talk is all it's been. Otherwise there's just been a bend-over-and-take-it kind of attitude. I've been hoping *someone* would have the gumption to stand up and play the hero, and it's funny but I did have a sneaking feeling that that someone would be you. You, the person who looked like he'd have most to gain from keeping his head down and staying put. The one man here who might have cause to be grateful to the Bulldogs. You know when you told me earlier that you thought I didn't like you very much? And I said, 'Not necessarily'? Well, that's the truth, Morris. Don't get me wrong, I don't want you as my friend or anything, but that isn't to say I *dis*like you. I think you're tightly-buttoned, a little self-satisfied, a little priggish. I think you actually quite enjoy living in England the way it is now. You're one of those people who believes suffering is good for the soul. Hardship maketh the man. But I think there's also something else to you, something more. And I think that that's what I'm being shown right now. So yes, I admit I shouldn't have got you to talk about your marriage and your wife's pregnancy; I shouldn't have tried to make you use that as a bargaining chip. Consider it a test. An oral exam. I had to be absolutely sure you weren't wasting my time and that I'm giving my permit to the right person. And now I *am* sure."

"Has anyone ever told you, Cruikshank, that you're an absolute shit?"

"Plenty of people," Cruikshank replied with a shrug. "It's not my policy to be adored. In fact, I consider it a mark of honour that I can be universally unpleasant and get away with it. I was like that when I lived in London, and still everyone rallied around when my sight started to go. That's how I got my permit, how I got down here. I was, as you so rightly put it, an absolute shit, yet people still took pity on me. You could say that by being the worst I can be, I bring out the best in others."

"You could, if you were desperately trying to justify your shortcomings as a human being."

Cruikshank gave a dry, crackling laugh. "Careful, Morris. It's not too late for me to change my mind, you know. Now just wait there. I won't be a moment."

The old man groped for the staircase banister and clumped up to the next floor. Fen heard him overhead, moving around, rummaging. A short while later he reappeared, a quarter-folded piece of white paper in his hand, and cautiously descended.

"There," he said, when he had reached the bottom of the stairs. He proffered the piece of paper to Fen.

Fen unfolded it. It was a brittle photocopy, marked with a faint blue stamp that said "London Council". The text on it was brief and to the point:

> This entitles the bearer to access to and from the Greater London area. Any resident/citizen presenting this permit to the appropriate authorities at a designated checkpoint shall be allowed free and unhindered passage except if at the discretion of the authorities that person be deemed undesirable or a threat to civic safety.

Fen read the words a couple of times, then carefully, even reverently, refolded the permit and inserted it into his breast pocket.

"So there you have it," said Cruikshank. "Your way in. Piece of advice, though. That bit at the end? About being 'a threat to civic safety', or whatever it says? The checkpoint guards usually use that as an excuse to extort a bribe, so I'd take something with you, something valuable, just in case."

"All right. Thanks. I will."

"Now fuck off out of here."

"Mr Cruikshank—"

"No schmaltzy nonsense, please!" snapped Cruikshank.

"I was just going to say, I *will* bring this back to you." Fen patted his pocket, then realised the action was probably lost on Cruikshank. "Your permit. I swear."

"Bollocks you will. You stand a cat's chance in hell of getting your wife out of London. You're on a fool's errand, you're as good as dead, and you know it. So don't give me any 'coming back' bullshit."

"I am going to try, though."

"Of course you are. Now bugger off and never darken my door again!"

Awake again. Blackness. Slept for... one hour? Two? Body aching. Thirsty. Hungry. Hunger like a *thing* inside me, a squatting presence, filling a vacancy with pain.

The floorboards. The reek of other bodies. The stench of our waste products.

Still here. This place. This house with bricked-up windows. This room I know by feel alone. How long has it been now? Two days? Possibly three. And what time is it now? I have no idea.

I sit up and try to knead some of the stiffness out of my muscles. There's not a stick of furniture in the room, unless you count the tin bucket we've been given to relieve ourselves in. Nothing to sleep on or under, not even a blanket. It's all bare and raw. The floorboards are gritty and splintered. The walls have holes in them, patches where the concrete beneath the plasterwork has been exposed. I've explored them with my fingers. They're shallow, like moon craters.

While massaging my back and legs, I become aware of one of the other women sobbing. Gasping into her hands. It sounds like she's suffering some kind of fit. I know I ought to go over and touch her, hug her, comfort her, but I lack the energy, the will. There are four of us in here. Are both of the two who aren't sobbing asleep? Maybe. Or maybe they're just lying there, thinking the same as I'm thinking: *I can't be bothered to help her. I don't see the point*.

We've had no contact with any of the other women since we were thrown in here and the door was shut on us. Presumably they're in other rooms in this house, sitting there scared like us. We've had no contact with our captors either. No one's even walked by in the corridor outside, or at least we haven't heard anyone. It could be that we've been locked in here and abandoned, left to rot.

But I don't think so.

I think this is a cunning little ploy our captors have devised. Put the women in rooms. No food, no water. Leave them there for a few days. Weaken them. Break down their resistance.

A culinary analogy comes to mind: tenderising the meat.

And with that thought the fear returns, the fear that I've been grappling with on and off since they pulled me into that van, and I feel helpless and numb and craven and I want to sob like that other woman, just surrender and let it all gush out. I think of the men in the van, and the other men who were waiting for us here when we arrived and watched us as we were shoved and herded across the compound to the building we're in. Their brutal muscularity. The light in their eyes. You could *feel* the avarice coming off them. It wasn't just desire, it was a need so strong it was almost a hatred. Their stares could have punched through wood. As we were being paraded past them, I thought they were going to grab us then and there and tear us to pieces. I never knew what "vulnerable" truly meant till that moment.

Those same men will be coming for us eventually, probably sooner rather than later, bringing with them violence and violation...

And now the fear has a tight grip on me and won't let go, and I ask myself, trying to be rational, what's the worst that can happen to me, and I think of several answers and the fear grows worse.

I try to reach for a memory. This is the trick I have developed in recent months. In order too escape the present, reach for something from my past, an image, a perfect, gemlike moment to contemplate, to find refuge in. Like that afternoon on the clifftop with Fen.

This time, however, it doesn't work. The hunger and fear in combination are too great. I grope for a happier time but all I come up with is myself screaming through labour, writhing under Anne Chase's grasp, her hands on my shoulders pushing me down onto the bed while she tries to soothe me, telling me everything's going well, breathe through the pain, breathe throooough the pain, but I know everything *isn't* going well, there's a deep and terrible wrongness to all this and I can see it in Anne's eyes, although I don't need to see her eyes to know it because I can feel it too, because deep down inside me everything's all twisted up, all sickly and rebellious, and I know I'm not giving birth, I'm giving the opposite of birth, and all this screaming and breathing throooough the pain is futile because what's coming out of me doesn't want life, never did, and then at last it emerges, the first one, in a few long, tearing minutes of agony beyond agony, and I see it and it's not moving, not making a sound, it's just lying there, stillborn.

Stillborn.

Born.

Still.

Fen holding it. Fen's hands dripping with blood, as though *he* is its murderer, *he* is the one who has killed it. Fen crying and talking to it through his tears, somehow trying to get it to live, force it to draw breath just by speaking to it and cradling it and urging it, but there's nothing he can do, he's not a miracle-worker, it's useless, and then the other one arrives, my body spitting it out into the world like it's poison, pus, something to be rid of, but Anne wraps it in a towel and offers it to me anyway, as if I would *want* to take it in my arms, as if I would *want* to embrace something my body has just rejected...

And now I give in to the fear, because that's all I can do, and as it surges through me I crawl over on all fours towards the sobbing woman. Plaster granules crack and crunch beneath my palms. I locate her by sound alone. Not knowing which of the other three she is, I latch on to her and she instinctively reciprocates. Our arms fumble, and then we have each other and we're trembling and sobbing together in the lost, awful dark.

A STORM WAS brewing.

The long spell of good weather had reached its inevitable conclusion, its climatic climax. The heat had become weary, the sunshine old, the clear skies stale. The air, humid and hayfeverish, was crying out to be sluiced, changed, renewed; this, and more, the storm promised. From dawn onward it loitered on the horizon, a swathe of dark grey cloud hung with filmy tentacles of rain. Rumbling. Biding its time. It would move in over Downbourne when it was good and ready. Until then, it was content to portend.

And the townspeople were more than happy for it to come. Their rainwater butts begged for replenishment; their gardens gasped. They wanted a downpour. They wanted the world to be washed and returned to them sparkling and as new. They wanted pluvial England yet again to provide.

And there was another reason why the townspeople welcomed the storm's ominous rumbling and the veiled sunlight and the taste that hung in the air, the teary, back-of-the-throat taste of impending rain—because today was the day they buried Michael Hollingbury. In the graveyard of St Stephen's, the hole had been dug (a pagan icon, yes, but Hollingbury had been a churchgoer too, most of his life). In a winding-sheet made of old bedclothes, lodged in a small side-room at the town hall, the body waited. The service was scheduled for noon. By eleven, the route from the town hall to the church was already lined with people. They turned out to pay their last respects to their slain mayor, but they turned out, too, to mourn the passing of something else, though they weren't sure what. A kind of innocence, perhaps.

The body was carried to church on a bier that, in another life, had been a kitchen door. Resting on the shoulders of six solemn bearers, including Henry Mullins, it wended its way past the silent crowds, up to St Stephen's, through the lychgate, across to the grave site. The vicar, the decrepit Reverend Cave, conducted the service, his quavery ceremonial intonements punctuated by the distant growls of the storm. The body was lowered. Handfuls of soil were thrown. There was, and would be, no headstone. All that marked Hollingbury's final resting place was a cross consisting of two lengths of wooden stake lashed together, the lateral one etched with his name. There were several dozen such crosses scattered about the graveyard, in various states of decay. Dating from after the Unlucky Gamble, they were as impermanent as the headstones from before then were lasting.

And it was while the townsfolk's attention was on the funeral, and concomitantly on themselves, that Fen emerged from the front door of 12 Crane Street with a knapsack on his back and the solidest pair of shoes he owned on his feet. Closing the gate behind him, he turned and took one last look at the house, the front garden, the meticulously clipped hedge, then turned again and set off up the road, northwards. His expression was, other than a slight jut to his jaw, impassive. In five minutes he had reached the outskirts of town. In another five minutes he was passing the signpost on which, facing away from town, the name of Downbourne was still just discernible through a film of green mould. The road ahead was craggy and overgrown, in places festooned with weeds, a decaying ribbon of tarmac that wound downhill to a copse of trees and emerged beyond into open countryside. He had travelled just over a mile along it when the first fat raindrops started to fall.

2.
On the Rails

After the rain, the sun. The road steamed, and as if from nowhere gnats appeared, swirling in the damp air, cycling endlessly, endlessly upwards. Fen walked past dripping trees and fields of glistening crops and great swathes of pasture where cattle munched and defecated loudly, his soaked clothes slowly drying. For a while he felt a greater optimism than he ever expected his misgivings would allow him to feel. His spirits, like the gnats, while not actually rising, at least pretended to the ascendant.

His hope was that, *en route* to London, he would be able to depend—like Blanche Dubois—on the kindness of strangers. For the first two days of his journey, however, he encountered strangers aplenty but very little kindness. The villages and small towns he passed through, many of them not much more than collections of houses sprinkled along the road, were places where itinerants were greeted with, at best, wary looks, at worst thinly disguised hostility, the latter becoming the more common reaction the further from Downbourne he went. Fen had not appreciated—perhaps, through accustomedness, had forgotten—that Downbourne was in many regards exceptional. Blessed by its location and by its adoption of a strong, charismatic leader, it was a lucky little oasis that had held steady, maybe even prospered, while everything around it fell apart. He was soon reminded that, beyond Downbourne's radius of influence, life was very different. People had less, and guarded what little they had jealously.

On the two occasions when he stopped at a house and requested water for his canteen, it was once given grudgingly and once, without apology, refused. When, in one village, he settled down on the central green to unlace his shoes and air his feet, he was approached by a delegation of five locals, one of them bearing a pickaxe, another with a Staffordshire bull terrier on a leash, and was asked—in a manner not anticipating a refusal—to move on. And when, as dusk was falling on his first night away from Downbourne in nearly a decade, he began to look for somewhere to sleep, it was not until after he had knocked on several dozen doors (and once been threatened with a shotgun) that he finally found someone prepared to offer him a bed.

"Bed", it turned out, meant a stretch of floorspace in a garden shed, but despite the pervasive reek of fertiliser, the lack of any mattress or coverlet, and the dangerous-looking array of horticultural implements hung around the walls, the place was surprisingly cosy, and Fen, exhausted from walking, slept soundly. The next morning he bandaged his blistered feet using the roll of sticking plaster that Greeley had given him, and set off again.

The road he was following was an A road which, in the days when everybody had a car and fuel with which to propel it, would have got him to London in a couple of hours if the traffic was good. How many times had he driven up and down its snaking length, on shopping trips to the West End, visits to the theatre, to see friends? Too many to count. He remembered how he used to seethe with impatience if his speed dropped below thirty because he was stuck behind a lorry or some lumbering farm vehicle; how he would drum his fingers on the steering wheel as he waited at one of the many bottlenecks along the way—crossroads, traffic lights, roundabouts. That was all the road had been then, a two-hour shuttle between home and the capital, with various obstacles to be negotiated along the way, some moving, some stationary.

On foot, it was a different entity. Its landmarks were hours, not minutes, apart. Its rises and falls, twists and turns, segued into one another, so gradually that at times Fen thought he had strayed onto the wrong road by mistake, since this one was unfurling prospects that did not accord with his recollection of it. He was used to seeing the scenery from car windows, condensed by speed. He was not used to seeing it evolve incrementally and fluently from one section to the next. Compounding the impression of unfamiliarity was the fact that, between the last time he had travelled this way and now, sizeable changes had been wrought by neglect and nature. The vegetation on either side of the road had encroached, at times narrowing it to half its width. Tree roots had thrust up through the camber, cracking the tarmac like reptile hatchlings breaking out of their eggs. The countryside around the road had altered, too. The hedgerows between fields had grown shaggy and rank so that there were no neat divisions; one field seemed to sprawl into another. It wasn't rare to come across a service station whose petrol pumps and forecourt were wreathed with weeds, or an isolated pub, now abandoned to the elements and half engulfed by rampant greenery. Everywhere, the slow capitulation of man to Nature, and Fen could not help thinking of Michael Hollingbury's death—his murder—and how this had been an inversion of the process he was seeing around him. Nature's representative destroyed on a pyre of manmade detritus, a small setback in a war which Nature was everywhere else winning handsomely.

NEAR THE END of the second day, Fen halted at the beginning of one of the road's infrequent stretches of dual carriageway. Sitting down on the verge and leaning his back against the signpost that encouraged overtaking for the next four hundred yards, he inventoried the contents of his knapsack and was dismayed to discover that he had consumed well over half of the dry rations supplied by Alan Greeley. The dry rations had been intended as a supplement to the warm, hearty meals Fen was to have received from warm, hearty homeowners whom he had anticipated would welcome him eagerly into their warm, hearty homes and offer him a place at their warm, hearty tables. He knew now how naïve this expectation had been, but that did not alter the fact that he was going to run out of food within a day or so unless the level of stranger-kindness improved dramatically (which, on the evidence so far, seemed unlikely, and he predicted that, with London on the horizon, it was only going to deteriorate further). He realised he was reaching, if not actually at, the point of no return. Turning back was the only sensible option.

But then—he reminded himself as he clambered wearily to his feet again—since when had "sensible" ever been a factor in this enterprise? Indeed, if anything characterised what he was up to, it was surely an utter lack of sense.

Coldly consoled by this thought, he resumed walking.

Near the end of the stretch of dual carriageway, just before it funnelled down to a single lane again, the road traversed a railway cutting. As Fen approached this, he became aware of a delicious aroma—or an aroma that would have been more delicious had it not carried for him a memory of the Green Man's demise. Roasting meat. At first he could not pinpoint where the smell was coming from, but then he saw a narrow plume of smoke twirling up from down in the cutting. He moved to the safety fence at the edge of the road and peered over.

Two parallel sets of rust-dulled railway tracks curved away into the distance. On the left-hand of the two, parked a dozen yards along from the road bridge, was a train, or rather part of a train, a single carriage. It was painted extraordinarily, a colourful, hectic mélange of figures and patterns adorning every inch of its bodywork, even the roof; and beside it, sitting on the shallow-raked embankment, was someone in a railwayman's uniform, a man, black-bearded, brown-skinned. He was squatting in front of a cooking fire, absorbed in the task of turning a spitted animal on a steel rotisserie which had once been part of a barbecue set. The animal appeared to be a rabbit, divided into halves, front and back.

Fen watched the bisected creature revolve, its skin gently charring, sparks of dribbled fat fizzling in the fire, and all at once his mouth was awash with saliva. His stomach, having had nothing to digest over the past thirty-six hours but peanuts, raisins, banana chips, and some chunks of pepperoni dipped in mustard, grumbled greedily. Hunger vied with caution. There was no reason to suppose the railwayman was any friendlier than anyone else he had met on his travels so far. Caution won. Fen was just about to back away from the fence and continue on his way when the railwayman, happening to glance up, caught sight of him. Immediately, a smile broke through the man's beard, like a sudden white moon. He raised a hand.

"Hello, my friend!"

And that was how Fen became a passenger aboard the *Jagannatha*.

Ravi Wickramasinghe had been a train driver for a decade and a half until the Unlucky Gamble sent England spiralling into freefall. Throughout that period he had been a diligent servant of the rail industry: never once missed a shift, often filled in for sick colleagues, did his utmost to ensure his trains arrived at their destinations on time, and if running behind schedule apologised over the intercom system in such a profuse and elaborate fashion that few of his passengers disembarked disgruntled. Indeed, his late-arrival announcements, he told Fen, had become legendary among commuters on his routes. He had heard from ticket inspectors that people often claimed they looked forward to delays, simply so that they could hear their driver offer contrition and furnish them with a not necessarily honest reason for why they were not where they were supposed to be at the time they were supposed to be there. Instead of the usual dreary litany of signalling failures and engine breakdowns and adverse leaf/track interfaces, Wickramasinghe used to offer preposterous excuses—less truthful but also less aggravating. An escaped elephant on the line was one of his favourites. "And what is it doing on the line? It is making a trunk call!" Another classic (to use Wickramasinghe's own description) was the somewhat surreal "We have not slowed down at all; rather, the world has speeded up around us." And then there was: "For those who expected to reach the terminus by eight forty-seven, I regret to say we have not met our Waterloo."

And everything had been fine, and then everything had gone to pot. Rail services had stumbled on, growing more erratic and unreliable with each passing day, and Wickramasinghe had done his best to keep his passengers entertained and amused even as their numbers dwindled and the frequency of hold-ups, curtailed journeys and cancellations increased. Inevitably, though, the situation had got to the point where the rail networks had had to begin laying employees off. And who had been one of the first drivers to go?

"You," said Fen, through a mouthful of rabbit meat.

"Me," Wickramasinghe confirmed. "The commuter's friend. They tossed me aside like I was nothing. 'Oh, let's lose the bloody Paki. No one will miss him.'" His tone was one of regret rather than rancour, the tone of someone who has shouldered more than his fair share of prejudice and abuse.

"You're Indian, though, aren't you?"

"Still a 'bloody Paki' as far as most people are concerned."

"And this." Fen indicated the single rail carriage. "This is where you live now."

Wickramasinghe shook his head, beaming a splendid grin. "I live," he said, "everywhere."

It took Fen a moment to divine the meaning of this gnomic pronouncement. "It runs?"

"She's called the *Jagannatha*, and we travel the rails together, she and I."

Fen peered at the carriage. It was a venerable piece of rolling stock, at least forty years old, but looked younger, and jauntier, thanks to the illustrations with which it was adorned. Here and there a scrap of its original livery was visible, but mostly this was obscured beneath dramatic representations of the pantheon of Hindu gods and goddesses. Here was blue-skinned Vishnu, seated on a throne of cobras. Here was ten-armed Shiva, sword-wielding and ferocious. Here was four-headed Brahma. And here were others whom Fen could not identify, all of them interlaced with strips of curlicued Sanskrit text that wove in and out of their dramatic poses like strains of music. It was a beautiful piece of work, and he said as much to Wickramasinghe, who took the compliment well.

"I am not an artist. I had never tried anything like this before, but my hand, it seemed, was divinely guided. Ganesha, god of new ventures, blessed me."

"Ganesha. He's the one with the elephant's head, isn't he? I don't see him."

"He's on the other side. When you have finished eating, I will take you on a tour."

An idea was forming in Fen's mind, a possibility. "You know, I'm surprised you can actually move about. I really had no idea there was still electricity in the rails."

"Oh yes, oh yes. In and around London there is. The Council has even managed to establish some regular services. I do not know how many people actually use them. I think they are a token gesture more than anything. Nevertheless..."

"So it is possible to get in and out of London by train."

"It can be done, yes. This is where you are headed? London?"

Fen nodded.

"May I ask why?"

Fen told him why, gnawing rabbit all the while. Rabbit had become a dietary staple in England since the Unlucky Gamble, its stringy gaminess no longer a deterrent to its enjoyment. Hare, mink, stoat, ferret—these too had been added to the nation's gastronomic repertoire, along with most types of bird, with the inevitable consequence that English cuisine was now more of an international laughing-stock than ever, and not only that but subject to all sorts of exaggerated and distorted rumours. In the United States, for instance, it was believed that American fast-food concessions in England served a "badger burger" (untrue, of course, since the fast-food conglomerates had closed down their English operations years ago, and it was anyway doubtful any of them would have been quite so honest about the meat content of one of their products), while in France, where just about any creature higher up the evolutionary ladder than the earthworm was considered edible, jokes about *les Anglais* and mouse pies were considered the height of topical humour. Or so it was alleged, at any rate. The provenance of such stories was dubious, and what they seemed to offer, more than anything else, was a reflection of the English attitude to foreigners' attitude to the English.

Thanks to his hunger this particular rabbit tasted better than usual to Fen, and he took frequent breaks from his account of the raid by the British Bulldogs and Moira's abduction to avail himself of fresh morsels of its flesh, which he chewed and swallowed with relish and which his stomach received with gurgling gratitude. Wickramasinghe listened attentively, eating rabbit himself but leaving the lion's share to his guest.

The rabbit was nothing but bones by the time Fen's narration was finished.

"A terrible state of affairs," opined Wickramasinghe, sighing. "I admire you for what you have undertaken. I know of the British Bulldogs. They have a fearsome reputation. You are a brave man."

"Not really," said Fen. "Are you married?"

"I was."

"I'm sorry. Is she—? Is your wife—?"

"No. No. Not dead. Daljit fled to India the moment things started getting shaky. Took our two sons with her and went to live in Calcutta with some cousin she barely knew."

"Oh, I see." It had been a common enough practice among England's immigrant community, renouncing your strife-torn adoptive land for the comparative security of the country from which you or your parents or your grandparents originally hailed.

"But I take your point," Wickramasinghe said. "In your shoes I would have probably done the same. What binds a husband to a wife is as powerful as it is hard to define, no? There is love. There is passion, at least to begin with. There is friendship, after the passion has faded. But there is more, too. A unity, a fusion of selves that takes place over the years, slowly, gradually, until you no longer know where you end and your other half begins. 'Your other half'—that pretty much sums it up, does it not? The part of you that is not you."

Fen murmured assent, licking rabbit grease off his fingers.

"Now listen, my friend," Wickramasinghe said. "I have a proposal for you."

Fen had an inkling of what the railwayman was about to suggest. It was, indeed, the very thing he had been hoping Wickramasinghe would suggest.

His answer could not have been anything other than yes.

THE *JAGANNATHA* WAS a home on wheels, neatly and narrowly self-contained. Up front was the driver's cab, which Wickramasinghe had decked out so that its interior resembled nothing so much as that of a Bombay taxi. A garland of nylon marigolds festooned the viewing window. Perched among the gauges and switches of the control desk were an incense holder (but no incense) and a small plastic figurine of Krishna playing the flute. To the pale-green walls had been added more lines of Sanskrit like those on the outside of the carriage—they were prayers, Wickramasinghe informed Fen—along with an intricately-petalled lotus and a reversed swastika. Wickramasinghe was quick to assure Fen that the latter was a fylfot, a Vedic symbol of wellbeing, and not anything more sinister. There were also two photographs on the wall, pinned in place. One was a formal portrait of a chubby woman, posed in her best sari, regarding the camera shyly, her hair centre-parted with almost geometric precision, her *tika* neat and round in the middle of her forehead. The other was a snapshot of a pair of mischievous-looking boys, hugging and gurning in a back garden.

"Daljit," said Wickramasinghe, pointing to the woman. He indicated each of the boys. "Sanjay. Naz."

"A lovely family," said Fen.

"It was."

Back from the cab, there were four first-class passenger compartments, one of which, with a blanket draped over the window for a curtain, was Wickramasinghe's sleeping quarters. To the rear of these was a small standard-class section, and right at the back of the carriage there was a toilet with a basin that did not work and a lavatory which Wickramasinghe had rigged up, by removing the base of the retention tank below, so that it emptied out straight onto the track without having to be flushed.

"Come and see how comfortable this is," Wickramasinghe said, ushering Fen into one of the spare first-class compartments.

Fen tested the springs of the plush banquette seats appreciatively. "I suppose I shouldn't ask, but I presume you stole the *Jagannatha* from your employers?"

"Not stole her," Wickramasinghe replied, firmly and with a touch of indignation. "Not stole. I took her from the yards because she is rightfully mine. After the way I was treated, it is only proper that I should have her. Besides, she was out of service at the time. No one will have missed her." His previous bonhomie returned. "But never mind that. Please make yourself at home. If there's anything you want, let me know."

"I will. Thank you."

"Tomorrow, we get started."

"Not tonight?" Only then did it dawn on Fen that he was being invited to bed down for the night in the train.

"Tonight? Oh no. I never travel after dark. Too dangerous. Tomorrow."

There was a decent amount of daylight left, more than enough to see them safely to London, but Fen refrained from pointing this out. It was Wickramasinghe's train, after all, and he considered himself lucky to have met the fellow. No point in pushing that luck.

"Very well then. Tomorrow it is."

"Crack of dawn," said Wickramasinghe.

He was as good as his word. When Fen opened his eyes the next morning, the sky outside the compartment window was a watery wash of pre-sunrise grey and the *Jagannatha* was throbbing tunefully, keen to be in motion.

He found Wickramasinghe in the driver's cabin, perusing a timetable and a map of railway lines.

"Fen! Good morning, my friend. You slept well?"

"Wonderfully well." Fen glanced at the timetable, which was a typically no-frills London Council production: a few photocopied pages of typed text stapled down the middle. "I take it this is to ensure that we don't crash head-on with the six-twenty out of Victoria."

"Exactly, my friend, exactly. One cannot simply gad about the network at random. Each journey, each step of a journey, must be carefully worked out beforehand. Not to worry, I know what I am doing. You are in safe hands."

"That's nice to know. Erm, before we set off—are you hungry?" He showed Wickramasinghe his knapsack. "Only, I have some peanuts, some raisins, other stuff, if you're interested."

Wickramasinghe gave a small cry of delight. "I eat almost nothing but meat," he said, "and it makes my bowels so raw. Peanuts, raisins... This will be marvellous! Such a welcome change."

And with that Wickramasinghe seized the knapsack and proceeded to wolf down much of what remained of Fen's provisions. Fen was not given a chance to object, or even to advise moderation. The railwayman just launched into the dry rations, opening packet after packet and guzzling the contents by the handful, and after a few moments of inner debate Fen decided he had no choice but to join in and match him gulp for gulp. It was only fair, he supposed. Wickramasinghe had been generous with the rabbit last night, and he *was* giving him a free ride into London. Fen mentally reapportioned the significance of the foodstuffs: not a survival necessity any more but his ticket into London, his train fare.

When they had both eaten their fill, Wickramasinghe gave a decorous little burp, patted his belly and thanked Fen for a most kind and thoughtful gesture.

"And now," he said, lowering himself solidly onto the driver's stool, "we commence our journey. Would you mind going back to your seat, Fen?" He jerked a thumb towards the rear of the carriage. "Passengers are not allowed in the cab while the train is in motion."

"Are you serious?"

Wickramasinghe looked at him levelly. "Quite serious."

"But what's the harm in my staying here?"

"You might distract me."

"But—but I'll be very quiet. You won't even notice I'm here. The thing is, this may seem silly to you, but ever since I was a kid I've always wanted to ride up front in a train." As a matter of fact, Fen had secretly been hoping that he might even be allowed to *drive* the train part of the way.

"I understand. I quite understand. Nonetheless I must insist that you go back and sit down. That is the proper thing to do."

"The proper thing."

"Please, my friend."

Bemused, and not a little disappointed, Fen returned to the compartment where he had spent the night and sat down next to the window, facing forwards.

A moment later, the *Jagannatha* started to roll. At the same time there was an electric pop from the intercom speakers in all the compartments, and Wickramasinghe's voice issued forth.

"A very good morning, ladies and gentlemen. This is your driver. As you can see, we are on our way again, and there is no reason to believe that we will not reach our destination as scheduled. For those of you who joined the train at the last stop, this is the London service, calling at London and several other places beforehand. Our estimated journeying time is four days, and I hope you will have a—"

"What!" Fen leapt to his feet and hurried up the corridor. Leaning in through the doorway to the cab, he tapped Wickramasinghe on the shoulder. "Did I just hear you right, Ravi? Did you just say four days?"

Wickramasinghe, directing a stern look at him, eased off on the power controller. "What did I tell you about passengers in the cab while the train is in motion?" he said, as the *Jagannatha* gently decelerated.

"Never mind that. Four days?"

"I don't want to have to lock the door."

"How *can* it be four days? We're twenty-five miles from London!"

Sighing, Wickramasinghe applied the brake, and the train juddered to a halt. "It seems I did not clarify the situation to you as I should have done."

"It seems you didn't."

"It is a very complicated business, Fen, making this journey. There are many factors to be taken into consideration." Wickramasinghe pointed at the rail map and timetable. "For one thing, as you already know, we must steer clear of other users of the rails. I am sure you can appreciate that that is of vital importance. And the only way we can manage that is by making certain detours and excursions, some of them quite prolonged and convoluted. We must thread ourselves in and around everyone else, you see, every scheduled train on the timetable, and in some instances that means going many, many miles out of our way, doubling back, all sorts of manoeuvres that may seem, to the layman, illogical. This, you understand, is simply so that we can make it to London in one piece. I am sure you are as keen as I am not to collide with another train at a combined speed of, oh, say a hundred miles an hour. I am sure you would rather we avoided *that*."

"Well, obviously."

"Then there is the matter of points. Not every junction will be aligned in our favour, so there will be occasions when we have to stop and wait for the automatic switching systems to change them, or we will have to, again, make detours in order to locate a set of points that *are* aligned in our favour. This, too, will add time. Not travelling at night, that is another factor to consider. As is damaged track. During the worst of the bombing our friends in the International Community, deliberately or otherwise, hit the network in several places. Some repairing was done, but not all the damage was fixed. Naturally we have to go around the sections that weren't fixed. Other rail users, points, not travelling at night, damaged track." Wickramasinghe checked the items off on his fingers. "Oh, and of course we must take into account the unknown. Specifically, stopping for food. I have made it my rule never to pass up any meal opportunities that come my way."

"Meal opportunities?"

"Like last night's rabbit," Wickramasinghe said, as though explaining something patently obvious.

"The rabbit?"

"Rail kill, Fen. How else do you think I came by it?"

Fen frowned. "I don't know. Trapped it?"

"I am no huntsman. I could not set a trap if my life depended on it. The rails provide for my needs. Either I run some animal over or it electrocutes itself on the live rail and lies beside the track waiting for me to discover it. You would be surprised, Fen, how much wildlife there is out there, eager to throw itself into my path. Why, just last week I hit a baby deer. That kept me going for three days, that did, and I must say it was most tasty!"

He smacked his lips, and Fen found himself feeling faintly queasy. It was clear now why the rabbit had been in two pieces.

"Oh, don't look like that!" Wickramasinghe admonished. "I will not touch anything that is not reasonably fresh. If I come across a carcass the birds have already had a go at—no way. And a train's wheels—*swish*! One could not ask for a cleaner, quicker death."

Wickramasinghe, Fen felt, had a point. If you could eat something that had lain in a snare for several hours or that had been raised in a pen and slaughtered by having its neck wrung, then you could surely have no objection to eating something that had been shocked to death by a few hundred volts of electricity or instantaneously bisected by the front bogies of a speeding locomotive. "Fair enough," he said. "I accept that this isn't going to be half as straightforward as I thought. But really... Four days? I could walk it in one."

"If Ganesha does not smile on us, it may even be as much as five," Wickramasinghe said, eyeing the timetable ruminatively.

"Then much though I hate to do this, Ravi, I'm going to have to decline your offer after all. It was very kind of you to say you'd get me to London, and I'm grateful for the hospitality you've shown me, but—"

"Of course there is one major advantage to sticking with me," said Wickramasinghe, butting in as though Fen had not been speaking at all. "I know where the British Bulldogs live. Lewisham. And my intention is to take you to Brockley Station, or perhaps Ladywell. In other words, virtually to their doorstep. Which, of course, means you will not have to cross most of south London by yourself and on foot—which, take it from me, as a one-time Londoner, is no easy thing. I will be saving you from the most hazardous part of your journey. And there is always the possibility that if, no, *when* you find your wife, we could meet up at some prearranged rendezvous and I could escort you both back out of the capital. How about that? Does any of that give you reason to reconsider?"

It did. Wickramasinghe had not mentioned anything before to Fen about taking him right to the Bulldogs' lair. No question, that would be a bonus. And a chance of a return trip to boot?

All at once Fen saw that his options were amplified. Assuming for a moment that he *was* able to wrest Moira from the Bulldogs' clutches—a massive assumption, but there you go—wasn't there a possibility, at least a small one, that he might be able to rescue the other Downbourne women at the same time? He might if Wickramasinghe was on hand with the *Jagannatha* to get them all safely home. The *Jagannatha* could carry them a good half of the way to Downbourne, perhaps even further, perhaps even as far as the station at Wyndham Heath, and although it probably would not be a quick journey, it would at least be a relatively comfortable one.

He was well aware that what he was now contemplating was a task several orders of magnitude harder than the already hard task he had set himself. On the other hand, if he succeeded in pulling it off, he would restore the status quo not only in his own household but in all of Downbourne. And he was not so deficient in self-interest that he didn't quietly relish that prospect of being hailed a hero by the entire town.

"OK, let's get this straight," Fen said to Wickramasinghe. "It's going to take a bit of time, but you can get me all the way to where the Bulldogs live and back out of London again."

"Certainly the one, probably the other."

"All right. And—well, I'm not sure how to put this, but in return you get...?"

"Nothing other than your company and a chance to play the Good Samaritan."

That settled it as far as Fen was concerned.

"Then I shan't hold you up any longer. Onwards."

Wickramasinghe grinned, then pointed down the corridor.

Obediently Fen returned to his seat, and the *Jagannatha* resumed rolling.

First, water. Then, some time later, food.

The water comes in two bottles that, by the feel of them, are the type that used to contain mineral water—although wherever the stuff that's in them now is from, it didn't come bubbling up from some scenic mountain spring such as the one that's undoubtedly depicted on the label.

As for the food: hard cheese which, if we could see it, would probably have flowers of mould on it, and some chocolate that's been in the sun and melted and resolidified. Probably more than once.

Susannah takes charge. Apportions out the food. Makes us go easy on the water, not gulp it down as we'd like to. Someone's got to do this, I suppose. Someone's got to be the practical one, the one who decides to make the best of things. I can almost hear her thinking: *I'm a town councillor, it's what's expected of me*. Maybe it helps her deal with the headachey thirst, the pain of hunger, the fear.

So we sip the water in measured doses (warm, brackish, chloriney). We chew the cheese and nibble the chocolate like we're wainscot mice. And we wait.

That's all there is to do.

That's the only way to pass the time.

Wait.

I think we're over the worst of it now. The worst of it was the anticipation of what's going to happen to us. The uncertainty of when, where, how. We're resigned to it now. We've subsided into a kind of acceptance. In a way, we're quite impatient. *Come on. Let's get it over with*.

It's Zoë I feel sorriest for. I feel sorry for myself, of course, but Zoë... They're bound to take her first. Young, pretty thing like her. Teenager. I can just imagine them rubbing their hands, grinning razor-sharp grins. Boasting how they're going to "break her in".

Then there's Jennifer. She was the one sobbing, the one I hugged. Jennifer Franklin. She's gone all but mute now. Catatonic. She's pissed her knickers—you can smell it on her—and just sits in the dampness, not caring. She won't put up any resistance when they come for her. She'll just let them do what they want with her. Shut them out. Maybe it'll seem to her that they're doing it to someone else, someone miles away.

Susannah, I think, will fight.

I certainly am going to fight.

I'm going to fight them with all the strength I have. Weakened as I am, I'm going to kick and punch and spit and scratch and bite. They'll have me, but they won't have me easily. I'm going to make them pay for it, every second of it. If I can, I'm going to make them regret it.

In the meantime...

Wait.

I'm good at waiting.

"You waited for me," Fen once said. He was being coy. Romantic. He meant because I'm a few years older than him. Because I remained single as if anticipating his arrival in my life. Because even before I met him, even though I had no idea he existed, I somehow knew he was on the horizon and so didn't become permanently attached to anyone else.

A nice conceit. Good for his ego. I didn't contradict him. I let him believe it was true.

The truth is, I wasn't holding out for him. Wasn't waiting. I wasn't some silly soppy girl with dreams of Mr Perfect. The truth is, Fen came along at the right time. I'd done with the half-arsed dates, the half-hearted boyfriends, the on-off relationships with men who couldn't make up their minds, the good-lookers who thought they could get away with murder, the ugly-bugs who couldn't believe they weren't God's gift to womankind, the so-called sensitive ones who pretended to be interested in my personality when all they were interested in was my pussy, and the married bastards, good God, the married bastards who'd swear on their children's lives that they were unattached. I was fed up with all the lies, the evasions, the meaningless flattery, the disappointing sex. I'd had enough of all that. I was tired of being available. I was tired of being Girl About Town. That's why I gave up working full-time at the magazine, went freelance and moved out of London to Downbourne. Here was a place, I thought, where I'd get a bit of peace and quiet. Here was a place where I might meet a decent man, an honest man.

And I did.

There he was, this unassuming little country schoolteacher. Handsome enough. Thoughtful in a way that London men don't have time to be. I met him at that drinks party—who gave it? Can't remember. He was introduced to me as "Downbourne's most eligible bachelor", can you believe it. Probably true, though. I met him and I took one look at him and I thought, yes, you'll do.

No, let's be accurate here. I was introduced to him and what I thought was: Fenton? What kind of a name is that? Fenton Morris?

And shortly after we got engaged I remember thinking, Moira Morris? What kind of a name is *that*?

He told me what Moira means. At the party where we met. His artless way of chatting me up, I suppose. I'd had no idea that the name had a meaning. Mum gave it to me to remind me of her ancestry, my Irish heritage, and I'd thought that that was all it was: an ungainly, unfashionable forename that I'd been saddled with, the Celtic version of Mary.

But Fen said, "Moira. That's Ancient Greek for 'destiny'. Did you know that?"

I said no. I think I might have laughed. I think I was impressed. No, I *was* impressed. And charmed.

Smart-arse, I thought. But affectionately.

A decent man. A man with a brain. Handsome enough. No dress sense, but that could be sorted out.

I didn't wait for him. He was there in the right place at the right time.

They come.

The door unlocks, rattles open. A torch beam flares in, blindingly bright.

"Her."

It's Zoë, like I thought. They seize her by the arms. She cries out. She writhes.

I should attack them, but what good will it do? I need to conserve what little strength I have left. For when they come for me.

Zoë screams and pleads. The torch beam waves wildly around, and in its dazzle I see Susannah's face—grubby and pinched and flinching. Jennifer's face—lost. Zoë's face—a mask of terror and misery. The faces of the men—grim, greedy.

Then they're gone, Zoë with them. The door slams. The darkness is smeared with acid-green after-images. Torch flashes like Chinese script. Glowing skeletal faces.

Zoë's voice echoes along the corridor outside, growing faint, like someone drowning, slipping beneath the waves.

Who will it be next?

No idea.

But if it's me, they won't have me cheaply.

SO THEY TRAVELLED, Fen and Wickramasinghe, shuttling around the maze of rails, brushing London like a moth flirting with a light bulb, now coming close, now darting away again. From his compartment window Fen watched the landscape change, shifting back and forth between satellite town and countryside. The distinction between the two was not easy to perceive any more. The Green Belt was far greener than anyone ever could have predicted back when the term was coined. (It was, in fact, no longer something so orderly and constrictive as a belt. Rather, Fen thought, a Green Wreath.) The parcelled-out regularity of the satellite towns had erupted into a rough verdant anarchy, so that with their unmown lawns and unmanaged parks they merged raggedly with the farmland and forest around them. And here and there was a destroyed power station, a flattened factory, even a bombed-out church, all adding to the general impression of civilisation knocked loose from its moorings.

In its roving the *Jagannatha* passed both of the capital's principal airports. Both were ruined almost beyond recognition, scorched wastelands with the shells of ruined jumbo jets lying around like used and discarded Christmas crackers. The train also passed a couple of military bases, their huts and hangars charred skeletons, their runways cratered, their parade grounds pounded to smithereens. The International Community's cruel-to-be-kind ministrations were evident everywhere, like the blundering efforts of a mad, myopic surgeon, trying to cut out a cancer he cannot find.

The journey was a stop-start affair. There was no flow to it. The great majority of the time was spent at a standstill, often in sidings where the track was barely visible among plantains and foxgloves, or else at small rural halts—cobwebbed ticket halls, waiting rooms with rotted benches, platforms wind-scoured and bare. Between, there were short hops from one place of refuge to the next. And then there were the unplanned halts, when Wickramasinghe would jam on the brakes and leap from his cabin with a yelp of predatory glee, having spied some potential repast lying defunct at the trackside. As he had told Fen, he did not touch any animal that was not reasonably fresh. He also drew the line at cats and dogs, the latter of which turned up with some frequency (hardly surprising given the number of rogue dog packs—once-domesticated canines and their descendants—which now roamed the land, a hazard to livestock and, on occasion, humans). With these exceptions, anything was considered consumable, and normally *was* consumed.

Fen's mustard went down well at mealtimes. "Such a rarity, such a delicacy!" Wickramasinghe enthused as he slathered the condiment over pieces of whatever luckless mammal they were eating. In fact, Fen's presence in general seemed a source of continual pleasure to the railwayman. For one thing, as he admitted to Fen, it gave him an excuse to make the intercom announcements he was so proud of. Seldom did a leg of the journey pass without at least one wisecrack or witticism from the driver's cabin. But Fen was also someone to talk to, company, *intelligent* company—such a bonus! Wickramasinghe had been happy enough on his own, riding the rails, going wherever the whim took him, and although he would meet people occasionally, spend perhaps an hour or two with them, share some food, he had never actually offered anyone a lift in the *Jagannatha* before. He was glad that, in Fen's case, he had taken the plunge. He would not have done so if Fen had not been so friendly, or for that matter so deserving of his assistance. It was gratifying, he said, to be helping out someone so educated and so courageous.

Wickramasinghe was certainly a talkative sort, but Fen didn't mind. Often the topic of conversation was Daljit. How beautiful she was, and how cruel she had been to abandon him like that, dragging Sanjay and Naz with her off to India, where neither of them belonged or had even visited before. It was not right for a wife to behave in such a manner. However, Wickramasinghe had found it in his heart to forgive her, and he was sure that when things in England settled down again, as they were bound to sooner or later, she and the boys would return. Fen agreed that this would happen, yes, definitely. Once things in England settled down. He did not add that he believed England wasn't going to be readmitted into the global fold for some while yet. Too many other countries were enjoying its plight. Not only did these other countries get a kick out of seeing a major-league player brought low, but England's plummet from First to Third World status was a salutary reminder of what could happen to any industrialised nation if its leaders were not careful. England was an object lesson in how *not* to handle an economic crisis, not to mention an example of just how fragile the constraints of civilised society were, and for these moral and instructive reasons the International Community had a vested interest in ensuring that its rehabilitation was not allowed to begin any time soon.

It hadn't escaped Fen's attention that Wickramasinghe was a little odd. He took the view, however, that the railwayman's eccentricity was an unavoidable by-product of his chosen lifestyle. Too much time spent in his own company had impaired his social skills, so that he had forgotten how one was expected to behave when around others. In addition, he was lost in a mild delusion of former glories, locked in the habits of the period of his life when he had felt the most functional, the most fulfilled. In this respect he reminded Fen of Reginald Bailey, or rather of Donald Bailey's frank assessment of his younger brother, as someone who chose not to think about anything that was going on around him but just let it happen. Wickramasinghe appeared to have slipped into a similar kind of fugue state, existing independently of—and immune to—the outside world, interacting with it only as far as necessity required. Denial of the present was a means as valid as any other of holding on and surviving, and Fen could not foresee a way in which, in this instance, it would entail any unwelcome consequences for himself.

In the evenings, after pegging out sheets of polythene on the ground to catch dew for drinking water, Wickramasinghe would spend a good half-hour or so poring over the rail map and timetable, plotting the next day's travels. At no point did Fen actually catch sight of any of the other users of the rails whom Wickramasinghe was at such pains to avoid, but when he mentioned this to the railwayman, saying he was surprised that he had not seen even *one* train pass by during one of their many stoppages, Wickramasinghe's reply was straightforward and credible enough: "I have to leave large margins of error, Fen. Who can trust a timetable completely? If we are close enough to see another train, then we are too close for comfort."

Fen took the point, and although he found it frustrating to travel in this way, in fits and bursts, with only the vaguest sense of his ultimate destination growing nearer, he soon began to settle into the journey's fractured rhythm and to enjoy the opportunity, enforced as it was, to see more of the nation than he had seen in ages. He was amused by the looks the *Jagannatha* drew from the people it passed—a few paid no attention, but a moving train was still a novelty and a moving train that sported a paint job like the *Jagannatha*'s even more so—and he began to understand the attraction to Wickramasinghe of a life perpetually on the move. Everything was there outside the train windows, England in all its crippled tenacity. Everything was there, but at one remove, and never for long.

He thought of Moira, of course. Every time there was a delay and every time there was not. When the *Jagannatha* was stationary, he would fall to wondering where she was and how she was, and he would itch for the train to be on its way again; and when the *Jagannatha* was rolling and he found himself gazing contentedly out at the view like some idle tourist, there would sometimes come a pang of guilt. How could he sit here enjoying himself when his wife was a captive of the British Bulldogs, suffering God knew what at their hands? The pangs of guilt were short-lived, however, and disturbingly mild. And grew milder still as time went on.

On the evening of their third day together, tucked away on a spur of a branch line somewhere in the depths of Berkshire, Fen and Wickramasinghe ate a dinner of spit-roasted pheasant. Wickramasinghe was in ebullient mood, pronouncing himself highly satisfied with their progress so far. "We are, you might say, well on track," he told Fen. "Two more days, I should think."

"Two. You're quite definite about that."

"Oh, indeed. Three at the very most."

This, of course, represented a significant upward revision of Wickramasinghe's original estimate of four days, but Fen was content to believe that the railwayman knew what he was doing. He retired to bed confident that within three days' time he and Moira would be reunited.

Not long after he got off to sleep, he was startled awake by the sound of the compartment door being rolled open.

"Ravi?"

Wickramasinghe was standing in the doorway, picked out in sharp relief against the dark blue, star-flecked sky that filled the corridor window behind him. Clad only in white Y-fronts, the railwayman stumbled into the compartment and sat down heavily on the banquette opposite. He heaved a sigh. All at once his shoulders began to jerk up and down, and Fen realised he was sobbing.

"Ravi, what's the matter?"

It took a while to coax out an answer.

"I miss her, my friend," Wickramasinghe said.

"Daljit?"

Wickramasinghe nodded. "I have just remembered—tomorrow is her birthday." And he started blubbering again, helplessly, like a little boy who has fallen and barked his shin.

Fen sat up, gathering the blanket under which he had been lying and wrapping it around his waist and thighs. He, too, was wearing just his underpants. He hesitated, then reached across and laid a consoling hand on Wickramasinghe's knee.

"It must be difficult," he said. "I know how you feel. To be apart from someone you love... Believe me, I've been there. Not in the same way, but close enough."

Wickramasinghe drew in a long, sniffling breath. "I had a feeling you would understand."

"But perhaps now's not the time to dwell on it. Like they say: everything seems worse at night. You should go back to bed, try and sleep. I'm certain it won't seem so bad in the morning."

"I miss the touch of her. The feel of her hair. Her smile. The way she used to kiss me. The way we used to lie together in bed." Wickramasinghe patted Fen's hand, and then his hand came to rest on Fen's, cupping it warmly, clammily. "My life is such a lonely one," he said. "Sometimes I forget how much I need human contact."

Very slowly and deliberately Fen extricated his hand. "Ravi, I don't think—"

"Don't you ever feel like that too? In need of human contact?"

"This probably isn't the time and place to discuss this," Fen said, all too conscious of his near-nakedness, and of Wickramasinghe's.

"More than just conversation. Physical contact."

"I really think we'd be better off—"

"I'm only asking that we lie together, Fen. I'm not suggesting anything dirty. I'm not that way, not at all. But just the feel of skin on skin, body next to body... I think it is essential to us humans. Animals do it all the time, snuggle together for warmth, closeness, connection. Why not us?"

"Ravi, please. Just go back to your compartment."

"You won't even consider the idea?"

"I'm not at all comfortable with the idea."

"But don't you see—"

"The seat's too narrow, Ravi, and perhaps I'm too narrow-minded, because I take your point about animals and all that, but I'm not prepared to do it."

Wickramasinghe gazed at him across the compartment, eyes glistening with tears which reflected the starlight. "Too English, then," he said, sombrely and somewhat bitterly.

"If you like."

"Too stiff-of-lip. Too puckered-of-arse."

"Try not to take it personally or anything."

"Had I been a woman, you would not have thought twice about it."

"But Ravi— Oh, fuck it, what's the point? Ravi, just go back to your compartment. That's that."

For a while Wickramasinghe was silent and didn't move, and Fen wondered if this was going to turn nasty—if the railwayman's desire for cosy physical contact was going to turn into a desire for not-so-cosy physical contact. Thanks to his experience at the hands of the British Bulldogs, Fen was better prepared than he otherwise would have been for the likelihood and the result of an assault on his person. He didn't know how to fight now, any more than he had known back at the festival when the British Bulldogs had gatecrashed, but he did know what to expect, what being hit felt like, and so in that sense, if in no other, he was combat-hardened. And since Wickramasinghe did not appear to be in particularly good physical shape, lacking anything like the menacing, brutal toughness of a Bulldog, Fen thought that, if it came down to it, he had a good chance of successfully defending himself, and might even be able to wrestle Wickramasinghe into submission.

In the event, no violence occurred. Wickramasinghe, coming to a decision, got to his feet and, without another word, strode out of the compartment, returning to his own. Fen heard him stretch himself out on his banquette, and for a long time afterwards he sat, wide awake, listening intently, expecting Wickramasinghe at any moment to get up and come back and try again. He pictured the railwayman lying on his banquette, listening too, hoping Fen would have a change of heart and relent and come and join him. The silence that filled the *Jagannatha* seemed to effervesce with embarrassment and urgent longing.

Then Fen became aware of deep, low breathing coming from Wickramasinghe's compartment, unmistakably the thick, leisurely respiration of someone fast asleep, and he relaxed, sank back in the seat and wondered what the hell he should do. He was tempted to get dressed there and then, sneak out, get as far away as he could from the *Jagannatha*; but there were, he quickly realised, several drawbacks to this plan, the main one being that he had no precise idea of where he was. Somewhere in Berkshire, he knew, but that could mean as far from London as Downbourne was, perhaps further. If he was going to abandon the *Jagannatha*, he should at least do so when he was within spitting distance of the capital. Otherwise nearly a week's worth of travelling would have been in vain.

He felt, too, that there was an acceptably slight risk of the episode that had just taken place being repeated. And Wickramasinghe's intentions *had* been innocent, hadn't they? He missed Daljit; he simply wanted the proximity of another warm body. That was all it had been, right? And if it did happen again, it could be dealt with by the same method—gentle but persistent dissuasion.

So Fen talked himself into staying. In truth, he didn't much fancy the idea of setting out on foot in the dark, in the countryside, with no clear notion of where he was going. He decided that for the time being he was safer, on balance, remaining where he was. His best bet for getting to Moira lay with Wickramasinghe and the *Jagannatha*.

But from then on, till dawn, he slept like a cat, nervy and wire-taut, on the alert for the slightest sound.

THE FOLLOWING MORNING Wickramasinghe acted as if nothing had happened. Sunny and cheerful, he peppered the day's travels with the usual amusing announcements over the intercom, and during each break in the journey he left the cab and came back to chat with Fen. If there was any discernible alteration in his behaviour, it was that he was even more solicitous towards his passenger than previously. As if to reassure Fen that all the delays and meanderings had a purpose, he kept him continually up to date with where they were on the rail map and where they were aiming for on their next stint, and when, at lunchtime, they came across a plump dead pigeon sprawled on one of the sleepers in a fluster of bloody feathers, Wickramasinghe deemed this a very good omen. "A city pigeon," he said, as he started to pluck the bird and prepare it for cooking. "There'll be more of these in days to come."

Fen was encouraged. Maybe it was his imagination, but it *had* seemed to him that they were passing through built-up areas more and more that morning, that he was looking out at countryside from the window less and less—as though, rather than the *Jagannatha* homing in on London, London was reaching out towards the train, enticing it, beckoning it with arms of concrete and brick and glass.

As they ate the pigeon, Fen quizzed Wickramasinghe about entering the capital by rail. Were there checkpoints on the rail routes, as there were on the road routes?

Wickramasinghe confirmed that there were, and predicted that the vagaries of the network were finally going to allow the *Jagannatha* to reach one tomorrow, some time in the late afternoon if all went according to plan.

"You do have a permit, don't you, my friend?" he asked.

Fen assured him that he did.

Once through the checkpoint, Wickramasinghe continued, they would pick up speed. Inside the city's perimeter the journey would become markedly easier.

"Easier? Surely there'll be more trains about."

"Ah yes, more trains, but also more track and junctions, therefore a greater number of different routes we can take."

Later, when they were under way again, Fen fetched his knapsack down from the luggage rack. Cruikshank's London permit was lodged in an inside zip pocket, wrapped in a polythene bag for protection. With it was the bribe, the "something valuable" which Cruikshank had recommended Fen should bring along just in case. Fen had deliberated for a long time over what to take, what was easily portable and at the same time self-evidently costly. Now, he extracted the chosen item from the polythene bag and held it in the palm of his hand, studying it.

Moira's gold wedding band.

She had stopped wearing it—when? A few months ago, shortly after New Year. He couldn't pinpoint the exact day she removed it and its companion, her diamond engagement ring, from her finger, since he had not registered the rings' absence straight away, not consciously at any rate, and she herself had not drawn attention to what she had done. For a while he had sensed that there was something different about her, something indefinably *wrong* about her appearance, and the anomaly had nagged at him and nagged at him, until one morning, when, as he was bringing her breakfast, he had caught sight of her left hand resting pale on the counterpane, and had noticed its bareness... and there had been a row. It was the first time since the stillbirth that he had raised his voice to her, one of only a few times in their marriage when he had gone so far as to lose his temper. In retrospect he could see that that was exactly what she had wanted. Taking off the rings had been an act of provocation. At the time, though, he had been too enraged, and too hurt, to realise this, and had thus played right into her hands. Such a small gesture, the removal of the rings. Physically so insignificant. Yet what it had represented...

He remembered going to buy the rings from a jeweller's in Wyndham Heath. The engagement ring first, of course, which he had purchased on his own, and then the wedding band, which Moira had gone along with him to choose. After lengthy deliberation she had plumped for one in red gold, and it had been at the upper limit of his budget, and he had wanted it engraved, which had added to the expense, but he had not begrudged the money, not a single penny of it.

There it was, the engraving, three words in an ornate typeface around the inside of the ring:

Moira My Destiny

And this was the object she had one day decided—on a casual, callous whim—she no longer wished to adorn her, and had stowed in her keepsake box on top of the chest of drawers, along with her engagement ring, as though the two items of jewellery were suddenly of no greater importance to her than any other. A calculated insult. If Fen had been sensible he would have ignored it. Since the stillbirth Moira had not been herself. She had been another Moira, embittered and aloof, a woman angry at the world, a woman robbed. He should simply have accepted the taking off of the rings as another manifestation of her illness, her depression. But it had stung him; it had wounded him to the quick. She had even tried to make out that somehow *he* was in the wrong for not noticing sooner what was missing from her hand. No wonder he had had a go at her. You can take forbearance only so far.

He held the wedding band up to one eye and watched the scenery outside chunter past, framed by the ring's circle, blurrily reflected in its russet surface. An embankment capped with crazed hawthorn. The film-reel stutter of a fence. Some tumbleweed tangles of barbed wire and then a farmhouse, apparently deserted, holes in the roof, shattered hollows for windows. Now under a brick bridge, temporary darkness. Daylight again, and what looked like an expanse of heathland until the presence of sand bunkers revealed it as the palimpsest of a golf course...

Then the *Jagannatha* began to slow down again for another of its spells of idleness, and Fen returned the wedding band to the polythene bag and the bag to the pocket in the knapsack. He felt—and he did not know why—that it was better if Wickramasinghe didn't find out that he had such an item with him. At the checkpoint, he would produce it only if necessary.

He wondered if Moira would appreciate the irony—as he himself did, in a grim way—that the wedding band that she had so spitefully discarded all those months ago had now been designated a major role in saving her. There was a certain aptness to that, after all, a certain inverse symmetry.

Perhaps she would not. Perhaps, when he informed her what he had used the ring for, she would not even care.

SUSANNAH DOESN'T STRUGGLE. I really thought she was going to. We talked about it after they took Zoë, a quick, whispered discussion, and she seemed to agree with me—why make it easy for them? But when the time comes, she lets them lead her away, meek and compliant. And I can understand why. Rationally, it's the wise thing to do. Resistance will only bring more pain than necessary.

I can't help feeling betrayed, though. Betrayed and dispirited. If Susannah hasn't fought back, why should I?

So now it's just me and Jennifer in the room, in the dark. Dumbstruck distant Jennifer over in one corner. A few yards—and several worlds—away.

So really it's just me alone in the room.

Alone, and hating the smell of myself, the reek of my hair, my breath, my unwashed body. Alone, and sore all over from sitting and lying on bare floorboards. Alone, and thinking what's the point? What's the point in putting up a fight when they come to take me? The principle of the thing? Bugger that! Principles aren't going to improve my situation one bit. Principles are a luxury for people who aren't being held captive, who aren't waiting to be dragged out and raped.

Time pulses erratically. I try to count out sixty seconds. It seems to take an hour.

At one point I find myself scratching madly at the walls with my fingernails. I don't remember making a decision to do this. I just start doing it, spontaneously. Scratch-scrabble-scratch, like the hamster I used to have when I was small. He used to burrow furiously at the metal base of his cage. The noise used to drive me crazy. I keep going, honestly convinced I'm going to break through the wall and there'll be freedom beyond, and I recall the crater-like depressions I felt in the plaster when I first got here, and I realise I'm not the first to have tried this. Others have knelt here clawing, just like me, just like my hamster. Without success.

Some time later I realise that I've given up. My fingertips are throbbingly raw. There's no escape from here, not that way.

But...

Escape.

I'm calm now. Thinking hard.

Escape.

I try to recall what I saw as I arrived here. Not much, just glimpses by the light of the vans' headlamps. A sort of courtyard area surrounded by small, cubic houses. Ordinary housing-estate houses. I was aware we'd just come through a huge, heavy gate with spirals of barbed wire along the top. I was aware of walls—barricades, really—adjoining the gate. A stockade, twenty feet high, built from all kinds of household junk. After that I kept my head down and concentrated on the ground in front of me, so as to avoid the men's stares, to avoid catching anyone's eye. As we were hustled away from the courtyard, I saw only the tarmac underfoot, then threadbare grass, and then this house. This house with all its windows bricked up, blind.

So I know this is a kind of compound I'm in. A section of a housing estate commandeered by these men for themselves, cordoned off, secured. Beyond that, however, I'm in the dark (ha ha ha, very funny). I don't know how big the compound is, how many houses it contains, how far its perimeter extends. I don't even know what area of London I've wound up in.

What I do know is that escaping is a far better plan than resisting when the men come to take me. More realistic, not so short-term. All I need is a clearer idea of the layout of this place, and an opportunity. Both, I am certain, I will have soon. And then I will make my bid for freedom.

I'm so buoyed up by this new resolution of mine, this new goal—why didn't I think of it earlier?—that I feel the need to share it with Jennifer. Maybe it'll have a similar effect on her, stirring her out of her despair. Giving her something to hope for, a chink of light in this unrelenting darkness.

I crawl over to her.

When I reach her...

When I touch her...

I know.

I know almost before my groping hand finds her arm and I feel how cold her skin is.

Jennifer has found her own method of escape. A permanent one.

OVER THEIR EVENING meal, another rabbit, Fen recalled what Wickramasinghe had said during his nocturnal visit, that today was his wife's birthday. He hesitated about bringing this up, not wanting to be responsible for triggering another bout of lachrymose neediness, but decided there could be no harm in mentioning it. Wickramasinghe had been nothing but upbeat and good-humoured all day, more so than usual perhaps *because* it was Daljit's birthday.

The subject was delicately broached, but Wickramasinghe responded in a puzzled—and, to Fen, puzzling—fashion.

"My wife's birthday? No, no, my friend. Whatever gave you that idea? November. Daljit was born in November."

Fen, against his better judgement, pursued the matter. He insisted that Wickramasinghe had told him that today was Daljit's birthday.

"When did I tell you this?"

"When you... You know. In my compartment."

Wickramasinghe drew a blank. "What are you talking about? When was I in your compartment?"

Nothing in the railwayman's expression intimated deceit. It seemed he genuinely had no recollection of the incident.

Immediately Fen backtracked. "Oh no, wait, hold on," he said, scratching his chin in feigned confusion. Several days' worth of stubble crackled under his fingernails. "Now that I think about it... Yes. Yes, actually it was a dream I had."

It had to be one of the poorest pieces of dissembling ever committed, almost childlike in its clumsiness. Fen could not believe Wickramasinghe would fall for it.

Happily, he did.

"A very strange dream. I came in and told you about my wife's birthday? Most peculiar." And the railwayman gave a little *hmph* and nodded to himself in amusement.

Darkness fell and the two men turned in. Compartment door firmly shut, Fen took off his shoes and, without divesting himself of any other clothing, lay down on the banquette and drew the blanket up over him.

After a moment's thought he pulled the shoes to within easy reach. They were the only objects he had with him that could, if necessary, be pressed into service as weapons.

He waited.

He fell asleep.

He awoke after an uninterrupted night and, looking at the shoes and at himself, fully clothed, was ashamed. As he stretched vigorously, working out various kinks and stiffnesses in his muscles and joints, he asked himself if there had really been a need for such precautions. Wickramasinghe was harmless. If what he had said was true and he had no memory of entering the compartment the previous night, then most likely he had been sleepwalking—and sleepwalkers are a danger to no one but themselves.

Perhaps, he reasoned, he was feeling awkward and on his guard because he was so much at Wickramasinghe's mercy. He had surrendered his fate to a man he barely knew, all on the basis of a quick smile and a barbecued rabbit. Perhaps—better late than never—a sense of proper caution had caught up with him.

If so, it wasn't worth heeding. He put on his shoes and stood up and slid back the door, suffused with faith and confidence. Today: the checkpoint. Tomorrow, or possibly the day after: Moira. Wickramasinghe was unquestionably going to deliver on all that he had promised.

The *Jagannatha* was silent. From the quality of the silence, its deadness, its absoluteness, Fen knew that he was the only person aboard. He searched for Wickramasinghe anyway—the cab, the first class compartments, the standard class section. He knocked on the toilet door. No reply, and the "Engaged" sign was not showing in the slot. He opened the door. No one there. Outside, he circled the carriage. No sign of Wickramasinghe. He peered along the track, shading his eyes. He turned and peered in the other direction. A lukewarm morning breeze tickled the trees around him and set the trackside weeds quivering. Wickramasinghe was nowhere to be seen.

He remained nowhere to be seen all morning. Fen spent the time sitting in his compartment and making brief exploratory forays into the surrounding woodland, both activities carried out with mounting frequency and impatience. When he was in the *Jagannatha*, he felt he should be out searching for Wickramasinghe, but when he was out searching for Wickramasinghe he wondered why he was bothering—it was a waste of time, he wasn't going to find him, he might as well stay with the train.

The sun climbed, the day grew hot, and Fen began to worry. Not about Wickramasinghe. He was quite convinced that wherever the railwayman had gone, he had gone of his own accord, on some obscure personal mission. It was about his own mission that he began to worry. Wickramasinghe's disappearance was surely going to muck up their journey plan. If they didn't make the checkpoint today, how long until the next opportunity arose to get to one? How many days was this going to delay them?

By midday Fen began to experience the first dim stirrings of concern. It occurred to him that if Wickramasinghe *was* a sleepwalker, he could have blundered out of the carriage during the night and got lost. He hurried outside again and patrolled up and down the track, calling Wickramasinghe's name. The trees swallowed his voice. Having yelled himself hoarse, he clambered disconsolately back into the *Jagannatha*. He was very hungry by now, and there was not a scrap of food left in his knapsack other than the mustard. Motion, he realised, was vital to survival when you rode the rails. "Meal opportunities" did not come your way if you stayed put. He headed forward to the cab. A few evenings ago he had prevailed on Wickramasinghe to give him a brief explanation of the workings of the control desk, in the hope that an invitation to drive the train might, as a natural consequence, follow. It hadn't, but he remembered well what he had been taught. There was the power controller. There was the brake valve handle. There was the slot for the control key...

But no control key.

That was bad news, of course, in that it meant he could not start the *Jagannatha* even if he wanted to. It was good news as well, however, in so far as it eliminated the sleepwalking hypothesis. Wherever Wickramasinghe had gone, he had gone on purpose, and that meant he would, surely, at some point come back.

Noon mellowed into afternoon, and Fen prowled inside the carriage and along the track for a hundred yards in each direction, walking to keep his mind off thoughts of food, to distract himself from the grizzling of his famished stomach. He alternated between cursing Wickramasinghe and praying for the railwayman's swift return. Back and forth he strode, inside the *Jagannatha* and outside, clocking up mile upon mile of useless distance.

It was nigh on four-thirty when Wickramasinghe finally reappeared. Fen had just stepped out of the *Jagannatha* for yet another quick turn up and down the track, and there was Wickramasinghe, sauntering towards the train like someone returning from a pleasant and bracing stroll.

By now Fen had worked himself up into a state of some agitation, and this, exacerbated by his hunger and by Wickramasinghe's manifest insouciance, boiled over into anger. As soon as the railwayman was within earshot, Fen set about lambasting him. Accusations spilled forth in a furious torrent. "What the fuck...?" "Who the hell...?" "Where in the name of God...?" Wickramasinghe continued to approach, unperturbed. It was as though such a welcome was no more than he had anticipated. When there was less than a couple of yards between them, he came to a halt and Fen stopped shouting, and for a while they stared at each other, the one red-cheeked and wild-eyed and panting, the other calm. Then Wickramasinghe said, simply, "See?"

"See what?" Fen spluttered. "What is this? What am I supposed to see?"

Wickramasinghe shrugged and carried on towards the *Jagannatha*.

"This was some sort of test?" Fen asked him. "A show of strength? So we know who's boss here?"

Wickramasinghe reached up and hauled himself through the rear doorway of the carriage, between the stern sentinel figures of Shiva the destroyer and monkey-featured Hanuman with his war club.

Fen followed him inside, not prepared to let this go just yet. If Wickramasinghe had been trying to prove a point, it was useless if he didn't make explicit what that point was.

He cornered the railwayman in the standard class section.

"Listen, Ravi," he said, reining in his temper as best he could, "would you at least tell me what you've been up to? Where you've been all this time?"

The railwayman glanced up at the ceiling, stroking a thumb through his beard. Then, lowering his gaze, levelling it at Fen, he said: "My friend, I fear you do not trust me."

"Now, that's not true."

"No?"

"No. In fact, when I got up this morning, the first thing I thought was, 'Today Ravi's going to get us to the checkpoint, just like he said he would.'"

"But if you trusted me, genuinely trusted me, you would not even have to think such a thought."

"For God's sake, what chance does *that* give me?" Fen said, raising his hands and letting them drop to his sides.

"I get the impression, Fen, the *distinct* impression that you believe that I am leading you on a wild goose chase. That I am deliberately prolonging this journey. That I have invented all this stuff about avoiding other trains and junctions and damaged track and so forth."

"Why would I believe that? Prolonging the journey? Even if you were, I can't imagine what you'd gain from it."

"More time with you. Your company. Friendship. A purpose. I am a train driver, after all. Transporting people was what I did, was how I felt useful. Transporting *you* has made me feel useful again. It makes sense that I would try to keep that going as long as possible. To prolong my usefulness."

Fen looked at him askance. "Are you saying that *is* what you're doing?"

"You see?" Wickramasinghe said, with an accusatory flick of his hand. "No trust."

"I never said that! Although you have to admit, wandering off like that without telling me, leaving me here to stew... You have to see how that could make me wonder about you. And then—" Fen checked himself.

"And then?"

"Nothing."

Wickramasinghe nodded, eyes narrowed. "You were going to say, 'And then there was that time you came into my compartment in just your underpants and asked to sleep with me.'"

"You lied," Fen said, high-voiced. "You told me you didn't remember doing that."

"No, *you* lied. You pretended you dreamed it."

Fen shook his head, flabbergasted. This was daft. Ridiculous. Wickramasinghe had it all back-to-front and inside-out and wrong-way-round.

"The fact is, my friend," the railwayman said, "you are willing to take nothing on faith. You want proof, don't you? Proof that I have not been stringing you along these past few days."

"I don't—"

"Fair enough. I shall give you proof."

With that, Wickramasinghe spun on his heel and marched towards the front of the carriage. Fen remained where he was for several moments, digesting this turn of events. He heard the engine whirr, and then the *Jagannatha* gave a lurch forwards and began to pick up speed. Fen rushed out of the standard class section and along the corridor, not sure what Wickramasinghe had in mind but sensing that, whatever it was, it wasn't going to be good.

"Ravi, what are you doing?"

Hunched over the controls, Wickramasinghe intoned, "No passengers in the driver's cab."

"Come on, stop the train. Let's discuss this."

"No passengers in the cab."

Fen stepped back so that no part of him projected past the doorway. "Right. I'm not *in* the cab. Now please—what's going on?"

"A demonstration," Wickramasinghe said, nudging the power controller a few degrees further round. The *Jagannatha*'s wheels were chattering busily on the track. In the viewing window in front of Wickramasinghe, sleepers were laddering down out of sight at a rate of several per second.

"Of what?"

"That I have not been stringing you along. That these"—he waved a hand at the timetable and map—"are not for show."

Fen gave an incredulous laugh. "What, you're going to arrange a near-miss with another train?"

Wickramasinghe turned, his face a mask of seriousness. "That is precisely what I am going to do. At our current speed and direction, we are on a collision course with the four-eighteen out of Paddington. Our path and its will intersect at a junction approximately twelve miles from here. If my calculations are correct, we should pass each other with perhaps a hundred yards to spare. You want to see why it is taking so long to get to London, Fen? Well then, let me show you!"

Bluffing, Fen thought. He's bluffing. Trying to rattle me. He feels unappreciated. Rejected. He wants his efforts acknowledged. He wants gratitude.

But something—perhaps pride, perhaps petulance—prevented Fen from giving Wickramasinghe what he wanted.

"All right," he said. "Enough. This is daft. Suppose I believe you and there is a train heading this way. What if your calculations *aren't* correct? What if there *aren't* a few yards to spare?"

"Then," said Wickramasinghe, "*boom*."

"You'd kill us both, and maybe a lot of other people? Just to prove a point?"

"If that is what it takes."

The *Jagannatha* continued to accelerate, urging itself forwards with an intrepid eagerness. The world in the windows on either side had become a blur.

"So this is why you've been gone all day," Fen said. "To get the timing right."

"How astute of you."

"Or else to make me think that."

"If you like. You obviously will not be convinced until you see the other train bearing down on us at the junction."

Fen weighed this up. Wickramasinghe was right. Perhaps he would not be convinced until then. But why let it come to that?

Launching himself into the cab, Fen made a lunge for the control desk. Wickramasinghe, having anticipated this, raised an arm to fend him off. He managed to shove Fen backwards. Daljit's photograph was dislodged from the wall. Fen recovered his footing and went for the desk again, grabbing for the power controller. Fingers slithered over bunched knuckles. Wickramasinghe dug an elbow into Fen's stomach and pushed him away. With his free hand Fen wrenched at the railwayman's collar, intending to haul him off his stool. Wickramasinghe responded by yanking on the brake valve handle. The brakes were abruptly engaged, and Fen was thrown off balance and went lurching into the viewing window with head-cracking force. Sparkles and pain. The *Jagannatha* squealed deafeningly, shuddering to a complete stop. Fen, dazed, felt arms around him. He felt himself being manhandled. Then he was tumbling back into the corridor, rolling to the floor, and there was the sound of a door slamming and a bolt being shot home.

He looked up, skull throbbing, blinking through dizziness.

The door to the driver's cab was shut fast, and the *Jagannatha* was once more trundling along, gathering speed.

They took Jennifer away a while ago. An hour? Half a day? I don't know any more. I don't know what's when or who's where or the whys and the hows of anything.

They came in and took one look at her, pale and still in the torchlight, and one of them sighed, "Oh, for fuck's sake," while the other clucked his tongue. He didn't sound appalled, just annoyed, like someone coming out of a restaurant to find his car has been broken into.

The torch beam swung around until it located me, cowering.

"Well, at least *she's* still alive."

Then they picked Jennifer up between them and carried her out. Where they took her, I've no idea. Disposed of her somewhere, I suppose. Somewhere outside the compound. Dumped her like rubbish.

How long had she been dead when I touched her? How long was I sharing the room with a corpse?

This is what I've been trying not to think about, and it is all I can think about.

Jennifer, silently willing herself to expire. Making this room a tomb.

Me, unwittingly present at her final moment. Inhaling air molecules she exhaled with her last breath.

The darkness enclosing me has become deeper, *thicker*, than I can bear. What I wouldn't give just to see the sun again. What I wouldn't give for warmth and light and just knowing what time of day it is, what *day* it is.

Be strong, I tell myself.

I can't.

Hold it together.

I can't.

I can't even tell if my eyes are open any more. What I see when I stare out—they may as well be tight shut.

There's floor. That's down. There are walls. That's sideways. There are legs and a torso and arms and a head and hair, and I can touch them with my hands, and that's me.

This is all I know.

It was foolish to think of escape. I'm never going to escape. I'm never even going to get out of this room. This is all I am going to know for ever. This is *my* tomb too.

I would scream, if I thought anyone could hear, anyone who cared.

Fen would care. If he heard.

Fen would. Or would pretend to, at any rate.

Where is he now? What's he doing now?

Having a party. Celebrating. He's rid of me. His millstone. He's a free man. He'll be out and about in Downbourne. Having a good time.

(This is the first time since I was captured that I've thought about Fen in the Now. Not as a figment of memory. As a living person.)

"Lucky Fen," everyone'll be saying. "Lucky old Fen. Those blokes from London did him a favour."

(He's better as a memory. I like him better then, because he liked me better then. There was nothing false or brittle about him then. No pretence. No call for it.)

Dancing through the town. A happy future for Fen.

Not darkness. Not limbo. Not like me.

Come *on!* What are you waiting for, you bastards? Come and get me! I don't even care any more what you want to do with me. I want out of here! Come and *get me!*

HAMMERING ON THE door produced no response. Shouting to Wickramasinghe produced no response. Reasoning with him, haranguing him—no response.

It was a bluff.

It wasn't a bluff.

The *Jagannatha* raced along, eating up distance, rocking and shimmying, its wheels beating out an implacable steely tattoo on the rails.

Fen pounded on the door again. This time he did get a response, though not an encouraging one. The intercom crackled, and the carriage was filled from end to end with the sound of Wickramasinghe intoning a poem in a loud, singsong voice:

> The guard is the man,
> The man in the van,
> The van at the back of the train.
> The driver up front
> Thinks the guard is a cunt,
> While the guard thinks the driver's the same.

"Ravi! Ravi! Come on! Stop this. This isn't funny."

The intercom clicked off. Silence again.

Fen pounded on the door one last time, then took a step back, breathing hard.

OK. OK, think.

Was Wickramasinghe really going to go through with his plan? Was he that much of a nutcase? Or was this nothing more than a ploy, a way of putting Fen in his place, of reminding him who was the driver here, who the passenger? Would Wickramasinghe halt the train after another mile or so and come out of his cabin expecting contrition from Fen, abject apology?

He recalled the look on Wickramasinghe's face as he had outlined his intentions. He recalled the frank, almost dismissive way in which the railwayman had acknowledged the possibility of a collision: "Then *boom*."

This was no bluff.

He had to get off the train.

Turning, Fen made his way to the rear of the carriage, staggering against the judders and buffets of the train's motion. He grasped the handle of the rear door and tugged inwards, and all at once there was roar and racket and vertiginous speed. The track whisked away from beneath his feet, sleepers passing too fast to distinguish one from the next. Wind sucked at his hair.

No way. No way was he going to be able to jump out at this speed. Not without breaking his neck.

But what choice did he have?

He braced himself in the doorway. It was this or take his chances staying on the train. Either way, not an attractive proposition.

The London permit.

Shit!

His knapsack. The permit. The wedding band.

He stumbled back up the carriage to his compartment and snatched the knapsack down from the luggage rack. As he flipped the bag onto his shoulders—it weighed next to nothing now—he glanced out of the window and saw embankment rushing past, a hectic smear of green.

Of course.

Not from the rear of the train.

From the side.

A much softer landing. A better chance of not hurting himself.

The side doors had external handles only. Back in the standard class section, Fen fought with the window of one, leaning on the metal rim-catch, struggling to shunt the thick pane of glass down. Finally! He groped for the handle. Found it. Battled to get the door open against the hurricane rush of the *Jagannatha*'s momentum. Succeeded, the door slamming back flat against the side of the carriage.

The track's gravel bed was a grey flurry at his feet. The embankment lay just an exaggerated footstep away, thick with bushes and brambles—natural shock absorbers. The embankment's height was decreasing, its gradient beginning to flatten out. Now was the moment. If Fen was going to do this, he would not get a better opportunity.

Just as he tensed, ready to leap, the sound of the train's wheels changed, becoming hollower, tinnier. All at once there was no embankment any more, instead a low brick parapet and, beyond, an unfurling vista of fields and copses, here and there a house, a barn, a glimpse of lane.

Fen shrank back from the doorway, his heart stuttering, his breath coming in short, constricted bursts. A viaduct. He had almost hurled himself over the side of a viaduct. Fuck! Fuck fuck *fuck*!

The landscape peeled by, a swooping beautiful valley, the kind of view the railway companies used to use to advertise the joys of rail travel, wanting you to believe that every mile of every journey revealed awe-inspiring sights such as this. *England, my England*. Then a hillside swelled up to meet the end of the viaduct's span and the view was whisked from sight. Fen could see no further than a hedgerow at the far end of a field, then a bell curve of embankment again, then another hedgerow at the far end of another field.

He gripped the door frame once more, and once more tired to nerve himself to jump. After his close shave at the viaduct, it was harder than ever to summon up the courage. His mind was all hysteria, his thoughts yammering in time to the wheels on the rails: *You'll kill yourself! You'll kill yourself!* It seemed to him that the *Jagannatha* was still accelerating and that the odds on him surviving the jump intact were lengthening with every passing second. Maybe he should just stay aboard. Maybe Wickramasinghe knew what he was doing. Maybe the man was not mad.

Then, distantly up ahead: a two-note blare.

Another train, sounding its horn in warning.

Jesus! No doubt about it now. He *was* mad.

The blare came again, the notes spaced much closer together this time. More urgent.

Squeezing his eyes shut and clenching his teeth, Fen leaned back. He bent his legs and, with a shout that was half scream, half prayer, propelled himself out of the doorway.

3.
The Poppy Field

THE RED ADMIRAL bumbled along on a spiralling, intricate flight-path. For days—a lifetime—it had been searching for hints of pheromone in the air, sky written come-ons, the lonely-hearts ads of its species. Wanting to mate, existing for no other purpose, it had quested and roved and flirted with the wind currents, so far in vain. Luck had kept it out of the beaks and webs of predators. The sexual imperative drove it onward.

In the soft glow of a quiet evening, the red admiral's peregrinations brought it to a field of rampant couch grass where wild poppies flourished in clusters, archipelagos of scarlet in a yellow-green ocean. At the field's edge, where it terminated in a steep, brambly embankment that led down to a railway track, the butterfly homed in on a particular stalk of grass. Descended. Settled, flattening its wings together like a penitent's praying hands.

Its weight, such as it was, caused the grass stalk to bend.

The stalk's seed-feathery tip touched the cheek of the human who lay close by, sprawled, motionless.

Briefly, Fen awoke.

A tiny, scratchy tickle on his face, but it was enough to stir him from insensibility, sparking a glimmer of consciousness in his brain.

His eyelids fluttered, not unlike a butterfly's wings.

He glimpsed hazy daylight and a jungle of grass. Heard the zip-zing-zither of crickets.

Then agony jolted up from his left leg, agony that surpassed any he had known before.

It was safer down in the dark. There was no pain there.

He happily surrendered to oblivion.

The red admiral took off, swirling back up into the air. Its search, its lust-wander, continued.

DUSK. A BURNT-UMBER sunset. It almost blinds me. I can barely walk. A controlled stumble. Two men holding my arms, helping me along. City odours, oddly nostalgic. Grass, urban turf—acrid. Fossil-fuel fumes. Rotting things, organic matter, fruit, vegetables. I think of market stalls and summer Sundays in the park, the heady rumble of traffic and getting drunk in bars. Maybe it's because I used to be a Londoner.

We go from the bricked-up house, confinement, the place where captives get the defiance knocked out of them—we go from there across the compound. I'm grip-hauled all the way. Hurts. We go between two houses, and an Alsatian on a chain lunges at me, snarling. We pass a flotilla of white vans parked all hugger-mugger, and nearby there are jerry cans of petrol stored in neat stacks, covered in tarpaulins, hundreds of gallons of the stuff. We go towards a house that seems larger than all the rest. That's the impression it gives, though this is—was—one of those estates where every residence is identical, plonked down one after another in rows as if deposited from the rear end of some gargantuan house-excreting machine. The other houses are shabby and tumbledown. This one seems larger because it has had some effort expended on it. Someone's done up the paintwork. Someone's neatened up the small square of front garden. Someone's kept the windowpanes scrubbed and the curtains hanging straight.

The front door is open. Looks like we're expected.

In the hallway we're greeted, not by a man as I thought we would be, but by a woman. I don't recognise her. She's not from Downbourne. She has prominent yellow teeth and one of those complexions that looks like dirt is permanently engrained into her skin. Her hair is long and lank, a muddy shade of ginger. She looks thirty but she's probably younger. She might have been pretty once, back when she was a girl, back before she became so etched, so whittled, by life.

She appraises me, trying to appear indifferent. But I've spotted the flint-spark of resentment in her eyes.

"This is her?" she says to the men holding me.

"Yeah."

She gives a small sniff. "Nothing special."

"You can make her nice."

"I can try." She fixes the men with a haughty look. She obviously has some power here, some status. "All right. I'll deal with it from here."

They let go of my arms. Blood flushes into the flesh where they were holding on—pins-and-needles tingle.

"If she gives you any trouble..."

"Don't worry. She won't."

The men leave. It's just me and this woman. She does a circuit around me, looking me up and down, and I can't believe she doesn't know she's acting like a madame in some bad period drama, inspecting the ingenue heroine, the whorehouse's newest recruit.

"I'm Lauren," she says, finally. "I've been here three years. I've survived. And I've survived because I'm a hard bitch and I don't take shit from no one. You'd do well to remember that. There's been lots like you. Craig gets through you like Kleenex. You come, you go, but I'm still here. So don't get any funny ideas. Don't get thinking you could replace me. You can't. You won't. Try it and I'll kick your fucking ass."

She isn't American. She's London through and through, and "ass" sounds wrong coming from her like that, but I suppose she was brought up on American TV and movies; culture-bombed into believing that everything American is cool. A brave (or a stupid) belief to maintain, given which country has been the most enthusiastic advocate of the International Community broadsides against England.

"First thing I'm going to do is get you cleaned up and sorted out," she continues. "You look a mess, and you're no good to anyone looking a mess. Then I'm going to fill you in on what's expected of you. Craig's away at the moment. Will be for the next couple of days. So I'm going to show you around, get you familiarised with how things work round here, get you ready for him. What you have to realise is that from now on pleasing Craig is what you're all about. As long as you please him, there won't be any trouble. *Dis*please him, and... Well, I don't think you'd be that stupid." She flashes a smile that isn't meant to be friendly. "I suppose I should ask your name."

It flits across my mind to give her a false name. I don't know why. Maybe just so as not to make things easy for her. Maybe a false name will somehow give her less of a hold over me. But I decide it isn't worth it.

"Moira."

She raises an eyebrow. Not disdainful. Mildly surprised. "I had you pegged as a Kate or a Jane. 'Moira'. Makes me think of somebody's aunt. 'I'm going to visit my Aunt Moira for tea and scones.'"

She's clearly missed her calling as a comedienne.

"OK, Moira. Come with me."

We go upstairs. I'm finding this all a little disorientating. Partly because I'm so damn weak (lack of food, and all that time spent in the dark—how many days?). Partly because I thought I'd be being raped by now. And partly because I'm here in a house that's done up like someone's idea of a perfect starter home—clean white walls, a framed print here and there, chintzy curtains—yet it's sitting smack-dab in the middle of a barricaded compound inhabited by a bunch of crop-haired bullyboys who kidnap women for sex. And now—Jesus—here's a bathroom with avocado-green fixtures, brass fittings, a nice clean mould-free shower curtain, and Lauren spins the bath taps and water comes out of the mixer spout and it's steaming! Hot water! Hot water pouring into a bath!

"Take those clothes off."

And I do. As if in a dream, I strip naked. Off come the grubby, reeking shirt and jeans and underwear, off into a pile on the floor.

A hot bath.

I can barely believe it. When the water's good and deep, I step in, and the warmth surges up my legs, and the sensation is sublime, and I'm transported back in time to when things like this were normal, when you could take a hot bath any time you felt like it. Not even a luxury. An activity you gave no more thought to than buying a newspaper or sticking a CD in the stereo. Something you did because you could. I sink down, immersing myself. Lauren watches me, sees the sheer bliss on my face, thinks I'm pathetic. I don't care.

"There's soap," she says, "and a face-cloth. Wash yourself. I'm not damn well doing it for you. When you're done, come downstairs."

She leaves me to it, taking my clothes with her. I scrub myself thoroughly, removing what feels like an inch of grime. The water goes grey. A filthy soap-scum forms on the surface. When I don't think I can be any cleaner, or have ever been so clean, I lie back, water-supported, near-weightless.

There's a small window. Edges fogged with condensation like an Edwardian photograph, it frames a rectangle of London sky. There are a couple of plump, brown-orange clouds up there. A distant tower block, sporadically lit. A single star.

I gaze out.

Bizarrely, incredibly, I'm almost happy.

A SUDDEN SHARP twisting twinge, then grisly pain. It couldn't be denied any longer. He couldn't shelter from it in unconsciousness any longer.

Surging up into self-awareness, Fen began to turn himself over. A hundred white-hot daggers gouged into his left thigh, working away with sawtooth fury. He screamed and groaned and gasped out half-words, empty glottal syllables. Fingers clawing the ground, he writhed like a severed worm.

He thought: I can't endure this. I'm going to die if this doesn't stop.

It didn't stop. Gradually, though, the pain grew less jarring, less alien, becoming acquainted. It settled in, a dull, enervating throb. Fen's breathing steadied. He regained control of his thoughts. Took stock.

He had broken his leg.

Put like that, it did not seem all that drastic.

He had jumped from the *Jagannatha*, and he was all right, he hadn't killed himself. He had only broken his leg.

People were breaking bones all the time. Alan Greeley had had his wrist fractured just the other day. All things considered, Fen was lucky it was *only* his leg that he had broken.

He tried to remember what had happened, but everything after leaping from the doorway of the train was hazy. He had a vague recollection of being *bounced* like a rubber toy, of pinwheeling upwards. It made him think of footage he had seen of motorcycle racers hitting the hay-bale crash barriers, bodies yanked over the handlebars and whirling, end over end, like human boomerangs. It had always amazed him how often they escaped with nothing worse than scrapes and bruises. Helmets and padded leather accounted for some of the lack of damage, to be sure, but even so the human frame was, when put to the test, remarkably resilient.

So here he was. It was dark, and he was lying sprawled on the brow of the railway embankment, left femur fractured. How badly? The section of his jeans surrounding the thigh felt tight, the thigh swollen, but he didn't think that bone had pierced through skin. A simple rather than a compound fracture. And (he performed a swift self-inventory) there seemed to be no other significant injuries.

Had the *Jagannatha* missed the other train? He couldn't see the track from where he was, but surely if there had been a collision he would know about it. There would be the audible aftermath of carnage, the sound of flames still burning perhaps, at the very least people injured, groaning, calling out. In the event, he could hear nothing except the sibilant hush of night-time countryside.

He glanced around. He was encircled by long, dry grass, and rising taller than the grass he could just make out the heads of flowers of some sort—poppies? At his feet lay a thicket of brambles which marked the top of the embankment. His right leg, his undamaged leg, was hooked up on the brambles, the cuff of his jeans snagged on thorns. His other leg lay stuck out to the side.

All right. First things first. To be stretched out like this, prone, chin pressed into the grass, was not exactly comfortable. If he could get himself sitting upright, that would be a start. A small improvement in circumstances.

He contemplated what he would have to do. He knew it wasn't going to be pleasant. Why not just remain as he was? It might be uncomfortable, but it was nowhere near as bad as moving himself was going to be.

The more he dwelled on it, the less eager he became to put his scheme into action.

Finally: sod it. He would give it a try.

He tugged his right leg, carefully disentangling it from the brambles. His left leg tolerated this, grumbling only a little. Next, he spread both hands on the ground, palms down, fingers splayed, as though about to do a press-up. Gently, with an even downward pressure, he raised his upper body a few inches, then lodged his right elbow under his ribs, angling his torso sideways. So far, so good. The leg was protesting, but the objections it was raising were bearable. Its voice had got a bit sharper, that was all.

He gritted his teeth and prepared to roll over onto his right side. He could do this, he could do this.

One.

Two.

Three...

Fen let out a howl that, had he himself been in a fit state to hear it, he would not have recognised as originating from his own throat, or indeed from the throat of any human. The howl frayed into a sob, and the sob dissipated into guttural, rasping bleats. Nothing, but nothing, was as horrible as this pain. No one on earth had ever suffered its like before. He collapsed back flat on his stomach, gritting his teeth, grimacing.

In time, his leg concluded that it had chastised him enough for having had the insolence to put it to the test. The awful agony became merely agony, and Fen was able to stop breathing in fits and bursts through his nostrils and just pant and gasp instead. He spat out a few grains of soil that had found their way into his mouth, then twisted his head round so that his ear, rather than his nose, was bearing the weight of skull and brain. His eyes burned with tears. He felt abject misery—how unfair this was, how viciously fucking *unfair*—but underlying the misery there was something else.

An inkling.

An inkling that, as bad as his situation was, it could very well get much, much worse.

Dressed in the white towelling bath-robe that I found hanging on the back of the bathroom door, I go downstairs, following sounds of activity. In the kitchen, a washing machine is churning—my clothes sloshing around and around in the window—and Lauren's preparing a meal. Nothing spectacular. Spaghetti hoops from a tin. Still, I'm all but drooling by the time it's ready. We eat sitting on opposite sides of the kitchen table. This is all so disturbingly *not* what I expected would happen, and there are dozens of questions I want to ask, but at the same time I'm not sure I want to know any of the answers. So, silence for now. Enjoy the respite.

"So where're you lot from?" Lauren asks as she chases her last few spaghetti hoops around her plate. There's a splat of tomato sauce on one corner of her mouth. Someone who liked her would point this out to her so that she could wipe it off. "Somewhere down south, isn't it?"

"Yes. Small town, not far from the coast. Downbourne. You won't have heard of it."

"Nope. Nice place?"

"Quiet. Primitive. Doesn't have anything like you have here—electricity, hot water. We haven't managed to get things running again. Haven't had that chance."

"Mm," she says, not really interested.

"I'm from London originally, though."

"Oh?"

"Barnes. Then Islington. Lived there till my late twenties."

"So this must be a bit like coming home for you."

She says this entirely without irony, entirely unaware of how crass it is, and it strikes me that she's actually quite stupid. Or perhaps a bit simple. Not all there. Maybe that's how she has, as she put it, survived. Not by being a hard bitch. By not fully understanding things. Ignorance as armour.

"You?" I ask.

"What?"

"You from round here?"

"Oh. Uh-huh. Not far."

"This may sound daft, but where *is* here?"

"South-east London."

"Can you be a bit more specific?"

She becomes wary. "Why d'you want to know?"

"No reason. Just nice to have some sense of where I am, that's all."

"Lewisham," she says finally, having thought about whether it'll make any difference if I know this information or not.

"And those men—who are they?"

"The British Bulldogs." This she says with some pride, like a cheerleader naming her team. "You've heard of them, I suppose."

"Not actually."

She rolls her eyes. "Well, you should've. They run this borough."

"In Downbourne we were a little, you know, out of things."

"Yeah, I reckon you were."

I volunteer to do the dishes. It's almost absurd how gratifying it is to run warm water into a sink, add a squirt of washing-up liquid, scrub cutlery and crockery under a layer of soap bubbles and place them rinsed and sparkling in a drying rack. I feel like one of those TV-commercial housewives discovering some wonderful new cleaning product and experiencing domestic-chore epiphany. I have to fight the urge to grin and giggle.

Afterwards, Lauren produces a beaten-up packet of cigarettes, some Dutch brand I've never heard of. She thinks about it, then holds out the pack to me. I haven't smoked in ages. I gave up before the Unlucky Gamble meant I had to give up, when the tax on fags rose to 150%. But it would be impolite not to accept. Impolite, and God, yes, why not?

The first drag makes me cough, but after that it's as if I never stopped. My system opens up to the nicotine, embracing an old friend. We used to smoke like chimneys at the magazine. None of that smoke-free office nonsense at *Siren*, no sir. Editorial meetings were conducted through a thickening tobacco haze, and at my desk I'd light up every time the phone rang, just about. It was almost a conditioned response. I didn't feel right taking a phone call if I wasn't firing up a cancer stick at the same time. I even penned a semi-flippant article about it for the magazine. "Pavlov's Beagles" was the title.

So we smoke, Lauren and I, and again I think how incongruous this is. In the midst of such a shitty situation, to be doing something as normal as having a fag in somebody's nice clean kitchen...

"This Craig you talked about," I say to her. "Who is he? Does he run things around here?"

Lauren gives me a look, like: how thick *are* you? Don't you know *anything*? "He's the King, ain't he?"

"The King?"

"King Cunt."

"Oh. Lovely."

"That's how 'most everyone else knows him. I'm one of the few who get to call him Craig."

"So what should *I* call him, when I meet him?"

"Whatever he tells you to."

"'Cunt' for short?"

She tips her head back and blows out a smoke ring. "I wouldn't be that way around him, if I were you."

"What way?"

"Clever. Craig doesn't like that at all."

"OK. Thanks for the warning. I won't be clever then."

"Just do like I said. It's not difficult. Please him, and you'll be fine."

"And when's he coming back, did you say?"

"Weren't you listening? Couple of days. He's off negotiating with the Frantik Posse over in Camberwell. There's been a bit of friction between them and that lot in Peckham, the Riot Squad, and Craig thinks he can score points with the Frantiks if he sides with them against the Squad. Not actually makes an alliance with them. Just keeps in with them in a"—she gropes for a suitable term—"diplomatic sort of a way. The Riot Squad aren't that strong at the moment. Been in a bit of trouble keeping people in their borough in line. So if the Frantiks try for a takeover, which they will, and they'll succeed, then we'll be in a position to take advantage of it. Expand our territory in that direction, if possible. The Frantiks won't mind because we were on their side and most of Peckham will be more than enough for them to manage. It's politics, you see."

"I see. And what does the London Council make of all this?"

"Nothing," she replies, quizzically. "What's it got to do with the Council?"

"A lot, I'd have thought."

She gives a steely little laugh. "You really don't have a clue how things work around here, do you?"

"I think I'm beginning to."

"The Council's there to keep the folks in the suburbs happy more than anything. It gives them the sense that everything in the inner city is fine, all under control. But the Council answers to the boroughs, not the other way round. If we need it to turn a blind eye, it always will."

Later, Lauren asks if I'm tired. I take the hint. I *am* tired, anyway. She shows me to an upstairs room that I can only assume is the guest bedroom. She herself normally uses this room, but while Craig's away she's been sleeping in the master bedroom across the landing. The bed's more comfortable there, apparently.

The guest bedroom isn't big. There's a single bed, a small window, some of the ghastliest wallpaper I've ever seen—but it's homely, the bed linen is clean and smooth and soft... We did our best in Downbourne with cold water and hand-scrubbing, but it isn't the same as soap powder, proper laundering, ironing... I lie down... Lauren switches the light out... There's darkness, and then there's...

He shouted for an hour. He shouted until his throat was sore and his yells had turned to feeble, pitiful rasps. He shouted into the night-time emptiness around him, into the whispering countryside, into the hollow cauldron of star-studded sky above. He shouted, and not even an echo answered. Nothing that heard his cries understood what they meant, or cared. Nocturnal fauna went about its business unheeding. Those that prowl prowled. Those that scurry in darkness scurried in darkness. Those that watch from tree boughs watched from tree boughs. Flowers were closed; the world was closed. Fen was stranded and crippled and almightily alone.

Still lying prone, afraid to attempt to move himself again, he struggled to marshal his thoughts, get them in some kind of order. Panic kept welling inside him, threatening to overcome him, reduce him to a quaking, witless wreck. The panic could be suppressed, but only with effort. He had to be rational. Rational thought was the control rod that kept this particular reactor from meltdown.

He was not going to die.

That was the priority here, the fact he knew he must keep at the forefront of his brain.

He was not going to die. He wasn't in some vast, uninhabited area. This was no Sahara, no Himalaya. This was England. South-east England, to be precise. The Home Counties. One of the most densely populated regions on the surface of the planet. Not as densely populated as it used to be, for sure, but still a place where you could not go a mile without coming across some sign of human habitation. It was inconceivable that *someone* would not hear him shouting. If not now, then in the morning. There must be someone who owned and farmed the land around here. There must be a village or a town reasonably close by whose residents, for one reason or another, were wont to venture in this direction during the daytime. If he started yelling again tomorrow morning, someone would surely hear him. Come to investigate. Go and fetch help.

He was not going to die.

And he was right next to a railway track. Trains would be passing—if not tonight then sometime tomorrow. If just one person glanced out of a carriage window and spotted him lying there, obviously in difficulties, that person could raise the alarm, and in no time...

In no time *what*? This wasn't, as if Fen needed to remind himself, the old England any more, the old England that had had a functioning infrastructure of telecommunications networks and emergency services, where you were never more than a phone call away from a police officer or an ambulance. Such commonplace certainties were a thing of the past.

Fair enough, but it was still conceivable nonetheless. A passenger in a passing train *might* try and get assistance to him. And what if Wickramasinghe came back in the *Jagannatha* to find out what had become of him? How about that? Not terribly likely, but a possibility.

All he had to do was last out the night here. Grit his teeth, endure the pain.

A few hours, that was all.

He was not going to die.

SELDOM HAD A few hours seemed so long. Lacking a watch, Fen's only guide to the passing of time was the moon, and the moon appeared in no hurry to go anywhere. Each time he peered up to check on its position, it was exactly where it had been the last time he looked. Even when he forced himself to wait, leaving as long an interval as he could before looking again, the moon stood still. Partially occluded on one side, its grey-shadow face leered at him like a clown peeking out from behind the circus curtain, laughing at him as though this was all just the merriest prank: Fen Morris lying helpless on the ground, waiting for a dawn that was not going to come.

The countryside was all rustle and activity. Every so often some animal or other would cough or hoot or yicker or wail. On one occasion Fen heard a creature shuffling and snuffling about nearby, sounding like something huge even though it must only be a hedgehog or a rabbit or a stoat. For a while a bat flitted overhead—its sonar chirrups were like a tiny wire being plucked inside his middle ear. Breezes swooshed through vegetation. This was the noise of the world when humankind was silenced. Raucous as any city, any factory, any rock concert.

And then the cold.

The cold seeped through his clothing, lowering his body-temperature degree by imperceptible degree. Fen began shivering before he was aware of doing so. The shivering intensified, his lips turned to rubber, and his throat started making small, involuntary stammering noises. The pain from his leg, which the cold might have been expected to numb, instead sharpened, becoming a glassy, crystalline, grating.

He bore it as best he could. He told himself over and over that it was just this one night, that once day broke this would all be over. All he had to do was hold out till then. Several times, though, he gave in and wept, grinding his face into the grass in despair. A similar number of times he cried out again for help, help, please, somebody, help—in the vain hope that his voice would carry to someone somewhere, some night owl, some insomniac. Once, though he was not aware of doing so, he even cried out for his mother.

An eternity later, the sky began to lighten.

No. Just a trick of the imagination. The night remained as dark as ever.

Another eternity passed, and then the moon was gone, having taken refuge at some point when Fen wasn't looking, and yes, there, distinctly, a greenish greyness to the black. The stars ever so slightly fainter, losing their lustre. A pallid glow encroaching from the east.

And at last—mundane miracle—a bird twittered.

Fen could not recall when he had heard a sound quite so welcome or quite so wonderful.

The bird was silent for a long while, as if it feared it had made a mistake. Then, tentatively, it twittered again, and some distance away, another bird responded.

After breakfast, Lauren takes me on a guided tour.

The compound covers about half a mile square, I reckon, although I'm not that hot on gauging such things. The fortifications are solid all round, nowhere less than twenty feet high. They're constructed from bits of old furniture and things like fridges and ovens, breeze blocks and heavy timber, car parts, all jumbled together, stacked high, packed tight. In most places there's barbed wire along the top or sections of spiked iron railing appropriated from the front of some town house, or else some more improvisational anti-climbing measure such as arrays of sharpened chair legs, side by side like the teeth of a comb, and planks of wood with shards of broken bottle glued to them. You could get over if you were really determined to, but not without risk of serious injury. There are a couple of lookout posts too, one beside the main gate, the other at the opposite end of the compound. They're little open-topped turrets knocked together from scaffolding and planks, accessible by ladders. Though I don't see anyone in either of them, Lauren assures me they're regularly manned.

In the centre of the compound there's the van park I passed last night—I count about twenty vehicles in all—and near that there's a kind of communal area, an expanse of open ground that was probably a children's playground when this was just an ordinary housing estate. It's got a large brick-sided barbecue pit and several tables and benches. The grass is littered with food packaging, fruit rinds, beer cans. It's a warm, bright morning, and quite a few of the British Bulldogs are out here, eating and drinking and amusing themselves. One of them is getting a new tattoo done, trying not to wince as a skull with a rose clenched between its teeth is jabbed out on his shoulderblade with the point of a compass. Another of them is giving a martial arts lesson to a few of his colleagues, demonstrating a kick technique that looks (to my untrained eye at least) just like an ordinary kick, although the Bulldog seems to think it's a move which must be studied and practised for years before it can be mastered. As Lauren and I go by, we are subjected to stares and leers and the odd building-site comment, although the men are definitely deferential to Lauren. I can't quite figure our her relationship to this King Cunt person—wife? housekeeper?—but whatever it is, her association with him protects her. Me, the men are quite happy to treat as though I'm just a vagina and tits on legs—although I get the feeling they're not being as coarse towards me as they could be. Why? Because I'm with Lauren? Because I'm under King Cunt's protection too?

What I don't see on the guided tour is any of the other women from Downbourne. I ask Lauren about this.

"Oh, they'll be indoors," she replies casually. "Sleeping, if they've got any sense. Getting their strength back."

"Getting their strength back for what?"

Lauren rolls her eyes. "What d'you goddamn think, honey?"

I'm completely dumbfounded by that. Not by what Lauren has said but the way she's said it. It doesn't seem to impinge on her—what's being done to these women, members of her own sex. She doesn't seem to care in the least.

"Where are they?" I ask.

"There are a couple of houses set aside."

"Brothels?"

"Well, no, actually, Moira. Duh. And here was I thinking you were all smart and knew, like, words an' shit. Brothels. Women in brothels get paid, don't they? And that's not what happens here. Craig's name for them is recreation zones."

"Not 'comfort battalions' then?"

"I don't get."

I didn't think she would. "And the Bulldogs can go there any time they like?"

"Pretty much. It's necessary, see. Craig calls it a release valve. Lets out the pressure. Keeps the boys happy."

"Christ. I mean... Christ. That's horrible."

"Honey, it's life," Lauren says, with a nonchalant shrug. "It's the way things go around here. I wouldn't spend any time worrying about it. There's nothing you can do."

"But one of the women from our town—well, she's not even a woman. She's a fifteen-year-old girl. A *child*."

For an instant—the merest instant—I think I glimpse something behind Lauren's studiedly casual façade, just a hint of something deeper than indifference. It's there, then it's gone. "Well, serves her right. Shouldn't have got caught, should she?"

I ask if she'll point out to me which houses are the "recreation zones", but she refuses.

"Think I've shown you enough for one morning. Let's go back."

As we make our way back to the house, we pass within sight of the lookout post by the gate. There's a Bulldog in it now, lounging, enjoying a cigarette and gazing out over whatever lies beyond the walls.

That's the route out of this place, out of this fort. Not the gate, not the barricades—the lookout post. That's how I'll be getting out of Fort Bulldog.

A FLOCK OF starlings passing a few feet overhead awoke him. The rippling flap of wingbeats, the sough of wind through feathers—he opened his eyes in time to see the last of the birds disappear from view beyond the grass-bordered limits of his vision. A momentary sense of dislocation. Where? How? Then it all tumbled back into place. His leg. His throat, raw from shouting last night and again at various intervals throughout the morning. His dry mouth. Hunger—deep-rooted, throbbing hunger. The smells of sun-warmed grass and earth strong in his nose. All the components of the hellish situation he was in. And now an additional problem: he needed to urinate.

He needed to urinate quite urgently, in fact, and since he wasn't going to be able to attempt this lying face down, flat out, he knew he would have to try something drastic. He knew he was going to have to do what he had failed to do yesterday and turn over.

It was half an hour before he was able to screw up sufficient nerve to attempt the manoeuvre. It helped that in that time the urge to urinate had become a critical necessity. His bladder was hurting, and if he didn't do something about it *now* he was going to wet his pants, and that would be an indignity too far.

He assumed the position he had tried before, that sort of press-up position, bent his torso up off the ground and wriggled his right elbow into the gap between hip and ribs. Then he clamped his teeth together and squeezed his eyes shut, in expectation of the unutterable, blinding pain to come. He sent up the prayer that all agnostics resort to *in extremis*, the if-you're-there-God prayer, the bet-hedging plea for special divine intercession. Then he shunted himself sideways using his elbow as a fulcrum, the plan being that his right leg would pivot where it was and his left would be pulled across it and fall into place, knee upwards, beside it...

...lightning detonated in his left thigh...

...he was on his back but the leg was stuck, canted across the other one...

...the thigh being bent...

...femur fracture flexing...

He groped for the leg to shift it by hand. He was grimacing, thrashing his head up and down, ululating inarticulately. His hands found his left knee and pushed it sideways...

...another lightning-burst...

He slumped back.

Passed out.

Pissed himself anyway.

"It's quite straightforward," says Lauren. "If he wants to fuck you, you let him fuck you. If he just wants to talk, you talk. You do as he says when he says. Don't do as he says, and he'll beat the shit out of you. Couldn't be simpler, could it?"

We're in the back garden of the house. It's turning out to be a gorgeous day. London sunshine—hotter, harder, less forgiving than country sunshine, but always, as I remember it, more of a gift: bleaching away the sins of the city, coaxing shut-ins outdoors, putting smiles on otherwise smile-free faces. Lauren's got me on my knees beside her, digging weeds from a bed of pink busy lizzies. I haven't done work like this in ages, and the months of inactivity—convalescence—are catching up with me. I have to stop every other minute to rest. Sweat trickles from my armpits, and I think of the bath I can have when this is done, if I want. How did I put up with it in Downbourne? The deprivations, the inconveniences? How?

That's when Lauren sets out, in the clearest terms yet, the cost of staying here. What I'm going to have to do if I want to keep enjoying hot baths and clean clothes and plentiful food.

I look at her. She looks at me.

"Is that how it was with you? When you first arrived?"

She nods. "That was my job. For about six months."

"King Cunt's concubine."

"Concubine?"

"Mistress. Bed-partner."

"Yup."

"And then?"

"Then I'd have been thrown on the scrapheap like the rest, only Craig'd taken a shine to me because I made myself useful around the house, kept the place nice and tidy, cooked for him and all that, which none of the others had actually done before, so he let me stay on. He didn't come out and *ask* me to stay on. He just didn't tell me to go, so I didn't go."

"But you could have gone if you'd wanted to."

"Oh yeah. But I mean... I'm safe here. Life's better for me here than it ever was out there. Here, I don't have to worry about when or what I'm going to eat, and I get respect from everybody, and—and it's just better, you know what I mean?"

I do know. I can understand her point of view exactly. It's gutless and it's venal, but I can understand exactly why she's made the choice she has.

"Can I ask, then—why me? Why have I been singled out from all the others?"

"What, you mean why have *you* been chosen to be Craig's... What's that word again?"

"Concubine."

"Concubine. Yeah. Well, it's obvious, ain't it?"

She strokes her hair.

I give her a blank look.

She strokes her hair again, then points to mine. "Craig has a thing about redheads."

"You're kidding me."

"Straight up. It's the only kind of girl he'll sleep with."

"Do you know why?"

"No idea. He just does."

I remember the Bulldogs in the van discussing my hair. Saying "he" would like it. They saw me in the street, stopped for me—a present for their boss. A red-haired gift. Jesus Christ. Now I understand. Of all the crappy, stupid reasons for this to have happened to me—a quirk of pigmentation! Were I a blonde or a brunette, they'd have passed me by. But I'm not, and that's why I've wound up here, and how ridiculous is *that*?

I'm laughing before I realise I'm laughing.

"What's so funny?" Lauren asks, suspiciously.

"Oh, nothing. Nothing at all."

But I keep laughing, rejoicing in the absurdity of it, tickled pink at how the worst of things can happen for the most meaningless of reasons.

I'm sure Fen, if he were here, would find it funny too.

THIS TIME IT was discomfort in his back that brought him round. Something protruding into his spine. Felt like a stone. No. He was lying on his knapsack. His water canteen.

Left thigh pulsing. Pain like a jellyfish wafting with the tide: clench and relax, clench and relax. Unbearable, then bearable.

Clammy wetness in the crotch of his jeans.

He fumbled with the knapsack straps, dislodging first one then the other from his shoulders. With a certain amount of judicious contortion he extricated each arm from the straps, then tugged the knapsack out from under him.

That was better.

He drew the knapsack onto his chest, undid the flap and removed the canteen from inside, hoping against hope that there was still some water left in it, even if it was no more than a trickle. Just enough to moisten his lips with would be nice. But the canteen was dry. Fen remembered shaking the last few drops from it into his mouth during Wickramasinghe's protracted absence yesterday.

Yesterday? Several decades ago!

He returned the canteen to the knapsack and fished out the only other item the knapsack contained, the mustard. This was all he had left of his provisions, thanks to Wickramasinghe. Half a pot of mustard. Not much use by itself, but still...

He unscrewed the lid, inserted a finger and hooked out a grainy ochre blob. Licked at it. Felt the tip of his tongue singe.

No, he wasn't going to be able to do this. Eat mustard raw. Not yet.

Besides, there *was* something to eat here. Earlier, he had noticed that the brambles at his feet were hung with blackberries—blackberries which ran the gamut of ripeness from tight green to swelling maroon to bloated purple-black. He was hungry enough to try one now.

He hauled himself up, stretched forwards, and plucked the largest of the fruits within reach. He popped it into his mouth and crushed it between his teeth.

Acid-sour.

He spat mashed blackberry out onto the grass. Somehow he had known that the blackberries would not be edible. Not just because it was too early in the year. A source of nourishment so close to hand would have been too much like divine providence, wouldn't it? Too much like a stroke of good fortune.

He lay back.

The sun was high and searingly hot.

No train had passed yet.

Time. He told himself it was only a matter of time.

By the time a train did come, Fen had lapsed into a kind of semi-doze, neither asleep nor wholly awake. It was as if he had withdrawn into a cocoon, somewhere where he was no longer exposed to the full glare of the sun, where the relentless grating throb from his leg was dulled, where pain and thirst and heat and hunger were problems but not *pressing* problems. He was detached from himself, at one remove from his senses. Somebody else who was feeling and hearing and experiencing all that he was feeling and hearing and experiencing.

The cocoon was a fine and private place and he would gladly have stayed there for ever, but then he heard the rails start to sing out a high-pitched whine and he knew this meant something, something important, something worth emerging for. Reluctantly he roused himself, re-entering the world of dry grass and parched lips and fractured thigh and burning sunshine, the harsh world he hadn't really left at all.

The rails were humming hard, the tines of a giant tuning fork, vibrating with the approaching tonnage of the train. Fen struggled up onto his elbows, and here it came, shoving a cushion of hissing air before it...

Whump!

The front carriage shot into view, and the trackside foliage writhed and surged like an appreciative crowd. Windows flickered by, some with passengers' faces in them, and then here was the second carriage and only now did Fen manage to raise a hand. A third carriage, and he waved hard, urgently—*here I am, I need help*—but the passengers were being whisked past too swiftly for him to tell whether any of them even registered his presence up there on top of the embankment. A fourth and final carriage, and then Fen was waving at empty space, at the trackbed weeds shivering in the train's slipstream, at the rails now relaxing into a relieved diminuendo, sighing, subsiding into silence.

He lowered his hand. He had done what he could. He only hoped someone aboard the train had seen him and had ascertained that he was in trouble. He realised that his waving could quite easily have been mistaken for a greeting. People did that, cheerily and thoughtlessly waved at trains going by. They had at the *Jagannatha*. But it should have been obvious that that was not what he had been doing.

He settled back stiffly into the grass, which had taken on a rough imprint of his body, a coffin-shaped silhouette picked out in flattened stems. He lay there and stared upwards at a patch of sky framed by the spikes of grass and a couple of nodding poppy heads. Soon his eyelids were drooping and the sky's blue was blurring and he was sinking back into the cocoon.

Safe here. Beyond harm here.

But then a sound. A strange, succulent sucking sound, liquid and living and lively, emanating from all around him. He opened his eyes. The couch grass was growing. Right in front of him as he watched. Struggling effortfully upwards. Stems writhing, multiplying, ramifying, breeding other stems, which bred yet others. Rising with time-lapse rapidity around him, deepening the depression in which he lay, limiting his view of the sky, shutting out the light, shrouding him in shadow. He tried to reach up to claw a hole through the grass. He felt like he was suffocating, drowning. But his arms would not move. The grass was vastly tall. The stems intertwined, interlocked, closed over him. Suddenly he was in green darkness, like that of a rainforest, canopied, cool. He was paralysed. He was frightened. It was like being buried alive.

Then there was someone beside him, standing over him, framed against the meshed vault of grass, looking down.

Michael Hollingbury.

It was unmistakably Hollingbury. Downbourne's Green Man in all his green finery. Yet he looked different. Greener, for one thing, as though he had daubed on several extra coats of vegetable dye, steeping his skin in the stuff. Somewhat plumper, too, than Fen remembered. And there was a peculiar quality to his hair, beard and eyebrows. Fen was reminded of chives—thick strands, juicy with chlorophyll. And Hollingbury's eyes... The irises were green, a deep, sparkling jade green, and Fen was almost certain they used to be blue.

All very perplexing, but not as perplexing as the fact that Michael Hollingbury was dead. Fen had watched him die. Had watched the British Bulldogs hurl his battered body into the festival bonfire. Had heard and smelled him burn.

With a certain pardonable circumspection, Fen offered this apparition a hello.

"Ah, Mr Morris, yes." Hollingbury smiled, shaking his head. "Not the most marvellous of situations, eh? But then we all of us make bad choices now and then."

"Do you think you could—?" Fen stopped. "No, I don't even know why I'm asking. You can't help me. You're dead."

"Am I?" Hollingbury's green eyes glinted.

"Of course you are."

"If you say so. I, however, would beg to differ. And the evidence of your own eyes ought to furnish all the disproof you should need. Do you really think I'm so easily despatched, after all the centuries I've lived?"

"I don't know. No, I suppose. Or yes. Maybe yes."

Hollingbury chuckled. "I must say, Mr Morris, for a pedagogue you seem sorely lacking in certainty. A teacher should have all the answers, shouldn't he? The correct response ever at his fingertips." There was a teasing note in his voice.

"Well, if you aren't dead," Fen said, "what are you?"

Hollingbury squatted down on his haunches, resting his forearms on his thighs and clasping his hands together. Fen noticed that his fingernails were as green as the rest of him. Normally they had never taken the dye quite so well. His teeth were green, too, a dark green that was almost black, each like a little hard lump of cooked spinach. This would have made anyone else's mouth look ghastly and diseased, but in Hollingbury's case it seemed somehow appropriate, not to say healthy.

"There is no death." The Green Man's tone was perfectly matter-of-fact. "Existences end, but nothing ever truly dies. Take that tree over there." He gestured, and at the sweep of his hand the couch grass that had grown up around Fen was restored to its normal size, as if instantly and silently scythed.

Fen, no longer entombed, turned his head in the direction Hollingbury was inviting him to look and saw a huge, solitary sycamore, standing some hundred yards away. He did not recall the sycamore being there before. It spread its branches against the sky, its leaves fretted with light.

"That tree," said Hollingbury, "flourishes now, but at a certain point in time it will cease to be alive. Its sap will no longer flow, it will not grow any more, but even so it will remain standing, continuing to give support to the ivy that twines around its bark, continuing to provide a haven to the birds that nest in its branches and the squirrel that hoards nuts in its trunk. Then, when the tree does at last rot through and fall, the decayed wood will be food and home to insects, and eventually will be broken down into mulch and compost, sustenance for new plant life. No death is without rebirth, just as no suffering is without gain. Do you understand?"

It was classic Hollingbury, the sort of mystical nature metaphor that had been his forte.

"Well, yes," Fen said. "But a tree's a bit different from a human being, don't you think?"

"Not at all. There's no difference whatsoever."

"OK, fine, fair enough." There was no point in arguing. Logic seemed irrelevant anyway at this moment. "So let's accept that you aren't dead after all. Does that mean you can get me out of this?"

Hollingbury flashed him a dark green grin. "Alas not. But I am keeping an eye on you, Mr Morris. I am on your side. Don't forget that. And everything, good or ill, happens for a reason. Don't forget that either. You will survive this. You're going to be all right. I can't promise that you're going to have an easy time of it in the near future. In fact, the opposite. But you *will* survive."

From overhead there came a low rending sound, like scissors shearing through canvas.

Hollingbury glanced up. "Ah yes. Behold."

Fen glanced up too, and saw, traipsing side by side across the sky, a pair of warplanes. Sun-gold glinted on their nosecones and the leading edges of their wings. They were at too high an altitude for Fen to determine whether or not they had dropped their payloads yet.

Come, friendly bombs, and fall on Fen, he thought.

He turned his head in order to share the humorous misquotation with Hollingbury, only to find that the Green Man had gone.

But of course he had gone. He had never been there. That had been a dream, and Fen was awake now.

He refocused on the warplanes as they eased towards the edge of his field of vision. There was little left in England worth bombing, but every so often the International Community saw fit to flatten a warehouse or an office block as a reminder, the geopolitical equivalent of a clip round the ear—*we haven't forgotten you, we assume you're still misbehaving, and if you persist in refusing to toe the line then you must be prepared to pay the penalty*. Sometimes the planes weren't armed, but a reconnaissance mission was almost as effective an aide-memoire: *we're up here, we're looking down, we see everything.*

It occurred to him to try and attract the pilots' attention. He then laughed at his own foolishness. Even if the pilots *did* spot him, how insect-like he would look to them, how insignificant.

The planes disappeared from view, the roar of their jets fading soon after.

The sky was hazier than before, a hoary shade of blue. Afternoon was over and evening was coming on. Fen realised he had been out here at the top of the embankment for over twenty-four hours. Possibly, thanks to a passenger on the train that had passed, people were on their way to rescue him. Possibly. The odds were against it, though.

Hollingbury in the dream: *You will survive this*.

But that had been a dream, and this was not. This was reality, and in this reality a single thought had begun tolling in Fen's head, faintly but insistently, like a far-off church bell.

A single sentence, iterated over and over.

You are going to die.

After supper, I ask Lauren if I can go for another wander around the compound. Immediately she's suspicious. She doesn't know if she can trust me yet. For her, being trustworthy means being sufficiently intimidated, and she doesn't know yet whether I am. All afternoon I've been doing everything she's asked me to—domestic chores, helping her keep the house in tip top condition for King Cunt's return tomorrow—and I've tried my hardest to give the impression that I'm coming to terms with what's happened to me, that I'm learning to accept my lot. It's worked. She's lowered her guard—but not completely.

"Why?" she says.

"I just want to stretch my legs."

"I'll come with you."

"You don't have to."

But she thinks she does, and it doesn't make any difference to me. I just want to get a better idea of the lie of the land. So off we go.

There's a revelrous mood in the compound this evening. The Bulldogs are charging around, ragging one another. Mock fights are going on, fuelled by beer. A stereo is blaring from one of the houses, rock music, drumbeats like thunderclaps, and there's a small crowd sitting around outside listening to it, nodding along in unison as though the rhythm has all their heads on a string. In the communal area, what appears to be a weightlifting competition is in progress. Rusty barbells get shunted up and down, propelled on their way with elephantine grunts. Extra weights are clamped on, and faces get redder and the veins in necks and temples get fatter. Everywhere, the braying, bassy laughter of men. It's a cliché but the air really does seem charged with testosterone.

As Lauren and I are wandering towards an area of the compound I didn't get to see this morning, one of the Bulldogs comes striding up to us. I recognise him from the night I was captured. He was the one giving orders as we were unloaded from the vans. I remember his gold tooth twinkling in the headlamp light.

"Lauren."

"Neville."

There's wariness in her voice. Lauren doesn't like this man. I don't think he much likes her either, but whereas she's possibly a little frightened of him, his dislike for her seems more a kind of impatience, as if he can't understand why she's still here, why she insists on hanging around when she's so clearly surplus to requirements. That, at any rate, is the impression I get from how each says the other's name and from the fact that Neville, without any further preamble, starts asking Lauren about me—how I'm shaping up, does she think Craig will like me.

Lauren's judgement is that I'm acceptable material, OK-looking, a bit inclined to speak my mind but I'll soon get out of *that* habit.

Neville eyes me up and down, then reaches out and, just like that, grabs one of my breasts. I'm too startled to protest. He paws the breast, palpating it, kneading it, and the look on his face is half sober appraisal, half smutty little schoolboy. Finally he gives the breast a tweak where he thinks the nipple ought to be (he's off-target by about an inch) then lets go. I'm still speechless but it's probably all for the best that I didn't voice my outrage or slap his hand away as I was minded to. I think I would have earned myself a punch that way.

"He likes 'em a bit bigger than that," is Neville's assessment. "But they'll do."

"He wouldn't have dared if Craig was around," Lauren confides a few moments later, after Neville's left us and we're walking on. She's indignant, although not, I feel, on my behalf. "He wouldn't have dared lay a finger on you."

I touch my manhandled breast. Sore. "Who is he?"

"Neville? Craig's second-in-command, I suppose you'd call him. They used to be friends at school, best pals, though now they're, like, not such good friends any more but Craig still keeps Neville around because Craig's thoughtful that way and because a lot of the guys think Neville's OK so it wouldn't be sensible to tell him to sling his hook. Which Craig ought to, 'cause Neville's a right pain in the ass, constantly having a go at him, bugging him about this or that. All the time he's like 'Are you sure, Craig, do you think that's a good idea?' I think he thinks he could do as good a job of running things here, maybe better."

"And could he?"

"No. Oh no. Nobody could replace Craig." This is Lauren's gospel, the central, unshakeable certainty in her life. King Cunt is king. It's sad how simply, how obviously, she adores him. "Anyhow," she says, "in case you haven't figured it out for yourself already, you want to watch that Neville."

"Thanks. I will."

Now we're coming to a house I know far too well, even though I had only glimpses of its exterior while entering and leaving. One look at the bricked-up windows and all of a sudden I'm back in the confines of that room—the gritty floorboards, the reek of human waste, the sobbing, the helplessness, the hopelessness, and Jennifer, dead Jennifer's cold corpse, lying near me for who knows how long. And I hate these men, these Bulldogs, for putting me through that. I hate them already but my hatred is redoubled, and I know that if it were in my power I would kill them all, every last one of them.

And around a corner I come across a sight that deepens that hatred still further.

Lauren would have steered me away from here if she felt I wasn't ready to see this. Perhaps I've succeeded better than I thought at convincing her that I'm subdued and passive and not likely to give any trouble.

Three houses, their eaves hung with strings of multicoloured light bulbs that cast a jaunty glow against the gathering dusk. The windows all curtained, the front gardens enclosed by chainlink fence, and in the gardens, women. Women standing. Women seated on an assortment of plastic outdoor chairs. Women waiting. About thirty of them in all, many familiar to me. There's Angela Pearson, one of the first people I met after moving to Downbourne, one of the first who was friendly and didn't view me with suspicion because I was From The Big City. There's Susannah Vicks. There's Rachel Jason, or is it Jacobs? I always get her name wrong. And there, oh God, is Zoë Fothergill, sitting and being hugged by Paula Coulton, who lost her daughter last year to an infection (Ginnie Coulton, eight years old, cut her hand open on barbed wire while playing with friends, got tetanus, and there was nothing anyone could do, not even Anne Chase, though God knows she tried). There they all are beyond the wire diamonds of chainlink mesh, and some have bruises on their faces and some have eyes that are sunk in dark-circled sockets, and all of them look hollowed and harrowed and bewildered, like survivors of a plane crash or high-street shoppers who were just minding their own business when the car bomb went off. They're waiting because there's nothing else for them to do. Waiting and trying not think about what they're waiting for.

Lauren stands back, arms folded. I don't know how she can't feel any empathy for these women, but she doesn't. Maybe she just can't afford to.

Me, I move forwards to the nearest of the front gardens. As I reach the padlocked gate, some of the women notice me. Their heads turn, alarm sparking in their eyes. They're expecting men. When they see I'm not a Bulldog, a couple of them turn away again, not even curious about me. Probably they assume I've been brought to join them. The rest keep looking, and then Susannah Vicks says, "Moira." She says it with a certain amount of interest, but mostly she says it in the lost, deflated tone of someone who doesn't care much about anything any more. It's a tone I'm very familiar with, having heard myself use it pretty consistently for a year and a half. She says, "Moira," the same way I used to say, "Fen."

I've no idea how to respond. I don't know what I can say to these women that won't sound fatuous or patronising or otherwise offensive. I can barely begin to imagine what they've been going through, I don't want to, and even though a similar fate lies in store for me when King Cunt returns, they're behind a fence and I'm not; they're incarcerated in these "recreation zones" and I'm walking around Fort Bulldog, not in any way free but nevertheless freer than they are.

"We've been told," Susannah says, and points to a woman I don't recognise. "Carla here has been filling us in. We know about the King and his redheads."

As she speaks I hear her groping for some resentment to put into her voice, but resentment demands just that bit more emotional strength than she has at present.

"Nice of you to pay us a visit," says Angela Pearson. She, too, is trying for something extra in her voice, in this case sarcasm. Trying and, like Susannah, failing.

I turn my attention to Zoë. Encircled by Paula Coulton's arms, she stares dazedly ahead, her face bereft of any of the liveliness you ought to see on a teenager's face. She has been hurled headlong into a world she could not have suspected existed, a world where men force and subdue and inflict hurt and disgusting humiliation over and over again. It has shattered her.

Susannah and Angela continue to snipe at me in that vigourless manner, trying to hate me for something they know isn't my fault. A couple of the other women join in. I should feel wronged, I should stick up for myself, but I don't. I ignore them, staying focused on Zoë, fixing in my mind how she looks: her slumped shoulders, every contour of her stunned, listless features.

Fuel for loathing.

We're halfway back to King Cunt's house when Lauren finally speaks. I'd forgotten she was even with me.

"I don't go there often, myself," she says. "Now you know why."

"What happens to them?" I ask. "I mean, they're not going to be held captive indefinitely, surely."

"Oh no. After a while the guys get bored. They want to see some new faces."

I should think that, where female physical attributes are concerned, faces come pretty low on the Bulldogs' list of priorities. "How long does that take, usually?"

"Varies. Anything from a few weeks to a few months."

"And then?"

"They go on another hunt."

"No, the women. What becomes of the women when they don't want them any more?"

"They get turfed out."

"Not... not killed, then."

"Did I say that? Just turfed out."

"And they have to make their own way home?"

"No, they get a taxi to take them wherever they want to go." Lauren sneers, despairing of me. "Of course they have to make their own way home!"

"But the women from Downbourne—we—live fifty miles away."

"And a lot of them won't make it that far."

"And what about the M25?"

"Moira, do you honestly think the guys here *care*?"

She has a point, of course. The British Bulldogs don't care about anyone but themselves. They live here in their little enclosed corral, doing as they please, taking what they need from the world outside. They certainly aren't likely to give a damn what happens to their "recreation zone" women after they're done with them. Shove them out the gate, get the next lot in...

I've learned more than I bargained for this evening, and everything has changed. I was intending to make my bid for freedom tonight, before King Cunt comes back tomorrow. Arm myself with a knife from the kitchen and scale the barricade via one of the lookout posts. If I was caught in the attempt, so be it. I'd take the consequences, whatever they might be.

But now I realise that I've been given an opportunity. I've been put in a position where I may be able to do more than just save my own skin.

I can help these women. Paula Coulton, Susannah Vicks, Angela Pearson, Zoë. All of them. I can help them.

It could be that this is just a pretext. It could be that I'm groping for some convenient excuse not to take the risk of escaping, and these women are it. But I don't think so. I can't in all conscience leave them here, can I? If somehow I can see to it that they're treated better, or at the very least that they're returned safely back to Downbourne when the time comes... well then, there's no question about it. That is what I must do.

THE DOG PACK found him not long after moonrise.

They had smelled him from miles away. The night-time air currents conveyed minuscule wafts of him to their noses, scents like phrase-fragments, gradually coalescing into an intelligible message. A human. A male. In distress. In pain. Injured. He had broken a bone. He had urinated on himself—perhaps in fear? The dogs detected the hotness of inflamed flesh. They understood that the human was hungry, tired, weakened. Their leader, a scar-faced Rottweiler, made the decision. Off he went, and the rest of the pack fell in behind.

Loping, surging, breasting, the dogs—a motley lot, all different sizes and breeds—made their way across fields, through hedgerows, along bridle paths, down tarmac lanes. Keeping to the speed of their slowest member, an elderly Jack Russell, they held their muzzles high, triangulating the human aroma as it grew stronger and richer. Soon they were within close proximity of their quarry and, as one, they slowed their pace, becoming cautious. Humans were unpredictable beasts, capable of a lot more than their ungainly, strangely furred physiques would suggest. Just a few nights back the pack had lost one of their number, a Labrador, to a human who kept chickens. They had been breaking into the chickens' cages when the human had emerged from his house, barking at them incomprehensibly and shining a small sun in their eyes. Then had come the deafening bang, and the Labrador had yelped and tumbled over, his ribcage devastated. The rest of the pack had scattered, and while fleeing had heard a second bang and, moments later, smelled the spilled-brains-and-shit odour of the Labrador's death. So humans could be very dangerous. But they could also, under the right circumstances, be eaten.

All of the pack members could remember, albeit dimly, a time when humans were their gods. They had lived in warm homes with humans, been fed regularly by them, looked after by them, governed by them, and all in return for loving worship. Loving worship—which came so easily to a dog. It had been a sweet deal. But then had come a fall, a period of anger and confusion and fear. Food had arrived less regularly, and then stopped arriving altogether. And soon after that, abandonment—a physical severance that was agonising, like being consigned to limbo. The dogs had each been part of a human pack, and suddenly they had become wild rovers, out on their own and having to fend for themselves.

They had come together slowly to form this new, dog-only pack. One by one they had added to its number, learning one another's scents and habits, establishing a hierarchy. Now they were of one mind, a single creature of disparate parts. A unit that had shrugged off all of the training instilled during the good years, the years of warmth and plenty, and embraced lawlessness and self-sufficiency instead. A unit that had learned to distrust and avoid humans but also, when they could, prey on them.

There was one among them that had never been close to humans, however, one that had been born into the feral life; and now, as the pack came to a halt less than a hundred leap-lengths from the human, it was this one who by mutual consent went forward to reconnoitre. The other dogs thought of her as the Sly Stranger, and she was a puzzling conundrum—a dog who didn't truly behave or smell like one but was one nonetheless. She had a narrow muzzle, reddish fur and a brushy tail, and most of the time she kept her distance from the pack, tagging along like an afterthought. She did, however, take an enthusiastic part in kills, and it was thanks to her that the pack had learned how to breach and raid the cages in which humans kept prey such as chickens or rabbits.

The Sly Stranger slunk towards the human through the couch grass, stealthy on her dainty black paws. Had the human shifted position or had the composition of his odour become tangy with anger or alarm, the Sly Stranger would have frozen, poised to retreat. But the human remained unaware of her approach, even after the Sly Stranger was close enough to view him clearly through the grass stalks. The human lay there, breathing irregularly, shivering...

An easy kill.

IF NOT FOR the fact that one of the pack—the Jack Russell—became overexcited and started yapping, Fen would have had no warning of the attack and would undoubtedly have ended up literally as a dogs' dinner. He was back in the cocoon, adrift inside the miserable, shiver-wracked body of Fen Morris, dreamily contemplating how easy it would be to die out here and at the same time how *miserable*—and then suddenly a small dog was yipping nearby and he could hear bodies moving through the grass.

His immediate thought was, They've done it! They've found me! Rescuers! Rescuers with sniffer dogs!

With all the energy he could summon, he began calling out, and although his vocal cords had been severely strained by earlier exertions, he nevertheless managed to produce a creditable level of volume. Relief and joy surged through him. He was saved. It was all over.

He kept shouting until it crossed his mind that no one was answering. Odd. Surely his rescuers would be telling him to hang in there, or yelling to one another, saying he was over this way, they'd located him. And then he thought: Wouldn't at least one of them be carrying a torch? Or, if they couldn't get the batteries, a lantern maybe? He saw no lights.

And then he heard growling.

A dark shape loomed through the couch grass to his right, something stocky and stout-bodied that stood not much higher than the grass itself.

All at once, Fen was staring into the face of a Rottweiler, and his surge of hope was snatched back down into a void of empty terror. In the moonlight he could make out the light-brown portions of the dog's features—jaw, jowls, pugnacious eyebrows. He saw, too, the onyx glitter of its eyes and the mesmerising white serration of its fangs. The Rottweiler continued to growl at him, and Fen, in spite of his fear, understood that it was studying him, perhaps perturbed by his shouts and wondering if he had been signalling to other humans in the vicinity. The growl was both intimidation and quizzicality, though more the former than the latter.

Peripherally, Fen became aware of other dogs lurking to either side of the Rottweiler, their eyes trained on him, glimmering through the grass stalks. Seven, perhaps eight of the animals. A pack. He kept his gaze steady on the Rottweiler. The Rottweiler had to be the alpha male. If it attacked, the rest of the pack would too.

Long seconds oozed past, the Rottweiler still indecisive. Fen's heartbeat banged in his ears, loud as timpani. The Rottweiler moved its head slightly, and he noticed that its face was crosshatched with scars. Pale little furrows across the muzzle, over the flat forehead. Wounds from old opponents, old victims. This was a dog that had fought and killed many times, yet for all its size and sinew it had not won every battle without some cost to itself.

Partly (Fen would realise later) the notion of hitting the Rottweiler was spawned by the sight of those scars. If other creatures had defied this brute in the past, why not him?

Mostly, however, hitting the Rottweiler all at once seemed the right thing to do. A reflex action but also, in a way, an irritable one. The only fitting riposte to such a turn of events, such a ridiculously unkind adding of insult to injury. A heedless, peevish *fuck you* to whichever deity had arranged this misfortune for him.

His fist lashed out. Perfect connection was made with the Rottweiler's nose. He felt the nose squash under his knuckles, mushroom-soft; heard a satisfying moist *whack*.

The Rottweiler yelped, about-turned and fled. The rest of the pack went scuttering after it, the grass stalks quivering in their wake.

Only when his lungs felt like they were about to burst did Fen remember to breathe. He sucked in air, exultant.

A pack of dogs. He had just been cornered by, and *seen off*, a pack of wild dogs.

He marvelled at his own audacity. Bashing one of them on the nose like that. A Rottweiler no less! If he had been a fraction of a second slower the damn thing would have had his hand off, but he had timed it just right, the Rottweiler hadn't known what was coming, his aim had been true...

He listened to the dogs racing across the field, rustling through poppies and grass, and he felt invincible. Having survived *that*, it seemed to him that he could survive anything. Broken leg? No problem. Not now. For a man who, with a single blow, was able to send an entire dog pack packing, what difficulties did having a broken leg in a remote spot present?

The rustling continued, and it occurred to Fen that the sound was not getting quieter any more. It wasn't getting louder, either, but the dogs were clearly no longer running away. At a fixed distance from where he lay, they were milling around. Regrouping.

His sense of triumph collapsed like a pin-popped balloon.

He hadn't won a victory with that biff on the Rottweiler's nose. All he had won was a respite.

Desperate, Fen groped around for a weapon, something he might use against the dogs, a rock, a branch, *anything*.

Nothing.

He had his knapsack with its empty water canteen and half-full mustard pot, he had two fists, one foot, that was it.

He heard the dogs distantly padding to and fro, and envisaged them planning a new attack. The group-mind of the pack, debating what to do. Stratagems of canine cunning. Their prey was alone and wounded, they were many. It wouldn't take them long to figure out that their superiority in numbers was their greatest asset against him. If they attacked him together, he couldn't ward them *all* off with blows to the nose.

Out there, beneath the icy stars and the laughing moon, Fen had never felt so defenceless or so alone. He felt trapped in a nightmare, not his own but England's, the nightmare of a nation that had believed that no more shocks lay in store for it. A nation that had, like some smug, ageing plutocrat, thought its future would be all comfort and civility and the nodding collusion of its peers. A nation that could never have foreseen the penury and upheaval and ostracism it was presently suffering. England was asleep and dreaming bad dreams, and Fen yearned for it to wake up.

The dogs stopped moving. At least he couldn't hear them any more.

He levered himself up and twisted round from the waist so that he could see up the slope of the field. Couch grass and poppies waved and rippled and undulated in the moonlight. The dogs might be lying still. Equally, they might this very moment be homing in on him like sharks through the shallows, their progress masked by the field's breeze-blown restlessness.

A dim, atavistic thought sparked in Fen's brain: hide.

But hide where? There was no shelter hereabouts, nothing to crawl behind or into or under.

His eye fell on the brambles.

Yes, there was.

The next instant, Fen was pushing himself with his hands and his functional leg, pivoting around on his backside in a series of slithering shunts. His bad leg first murmured, then whined, then shrieked as it was repeatedly dragged and buffeted, but he pressed his lips tight shut and kept going. The pain became so excruciating that he twice came close to giving up. He persevered. No matter how much this was hurting him, it could not be worse than being mauled to death by dogs.

Finally—he could scarcely believe he had managed it—he was sitting with his back against the brambles.

He allowed himself a brief rest, breath whistling in and out through his teeth. His thigh felt huge and hot, like a chunk of molten ore.

Not far off, he glimpsed a shadow cleaving slowly through one of the clumps of poppies.

He snatched up the knapsack and slung its strap around his neck. Then he drew his right foot in, dug the heel into the ground, and thrust himself backwards into the brambles.

His clothing snagged. Thorns pricked. Waves of incandescent agony radiated up from his thigh.

He drew his right foot in again and thrust with it again, penetrating deeper into the brambles.

He thrust once more, but this time made no headway. The thorns had a secure grip on him now. He was in the brambles up to his waist, permitted to go that far but no further.

He struggled to detach his sleeves from the thorns. He could now discern three of those shadows slinking downslope through the field, their trajectories converging on him. The nearest was less than a dozen yards away. He thrashed his arms, managed to free them, then looked about for something to grab hold of so that he could augment pushing with pulling. There was nothing within reach but brambles. No alternative—he grasped a bunch of stems with each hand, wincing as a score of needlepoints stabbed his palms. Nasty but, compared with his leg, trivial. He bore down with his right foot, hauled with his hands, and succeeded in burying himself in the brambles as far as his knees.

Nearly there. One last shove should do it.

In front of him, the Rottweiler broke cover. Its massive head reared from the grass, no more than a decent lunge away from his feet.

Beside it, the head of another dog appeared. Actually, not a dog. A *fox*.

Fen had just enough time to wonder at the anomaly—a fox as part of a dog pack, an alliance forged through some sort of distant-cousin kinship—and then the Rottweiler went for him.

Sheer panic lent him the power and the coordination to save himself.

Arms and good leg did exactly what was required of them. Bad leg, for the brief period that was necessary, ceased to hinder. In an ecstasy of fear Fen wrenched himself bodily backwards, hearing—*feeling*—the clunk of the Rottweiler's teeth as they snapped shut on the space where a half-second earlier his left ankle had been.

Then the world fell away beneath him and he was slipping backwards down the embankment.

It wasn't a smooth descent, rather a series of short, jerky slithers as brambles snagged him and, unable to sustain his weight, let go, passing him on. He was near the bottom when, finally, he came to a clump sufficiently thick to arrest his progress. He crunched head-first into it, and for a fleeting instant this seemed to be how he was going to stay, vertical and inverted. Gravity, however, had other ideas, and his body continued to slide, rotating slowly like the hand of a clock going from twelve to three, until he fetched up lying almost horizontal along the embankment.

He had a few seconds of stunned numbness in which to reflect on what he had done. In a sense, he had succeeded far better than he had hoped. He was even able to bemoan the countless scrapes and scratches he had received from the brambles. His face and hands stung all over. He felt grated. Lacerated.

Then his leg cut in, cancelling out these minor injuries as the sun cancels out the stars. The leg resumed its litany of pain with spectacular gusto, no longer merely drawing attention to itself but actively punishing Fen for his part in, first of all, fracturing it, and now aggravating it. The pain mounted in a massive crescendo, and Fen threw back his head and wailed.

He wailed, and he put everything he had into the wailing, hauling up the agony, dredging up every hurt and slight and wound ever inflicted on him and hurling them out through his voice.

He wailed until the sound seemed to fill the sky and there was no room for anything else in the world except this wordless exposition of suffering.

At the top of the embankment, the thwarted dog pack circled about, ears pricked and tails at half mast, uncertain what to make of what they were hearing. One of them decided to start baying, and suddenly they were all of them baying, all trying to beat the human at his own game.

Down below, cradled in thorns, Fen bawled like a baby, oblivious to everything but the tragedy of himself.

4.
Netherholm College

THERE WAS PURE blinding whiteness all around him, and he thought, so this is how it happens. You don't remember dying. Life stops and, hey presto, you're elsewhere.

Squinting against the brilliance, Fen discovered that the after-life was a somewhat more mundane-looking place than he had imagined it would be. He was in a long white room with three tall, arched, curtainless windows that afforded a view of trees and sky—a march of oaks beneath a swath of cloud-patched blue. The room was furnished with beds of the military-barracks variety, half a dozen of them, including the one he was lying in. Their iron frames were painted white, with black spots here and there where the paint had chipped away. Each had a white wooden cabinet next to it. The place—some sort of hospital ward—smelled of mildew and liniment, and in one corner of the cracked-plaster ceiling there was a spider in a web.

Perhaps, he thought, all this ordinariness was meant to reassure him, to ease the period of transition. Once he had acclimatised to the idea of being deceased, he would then move on to a part of the after-life that was altogether more... after-life-like.

He then noticed something odd. The after-life hurt. Apparently the world's religions had got it wrong. You *did* take your bodily aches and pains with you when you passed on. Your bramble scratches smarted, your sunburned skin stung, your hoarse throart throbbed, and your broken leg...

...was in traction?

Fen peered at the makeshift device that was strapped around his left leg, keeping it suspended at a forty-five degree angle from the bed. A sling had been fashioned from a section of bright orange canvas which had, by the look of it, once been part of a tent. Laced through brass eyelets in the canvas was a length of thick cord whose ends ran up to a pair of hooks screwed into the ceiling. Within the sling there were three planks of wood, underneath and on either side of the leg, providing the necessary stabilisation.

Interesting. So the after-life wasn't all that dissimilar from England, then—a place where, when the proper equipment was not available, you improvised.

But of course it had dawned on Fen by now that he was not dead. On the contrary. He was alive. Blessedly, wondrously, miraculously alive. He had been saved from the dog pack; he had been rescued from the railway embankment.

By whom?

As if in answer, vague memory-images bubbled up in his brain. People shouting to one another as he lay among the brambles on the embankment. Lights bobbing in the dark. Hands taking hold of him by the shoulders and ankles, preparing to lift him. More pain then than he had known what to do with. He felt as if he had dreamed these things. Who were the people who had found him? Where had they brought him? It didn't matter. Doubtless he would find out soon enough. It was sufficient, for now, to be indoors and no longer in peril of his life.

Resting his head back against the pillows, Fen gazed up at the ceiling. His eye was drawn to the spider he had noticed earlier. He could see now that the creature, one of the generic brown domestic variety, was dead. Its legs were huddled about its body and it had the look of something desiccated, spindly and autumnal, something that winter winds would blow away. Its web had become its bier.

Like some arachno-coroner, Fen studied the corpse in an attempt to determine how it had died. He decided starvation must be the answer. The spider was the web's sole occupant. It had cast its net into barren waters.

He chose to interpret the spider's death by starvation as an auspicious sign: a predator denied a victim, just as the dog pack had been deprived of the opportunity of making a meal out of *him*. He rejected the notion, wickedly offered up by some malicious mental sprite, that there was a parallel to be drawn directly between the spider and himself—both of them strung up in this ward, attached to the ceiling, immobile. The spider's fate a foreshadowing of his own? That was a ridiculous idea. There was nothing to be gained by thinking like *that*.

THERE'S A SHOUT from outside the house.

"Oi, Lauren! He's on the approach road!"

Lauren snaps to her feet and rushes, I swear, *rushes* to the mirror in the hallway to check her face. She put makeup on after breakfast, since when she's been examining it at every opportunity. The mascara's applied too thickly and the lipstick isn't her shade, but frankly it doesn't matter—she has makeup, and that puts her one up on most other women in the country. And now, for the umpteenth time, she primps and preens in the mirror. She teases a lock of hair to one side, she fingernails a crumb of mascara away and she thumb-buffs the corner of her mouth, and then she gives herself a settled-back, approving look. *Yes, I'm all right really*. Then: "Moira, let's go."

Three days King Cunt has been away. Three days making overtures to the Frantik Posse, lords of Camberwell. A delicate mission, as I understand it from Lauren. The Frantiks, touchy at the best of times, don't take kindly to outsiders coming in with offers of alliances. Especially *white* outsiders. That they agreed to a meeting with King Cunt at all is, I've been assured, remarkable, a sign that even they have respect for his reputation and that of the Bulldogs. But this respect will not have been enough. In order to convince them to hear him out, King Cunt will have had to prove himself to them first, undergoing a kind of test of his manliness. Hence the negotiations taking three days. King Cunt has had to party with the Frantiks. Party hard. That's how the Frantiks take the measure of a man. King Cunt will have had to drink as much booze as the toughest-livered among them drinks. He will have had to smoke as much ganja as the biggest dopehead among them smokes. He will have had to satisfy as many of their women as their most priapic Mr Lover-man satisfies. He may even have had to engage in a round or two of "friendly" combat with one of their top cruiserweight bruisers. He will, in short, according to Lauren, be arriving home absolutely knackered.

So I'm expecting some bedraggled, bloodshot-eyed wreck to come staggering in through the compound gate. And I'm thinking he'll be a small man. I don't know why I've pictured him that way—Napoleon complex, I suppose. I see him as stocky, bullet-headed, bow-legged. This is the image of him that's built up in my mind over the past couple of days. I think that, when not "absolutely knackered", he'll be cocky and coarse. Come on, anyone who calls himself King Cunt is hardly likely to be a model of sophistication. I think that, the moment I see him, I will know how to feel contempt for him and why.

All the same, I can't deny that I'm curious about him, and that I'm slightly—*slightly*—looking forward to meeting him. From an almost anthropological viewpoint he interests me. From a pragmatic, self-centred viewpoint as well. This is the man, after all, whose girlfriend I was brought here to be.

The Bulldogs converge on the entrance to the compound. They saunter, not wanting to be seen to look eager. But the eagerness is there, in clenched fists, quick grins. The King. The King is returning. They assemble just inside the gate, and jostle about, trading quips, nudges, suppositions. "D'you think he pulled it off?" "I think one of those curvy little Frantik girls pulled it off *for* him, ha ha ha! Know what I mean?" Then there's the rumble of an engine outside, a toot on a horn, and the man in the lookout post gives the OK signal.

Three Bulldogs heave aside the thick bar of timber that secures the gate. Another two haul the gate inwards, revealing a bare street, ramshackle houses, a few locals peering nervously from various vantage points, and of course King Cunt's van. Purring and travel-dusty, the van—which is a Mercedes, white of course—noses into the compound, the Bulldogs moving aside to make way for it. As the gate closes, the van glides to a halt, and the gold-toothed Bulldog, Neville, steps forward from the crowd.

"All right, lads. He's back. Let's hear it for the King."

The chant starts up straight away, from a dozen throats, then several dozen. At first I think what they're saying is "Fucking cunt! Fucking cunt!", until I realise it's a sort of pun. They're chanting "For King Cunt! For King Cunt!" and the resemblance of this to "fucking cunt" is intentional but, at the same time, not disrespectful. In fact I have a feeling the joke is, in a weird way, the opposite of disrespectful.

The chant gathers volume. Fists, Neville's among the first, start punching the air in time. "*For* King *Cunt*! *For* King *Cunt*!" The Bulldogs cluster around the van. The driver's door opens.

Out he comes. He *is* small. Small and, I have to say, quite ugly, with a hook nose and a head too large for the rest of him. He acknowledges the Bulldogs' acclaim with a humble, shoulder-shrugging wave, and bows as if to say *I'm not worthy*. It beats me how this little gnome of a man can command all these individuals much bigger than him. He has no obvious leadership qualities, no *presence*.

I turn to Lauren to make a comment to this effect, and it's then that I realise my mistake. Her face is the giveaway. The little man doesn't interest her in the slightest. She's looking to the passenger door of the van. The gnome isn't King Cunt at all.

The passenger door opens, and the chanting dissolves into cheering.

The van tips to one side as he emerges; springs level again as his feet touch the ground. He's massive. He has the body of a comic-book superhero. The inverted-cone torso, the muscle-clotted arms, the swooping thighs. As with the rest of the Bulldogs he has cropped hair and is dressed in sports casualwear (his shirt is the red strip of what was once the country's most popular football team). Unlike the rest of the Bulldogs, however, he doesn't look like a thug. Oh, he has all the tangible attributes of a thug—the physique, the haircut, the jawline—but what he doesn't have is the *demeanour*. He doesn't hulk and slouch, and his face, his eyes—there's more going on there. There's an alertness. There's, dare I say it, an intelligence. He surveys the cheering throng, and he looks suitably gratified. He holds a hand aloft. He grins. He accepts the men's approbation and rewards it with precisely the right level of leaderly indulgence. But it's clear he's their superior in more than just rank. He is a different order of human being altogether. He is someone who has stratagems. Who has plans. Who has *vision*.

Or does he seem so superior simply because of who he's chosen to surround himself with? A carp amongst minnows. An ordinary man amongst pygmies.

Lauren gazes at him, rapt as an infatuated schoolgirl, and the cheering goes on, showing no sign of abating. Neville trots forward, and he and King Cunt shake hands. Lip-reading, I see Neville say something like "Welcome back, mate," and he claps King Cunt on the biceps. King Cunt reciprocates the gesture—but is there just the briefest of hesitations before he does so? Or am I, thanks to what Lauren's told me about Neville, simply reading too much into things?

And still the cheering goes on.

And then King Cunt looks past his men, and he catches sight of Lauren, and the next instant he's looking at me.

And he smiles.

Luckily I catch myself in time. But it's a close-run thing.

I nearly smiled back.

Suddenly it was evening. Fen awoke to find that the white room had taken on a rosy twilight blush. He blinked around, wondering why no one had come to check up on him yet. He listened, but there was nothing to be heard other than his own breathing and the distant, rustling tumult of the oaks outside. For all he knew, he was alone in the building. His rescuers had brought him here and fixed up his leg in a home-made traction apparatus, and had then abandoned him? It seemed unlikely—not unless he had been made the victim of some bizarre, incomprehensible practical joke.

He noticed something that had escaped his attention earlier. His clothes lay in a pile, neatly folded, on a chair nearby. They appeared to have been laundered. With them hung his knapsack. The chair was within reach, so he was able to grab the knapsack and look inside. Its contents were all present and correct—wedding band, London permit, not forgetting the pot of mustard. Clearly the people looking after him, whoever they were, were as honest as they were solicitous.

So where *were* they, these saintly saviours of his? Perhaps they had assumed that, when he regained consciousness, he would shout for their attention.

He tried. He put all he had into it, forcing the breath up from his lungs as hard as he could, but the best his throat was able to produce was a pitiful, aerated squeak that even someone in the same room might not have heard. His voice was ruined from all the yelling and screaming he had done during those awful hours out in the open, when it had seemed all too possible that he was going to die. His vocal cords, for the time being, had nothing left to give.

Plan B: thumping on the wall. But the wall proved solid, unresonant, dulling the smack of his fist.

Then he hit on the idea of thumping the bed frame.

The bed gonged with each blow, and the whitewashed floorboards acted as a sounding board, amplifying nicely. For half a minute Fen hammered out a sonorous irregular peal, then stopped and waited.

Someone came.

SHE WAS A short woman, round-faced, wearing spectacles with lenses as thick as ice cubes, through which her eyes peeped like a pair of tiny asterisks. Her hair was wiry and brown and held in place by plastic clips, and there was something both brisk and anxious about the way she crossed the room—swift little strides, stubby arms swinging tautly.

"There you are!" she said. "Back in the land of the living. I take it all that banging was to summon me."

"I'm sorry," Fen rasped. "I would have shouted, but..."

"Ah yes. Lost your voice. And otherwise? How are you feeling generally?"

"Sore." He nodded at his leg. "Very sore."

"Well, we haven't got any painkillers for you."

This brusqueness, Fen thought, was a cover for shyness. The world snapped at this woman; she snapped back.

"It's all right," he said. "I'm not complaining. I'm just glad to be alive. This place." He gestured at his surroundings. "A nursing home of some sort? A hospital?"

The woman cast an amused glance around her. "Does it look like a hospital?"

"Sort of."

"As it happens, you're in the sanatorium of a school."

"A school?"

"Netherholm College. Boys only. Ages thirteen to eighteen. Boarding. You won't have heard of it. It wasn't one of the major ones. And it isn't a school any more, of course. Closed down years ago."

"Were you the matron?"

"Oh no. No, no." The idea tickled her.

"But you obviously have some medical training."

"Fourteen years with the St John Ambulance. Hold still a moment." She pressed a firm, dry palm against Fen's forehead, then took his pulse, timing it against her wristwatch. Satisfied with the results of both diagnostic procedures, she plumped up his pillows. "You'll be hungry, I expect. I'll bring you some supper in an hour or so. In the meantime, do you need to do a business?"

"Do I need to—? Oh. Yes."

"Urine? Stool?"

Fen nodded.

"Well, which is it?"

"Just urine, I think."

"Back in a mo."

The woman returned with a kidney-shaped enamel dish, which she slid, with little ceremony, beneath Fen's backside. The dish's rim was shockingly cold against his skin.

"There. It's none too easy if you haven't tried it before, but keep at it. You'll soon get the hang. When you're done, leave the dish on the floor. By the way, do you have a name?"

"Fen. Fen Morris."

"Hello, Fen Morris. I'm Miriam."

"Pleased to meet you, Miriam."

"Likewise. Welcome."

He's been asleep all day, flat out on the double divan in the master bedroom, fully dressed on top of the covers. Lauren and I have been tiptoeing around his presence like deer around a slumbering tiger. We haven't spoken much, and when we have it's been in whispers. The house is changed for having him in it. I was beginning to think of it as ours, mine and Lauren's. Now it is quite unmistakably King Cunt's. In the unlikely event that either of us were to forget that, there are sporadic bouts of heavy snoring to remind us.

My mind is a conveyor belt of different emotions, one trundling after another. Mainly I'm scared. I'm dreading what will happen when he wakes up, what he will want then, what he will demand. I'm also relieved, because I've seen him now, I know what he looks like now, and he's nowhere near as bad as I was expecting. He's physically impressive. He's even—in a beetle-browed, heavy-chinned way—handsome. I'm alarmed at myself for thinking about him in this manner, for even considering that he might be attractive, and then I'm cross with myself for trying to deny something that I honestly feel, and then I'm angry with myself because it doesn't really matter what King Cunt looks like because it won't make what I'm going to have to let him do to me any more bearable. Rape is rape, whoever's committing it, whatever the circumstances in which it's carried out.

I'm jittery with these conflicting feelings, and with the cigarettes I've been nabbing off Lauren throughout the day. Each time I ask her for another she says, "Get your own darn smokes," but then lets me have one anyway. I'm awash with nicotine in a way I haven't been for years. It's a darkly nostalgic sensation. Part of me keeps expecting a wad of page proofs to be dumped in front of me for final inspection, or someone to ask me what I'll be having to drink.

Finally, around seven p.m., King Cunt stirs. There's a lot of groaning and grunting and yawning, and then the sound of footsteps across the floorboards as he heads for the bathroom, and then the loud, echoey rattle of a man peeing. (They can never do it quietly, can they? Always right into the centre of the water, where the toilet-bowl acoustics are at their resonant best.) Then the flush, and then King Cunt comes clumping barefoot down the stairs.

Lauren's standing at attention to greet him. She clucks and fusses over his right hand, which is wrapped in a ragged strip of cloth that's brown with dried blood.

"Was it a fight?" she asks.

King Cunt glances uninterestedly at the hand. "Nah. Just a bit of ritual malarkey. I am now, officially, a blood-sworn member of the Frantik Posse." He turns to me. "Hi there. We didn't get a chance to talk earlier. You are...?"

I tell him, in a voice that doesn't sound quite like my own. I wait for that daft face that people usually pull when they hear *Moira*. I don't know why my name has that effect. It just does.

But not on him. King Cunt is one of the rare exceptions, just as Fen was. "Moira, huh? Don't tell me—Scottish mum."

"Irish."

"Dah! Had to be one or the other. Well, nice to meet you, Moira. I hope Lauren's been looking after you."

"She has. We've been getting along fine." Past King Cunt's shoulder Lauren fires me a quick, grateful smile, as though I've done her a favour. But what I said wasn't a lie. We're never going to be firm friends, she and I, but all things considered, she could have been treating me a lot worse.

"Yeah, Lauren's a treasure, isn't she? Couldn't manage without her."

Lauren positively squirms with joy.

"Now, Moira, the question that's probably uppermost in your mind is, What the fuck am I supposed to call this bloke?"

I nod. It's certainly *one* of the questions uppermost in my mind.

"Craig'll do. Most girls don't much like using the word 'cunt', do they. I can understand why. It's not one of *my* favourite words, to be honest with you. But it does the business. King Cunt—'cause I'm more of a cunt than anyone else. It's a name people remember. They hear it once, they don't forget it. But you stick with 'Craig'. Or 'King', if you'd prefer. That's what most of the lads call me. Another question you're probably asking yourself, I reckon, Moira, is: Is he going to hurt me? Because I'm guessing you've formed the impression that I'm a bit of a bastard and I don't like it if I don't get my own way. And I'm betting Lauren's told you something to that effect too. She usually does. Don't you, Lauren?"

Lauren shrugs.

"She likes to make me out to be nasty, a bit of a harsh taskmaster, bless her. And I'm not. At least, I don't think I am. I think what I am—and I'm being serious here—is moral. You don't do anything to upset me, you'll be fine. Cross me, and you won't be fine. You'll be anything *but* fine. OK?"

"OK," I say.

"Glad we've got that sorted. Now, one last thing... Actually, Lauren love." He pats his flat abdomen. "I could do with a bite of something. Would you go and get dinner started?"

Lauren sidles off to the kitchen and begins clattering utensils around more loudly than she needs to. King Cunt moves closer to me.

"Listen, Moira," he says, voice lowered, "what I don't want you to do, most of all, is be scared of me. I want everyone else to be scared of me. The lads here, the other gangs, everyone in south-east London, everyone in *London*. But not you. Because it doesn't work if you're scared of me." He steps back, and I realise he has just bared his soul, or come as close as he perhaps ever will to doing so. "I don't expect you to like me. I certainly don't expect you to love me. But if you can just see your way to not being scared of me... well, that would be great."

I don't know what to say. I mutter something like, "I'm sure that can be arranged," and after that we stand there for a while, facing each other. King Cunt looks searchingly into my eyes, and it's like he's imploring me for some kind of absolution in advance. I stare back, not softening, not allowing him even a glimpse of what he's after, fearing him too much not to despise him. I don't know why but I feel oddly guilty about doing this, about not giving him what he so desperately wants.

He waits a moment longer, then, understanding, drops his gaze. Off he goes to the kitchen to chat with Lauren while she cooks, and I'm left wondering if I haven't just made trouble for myself.

Maybe I have. But maybe not.

"How was the meal?" Miriam asked.

The scraped-clean bowl and empty sideplate told one story, the gist of which was that Fen had wolfed down his vegetable soup and chunks of bread. Fen corroborated the story by pronouncing the meal delicious.

In truth, starving-hungry though he was, the meal had been anything but. The soup had been thin and tasteless, the bread gritty. He had eaten out of necessity and to a lesser degree politeness, but he had not eaten out of pleasure.

"Good. We're not exactly flush with provisions here but we make do."

"Well, your chef's done a good job, whoever he is. Please pass on my compliments."

"Better not. It was Derek's turn today, and his head's swollen enough as it is." Miriam chuckled, her spectacles glinting softly in the light of the candle by Fen's bedside. "Now, before I leave you for the night, is there anything else you want? Anything you need?"

"Just a couple of questions answered, Miriam."

"Go on then."

"How long do you think it's going to take for my leg to get better?"

"As far as I can see, it's a straightforward fracture, very little damage to the surrounding muscles... I'd say we'll have you on your feet in a week."

"A week? Really?"

"But that's just to exercise the leg. I don't think you'll be walking any great distances on it for a month or so."

A month or so.

"OK. But is there any chance someone here could get me to London, broken leg notwithstanding?"

"London?" Miriam frowned, as though he had just said Constantinople or Timbuktu. "Well now, I don't know about that. I don't know about that at all. I take it you're hoping we have some form of transportation here—a horse and cart, maybe even a car. We don't. There are bicycles, but few of them work properly any more. Tyres gone, brakes rusted. Mostly we get around using good old-fashioned Shanks' pony. So I'm afraid, Fen, you're stuck with us for a while. Best get used to the idea."

"And that's my second question. Who's 'us', Miriam?"

"We're friendly, Fen. That's all you need to know."

After Miriam had taken away the supper tray and extinguished the candle, Fen lay in the dark and pondered. On the one hand, he was alive and being looked after by someone who seemed to know what she was doing, which was indisputably a good thing. On the other hand, his journey to London was on hiatus for at least a month, probably much more, and that was not such a good thing.

It was only then that he realised that he had not thought of Moira since... since leaping off the *Jagannatha*. All that time he had lain out in the open, she—the entire purpose of his journey—had not once even crossed his mind. He felt a prickling of guilt, which he absolved himself of by reasoning that he had been alone, in pain and in fear of his life. He had had, in short, other things on his mind. And with this comforting rationale came a renewed determination to reach Moira just as soon as he was able to. However soon that was.

He could see, with hindsight, that everything had started to go wrong the moment he accepted the offer of a lift from Wickramasinghe. Had he continued on towards London on foot, he would almost certainly have been reunited with Moira by now. He and she would be heading back to Downbourne together, Moira brimming with new-found admiration for the husband who had come such a distance, risked so much, in order to rescue her.

That was one possibility, at any rate. Another was that he would, by now, have reached the British Bulldogs' lair and be returning to Downbourne empty-handed and dismally alone, having failed to persuade Moira's captors to let him have her back. Another, yet worse possibility was that he, too, would have been taken prisoner by the Bulldogs, and would be undergoing God-knows-what kinds of abuse and mistreatment. He might even be dead.

Could it be that maybe, just maybe, he had never had any intention of reaching London at all? Could it be that he had accepted a lift from Wickramasinghe, and then thrown himself from the *Jagannatha* while it was travelling at high speed, simply in order to furnish himself with an excuse for not continuing with his rescue attempt? In other words, could he have deliberately (albeit subconsciously) sabotaged his own mission?

If so, a broken leg was a pretty drastic way of going about it.

Then again, anything less drastic than a broken leg would have been insufficient to waylay him. At least he could now say to himself, "Well, I tried, didn't I? I gave it my best shot," and, with a clear conscience, abandon the whole enterprise.

Yes. Except that he could not.

Broken leg or no, the fact remained that he had set out to rescue Moira, and he was damned well going to. Even if it took him, in the end, several weeks. Even if, by the time he got to her, she had given up all hope of ever seeing him.

He pictured Moira, in some imprecisely-realised urban setting, scanning the horizon for a sign of him. Penelope on an Ithacan promontory, praying for a glimpse of Odysseus' sails.

She isn't waiting for you at all. It hasn't even occurred to her that you might be coming.

But that was untrue.

Fen was convinced it was untrue.

Almost completely convinced.

HERE WE LIE, like husband and wife. His weight doesn't just tilt the mattress, it seems to tilt the entire house, as though he is a collapsed star, concentrated gravity. His left arm rests across my midriff. Rests? It bears down on my stomach muscles, heavy as a slab of marble. It makes breathing difficult, but I don't want to move it off me. If I move it, he might wake up, and if he wakes up...

His deep, slow, ponderous breathing fills the darkness. It's like lying next to an ocean cave, the waves surging in, the waves surging out. I am not going to sleep tonight. I may never sleep again.

Nothing has happened. This gives amazement and anguish in equal measure. Nothing has happened, he just turned the light out, put his arm across me and went to sleep, and I'm relieved, God yes, but I wanted it over with too, so that I wouldn't have to keep wondering what it's going to be like, how it's going to make me feel about myself. In the past, I've had sex when I didn't want to—when I wasn't in the mood for it, or just to stop a man pestering me for it. There was even that one occasion that would probably qualify as rape, in that I was too drunk to give my consent, or at least to refuse coherently. (I paid the bastard back the next morning, when I phoned his wife using the speed-dial on his mobile and told her where he was.) But I've never had sex when a man has forced me to against my will, using his superior strength or the threat of violence to subdue me, taking what will not be willingly given. I've resigned myself to enduring it with King Cunt, for the sake of the other women, for Zoë's sake most of all—but I have not had to endure it yet. Having spent all day readying myself for it, having followed King Cunt up to the master bedroom with a belly full of dread, here I am with the awful event still unrealised. He lies beside me, a giant in football shirt and boxer shorts, as dead to the world as a sleeping infant. The mattress inclines me to him, his arm denotes me as his property, but he has not yet used me for the purpose for which I am in his bed.

Perhaps he is still exhausted from his three days of exertion over in Camberwell. Perhaps the women there slaked his urges for the time being. I don't know. I don't understand this man at all, this King Cunt, this Craig. He is quite unlike any other man I have ever known. He has fists that could crush bricks and yet there's an articulacy to him, and a vulnerability, that I would never have suspected. I think of him earlier, begging me not to fear him. Does he want that in order to make things easier for me, or easier for him?

Awake in the dark, I can only wonder.

OVERNIGHT, THREE BOOKS had manifested on Fen's bedside cabinet. It was as if elves had placed them there while he slept. All three were paperback novels, two of them of average thickness, the third very thick indeed. Their spines were well creased and their page edges were coffee brown with age.

The very thick one was a science fiction novel called *Falling Across Forever* by Jeremiah S. Coburn. Its cover showed a spaceship in orbit around a planet. One section of the spaceship was exploding, and the planet's atmosphere was a seething swirl of reds and purples. The image promised Excitement! Adventure! Intergalactic Derring-Do! According to the publisher's blurb, *Falling Across Forever* was the second volume in "the epic, universe-spanning *Farways* saga".

The other two books were in the larger-dimensioned paperback format that traditionally denoted more literary fare—subtler cover design, better quality paper and printing—higher production values for a higher-brow content. Both were by someone called Jeremy Salter, who, if a reviewer for the *Daily Telegraph* was to be believed, was "one of the foremost living exponents of the comedy of manners". The name rang a faint bell. Fen thought he might have come across it in a bookshop once; might have briefly considered a book by that author before discarding it and picking up one by somebody else.

Idly curious, he started thumbing through the slimmer of the two Salter books, *A Charmed Life*. The novel was set at Oxford University in the early 1970s and (Fen quickly gleaned) concerned the lives and loves of a group of undergraduates at the fictitious Haldane College. A precocious lot, not to say precious, they spent most of their time drinking coffee and wine and discussing the sociopolitics of the day and, with greater enthusiasm, who among their circle of friends was bedding whom. The main protagonist was Charles Buck, devilishly handsome and something of a cad, as devilishly handsome men often are, because they can afford to be. Women were drawn to him "like paperclips to a magnet", as one of his friends put it, and were content to take what they could get from him, whether it was a one-night stand or even just a fond, condescending smile.

His romantic misdemeanours—and they were many—were invariably forgiven, as were his academic misdemeanours, for he repeatedly turned up to tutorials with no essay prepared and his dons never reprimanded him for it. He seemed to exist (at least up until page 27, which was as far as Fen read before Miriam arrived with his breakfast) within a cloud of irresponsibility, sowing trouble and never reaping the consequences. *A Charmed Life* indeed.

"Ah, started already," Miriam said as she set the breakfast tray on Fen's lap. On the tray were a mug of herb tea and a bowl of porridge. The tea smelled faintly of horse stables, the porridge looked a gruelling proposition. "Enjoying it?"

Fen eyed the book, front cover and back, keeping his place with his thumb. "It's all right. Not really my sort of thing, to be honest."

"Oh." Miriam was inordinately dismayed by this response, as if Fen had told her the novel was absolute rubbish and so was she. It was clear she held the work of Jeremy Salter in very high regard.

"I mean, it isn't *bad*. Just not... Well, I think Bradbury and Lodge have done the whole university thing better. Larkin, too, in *Jill*." As he did his best to backtrack, Fen found that everything he said seemed to condemn *A Charmed Life* further. "It's quite funny, I suppose. Funny in a droll way. You know, a quiet sense of humour to it. Not belly-laugh funny. Isn't it?"

Apparently the book was not supposed to be funny at all. "It *was* his first published novel," Miriam said, by which Fen took her to mean that *A Charmed Life*, though still an excellent piece of work, wasn't her favourite author's finest hour.

"Well, there you go. His later stuff's probably much better."

"It's also his most autobiographical."

"Ah."

"Maybe," said Miriam, "you'd get on better with *Falling Across Forever*. For sci-fi, it's quality stuff. And much less challenging than Salter's mainstream fiction."

Fen got the point. *A Charmed Life* was too difficult for him. He had misunderstood the novel, failed to wrap his head around its complexities. Perhaps a piece of SF fluff was more his level.

He didn't think it wise, bearing in mind his and Miriam's respective positions as care-receiver and care-giver, to try to correct her misevaluation of his intellectual capabilities. Instead he said, "Same author, then? Jeremy Salter *is* Jeremiah S. Coburn."

"Coburn was his mother's maiden name. He used the pseudonym so that fans of his mainstream work wouldn't pick up the *Farways* books expecting more of the same."

"Or perhaps because he didn't want his sci-fi readers picking up his literary stuff," Fen said, with a quick smile.

Lost on Miriam. "Although, despite the sci-fi trappings, the *Farways* books are unmistakably his work. Well-judged dialogue, fine prose, an unparalleled grasp of character... and, of course, the philosophy."

"The philosophy?"

Miriam gestured at the tray. "Eat up before it gets cold."

Perusal of the first few chapters of *Falling Across Forever* revealed no "philosophy" that Fen could discern. Rather, it revealed a mediocre (at best) literary talent, all at sea within a genre that was not his natural environment. The novel made Fen think of a space explorer who had stepped out onto the surface of an unfamiliar planet, opened his helmet visor, and was staggering around, suffocating in an unbreathable atmosphere. The characters spoke in a hideously dated and clunky "future" argot; the aliens were humanoid and seemed more like people from another country than beings from another solar system; there were spaceship battles that, but for a few differences in technical terminology, could have come straight from C.S. Forester; every female was consigned to a subsidiary role and judged according to her bra size (big chest good, flat chest bad); and even Fen, whose scientific knowledge was confined to what he had learned at school, with the addition of what had boned up on in order to teach to his class at Downbourne, could tell that Jeremiah S. Coburn's grasp of certain principles of biology and physics was not as sure as it might have been.

As undemanding fodder for adolescents and adults still arrested at the adolescent stage, *Falling Across Forever* just about passed muster. By any other standards, it was nonsense. And if, as Miriam seemed to imply, the book expounded some particular system of beliefs, a life-doctrine, then it was so deeply embedded within the text as to be imperceptible.

By page 30, Fen was contemplating giving up on the novel. At page 51, he did so. Nothing compelled him to read further. He wasn't in the least interested in finding out whether grim-jawed hero Paul Cordwainer was going to be able to rescue his lover, the beauteous and vastly buxom Maya, from the clutches of the evil aliens, the Ch'ee-Lan, who had kidnapped Maya in revenge for Cordwainer's destruction of their home planet, which had apparently been the climax of the previous *Farways* novel. There was no doubt that Cordwainer would succeed, and Fen wasn't even curious to know how the rescue was going to be pulled off. He had a rule regarding art and entertainment: if it doesn't show you something new, it isn't worth your time. And *Falling Across Forever* contained nothing that was not hand-me-down, predictable and stale. A novel without novelty.

When Miriam next visited, she brought with her a bucket of warm water, some soap and a cloth, and invited Fen to wash himself. He obliged, using the water as sparingly as possible so that he would not have to lie in damp bedclothes afterwards. When she returned for the bucket, he asked her if by any chance she had something else he could read.

"You haven't finished already?" The incredulity in Miriam's voice contained more than a dash of scepticism.

Fen thought his best tactic was to be truthful. Truthful, and at the same time not unconditionally candid. "I've never really been into spaceship stuff. However well it's done, it's just never grabbed me."

"I told you to look beyond the sci-fi aspects of the book, didn't I? To delve deeper."

"I tried, honestly I did. But, well, the spaceship stuff got in the way." He fixed her with an appealing gaze, hoping to convince her that the fault lay with him and not the book's progenitor.

"And you haven't even considered *Noontide*?" Miriam was referring to the last of the triptych of novels, the other Jeremy Salter offering.

Fen gave a hapless shrug. "Just not my cup of tea, your Mr Salter. My loss, I'm sure. Isn't there *anything* else to read here? I mean, this is a school. Surely there's a library."

"A library?"

"Yes. You know, big room, full of books."

"Thank you, Fen, yes, I do know what a library is."

"Well?"

"Well what?"

"Is there one?"

"Burned down," said Miriam. "To the ground. Terrible thing. One of the pupils was responsible, apparently. The very last term, before the school closed down. Some kind of protest, I think."

"Really?"

"Yes. Really."

Fen knew she was lying. What he couldn't work out was why. He didn't, however, have the opportunity to pursue the matter. Before anything further could be said, Miriam snatched up the Salter books and flounced out of the room. Fen did not see her again until evening.

I FOUND OUT a little more about King Cunt today. (Craig. I must try to think of him as Craig.) First, like any leader he likes his sycophants. Second, I think that secretly he hates gold-toothed Neville.

There was a meeting at the house this afternoon. Neville attended, as did Mushroom, the ugly little gnome who was King Cunt's—was *Craig's* driver yesterday. A couple of others came along whose names I didn't catch. Mushroom's called Mushroom not because he looks like he ought to live under one but, or so I've been reliably informed by Lauren, because of the shape and size of his penis. Which means I now have a particularly repellent mental image that I really wish I could get out of my head: a small, bulbous-headed penis attached to a small, bulbous-headed man.

The aim of the meeting was to discuss Craig's trip to Camberwell, and they held it round the table in the living room, while Lauren and I, in the kitchen, eavesdropped. Craig was soon describing how he finally won the trust of the Frantiks' main man, Eazy-K, by knocking cold one of Eazy-K's lieutenants in a fight that lasted all of three seconds.

"Big beast he was and all. Six foot eight if he was an inch."

"Closer on seven foot," Mushroom offered.

"Nah, he was never seven foot."

"Looked that way to me."

"Everyone looks seven foot to *you*, Mushroom," said Neville, and they all laughed, even Mushroom.

"Anyway, bastard came at me like a windmill," Craig went on. "You know, arms all like that. Wurrrr! So I just ducked inside his reach, pow, one shot under the chin, and down he went. Like a chopped tree."

"It was poetry," said Mushroom. "Sheer fucking poetry. Eazy-K almost popped a gasket. His face was like, 'I do *not* believe this!'"

"But full credit to him, full credit to him," Craig said, "he came up straight afterwards and put his arm around me and called me his brother and said big respect. He meant it, too."

"And that was that," said Mushroom. "Now the British Bulldogs and the Frantik Posse are the best of friends."

"Of course, that doesn't mean they won't try and fuck us over at a later date," Neville observed.

One of the other Bulldogs—Dean, I think his name is—asked him what he meant by that.

"Think about it for a moment. The Frantiks move in on Peckham, fine. They get control, send the Riot Squad packing, everything's cosy and rosy and nice. We're their mates, they're not going to bother us. But now we've got them bang next door, and what if they think to themselves, well, those Squadders weren't much cop, how about those Bulldogs then? Why don't we try and move in on their patch too?"

"Because now we've got a non-aggression pact with them," Mushroom said, as if explaining the obvious. "Because they've met the King and he impressed the fuck out of them and they're not going to take us on because they've got to be thinking, shit, if they're all like *that* where he came from..."

"I understand that. I'm just saying we can't trust them to keep to their side of the deal."

"But they will if they think we're harder than them, which they do, and which we are. You don't make a non-aggression pact with someone you think you can beat, do you?"

"Maybe they're bluffing. Maybe they want us to drop our guard."

"You weren't there, Neville. Believe me, by the end of it the King had them eating out of his hand."

"I might not have been there, Mushroom, but I do know that you can't trust anybody and especially you can't trust a bunch like the Frantiks."

"What, because they're black, Nev?" said Craig.

There was a pause before Neville replied, and I could imagine him darting a look of annoyance at Craig. Equally, I could imagine him smirking. "Because they're ambitious bastards. Because they've got designs on Peckham so what's to stop them having designs on another borough as well? And yes, because they're black. That's a factor."

"All right." Craig's tone was lofty, cool. "The point is made. The thing is, Mushroom's right. I impressed them. Intimidated them, even."

"Did a blinding job of it."

"Yes. Thank you, Mushroom. Did a blinding job of it. And they swore me in as their blood brother, too. So we have to assume that they're not going to risk moving in on our turf. I suppose to some extent we ought to pay attention to what Nev's saying. If the Frantiks get Peckham—and

I say 'if' because it's not a foregone conclusion—then we'll need to stay vigilant. If, as a thank-you, they want to give us some of the territory they gain, then great. We'll take it. And if they don't, well, nothing lost. But if we start hearing reports that they're muscling in on Lewisham, interfering with our supply routes, trying to shake down people who expect us to look after them because that's what they're paying us tribute for... If we get to hear about any of *that* shit, we come down on them like a ton of bricks."

"Thanks, Craig," said Neville, satisfied.

"Mushroom *is* right, though. You weren't there. I think we've got the Frantiks where we want them."

"We'll see, won't we?"

"Yes, Nev. We'll see."

"Only Neville would dare talk to him like that," Lauren whispered to me. "Only Neville."

Well, that's what longstanding friends are for, isn't it? To say the sort of things to you that others won't or daren't.

But I get the impression that Neville's less a friend to Craig these days and more a thorn in his side. If what Lauren said is true and he's after the King's crown, I can't see him challenging Craig for it head-on. He wouldn't win. But by constantly undermining Craig's authority, chipping away at his pedestal...

Anyway, what do I care?

I care enough, evidently, to broach the subject with Craig now, as once again, just like last night, he switches out the bedroom light and climbs into bed beside me. Maybe it's just that I want to talk in order to postpone the inevitable. Tonight, I'm sure, he's going to want to claim what he feels is rightfully his. Zoë, I'm thinking. Susannah. Paula. All of you...

"Lauren says you and Neville have been friends a long time."

"Since primary school. Why?"

"You must like him."

"He's stuck by me through a lot of shit."

"And he still sticks by you now."

"Oh yeah." He sounds definite, and perhaps surprises himself with this, because the next moment he says, "Pretty much. We don't always see eye-to-eye. Why do you want to know about Nev anyway?"

"No reason. Just making conversation."

"Lauren's told you to steer clear of him, hasn't she? I swear, that girl. She really has it in for poor Nev. She's got it into her head that he's after my job."

"Which he isn't." I make it sound like I'm not questioning him.

Question or not, he avoids a direct answer. "It's just Lauren being overprotective of me. Nev has a go at me now and then, yes, but that's Nev for you. If he really got uppity, I'd slap him down. If I thought he was, you know, out of line. But I've never had to yet. No, tell a lie. I did once."

Lauren's advice: *if he wants to fuck you, you let him fuck you. If he just wants to talk, you talk*. "What happened?"

"It was a while back. Me and Nev, we weren't much more than kids. Nineteen, twenty. Proper pair of tearaways we were. Always mixed up in one iffy scheme or another. Selling stuff that we didn't ask who we bought it from where it came from. Doing a bit of unofficial bailiff work, recovering debts from people who owed money to people you shouldn't owe money to. That type of thing. Nothing against the law, technically, but you know—treading a fine line. For a while we organised raves. That was about the most legitimate we ever got. Remember raves? Hundreds of kids in a barn or warehouse somewhere, off their tits on chemicals and dancing and hugging each other?"

"I remember. I never went to one myself."

"Didn't think it'd have been your thing. Not someone like you. Wasn't my thing either, to be honest, but Christ, the money you could make. Silly money! There was three of us doing it. Nev, me, and this girl I was seeing at the time, Kirsty. Kirsty was the brains of the outfit. She did all the promoting, put out the flyers, signed up the DJs, greased the right palms to get licences and permits and what-have-you. Me and Nev were mainly there in case anyone she was dealing with got the wrong idea and thought they could rip her off. That's when we'd step in and, as they say, persuade whoever it was to see the error of their ways. It was a good system. Worked a treat. Kirsty was a looker as well as smart. She was the presentable face of the business. Me and Nev were the ugly fuckers who backed up her smile with force. We did well for a year or so, and then..."

A slow silence. I think he's not going to continue, and then he does.

"It was all a bit silly, really. Nev just kind of overstepped the mark one night. One of our raves. Sun was coming up, things were winding down. I'd gone off to talk to some local police who said they were there to arrest a few dealers but were willing to reconsider in return for a small incentive, nudge nudge. Bent coppers. There's nothing worse. Leave you feeling slimy all over, like you need a shower. I came back from sorting that out, anyway, and there was Kirsty looking all huffy and annoyed, and I asked her what was the matter and she said, 'Nothing,' and I hate it when there's obviously something the matter and people pretend there isn't, so I got a bit insistent with her, probably a bit angry actually, and I told her to tell me what was up, and she wouldn't, but eventually I pissed her off enough so that she did tell me. And I can remember her exact words: 'You don't want to hear this, Craig, but because you're being such a prize prat... Neville came on to me. I told him to shove off but he wouldn't listen, and now he's out by his car nursing a sore pair of nuts.' Now, any other occasion I might've thought this was funny, but I'd just had to handle those cops and I'd worked up a bit of a head of steam because Kirsty had been so evasive, and things had generally been pretty hectic and I hadn't slept for a couple of days, and..."

"You went and found Neville and beat him up."

"Didn't beat him up. Just decked him. One punch to the gob. Took his tooth out. I was *that* fucking pissed off with him. But as soon as I'd landed the punch, all my anger went. Stupid twat. I just felt sorry for him then, lying on the ground, holding his mouth, blood trickling through his fingers. I mean, he's never ever had much success with women, and to try it on with his best mate's girlfriend—I mean, how daft is that?"

"Seems like he deserved what he got. Both from you and Kirsty."

"Yeah, but... He was my mate. It cost me to hit him. Literally, because I paid to have that gold tooth put in. But it cost me in other ways too, because not only did I lose face with him, I lost face with Kirsty too. And then... just lost her. Not straight away, but over the next month she just sort of grew more and more... detached from me. She wasn't one of those girls who get a kick out of men fighting over her. She wasn't that stupid. But she thought I'd disrespected her. She'd given Nev a kick in the nads, that should have been enough, and then off I went and laid him flat and she thought that was unnecessary. Macho bollocks. So finally she left me, walked out on me, and our little business empire broke up, and it was just me and Nev again, the two of us, doing we'd been doing before, ducking and diving, and that was that."

"So he forgave you."

"For decking him? Oh yeah. He knew he'd done wrong." Craig yawns. "But it was all a long time ago. Water under the bridge. I'm going to try and get some kip now, Moira. Goodnight."

The arm extends across me, clamping down. Within a couple of minutes he's away and snoring.

Funny little story. A classic of its kind. Two close friends and the girl who comes between them. *Jules et Jim* in the world of cash-only business deals.

But I wonder if Neville didn't know exactly what he was doing when he came on to Kirsty. I wonder if he didn't know precisely what the outcome of his actions would be.

And I'm willing to wager good money that Kirsty had red hair.

"'...TURNED JUST IN time to see Charles Buck pedal off with a valedictory trill on his handlebar bell, disappearing into the mists that seethed and swirled along the Banbury Road.'"

Roy Potts looked up from the book.

"There we go. End of chapter seven. More, Fen? Or have you had enough?"

Fen refrained from saying what he wanted to say—that if he had to listen to another word of *A Charmed Life* he would probably scream. Potts possessed an air of hard-won and undependable enthusiasm, the kind that was like a confection of spun sugar, liable to crumble to pieces unless handled with the utmost delicacy. To hurt the feelings of this slouchy, insecure little man, tempting through it was, would have been ungrateful. No, worse than that. Would have been uncharitable.

"As a matter of fact, I am quite tired," Fen said, and stifled a bogus yawn.

Potts closed *A Charmed Life*, having marked his place by dog-earing the page corner. "We'll carry on later."

He didn't leave, however. He continued to sit where he was, on the edge of the bed adjacent to Fen's, hunch-shouldered and hopeful, as if anticipating some reward.

"Thank you for reading to me," Fen said, but this, it seemed, was not what Potts was after.

"Do you see it yet?" he asked.

"See what?"

"What the Master is getting at."

"The Master?"

Potts held up the paperback and underlined Salter's name on the cover with his index finger.

Somewhere deep inside Fen, there was a sudden heavy click of comprehension. He felt both relieved and irritated, the way you do when you realise you and another person have been talking at cross purposes for a while. All at once the fundamental misconception becomes obvious, and you wonder, exasperated, why neither of you spotted it sooner.

When Potts had knocked on the door a couple of hours earlier, introducing himself and saying he had come to help keep Fen amused, it had seemed reasonable to assume that the book he brought along for this purpose had been chosen by Miriam—a fresh attempt by her to kindle in Fen a love for the work of Jeremy Salter. All right, Fen had thought, let's give *A Charmed Life* another crack. On the whole, when someone proselytised as vehemently about an author as Miriam was doing, that author had to have *something* to recommend them.

Now he understood that Roy Potts was a Salter fan as well. More than that. "The Master". A passionate admirer.

And...

Oh God. Surely not. Surely it wasn't possible.

"Roy?"

"Yes, Fen?"

"'The Master'."

"Yes, Fen?"

"I don't know quite how to put this, but..."

"Yes, Fen?"

"Well, there's a group of you here, right? At Netherholm College?"

"That's correct."

"How many in all?"

"About fifty."

"Fifty. And all fifty of you live here, have established a community here, because..."

"Yes, Fen?"

Fen gestured at *A Charmed Life*. "Because of him. Am I right?"

"You are, Fen."

"Because you really like what he writes."

"Yes, Fen."

"It... it speaks to you in some way."

"Very much so." Potts's eyes gleamed. He leaned forward on the bed, narrowing the gap between him and Fen. He was clasping the novel between his palms as ardently as a priest with his psalter. "The Master—Jeremy—isn't simply a great writer, you see. He's a great teacher. A great thinker. This is something we all believe." He paused. "And it's something we'd like you to believe too, Fen."

There were a dozen things Fen could think of to say by way of a reply, but none of them seemed appropriate, so all he said was, "Ah," following this up with an equally noncommittal "Oh".

"Let me put it this way," Potts said. "We've no interest in how you came to be where we found you, in the state that we found you in. That's not how we operate. Anything you did before we met you is none of our business. But we do think that there's a reason we found you, Fen. A reason you wound up injured in a place where we would hear you. Or rather, hear those dogs that had cornered you howling."

"The reason being?" Fen said, although he wasn't sure he wanted to hear the answer to the question.

"In the past, we've had a number of strangers come our way. Not many, but in each case, once the person has stayed with us for a few days, been looked after by us, seen how welcoming we are, he or she realises that they were directed towards us. Were brought here. Something impelled them—some need, some absence in their life—to make their way to this neck of the woods. We call this type of person someone who's lost the plot."

"Charming."

"It's not an insult. No. All it means is they've lost sight of the overall direction of their life. Somehow or other, they can't see where they're headed any more, what everything they do is leading to."

"Quite a common phenomenon, I'd have thought. Especially in England these days."

"I agree."

"No one's making plans."

"And why should they?"

"It's all hand-to-mouth and moment-to-moment."

"Indeed."

"There's a lot of drift and uncertainty."

"Quite, quite."

"But you've got the solution to that."

"We like to think so."

"A way of... reorganising your life. Rediscovering your purpose."

"A rather simplistic way of putting it, but yes."

"And what if I said I'm not interested, Roy? In fact, what if I said I already had a purpose? Discovered one quite recently, as it happens?"

"I'd believe you. But then I'd have to ask you, why are you lying there in that bed?"

"Because I have a broken leg."

"No, Fen."

"But I do."

"But that's not why you're there. You need to dig below the surface of things. You need to look for the subtext."

"The subtext. This sounds like literary criticism."

Potts nodded encouragingly.

"Literary... as in Jeremy Salter."

Again Potts nodded, and Fen was reminded of the way he himself would elucidate an answer from one of his pupils, coaxing the child towards the correct solution with pertinent questions, and in the process fostering, he hoped, the capacity for deductive reasoning.

"Salter's books. His thinking. His 'philosophy'. He's taught you to treat life as if... as if it's a novel?"

Potts looked pleased, not just with Fen but with himself.

"A novel," Fen continued, "and each of us is the main protagonist. We're walking works of fiction. The plot runs from birth to death."

"There. You see? It's been there all along, inside you, like a buried seed. The knowledge. A few pages of the Master's prose to water the soil, and bingo, suddenly up it comes."

"All I'm doing is extrapolating from what you've said."

"No, you *think* that's all you're doing."

"No, I *know* that's all I'm doing."

"Oh, Fen," Potts said, shaking his head, "we still have some way to go with you, I can tell. But not to worry. We're nothing if not patient." He stood up. "I've given you something to think about, at any rate. I'll leave you to get some sleep now. You did say you were tired."

"Oh, I am." Fen thought about feigning another yawn; decided it would be over-egging the pudding; opted instead for a slow, sleepy blink.

"You're fortunate to have fetched up where you have, you know." Potts waved *A Charmed Life* at Fen. "You'd do well to remember that."

"I will," Fen replied.

He would also, he decided, do well to remember the way in which Potts had said, "We're nothing if not patient."

He didn't want to think of terms like prisoner. Captive. Helpless victim. He didn't like to compare the bare white sanatorium room to a cell, the makeshift traction apparatus to shackles. He didn't relish the scary little notions that kept popping into his head—that he was trapped, that his hosts weren't entirely *compos mentis*, that what had first seemed like salvation was beginning to look more like the opposite.

He tried, instead, to adopt a positive outlook. Tried to feel that this situation was something he could endure, something he could survive so long as he kept a sense of humour and a sense of perspective. Potts, Miriam, the rest of the people at Netherholm College, these disciples of author Jeremy Salter, these literary acolytes, these Salterites—they were just human beings. Being members of some odd little sect, some weird hybrid of fan club and secular cult, didn't necessarily make them mad. Or bad. Or, for that matter, dangerous to know. It just made them different, and perhaps a little more difficult to deal with than ordinary people. But he could deal with them, as long as he kept his wits about him.

The trick would be to remain friendly and, if he could, open-minded. He knew Potts would be back to evangelise further about the wonderful credo he and his friends lived by. All he had to do was smile and nod and keep saying how very fascinating it all was while at the same time make clear that what was being advocated, this fiction-based method of making sense of life, was not for him. Potts would get the message soon enough.

Fen was wrong, however. He was right about the evangelising, but he had underestimated the Salterites' persistence.

It became a kind of siege.

The first few exploratory forays had already been made, testing the strength of Fen's fortifications—Miriam with the paperbacks, Potts giving a reading. Now, the assault began in earnest. Potts returned the following morning to give another reading, picking up from where they had left off. Two more hours of *A Charmed Life*, and then a further two later that same day. With the book nearly finished, Fen professed—lying—that he had found it enjoyable, much more so than he might have expected.

"Enjoyable," said Potts, "and illuminating?"

"Perhaps."

The next day Potts polished off the last couple of chapters, and not long after he left, someone else turned up to begin another Salter novel. This new person was stiff, elderly Leonard, who suffered from an infrequent but severe tic that caused the whole of the left side of his face to crease in spasm, eye winking, mouth wrenching up at the corner. Naturally, this condition interfered with his reading. Without warning, Leonard would break off in the middle of a sentence, sometimes between syllables of a word, and twitch silently for anything up to a minute before resuming his recitation, his mind entering stasis while his facial muscles danced their little jig. The marvellous thing was that he never gave any indication of having halted. He carried on after each hiatus just as if it had never happened, not losing the cadence of the prose. It was like somebody randomly pressing the pause button while a spoken-word CD played.

Fen took a shine to Leonard but not to the book he was reading, *The House of Janus*, which was intended as a satire on the publishing industry but came across more as the peevish rantings of someone who had not attained the level of success and renown that he felt he merited. It was a tale of two authors, boyhood friends who tirelessly encouraged each other in their fledgling literary efforts until one day one of them sold a novel which, when published, became a best-selling sensation. Then the cracks appeared in the friendship, as the successful author failed to honour the pact the two of them had made when young, that if either hit the big time he would do all he could to help the other's career. Festering in a mire of bitterness and rejection slips, the unsuccessful author—by far the more sympathetically drawn of the two characters, not to mention (oh, irony!) the better writer—began to plot his estranged chum's downfall. This involved a bogus publishing imprint and a pair of jailed but still powerful East End mob boss brothers. The resulting shenanigans stretched credulity to breaking point. Towards the end of the novel Fen was praying that the mob bosses, the Kray twins in all but name, would go ahead and give the order to have both of the authors killed, thus putting *everybody* out of their misery.

He and Leonard discussed the book afterwards. Leonard was keen for Fen to see that *The House of Janus* was all about duality, the good and bad that existed in everyone, while Fen attempted to persuade Leonard that it was nothing more than a rather silly revenge comedy (although phrasing his argument somewhat more daintily than this). Leonard, of course, was not to be convinced.

Then came Pamela.

Pamela read *I Am Watching*, a dark, grimy little novel about a voyeur, as though it were an adventure story for children. It didn't help that she lacked breath control, so that she would accelerate towards the end of each paragraph and then gasp for air like a swimmer surfacing. Nor did it help that she had a naturally high-pitched and girlish voice, which rendered the seamier portions of the novel incongruously naïve-sounding. The disparity between her vocal style and the book's subject matter made the reading a deeply disconcerting experience. There were times when Fen felt as if he had side-slipped into a parallel universe, one where Enid Blyton's preferred topics were not faraway trees and gangs of intrepid junior detectives but lingerie, binoculars, and relentless masturbation.

Though she sounded unsophisticated, Pamela was anything but. She offered up a spirited defence of *I Am Watching* as an honest and uninhibited exploration of the sweatier crevices of male sexuality, while at the same time conceding that Fen's description of the novel as pornography might be justified.

"Not that there's necessarily anything wrong with pornography," Fen said. "Do you think the Master read a lot of it as part of research for the book? Or do you think all the dirty bits just came naturally to him?"

"I don't know, Fen. What do *you* think?"

"I can't say. I really haven't read enough porn to comment."

Then Leonard returned to deliver a pause-strewn rendition of the contents of Salter's one and only collection of short stories, *Inhuman Nature*. All of these were twist-in-the-tail squibs in the manner of Saki and Roald Dahl, and Fen's sole source of amusement while having them read to him lay in seeing how early on he could guess the upcoming "surprise" ending. More often than not, he had it within the first minute: the child was not telling lies, there really *was* a tiger in the back garden; the narrator of the story was neglecting to reveal one crucial item of information, namely that he was dead; the murderer managed to convince the jury he had not committed the crime when—ta-daa!—actually he had; and so on. The only yarn in the entire collection that displayed a modicum of ingenuity was one in which a cuckolded husband, having heard his wife's pet parrot squawk the name of her lover, went after the wrong man, persecuting and eventually killing innocent Phil Liphook instead of guilty Philip Hook.

Leonard insisted that there was a lesson to be drawn from *Inhuman*

Nature, something along the lines of you could never foresee the pitfalls that life might put in your path. Fen, though Jeremy Salter's pitfalls were anything but unforeseeable, didn't demur. He simply said that some shocks were greater than others.

Miriam manned the siege engines next, treating Fen to *Noontide*, which she deemed Salter's very best work. Her reading style was idiosyncratic, to say the least—a hectoring combination of pace and bombast that left Fen deafened and reeling. *Noontide* was a study of a young man's sexual awakening, the kind of coming-of-age tale that traditionally strives to evoke such epithets as "sensitive" and "moving". Whatever niceties and subtleties Salter might have woven into the prose, however, were bulldozed flat by Miriam. For her, it seemed, a nuance was a crease to be ironed out; a shade of meaning a weed that should be trampled. At times she was almost declaiming the novel, like an orator on a podium.

And so, with work of fiction after work of fiction, the pressure was applied, but Fen held out, refusing either to succumb or to retaliate. Like London during the Blitz, he maintained an attitude of cheery resilience in the face of constant bombardment. What else could he do? The Salterites wanted to open his eyes to the manifold and multifarious brilliance of their favourite author, but even if Salter had been indisputably a genius, Fen would have refused, on principle, to acknowledge it. There was a streak of bolshiness in him that responded badly to browbeating. At the same time, he wasn't about to risk offending his hosts—captors, assailants, whatever they were—by telling them to bugger off and leave him alone. Much though he would have liked to, his sense of self-preservation counselled against it. He remembered only too well what had happened when he had confronted Wickramasinghe and invoked the railwayman's wrath. If he had learned anything from that episode it was that you should never aggravate someone who has power over your continued health and wellbeing, especially if you suspect that person to be slightly unhinged.

Day by day, as the siege wore on, Fen felt his leg getting better. The pain was abating. On a number of occasions he realised that he wasn't noticing it at all. There was a sensation of healing, nothing he could precisely define, not a tingle or an itch or a glow, just the distinct impression that events were going on inside his thigh, the body's wondrous self-repairing mechanisms hard at work. Tiny fissures being bridged, damaged bone and tissue being microscopically patched up. A fizzing cellular industriousness. And with each day that passed and each incremental improvement in his leg, he was pleased to think he was getting closer to resuming his quest for Moira. He wished he could somehow transmit his thoughts to her. Psychically tell her to hang on, not give up hope, he was coming for her.

He knew the Salterites meant well. That was the most galling, the most frustrating thing about the whole situation. They weren't bad people. They were harrying him in the same way that the International Community was harrying England, with the best of intentions. They had something to share with him that they genuinely believed would improve his life. The novels of Jeremy Salter were not mere works of fiction but sacred texts, riddled with messages and lessons and meanings. In their pages, for those with the wit to perceive it, could be found the answer to everything. The scales presently covering Fen's eyes would fall away, the Salterites were sure, if only he were exposed to enough of the Master's prose.

How Salter had become their guru was revealed by Miriam on the evening she finished *Noontide*. As she and Fen talked the book over, he parrying her thrusts of argument with deft, sideswiping evasions, the conversation strayed into the arena of writing in general, whereupon Fen made a comment to the effect that the relationship between author and reader was a paradoxical one, at once intimate and distant.

"You don't actually know the person whose stuff you're reading," he said, "you've never met them, and yet it's like you've been given privileged access to the inside of their head."

Not at all an original opinion, but Miriam responded as though a major breakthrough had occurred, as though the Salterite battering ram had finally breached Fen's outer gates.

"Yes! Yes! Almost a kind of thought transference. You know the author better, I'd say, than if you actually met him or her in the flesh."

"Have you met Mr Salter in the flesh ever?"

"Of course."

"And what's he like?"

Miriam paused to think, her asterisk eyes contracting to full stops. "How to put it into words? It's not easy. Very relaxed, I suppose you could say. Very affable. Always ready with a smile. Modest. But behind that, an incisive intellect."

"Was this at a book signing?"

"The Master doing a book signing? Not likely. No, this was on his creative writing course."

"He held a creative writing course?"

"Every year here, during the summer holidays. It was a way for Netherholm College to make some extra money outside term-time. Two weeks of intensive study and practice of the literary craft. Cost a bit to attend, I can tell you, but it was worth every penny. I came four years running. I would have come a fifth, but the course was cancelled because... well, the obvious reason. The school had closed. All the posh families were fleeing the country. No point keeping a fee-paying school open when your fee-payers are emigrating."

"And this was something Salter did—teach creative writing—for the love of it?"

"Of course."

"And not for the income."

"That, too. The Master has never been one of those who can earn an acceptable living just from writing alone. Nothing to be ashamed of in that. Not many authors do, and those who can are the ones who produce dreadful tripe. Lowest-common-denominator stuff. The potboilers, the airport-lounge thrillers. It's one of the terrible ironies of publishing that the really good books sell poorly while the rubbish gets snapped up by the bucketful."

A debatable point, but Fen let it slide. He also refrained from commenting that Salter's Jeremiah S. Coburn SF novels had quite clearly been an attempt to tap into the lucrative "rubbish" market.

"But I do believe," Miriam went on, "that the Master taught the course simply because he wanted to impart his love of fiction to others, and because he wanted to share his vision with others." She nodded to herself. "I do believe that."

"So you studied under him. You learned at his feet."

"Initially I went along with a view to improving my writing skills. I had ambitions in that direction, as you can probably guess. But as the fortnight progressed, more and more the Master's lessons came to be about things outside writing, about the wider world and the role of fiction in it. And we liked that. There was a group of us, you see. I suppose you could call it a core. It had started forming the year before I went. I fitted in pretty quickly. We were all of us Salter aficionados already, and after the course was over we kept in touch with one another, and there were meetings. Informal at first. In pubs, people's houses. We'd get together and discuss the Master's work. And it just snowballed. Each summer we'd come back here and renew contact with the Master, and he saw how fervent we were about his books and how we were drawing life-lessons from them, and it was as though we had been searching for him and he had been searching for us. It was mutually beneficial. He realised from us what he could be, and vice versa. And that was why, as everything began to fall apart, that awful time, the riots and lawlessness, and then the bombing..."

Miriam shivered, and Fen shivered too in entirely sincere fellow-feeling. The events that had followed immediately after the Unlucky Gamble had left a scar in every Englander's psyche, a communal trauma that still ignited nightmares and haunted waking thoughts. No one talked about it much. No one had to.

"Netherholm College seemed to us a safe place," Miriam said. "Remote. Self-contained. No one else wanted these buildings. Why shouldn't *we* use them? So we just converged on here, and here we've stayed ever since, quietly getting on with things."

"And the Master?"

"What about him?"

"Do you know what's become of him?"

Miriam changed the subject as clumsily as a learner driver shifting gears. "I think tomorrow we should get you up and outdoors, Fen. Put some colour in those cheeks."

"Sounds good to me."

"Can't have you wasting away in bed, can we?"

"You don't actually know where Salter is, do you?"

She let out an impatient huff. "I know that he's fine and that he's hard at work on a new novel."

"Really? A new one?"

"Oh yes, and we're all looking forward to it immensely. It's going to be his greatest literary endeavour yet. His masterpiece."

"Well, that's something. Beavering away amid all this mess. He must reckon the country's going to be back on its feet soon, then."

Miriam's eyebrows popped up, inquisitively, above the rims of her spectacles. "What makes you say that?"

"Stands to reason. If he's writing a book, he must expect someone's going to be able to publish it for him when it's finished." Fen kept to himself his astonishment that Miriam could imagine even a leaflet being published in the present circumstances, let alone a full-blown novel.

"Fen"—suddenly Miriam was beaming—"you are so right."

"I am?"

"The Master wouldn't write a book that nobody would get a chance to read. Sometimes I've had my doubts. You wonder, don't you, if what you're waiting for, really waiting for, is ever going to come. But then... Thank you, Fen. Thank you."

"No problem," said Fen, bemused, not sure what he was being thanked for. "Glad to be of service."

It's hardly a routine, but I really don't know what else to call the shape of our days here. We've fallen into a pattern. It's not a smooth one, there's no strictly-adhered-to timetable, but still, things go in their habitual order. I wouldn't say life is dull. My nerves are at full stretch and I feel like I'm walking on tiptoe all the time. There's something a little anticlimactic about all this, however, as if I've turned up at a theatre expecting to see a Webster play and they've put on Pinter instead. Not that I'm not grateful. Who would prefer blood-and-guts over drab domesticity? It's just that I keep expecting the sudden explosion, the whirr of action, the descent into nightmare, and it hasn't happened. Is this the lull before the storm, or is this simply how things are *chez* King Cunt, one long perpetual round of unreleased tension? The undercurrent of threat always there. Just like in Pinter.

Craig wakes up around seven-thirty. More often than not I'm awake already. Lauren makes breakfast for all of us. Craig then goes out, mucks around with the lads, works out with the barbells, maybe does a little sparring. Lauren and I, like a pair of redheaded charladies, clean the house. Craig likes a clean house, he does. We get lunch ready for him and whomever he feels like inviting over, usually the charming Neville, often Mushroom too. After lunch, he carries out his official duties as man in charge of Lewisham. He receives tribute from the locals, in the form of food, petrol, clothing, other essential items. God knows how these people get hold of the stuff, what they have to do in exchange for it, but some of it has to come Craig's way, a kind of tithe. And in return, he extends them the Bulldogs' protection. It's a version of the feudal system, and whether or not it's right and just, I have to say it seems to work. All across central London these little fiefdoms maintain a delicate, interconnected balance, keeping the heart of the city tamed and under control.

Sometimes Craig's called upon to judge disputes among his "subjects". Like some latterday Solomon he listens and arbitrates, and his word is law, his decision binding. Sometimes he has to punish, although this hasn't yet occurred while I've been here. Lauren tells me there are occasions when nothing except a beating will sort a problem out. Craig is fair but, when he has to be, he is harsh too. When it comes to maintaining order, there's nothing like a short, sharp burst of violence, is there? It's an inoculation, a tiny dose of disease to stimulate immunity.

Come evening, Craig's back for his tea, and then he's out again, loose in the compound, seeing what the rest of the boys are up to. They watch movies on tape, I hear. Hollywood and Hong Kong action blockbusters. Someone's got a collection—aliens and killer robots and kung fu spectaculars and lone cops in skyscrapers battling terrorists, a classy selection, only the best. The Bulldogs have watched them over and over till they know every line of dialogue and the tapes are so worn there's more snow on-screen than image. Or they sit around and listen to music and drink beer. Or they mess about with the engines of their vans, ostensibly to keep the vehicles running, really because they just enjoy having the bonnets up and being able to tinker around and talk in motor-speak. It makes them feel skilled and arcane, like initiates into a mystery, a cadre of mechanic-Masons.

Around nine or ten, Craig comes home and we go to bed. Usually I can smell alcohol on him, but he never has so much to drink that he's drunk. I don't think he likes the lack of self-control that comes with being drunk. I think for Craig self-control is very important, the attribute he prizes the most. It wouldn't do him any good to be pissed and incapable in front of his Bulldogs, of course. He would lose face. But also, I'm not sure he wholly trusts himself. That story about punching Neville suggests his temper is fearsome when aroused and so he has to keep it buried deep where it won't easily be disturbed. Being drunk and uninhibited carries too many risks for him.

The other Bulldogs, at this hour, troop off to the recreation zones to round off their evenings with some coerced sex. Craig has that option here at his house—I wouldn't be able to fend him off if he forced himself on me—but he doesn't take it. We get into our nightclothes discreetly, keeping our nakedness from each other. The light goes out. Sometimes we talk, sometimes not. When we do, it's Craig telling me about his day, what he's been up to, the decisions he's had to make. He doesn't ever ask me about me. He doesn't ask about where I come from or what I used to do for a living or anything like that. He hasn't even asked if I'm married or not. Does he know already? I don't see how he *can*. Perhaps it doesn't matter to him. Perhaps he assumes I'm not. (I'm not wearing a ring, am I?) Or perhaps it's simply that he doesn't want to know either way.

If he did ask, I've no idea what I would tell him. *Yes, I am married*. Technically, that's true. *No, I'm not married*. Emotionally, that's true. Fen and I were in a state of separation. There was a distance between us that might as well be called a divorce.

But, for whatever reason, the question doesn't arise. All I do, when we talk in bed, is what's expected of me: listen; comment occasionally; let Craig unburden himself until he's ready to go to sleep. And then we go to sleep, and another day is over.

After more than a week of this, I have to confess I'm starting to become restless. Keeping house may be all right for Lauren—I think she actively enjoys it—but I'm nobody's skivvy. The idea of escape suggests itself again, but I remind myself I've resolved to stay and help the others, the women from Downbourne, if somehow I can. The problem is, now that it comes down to it, I really have no idea what I can do for them. I've been racking my brains and come up with nothing. According to Lauren they get fed regularly, they have bathing and clothes-washing facilities, and Craig is adamant that his men always use condoms. Anyone reported not to be doing so will, I am assured, "get the living shit kicked out of him". What I really want, of course, is these women freed and got back home safely. I know that I'm in a position of influence here. I have the ear of the Bulldogs' leader every night. I just haven't yet figured out how to take advantage of that.

An idea will come, I'm sure. All I have to do is bide my time, tread softly through the days, be alert, be aware, wait, watch, not cause any trouble, above all be patient. An idea will come.

NETHERHOLM COLLEGE WAS laid out like a university campus, with large buildings separated by quads and lawns. But there was, too, something of the monastery about the place. Windows were arched, doorways likewise, and everywhere there were cloisters through which Fen could picture well-scrubbed boys filing on wet winter days, books in hand, as pious and orderly as friars going to prayer.

A buttressed clock tower, resembling a sort of brick rocket, was the school's geographical epicentre, the hub from which all else radiated. Predictably no longer functioning, its four dials told an eternal twenty-five to six. Immediately adjacent was a dining hall, and, set at right angles to this, a chapel. From outside, both edifices looked the same, both lofty, boastful, conscious of their importance. A small spire topped by a stone crucifix identified which of them was the venue for the taking of spiritual, as opposed to physical, sustenance.

To the south lay a long driveway which sloped downhill to a distant gate. Next to the driveway there were playing fields, an expanse of greensward still set up for the rugby season. The grass had grown shin-high and several of the goalposts had lost their crossbars or else collapsed completely. Nonetheless it was possible to envisage packs of pink-legged youngsters out there chasing balls to and fro, clustering, yelping, heaving, rucking, covering themselves in mud and sometimes in glory, while classmates, house masters and parents stood scarf-wrapped and huddled on the touchlines, filling the air with vaporous cheers. *Come on, Netherholm! Get in there! Tackle him! Tackle him! Pass the ball! Pass it! Yes! Yes!! Yes!!!*

In every brick, in every architrave and flagstone, in every finial and stained-glass pane, in every single swipe of mortar that had gone into its construction, Netherholm College embodied tradition, but more than that, changelessness. Nothing had been different here for ages. Oh, doubtless there had, every now and then, been concessions to modernity. The innovations of the outside world would have to have been acknowledged, some of them even incorporated into the fabric of school life, but invariably they would have been embraced with circumspection, looked on as passing fads, trinkets that paled into insignificance beside the jewels of hierarchy and religion and rote-learning. Netherholm College was a place designed to stand the test of time, founded on immutable values, rooted in certain solid, unquestionable verities. It struck Fen as more than apt that the hands on the dials of the clock tower now stood still.

While Miriam pushed him around in a wheelchair, showing him the sights, he kept drawing comparisons with his school back at Downbourne, then chiding himself for doing so. It was no contest. Netherholm College was in an altogether different league. Macmillan-era modesty could not hope to compete with Victorian grandiosity. Establishment wealth trumped post-war state funding every time.

All the same, he could not help wondering what he might have done, as a teacher, with facilities such as these. He had never once entertained the notion of entering the independent sector. Fresh from obtaining his PGCE he had had only one goal, to educate ordinary kids and make them the best they could be. He had known that he was choosing the harder of two options. He had known that a more comfortable and lucrative existence awaited in places like Netherholm, where the pupils arrived eager to learn, having been brought up with the understanding that this was what they must do in order to be awarded the bright futures that gleamed alluringly on their horizons. So much easier it would have been for him to slip into this well-pelfed world, to coast through the short terms and long holidays, to rise gradually, effortlessly, through the common-room ranks to the top. He could have done it. But why? Why, when there were pupils from normal backgrounds, normal homes, many of them with no inculcated desire for an education, who needed him more? A job at a public school was a sinecure. A job at a comprehensive was a vocation. It was a rougher, rowdier existence, to be sure, but the sense of achievement was commensurately greater. The extra effort you had to put in made every success, every good exam result and university place, that much more gratifying.

He had no regrets about the career path he had chosen to follow... and yet these immense, impressive buildings, these huge spaces—what power they might have conferred on him. What pedagogical muscles they might have allowed him to flex. The things he could have done with the minds of the scions of the well-to-do. The difference he might have made.

Miriam halted the wheelchair. The tour of the school premises had come full circle, ending where it had begun, at the entrance to the sanatorium.

"You're very quiet," she remarked. "Leg bothering you?"

Fen glanced down. The leg stuck out in front of him, still in its sheath of canvas and plank, pointing the way forward like a tank's gun barrel. The cord that had tethered the sling to the ceiling hooks was now wrapped tightly around it, binding the whole package together like parcel string. By this simple expedient, traction apparatus had been transformed into cast.

"It feels fine. I've been thinking, that's all."

"Anything you want to tell me about?"

Fen felt a flash of irritation. Weren't his thoughts his own business? Then he remembered that this was a woman who, at least twice a day, carted away his bodily waste products in a dish. Hardly surprising that she should feel a proprietorship over him, a right of access to his inner workings.

"I was just wondering why we haven't seen anybody." Well, it *was* something that had crossed his mind. "I'd have thought, what with there being fifty-odd of you here and it being such a nice morning and everything, we'd have bumped into *someone*."

"This is writing time," Miriam replied. "Between nine and one, we stay in our rooms and set down on paper what we did yesterday and what we're thinking about and where we feel the shape of our current personal chapter arc is taking us." (Fen didn't interrupt her to ask what "personal chapter arc" meant. The term seemed pretty self-explanatory.) "I, of course, have been given special exemption from that while I look after you. As have the people who've been reading to you."

"But doesn't it get a bit, well, repetitive? Don't take this the wrong way, but I can't see that an awful lot actually happens here to write about."

"We're encouraged to elaborate in our writing. To fantasise. It's all part of the process. Fabulating the real, we call it."

"I see. And the afternoons? What do you get up to then?"

"There are chores, of course, but once those are done we gather in the dining hall to read out what we've written, and then workshop it together, suggesting changes, improvements. The point isn't so much the writing itself, you see, as the act of giving definition to our lives."

"And the ritual of it too, I imagine."

"The ritual," Miriam said, construing the word to mean what she wanted it to mean, perhaps deliberately, "is the Master's own. He himself has always done his first-drafting between nine and one every day. That's his discipline, so we observe it too."

"It's really made a difference to you, hasn't it? Being a Salterite."

"A what?"

"Sorry. Just a name I came up with."

Miriam tried it out for size: "Salterite. I like that. We've never called ourselves anything. When something occurs so spontaneously, like us, a name doesn't really seem necessary. Salterite."

"I thought of 'Jeremiads' as well, but..."

"No, Salterites is better. Much better. I'll mention it to everyone this afternoon, see what they think. Well done, Fen. Very good." She bent down and—what he was least expecting—planted a kiss on his cheek. "You certainly fit in here. And being a Salterite is really going to make a difference to you too."

It was then that Fen understood, once and for all, what he was going to have to do. That kiss. That remark about fitting in. He was going to have to get the hell out of Netherholm College just as soon as he could.

HOW, THOUGH? THAT was the question. As Miriam helped him out of the wheelchair and then provided a supportive shoulder while he hopped in ungainly fashion backwards up the sanatorium stairs, Fen felt more acutely than ever his crippledness, his dependence on others. I am Gilbert Cruikshank, he thought bitterly. Surrounded by people I regard as simpletons. Obliged to rely on them for my survival.

In the ward, he lowered himself onto his bed, then watched as Miriam unwrapped the cord from his leg and set about reconnecting it—him—to the ceiling hooks. He reckoned that, if it came to it, he would be able to unpick the cord from the sling and detach himself. He would probably able to hobble downstairs, using the banister for support. But thereafter...?

Miriam had told him she had searched the whole school but had failed to locate a pair of crutches. The wheelchair had been a lucky find, folded away at the back of the props cupboard in the school theatre. (Fen postulated that it must have been used in a production of *The Man Who Came To Dinner*.) Crutches, however, would have been preferable. With crutches, he would have been able to make a reasonable stab at a getaway. Why couldn't the Netherholm College drama society have put on *Richard III* instead?

Of course, the wheelchair itself was a potential means of escape. He pictured himself struggling into it, then propelling himself out of the sanatorium, down the driveway, out through the front gates, off into the wild blue yonder...

And then? Realistically, he was not going to get very far in a wheelchair on roads that were only just passable on foot. And what if he came to a steep hill?

But then that wasn't really the point. The point was liberating himself from the clutches of the Salterites. Whatever hazards and difficulties lay beyond the boundaries of Netherholm College, he was surely better off taking his chances out there than staying here among these people, these kindly but deluded bookworms. How long before their persistence wore him down? How long before he started swallowing all this guff about "personal chapter arcs" and "fabulating the real"? How long before they succeeded in making a brainwashed convert out of him?

Hell, the process might already have begun. How would he know if he wasn't already secretly succumbing to the Salterites' influence? Mad people kept believing they were sane, didn't they? They were never aware of going mad. And the same here. The mutation in his thought patterns could be creeping over him silently and surreptitiously. He could be sliding into convertdom without even realising it. Turning into a Salterite while remaining convinced he was perfectly all right and normal. That was how cults operated, wasn't it? An insidious drip-drip-drip, wearing the subject down without his knowledge.

One mark of his resistance was the subtle digs he kept working into his conversation, as just now, that comment he had made to Miriam about not an awful lot happening at Netherholm College. Little sniping potshots fired from behind a camouflage of disingenuousness. Verbal barbs the Salterites were too blinkered to notice, too thick-hided to feel. As long as he kept those up, he was fine. Right? It meant he was still himself, still wary, sceptical old Fen. Still the same person who had all his life avoided the octopus embrace of any one particular creed or philosophy, who had dodged dogma, ducked doctrine, steered his own course through the world, striven to remain individualistic and ideology-free. Right?

The fact was, he did not know how much longer he was going to be able to last. His determination to escape, however, was outweighed by the obstacles that stood in the way of that escape being a success. Which was definitely a problem. But it was not, he was certain, going to be a problem for ever. Sometime soon, he would have absolutely no choice but to flee. Something would provide the impetus he needed, the shove to set the ball rolling. He could not know what that something would be. He could only hope that he was in a fit state of mind to recognise it when it came along.

And then, just like that, we go from Pinter to Webster.

Everyone in our happy little household is getting ready for bed when Mushroom arrives hotfoot with the news. He hammers on the front door. Craig opens the bedroom window and sticks his head out.

"What's up?"

"Trouble at the recreation zones, King."

As Craig pulls on his shoes and tracksuit bottoms, I ask him if I can come along.

"What for?"

There's no obvious answer to that. I'm curious? I want to help?

He decides it doesn't matter. "Oh, all right then. Get your kit on. Hurry up."

I'm only partially undressed, so it doesn't take me long to get ready. On our way out, we pass Lauren, standing in the doorway to her bedroom. She perceives instantly that I'm not merely accompanying Craig to the front door, that I'm going outside with him. I ignore the look she gives me, half envy, half spite. Ignore it, and at the same time am amused by it.

Across the compound Craig and I go, following Mushroom, who bounds impatiently ahead of us, like a spaniel.

At the recreation zones, in the jaunty glow of the coloured light bulbs, I see clusters of Bulldogs, clusters of women, standing, murmuring. Their attention is focused on the rightmost of the three houses, and specifically on a small group of people in that house's fenced-in front garden. A trio of Bulldogs, several women. One of the Bulldogs is slumped in a chair, clutching the side of his face and letting out a stream of pained profanities. There's blood running down his neck, glistening like fresh paint. The top of his T-shirt is soaked with the stuff. The other two Bulldogs are hurling abuse at the women, who shout back. The women are fearful but defiant. There's an insane look about them. Women cornered, with their backs to the wall, become Furies.

"It's Gary," Mushroom says, pointing to the bleeding Bulldog. "Seems like one of the bitches went berserk on him."

A Bulldog stationed outside the fence gate unlocks and opens it. Craig strides through, closely followed by Mushroom. Although I'm not invited to go with them, I'm not instructed to stay put either. I approach the gate with a sufficiently authoritative air that the Bulldog guard doesn't think to bar me from entering.

The moment they catch sight of King Cunt, the shouters fall silent. That's presence for you: the ability to bring hush without even saying a word, just by being there.

"Gaz? How bad is it?"

"She just fucking went for me, King!" Gary moans. "I didn't do anything. Honest. She just—"

"I didn't ask what happened. I asked how bad is it."

Gary takes his hand away from his face. There's a hole in his cheek like a crimson rosette, a chunk of skin and flesh missing, ragged meat revealed. Blood's still oozing out.

Craig glances round at Mushroom. "Get the first-aid kit, will you?" As Mushroom scuttles off, Craig turns to face the women. "OK, which of you was it?"

The women exchange glances. One of them raises a trembling hand. It's Paula Coulton.

Craig studies her for a moment, then sighs. "Which of you *really*?"

"Me," Paula insists.

"Don't fuck me about, eh?"

Paula hesitates, then lowers her head, and then her hand. Another hand goes up. Someone at the back of the group of women, hidden by the others. They part to reveal her.

Zoë.

Craig seems startled. It never occurred to me that he might not know that one of the recently gathered crop of "bitches" is so young. I assumed Neville, or one of the others, would have bragged to him about it. Apparently not.

He beckons her forward. Zoë looks tiny and wretched in front of him, barely half his size.

"What's your name?" he asks her.

"Zoë. Zoë Fothergill."

"Why did you attack this man, Zoë?"

Zoë shakes her head.

Craig repeats the question, more sternly this time.

Finally Zoë says, "I didn't want him touching me." The words spill out. "I hate him. I hate all of them. I'm sick of them and what they do. I don't want any of them touching me ever again."

"She bit me," Gary interjects. "We went up to a room and the little slut just turned around and *bit* me. I hadn't even done anything. She's a fucking animal!"

Well, of course she is. She's a *bitch*, isn't she?

"Zoë," says Craig, "you realise you're in big trouble, don't you?"

"Don't care."

"I can't have you—any of you—attacking my men."

Zoë mutters something.

"Beg pardon? I didn't catch that."

Loudly, in a burst of truculence, Zoë says, "Piss off, you horrid bastard."

There's a gasp from everyone watching. Myself, I'm appalled—doesn't she realise who this man is?—yet I can't help but admire her too. She has nerve, that's for sure. Nerve, and nothing to lose.

Then a voice calls out from the next-door front garden: "Oi, Craig! You're not going to let her talk to you like that, are you?"

Who else but Neville? He steps up to the intervening fence, showing us his grin with that glint of gold in it.

"Tart needs to be taught some manners, she does," he adds.

"Leave this to me, Nev," Craig says, and while his voice is steady and controlled, I can see the muscles in his right forearm flexing, as though he's having to fight the urge to make a fist. "Zoë? Best not make things any worse for yourself than they already are."

Zoë shrugs, resigned to her fate.

"I'll do it if you want," says Neville. "Dish out the beating. If you're too squeamish."

"I said, Nev"—now Craig's patience is really being tried—"leave this to me."

"Keep your hair on. I was only offering."

"She doesn't need to be punished."

Who said that? Was it me? Jesus Christ, it *was*.

Craig spins round. Stares.

My heart's in my belly, kicking there like a rabbit.

Everyone's looking at me.

In a much feebler voice, the sound of someone who knows it's too late to backtrack now, I repeat myself: "She doesn't need to be punished." And add: "She's fifteen. She ought not to be here. She's suffered enough."

Craig's eyes go from wide-surprised to narrow-shrewd. I see him considering. Appraising. He realises what I've just presented him with. A face-saver. A get-out. I could tell he didn't have any stomach for giving Zoë a beating. He'd have gone through with it if he felt he had to, but this way he has a choice. It all depends on whether he can make it look as though he was already thinking what I said, as though I've merely articulated what was already on his mind.

If he doesn't think he can pull it off, then not only will Zoë have to be punished but so will I. Can't have a bitch mouthing off like that. Especially not King Cunt's bitch. Sets a bad example to the rest, doesn't it?

"Fifteen," he says.

I think what I am, he said the other day, *is moral*.

"Nev?"

"Yeah?"

"Did you know how old she is? First time you saw her?"

Neville senses which way this is going, and replies, "I'd no idea. News to me." Whether this is the truth or not, it's a sensible stratagem. Backside firmly covered. "Some girls, you know, they look more mature than they are."

Craig studies Zoë. Now, after all she's been through, she seems older than her years, but before, back in Downbourne, no one could have mistaken her for anything other than the age she is.

"She doesn't belong here," he says finally. "She shouldn't have been brought here. It was wrong." He turns to me. "Moira? She's coming back to the house with us. She's your responsibility now. All right?"

I want to smile. I want to sink to my knees with relief. I don't do either. I simply nod.

"She's still going to be punished, right?" says blood-drenched, grimacing Gary.

"No."

"But, King! My fucking face!"

"I said no, Gaz."

Gary gets to his feet. "I'll do it myself, then."

He takes a step towards Zoë.

If he wasn't so angry, and in so much pain, he'd never have been so stupid.

I don't even see Craig's arm move. There's just a sudden, meaty *smack*, and then Gary's on the ground, doubled up and writhing.

"Don't," Craig says, standing over him, "you ever fucking do that again. Don't you ever even *think* about it. I say something, it's an order, you little shit-head."

"I'm sorry, King," Gary mewls. "I'm sorry, I'm sorry."

"Yeah, you are now."

"It won't happen again, I swear."

"Too sodding right it won't." Craig looks up. Looks around. Sees that his authority has been reasserted. The brief, one-man mutiny has been quelled with sufficient speed and force. No one is in any doubt that King Cunt is still boss around here. Not even Neville. At least, whatever Neville's really thinking, his expression displays nothing but approval for the King's action.

"OK, everyone," Craig says. "As you were. Show's over."

Mushroom arrives with the first-aid kit, now needed by Gary more than ever.

Paula Coulton guides Zoë over to me. "Look after her," is all she says. I take Zoë's hand and nod.

Craig stalks out of the garden. I want to say more to Paula, but I think it's best to leave. Get out while the going's good. I offer her what I can in the way of a reassuring look—*there, you see, I'm on your side, I'm trying to help*—and she seems to understand.

All the way back to the house, Zoë by my side, I feel the breathless exultation of a gambler who's staked everything and won. It's not the jackpot by any means, but it's a start. A victory I can build on.

I make up a bed for Zoë on the sofa in the living room. Exhausted, traumatised, she lies down and goes to sleep almost immediately.

Upstairs, Craig's waiting for me. He's sitting on the edge of the bed, looking... *discombobulated* is the only word for it.

"You stuck your neck out there, Moira."

"I know."

"Big risk."

"I realise."

"Thanks, though."

"I did what I felt I had to."

"Thanks anyway."

"That's OK."

He pauses, then: "You're still scared of me, aren't you?"

"I'd be foolish not to be." The honest answer.

"Ah well. Never mind."

"I'm sorry."

"It's OK. I just hoped that... Forget it." He shrugs, turning his head away.

I spy an opportunity here. "Craig, can I say something?"

"Yeah?"

"The recreation zones..." I hesitate.

"Yeah. Yeah. I know what you're going to say, Moira. Not humane, not right, blah blah blah. If I'm being honest, I'd have to agree with you. But we have to have them. That's all there is to it. Have to. No choice. Now look, I'm tired." He yawns and begins to undress. Conversation terminated. Subject closed.

And so to bed.

Tonight, however, no arm comes over to pin me down.

Strangely, I find myself missing it. The contact.

And so, once Craig is sound asleep, I reach over and gently rest *my* arm on *him*.

The weight of my arm is so light, and he is so massive, that I don't think he'll notice. But he does.

Briefly, ever so briefly, my touch makes him stir.

Two days later, Miriam wheeled Fen out into afternoon sunshine and steered him past the clock tower to the dining hall.

There, surrounded by linenfold oak panelling and glowering oil portraits of past headmasters, he was introduced to the entire Salterite contingent, all fifty-plus of them. They were as jumbled and shamblesome a collection of human beings as he had ever met, the odds and ends from God's attic trunk. Everywhere he looked he saw protruding teeth and flustered hair, chewed fingernails and patterns of beard that could just as likely have been accidental as intentional. There were unusual sartorial combinations of waistcoat and T-shirt and full-length skirt and knee sock and sandal; there were hats—deerstalker, fedora, Tyrolean, Homburg, kepi—worn as badges of individuality, headgear that protested *I am different, I am special, I am not run-of-the-mill;* and there were spectacles, dozens of pairs of them; thin, thick, large, small, round, rectangular, bifocals, trifocals, bottle-bottom, rimless, a large proportion with sticking-plaster or scotch-tape repairs to their frames, a whole glinting thicket of optical aids.

The Salterites smiled at Fen. He smiled back, paying particular attention to the three of them he already knew—Pamela, creaky, twitching Leonard, hunched-up Roy Potts. He kept smiling, and tried not to feel like some anthropological curiosity, presented before a gathering of scientists for study and dissection.

It was Roy Potts's turn to moderate today. He got the proceedings under way by extending a formal welcome to the new addition to their group. (Fen winced inwardly: *new addition.*) The Salterites were invited to greet Fen with a round of applause, which echoed ripplingly up to the hall's high rafters.

"This is the man," Potts added, "who has christened us."

There was more applause, and a few shy cheers.

Then it was down to business.

One after another, the Salterites stood up and read aloud their morning's work. They wrote in exercise books with the Netherholm College crest on the front cover. They wrote with pencils and ballpoint pens obtained, evidently, from the same bountiful stationery cupboard as the exercise books. They wrote about themselves, but what they wrote was not mere autobiography. As Fen had surmised, not enough went on at Netherholm College to make a straightforward chronicling of each day's events worthwhile. Instead, the Salterites cast themselves as first-person narrators of novels, recounting the minutiae of their daily exploits in story form, with all the heightened drama and tension that it entailed. They replayed conversations they had had, the prism of imagination transforming what must have been banal exchanges of dialogue into colourful cut-and-thrust repartee. They took mundane rituals—washing, cooking, eating, cleaning, digging out weeds in the kitchen garden—and developed them into allegories, extrapolating macrocosmic struggles from microcosmic endeavours, the ordinary becoming extraordinary, the humdrum Herculean. Some of them, perhaps inspired by Blake's line about seeing a world in a grain of sand, described in intense detail, at often enervating length, a scene or object they had come across. Several related their dreams (in Fen's view, there was nothing more fascinating than your own dreams, and nothing more boring to other people). A few offered up poems, lolloping doggerel mostly, or free-form meditations that borrowed clumsily from the Beats—the angst, the heart-cry, the repetition, yes, the repetition. One man seemed to think he was Raymond Chandler, another James Joyce, while among the women there were a couple of Dorothy Parkers and one Jane Austen wannabe. What they all had in common was that every one of them, without exception, believed that he or she was the most important entity on Earth, the focal point of everything. The world revolved around each of them. They were the heroes of their own lives.

The readings were breathtaking in their solipsism and self-absorption. Breathtaking, too—though for a different reason—was the workshop session that followed each one. The frankness of the Salterites' criticism of one another's work verged on the lacerating, and Fen quickly discerned that they were anything but objective in their opinions. In the guise of honest commentary, scores were being settled, feuds waged, rivalries aired, personal animosities given vent. The Salterites were not the happy, collaborative bunch they might like to think they were. When one of them found fault with another's use of, say, metaphor and alliteration, what was really at issue was neither of these things but the writer himself or herself. Because writing and individual were so closely linked, it was impossible to discuss the one without discussing the other. As a result, tempers frequently flared. Umbrage was taken. Voices were raised. "There's nothing wrong with my adverbs!" "Nothing that cutting half of them wouldn't cure!" "You wouldn't know a decent simile if it came up and hit you in the face!" "I would if it hit me like a wet ten-pound salmon!" And so on. It was a critical bear pit, and several of the Salterites were reduced to tears by the maulings they received. They would sit and sob while the next member of the group read, and then they would, often as not, lay into that person's work, alleviating their hurt feelings by hurting someone else's. What surprised Fen was that no one stormed out and no one declined to read. Willingly the Salterites exposed their writing, and themselves, to the harsh scrutiny of their peers, perhaps in the belief that there was no gain without pain. He couldn't make up his mind whether this was inestimably brave or inestimably stupid. Probably, he decided, both.

It went on, this brutal, bruising exercise, and on. After a couple of hours, whatever mean-spirited delight Fen might have derived from watching the Salterites verbally savage one another had evaporated, and all he wanted was fresh air and silence. The baton of reading passed to a man called Roger, a sallow, lizardy type whose spectacles had tinted lenses (tinted lenses always made the person wearing them look—Fen had no idea why—like a pervert). As Roger launched into an elaborate account of making his bed that morning, Fen realised he couldn't stand any more of this. He nudged Miriam and whispered that he needed to be excused.

"Can't it wait?"

He indicated, with a grimace, that it could not. "But look. I can wheel myself out."

"Are you sure you'll be able to manage?"

"Wheeling? Of course."

"Relieving yourself."

"I'll just find a patch of grass and slide myself down and... you know. I only need to pee. I'll be fine. Really."

Miriam looked doubtful, but he could tell she had no desire to leave before the readings ended. She had proved to be a vituperative judge of others' work, her tongue one of the most caustic in the room. Fen wondered if this had anything to do with the fact that, thanks to her special exemption, she herself had no piece of prose or poetry to offer. She was, for the time being, safe on the sidelines, a commentator rather than a participant. She could shoot down without fear of being shot down in return. Then again, perhaps this was how she always was.

"All right," she said. "But don't go far."

Fen began nudging the wheelchair slowly backwards, hoping to make a discreet exit. Unfortunately, Roger spotted him, and interrupted a digression on various symbolic interpretations of folding a hospital corner in order to say, "Excuse me, Fen, is there something the matter?"

Fen halted. All eyes were on him. "Call of nature. Sorry. Please, carry on."

Roger was haughtily dismayed. "It's not considered polite to leave in the middle of someone's reading."

There were mutters of agreement, a few tuts. Fen sensed that among the Salterites his stock had just fallen sharply. Well, so what? Fuck them.

"I'll be as quick as I can," he said, and turned the wheelchair around and aimed for the door. Reaching it seemed to take forever, and then the handle proved hard to budge, and then there was the whole rigmarole of shunting the door open and manoeuvring the wheelchair through the gap, and meanwhile he could feel fifty-odd gazes fixed on him, the back of his neck tingling as though under hot lights... but finally he was out of the dining hall, out in the open, out in the late-afternoon brightness, out, thank God, out!

He rested a while, sun on his face, sturdy and silent clock tower beside him. Then a thought came: here was his chance. While the Salterites were busy with their vicious group-therapy. He should aim for the driveway and just keep on going. See where he ended up by nightfall. Surely he would find someone out there who would offer him board and lodging, someone who would take pity on a poor, wheelchair-bound gimp.

But no. Damn it. He didn't have his knapsack with him. It was still hanging on the chair in the sanatorium. And he wasn't going anywhere without his knapsack, or rather what it contained.

He decided, instead, to take the opportunity to explore the school further. Apart from anything else, if he was going to escape at a later date, he needed some practice with the wheelchair.

He circumnavigated the clock tower a couple of times, then trundled past the squash courts and the tuck shop and took a left into one of the larger quads. A dead fountain stood in the middle, pretty but incomplete without its plume of water, like a vase without flowers. He pulled up beside a window and peered in through a grubby pane. A classroom. Desks waited in their rows, marshalled and forlorn. On the blackboard somebody had scrawled *SEE YOU NEXT TERM*—a promise not kept. Geography had been taught in this room. There was a globe on the teacher's table, and a couple of maps on the wall, one of the world, the other of the British Isles. On the latter, three thick red lines had been added by hand, denoting the new, fortified frontiers between Scotland and England, Wales and England, and St Piran's Peninsula and England. Hadrian's Wall was now a rampart, Offa's Dyke a trench, and the Tamar river a guard-patrolled moat, for the Cornish took their secession as seriously as anyone else. There ought to have been a fourth line, a red ring around London, and Fen could only assume that the capital's self-isolation had occurred after Netherholm

College broke up for the final time. Yes, that would make sense. Whereas Scotland and Wales devolved from the union almost overnight after the Unlucky Gamble, and Cornwall soon followed suit, the M25 became a cordon only after the London Council was formed, and that was a little less than five years ago, after things had settled down in the city and all the central boroughs had become established as pocket principalities, firmly under the control of quasi-militias like the British Bulldogs.

London. Bulldogs. Moira.

Fen put his hands to the wheel rims and rolled himself disconsolately on. Some rescuer he had turned out to be. But he would, of course, be resuming his journey to the capital any day now. Just as soon as he felt completely fit and well and ready to do so.

In flagrant disregard of Miriam's admonition not to go far, he crossed the quad and propelled himself through a vaulted passageway, emerging into another, smaller quad. It was not one he had visited with Miriam during the tour the day before yesterday. There was a great, chunky, bolt-studded door at the far end, with a row of curtained windows on either side. The door seemed to indicate that what lay inside was of some importance. The curtains too, closed against prying eyes. Fen couldn't resist the temptation to investigate.

The handle rotated rustily. The door swung ponderously inward. Along the threshold there was a low lip of stone, which Fen managed to negotiate without too much difficulty.

Towering bookcases, densely tomed. The piquant bouquet of decomposing paper. Buttoned-leather armchairs, designed for the long, lounging perusal of text. A lectern with a huge venerable volume laid out on it, pages spread like angel wings.

The school library.

The place Miriam had said had burned to the ground.

Echoes of the door's opening skittered through the gloom, disappearing into far-off corners, book-shadowed deeps. Fen edged tentatively forwards, waiting for his eyes to adjust to the lack of light. There was something that didn't seem quite right here (other than the fact that Miriam had lied to him so flagrantly about the library's continued existence). He had every reason to think that he was alone, yet he sensed somehow that he was not.

"Hello?"

Silence. Yet it was a stifled silence, not pure absence of noise but noise being withheld. The sound of someone listening.

"Hello?"

Finally, a distant answer: "What, is it supper time already?"

Fen, now more curious than ever, headed in the direction the voice had come from.

Deep within the library's dimness he passed a bookcase aisle in which there was a camp bed, a sleeping bag draped over it like a slab of melted cheese over a slice of toast. A little further on he came to a double row of carrels. A man was ensconced at one of them, reading by candlelight. Probably in his early sixties, he was wearing leather slippers and a silk dressing gown that was threadbare, with seams split at one armpit and on one pocket. He hadn't shaved in over a week, and his skin had the pallor of someone who had not seen the sun in ages. As Fen came into his line of view, he looked up and blinked, mole-like.

"Who are you? I've not seen you before."

"Fen," said Fen.

"Oh yes, the new boy." The man appraised him: face, wheelchair, splinted leg. "Where's my meal?"

"Meal?"

"You aren't here to bring me my supper?"

"Sorry, no. It's a bit early, actually."

The man consulted his wrist—a reflex action, since he wasn't wearing a watch. "Yes. So then why aren't you with the others, workshopping?"

"I bailed. I was finding it a little... wearing."

The man laughed.

"Why aren't *you* there?"

"I used to go. Regularly. But like you, it got on my nerves, so now I just leave them to it."

"Seems wise."

"I don't know how they do it. Every day, including weekends. How do their egos survive?"

"Flagellants."

The man laughed again, warmly this time. Fen sensed a kinship kindling between them, both of them outsiders, positioned by choice at the periphery of the Salterite flock.

"How did that happen?" The man pointed at Fen's leg. "No one here seems to know."

"No one's asked. It's a long story."

"Go on. I like long stories."

Fen saw no reason not to tell him. He began with his adventures aboard the *Jagannatha*, then filled in the background—Downbourne, the arrival of the British Bulldogs, Moira's kidnap—and concluded with his time spent out in the wild, broken-limbed and helpless.

"Nasty," said the man, with a wince of sympathy. "Still, at least you're alive and, after a fashion, kicking. And lucky you were found by such nice people, eh?"

"Very lucky," said Fen, surprised by the other's note of sarcasm and only too happy to match it. "So how come you've managed to not be a part of all this? To keep your distance? I mean, you're here, but it's obvious you don't really belong."

"Is it? Don't you know who I am?"

Fen didn't until that moment. As soon as the man asked the question, the penny dropped.

"Jeremy Salter?" he said. "*You're* Jeremy Salter?"

"Don't look much like my jacket photograph, do I?"

"I haven't seen your jacket photograph. The only editions of your books I've seen are paperbacks."

"Take it from me, it doesn't do me justice. And of course, it is rather out of date. That's the beauty and the tragedy of jacket photographs. They're ageless, while their subject ages. It's often a bit of a shock for readers, first time they meet you. I see it in their eyes: *blimey, he's old!*"

"Jeremy Salter." Fen shook his head, bemused. "I've got to say, it never even occurred to me you'd be hanging around this place. I pictured you in, I don't know, a nice little cottage somewhere on the coast. Book-lined study, desk, typewriter, view of the sea."

"How about a one-bedroom flat in Hackney with a view of a Turkish restaurant?"

"That would have been my second guess." Fen threaded a chuckle through the remark.

"Believe me, if I had a cottage like you describe, I'd be there right now."

"I don't know. Hackney's not so bad, is it?"

"It used to be fine. I liked it. But rumours are, there was trouble there a couple of years back. An outbreak of fighting. The International Community weighed in. Now most of the area is rubble."

"Better off here then."

"Quite. I have peace and quiet, my meals brought to me, and all the books I can read."

"Plus lots of time to work on your new novel."

"Ah, you know about that."

"Miriam told me. She said you're hard at it." He saw Salter flinch slightly. "Aren't you?"

"Miriam," said the novelist, with a sigh, "would like to believe I am. They all would. They're all looking forward to it desperately. Salivating at the prospect. The new Jeremy Salter. It's an article of faith for them, that that book is coming. And a sign."

"A sign?"

"When the novel is ready for publication, that will be when England returns to normal. Didn't Miriam explain that bit?"

"Not exactly." Although she had hinted, hadn't she? When she had talked about waiting for something, wondering if it was ever going to come.

"Well, she probably thought you weren't ready." Salter stood up and ground his knuckles into his lower back, baring his teeth with the ache. "Jesus. Bad posture, that's my trouble." He glanced down. His dressing gown had fallen open, and he was wearing nothing underneath. A glimpse of pubic hair and peeping pink. He tightened the cord to restore his modesty. "It's really very simple," he said. "To them, at any rate. Once my book is finished, all will be right with England again."

"How do they reckon that?"

"Because when the book is ready, there *has* to be a publisher to publish it, because it's a book by me, Jeremy Salter, the Master. And if there's a publisher to publish it, there must be booksellers to sell it, and if there are booksellers then there'll be other shops, and if there are other shops... and so on and so on."

"Very logical."

"Isn't it? The whole country will spring back to life, just like that, because of me. There'll be petrol and electricity and cars and buses again. There'll be supermarkets full of food, and the BBC back on the air. Phones will work, and you'll be able to listen to the shipping forecast once more. You'll be able to go on holiday once more. You'll be able to visit the chemist's to buy your toothpaste and your tampons and your headache tablets. There'll be doctors and 'flu jabs, pub landlords and sandwich shops, dustmen and plastic carrier bags..."

Salter shook his head, the vision vanishing.

"Albion will rise again," he said, "just as soon as my book is done."

"And you don't believe it."

"No, of course I don't believe it. It's just a fucking book we're talking about. Its appearance isn't going to change things overnight, like waving a magic wand."

"So why haven't you told them that? Everybody here?"

Salter, with a rueful laugh, picked up the book he had been reading, closed it and searched for a slot on a shelf to insert it into. "As if they'd listen."

"But you're nothing short of a religion to these people. Miriam, Leonard, all of them. They've organised their lives around you."

"Tell me about it. It was never my intention. It's these damn times we're living in. People are desperate for new leaders, new gods. Anyone'll do, anyone who even vaguely fits the bill. Even a washed-up and never-very-successful author. Whatever offers them just a little glimpse of stability, they'll take it. Don't think I don't know I'm the proverbial 'any port in a storm'."

"But what I mean is, they'd listen to you. If you told them their book might not be coming. They'd listen to you and they'd understand."

"Really? And even if they did, how can I do that to them? I'm Jeremy Salter. I'm their Master. They love me. I can't let them down. Can't disappoint my fans."

"Have you even started this novel?"

Another rueful laugh.

"Writer's block?"

"To a certain degree, yes. I've been 'silent', as they say, for a while. Not produced anything of any note. Bred 'not one work that wakes'."

"Hopkins."

"Well done. Mainly, though, it's the weight of expectation. I can hardly deliver the book, can I? Not when my devotees have so much hope invested in it. What happens when I complete a manuscript and nothing changes, England just continues to stumble along in its buggered-up way? How crushing is that going to be for them? The Master promised the country's rebirth and it didn't come. Not that I *did* promise it. It's just an idea they got into their heads: delivery of new novel equals dawn of new era."

"I see," said Fen. "That does leave you rather up the creek, doesn't it?"

"I should say so. Even if I could write a book, I don't dare. And so this is what I get up to instead." Salter gestured around the library. "Read. Look busy. I tell them I'm doing research. Seeking wisdom and inspiration among the words of others. Preparing the ground. Stoking up my creativity. And writing too, although that part's a lie. Not a *complete* lie. Occasionally I do jot something down, maybe in the margin of a book—an idea, a fragment, a line or two, a character sketch, a few paragraphs of cross-talk. But usually it's no good, or else I lose the book or the scrap of paper I've written it down on. By and large, I just kill time. There's a lot of interesting stuff on these shelves. Some absolute crap, too. You'd be amazed the kind of junk a public-school library accumulates over the decades. Cricketing almanacs from way back when. Obscure novels by even obscurer novelists. Bound collections of Victorian-era *Punch*. Some of the most recondite non-fiction works you can ever imagine. Who'd have thought somebody would have written, let alone published, a survey of British gas-lamp designs, eighteen-fifty to nineteen-twenty?"

Fen's next question—*How long have you been here?*—he decided against asking. He didn't think he wanted to know the answer. He rolled himself closer to Salter, not by much, just a couple of wheel revolutions, and lowered his voice, as if someone might be eavesdropping, as if books had ears to go along with jackets and spines.

"Leave," he said. "I hear what you've been saying, but leave. You don't have to stay here. Come with me. We'll go together."

Salter peered round at him, frowning. "You're deserting Netherholm? Already?"

"I've been putting it off, but yes. I can't stand it here, and I've been sidetracked long enough from what I have to do."

"But your leg..."

"Won't be too much of a hindrance. Not if I have your help. Come with me."

"What about"—Salter gestured in the general direction of the dining hall—"them?"

"What *about* them? They'll be upset to lose you, sure, but I imagine they'll get over it. Eventually."

"I'm not so sure."

"You didn't ask to be their Master, Jeremy."

"I didn't exactly discourage them. I was... flattered by the attention they gave me. Not to mention the adulation. They really love my books."

"Fine. But you didn't ask them to make the nation's recovery your responsibility. They've elevated you to a role you can't possibly live up to. So forget them. It's time to move on. Don't you want to get back to your flat in Hackney?"

"If it's there any more."

"You can at least check up on it, see for yourself. I need to get to London too, remember. And if we go together..."

Was he being too forceful? Pushing Salter too hard? But Salter needed to escape, even if he didn't realise it, and with his assistance Fen's own bid for freedom would be markedly easier. Fen could see the pair of them, Salter at the handles of the wheelchair, wending their way towards the capital. (Presumably Salter had some proper clothes lying around somewhere—shoes, socks, trousers, all that. And a London permit. He must do, as an ex-Londoner.) It was perfect, wasn't it? Two predicaments solved at a stroke.

"I don't know." The corners of Salter's mouth were turned down in a grimace of reluctance. "They look after me here. I get fed. I get respect. I'll have to think about it."

"OK," said Fen. "Of course it isn't something you should rush into. But, not to put pressure on or anything, I do want to get out of here pretty soon."

"I understand."

"Perhaps I could come back and visit you tomorrow? Assuming I can find a way to."

"I can't say I'll have made up my mind by then."

"Nonetheless."

Salter deliberated for a moment, then said: "All right. Tomorrow."

When the Salterites emerged from the dining hall, they found Fen next to the clock tower. He was asleep in the wheelchair, or at any rate seemed to be, for when Miriam shook him by the shoulder, he acted very much like someone waking up—blinking, smacking his lips, squinting around him.

Miriam was not best pleased. Nor were the others. Fen had shown them great disrespect. It appeared he was not taking their way of life as seriously as he should. There were grumbles and murmurings—a definite discontent about the new addition's attitude.

Fen apologised and apologised. He was still not a hundred per cent well, and it had been such a warm afternoon—he had just nodded off, nothing he could do about it. Very poor show, he knew. Could they find it in their hearts to forgive him? Just this once?

The Salterites could, and in the end, impressed with his contrition, did. Miriam alone remained unmollified. Fen was in her care. He had embarrassed her. She wheeled him back to the sanatorium by the bumpiest route possible, jerking the chair around corners and braking sharply more often than was strictly necessary. Up in the ward, she tied his leg up to the hooks—tight knots—then left him for a long time with nothing to do except watch dusk gather outside, the sky purpling, the oaks clouding into silhouettes, a last twilight fling for the birds. Supper arrived, and then, when he had eaten, out went the bedside candle.

But tomorrow afternoon. Tomorrow afternoon he would know. Whether or not he had a new-found ally. A fellow escapee.

Fen opened his eyes, aware that he had just awoken from a very vivid dream. Dawn light, barging in through the curtainless windows, flooded every inch of the room, liquid brightness. Outside, the wind-busied oaks were all writhe and bluster, shouldering against one another, boisterous as drunken soldiers. It was early. Five, five-thirty. Today, he felt, was the day.

The day for what?

For fleeing, he hoped.

Through the windows he gazed at the oaks. He was both drowsy and nervously excited. He might sleep again before Miriam arrived with breakfast; he might not. Like a sea view, the oaks were comforting to watch: the graceful filigreed flutter of their leaves, and now and then a deep cavity appearing where the wind punched a hole. On one particular tree he could make out what looked like a face forming amid the heaving green. Yes, thanks to the configuration of its branches and the efforts of the wind, the oak definitely seemed to have facial characteristics. Sunken eyes, a thick nose, a mouth opening and closing. The more Fen searched for the face, the more apparent it became. Not just a nose but a nose with nostrils. Not just a mouth but a mouth surrounded by beard. And in the eyes... It was daylight showing through the leaves, but the resemblance to the gleam of real eyes was uncanny. There was a clear differentiation between white and iris. Remarkable. He would point the phenomenon out to Miriam when she came.

And then the oak spoke.

And its voice was Michael Hollingbury's. And so, Fen realised, was its face.

"Be ready, Mr Morris," it said.

The voice was vibrant and multifaceted, exactly as one might expect a voice to sound when formed from thousands of rustling leaves. It was shimmering and sonorous, both reassuringly familiar and disquietingly strange.

"Ready as the seed pod," it said, "waiting to be freed by a gust of wind."

Fen felt a chill run through him and he wanted the voice to be quiet; he didn't want to see and hear this tree talk to him, however much it looked and sounded like Hollingbury.

"Ready as the fungus spore, waiting for the raindrop that will burst it loose into the world."

He tried to ignore what it was saying. Tried, through disbelief, to will it into non-existence.

"Ready as the pollen grain for the questing bee."

Shut up! he yelled in his head. *Shut up!*

"Be ready for your opportunity."

FEN OPENED HIS eyes, aware that he had just awoken from a very vivid dream. Dawn light, barging in through the curtainless windows, flooded every inch of the room, liquid brightness. Outside, the wind-busied oaks were all writhe and bluster, shouldering against one another, boisterous as drunken soldiers. It was early. Five, five-thirty. Today, he felt, was the day.

The day for what?

For fleeing, he knew.

Through the windows he gazed at the oaks. The oaks had been part of the dream, integral to it. He remembered them as being sensible. Sensible, and familiar, and alarming. With some effort, because the dream was rapidly dimming in his memory, he recalled Michael Hollingbury's face appearing in the leaves and branches of one of the oaks, and then the face speaking to him. He recalled his fear at the apparition, and realised that the fear was still with him, an echo of itself, fainter but still resonating away in his insides.

Twice now. Twice he had been visited in a dream by Downbourne's dead mayor. Was it right that he should be dreaming so intensely about the man? Was it *sane*?

At least this time, instead of vague reassurances like last time, Hollingbury had had some practical advice for him. Something along the lines of...

What was it?

Be ready.

That was it. But what did that mean? In what way "ready"?

Ready as he had not been ready yesterday, when he could have made his getaway but for the fact that he hadn't had the London permit and Moira's wedding band with him.

A lack of foresight that was easily remedied.

Fen reached for his knapsack.

"'WHY?' I HAD to ask myself. 'Why has he chosen this moment, of all moments, to make his exit?' My flow was broken. I felt betrayed. This new member whom we had invited into our circle, clasped to our bosom, had had the impertinence, or so I thought, to make to leave whilst *I* was reading.

"'Fen, my lame-legged friend,' I said, peering at him coolly, 'I trust you aren't going anywhere.'

"How furtive he looked then, like a burglar caught in the beam of a policeman's torch.

"'I'm enjoying your piece immensely, Roger,' came the reply, and there was a murmur of assent throughout the dining hall, a general acknowledgement that, with these words, Fen had spoken for all. 'It's powerful,' he added. 'Almost too powerful. I need to go outside and ponder a while.'"

Fen managed to suppress a snigger, but it hurt to do so, like containing a sneeze. A couple of the Salterites seemed bemused by Roger's outrageously distorted version of yesterday's events, but most appeared not to find it extraordinary at all. They regularly performed the same kind of alchemy themselves, turning base reality into literary gold.

"I smiled at him," read Roger, "the warm, wise smile of a man who knows he has done his job properly. To provoke another to contemplation, to stir the depths of another's soul—this is the one true goal of the author. And so with Fen. It was his first-ever attendance at one of our meetings, and I had succeeded in—*oh, what now?*"

Behind the tinted lenses, Roger's eyes flashed with irritation. Who could it be, opening the dining-hall door? Who was the late arrival whose entrance meant that for the second day running his reading was interrupted?

Then Roger remembered that all of the Salterites were present and accounted for, so the late arrival could only be—

"Master," he gasped.

Jeremy Salter's head poked round the door. He regarded everyone nervously, debating whether or not to enter. After a moment he did, sidling warily into the room. An absolute hush had fallen. On every Salterite face there was mingled delight and disbelief. The Master, paying them a visit. Could it be that he had left the library for a very specific reason? Could he be here to give them a progress report on the new book? Might it be nearing completion? Might it even be—no, surely not, it was too much to hope for—be *finished*?

"Master," said Roger, "forgive me, please. I didn't mean to sound so annoyed. My temper got the better of me. I'm sorry."

Salter barely heard the apology. He was gazing around at his assembled acolytes, and Fen wondered when was the last time he had faced them all together like this. By the look of him, it had been a while. The devotion, the *need* of such a number of people, was overwhelming to him. He hadn't bargained for this when, willingly or otherwise, he had become their messiah.

It took him the best part of a minute to gather himself together. He toyed with one end of the cord of his dressing gown, coughed, thrust a hand into the dressing gown's unfrayed pocket, took it out again, looked down at his feet, looked up, ran his fingers through his hair, and finally summoned up the nerve to speak.

"Everyone," he said.

A long pause.

"Everyone, I have something to tell you."

A wordless whisper went around the room, a susurrant rustle as Salterite turned to Salterite, exchanged a look, nodded. *Here it comes. This is it.*

Fen, for his part, had the fear that Salter was about to land him in trouble. *This man came to the library yesterday afternoon and tried to talk me into abandoning you all.* He hated to think how the Salterites might respond. Beneath that meek bookishness ran a current of restive, ill-focused anger. He had had numerous glimpses of it yesterday, during and immediately after the workshop session. He could see it, given sufficient provocation, welling up and erupting. Violently. And here he was, in a wheelchair. Never had he been less capable of defending himself.

In the event, what Salter had to say gave hope to the perturbed Fen and perturbed the hopeful Salterites.

"For a while now, I've been distant from you," Salter said. "Hidden away in the library, I've left you to carry on pretty much under your own steam. You may feel that I've been neglecting you." There were cries of *no, no* and *of course not*. "You may feel that my aloofness has meant that

I want nothing to do with you." Again, the Salterites loyally contradicted him. "You may have found it insulting that I, your Master, have withdrawn from all contact with you save for brief meetings at mealtimes."

"We don't mind," said Pamela.

"You need your solitude, Master," said another of the Salterites.

"The fact is," said Salter, "it's true."

There was silence as the Salterites attempted to decipher this remark. *What* was true? That he needed his solitude? That he only saw any of them when they brought him his meals at the library? Or that...?

"Master?" said Roy Potts. "What are you saying?"

"I'm saying"—Salter looked both patient and scared, making Fen think of a saint in the throes of martyrdom—"I'm fed up with the lot of you. This is absurd. Crazy. I should never have allowed things to get out of hand the way they have. Look at yourselves. Go on. Take a good, long, hard look. What are you doing here? What are you achieving? What does writing about yourselves do for you? Where does it get you, putting yourselves through the mill like this day after day? Do you honestly feel better for it?"

Several of the Salterites nodded. They honestly did. The rest were just puzzled.

"And waiting for my next novel," Salter went on. "Waiting for it like it's some kind of magical solution, the talisman that's going to save the day. Here's a newsflash. It's not coming. It's never coming. I haven't written a word of it. I've been sitting there in that library with my thumb up my arse, pretending to be creating. I've been stringing you along, simply because I can. Because you've let me. And it's time this whole... this whole *charade* was at an end. I'm not what you think I am. Nor am I what you hope me to be. I'm just an ordinary person who's been promoted way above his station and who's sick and tired of being hailed as something he isn't. Let's stop this now. Let's call it a day and go back to our homes. It was fun while it lasted; now it's over. And I'm sorry. I hope we can still be friends after this, but I appreciate that's most likely impossible. I'm sorry I misled you. I'm sorry that we all got into such a mess. But there you are. It's all over. Please, let's just agree that it's all over."

The Master had delivered this illusion-shattering speech in such a hesitant and understated manner that for a while the Salterites wondered if he was genuinely telling them what he seemed to be telling them. A couple of them murmured something to the effect that this was a test of faith, an attempt to discover which of them were his true devotees and which merely playing at it. Another mentioned a scene in one of the Master's Jeremiah S. Coburn books wherein an evil Paul Cordwainer duplicate comes to Earth and tries to persuade the planetary government to call off the war with the Ch'ee-Lan. This, surely, was the Master acting out a similar scene, perhaps in order to establish how familiar they were with the *Farways* novels (as if such a thing needed establishing!). A few of them had simply not heard a word Salter had said, refusing to believe what their ears were telling them.

For most present, however, it became apparent soon enough that the Master was not fooling around. This was no attempt to wrongfoot them, to shock them into some precipitous and self-revelatory response. This was no demand for proof, no trial by fire. This was really happening. The Master had had enough of them. The Master was a sham. The Master had just confessed that he had been lying to them, leading them on, avoiding them because he thought them...

Absurd.

Ridiculous.

Contemptible.

And in that instant of dreadful realisation, the Salterites switched from adoration to loathing. Fen could feel the animosity lunge out of them at Salter. Salter felt it, too. He took an involuntary step backwards, as though recoiling under the impact of a physical blow. Behind dozens of pairs of spectacles, eyes went narrow and dark. The atmosphere in the dining hall drummed with dissident rage.

Roy Potts stood up. "You shit," he growled. "You absolute *turd*."

Then Leonard got to his feet. "How could you have"—half of his face jerked and writhed for several seconds—"done this to us? All we did was"—more jerking and writhing—"admire you."

Now Roger: "A joke. That's all we've been to you, isn't it? A big stupid joke."

Salter was shaking his head. He was suddenly calm. Surprisingly so, Fen thought, given the circumstances. "Please understand," he said, "it was never my intention to hurt anybody's feelings. This has been long overdue. I had to get it out into the open. For all our sakes. I couldn't go on deluding you, letting you delude yourselves."

"We were happy!" someone shouted.

"You've ruined everything!" someone else shouted.

All the Salterites were on their feet by now. Slowly, menacingly, they began to move on Salter. Some were yelling and gesticulating, others were grimly tight-lipped. Among the latter, Miriam looked the grimmest and tightest-lipped. Her face was white, her mouth a barely visible slit. In her asterisk eyes Fen saw pure murder.

It did not take a psychic to predict that the situation was about to turn very nasty. Certainly Salter seemed aware what was going to happen, but, although he retreated before his acolytes' advance, he did not turn and attempt to flee. It was almost as if he had been expecting something along these lines. Almost as if he welcomed it. As he backed up against a wall and the Salterites encircled him, he looked relieved that the option of escape was no longer available. It was out of his hands now. He had set a train of events in motion. He had no choice any more but to ride it to its final destination.

Briefly Fen considered intervening. But what could he do, wheelchair-bound as he was? The expression on Salter's face decided him. The resigned acceptance. A price was about to be paid. Fen aimed the wheelchair for the door, which Salter had left ajar. The last thing he saw before he propelled himself through it was the Salterites pouncing on their disgraced, dressing-gowned Master. The last thing he heard was a howl from several dozen throats, a cry of pure, maenad fury.

And then he was off, hurtling past the clock tower, past the science block, onto the driveway. Thrust, thrust, thrust with his hands, the wheelchair jouncing and juddering over uncertain tarmac. In his trouser pocket: Gilbert Cruikshank's London permit, Moira's wedding band. Farewell to the knapsack—he had had no choice but to leave it on the chair in the sanatorium, but it wasn't such a great loss really. Frantically down the driveway, with the Salterites' howl still echoing in his ears. Were they following him? Were they behind him? Or were they still in the dining hall, exacting their terrible revenge on Salter? He didn't dare look. He should have helped Salter. No, he couldn't have done a thing. Wheel spokes a blur. Palms and fingers slipping on the steel rims. Breathing rough. But thrust, thrust, thrust, and out through the gateway and into the world beyond Netherholm, and on, and on, as if all the devils in hell were giving chase, on along a pocked, pitted road, with no direction other than Away, no goal other than putting as much distance as he could between him and the school. And on into the emptiness of England, and on.

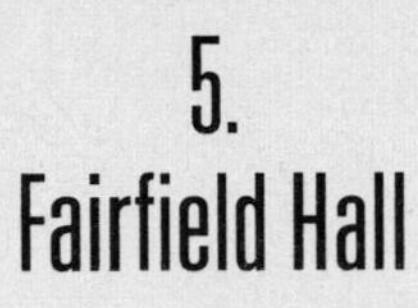

5. Fairfield Hall

HANDS BLISTERED, ARMS aching, Fen homed in on the hum.

He had been two and a half hours on the road. Urgent impetus had become painful effort had become exhausted trudge. The going had not been as difficult as he anticipated, but neither had it been easy, thanks to one of the wheelchair's front castors, which had developed shopping-trolley syndrome, that propensity to stick when least expected and least wanted. More and more, with his shoulders tiring and his palms turning raw, Fen had had to fight against the chair's leftward veer and force the damn thing around right-hand bends. Wearisomeness adding to weariness.

Then, the hum.

Shortly before he first heard it, he had been reconciling himself to two uncomfortable facts: that evening was coming on, and that he was hopelessly lost. From Netherholm, he had hurtled headlong into a network of country lanes, single-track, high-banked, an open-topped labyrinth. At junctions there were signposts—the old-fashioned kind, wooden with black lettering, not needing to be replaced by anything newer, their mile-truths still accurate—but the names on them were of no help to him. The signposts weren't giving directions to any major towns, merely offering guidance to the immediate vicinity. Evidently you weren't supposed to enter this rural backwater unless you already had some idea where within it you were headed.

There had been hills, but none steep. There had been ruts and potholes, nothing he could not steer the wheelchair over or around. But then, as the light began to fade, the despairing sense had crept into him that he was getting nowhere. Where were the houses around here? Where *were* the villages named on the signposts? Hemmed in by tall hedgerows, he was afforded no prospects, no glimpses of a potential destination. It could be that he was going round in circles. What if he wound up by accident back at Netherholm? Netherholm, and those betrayed bookworms who had vengefully turned on their god. Not an appealing thought.

Then he had come to the wall—mossy brick, waist-high, round-capped, portions of it collapsed, other portions sagging with intent to collapse. The wall curved with the road, extending a protective arm around a deep margin of woodland. Wall meant habitation. Fen, with renewed vigour, had followed its course, and after quarter of a mile had become aware of the first faint strains of a threnodic thrumming, as though a distant choir of bass singers was intoning a minor-key chord. The sound originated from up ahead, further along the path of the wall, and as Fen shunted himself closer it deepened and intensified and developed weird harmonics, skittering piccolo trills like a knife scraping ice. Closer still, and the world seemed to shiver with it—sky, trees, lane, trembling to its eddying vibration and swirl. A power drill? A chainsaw? What?

He rounded a corner, and the wall rose in a swooping parabola and became a pillar, crowned with a limestone lion. Five yards on, there was an identical lion atop an identical pillar, after which the wall resumed at its previous level. Between the two lions, a pair of imposing gates might once have stood, but now there was just an open entrance. On each pillar a brass plaque was attached, and on each plaque were etched two words, still legible under the verdigris:

FAIRFIELD
HALL

Fen eased himself onto the incurving apron of gravelled tarmac which, beyond the gateway, became a winding drive. The source of the hum lay along the drive, somewhere past the point where the margin of woodland ended. The wheel rims were tacky with blood from his flayed palms. His knitting, splinted femur throbbed from all the jostling and bumping it had had to endure over the past few hours. His arms ached so much, they no longer felt part of him; they were hollow, unwieldy prostheses. What kept him going was the thought that the hum, whatever it was, had to mean human activity of some sort, human industry, consequently someone on whose mercy he could throw himself.

A hundred yards of stiff, wincing progress brought him clear of the trees. He was at the top of a rise. The drive wound downwards, into a valley. All Fen could see of the house to which it led was a dozen red chimney tops, standing proud amid a cluster of cedars. Beyond was a flank of green hill where sheep, tiny as maggots, grazed.

A bee buzzed across his field of vision. He turned to look in the direction it had come from.

Of course.

Hives. A couple of dozen wooden hives, like miniature white tower blocks, each with a cloud of bees cycling attentively around it.

And next to one of the hives, a man dressed in a beekeeper's veiled hat and thick, tight-cuffed gloves.

The man had removed the hive's top two levels. As Fen watched, he leaned down, extracted a frame from inside the hive and held it up to peer at the comb it contained. Drones and workers crawled off the frame onto his gloves, like a glossy black contagion, but the man seemed unconcerned, his the fearlessness of someone who has been stung often, or never stung at all. Having satisfied himself that all was as it should be with the comb, he slotted the frame back into place and commenced the delicate task of removing the bees from himself. It was while he was doing this, gently wiping one hand against the other, that he noticed Fen.

He let out an oath, more in bemusement than in shock. Next moment, he began laughing—a rich, throaty chortle. His whole body, which was of some considerable size, rocked and wobbled, and the last few bees still clinging to his gloves took flight, dispersing agitatedly.

Fen, for all his various pains and discomforts, could not help but smile. The man's laughter was so unexpected and so obviously heartfelt that it was impossible not to relish it. Even though he, Fen, was its cause—and he realised how absurd and incongruous he must look, broken-legged in a wheelchair, here in the heart of the countryside—he was not offended. Rather, he was relieved that he had given the beekeeper something to laugh about. A better response he could not have hoped for.

The man carefully reconstructed the hive, then walked over to Fen, lifting his veil as he went and securing it over the hat brim. Something about his revealed face made Fen instinctively want to trust him. He was somewhat surprised that, given his experiences with Wickramasinghe and the Salterites, he still had it in him to trust a complete stranger. Nevertheless...

"I need some help," he said.

"I'll say you do," the man replied, and not long after that he was wheeling Fen down the drive, away from the hive hum, through the stately acres towards the house where Fen was to spend the next two months of his life.

FAIRFIELD HALL HAD been Beam's family's principal residence since the Restoration. Legend had it that the duke who built it was given the land and the funds for its construction by Charles II himself as a reward for his loyalty and financial support during the king's exile. (Legend also had it that the duke was one of the royalists who helped hide Charles after his defeat at Worcester, although in Beam's view this was merely an instance of the family lily being gilded.) The one condition attached to the king's munificence was that he was entitled to visit the house whenever he wished and have his way with the duke's wife, by all accounts a great beauty. Such an arrangement seemed to suit the duke, no doubt because he, in turn, was exercising *droit du seigneur* over various of his female servants. As for the duchess, she got a large and impressive country seat out of the deal, and what woman of that era, or indeed any era, could resist the blandishments of the monarch? Besides, when the king was not around and her husband was otherwise engaged, there was always a discreet footman or a handsome, horny-handed stable lad whom she could, as it were, fall back on.

So licentiousness had reigned in the household, and had continued to reign for several generations, with the result that the routes by which the Hall passed from one owner to the next were not necessarily the most direct and straightforward. Every time a resident duke died, he left behind at least two heirs, usually more, each with more-or-less equal claim to his title and estate. For a couple of centuries the family tree was a tangle of half-siblings and bastards and bigamy and morganatic marriages—less a tree, in fact, more a briar patch—and often the question of inheritance could only be settled by who was the better shot in a duel, or, as time went by, who employed the better lawyers.

By the middle 1800s things began to settle down, as conventional morality asserted itself and the system of eldest-son-of-sole-spouse-gets-everything became the norm—generally a more satisfactory method of establishing right of succession, and less costly in terms of both money and life. The promiscuity that had characterised the early years of Fairfield's existence was eschewed, and a prudish veil drawn over that era of the house's history. A shame, in Beam's view, but there you go. The Victorians were unlikely to believe, as he did, that not only had the family benefited from the misbehaviour of its first owner and his immediate descendants, the Hall itself had too. The house, he reckoned, had received a kind of erotic christening, an infusion of energy from the sexual shenanigans that had taken place within its walls during its formative years, a baptism by fornication that had imbued it with a vibrant, playful atmosphere of the sort you wouldn't find in, say, a cathedral; while the admixture of commoner genes to the bloodline meant that, whereas many an aristocratic family dwindled away through inbreeding and hereditary disorders, becoming an anaemic ghost of its former self, Beam's had remained robust and vital down through the decades. For an example of this, you only had to look at his grandfather, who had survived appalling wounds at Anzio and a three-bottles-of-claret-a-day drinking habit to live to the ripe old age of ninety-four. War took one of his arms, alcohol-related circulatory problems cost him both of his legs, but he had soldiered on regardless.

"When I was young, it used to be my job to push the old bugger around in a wheelchair," Beam told Fen as they trundled down the drive. "Just like I'm pushing you now. I was only a strip of a lad, but it wasn't that hard work. So much of him was missing, he hardly weighed a thing. We got along great, Grandfather and I. He taught me all the dirty jokes I'll ever need to know. But d'you know what impressed me the most about him? How he never let his disability get in the way. He'd shoot game, uncork bottles, rattle off long, choleric letters to the *Spectator* on his typewriter... No mean feat if you've only one functioning limb. Fondled the ladies, too, and always knew he could get away with it because they couldn't possibly slap a one-armed war veteran in the face, could they? Naturally enough, I grew up wanting to be exactly like him."

"With all your parts intact, of course."

Beam laughed, in the very same way that he had laughed when he had caught sight of Fen at the hives. Fen got the impression that Beam laughed a lot; a lot of things amused Beam. His face seemed designed for little else: the small, twinkling eyes; the clownish bulb of nose; the nub of chin that rested on a roll of dewlap; the parallel grooves in his jowly cheeks that reminded Fen of a cut of meat from the butcher's, segmented with string. A face that was the very epitome of the term jovial.

"My father was much the same," Beam continued, after his laughing fit had run its course. "When he took over the Hall, we were getting fucked five ways to Sunday by the government. Taxes on this, taxes on that. At the time, they were treating the landed gentry like a disease that had to be eradicated. And who knows, maybe they're right. Maybe we are. But that's another argument. The thing is, Dad refused to let it get to him. I never once heard him even grumble. You'd see these arsehole politicians come on the television and talk about social equality when what they were really talking about was paying off their debts at our expense. And Dad would just smile. He took the view that we'd been around for a while, and we'd continue to be around for a while, come what may. That's what lineage does for a family: roots it hard, like an old tree. So a few paintings, a few heirlooms, went off to the Middle East and Silicon Valley. It was sad to see them go, but they saved us. A small portion of our past bought us our future. I think there's a kind of justice in that, a kind of balance. And it meant Fairfield didn't have to become a country-house hotel, the way so many other stately homes did."

Fen asked, in the tone of someone both amused and baffled, how Beam had come to be called Beam.

"Because it's my name," was the straightforward reply. "Well, part of my name. Part of one part of my name. I've got more barrels than a brewery. Beam's a useful shorthand. That's how everybody knows me. And I think it rather suits me, don't you?"

It did, Fen thought. Beam, as in ray of light. Beam, as in big smile. Beam, as in "broad in the...".

"But perhaps we should steer clear of the subject of unconventional names, *Fen*."

Now the drive was flattening out, settling in for a final long, straight run. The Hall itself was still masked from view by its stockade of cedars but Fen saw outbuildings, stables, which had been converted into an open-sided garage. He saw cars within, half a dozen of them in a row, snug under dustsheets. He saw a stream winding through a deep groove in the valley, decanting into a lake. He saw a great, undulating expanse of lawn on which clumps of rhododendron squatted, somehow calling to mind giant green armadillos. He saw a tennis court, and a huge ancient oak whose boughs played host to a rope-and-tyre swing and a ramshackle treehouse. He saw people. A group of children haring around in a field. Two men walking back to the house from the stream, toiling under the burden of filled buckets. Women sitting out on the grass, preparing vegetables, nattering. Everyone lit sidelong, gilt-edged, by the early evening sun. The women waved to Beam as he and Fen passed by. Beam waved back, and Fen, not knowing what else to do, waved too. One of the women shouted out, "What have you found there, Beam?" and Beam replied, "*He* found *me*."

Then, at last, the Hall. Aged. Pondering. Crimson beside the dusky blue of the cedars. Three storeys tall, with the chimney stacks adding the height of a further storey. A spread of ivy embracing most of one wing, like a viridian pelt. An interlocking to-and-fro of pitched roofs. Windows large and true. Something so solid, so sempiternal about the place that you could quite see Beam's father's point. What could destroy *this*? No act of Parliament, of International Community, even of God, had power sufficient. Netherholm College had been founded on principles, and in the end had failed to survive. Fairfield Hall had been founded on land and lust, earth and earthiness, and had endured.

A pair of Irish wolfhounds appeared from nowhere and came charging up the drive towards Beam and Fen, barking wildly. Fen gripped the arms of the wheelchair, his mind whirling back to that night on the railway embankment, the dog pack, the lunging Rottweiler. His heart was quick-thumping, and he would have, if he could have, stood and run.

The great grey shaggy beasts zeroed in on him and subjected him to the impertinent sniffing and slobbering with which domestic dogs traditionally greet new arrivals to their territory. Fen held himself utterly still, not wanting to give them the least excuse to take offence. He knew, he *knew*, the wolfhounds would not attack. Their tails were lashing to and fro. They were just being friendly. But they were huge creatures, and set into the grizzled muzzles with which they were probing him there were teeth. Huge, sharp teeth. And the smells of dog fur, dog breath, were rank, overpowering, all too horribly reminiscent...

"Crap! Piss!" Beam yelled, somewhat belatedly noticing Fen's discomfiture. "Off! Get off, you buggers!"

Obediently both wolfhounds moved away from Fen. Still wagging their tails, they circled round until they were flanking Beam.

"I do apologise, Fen. They don't mean any harm. Just very excitable. You're not a big fan of dogs, by the looks of things."

"Got put off them quite recently," Fen said, with a forced laugh. "Crap? Piss?"

"It's all they did when they were puppies. And chew shoes."

"So which is which?"

"Honestly don't know."

Beam left Fen by the front door, saying he would only be a moment. He disappeared into the house, but Crap and Piss, instead of following their master, remained with Fen, stationing themselves on either side of the wheelchair. Their heads were on a level with his. They peered at him with their big, rough-browed eyes, beseeching. He realised all he had to do was give one of them a pat and he would have a friend for life. He could not bring himself to. He kept thinking of the Rottweiler, of punching it on the nose. Someone else had done that, someone terrified to the point of recklessness. That someone was still inside him, and had sworn for all time to detest dogs, and no amount of logic was going to persuade him to change his mind.

Several minutes later Beam emerged, bearing a dusty wooden crutch. "My grandfather's," he said, brushing cobwebs off it. "Between losing one leg and losing the other. He used to race around the house on this. It's been in the attic a few years. I hope it's still all right." He banged the rubber ferrule on the ground. "I mean, it seems pretty sturdy, and I can't see any signs of woodworm. But if you don't want to take the risk..."

With Beam's help Fen eased himself up out of the wheelchair. He lodged the crutch under his left arm. He took a few exploratory steps, with Crap and Piss padding alongside, perhaps thinking they were being helpful. The crutch creaked but did not seem in any immediate danger of snapping. It felt strange. His first independent steps in over a fortnight. It felt good.

He turned around and headed back towards Beam, gaining confidence with the crutch.

Beam, he saw, was beaming.

Fen started beaming, too.

SUPPER WAS A raucous, convivial affair. Only then, with the full complement of residents gathered in the dining room, did Fen begin to appreciate how things worked at Fairfield Hall and what Beam had achieved here.

All told, adults and children, there were thirty people present. The table they sat around was a great long slab of mahogany, scuffed and coarsened, the wood slowly reverting through usage to a semblance of its original raw state. They ate off ironstone china, using good silverware. They ate well. And there was wine—wine!—from a cellar stocked so generously that, by Beam's reckoning, it would take a decade of hard boozing to empty it. His grandfather's legacy. The old bugger had acquired the stuff even faster than he could guzzle it. He'd had a morbid fear of the house running dry. There was water on offer, too, cool and clear from the stream. Perfectly safe to drink, Beam assured Fen. The stream had its source a short way up the valley, bubbling up from a deep underground spring, so unlike most waterways in England it hadn't been polluted by the outspill from destroyed factories and power stations. Proof? They were eating the proof. Trout from the lake. Lake was teeming with the buggers. So many, you got a bite almost before your bait hit the surface.

The wolfhounds hunkered by Beam's chair, waiting for scraps which he fed them even while scolding them—*greedy devils!*—for begging. Beam, as you might expect, was seated at the head of the table. Fen was accorded the guest of honour's place at his right hand. And throughout the meal everyone chattered and bickered and hooted, filling the room with noise. The adults discussed the day just ended and what needed to be done tomorrow, and teased one another about working too hard or not hard enough, while the children yelped and squabbled and, between courses, played hide-and-seek under the chairs. Gradually Fen picked up names. Annabel, Simon, Ed, Lucinda, Corin, Jessica... He chatted with a couple of them, but Beam monopolised him, wanting to know all about him, genuinely interested. A dessert course—honey pudding—was brought in, fresh from the wood-burning range in the kitchen, still warm. More wine. Yes, he was a schoolteacher. Lived down south, not far from the coast. Yes, yes, he *was* a long way from home. Thereby hung a tale. Tell me, said

Beam, so yet again Fen rehearsed his litany of travels and tribulations, not forgetting to tack on the latest addition at the end, Netherholm College. Oh, Beam knew about those people over at Netherholm. Everyone around here just left them to get on with it. All sorts of rumours. Artists' colony of some kind. Writers, eh? And they had done *what*? Killed someone! *Maybe* had killed someone. Ah yes. So Fen hadn't seen this Salter fellow actually die. But he was pretty sure the chap had met a sticky end. Brrrr. How ghastly. Still, Fen had got away from 'em, and by the sound of it he'd had a lucky escape.

In the windows the tail-end of twilight deepened into night—violet, indigo, black. Candelabra were lit. The children were taken up to bed, each having kissed Uncle Beam goodnight. It was like a family, Fen thought, a big, rumbustious family, presided over by a portly, avuncular patriarch. He had established that the majority of the people here were old friends of Beam's. As the effects of the Unlucky Gamble began to take hold, they had gravitated towards the Hall. Before, they used to come for weekends, for a break from their pressured working lives. A place of refuge then. Now more so. Beam had welcomed them in under his roof. Then had come one or two outsiders, drifting in as Fen had drifted in: friends of Beam's friends, who knew of the Hall and had made their way there in the hope of finding sanctuary too. They had been welcomed, of course. There was room enough. As long as you did your bit, you could stay. That was the one rule here, according to Beam. The only rule. There was always work to be done, and as long as you chipped in, you fit in.

"Seems a fair system," Fen observed.

"Probably isn't," came the reply, with a wink, "but I like to think it is."

More wine, and still more. The candle glow mellowed, refracted. The faces ranged around the table were golden moons. A little boy came downstairs in his pyjamas, unable to sleep. He sat on Beam's lap and everyone listened as Beam told a story about a chocolate moose. The boy had no idea what a moose was and only a vague concept of chocolate, but he loved the story, which Beam made up as he went along and which contained very little plot other than the various different methods the moose employed to keep from melting in the sun. The wolfhounds snored at Beam's feet.

Later, the dribs-and-drabs decampment to bed.

Later still, Beam and Fen stood on the Hall's west-facing terrace, last survivors of the evening. Crap and Piss busied themselves, dim loping shapes in the dark, carrying out their eponymous bodily functions. The night was black and brilliant, the bowl of the valley crisply silhouetted against the stars. A barn owl screeched. Other than that, the world was so hushed and still that Fen could hear the wolfhounds' panting, the bump of their paws on the grass, and his own heartbeat, accelerated and erratic from the wine, bounding in his ears. Everything that had happened to get him here suddenly seemed remote, someone else's sufferings. Even Downbourne seemed remote. And what seemed remotest of all was Moira. He pictured her face. The last time he had seen her. It felt like long, long ago.

"Lovely out here, eh?" Beam said.

Fen concurred. "And what a meal. It's ages since I've eaten that well. I'm so full my trousers are tight."

"Better than being so tight your trousers are full!"

Beam laughed mightily at his own witticism. Fen joined in.

"So tell me," Beam said, "any idea what your plans are? I mean, in the immediate future?"

"London," Fen replied. London, in his drunkenness, seemed all at once the London of old, the London of cliché, red double-deckers and Tower Bridge and pigeons and Hyde Park and newspaper vendors barking out headlines on street corners. Disney London, Swinging London, Ealing Comedy London. Faraway and lost. Big Ben chiming through the fog. Black cabs on rain-glassed roads. A fantasy capital that he could no more reach than he could reach Xanadu or Shangri-La.

"But not straight away," said Beam.

"I suppose not." Why not? Moira was there, and he wasn't a captive here as he had been in the *Jagannatha*, on the embankment, at Netherholm. He could leave any time.

"Even with a crutch."

"Yes. Even with."

"We're happy to have you here for as long as you want to stay. That's what I'm trying, in my clumsy way, to get at."

"Thank you. But I'm not sure..."

"Not sure...?"

Not sure he should stay. "Not sure what work I can do." He tapped the crutch.

"Teaching," Beam said, with a shrug, as if it was the most obvious thing in the world. "Take that mob of little tearaways you met this evening and knock a bit of knowledge into 'em. Think you could manage that?"

Fen thought about it. Thought he could. But: "It'd only be until my leg's useable. Would it be worth it?"

"A little bit of learning's better than none. Might stop 'em from turning into *complete* savages. We have books. The library can be your classroom. What d'you say?"

As Fen said yes, OK, he saw Beam grin and nod to himself. Though it might have been a trick of the starlight, he thought he glimpsed not just satisfaction in the grin but also regret, as if Beam was acknowledging some brief, private twinge of pessimism—the impossibility of bringing children up wise and true in a shattered, unmoored country like this one. Fen himself had had to battle with this pessimism on a regular basis. He laid a hand on Beam's shoulder.

"I'll do what I can in the time available."

Beam did not speak for a while, then said: "Words we should all live by. 'Do what you can in the time available.' A good philosophy. Yes."

Coming back through the dark from a tour of the borough's borders. Mushroom and me crammed together on the Mercedes's passenger seat, which is wider than a single but not quite a double. Craig at the wheel, peering ahead into the headlamps' projected glare. Slow going, the roadways treacherous at night, hidden holes, lumps of debris, a minefield of obstacles. Every so often, a glimpse of a figure scuttling into a doorway or down an alley, scared by the van. Like cockroaches running for cover when the kitchen light comes on. Lewisham eerie after nightfall, fitfully illuminated by the few streetlamps that haven't been vandalised, the occasional stray chink from an uncurtained window, the jump-and-flicker of a dustbin fire. A shadow land. Shadows folded over shadows. King Cunt's kingdom, but after sunset it belongs to others too, or so it seems. Furtive fugitives engaged on errands I don't dare speculate about. Sealed in the white van, we thread our way cautiously. I keep reiterating a small prayer: *thank God Craig's with me, thank God I'm with Craig*.

We've spent the day over by the western edge of Lewisham, where it folds into Peckham. Honor Oak Park, Brockley, and up towards New Cross, St Johns. Partly a state visit, partly an intelligence-gathering patrol. Word has come: the Frantiks have finally made their move. And so Craig's been consulting the locals. What have they heard? What have they seen? There are rumours. Running battles around Peckham Rye Common and Nunhead Cemetery. Fires towards the south, down Dulwich way. Nothing substantiated, but no reason to think the rumours aren't true. Everybody, understandably, is pretty anxious. Where reassurance is called for, Craig has reassured. Where scolding is called for, Craig has scolded. King Cunt has the situation under control. Lewisham is not going to be affected. The Frantiks and the Bulldogs have an agreement. O ye of little faith! The King is looking out for his subjects. He has their best interests at heart. Never fret. Never worry.

Beside me, Mushroom picks his nose, coring out a long brown rind of dried snot. Either he thinks I don't see or he doesn't care if I do. He studies the snot, turning it this way and that on his fingertip, then pops it into his mouth. Yum. I really hate Mushroom. But I'd far rather it was him sitting squashed up against me than, say, Neville. Mushroom, at least, is openly repellent. With Neville, it's worse because it's all inside. He makes my skin crawl.

Craig seems all right with what we've found out today. Nothing more or less than he expected. He estimates that Peckham will be fully under the Frantik Posse's control within a fortnight. Those members of the Riot Squad that the Frantiks don't kill, they'll chase out. Some of them, inevitably, will fetch up in Lewisham, where they'll get pretty short shrift from the locals and from the Bulldogs.

The only thing that troubles him—slightly—is the International Community noticing what's happening. It's a slim possibility, but all it takes is a chance flyby, a wink from a spy satellite, and down will come fire and great punishment from heaven. He doesn't give a shit about Peckham getting pounded, but the International Community isn't noted for its pinpoint accuracy. The odd stray missile may land on Lewisham. All the same, a slim possibility. A risk factor he can live with.

At last the gate to the compound comes into view. I never, ever thought I would be glad to see it. It opens as we approach; Craig doesn't even have to decelerate. We glide through, we're in. The gate closes. Safe.

A vague thought: *I'm trapped again*. But it doesn't feel like that any more. It feels like that less than ever. This trip outside has been instructive. Apart from making me realise I'm safer off here in Fort Bulldog than out there in the wilds of the city, it's also made plain the extent to which Craig trusts me. There were several times today when I could have made a bid for freedom. Craig was busy talking to people, and Mushroom, obviously at Craig's instruction, was hovering close by me all the time, but I'm pretty sure I could have given him the slip and outrun him if I'd wanted to. And I'm pretty sure Craig knew that. He also knows I wouldn't leave Zoë behind. But still, he trusts me. And he wanted me to come on the trip. He asked me to. He wanted me to see him at work. And every now and then he's asked me for my opinion. A vote of confidence there.

There's something going on between us, that's for sure. Developing. I just have no idea what it is. The closest I can get to a name for it is an *understanding*. Not like in a Jane Austen novel, though. "Reader, it seemed that Mr Cunt and I had come to an understanding which would, when in the fullness of time it reached fruition, grant the both of us much happiness." No, not like that at all. But an understanding nonetheless.

Soon as we've parked the van, Craig heads off to share with the lads the info he's gathered today. Mushroom goes with him. I traipse back to the house. *Our* house.

Lauren's taking a bath, running through a medley of tunes as she lies soaking. *La la, tum de tee, mmm-mmmm, will always love yoooou*. She hasn't got a bad voice, just not as good as she thinks it is. I find Zoë in the living room. She's flicking through one of the magazines she found yesterday. There was a whole stash of them at the back of a cupboard. Time capsules from a healthier, wealthier age. Including an issue of *Siren*, one I worked on. I checked for my name in the contributors' credits. There it was: Deputy Chief Sub-Editor—Moira Grainger. It was like finding an old snapshot of myself. *God yes, that's me*. No, it didn't have quite that sense of familiarity. It was more as if I'd come across a name in print that just so happened to be the same as mine. Who was she, this Moira Grainger? Well-paid, career-obsessed, determined to succeed, enjoying a hectic social life, interested in nothing but the world immediately around her, happy with that. If we met, the two of us, we'd hardly recognise each other.

The magazine Zoë is reading is one of those teen-girl titles. (There were several of them in the stash. A girl Zoë's age must have lived here, before.) Garish fluorescent layout. All those hunky pop stars, those fashion tips, those tricks for losing weight, those photo-love stories. Messages from another planet, to Zoë. When I come into the living room, I see she's looking at the problem page. No agony aunt could offer advice for what *she* has been through.

"How are you, Zoë? How's your day been?"

"Oh, fine. Bit boring."

Boring's good. Thank heaven for boring. Once again I marvel at how well she's bearing up. She seems to sleep a lot, but otherwise there's little outward sign of trauma. She says she barely remembers anything that happened to her in the recreation zones. Perhaps she believes this. Perhaps it's even true.

She asks how the trip went. I tell her about it. She isn't that interested, but listens anyway.

"Will we be all right? The fighting and that?"

"We'll be fine. Are you hungry?"

"Yeah. Lauren said it's your turn to cook tonight, so we've had to wait for you."

She accompanies me to the kitchen and for a while just watches as I put on a pan of water to boil and start cutting up some potatoes. I don't know teenage girls. I used to be one but I don't remember it well enough. I don't realise that Zoë wants to talk about something but requires some cue from me to get her going. Eventually, seeing she's not going to receive it, she starts talking anyway.

"Moira... I heard something today. Something I wasn't supposed to."

"Oh?" It comes out more curt than I intended. I'm just about to hear some trivial piece of gossip, aren't I? Some comment Lauren made about me, probably not complimentary.

"Um, yeah. That bloke came round this afternoon. That one who was in Downbourne. He was the leader there. The one with the tooth."

"Neville." Now she has my attention. "He came round? But he knew Craig was out today."

"He wanted to see American Lauren." Children have a knack for nicknames. They never come up with anything subtle, but they always get it dead-on. "I was having a snooze. At least, I was till Neville arrived. I woke up when I heard him come in. He asked Lauren if they were alone. She said hold on a moment and came upstairs and looked in on me. I was in your room, because you said I could go in there during the day if I wanted to?"

She's checking to make sure the offer is still valid. She has to sleep on the sofa down here at night, so I made sure with Craig that she could use our bed in the daytime, somewhere more comfortable if she wants a nap. I nod.

"I pretended I was still asleep," she continues. "Lauren said my name but I didn't move or anything. So they went out into the garden and they started talking. They thought they were being quiet but I could still hear them, because, well..." Here she looks guilty. "Because I went into the bathroom and listened. The window was open. I knelt right by it. I know I was being nosy, but it was strange him visiting, Neville, because Lauren always says how much she doesn't like him, doesn't she, and here he was being all friendly and nice and wanting to talk to her and that. And I think it was good I listened, because what they talked about was you. You and Craig."

I hold up a hand—*ssh a moment*. I listen at the kitchen door. Upstairs, Lauren's still warbling away.

"All right. Go on. Just keep it low. Me and Craig?" I still have a vague feeling that this is going to be just gossip, Neville saying he doesn't think much of me, something along those lines. I still have that feeling, but it's more hope than expectation.

"I didn't catch every single word of it," Zoë says. "They *were* being quiet. Especially Neville. But they chatted about this and that for a while and then he asked Lauren about you, what she thought about you, and she said... you're not her favourite person in the world."

Can't fault Zoë for her discretion. I'm sure what Lauren said about me was a lot less polite. "Well, she isn't mine either, so that's all right."

"She said she thinks you're bad for Craig."

"Did she say why?"

"She might've. I missed a bit. Someone in one of the other houses turned on some music very loud, then turned it down, and then she was talking about me, not you any more, about how it was a 'pain in the ass' having me here because the house isn't big enough for all of us. And Neville said yeah, like he didn't really care, and then he started going on about the other night, you know, at the houses where all the women are, when you and Craig came, and there was that arguing because I'd..." She shies away from mentioning what she did. She doesn't want to think about it. "He said because of me you'd made Craig look stupid. Stupid and... 'pussy-whipped'?"

"It's another way of saying stupid."

"Oh." Not quite convinced, but she gives me the benefit of the doubt. "And he said a lot of 'the boys' have been grumbling about you. And about Craig. Apparently they think he should never have made a pact with that lot in Camberwell, and he's losing his edge. They aren't respecting him as much as they used to."

Is that true? Or is it just what Neville wants to believe? "I bet Lauren stood up for Craig."

"Well, she did, but it was funny because it was like she really had to try. Like her heart wasn't in it. She said she was surprised by herself but even *she* was beginning to wonder about him. And she said she thought you were to blame. She said if there was some way to get rid of you..."

A soft, sudden chill. "Get rid of me?"

"I don't think that was exactly her words. Maybe get you out of the house. Away from Craig. Anyhow, Neville said he didn't think Craig would stand for that, and besides the problem was more him than you, and Lauren said, 'There's a problem?' and Neville said, 'There's definitely a problem.' I remember that clearly. 'There's definitely a problem.' And Lauren had a cigarette then because she needed to think, she said. And while she was thinking, Neville went on about the Bulldogs getting more and more unhappy with the way things are being run here, and about how there's talk of maybe someone should make a challenge for the leadership, and about how if that was going to happen then now would be a good time, or soon, while this Peckham business is going on, while Craig's distracted. And... That's about all I can remember. Yeah."

"You're sure? Nothing else?"

"Yeah. At the end, though, Lauren was being much nicer to Neville than when he arrived. When he arrived she was all 'Craig's not in, what do you want?' but when she was showing him out she was more 'Well, you know, I'm glad you came and told me all this, I don't know if there's much we can do but maybe we should have another chat soon, honey'. She didn't say 'honey' actually, but it was kind of like when she *does* say 'honey', you know, when she's talking to Craig, all soft and caring."

Good old Lauren. I doubt she really believes the King's throne is under threat. I certainly don't think it is, and she's ten times more loyal to him than I am. But still, it never hurts to keep on the pretender's good side. Just in case.

"Does this mean you're in trouble, Moira? Over what you did for me?"

"I don't think so."

"Because if you are, I'm really sorry."

"Don't worry about it."

"What about Craig? Is *he* in trouble?"

"If he is, it's nothing he can't handle."

"So are you going to tell him?"

A very good question. Am I?

"I don't know, Zoë. We'll have to see."

THEY TESTED HIM at first, but this was no more than he expected. It was what children, in groups, did when someone new was put in charge of them. That exploratory prod-and-probe. *How much can we get away with?* The trick, he knew, was not to let them rile him. Rise above it. Assert his authority gently, calmly. Allow them some leeway to begin with, not put them in their place too soon, give them the sense that he was patient, amenable, draw them up to his tolerance threshold and slightly over, so that they would never be quite sure where it was, then snap them back down with a single, sharp, well-chosen comment. That was how it worked. That was how you turned a mob into a class.

In this instance, it did not work.

The seven children at Fairfield Hall were not a *tabula rasa*. That much Fen swiftly established. From the youngest, five, to the oldest, thirteen, they were numerate and literate. Some parental educating had gone on so he did not have to start from scratch, which was a relief. But they were part-feral, too. With the adults preoccupied with planting and cultivating and gathering, pickling and preserving and cold storing, herding and hewing and generally keeping on top of the basic necessities of existence, the children had been left pretty much to their own devices. And children who have been left to their own devices will, as Golding, Barrie, Ballard and others have shown, run wild.

So they did not like being cooped up every morning in the library with Fen. They did not like being read to and having to read. Being made to do sums. Being made to learn about England and Europe and the other nations and continents of the world. Being asked to wrap their tongues around the strange new syllables of French and German. Being expected to find interesting such outlandishly irrelevant concepts as atoms and history and moon landings and monarchic succession. Where was the fun in all that? It wasn't anywhere near as exciting as, say, climbing a tree to its topmost branches, or watching a lamb being born or slaughtered, or damming up the stream, or swimming starkers in the lake, or investigating the Hall's many attics with their plethora of dust-coated artefacts (always something new and inexplicable to discover). The children fidgeted and champed and chafed, and at the end of each morning, when Fen finally allowed them to leave, they exploded out of the library like peas out of a malfunctioning pressure cooker.

He thought the problem would right itself with time. If he just hung on, the children would soon come to realise that the lessons were to their benefit.

Then they started not turning up.

The first time, it was just the one absentee, the eldest child there, the leader of the pack, Christopher. Fen decided not to waste time looking for him. The boy could be anywhere. He taught his remaining six pupils as normal, as if nothing was awry, and later, when Christopher put in an appearance at lunch, he took him aside and had a gentle word. Shouldn't set a bad example to the rest, et cetera.

The following day, Christopher dutifully showed up, but three of the others were missing. This was unacceptable. Fen enlisted the four attendees' aid in finding them. The hunt took up most of the morning, and everyone except Fen found it hilarious. Up in the attics, out among the rhododendra, down by the stables—to the children it was one big romp, a supervised version of the games they normally played. One after another the truants were rounded up, and in the hour remaining before lunch Fen drilled the class on *être*, *avoir* and *aller*, making them chant the conjugations till they, and he, were heartily sick of irregular French verbs.

"I'm not sure about this," he confessed to Beam that afternoon. They were down in the damp of the wine cellar—vintage-packed vault leading to vintage-packed vault, like the tomb of some bibulous pharaoh. "I don't know if it isn't too late for these kids."

"Hmmm," said Beam. It was unclear whether he was musing on what Fen had just said or on the bottle of Beaujolais whose label he was examining by torchlight.

"They're just not responding to me. They're bright, all of them, very bright, but they've no discipline, no attention span."

"Perhaps..." Beam said.

"Perhaps...?"

"Or perhaps not." Beam returned the bottle to its place in the rack. "Too flowery. One needs something 'bigger' with lamb casserole."

Beam, to Fen's chagrin, did not seem in a mood to discuss the subject of the children's education. It wasn't until they were leaving the cellar, each carrying as many bottles of Cabernet Sauvignon as he could, that

Beam gave any indication he had been listening to Fen at all, and then all he said was: "Keep at it, old chap. I know you can do it. Be prepared to meet them halfway."

Fen was of the opinion that he had already met the children halfway. Had, indeed, gone further than that. But he resolved to persevere with the lessons. He owed it to Beam to keep trying, at least.

The next morning, all seven pupils failed to show. They had got it into their heads that hiding from their teacher was not only an enjoyable exercise but an honourable one as well, and perhaps even an educational one. They set themselves the goal of finding places to stow away that were so abstruse, so cunning, that they would remain undiscovered all morning. It was a test of their wits against Fen's, their ingenuity versus his perspicacity.

They won. And, in another sense, they lost.

Fen did not go looking for them. He stayed in the library, quietly thumbing through a copy of *The Jungle Book*. He stayed there even through lunch. When he didn't appear for the meal, and his absence was remarked upon by the adults, the children exchanged questioning glances. Afterwards, *they* went searching for *him*. Perhaps he had chosen to turn the tables. Perhaps *he* had gone hiding, expecting to be found.

The last place any of them thought to look, because it seemed too obvious a place for their teacher to hide, was the room in which he taught them. But one by one they eventually wound up at the library, having exhausted all other possibilities. Each entered, saw Fen sitting, calmly reading, and went straight to the big table in the middle of the room and pulled up a chair. They none of them could understand why, precisely, they did this. Something to do with the way Fen had been waiting for them, the way he said nothing when they came in, the way this made them feel. Awkward. A bit unhappy. They sensed they had hurt his feelings. They had never meant to hurt his feelings.

From then on, there was no more playing truant. A lesson of a different kind had been taught, and learned. The children began to take to Fen, and to tutelage. They recognised that he had out-psyched them, and it earned him their admiration. If he could beat them at their own game like that, he must have *something* going for him, therefore his lessons must have *something* going for them too, therefore it might be wise to pay attention.

For his part, Fen began tailoring his usual teaching style to accommodate this group of children's particular waywardness. He took them out of the library whenever he could, giving them fresh air and sunshine and a sense, if not the actuality, of freedom. He encouraged exploration of the environment, drawing instructive examples from trees and fields and buildings and animals and the contents of the Hall's attics. He chaired round-table discussions, nudging the proceedings along with simple, reflexive questions that were intended to lead his pupils to an understanding of their own ignorance—the Socratic method. He kept rote-learning to a minimum. And he began to enjoy his job in a way he had not for years. At Downbourne teaching had become, while not a chore, something he did only because he was not fitted for much else. Sometimes, especially after Moira lost the babies, he had had to drag himself to school in the mornings. What good was it, he had wondered, instilling knowledge in kids who might never get the chance to make use of it. The hope of every Englander was that present circumstances could not pertain for ever. That was just about all that kept people going, belief in an inevitable end to the hardships and exigencies of post-Gamble life. But what if there was never going to be any end? What if the International Community kept up its war of attrition indefinitely, whittling and whittling until England was no more? Why bother, if that was the case? Why bother teaching? Why bother doing anything? He had grappled with these doubts. Everyone had to. And most of the time he had got the better of them, but sometimes they had got the better of him.

Now, he was sure—as sure as he could be—that his efforts were not in vain. Christopher, Toby, Megan, little Scarlett—he felt them burgeoning under his care. Hungry young minds opening like flowers. William, who had a surreal sense of humour. Gap-toothed Serena, away in her own little world half the time. The aptly-named Storm, with his touchpaper temper. Fen forged a relationship with them closer than the usual teacher-and-class. The seven-strong gang embraced him. He became one of them, their eighth member and, Christopher graciously abdicating the role, their leader. He assumed responsibility for organising their afternoons as well as their mornings. A tennis racquet and ball, unearthed by Beam at Fen's request, provided—along with some wooden fence-stakes—the wherewithal for games of cricket and rounders. Crutch-hampered, Fen umpired. The other adults postponed their after-lunch labours in order to spectate. Usually one of them could be persuaded to take part, making up numbers so that there were two even teams. On a couple of occasions the adult was Beam himself. Not much of a runner, it must be said, but the children made allowances, fielding in slow motion so as to give him time to waddle and huff his way between the wickets or from rounders post to rounders post. Crap and Piss liked to join in too, but since their involvement invariably culminated in one or other of them making off with the ball and refusing to give it up, it was soon agreed that they be banished indoors for the duration of play.

Dealing with the children full-time, being one of them, took a lot out of Fen. Every night, he would clump upstairs to bed exhausted, his left leg a symphony of aches. His room lay at the far end of the Hall's west wing, two doors down from where Megan and her parents, Ben and Sally, were quartered. He slept in a creaking four-poster with a capacious trough in the middle of its mattress. He never closed the curtains. He liked to drift off watching the night outside, pure and ancient, with the window casements left open so as to invite in breezes and the countryside's whisperings.

Gradually the sufferings he had endured prior to arriving at the Hall began to fade, slipping into that recess of memory in which everything seems to have been exaggerated and you're pretty certain that what happened to you was nowhere near as bad as it felt at the time. He could almost laugh now about being beaten up by a Bulldog, and about the non-physical, though no less thoroughgoing, assault he had undergone at the hands of the Salterites. Ordeals were metamorphosising into anecdotes. He was incorporating his recent experiences, becoming someone shaped by them rather than someone still reeling from them. It was amazing what a difference a few days, a regularly filled belly, beautiful surroundings, and a renewed sense of job satisfaction, could make. It was as if he had entered a whole new country; had, just a handful of miles from the railway embankment and Netherholm College, crossed a border into a realm so utterly unlike either of those places that it was hard sometimes to believe it even existed.

There has to be a catch. Something, somehow, has to be wrong with this situation.

But the days passed and no fly garnished the ointment, no bump appeared in the road, no serpent hissed in Eden. Fairfield Hall was nothing other than it appeared to be, and thank heavens for that.

For Fen felt he had found something here. Something like home, but not quite. Something more fundamental than that.

Increasingly he found himself thinking, *I could stay here.*

Not just till his leg was better.

I could stay here for good.

THE FOUR RIOT Squadders kneel on the ground and weep and beg for their lives.

You'd think they were tough nuts, to judge by their thick necks, their combat trousers and boots, the ragged red "R" of scar tissue that each of them sports on the underside of his left forearm, razor-etched there. Hard as nails. You'd think they wouldn't even know *how* to cry. But they're crying now, like four man-sized babies. Blubbing and pleading with King Cunt. The Frantiks have overrun Peckham, they tell him. They're killing any Riot Squadders they find. The "R" on their arms is as good as a death sentence. Please, they implore. They'll do anything. Join the Bulldogs, anything. Just please spare them.

Unfortunately for them, Craig isn't going to. Unfortunately for Craig, he has no choice in the matter.

It wasn't easy, letting him know about Neville's conversation with Lauren. It wasn't easy finding a way and an opportunity to broach the subject. For one thing, he's been hellishly busy with the Peckham situation this past couple of weeks—sifting through the reports coming in from the borough border, sending out Bulldog patrols both to repel fleeing Riot Squad members and as a show of strength to reassure the local populace, keeping channels of communication open with the Frantik Posse, marshalling his resources so that he'll be able to take advantage of the Riot Squad's capitulation when it comes (and it's pretty much a foregone conclusion now; Craig just requires confirmation of the fact from the Frantiks themselves). We've barely had a quiet moment together, he and I, since the Frantiks' attack was launched. At night, he comes to bed so late that I'm already asleep, and, if I happen to be awake, he zonks out as soon as his head hits the pillow, without time for much more than a mumbled "g'night".

But the problem didn't only lie with how busy he's been. It lay with me, too. The number of times I almost came out and told him, and then balked. Neville's his friend, his best mate. Would he believe me if I told him his schoolboy pal was plotting against him? And my source being Zoë—it's not as if she doesn't have an axe to grind. Neville was the one who took her captive in the first place, the one who offered to beat her up at the recreation zones when Craig wouldn't. *I* have no reason to think she made up the stuff she heard, but Craig might.

There was never the right moment.

Then there was.

Last night.

It wasn't premeditated.

In fact, nothing about last night was premeditated.

It just happened.

And I'm not ashamed of it. Any of it.

It was the way Craig looked as he was getting undressed. The hour was late, past one, and he thought I was asleep and so, as usual, he didn't turn on the main bedroom light, just left the bedroom door open and used the light coming in from the landing to see by. Courteous.

And it was the tiredness of his actions, the clumsy way he removed his football shirt, fumbling it over his head as though it was a conundrum whose solution he could not quite fathom.

And it was the contours of his torso—that magnificent torso—combined with the slight stoop in his shoulders that I hadn't noticed there before: the weight of care, the burden of leadership.

And it was the lost look on his face, the expression people get when the only thing that'll help them is the oblivion of sleep

I felt sorry for him.

I wasn't scared of him, not now, not any more.

I wanted to comfort him.

It just happened.

He got into bed. I took the initiative. I reached across. My hand between his legs. Took hold of him. Kindled him. Quickened him. Straddled him. Rode him. It was over with in no time. He took part, distantly, a little puzzled, but his hands were strong on me, and the digging grip of his fingers deepened, and he gasped, and it was over with. I can't say I found it earth-shattering, but I can't deny there was pleasure in it. The sight of his face relaxing afterwards, tension ebbing out, tightness unclenching. This giant underneath me, eased by my ministrations.

I thought that, after I rolled off him, he would doze off straight away, but he didn't.

"You know why I'm called King Cunt, Moira?" he said, after a minute or so of silence.

"You're 'more of a cunt than anyone else'."

"Yeah. Yeah, that's what I tell people. It's less complicated. Saves bother. It's not really why, though."

For one terrible moment I think he's going to start boasting about his sexual prowess. Talk about inappropriate!

But he says: "You've heard of King Canute, right? 'Course you have. Bloke who sat on a beach, commanded the tide to go back, got his feet wet. Every schoolkid knows that story. Well, I read about him once, in a magazine, or maybe a book. Or maybe it was something I saw on the telly. Can't remember. Anyway, apparently the way we spell his name isn't the way his name's supposed to be spelled. You know, we spell it 'can-yoot', but actually in Norwegian or whatever, it's 'ker-nut'. See, en, you, tee. Now, I'm a bit dyslexic. I look at a word and the letters sometimes kind of float around a bit. So I'm looking at 'Cnut' and what do I see? Cunt. Amazing what a difference swapping two letters round can make to a word. And I thought it was quite funny. 'King Cunt'. It just stuck in my head. One of those things you don't forget. One of those things you tuck away for later use and you don't know why. And then, when things started falling apart a few years back... It was like a tide. A tide of chaos. Remember?"

I remember.

"Crashing over everything. The country going mad. England going under. And as things began to fall apart, I realised... If I say I realised my destiny, I'll sound like a total ponce. I realised what I had to do. Somebody had to pull things together. Somebody had to try and hold back that tide. But it had to be by force. That was the only way it could be done. Just words alone, grand gestures, wouldn't work."

"As King Canute showed."

"Yeah. Exactly. And I knew that, even by force, I couldn't bring the whole of London under control, let alone the whole country." He laughs at the absurdity of *that*, which suggests to me that at one point he did consider it. "But maybe a small area of London. Maybe where I lived, here, Lewisham. Maybe with foot-soldiers under me, a small army, I could do it. I wasn't alone in having this idea, of course. The Unlucky Gamble gave rise to a lot of people like me, especially in the big cities. Selected us, in a way. Remade us. Moulded us into the thing we had to be. People who under other circumstances probably wouldn't ever have made much of an impact on the world—suddenly it was our time.

We were needed. Here, in London, we were needed most of all. And so I stopped being Craig Smith and started being someone else."

"King Cunt."

"Seemed like the right name for the job. And it worked. The whole thing worked. The name, what I wanted to do. It wasn't easy. God, all that fighting, that staking out territory and defending it. Getting the Bulldogs together, moulding them into shape, giving them an identity they could be proud of. And then seeing off other gangs. One long constant struggle. But eventually the effort paid off and things settled down, and I'd achieved something. I knew it. I'd brought some stability and order back into people's lives. I hadn't made things perfect again, but King Cunt had done what King Canute couldn't do. He'd held back the tide. Only, now it looks like..."

All at once he seemed to be speaking from deep inside himself, his voice thick, cracked with exhaustion.

"I'm trying to keep it all together, Moira," he said. "You can see that, can't you? I'm trying to, but it's not easy. It's not enough just to make the right decisions. You have to make the *best* decisions. All the time. Or else you lose respect, and then you lose everything."

And I realised I'd never heard him so vulnerable.

"They want you to be infallible, and if you're not, they'll turn on you. One wrong move is all it takes, and it's gone. Everything you've worked for, fought for. Gone."

Or so lonely. I never realised how lonely till then.

"You think you have trust. You don't. All you have is whatever people find it convenient to give you."

Now.

"I think there's something you should know about Neville..." I began.

I didn't have to say much more.

Craig wasn't angry. I'd expected rage, I'd expected cursing, but all that came was bitter acknowledgement. He told me how he'd been aware for some time that all was not right within the Bulldog ranks. He told me that Neville was the main source of the unrest, Neville waging a covert campaign against him, Neville spreading discontent through the compound, but doing it quietly, subtly, insidiously, planting a seed of doubt here, a seed of doubt there, always with the knowledge that, as King Cunt's best friend and second-in-command, he was above suspicion, no one in their right mind would believe *him* capable of treachery, not *Neville*.

Craig, it transpired, had known about all this for quite some while.

And when I asked him why he hadn't taken steps to remedy the situation, he said he couldn't, at least not openly. "The lads see me and Neville as inseparable. He's been with me right from the very beginning. I can't turn on him. I'd be finished for sure if I did. Reputation would be shot to shit. The only way I can handle what he's doing is by being better than ever at my job. Keep the lads on my side by continuing to set an example."

And I saw then—and see even more clearly right now, with the four captured Riot Squadders awaiting King Cunt's verdict on whether they are to live or die—how well Neville has manipulated things. He's manoeuvred Craig onto a narrow, knife-edge pathway, with a sheer precipice either side. Craig has no choice but to keep going forwards, to prove himself time and time again to the Bulldogs, to be more and more the King Cunt they expect him to be, ruthless leader, hardest of the hard, to continue to pull off this precarious balancing act. Because the slightest misstep now, and he will fall.

And Zoë. She, I understand now, was part of it, part of Neville's scheme. A test. A provocation. How would King Cunt react when he found a fifteen-year-old in the recreation zones? He reacted, with my help, according to his sense of morality... and the decision gave Neville yet more ammunition against him.

Which is why these four members of the Peckham Riot Squad have to die. It's their lives against Craig's credibility. And while he could show leniency towards a fifteen-year-old girl and just about get away with it, he can't do the same with members of a rival gang.

It's there in the Bulldogs' eyes as they look on. It was there before, but I mistook it for admiration. It's zeal. Fanaticism. Thanks to Neville's machinations, the Bulldogs now believe in King Cunt, the ideal, far more than in King Cunt, the man.

Which makes him more, not less, vulnerable. A man cannot disappoint. An ideal can.

The Bulldogs need Craig to be what they want him to be. As they stand here in a ring around the Riot Squadders, restless, bloodthirsty, they're waiting for King Cunt to give the word, waiting for him to demonstrate that he truly deserves their worship.

And he does give the word.

Because, this time around, he has no choice.

"Do it."

There's a roar of approval, and the Bulldogs move in on the four Riot Squadders.

The compound was formerly a housing estate. There are lamp-posts. The Bulldogs have rope.

I don't stay to watch. Neither does Craig. As the Riot Squadders are hauled off struggling and screaming, he stalks away, head down, not looking at me, not looking at anyone. I go with him, but I might as well be walking alone.

It doesn't take long. I hear, behind me, four separate sets of jeers and yells, and then it's over with.

Afterwards, a sated silence descends on the compound.

The British Bulldogs are content again.

For now.

It got better.

Christopher's mother, Jessica Myers, was a divorcee. At first Fen assumed she was Beam's girlfriend. The two flirted constantly, teased each other brutally, were often to be found in a conspiratorial clinch, giggling over some private joke. She was a small, robust woman, very pretty, with big round eyes that gave her a look of perpetual wonderment. (Fen found out later she was severely short-sighted but too vain for spectacles.) Among her faults, she had a laugh which, had she been any less pretty, would have made you want to throttle her. Indeed, when she laughed it sounded as though she *was* being throttled. Torture to listen to. She was, moreover, one of the most artless and tactless people Fen had ever met.

And yet, and yet...

It soon became clear to him that she was not Beam's girlfriend. She and Beam had known each other since childhood. Theirs was an intricate intimacy, established during innocence and adolescence, playful and sexually charged but always quite perfectly platonic.

And as the only unattached woman at the Hall, it was not long before she was sizing Fen up as a potential partner. She knew about Moira, of course, but Fen was nonetheless, to all intents and purposes, unattached too. It was not as if Moira was anywhere nearby. London was another country, another *world*. Nor was it as if Fen was likely to be departing for the capital any day soon. That, indeed, was looking an ever more remote prospect. Everyone at the Hall could see that. They could see how Fen was settling in, how comfortable he was becoming in his role as the children's pedagogue-cum-ringleader. He was fitting quite nicely, thank you, into the warp and weft of Fairfield life. They could sense his growing desire to remain, his dwindling eagerness to leave. He was mentioning Moira and London less and less. His mission, his quest, was receding in importance. Perhaps he had already abandoned it but had yet to admit this to himself.

So, by this way of thinking, Jessica was perfectly entitled to go after him if she wanted to. And he, in turn, was perfectly entitled to reciprocate.

He didn't, though. At least, not to begin with. He was flattered by her advances. Jessica was, her laugh notwithstanding, an enticing proposition, and it gave him a delicious and queerly nostalgic thrill to be the target of a female's attentions once again. As a husband, you kind of got out of the habit of thinking that just any woman could find you sexually desirable. You took it for granted that your wife did, and there seemed little need to consider the prospects any further than that. To be reminded that you were appealing to a broader section of womankind, that you were, besides all else, a *man*—this was not an unpleasurable thing.

All the same, he *was* married, that fact had not changed, so for a while he kept Jessica at arm's length, and this he did through a combination of evasion and obtuseness. He pretended to be oblivious to her interest in him. Though her intentions could not have been more obvious, nor her overtures less subtle, he still managed to give the impression that he had no idea what she was up to. When, for example, she told him that there was nothing sexier than a man who got on well with kids, he replied, "And nothing more likely to get that man arrested." When she complained one evening about the size of her bed—"I can't think of anything more depressing than a double bed with only one person to occupy it"—he suggested she get Crap and Piss to join her in it. When she expounded a philosophy to the effect that nowadays, with England in the precarious state it was in, people shouldn't hang about, there was no point putting off till tomorrow what you could do today, "gather ye rosebuds" and all that, Fen's reply was: "You know, I always used to think *carpe diem* was Latin for 'death to fishes!'"

There was, he could not deny, some delight to be had in frustrating his admirer like this, in being so deliberately knuckleheaded. However, the fun wore thin pretty quickly, and at the back of his mind there was always that feeling of *why not?* Jessica fancied him. She was lonely. She was lovely. Moira was miles away and probably lost to him for ever; had, in a sense, been lost to him a long time back. Why not take advantage of what Jessica was offering? Why not treat himself to her? Why not? Why the damn hell not?

LATE ON A drizzly Sunday afternoon, Fen and Beam were playing billiards in the games room. Low leaden light came in through the rain-ticked windows. Crap and Piss were sprawled in a corner, with only the occasional whistling sigh from either to prove they weren't completely comatose. Throughout the house there was a similar air of profound repose. Sunday was, by Beam's decree, a day of rest. No work, other than culinary-related activities, could be done on a Sunday.

"A lack of real responsibility," Beam said, squaring up for his next shot. "That's always been the problem." With a deft, deceptively soft thrust of his cue he ricocheted the red ball into one of the side pockets. "Fourteen."

Fen fished the ball out of the pocket and placed it on its spot. This task, along with supervision of the scoreboard, was pretty much the extent of his involvement in the game. Beam was a billiards expert, his skills honed by a lifetime of practice on this very table. Fen had played pub pool a few times, but to no great success, and anyway billiards, as Beam said, was an altogether higher order of game, as far removed from pool as Picasso is from painting-by-numbers. A game of refinement, of space and angles, of rebounds and strategy and a wonderfully pure simplicity. A game that demanded an archer's eye and a surgeon's hand. Whereas pool—well, pool was, for want of a better word, *American*.

"You mean politicians aren't directly accountable for anything they do," Fen said.

"Precisely. Precisely." Beam moved around the table, sized up his options, leaned over, and assertively scored a cannon. "Take this last lot we had," he said, as the balls rolled to a rest. "Perfect example. The ones who buggered everything up for everybody. The ones to blame for the mess this country's in. Where are they now, eh?"

"Bermuda, last I heard."

"Exactly. Bermuda. Holed up in the tropics. Soaking up the sun while the rest of us get shat on."

"'Parliament in exile'."

"Ah, yes." Beam recognised the quotation, part of the speech made by the Prime Minister shortly before the House of Commons voted *nem. con.* to up stakes and relocate to the Caribbean.

"'Waiting until national circumstances are conducive to the re-establishment of effective control'," Fen added.

"Ha!" Beam careened his cue ball off Fen's and into a corner pocket. "Eighteen." He stepped back, appraising, while Fen returned the ball to the baize. "Always were a lying, weaselly lot, weren't they? Trouble is, that's par for the course where politicians are concerned. Like I said, a lack of real responsibility. Tell me, when was the last time you saw a cabinet minister get it in the neck because of some poor decision he made, some catastrophic error of judgement that ruined dozens, perhaps even hundreds of lives? I mean *really* get it in the neck?" He allowed Fen a second to answer, or rather, not answer. "I'll tell you. Never. At worst he might have had to resign, but even then you can bet there'd be some other government post waiting for him, or a seat on the board of a blue-chip corporation, a job in broadcasting, a lucrative publishing deal for his memoirs. Something like that to cushion his fall. And he might show remorse for his mistakes, might even *feel* remorse, but he's still got away scot-free while the people he shafted are left to suffer. If the owner of a business screws up, his livelihood is on the line, isn't it? If a sea captain blunders, his ship goes down and most likely him with it. But a cabinet minister?" He bent down, his belly doubling over the cushion, and lined up his cue. "See my point?"

Fen dutifully asked the question he knew Beam wanted him to ask. "So how would you do it? How would you go about introducing a level of accountability into government?"

Beam stroked the cue back and forth, as if storing up kinetic energy for the shot. "Simple. Link every politician's fortunes intimately with those of the nation. If a Chancellor of the Exchequer, say, wastes taxpayers' money—and we're all too painfully aware that Chancellors of the Exchequer can and do, to a disastrous degree—then instead of him using nothing but more taxpayers' money to make up the loss, he ought to have to contribute a significant sum out of his own pocket, enough that he shares everyone else's financial pain. And the Defence Secretary. It should be decreed that, in the event of war, the Defence Secretary's nearest and dearest are flown to straight to the front line. That way, as it's *his* next of kin at risk rather than someone else's, he'll be much more inclined to choose diplomatic resolution over conflict. And the Home Secretary should be made to live in the most run-down, most crime-ridden housing estate in the land. Policing problems would be solved in no time!" At last Beam unleashed the shot, and there was a ripple of clacks as his cue ball met both the other balls and all three scattered across the table, rebounded chaotically and collided again. "Double cannon. Twenty-two."

"And the Health Secretary should never be allowed to go private for an operation," said Fen.

"Exactly."

"The Transport Minister should have to travel everywhere by bus or train."

"See? It's a very easy system to get the hang of."

"Never work."

"Why not?"

"Nobody'd be willing to become a politician under those conditions."

"Oh, I'm not saying it should be all stick. There'd be carrot as well. Financial incentives. Bonus payouts for particularly commendable pieces of governance."

"Decided on how? By whom?"

"An administrative body drawn from a representative cross-section of the electorate. They'd deliver annual reports on the government's performance and mete out rewards and punishments as they saw fit. What I think you'd get, you see, if this scheme were put into action, is a better class of politician. Men and women keen to do their best, to do what's right instead of what's expedient."

"I'm getting the distinct impression you don't think much of politicians."

"Line 'em all up and shoot 'em," Beam said cheerfully. "Of course, I don't ever expect to this little utopian fantasy of mine to come to pass. It's just a dream I have. A dream of leaders who do us justice rather than do us over." He fired off a quick shot which unaccountably failed to score and thus brought his break to an end. "Your turn, old chap."

Fen picked up his cue and hobbled over to the table. He had recently graduated from the crutch to a walking stick—a walking stick which, like almost everything else at Fairfield, came with a detailed provenance, an oral history. Beam's Great Aunt Ernestine had been its first user. Beam's father had availed himself of it next, as his arthritis set in. A venerable stick, a well-scuffed stick, now helping a third generation of the halt and lame to get about. Fen hooked it on the edge of the table by its deerhorn handle and, taking his weight on his good leg, crouched down with the cue.

"Bit of topspin," Beam advised, and it was good advice. "Well done!"

The game proceeded, and so did Beam's disquisition on leadership. For a model of sensible ruling, he said, one only had to consider the beehive, specifically the type he used, the British National Hive, in which the queen was confined to the bottom section, the brood chamber, by means of a partition which had holes in it big enough to let drones and workers through but not the queen herself, who was, of course, of somewhat larger proportions. Down there in the brood chamber, Her Majesty had two basic functions. One was to squeeze out eggs—up to a couple of thousand per day during spring, the equivalent of her own body weight—and the other was to send out a continuous pheromone signal informing her loyal subjects that she was alive and well. ("Like a Christmas Day message," Beam said, "all the time.") In other words, the queen was both the hive's figurehead and its most menial member. She was stuck in the basement with nothing to do except procreate and keep up morale. A true servant of the people.

"And you think a system like that would work with humans?" said Fen.

"Possibly. Possibly not. It's the interdependence of it that I find so alluring. The queen has a vested interest in the welfare of her subjects and vice versa. They cosset her, keep her sweet, and in return she works harder than any of them. She's both above and below them in the social order. Interesting, eh?"

Fen nodded, unconvinced. "With the greatest of respect, Beam..."

"Oh dear, *that* euphemism."

"...the trouble with nature analogies is that you can find one to apply to any situation, can't you, and that makes them essentially valueless. You can say a beehive is a good model for human society, and someone else can say yes, but a pride of lions is too. You know, the females do all the hunting and rearing while the males loll around, rousing themselves for a mating session every so often. Or a school of fish, which has no leaders at all and operates as a kind of mass entity, every member playing an equal part—pure communism. Or a flock of migrating geese, each taking it in turns at the head of the formation, doing its stint of the navigating and pace-setting, like a committee with a rotating chairmanship. Nature analogies are like biblical quotations in that respect. There's one to suit every occasion."

Beam found this highly amusing. He pointed his cue at Fen. "I *do* like you, Fen!" he exclaimed, chuckling. "Liked you the moment I laid eyes on you. You've a good heart and a good brain and you're not afraid to use either. I hardly need add that everyone else here likes you too. Apart from anything, the difference you've made with those children is remarkable. What is it, a month? And they're scarcely recognisable as the urchins who used to tear around the place and get up to no end of trouble. Quiet and thoughtful and polite as can be. Everyone's come up and said to me how much they appreciate what you've done. What you're doing."

"That's very nice to hear. Thank you."

Beam rested the end of the cue on the floor and leaned on it like a shepherd on his crook. His face was serious now, as serious as Fen had ever seen it. "But I think the thing we all want to know, old chap, is whether you plan to stay on or not. Your leg's definitely on the mend. I'd say you could be on your way in a fortnight or so. Now, I'm not expecting you to give me an answer right here and now. There's a lot for you to consider, I understand that. For my own selfish reasons I'd like to think you *are* going to stay, but that's not to put pressure on you or anything. Just a statement of fact. And, my God, it's your wife up there in London, and no one admires you more than I do for trying to go after her and bring her home. You're a braver man than I am, Gunga Din. But if you've come to the conclusion that rescuing her is a lost cause, no one here's going to fault you for it. Quite the opposite. And the children *do* think that you're the best thing since sliced bread. And"—Beam winked—"it's no secret that there's a certain lady here who's quite smitten with you. What I'm getting at is, you have good reasons for going and good reasons for not going, Fen, and I think now's the time for you to ask yourself, frankly, honestly, which you have more of."

A VISIT FROM Eazy-K.

The head of the Frantik Posse is tall, languid, graceful, and cocky (as well he might be, given that he's just masterminded the takeover of a neighbouring borough). He wears a dark blue bandanna tied around his head, gypsy-fashion. So do the two lieutenants he's brought with him. His eyes are profoundly bloodshot, their black irises surrounded by flaring coronas of red. He greets Craig with a complex configuration of handshakes. "My brother." He's all smiles and back-pats and compliments.

Then he and Craig disappear into the dining room together for a powwow. Eazy-K's two lieutenants are left to loiter in the living room with Neville and Mushroom. There are attempts at idle chitchat. They come to nothing. There's little love lost here. The roots of tribal rivalry run too deep.

As the women of the household, Lauren, Zoë and I are called on to play happy hostess. *Tea? Coffee? Snack of some kind?* "I'll have *you*," one of Eazy-K's men replies, leering at Zoë, a great creamy grin on his face. I pull Zoë out of the room before she, or I, can do something we might regret.

The powwow goes on for half an hour. Voices in the dining room rise. Tension in the living room grows. Another quarter of an hour. Then Craig comes out, fuming. Eazy-K saunters out after him. "Don't take it bad, man," he says. "We don't want much."

Craig whirls, and for one terrible moment it looks like he's going to hit Eazy-K, and I envision an explosion of violence, Bulldogs and Frantiks at each other's throats, with Zoë and me caught in the crossfire.

"We had," Craig says, spitting out the words, "a deal."

"Still do," comes the reply. "Only, it's changed a lickle bit."

"I swore blood loyalty to the Posse."

Eazy-K shrugs. "Yeah, well. You in't the right colour, knowah mean?"

"You're fucking with the wrong person here, Eazy. You do realise that, don't you?"

"I ain't fucking with nobody, man. I come here, I been straight with you... It ain't *my* problem you don't like what I'm offering."

"I think you'd better go." Craig jerks a thumb. "Go on, get the fuck out."

Eazy-K makes an air-patting gesture, his long fingers splayed. "OK, OK. I can see you need some time to think about this."

"I don't need any time. You try anything you shouldn't, and it's war. Right? Can I make myself any clearer?"

Eazy-K and his lieutenants leave the house, swaggering back to the stereo-on-wheels they arrived in. They drive out of the compound with rap music on at full volume, the car throbbing like a titan's pulsebeat.

Tight-lipped, terse, Craig sketches us in on the content of his and Eazy-K's discussion.

The Frantiks, it turns out, want some of Lewisham. They want Brockley. They have Peckham and they've decided to extend their new territory a little further east. They want to make Brockley Road the boundary between their turf and the Bulldogs'. Until now, the boundary between Peckham and Lewisham has always been, by common consent, the railway line.

"No fucking way!" exclaims Mushroom.

"Told you so," says Neville.

"They wouldn't dare," I say.

"Who asked *you*?" Neville snaps.

"Shut your face, Nev," says Craig.

Neville doesn't bat an eyelid. "I told you you should never have trusted them, didn't I, Craig. I warned you, but would you listen to me? Wankers! We should've kicked shit out of them while they were here."

"It wouldn't have achieved anything," says Craig. "Anyway, safe passage through each other's territory was part of the agreement."

"The agreement they've just broken."

"They haven't yet. Eazy-K was trying it on. Seeing how I'd react."

"Bollocks."

"Neville, unless you have anything constructive to say, kindly either shut up or piss off."

Neville strides up to his old friend, his former school chum, his leader, and thrusts his face up to Craig's and looks him straight in the eye.

"You've lost it, you know that, mate," he says. "You've let yourself get shafted. You've fucked everything up good and proper."

Craig towers over Neville. He could break him in two. He could crush his skull with his bare hands. For all that, it's easy to see which of them has the advantage right now. Neville has Craig right where he wants him.

"Out, Nev. Now. Go. Leave."

Neville turns to Lauren, who has been standing at the entrance to the kitchen along with me and Zoë, watching this drama unfold. "You want to stay here, Lauren? With Captain Loser? You still think he's such a big shot now?"

Lauren bites her lip, thinking hard. Her eyes flick from Craig to Neville, Neville to Craig. Finally, she comes to a decision.

"Let me get my things," she says, and pushes past Zoë and me.

Five minutes later, she's gathered up her belongings in a bundle. They don't amount to much—an armful of clothing and cosmetics. Neville's ready to leave, but Lauren keeps prevaricating. I know what she's waiting for. She's waiting for Craig to ask her not to go. All he has to do is say the word and she'll stay.

But Craig doesn't care any more. About Lauren, about anything. He sits slumped in an armchair in the living room, head bowed, hands locked at the back of his skull, gazing down at his feet.

Neville opens the front door. "All right?" he says to Lauren.

Lauren looks like she's about to have a last-minute change of heart. She's fighting back tears.

She peers through the living-room doorway at Craig.

Craig doesn't move.

She draws in a deep, self-strengthening breath and says, "Yeah, I'm fine. Let's get outta here."

Barely has the front door closed when Zoë taps me on the shoulder and whispers, "Does this mean I can have her room?"

Under other circumstances I'd laugh.

But this now—the way Craig is.

This is not good.

Early the next morning, Fen took himself down to the stream and sat for a while on the bank with his bare feet dangling in the limpid water. The valley, refreshed by yesterday's rain, was an exultation of green. Sheep bleated to one another distantly in the stillness. The lake reflected the emerging sun as a sheen of glittering gold, broken here and there by the small plopping roundel of a fish-rise.

A religious person, gazing around, might have called this spot God-blessed. A secular person like Fen could admire it as a sublime synthesis of Man and Nature.

How did he get here? He reviewed the chain of event and circumstance, the causes and effects, that had brought him to Beam's door.

A religious person could have unravelled a thread of divine intent from the tangle of error and impulse that was the story of the past few weeks of Fen's life. Fen himself could perceive only human will and the odd nudge from his subconscious, nothing that could be considered, even in retrospect, a supernatural plan.

What was he to do? *You have good reasons for going and good reasons for not going, Fen, and I think now's the time for you to ask yourself, frankly, honestly, which you have more of.*

A religious person could have prayed to his or her deity for guidance. Fen had only himself to consult, his heart and his gut instinct to put forward the various arguments for and against staying.

He found himself vaguely wishing for another appearance from Michael Hollingbury. Surely here, if anywhere, the Green Man would feel at home and be happy to manifest himself. Just some words of advice, that was all Fen needed. Just something to tip him in one direction or the other.

Don't be foolish, he chided himself. Don't be so childish.

The Green Man came only when he was asleep. The Green Man was a dream-vision. You couldn't expect him just to pop up out of the grass when you wanted him to, could you?

Could you?

Shadows steepened. Sunshine deepened. From behind him Fen heard the sounds of Fairfield Hall waking up—windows being opened, indoor shouts, the wolfhounds barking, the first stirrings of another day of cheerful industry. His feet went numb in the chilling stream. The damp ground soaked the seat of his jeans.

It was up to him.

What was life but a series of choices, some far harder than others?

These were exceptional times.

He had been through so much. Had he been through enough?

The wise man knew when to call it quits.

The unknown was sometimes more welcoming than the known.

Another shot at happiness.

A new leaf.

A fresh start.

And just like that, Fen realised that his mind was made up. He got to his feet, picked up the walking stick, gathered up his shoes and socks, turned towards the Hall...

Forgive me, Moira.

...and, feeling lighter inside than he had for a long time, ambled across the grass towards his new home.

THEN BEAM DIED.

Nobody had the least inkling that all was not well with the lord and master of Fairfield Hall until, one suppertime, he collapsed. More accurately, he *sagged*, since he was seated at the time and the arms and back of his chair kept him mostly upright. Those at the table who witnessed the actual event saw Beam slump forwards, saw his eyes close and his chin sink into its hammock folds of jowl, saw his fork tumble from his suddenly nerveless fingers, and assumed, quite reasonably, that he was playing a prank. No one, just then, was talking to him, and Beam dearly loved to be the centre of attention. Hence he had feigned falling asleep. A narcoleptic attack, brought on by boredom. Any moment now, once he was sure that people were looking at him, he would open his eyes and grin and wink.

Someone laughed.

Beam did not stir.

Someone else laughed, uneasily this time. Beam was taking the pretence a little further than was comfortable.

"Uncle Beam's not moving very much," observed one of the children.

An ugly silence fell.

Jessica was the first to her feet. She hurried to Beam's side, took hold of his arm and shook him. His head rolled and his eyelids fluttered and he murmured something. Thereafter he swiftly regained consciousness and, while protesting that they shouldn't make such a fuss, allowed Jessica and Sally to lead him out of the room and upstairs.

After he was gone, there was muted consternation. None of the adults, because there were children present, wanted to voice too much concern, but the children picked up on the general mood of anxiety and became fretful and agitated, demanding to know what was wrong with Uncle Beam and why he had had to leave the room like that. Since the meal was almost finished anyway, Fen proposed that the youngsters should go up, get into their nightclothes, come back down to the drawing room, and there he would read them a Sherlock Holmes story. The diversionary tactic worked, and an hour later the mystery of the Red-Headed League had been solved and the children trooped contentedly to their rooms, yawning hard.

Back in the dining room, Fen learned the worst. Jessica said that when she and Sally undressed Beam, they had found blood in his underpants. He was still bleeding. There was a chance it might just be a perforated stomach ulcer. That was the best they could hope for. But even a perforated stomach ulcer was hardly good news.

Fen asked—for the sake of asking, not expecting the answer to be yes—if there was a doctor living somewhere hereabouts, in one of the nearby villages perhaps. He was told there was not. In one of the big towns? Maybe, but the nearest of those was over ten miles away. Besides, how much help was a doctor going to be? To which Fen could only nod. As he himself knew only too well, under present constraints there were limits to what a medical practitioner could do, especially in cases as serious as this. Medicine had been thrown back to the days of poultices and cold compresses and faith in the body's ability to heal itself. At best a doctor could diagnose what Beam was suffering from, but as for treating him...

It was a long night. The adults sat downstairs, unwilling to retire to bed, as if to do so would constitute a betrayal, as if by staying up, remaining awake, they could somehow assist Beam's recovery. To keep their spirits up, they swapped Beam-related reminiscences—tales from before the Unlucky Gamble, from prelapsarian England, a more innocent age. That time Beam swam across the lake at night for a drunken bet and, when he came out, they had hidden his clothes, but he just spent the rest of the evening walking around naked, his revenge on them. That time he set up an abseiling rope on the side of the house and got into difficulties halfway down and was left dangling there for over an hour before anybody came looking for him. That time he drove his convertible Beetle up onto the terrace and crashed it into his mother's favourite urn, the one she had brought all the way home from a holiday in Sardinia, insisting on taking it aboard the plane with her as hand luggage even though it was nearly as big as she was. At first they found it invigorating to recollect Beam's life in this manner but after a while it started to feel ghoulish so they stopped. They drowsed. They waited. Upstairs, Jessica and Sally kept vigil at Beam's bedside. There was nothing anyone else could do. Drowse. Wait. The empty hours of darkness crept by.

At dawn, Jessica delivered the latest update. It was not encouraging. More blood, a lot of it. Beam was conscious, he was talking, but he was terribly weak. Things did not look good.

Life tried to go on as normal. Exhausted as they were from their sleepless night, the adults still had the children to consider and still had tasks to do. Breakfast was prepared and, in desultory fashion, eaten. Fen took the children off to the library and coached them for an hour on Venn diagrams. Their hearts weren't in it. Neither was his. Megan asked him if Uncle Beam was going to die. "Of course not," he said, and wondered if the children could tell he did not believe it.

The day was overshadowed. Always it was *there*, unspoken, unacknowledged, always *there*, the fact that Beam was lying upstairs in his room, not well, ill, deathly ill. The Hall was dulled, subdued, filled with hollow whispers and muffled echoes. Crap and Piss were not their usual exuberant selves. They sensed what was up, and skulked and moped, looking so mournful, so hangdog, that even Fen, recently confirmed canophobe that he was, was moved to ruffle their ears consolingly. Outside, the sun shone. Inside, the Hall was all the gloomier for its brilliance.

By evening, the prognosis was very bleak indeed, and the mood in the house likewise. Of all of them, only Beam was facing up to the inevitable with anything like equanimity. He had told Jessica he had suspected for some while that things weren't right with him. Odd cramping pains every now and then. A feeling of bloatedness that he had put down to his being, not to put too fine a point on it, a fat bastard with poor digestion and a fondness for the booze. If you really wanted to get down to the nitty-gritty: for several weeks now he'd been suffering from the most chronic wind. His farts had reeked like Italian bank notes. Always a bad sign, when you found the smell of your own farts offensive. Yes, he'd had a pretty good idea that something was up. He hadn't mentioned anything to anyone because, well, after all, who wants to hear about stuff like that?

All this Jessica relayed to the assembled household after the supper dishes had been cleared away and the children put to bed. She was doing her best not to cry. Beam had expressly forbidden any of, as he called it, *that weepy stuff*. "Not in my house," he had told her, "not from any of you, so long as I'm alive." She said he was resolutely upbeat, despite being in considerable pain. And she said he had requested that no one should see him except her and Sally. He wanted everyone's last memory of him to be of him as he always had been, not as he was now.

"What, no one see him at all?" said Corin. "We can't even say a goodbye?"

"It's what he wishes," Jessica replied firmly.

There was a numbed, silent exodus to bed. Fen, in his room, lay on his back and stared up into the shadowed recesses of the four-poster's canopy and tried not to think what would become of the Hall with Beam no longer alive. Cliché though it was, Beam was the place's heart and soul. Without him, would this oddly effective little community be able to survive?

He had no idea he had fallen asleep till he became aware of Jessica beside him, prodding him.

"Fen? Fen? Wake up. Beam would like a word."

THE SMELL OF death was in the room. Fen did not have to know it to recognise it. It was a smell as insinuatingly familiar as a door-to-door salesman or a prize-draw letter. With a leer on its face and your name on its lips, it greeted him like an old friend he never knew he had. *This is me,* it said, in silky, sickly tones, *and one day this will be you.*

Beam turned his head as Fen entered, and the smile he offered was a ghost of itself, a faint copy of the original. He looked half the man he had been. Still of the same proportions, but undeniably diminished, he sat propped up on pillows with his hands resting limp by his sides. His face was riven with lines, its slack pulled in by pain. The candlelight lent his skin a ghastly jaundiced pallor.

On the way here, Fen had decided that humorousness would be the best attitude to adopt. Do what he usually did with Beam: intelligently amuse him. But it took several moments to adjust to the sight of the reduced, wretched figure in the bed; to get over the changes that less than a day and a half had wrought, to tune out the death odour. It was an effort to come up with something suitably jaunty to say.

"Nice pyjamas."

"D'you like 'em? I think it's the monogram that gives them real class." Beam patted his breast pocket, on which was embroidered an elaborate "B".

"Oh, definitely. But you know, this hypochondria, Beam... Enough's enough. It's got a lot of people upset, and it's time you leapt out of bed and admitted you're just putting this on to get you some sympathy."

"Curses! Rumbled!"

"Nothing escapes my eagle eye."

There was more brittle banter, then Beam signalled to Jessica and Sally that he wanted to speak to Fen alone.

After the women had gone, Beam allowed himself to drop the mask of bravado. "Christ, this is fucking awful, Fen."

"I don't know what to say."

"Well, that's good. I don't want to hear any crap. Especially none of that nonsense about a better place and eternal life. I've never believed in any of that and I'm not about to start now."

"I've never believed in it either, if that's any consolation."

"Funnily enough, it is. Damn, this has all happened so quickly. I suppose I was in denial for quite some time, but even so."

"It *is* cancer, isn't it?"

"Oh, I think so. No question, really. I've been incubating a nice little tumour for myself. A nice *big* tumour, I should say. And it's bleeding me dry." Beam winced, although whether at a twinge of pain or merely at the thought of the homicidal growth he was harbouring inside him, Fen could not tell. "What I hate most," he said, "is having to leave all this behind. Life. Life's a marvellous old thing, really. There's so much to it."

"You've had a good one, Beam. Last night everyone was telling stories about you. You've had a lot of fun, by the sound of it. You've made people happy. You've done good things. This"—Fen waved around him, indicating the Hall—"is a good thing."

"You think so? I hope so. And actually, Fairfield's the reason I asked to see you, Fen. You see, someone has to take over from me. Someone has to keep the old place going. Someone— Why are you shaking your head?"

"Not me, Beam."

"Why ever not?"

"I can't. I'm the new boy. The others—they've known each other for years."

"And that makes you ideal for the job. You're from outside the circle. You have no history with any of the others. Think of the tensions it would cause if one of them was elevated above the rest. Would *you* like it if suddenly you had to start deferring to a long-standing friend of yours? Whereas an outsider..."

"Even so, they won't take kindly to me telling them what to do."

"It isn't about telling people what to do. Not really. It's about being there. Queen bee, Fen. Queen bee. Top *and* bottom of the social ladder. Overlord *and* underling. Ruler *and* drudge. You have it in you. I know you do."

"I know I don't. I'll happily carry on with the kids, but as for being in charge of everyone else... How about Jessica? Or Ben? Or Simon? Any of them rather than me."

"I want you to do it, Fen."

"Do I have a choice?"

"No. And if you continue to object, I'm going to have to pull rank on you. I'm the one dying. That means you're obliged to honour any last requests of mine."

"That's not fair, Beam."

"No, it isn't. Tough. You're my successor. I'm going to tell Jessica and Sally that when they come back. Like it or not, the job is yours. Now, we can keep arguing about it if you want, but that'll probably hasten my demise. Best you just accept, eh?"

HE LASTED ANOTHER three days.

He did not go prettily. He did not sink sighing into the embrace of everlasting sleep. He went writhing and groaning amid soiled bedclothes. He departed from life in much the same way as he had arrived, swaddled, blood-drenched, gasping for breath.

The day they buried him was a gorgeous one, summer in its full ripeness, with just a hint of the decline to come—autumn's bloat and shrivel—discernible in the air.

The wolfhounds keened from morning till dusk.

A BAD ATMOSPHERE. Not just in our house, throughout the whole compound. Perhaps because I'm looking for it now, I see it everywhere I go—anger, uncertainty, mistrust. The unity isn't there any more. Inside them, the Bulldogs sense the power struggle Neville's initiated; they feel it tugging them this way, that way. They want to stay loyal to King Cunt. They do. But Neville is talking to them, and he's being so persuasive, so convincing. And then there's the evidence. You can't turn ignore the evidence. The Frantik Posse, planning to make inroads into Bulldog turf. Mistake to have trusted them, wasn't it? And Lauren has moved out of the King's house. She's gone and shacked up with Neville. Lauren! Just in Neville's spare room, mind. He's not knocking her off or anything, just letting her stay with him (and in return she does his housework because that's what she does best, housework). But Lauren! If *she's* abandoned King Cunt, then something's got to be up with him, hasn't it? So maybe it's time to have a good hard think about who should be leading them. Maybe Neville's right. Maybe the King *is* past his best. Maybe—they can scarcely believe it—maybe they should be looking for someone to replace him.

Several of them, I notice, have taken to wearing football scarves around their necks, or long-sleeved shirts. Hiding their KING CUNT tattoos.

What's so ludicrous is, Craig could put a stop to all this if he wanted to, no trouble. All the Bulldogs need is to be reminded again who's boss, and he could do this easily, if only he had the will to. A show of decisiveness, a firm, forthright display of action. That's all it would take, and the Bulldogs would fall back into line.

Craig, though, hasn't been out of the house in days. Craig prowls about indoors, sullen, uncommunicative, eating, sleeping, mechanically going through the motions of living. He just can't be bothered any more. And I don't need to ask why. There's been too much treachery. He's surrounded by Judases. Neville, Eazy-K, Lauren. All he's done for his men, for Lewisham, and this is how he's rewarded. This is the thanks he gets. Craig has had enough. He just wants everybody to fuck off and leave him alone.

God, I've known exactly how *that* feels!

There's nothing I can say or do that'll bring him out of it, however. I try talking to him and get nothing in response but monosyllables. I try nuzzling up to him at night and get pushed away. Some nights I don't even get *that* much of a response, because he's drunk heavily, a couple of six-packs of beer at least, and by bedtime he's in a virtual coma.

Zoë does her best. She asks him questions, cracks jokes, even gently teases him about the way he's behaving, as if he were her big brother. Sometimes he looks at her and it's as if he'd like to be amused by her antics but can't bring himself to. Other times he looks at her and his expression is so murderous I have to warn her to give it a rest.

One small side-benefit. Now that I don't have Lauren breathing down my neck all day, and since I'm not able to achieve much with Craig at the moment, I've started paying regular visits to the recreation zones. I went along initially in order to keep the women there abreast of the situation within the compound, but they, it turns out, know as much as I do about what's going on, perhaps more. The men who screw them can be very talkative at times, so they're well aware how things have begun to deteriorate. Paula Coulton is my main point of contact. We talk through the chainlink. She says she and the others are worried what'll happen if Neville succeeds in overthrowing Craig. "At least he's the devil you know," she says, with reference to Craig. "That Neville, on the other hand. A bastard, he is. Although..." And then she tells me something we both have a good long laugh about. Neville, it seems, has a slight problem in the bedroom department. A bit of a *shortcoming*, you might say. He's a little too, as it were, easy to please. In fact, the women have taken to referring to him as Nine-Second Neville (although never to his face, of course). Nine seconds is his record, allegedly.

It's jokes like this that help keep them going, help keep them brave. I admire these women beyond all reckoning.

"There's a chance, of course, that we can turn what's happening to our advantage," I tell Paula one afternoon.

"Go on," she says, looking dubious.

"There's going to come a point," I say, "when Neville will have to make a stand. He's going to have to face Craig in front of all the other Bulldogs and tell him it's over and someone else is in charge. A public confrontation. That's the only sure-fire way Neville's going to be able to dethrone Craig and take his place."

"So?"

"So then one of two things can happen. Either Craig slaps Neville down once and for all, or he lets him win. It's not about what Neville does, you see. It's about how Craig responds, what *he* does or doesn't do. He can give in to Neville or he can sort him out good and proper."

"'Sort him out good and proper'. You're starting to sound like one of them, Moira."

She's right. I *am* taking on Bulldog cadences and inflections. Sometimes I catch myself at it. Mostly I don't notice any more. Camouflage, I tell myself. Blending in.

Fitting in?

"Yeah, well, when in sarf-east Lahndan..."

Paula tuts and rolls her eyes.

"Anyway," I say, reverting to the good middle-class tones I was brought up to speak, "my point is, Neville confronts Craig, Neville loses, all well and good."

"Why? Nothing will have changed."

"No, everything will have changed. Neville's no longer undermining Craig all the time, Craig has full control over his domain again, and then I can start to work on him. Get all this"—I indicate the recreation zones—"dismantled."

"You think you can do that?"

"I don't know," I admit. "But I can have a damn good crack at it. Craig trusts me. I think he's even quite fond of me. We have a working relationship." Is that entirely right? We've had sex once, and since then there's been too much going on for the event to be repeated, and Craig was so distracted at the time, and has been so distracted since, that I can't be a hundred per cent sure he even remembers it happened. A working relationship? Not right now, not in any real, practical sense. "And with Neville out of the way, Craig'll be much more amenable to listening to me. Much more open to my influence." That part, at least, I do believe is true.

"And if Neville takes over?"

"Then we have a chance—a slim one, but still a chance—to try and get out of here."

Now Paula looks openly incredulous.

"There'll be confusion for a while," I tell her. "Disarray. Neville won't be able to get a handle on things immediately. The transition won't be smooth. That'll be our window of opportunity. While the Bulldogs are adjusting to their new boss."

"I like the first alternative better."

"So do I."

"Escape just seems"—Paula shakes the fence—"a bit unlikely."

"Agreed. Which means what I have to do is make sure Craig *does* stand up to Neville when the moment comes. The mood he's in right now, I doubt he will. I think he'd much rather be shot of the whole thing."

"Then you have to work on him."

"If I can. I *am* trying, but he's not especially receptive at present."

"Then," says Paula sternly, "you have to keep trying."

And she's right. But I get back to the house and nothing's changed, Craig's still this hulking great thundercloud in the shape of a human being, all grumbles and brooding silences and pent-up menace, and I begin to wonder if anyone can do anything at all to stop Neville's challenge to the throne.

I'm scared what may happen if Neville takes over this place.

I'm especially scared what may happen to me.

Fen found Jessica at the grave. They had buried Beam close to the edge of the Hall's apple orchard, a spot he used to love, especially in spring when there was blossom on the trees and a mauve mist of bluebells beneath. In the grave's turned earth, a few shoots of grass had already appeared, fine as hairs.

Jessica didn't look round as Fen approached but signalled she had heard him coming by straightening her spine, squaring her shoulders and raising her head.

"How are you?" he asked.

"How do you think?"

He hesitated, then placed a hand on the lower slope of her neck, just at the base of her bobbed brown hair. A paternalistic gesture. He was trying—although he didn't like it and didn't think he was very good at it—to be exactly as Beam had been. Continuity, for now, was what the household needed, and he *was* Beam's replacement, no matter how undemocratically he had been appointed to the role.

Jessica's big eyes were red-rimmed and swollen. "It's not right, Fen. It's just not fucking right at all. Why him? Why, of all people, him?"

Because life's a bitch and fate's a bastard, Fen thought, but said, "At least it was quick. Relatively quick."

"No, 'quick' is a heart attack, a car crash, a fall off a cliff. Bang, you're dead. This was five days. Longer, considering he'd known a while back he was going to die."

Fen recalled his first evening at the Hall, him and Beam out on the terrace, Beam echoing a certain remark he had made: *Do what you can in the time available*. How could someone live with the knowledge of impending death like that and not crumble in despair? Out on the railway embankment, Fen had truly believed he was a goner and had been terrified. Yet Beam had been able to joke and smile almost to the very end. Courage? Or was there a certain point past which it became possible to accept what was going to happen, courage no longer called for? The two deaths Fen had hitherto had first-hand experience of, those of his parents, had been slow, incremental slides into oblivion, eased by medication. In hospital beds, drip-fed and cathetered and pumped with drugs strong enough to obliterate almost all conscious thought, first his mother and then a year later his father had slipped away, scarcely knowing where they were or why they were there. A miracle of modern science: the insensible demise. But now that that kind of easy get-out was unavailable and would probably not be available again for some time, it was necessary once again to face up to death as people had done down through the centuries, tackling it, taking it by the horns, wrestling it to its knees. Beam, it seemed, had managed this feat. Fen hoped he might learn from the example.

"I was just trying to say something positive," he said.

"I know, Fen." Jessica patted his arm. "I know. I didn't mean to snap. I'm sorry."

His hand was still on her neck. Her skin was soft, warm, faintly sticky from the summer heat. He felt a sudden, sharp uncoiling of lust. Shameful, at Beam's graveside, but there was nothing he could do about that. He wanted her. He knew that now for sure. If she was still keen, he wanted her.

"What did you come out here for?" she asked.

"Oh, no particular reason. See if you were all right. And to tell you that lunch is on the table, if you want some."

"How kind."

"Not at all."

"I've not got much of an appetite at the moment."

"You ought to eat *something*."

"Fen..." Hesitantly.

"Yes?" Expectantly.

She let him down with remarkable gentleness. All in all, for someone in the habit of just saying the first thing that came into her head, she was extremely considerate. She told him she had been doing a lot of soul-searching over the past few days. She told him her perspective on a lot of things had changed. She told him her outlook was different now. She said she felt the world was a great deal colder and emptier than she used to believe. More brutal, less favourably disposed towards human endeavours. Things one started might not necessarily finish well.

In that way that many foreigners regard as peculiarly English, she avoided direct mention of what she was actually talking about. She skirted around the subject like a swordsman around a practice dummy, taking oblique feints at it. By this method she hoped to spare herself, and Fen, feelings of awkwardness. To a large extent she succeeded. When she stopped speaking, all Fen had to do to acknowledge that he understood her meaning was take his hand from her neck and nod. He managed both actions with surprising ease. He was nowhere near as crestfallen as he might have expected. All at once he realised how little he in fact liked Jessica. What a shallow person she was! It said everything about her that her reasons for spurning him were so tenuous, so contrived. Did she honestly expect him to believe that she had only just now realised that life was unfair, that the world always worked against you, that everything always turned to shit in the end? How naïve of her to think he could think her so naïve.

All the rest of that day Fen was elated. He felt like he had dodged an assassin's bullet. Jessica's manners, her mannerisms, that wide-eyed look of hers that she thought so winning—come to think of it, he couldn't stand her. If they had started an affair, she would have driven him up the wall within days. A lucky escape he had had. Definitely. No question about it.

Besides, he was Beam now. Beam had not had a girlfriend. Accordingly, nor should Fen. He couldn't be allowed to play favourites, could he? He had a duty to run things impartially. Like Beam, he had to be wedded to the Hall. The Hall came first, his personal desires a poor second.

Brimming with self-justification, Fen began to feel that Beam's mantle might indeed fit him after all. He started to behave less like a copy of Beam and more like the version of himself that he thought Beam would have wanted him to be. He did not take on airs. He was rigorous with himself on that front. No swanning about the place acting as if he was better than everyone else. Humility was his watchword. The walking stick, he thought, helped with that. It accentuated his lameness, reminding the others that he lacked a basic function that they all retained, full mobility. He was unstinting with his courtesies. Pleases and thank-yous and words of praise were forever coming from his mouth. He was careful, at the same time, never to patronise. Above all, he worked as hard as anyone. Teaching the children remained his primary duty, but no longer was he able to supervise them in the afternoons as well as the mornings. The morning lessons continued in the library as before, but after lunch Fen went off and helped where he could around the estate, indoors, outdoors, wherever an extra pair of hands was needed. He handed dominion over the gang back to Christopher. Christopher accepted the returned responsibility without pleasure. He had quite liked not having to think on behalf of all the other children, most of whom, let's face it, were scarcely older than *babies*. He had also quite liked the way Fen used to discuss with him on what they all should and shouldn't do together. Being unofficial aide-de-camp to Fen had made Christopher feel rather grown up. Now, all of a sudden, he was just another kid again.

Miffed and a little betrayed, the children started to slide back into their old ways. Restive during lessons, unruly at other times, they punished Fen for, as they saw it, abandoning them. It was understandable, he thought. And it could not be helped. Sacrifices had to be made, and the children's untarnished admiration was one of them. They came up with a nickname for him—No Fun Fen—and he let them use it in his presence, or rather did not react when they used it in his presence, so as to demonstrate that he understood their feelings of hurt and sympathised. They could hurt him back if they wanted to, because then they might appreciate that he, too, was not happy about the way things had had to change. The children might be unfamiliar with the word *martyr*, but he was sure they would grasp the concept soon enough.

So Fen did his best to lead by example, and for a while the other members of the household seemed content to have him in charge. After the shock of Beam's death, the loss of an old, dear friend, they were stunned, numbed, rendered docile. They allowed Fen to take over because, yes, that was what Beam had decreed, of course, but also because none of them felt up to objecting. If Fen wanted to step into Beam's shoes, fine, go ahead, let him. It made sense. Fen wasn't suffering to the extent that they were. He had known Beam for a little over a month. His bereavement was nowhere near as great as theirs.

Gradually, though, the shock wore off, and that was when Fen's troubles really started.

Little signs at first, a grumble here, a muttering there, snippy remarks that Fen could ascribe to grief, that probably *were* the result of grief. On one occasion it was his choice of suppertime wine. His choice of wine! Someone said only an idiot would choose *that* wine to go with *this* main course. He overlooked the comment, treating it with the disregard it deserved. On another occasion, one of the wolfhounds stole an untended raw chicken from the kitchen table and left scraps of skin and flesh and gnawed bone all over the drawing room. For this misdemeanour Fen was expected to shoulder at least part of the blame. As if Crap and Piss were his dogs now. As if he was supposed to be able to control them. He didn't even like the bloody animals!

Little signs. Snippets of conversation that he happened to overhear and was perhaps meant to overhear. Was it proper that Fen should sit at the head of the table at mealtimes? Why had Fen given up minding the kids in the afternoons? Did Fen really think, when he was supposedly helping the adults, that he was actually being useful? With that leg of his he was more a hindrance than a help. Got in the way. He couldn't dig. He couldn't kneel. It was nice that he made the effort, you couldn't fault him for that, but all the same...

Little signs. People being curt with him. When he asked someone to do something, receiving a frosty reply, usually along the lines of "I was just about to" or "I'm not stupid, you know". Simon one day addressing him as *mein Führer*, meant as a joke, naturally, just a little tease, and Fen took it in good part, but others who were present laughed in that cackling, spiteful way which adults never grow out of using, no matter how many decades separate them from the school playground, and thereafter *mein Führer* and German accents were frequently to be heard in Fen's presence.

It was never open rebellion, and was all the worse for that. Open rebellion would at least have been honest. Instead, it was furtive, corrosive, a process of constant undermining, a campaign of dissent conducted behind smiles that were broad and fine and friendly and fooled no one. Day after day Fen endured the genial needlings, the snide provocations. At no point did he lose his temper, although several times he came close.

He forbore, he tolerated, and he hoped that, as time passed, things would settle down. But time passed, and the dissent only intensified, becoming an attitude of entrenched resentment. As autumn crept in, its drying touch turning first this leaf brown then that one, its chill slowing the ardour of growing, its dampness stiffening the air, Fen realised that his days as head of the household were numbered. Either he would have to step down or he would be deposed. Sooner or later, one or the other would have to happen. The situation could not continue as it was.

He was reluctant to step down. It not only smacked of failure but seemed a betrayal of Beam's dying wishes. Then again, Beam would not have wanted life at the Hall to carry on amid such an atmosphere of distrust and antagonism, nor would he have wanted Fen to remain in charge when everyone else was so against it. If only Beam had foreseen that Fen might not work out as his replacement. If only he had made provision for that possibility by assigning Fen a second-in-command, an obvious next-in-line should the need for one arise. But Beam, on his deathbed, had had a fixed, single-minded vision for the future of the Hall. It had been a consolation to him to believe that all would pan out exactly as he intended. He had not allowed room in his head for uncertainty. Perhaps had not dared.

Fen, by contrast, had room in his head for little else *but* uncertainty. The dilemma gnawed at him. Should he abdicate now or should he stick it out till he was forcibly ousted? Which would be healthier for the household as a whole? The latter, he suspected, for the simple reason that ousting him would require the others to organise themselves; it would require focus, a deliberate act of will; and in that act of will a new leader would emerge from their ranks, naturally, organically, as part of the process. One of them would inevitably come to the forefront as spokesman, voice of the aggrieved masses. That person would then, once the overthrow was successfully completed, find himself or herself being asked to take Fen's place. That was how revolutions worked. That was how new regimes were established.

Fen steeled himself for the impending coup d'état. He became impatient for it to happen, just so that it could be over and done with. Maintaining the pretence of business-as-usual was an effort. It would be a relief not to have to act the innocent any more, not to have to carry on as if he didn't know the others were going to rise up against him. He would be glad when the sniping stopped, when he was no longer the household's whipping boy, when it was no longer them versus him. Everything could then go back to the way it was before.

Except that it couldn't, of course. With Beam gone, nothing at Fairfield could ever be the same again.

This became clear the morning Ben and Sally left.

THEY TOOK OFF in one of the cars. Fen had had no idea the cars were still in working order. He had assumed that beneath the dustsheets they were mouldering away, becoming useless, static sculptures of perished rubber and oxidised metal. Nobody had told him, not even Beam, that efforts had been made to keep them viable, and that quantities of petrol were stored with them in the garage. Nobody had mentioned this to him because, it seemed, nobody had thought it of any importance. Beam had wanted the cars maintained for no other purpose than that they would not go to waste. There were a couple of vintage models, there was an E-Type that had belonged to Beam's father, there was Beam's beloved convertible Beetle—beautiful machines, all of them, well worth preserving. When the day came that England was allowed back on its feet again, Beam had wanted them driveable. It hadn't required much effort, turning the engines over every so often, keeping the batteries topped up, that sort of thing. However, the first Fen knew about any of this was when he and the rest of the household were rudely awoken one morning by the sound of a motor revving, followed shortly by the sound of a car disappearing up the drive.

Fen ran to his window but knew it was useless. There was nothing to see but cedar fronds. He listened to the putter of exhaust and the rumble of tyres, fading into the distance. When silence finally returned, it was a strange kind of silence. There was a feeling that something more than just the tranquillity of the morning had been broken.

Ben and Sally—along with daughter Megan, of course—had made off in Beam's MG. The note they left to explain their sudden departure was succinct, if also somewhat disingenuous:

> *We've borrowed the MG. Hopefully we can bring it back sometime.*
>
> *Things aren't working out. Maybe you'll be better off without us.*

Sorry.

—B, S and M

"Bastards!" exclaimed Corin, after the note was read out. "What utter bastards! How dare they!"

Similar sentiments were expressed by many of the others. Ed, a tall, rangy man whom Fen considered to be Beam's best friend after Jessica, was quick to point the finger of blame at Sally, saying she had never been entirely happy here. Whether or not this was true—and Fen was of the opinion that it was not—there was general agreement that Ben wouldn't have left of his own accord. He and Beam had been at school together. They had shared digs at university. And Ben loved Fairfield.

In no time at all, Sally had been transformed into an Aunt Sally. Everyone at the Hall, in her absence, turned on her, dredging up every slightly waspish comment she had ever made, every small *faux pas* she had ever committed, every cause for mild grievance she had ever given, treating these peccadilloes as if they were cardinal sins. In a way Fen was glad that, for once, someone other than him was taking the flak, but the novelty of this soon wore off, and as he watched Sally's former friends vindictively pull her to shreds, he realised—with a profound and wearying sense of regret—that Fairfield Hall was falling apart.

And it was nothing to do with him. It was not his fault. He had done everything he could to hold the household together, and the fact that he had not succeeded said nothing about his leadership qualities and everything about the depth of influence Beam had had over these people. They had not merely respected Beam, they had needed him in a manner so fundamental that not even they themselves understood it. He had been more than simply their friend: he had been their father-figure, their magnetic north, their confessor, their idol, their liege lord, their arbiter, their all. They had abdicated responsibility for their lives to him, and now that he was dead, they did not like having that responsibility back. They did not know what to do with it.

Fairfield was doomed. No matter what Fen, what *anyone* did, the community was not going to last. Ben and Sally had realised this a little earlier than everyone else. They had jumped ship while they could.

Who would be next?

Fen could see it in everyone's eyes. Even as they lambasted Sally, they were all of them thinking the same thought: *maybe I should leave too.*

It was a matter of days, he reckoned. A couple of weeks at most. No one would be willing to follow Ben and Sally's example straight away—how could you emulate someone you were so busy denouncing?—but after a reasonable interval had elapsed, perhaps forty-eight hours, there would be another departure. And then another, and then another. A steady trickling away that would rapidly become a gush.

And nobody would want to linger on after the majority had gone. Nobody would want to be the last one left here. The only thing sadder than an outdated dream was the person still clinging adamantly to it.

It was not difficult for Fen to decide what course of action he should take. Unlike the others, he did not care what anyone thought of him. Not only that but he felt he was owed something for the slights and resentment he had had to endure these past few days.

At first light the following morning, he was out at the garage, hauling the dustsheet off the Beetle.

6.
London

THE FIGHT BEGAN in the grass beside a rotted tree stump. Head to head, mandible to mandible, the stag beetles shoved and buffeted, each seeking advantage, each looking to flip the other over. It was, unquestionably, a grim battle—two males in mating season, horns locked in competitive fury—but there was something delicate in its execution, too, something dance-like: the stateliness of a waltz, the precision of a pavane. The beetles, for all the tenacity with which they gripped each other, seemed in no hurry for the contest to be over. Eventually, inevitably, one of them would have to triumph, but until then there were steps to follow, beats to count, a silent music to heed. Looking down on this minute minuet, one might even imagine the beetles were enjoying themselves.

From the grass, the beetles' pushing and pulling brought them out onto the rugged grey plain of a road. Whether they registered the change in terrain is hard to say. It would be tempting to conjecture that each was concentrating so intently on his opponent as to be oblivious to all else. Equally, the tarmac provided a clearer field of play than the grass. The stag beetles' movements became more surefooted, and they must, at some dim level of insect sentience, have been aware of this.

What they were not aware of was the possibility of imminent destruction.

It came with a roar too loud for the beetles' crude nervous systems to assimilate. It came at a speed that these deliberate little creatures, even when airborne, could never hope to match. It came with earthshaking suddenness, with thunder and immensity, like a fit of divine rage.

In the event, it took only one of them. A few millimetres further into the road and both beetles would have been obliterated, crushed to coleopterous paste. As it was, one was flattened and the other was sent scuttering away, fetching up on its back some yards distant. After much struggling, it managed to right itself. Moments later it was on its way, the fight seemingly forgotten.

The unwitting agent of the other beetle's demise drove on, whistling to himself, a blameless angel of death.

It was, Fen thought, a lovely morning.

THREE HOURS WAS all it took to reach the M25 from Fairfield. Three hours, travelling not very fast over road surfaces that varied in quality from passable to atrocious. Three hours, including time spent doubling back and detouring around obstacles—a fallen tree, a bomb crater, a town with such an antipathy to through traffic that the residents had erected barricades across the roads leading in.

Three hours.

Half a morning.

Fen drove with the Beetle's roof peeled back, the sun full on his head, and a sense of ridiculousness in his heart. Because getting to London was, after all, proving to be simple. Absurdly simple. *This* simple. And hadn't he made such heavy weather of it till now! All those mistakes, all those setbacks. Certainly, were it not for the mistakes and setbacks, he would not now be at the wheel of this car. But still, he had wasted so much time. Ten weeks, give or take. When he could have done the journey, there and back, in less than a day.

It was something to laugh about, self-deprecatingly, as the M25 neared. An irony that was palatable only because at last he was on the right track, at last things were going swimmingly.

Well, almost. The clutch on the Beetle was stiff and temperamental, not helped by the fact that Fen's left leg was still weak. On several occasions he was unable to push the pedal all the way down and his attempt at a shift in gears ended in an ugly, wrenching crunch of cog teeth. This, though, all things considered, was a minor inconvenience. Otherwise the car behaved itself impeccably. The miles clocked up on the odometer. And suddenly, almost before he knew it, Fen was within sight of the M25.

What he first saw was a watchtower, a teetering breeze-block edifice so poorly constructed that it seemed as much of a hazard to the lives and safety of the armed sentries who were posted at its summit as the armed sentries were to the lives and safety of anyone who might attempt to cross the motorway illegally.

The next thing he saw was the gridlock.

Stationary, bumper to bumper, they stretched in both directions as far as the eye could see—lorries, coaches, vans, cars, cars with trailers, cars with caravans, great parallel chains of multicoloured metal. At first glance they looked like part of some immense traffic snarl-up that would, in time, clear. But Fen knew this wasn't the case, and even if he hadn't known, the lack of noise was a clue. Absent were the sounds commonly generated by traffic at a standstill, the horn toots and the impatient shouts and above all the massed rumbling of engines in neutral. Hundreds of vehicles, sitting in stark silence, empty—it was a surprisingly eerie sight, like the chaos left behind after some unspeakable holocaust.

Which, in a sense, was just what it was.

The gridlock had, in fact, occurred years ago. Londoners, having withstood months of so-called "precision strikes" designed to bring them back into line, and having failed to be brought back into line, had been subjected to an all-out, no-holds-barred assault, an apocalyptic rain of high explosive that lasted a week and that left few of the capital's landmarks standing and many of the capital's citizens in no doubt that it was time to flee. This they all chose to do at once and by motorised means rather than on foot. Result: few of them got further than the M25. Accidents happened, junctions became blocked, fuel tanks ran dry, the orbital motorway seized up, and gradually it became clear to the would-be refugees that they were unlikely to make any further progress, and so, for lack of an alternative, they abandoned their transportation and trudged back home. Some of them, perhaps conditioned by the fact that hold-ups were once commonplace on the M25, or perhaps out of sheer desperation, had stayed put for days before at last allowing themselves to admit that the gridlock was permanent and irremediable. It was even rumoured that here and there along the motorway's circuit small pockets of humanity remained, communities that had adapted to their automobile-bound environment, using belongings they had brought with them and items scavenged from other vehicles to erect shelters that hid them from the prying eyes of the watchtower sentries. Fen was intrigued by the idea of people living this rat-like existence, scurrying secretly among the rows of immobilised traffic, but his feeling was that this particular rumour consisted far more of fable than of fact.

Inarguably, though, the gridlock had proved advantageous to somebody, namely the London Council. To those who might wish to enter or leave the Greater London area without valid documentation, six lanes (in some places eight) of packed-solid automobiles formed a daunting psychological barrier. The gridlock was the detritus of an abortive exodus, the husks of failed escape, and as such it was perhaps as efficient a deterrent as all the physical barriers—the watchtowers, the mined areas, the armed guards, the fifteen-foot fences that ran all the way around the motorway's inner perimeter—put together.

Fen had managed to get himself onto one of the A-roads that, if memory served, traversed the M25 on its south-western arc by means of a narrow bridge. He hoped that, since the bridge was one of the motorway's minor crossings, its checkpoint might be unattended, and that there might not even be a checkpoint at all. No such luck. Reaching the bridge, he entered a chicane of rock-weighted oildrums, and having negotiated this, he found two large piles of sandbags ahead of him, stacked on either side of the road so as to create a bottleneck just one vehicle wide. Drawn across the bottleneck were sturdy-looking sawhorses wreathed with barbed wire, and stationed to one side of this obstruction were three men with rifles.

They were ex-soldiers, and looked it. They wore camouflage uniforms that were patched and threadbare and hung tiredly off their bodies—drab fatigues displaying more than a few signs of drabness and fatigue—and they themselves were long-haired, rough-shaven and lean in a way that they would never have been allowed to become were they still in the army. Immediately, Fen felt a twinge of apprehension. As he came closer to the checkpoint, one of the men unshouldered his rifle and wandered out in front of the sawhorses, there to stand louchely with the weapon cradled across his belly, looking towards Fen with an expression that seemed to say: *who are you and why do I hate you?* Fen considered making a three-point turn and getting the hell out of there. But that, surely, would arouse the guard's suspicions, and he could not afford to arouse the suspicions of someone with a warrant to deploy lethal force as and when he saw fit. Besides, he had a permit, didn't he? And, if necessary, a bribe.

He continued forward, maintaining such a low speed that the needle on the speedometer failed to register it. As he drew to a halt in front of the guard, he put on a smile that felt face-crackingly false. He could feel his heart hammering away inside his ribs. Was it really possible for the human heart to beat that fast?

The guard came around to the side of the car and, as if this was no more than a casual meeting between two strangers, as if one of them was not in uniform and toting a loaded rifle, made some innocuous comment about the weather, to which Fen, warily, responded in kind. The guard eyed the

Beetle and said that it looked like a nice little runabout; Fen said it was. The guard nodded at Fen's walking stick, which was propped up against the passenger seat, and said that it looked like a nice stick; Fen said it was.

During this exchange of pleasantries, Fen dared to dart a glance at the other two guards. Theirs were the faces of people who have front-row seats at a show and are fully expecting to be entertained.

His apprehension deepened.

"Permit," said the guard beside the car, and Fen delved into his trouser pocket, slowly, cautiously, making the action as open and demonstrative as possible so that the guard would not somehow get it into his head that he was reaching for, oh, say, a concealed pistol or something.

He slid the permit out. Should he get out the wedding band too? No, not yet. Wait and see.

The guard studied the permit. He seemed to study it for a very long time. So long that it occurred to Fen that perhaps the permit was a fake. Had Cruikshank played a cruel trick on him? He wouldn't have put it past the old blind bastard.

He told himself the worst that could happen was that the guard would turn him back.

That was the worst.

The very worst.

"Hmm," said the guard, in such a way that it was impossible to tell whether he was pleased or displeased with what he was looking at.

"It *is* quite an old one," Fen said. "I haven't used it in a while." It had dawned on him that the problem might be that the permit was out of date. The London Council might have issued a new version of the document since Cruikshank left for Downbourne.

"Hmm," said the guard again, and his two colleagues shared a quiet snigger. Lording it over people at the checkpoint, tormenting them—it was one of the perks of the job. "Yes, well, it does look like it's been sitting in a drawer for a while. But I don't suppose that matters. Reason for journey?"

"Visit. I'm making a visit. Visiting someone."

"Who?"

A trace of indignation—just a trace—entered Fen's voice. "Is that relevant?"

"If it is to you, it is to me."

"It's..." There was no point telling him the whole saga. "A friend."

"Anyone I know?"

"Doubt it."

"Try me."

"London's a big place."

"Not as big as it used to be."

"All right, his name's"—*quick, think*—"Jeremy. Jeremy Salter."

Why this, of all names, should have popped into his head, Fen couldn't say. Possibly it had something to do with the fact that Salter had once lived in London. Fen had long ago learned that he was one of those people who could not lie plausibly unless the lie contained an element, however small, of honesty.

"Jerry Salter? You know Jerry Salter?"

Oh fuck.

"Fancy that!" The guard turned to his companions. "This bloke's a mate of Jerry's."

The other two laughed and nodded, and there was a lot of *Jerry this* and *Jerry that* and *ah, good old Jerry*.

And then the first guard said, "Never heard of him."

Fen, who had already worked out that he was having his leg pulled, said nothing, but quietly wished some horrible accident would befall all three of the guards. He wondered how many times they had perpetrated this feeble gag on people using the checkpoint. Not enough times, clearly, to have grown bored of it.

"All right, here you go." The guard offered the permit back to Fen. All at once he had become a smiling, beneficent presence, his manner saying don't mind us, just our sense of humour, bit of piss-taking, dull job, breaks up the routine, you know how it is.

Fen took the permit. He was relieved that the ordeal was over, but peeved, too, at the way he had been treated—so much so that the *thank you* he offered the guard, while as ingratiating as he could make it, was also not a little supercilious.

The other two guards began moving the sawhorses aside, shunting them with their booted feet on account of the barbed wire. Fen bore down on the clutch and was all set to put the car into gear when the guard beside him said, "Hang on."

Fen eased his foot off the clutch and looked round.

The guard had changed the way he was holding his rifle. A subtle but unmistakable repositioning. His left hand was now clamped around the barrel, while his right had moved to within twitching distance of the trigger.

"Now I might just be being over-sensitive," he said, "but d'you know what? I don't think you sounded all that grateful just now. For me letting you through."

Fen assured him he was grateful. He conveyed his gratitude with words, with tone of voice, with his eyes, his face, his entire body. He *radiated* gratitude. It was conceivable that no one had been more grateful to anyone in the history of the world ever.

"Well, still," the guard said, "I am a little hurt. Perhaps it'd make me feel better if you gave me something. Yeah. Something as compensation."

"Something as—"

"Like, for example, your car."

"My car."

"It's a lovely little car."

You can't have it, Fen thought.

But of course he could. The man with the rifle could have whatever he wanted.

"Or maybe your walking stick there. I quite fancy that, as a matter of fact. I'm no expert, but it looks like an antique to me."

Fen handed over the walking stick without a quibble. What choice did he have? None, and both he and the guard knew it.

He was sorry to lose the stick, but he would, he thought, be able to manage without it. For the past few days it had been more of a stage prop than a necessity, anyway, and seeing as he had a car now, he didn't anticipate having to do a great deal of walking in the near future.

The guard brandished the stick at him in a kind of ironic salute and waved him on his way.

AND AT LONG last, London.

Half a mile past the checkpoint, Fen could still hardly believe it. Finally, after all this time, he had made it into the capital. He steered his way through suburbs, maintaining a low speed partly because he had to—the quality of the roads inside London was little better than that of the roads outside—but partly because he wanted to. There was much to gaze at as he went, and gaze at it he did, with something of the curiosity of a tourist and something of the bewilderment of a dreamer.

Suburban London was, as it had always been, the overlap between two distinct modes of being. Once, those two modes had been city and country. Now they were past and present. So, while everywhere there was evidence of International Community intervention and of the civic disturbances that had prompted that intervention, there was also the clear impression of old ways having been re-established and, where possible, retained.

Houses were missing (Fen saw semi-detached homes that were now fully detached, and terraced rows with gaping absences like pulled teeth). He passed a shopping mall and several municipal buildings that had been reduced to blackened, burned-out skeletons. There were tower blocks which, with many of their windows patched over with sheets of polythene, resembled vast, three-dimensional crossword puzzles.

And yet, amid all the devastation and dereliction, there were high-street shops open for business, selling basic goods and supplies, including food tins retrieved from International Community airdrops. At intersections there were traffic lights that ran through their signal cycles for the benefit of road-users who, though there were too few of them to make it strictly necessary, obeyed the lights' instructions nonetheless. There were black taxis, grumbling along, their drivers likewise grumbling along, either to themselves or to their fares. There were pubs, and midday drinkers at tables outside, supping pints and shorts. There were schools whose playgrounds were thronged with howling, whirling, delirious children, some of them clad in uniforms, some in home-sewn approximations of uniforms. There were people who looked unmistakably like people with office jobs, and their suits and shoes might not have been of the newest but still they disported themselves with an air of tidy diligence as they strode along pavements or—Fen caught the occasional glimpse through a window—sat at desks and performed whatever clerical or administrative duties it was that they were paid to perform. If they *were* paid, that is. It occurred to him that they might visit their workplaces simply because that was what they had always done before the Unlucky Gamble. They were like rats navigating through a maze in a laboratory, even though there was no longer any cheese at the other end.

It was like some ghostly display, with phantoms of normality flitting to and fro against a backdrop of semi-ruin. Although Fen had known that in London, specifically outer London, life had got back pretty close to the way it was before, he had had no idea, till now, just how close. Hearing about the high standard of amenities and actually seeing it for himself were two very different things. Perhaps the most arresting symbol of the suburbs' regeneration he encountered was a municipal fountain in full working order. Drinkable water, that most valuable commodity in Downbourne, the resource the townsfolk assiduously conserved and prayed for, was here being jetted into the air in profligate amounts, merely for the purpose of providing a public spectacle.

No wonder Londoners had to have permits. No wonder they were so jealously protective about what they had. No wonder they had turned the M25 into their castle moat.

Weirdly enchanted, Fen drove on.

Thanks to Wickramasinghe, he knew where he was headed. Lewisham. The precise route he should take to get there he wasn't sure of, but he was familiar enough with the basic layout of the capital to know that Lewisham was somewhere in the south-east, not far from the Thames, somewhere around Catford, Greenwich, that area—so as long as he continued going northward and eastward and kept an eye on the road signs, he would eventually wind up in the general vicinity of his destination. And having got near, doubtless he would be able to prevail on some helpful passer-by to tell him where, exactly, he might find the British Bulldogs.

It was a nice, sensible, straightforward plan, and it might well have succeeded, had the Beetle not had other ideas.

One moment, the clutch was merely troublesome. The next, it was broken. Fen, needing to downshift from third to second in order to negotiate a sharp bend, put his foot on the pedal and pressed. The pedal did not budge. He pressed harder. Still the pedal would not budge. In a paroxysm of panic, he stamped on the brake. The Beetle juddered, stalled, swerved sideways, and went veering into the kerb.

Since he had not been going particularly fast, the impact, while shocking, caused no injury. He sat for a minute till his jangled nerves steadied, and then he unclamped his hands from the steering wheel and tried to restart the engine. He twisted the ignition key, and the Beetle gave an unhappy gargle and jolted into the kerb again.

Of course. Still in gear.

He wrestled with the gearstick but could not move it. It was locked in place.

Great. Absolutely great.

Fen swore at the Beetle for a while, leaving it in no doubt how he felt about it. He hammered on the clutch pedal with his good foot, hoping that brute force might solve the problem, as brute force so seldom did. Neither the verbal nor the physical assault yielded results. The car was useless. Beam's pride and joy, Fen's easy means of getting to Lewisham, had become an inert, inoperable heap of junk.

So IT WAS back to walking again. As he had commenced his journey, so he would complete it.

After a brisk-paced mile, Fen remained confident. His left leg was bearing up. He was beginning to regret that he had not had the foresight to take some food with him from Fairfield, but he couldn't have known that the car would break down, could he? Besides, he was only slightly hungry. Otherwise he was in good spirits.

After two miles, he was wishing he still had his stick.

Three miles, and he was limping, and he was very hungry indeed, and he had no idea where he was. Somewhere north of Croydon, but that was as accurate as he could be. He had entered the zone where outer London shaded into inner. True suburb was behind him and, with it, the orderliness he had found so remarkable. Here, the city looked depressingly as he had expected it would: worn-out, bombed-out, scoured, rubbled, harrowed. Little was as he remembered, little readily identifiable. Now and then he would come to a section that was sufficiently intact for him to recognise it, but it was like finding a patterned shard amid a heap of broken chinaware, familiar but no longer integrated.

He soldiered on, noting as he went that there were considerably fewer people out and about compared with the suburbs, and they walked quickly and purposefully, those that *were* out and about, and kept their heads down, and resisted catching anyone's eye.

At around the same time as this, he became aware of a piece of graffiti. When he first spotted it, he thought nothing of it. He soon realised, however, that it was everywhere. On walls. On signposts and shop façades. On the hollowed-out frames of phone boxes and bus shelters. Across the torn scraps of poster that still clung to advertising billboards. Spaced out down the white sections of a Belisha beacon pole. A single word, scrawled in marker pen or clumsily spray-painted:

RAZORBOYS

What the graffiti actually signified did not become clear to him until, as he was sitting perched on the wall of somebody's front garden, taking a rest, a couple of young men came strolling by wearing T-shirts with the same word emblazoned across the front. The young men scrutinised him as they passed, subjecting him to the sort of stare that manages to be both appraising and contemptuous, the sort of stare that policeman and security guard and doorman and every other thug with authority struggles to perfect, and all at once it dawned on Fen that they were looking at him in this way because he had strayed onto their territory. He was now in that region of London that was nominally under the control of the London Council and really under the control of people like these two. The graffiti marked the area as theirs. Their T-shirts confirmed the fact. They were entitled, by dint of proprietorship, to look at him in whatever way they wanted.

In the event, the two Razorboys did not give him any grief, although undoubtedly they would have if they had felt the urge. They sauntered on by, and then one of them let rip an immense fart, which prompted his friend to punch him and call him a disgusting pig and say it sounded like he had bust his ringpiece, and this kept them both guffawing all the way to the end of the street and around the corner.

From there on, Fen proceeded with extreme caution. He was in the badlands now, and frankly, it scared him. Taking his cue from the other pedestrians, he moved like a shuffling tramp, gaze fixed on the ground, spine hunched so that he would seem small, unimportant, beneath notice. Northward still, and eastward, he zigzagged through the shattered capital, pausing every so often to take his bearings from the sun, or try to, for the sun appeared to want no part in his plans and dodged erratically across the sky, travelling in any direction except, it seemed, west. Soon its light was filtering sideways, and the city took on a skewed geometry, jagged purplish shadows everywhere. By now, Fen was ravenous, but hadn't a clue what to do about it. He traipsed past restaurants, and what remained of the frontage and decor of each evoked pangs of hunger strong enough to make him groan. A curry house: he could taste the spices. A Chinese take-away: what he wouldn't have given for a heaped-high plate of chow mein. A burger bar: Christ, french fries, french fries, *french fries!* In the partly-demolished interior of a pizza parlour he rooted around for half an hour in the hope that somehow, by some miracle, some item of non-perishable foodstuff had survived, tucked away in a corner, in an undiscovered store cupboard—a tin of tomatoes, some vacuum-packed meat product, *something*. All he turned up, however, was a menu, which he tortured himself by reading and then reading again. The menu even smelled of the various permutations of pizza toppings it advertised, its cardboard impregnated with the wondrous aromas that at one time had swirled wantonly around it. He put it to his nose and inhaled and inhaled and inhaled.

It was hard to concentrate on finding his way when an unfilled stomach commanded so much of his attention. Obtaining something to eat was now a dark, hounding obsession. He approached strangers in the street—people who looked safe—hoping to cadge a meal, but no one was prepared even to listen to what he had to say. It was all too obvious from the way he approached that he was going to ask a favour, and whatever the favour was, they weren't in a position to grant it. It wasn't that kind of world any more. Maybe it had never been. They shooed him away like a stray dog.

Lost, light-headed, despairing, he stumbled on into the thickening haze of evening. A few streetlamps popped into life and brightened from buzzing pink to silent amber. Stars blinked awake in the dirtying sky. Blinds were drawn, hatches battened. In the gathering dark London did not come to life with light and activity as it had used to. It hushed and grew still. And then nightfall.

With the onset of night, Fen knew he had to find shelter. Somewhere to hole up, hide, sleep. He came to a set of railings in front of a church. The church was still used for worship but its door was not locked. All that was worth stealing from inside had been stolen long ago.

He drank from the font, spooning holy water into his mouth with a cupped hand. The water filled his belly, and that made things better.

Curled up on one of the pews, a hassock for a pillow, he fell asleep to the rustle of pigeons in the rafters.

I HAD A dream last night that Fen came for me. He fetched me away from here, whisked me back to Downbourne, and everything was well. Downbourne was its old self, unbusy little country town. I filed my articles—detox this, de-stress that, how to improve your love life, bigger breasts, firmer buttocks, the usual. Fen taught his kids. We got by. We got along. Everything was well.

This morning, everything is *not* well.

It turns out I underestimated Neville. Or rather, I overestimated how bold he would be. I fully thought he would offer some sort of formal challenge to Craig. Not so. He's sidestepped that whole process and crowned himself king anyway. So no Neville/Craig confrontation. Nothing to force Craig to get off his backside and *act*.

Neville, to all intents and purposes, is the new leader of the Bulldogs.

"Men," he says. He's standing on one of the picnic tables. In front of him, an eager, milling throng—dozens upon dozens of close-cropped haircuts, of muscled necks, of transfixed eyes. Weapons are carried. Bats and two-by-four at the ready. Neville has these men in the palm of his hand. Perhaps he's learned a trick or two hanging around Craig. He speaks with the skill of a practised orator, and he looks—I wish I could deny it but I can't—he looks statesman-like.

"This is the time," he says. "This is the hour. This is when we decide whether or not we're going to allow ourselves to be pushed around. Because let's not be under any illusion here. The Frantik Posse are taking the piss. Somehow"—ironic emphasis—"they've got it into their heads that we're a bunch of pushovers. Somehow they seem to think they can just waltz in and steal a piece of our turf and we won't do anything about it. Now, is that true?"

The assembled British Bulldogs mutter and grunt and grumble their negatives.

"No," says Neville, "it isn't fucking true, because that's not how things work around here. That's not how we are. That's not *who* we are. We're called Bulldogs for a reason. You mess with us, we'll bite your sodding leg off!"

Laughter. Some cheering.

"So listen. We all know what's happened. The Frantiks have gone into Brockley, like they said they would, they're lah-di-dah-ing around like they own the place, and I don't even want to get into why they thought they could do this and get away with it, because, well, it's not a subject I much enjoy talking about."

He leaves a pause there, so that the Bulldogs can appreciate not merely what he's referring to but his tact in referring to it so obliquely.

He then makes a minor misstep by deciding to go into detail. "King Cunt thought he was doing the right thing by striking a deal with Eazy-K. All along he was being warned against it but he went and did it anyway, and now that he realises he made a mistake, where is he? What's become of him? Why haven't we seen him lately? I'll tell you why. Because he can't face us. Because he's ashamed."

Some of the Bulldogs sound appropriately disgusted, but a few speak up in favour of Craig. One of them's Mushroom, who—bless his stubby little penis—says: "Fair do's, Nev, he thought he was doing what's best for us."

Neville realises then that he would have been better off not mentioning Craig directly; leaving unsaid what he said would be unsaid. Briefly he flounders, lost for words, and I think (but it's more of a hope than an expectation) that his whole scheme is going to unravel there and then, and the Bulldogs are going to turn on him and heckle him off his makeshift podium and chase him out of the compound and that will be that.

But he recovers. This is his moment. He knows it. His self-belief is riding high. He's silver-tongued. Unstoppable.

"Craig did think that, yeah. His intentions were good. But let's face it, good intentions and smart decisions don't always go hand-in-hand."

He allows time for the epigram sink in. You can see the Bulldogs working it through. *Good intentions. Smart decisions. Oh yeah. Huh. Clever.* They stop scratching their heads and start nodding them.

"And here we are," says Neville. "Left with a right mess to tidy up. We've got people inside our borders who shouldn't be inside our borders. Today it's Brockley. Tomorrow, who knows? Crofton Park? Loampit Hill? Hilly Fields? *Here*? Because that's what's going to happen. You mark my words. The Frantiks aren't going to stop at Brockley. They'll come all the fucking way in, just like they did in Peckham. Or they will if we don't send them packing."

He has the Bulldogs back under his sway again. All of them, even the Craig loyalists like Mushroom, I think. He's appealing to their instinct for self-preservation, their desire to keep the good times rolling for themselves, above all their innate love of a good scrap. What he's also doing—a tactic beloved of monarchs and emperors and politicians throughout the ages—is creating a distraction from an internal problem by directing attention elsewhere, onto an external problem. The Frantiks are a genuine threat to the Bulldogs, no question about it, but for Neville they're also a convenient bogeyman. They're there and he can use them to rally the Bulldogs behind him and in the process cement his popularity as leader, and so that's what he's doing. And he's doing it well, damn him, he's doing it very well indeed.

"What I'm asking from you lot," he continues, "is nothing more than you'd be happy to do anyway. Kicking the Frantiks' arses. They won't be expecting us to come after them. They certainly won't be ready for it. And look at us. *Look* at us. Look how fucking tough we are. I get the shits just seeing all you lot's ugly faces."

That one gets a huge round of laughter.

"And them? Bunch of fucking dopeheads. 'Yah mon, jus' wait till I roll dis spliff before you kick shit outta me, a'right?'"

This time the Bulldogs' laughter is more like a snarl.

"So what are we going to do? I'll tell you what. We're going to hit 'em like a lightning strike. Swift. Sharp. Clean. Sudden. Like we're fucking cobras."

The snarl again, rising in tone, deep, like magma welling up in a volcano.

"Shove 'em back into Peckham. Further, if we can. That's what we're going to do. But I need to know, lads, I need to hear you tell me, are you ready for this?"

A massed assent, an enormous, greedy *YES!*

"Are you ready to give the Frantiks the kicking they deserve?"

Again *YES!*

"Are you sure?"

One more *YES!*—yelled, howled, roared, thundered.

Neville raises his fists aloft, like a demagogue, a dictator. On his face there's a passionate, an almost beatific smile. "Then let's go *get* the fuckers!"

And for a while it's all stampede and frenzy and weapons aloft, and when the dust settles there's just me left behind and, I discover, Lauren. The two of us, standing on opposite sides of the space where, a few moments ago, the Bulldogs were congregated.

We eye each other awkwardly, warily, and then Lauren decides to give me this weird, superior waggle of the eyebrows, like she's someone who's just won a crucial point in a debate. "He was good, wasn't he?" she says.

I feel the urge to call her all sorts of names. Stupid cow. Silly bitch. Can't she see what Neville *is*? He's not a true leader of men, like Craig. He's a rabble-rouser. A shrewd little opportunist who's bided his time and got lucky. I want to say this to her, but then I realise if I do, I'll sound just like she used to before she changed allegiance, before she became Neville's live-in skivvy rather than Craig's. I'll sound like I'm just as head-over-heels about Craig as she used to be.

So instead I say, "Lauren, this isn't going to end well. You know that. For either of us. For all of the women here."

"How d'you reckon that, Moira?"

"Neville's dangerous."

"Oh really?"

"And declaring war on the Frantiks—he may have bitten off more than he can chew."

She sneers at me. "D'you really think that, Moira? Or are you just saying that because you're stuck with Craig? Because Craig's a waste of space now and you just can't bring yourself to admit it?

"A waste of space?"

"You know it, I know it. But only one of us has had the guts to do something about it. Am I right, huh?"

She's got me there. But not in the way she thinks she has. Doing something about Craig—yes, I haven't had the guts. But that's because what I have in mind to do about Craig isn't run away, à la Lauren. What I have in mind is a great deal harder and riskier, which is, of course, the reason I've been putting it off.

I know now that I can't put it off any longer.

"Lauren." I inject defeat into my voice. Let her think she's won. Simpler that way. "You're right. Nailed my colours to the wrong mast. I'm a fool."

"Oh, don't be so hard on yourself, Moira." She sounds almost genuinely sympathetic. "I'm sure you'll get on fine in the recreation zones. Craig's ex-concubine." Well done her, mastering that word.

"You'll be amazingly popular. The guys'll be queuing up for you."

With that, she flounces away.

Queuing up for you. Nice image.

I begin trudging back to the house.

I've gone over this and over this, and it's the only method I can think of for getting Craig to come to his senses.

Am I happy at the prospect of what I'm going to have to do?

I think not.

Is there an alternative?

I think not.

He found a dead pigeon lying on the floor in the nave. No obvious indication of how it died. Just lying there on the flagstones, as though it had quite literally dropped off its perch. He thought it was a dove at first, and the symbolism seemed too absurd to be true. Closer to, he realised the bird was just a pigeon after all, a freakishly white one with a few tiny specks of brown in its plumage.

He didn't eat it.

He was tempted. He picked it up. Weighed it in his hand. Plump, limp little body. Lolling head. Contemplated how he might pluck its feathers, tear its skin open, pull off bits of its flesh, shove them raw into his mouth...

But he didn't.

Repulsed by the idea, and by himself for entertaining the idea, he threw the bird down and stumbled out of the church into the daylight.

It was an overcast morning. Warmish but not warm. A light wind gusting. Mealy-coloured clouds lidding the city. He began walking straight away, at first to put distance between him and the church (and the pigeon, and the temptation) but once the church was out of sight he kept going because he was already in motion and it seemed easier to continue than to stop. Then he did stop. After half a mile, he felt a sudden, hollowing onrush of dizziness. Weak-kneed, woozy, he looked for the nearest thing to sit down on, which was the stump of a tree. Since the winter that followed the worst of the bombing, very few trees in the inner London area had been left standing, arboreal beautification having had to give way to the need for firewood. He lowered himself onto the stump and stayed there till his head cleared and he felt strong enough to carry on. In the interim, he watched the wind pluck at the edge of a bin-liner that had been fixed, none too securely, over a hole in a roof. The bin-liner wavered, lifting, descending, lifting, descending, never quite touching down, like a nervous lover's hand. Fen was mesmerised. He could have sat and watched it all day.

But on he went.

It was all he could do. All he had left to him. He had come this far. To give up now was unthinkable. He knew that she was somewhere near. Moira. Somewhere near. If he kept going long enough, if he could just keep going long enough, he would find her.

Right foot, then left.

Along buckled roadways, over uneven pavement, treading the contours of London's hills—on he went.

Right foot, then left.

Momentum propelling him. The accumulated weight of the distance he had travelled to get to here. A last few ergs of inertial energy, spinning themselves out, bearing him along on their ebb.

Right foot, then left.

A final, desperate, all-or-nothing push. No sense of direction, only purpose. No sense of destination, only hope.

Right foot, then left.

He paid no attention to his weaker leg, which pleaded with him to stop. He blanked out the hunger, miserable in his belly, that dragged, nagged, ached, enervated. Mind over body. Him versus himself.

Right foot, then left.

And on, and on, and on. One step after another. Thinking no further ahead than where to place which foot next.

Right foot, then left.

Who was he? Not Fen Morris but gradually, receding, now, an entity inside Fen Morris. Sharer of his own body. Passenger in his own skull. Staring out.

Right foot, then left.

Viewing the world like a rider on horseback or a sailor on a ship's deck. Watching the scenery sway up and down, lurch from side to side. Watching people pass by as indifferent to him as stalks of corn in a field.

Right foot, then left.

A bus depot. Every one of the parked red double-deckers with its windows and headlamps smashed. Methodical, systematic vandalism.

Right foot, then left.

A flyover, broken in two. A landslide of concrete boulders. Snapped reinforcement bars protruding from their sheared edges, like iron bristles. Some children treating the rubble as though it had been put there for their benefit, a place to clamber over and explore.

Right foot, then left.

A shanty village occupying what had once been a construction yard. Huddled, ramshackle shelters cobbled together from pieces of plywood, timber, corrugated iron, other scavenged scraps. Leaning against one another, mutually supportive. Homes for the displaced, the dispossessed, the despondent.

Right foot, then left.

A rat, hunkered inside an overturned dustbin like a bear in its cave. Doing what Fen had not been able to bring himself to do: gnawing on the corpse of a pigeon. Blood on feathers. Tiny yellow incisors. Little jealous eyes.

Right foot, then left.

A bomb crater on a common, as though some gigantic hand had reached down with an equally gigantic trowel and scooped out a section of the planet. And not far away, another missile that had landed but, unlike its fellow, failed to detonate. Embedded nose-first in the earth. Surrounded by a carpet of weather-worn offerings: flowers, keepsakes, handwritten messages, items of clothing, cuddly toys. Propitiatory tributes at a shrine.

Right foot, then left.

A municipal park. Shorn of trees. Stripped, too, of the play apparatus in its children's activity area. Swings, seesaw, slide, climbing frame—all dismantled, taken away for use elsewhere, leaving just empty oblongs of rubbery all-weather base, dented by the impacts of a thousand minor tumbles.

Right foot, then left.

The Thames. Surly and slow and grey-green. Easing eastwards. Its waters swirling in lagoons where the river bank had been breached by bombs. On the foreshore, mudlarks scavenging.

Right foot, then left.

Canary Wharf tower, rising high above the rooftops. The immense glass-and-steel obelisk having been used, it would appear, for aerial target practice. Gouged, bruised, scarred.

Right foot, then left.

A street with few pedestrians about, and then an adjoining street with ever fewer. A feeling. Something he could not put his finger on. An tingle in the atmosphere. The sense that there was a reason why people were suddenly not around. A rhythm he was not attuned to but they were. Invisible signs he did not know how to read.

And then, around a corner: men, fighting. Scuffles up and down the length of a street. Black men with dark blue bandannas knotted around their heads. White men with next to no hair. Laying into one another with brutal intensity. A clamour of shouting. Bared teeth. Bloodied, pummelling knuckles. Contorted faces. Pistoning arms. Weapons pounding. Combatants running to and fro, seeking fresh opponents, launching themselves frenziedly into existing brawls. Black against white. White against black. A rhythmless choreography of fist, knee, foot, elbow, forehead, wood on flesh, impact, impact, impact. And there: a nose getting mashed by a hard, sharp, sidelong chop with a broom-handle truncheon. And there: a man on his knees, clutching his groin, ashen-faced, vomiting. And there: someone yelling defiance even as his arms were pinioned behind his back by one opponent and he was punched repeatedly in the mouth by another. And there: someone on the ground, having his fingers whacked with a baseball bat until every one of them was broken. And there: an ear being bitten, an indignant scream, a chunk of cartilaginous flesh being spat out...

And now Fen, being seized by the arm, being yanked into a doorway, through the doorway, inside.

Door slamming.

"Jesus Christ! You ruddy great moron, are you *trying* to get yourself killed?"

THE MAN WAS angry. Angry like a father whose child has just performed some staggeringly foolish stunt and avoided injury thanks only to a timely parental intervention. He bolted the door and went off muttering, leaving Fen alone. *And you can stay there while you think about what you've done*. Outside, the fighting raged on, dimly, a conflict in another world. Fen peered around. A large room. Windows on two sides, boarded over. The shapes of furnishings gradually loomed into visibility through dust-hazed stripes of sunlight. Chairs and tables, leafy anaglypta wallpaper, the squarish bulk of what looked to be a jukebox, and was that a dartboard? And over there, filling out the far end of the room—a bar?

He pulled up a chair and dumped himself gratefully into it. His feet throbbed with relief; his bad leg, too.

Some time later, his rescuer returned.

"Listen." He was a raw-skinned, big-bearded man. Used to be professionally jolly, you could tell. Brawny, too. A laughing, no-nonsense type. Though not any more. "About earlier. Sorry. For shouting at you. But I mean, honestly, what did you think you were up to? Standing out there like a prize chump."

Fen couldn't think of a reply to that.

"The Frantiks wouldn't have known the difference, not with their blood up like that. Just one more white guy needing to have his face bashed in."

"Pub," said Fen.

The man blinked. "That's right, yes." Mentally downgrading Fen from berk to nutter, he took a precautionary step backwards. "A pub. Used to be, anyway."

"Yours?"

"Of course. And before you ask, no, I don't have anything to drink. Not a drop."

"Eat," said Fen. "What about eat?"

"Nor that either. I don't have anything except what I need to survive. Look, you're welcome to stay, but only till things calm down outside. After that, out. It's the most I can offer."

Fen nodded, accepting. It was the most he could expect.

SLOWLY THINGS DID calm down outside. The shouts and the stampeding and the unholy smackings of wood on flesh faded away as the fighting moved on elsewhere. The publican kept watch by the window, peering out through the gaps between boards. Fen sat in his chair with his arms wrapped tight around his belly, drifting back and forth between full consciousness and semi-trance. The numerous scratches and indentations on the tabletop in front of him, the crudely carved words, the stains etched into the varnish by alcohol spillages, all kept swirling before his eyes, forming themselves into patterns. Not just patterns but symbols, hieroglyphs whose meaning, if he could only interpret it, would, he knew, explain everything he had ever wanted to know. He was forever on the brink of a great understanding, but then the patterns would break up, dispersing back into randomness, all intelligibility gone, and he would be left with the tantalising sense of a wonderful opportunity lost. He hoped, each time, that order might be extracted from disarray. Each time, he was disappointed.

Finally the publican said, "Well, that looks like that. All clear. Time you were on your way."

Fen rose to his feet.

Then he was lying flat on the floor.

How had *that* happened?

He heard the publican hiss through his teeth. "Fuck's sake! What is *wrong* with you?"

"Food," Fen mumbled. "Hungry."

For a while there was silence, and then he heard the publican sigh. It was the sigh of someone who has decided, against his better judgement, against every instinct he has, to do good.

The meal came from tins—baked beans, processed ham, peach slices in syrup—and was served up with the minimum of presentation. The publican opened the tins, handed Fen a fork, wielded another fork himself, and together they took it in turns, digging in, prising out, shovelling into their mouths.

It was hardly *haute cuisine*, but it was one of the best meals Fen had ever had the pleasure of putting into his body, and once he had finished he was appropriately grateful.

"Don't thank me, thank the International Community," said the publican. "It giveth as well as taketh away. Though not so often."

Fen now felt well enough to explain how he had come to be standing outside the publican's door in the middle of that pitched battle. In return, the publican explained how the pitched battle had come about and who the two sets of combatants were.

"Bulldogs?" said Fen. "*British* Bulldogs?"

"Our local landlords, you might call them. Although how long they remain that way is anybody's guess."

"But it's them." Fen felt a prickle of excitement. "They're the ones. They're the ones. There's only one gang in London called the British Bulldogs, right?"

"Far as I know."

"And this *is* Lewisham."

"Edge of."

"So they come from round here. I mean, they have some sort of headquarters here."

"About a mile due east."

Fen sat back. That was it, then. *A mile due east*. Half an hour's walk. Less.

"Will you give me directions?" he asked. "How to get there?"

"If you like. I don't recommend you try, though."

"Why not?"

The publican gestured towards the windows. "You've seen for yourself—we're in the middle of a territory war. Not sensible to get caught up in that. Again. And then there's the small matter of actually gaining access to the Bulldogs' lair. It's pretty much a fortress. Certain specific times, outsiders are allowed in. The rest of the time, not. What do you have in mind? Stroll up to the gate and demand entry?"

"Won't that work?"

"It might. Most likely not. Please understand, I'm not trying to pour cold water on your plans. It's just that you couldn't have picked a worse time to turn up. The Bulldogs are fighting to keep control of the borough, and word is that King Cunt's no longer in charge. Nobody's seen him in a while. I've even heard it said that the Bulldogs have kicked him out and he's left London."

Fen recalled the tattoos on the Bulldogs' forearms and necks. King Cunt. Their leader.

"All the same," he said.

"All the same," said the publican, nodding. "They took your wife. Here you are. The circumstances are far from ideal, but there's not a lot you can do about that. All right..." With a heavy exhalation, he stood up, left the room, and returned moments later with a pen. He peeled the label off the tin of baked beans and smoothed it out flat on the table, unprinted side up. "Here we go." He began drawing. "This is the pub, here. First off, you need to head down this way. And then..."

It was quiet as Fen stepped outside. The street seemed strangely unaltered by the violence to which it had played host just an hour earlier, as though human carnage were a phenomenon it was well accustomed to. There were spatters of blood here and there, already hardened and black, and a puddle of vomit which a scrawny, jittery cat was hurriedly lapping up. Otherwise, little trace. The wounded were gone. The street looked no more or less ravaged than any other street in the area. The fighting might as well never have happened.

The publican, in the doorway, wished him luck and godspeed. "If you don't make it," he added, "or they don't let you in, come back here."

Fen shook his head. "You've done enough."

"Hey. In for a penny..."

Fen smiled gratefully, then looked down at the map the publican had drawn for him and turned it till it was correctly orientated. When he looked up again, the publican had withdrawn indoors. He heard the sound of bolts sliding to.

He realised then—to his surprise and, it must be said, shame—that he had failed to learn the man's name. True, the publican had neglected to introduce himself, but that was no excuse. When someone helped you like that, the least you could do was find out who he or she was. It was only proper.

Well, he thought, if nothing else I can make sure I remember the name of the pub, which is...

His gaze travelled up to the long, narrow board on the side of the building, where faded gold letters on a flaking black background spelled out three simple words.

And he stared.

And then he laughed.

And then suddenly his amusement curdled, and a feeling of disquiet stole over him. It was all right to laugh, but not when there was a good chance that he himself was the butt of the joke.

A pub called The Green Man?

He looked across to the sign that hung from the corner of the building.

There, too, was the pub's name, along with a depiction of a man wreathed in foliage, with twinkling eyes, a merry smile, holding a foaming tankard aloft. He did not resemble the late mayor of Downbourne in any way, this apple-cheeked, boozy charmer whose features were criss-crossed with horizontal fissures where the wood of the sign had warped and split. Nor did he resemble the figure Fen had seen twice in his dreams, once on the railway embankment, once in the sanatorium at Netherholm: that transformed and transforming version of Michael Hollingbury, the first time a man with tree-like attributes, the second time a tree with man-like attributes. *This* Green Man looked exactly as a picture of a Green Man painted on a pub sign ought to look.

There was something about him, nevertheless.

The smile.

The knowing cast of his features.

No.

Rubbish.

It was easy to read too much into this sort of thing. Coincidences, Fen felt, existed solely in order to disprove the notion of a planned, rigid universe. If everything wasn't entirely random, if some guiding force did run the show, then coincidences would never happen, because a guiding force would never choose to be that obvious. Like the author of a novel, it stood to gain by remaining hidden, submerged within its material, its machinations well masked. To reveal itself time and time again was to jeopardise the illusion it had worked to hard to foster in humans—the illusion that their lives were their own, their destinies malleable, their decisions all a matter of free will; that they weren't puppets whose every action, from birth to death, was preplanned. In a universe that was entirely driven by chance, coincidences—by the laws of statistics and averages—*had* to happen.

In fact, looked at objectively, the manifestation of a Green Man three times in Fen's recent history was hardly worthy of being called a coincidence at all.

A couple of dreams and the name of a pub, that was all it amounted to. The memory of someone he had seen die horribly. A very common British pub name.

And just like that, Fen was able to dispel the eerie tingle he had been feeling. Nothing to it. Simply apply a bit of cold, hard rationality to the problem and it went away.

And he wasn't troubled as he walked away from the pub, following the route indicated by the publican's map.

Wasn't glad to leave the pub behind him.

Wasn't relieved when he turned a corner and there was no longer the pub's presence at his back and no longer the fear that, if he glanced over his shoulder, the man in the sign would have changed and his face would now very much resemble that of Michael Hollingbury. Or, worse, that of the publican.

None of that.

Oh no.

Not looking forward to this. *So* not looking forward to his.

Each step I take up the staircase—the condemned prisoner walking towards the electric chair.

Get a grip, Moira! Don't be so melodramatic.

But still...

Out of the corner of my eye I catch Zoë peering up from the living-room doorway. I wave angrily: *I told you, stay in there, keep the door shut*. She retreats, closing the door.

Good girl.

Craig's fast asleep on our bed. I wanted to wait till he woke up, but it seems he's out for the count. Which means I'm going to have to wake him up, which isn't going to help at all.

Deep breath. Here goes.

Nudge.

"Craig."

Another nudge.

"Craig."

A low, burbling murmur that ends with "Go away."

"Craig, we have to talk."

That does the trick. Four words every man dreads to hear from a woman: *we have to talk*.

He lifts his head from the pillows, puffy-eyed, not happy. "What the fuck is it?"

"We have to talk"—my mouth is so dry—"about Kirsty."

He looks at me like I'm mad.

Then he looks at me like I'm stupid.

Then he slams his head back down onto the pillow.

"Piss off, Moira."

I sense that this is the point of no return. My last chance to back out. But I can't. There's too much at stake. So:

"You gave up on her, didn't you?"

No reply.

"After that night at the rave when you punched Neville and she got cross with you for it. It all started to go wrong from there. Your relationship. All started to turn sour."

Still no reply, other than a brief, testy sigh.

"You loved her, though. You still do. She's the only woman you've ever really loved."

Now Craig looks up again, and his face is blank contempt, but I can see it in his eyes—I'm getting to him.

"Moira, I don't know why you think I'm interested in hearing any of this," he says, coldly, precisely, "but I promise you, I'm not. In fact, I promise you that right now this is the very last thing I'm interested in hearing."

The threat could not be more explicit. Leave him be or else.

But of course, what else can I do except forge on?

"That's why you have a thing for redheads. You can't have Kirsty back, much as you wish you could. So what do you have instead? A string of Kirsty substitutes. That way you can be reminded of her but, because none of us is ever going to be her, you don't have to worry about falling in love. We remind you of her just enough to remind you that we're *not* her. And falling in love is something you really don't want to do because look at all the hassle and the pain it brought you the last time you did. You can't bear to go through all that again, so best avoid it, eh?"

He waits a moment, then says, "Finished?"

I shake my head.

"Then, before you go any further, a word of advice. This isn't clever, Moira, this psychoanalytical bollocks. I don't know what you're hoping to achieve, but you're wrong on so many counts. So many counts. So just give it a rest, all right? For your sake, not mine."

"You gave up on her, Craig. You know you did. The moment things started to get difficult, you gave up on her. You let her slip through your fingers, and all because you were too proud."

"What?"

"Too proud to admit you'd done something wrong. Too proud to apologise. That's all Kirsty was waiting for—you to say sorry, to say that you acted like a big fat idiot, you shouldn't have, please forgive me. But you didn't. You couldn't."

"Moira..." Not so much my name, more a growl.

"She didn't leave you, Craig. Kirsty didn't give you the elbow. You let her go. And you did it knowingly, and it was the single biggest mistake of your life, and you've been bitterly regretting it ever since."

He sits upright, slides off the bed, stands, one swift agile movement. So big but so fast. Now I'm looking up at his face instead of down. Now we're one yard apart instead of three.

I'm within his reach. Within striking distance.

I should be terrified.

But I'm the woman the Bulldogs kidnapped and kept in a bricked-up room for God knows how many days. I'm the woman who's managed to survive all this time in Fort Bulldog and maintain her sanity and her dignity. Most of all: I'm the woman Craig has allowed to share his house, to accompany him on trips, the woman he has confided in, slept with, the woman he trusts, perhaps even respects.

He will not hit me. He will not.

"You were a coward. Big King Cunt, a coward."

His face reddens. His eyes bulge.

"You were a coward then, and you're being a coward now."

His fist clenches. A part of me can hardly believe I'm saying these things to him. Another part of me knows I have to, no matter what the consequences.

"And you know why you're a coward? Because whenever you have a problem, not a practical problem, an emotional problem, a *personal* problem, you refuse to face up to it. Oh sure, King Cunt can handle anything. King Cunt's the fixer, the fighter, the organiser, the ruler. There's nothing *he* can't deal with. But Craig? Once you get to Craig, it's a whole different story. Like now. Neville's stolen your empire right from under your nose, and you've let him. He's undermined everything you ever worked for, just like he undermined everything you had with Kirsty. You know this. You told me you've been wise to his game all along. But why haven't you done anything? Because Neville's your blind spot. Your great weakness. The flaw in this marvellous moral code you live by. You've let him stay with you all this time, tag along in your slipstream, because you somehow think you owe it to him. You think you need him, perhaps so that you won't forget where you came from, your youth, your background, your origins—or perhaps because every time he grins and you see his gold tooth you remember how it felt to lose control and hit him, how it felt to turn on someone you're still for some reason convinced is your best friend. Christ, Craig, that's what Neville plays on. That's his great advantage over you. He grins all the time when he's around you, have you noticed that? And you can bet whenever he does it, part of the reason is to make sure that tooth of his reminds you what you did to him. But then was it really so bad, hitting him? Didn't he deserve it? Wasn't he *asking* for it?"

I have to keep talking now, if only to forestall a reaction from Craig. Keep talking. Let it all come tumbling out. All these words that I've planned, rehearsed in my head over and over for days, but still somehow never expected to hear myself say out loud.

"If that guilt has been eating at you ever since, it's time you bloody well stopped letting it. You are King Cunt. Hardest of the hard. You are King Canute. You stood up to the tide, to a whole tsunami of troubles, and turned it back. You did that. You can do the same now. The only difference now is that this time the enemy isn't outside. It's in you. It's *you*. All that mess that's in your head, all those conflicts between what you think you ought to be and who you really are."

He raises his arm. Fist the size of a wrecking ball at the end of it.

"You can give up," I tell him, "or you can fight back. Which is it to be? Because it's not too late. Neville's running things for now, but you're still here and your Bulldogs still aren't completely convinced their future lies with anyone other than you. You can pull this back from the brink, even now. *If* you choose to. That's what it boils down to, Craig. You have to make the decision. You have to want your kingdom back, otherwise you won't get it."

No more. I've run out. I've stated my case. Nothing more to say.

His fist hovers in the air.

It occurs to me: in attempting to save my own skin, it could be that all I've done is put myself in line for a severe beating.

But I knew the risks in goading him like this.

I had to get him angry, and I've succeeded.

The fist hovers.

This is just a few seconds. This is forever.

No man has ever laid a finger on me before.

Craig will not hit me.

The fist hovers.

Pure silence. We are in a bubble, the two of us. There is nothing in the world but us.

I look him in the eye.

The fist hovers.

It will only be pain.

He moves.

I flinch.

He wheels away.

He lets out a guttural yell.

A lamp goes flying.

A bedside table does a backflip.

The bed is hurled over onto its end, covers sliding off, mattress bouncing.

The curtains are torn down.

He starts pounding the wall. Thump after thump after thump, until the plaster begins to crack and fall away in chips and then in chunks and then bare brick is exposed, and still he keeps pounding. As though he can break through. As though, if he keeps at it long enough, hard enough, he can bring the whole house down.

He curses all the while, spitting out a long chain of profanities, giving vent to the frustration he has been feeling, articulating the injustices that have been done to him, naming the principal source of his pain: *Nev, Nev, Nev...*

Women cry. Men cry out.

He grunts and swears and rails and pounds away, and the house reverberates to the damage being inflicted upon it, a huge sounding-board for King Cunt's anger and anguish.

He would not stop, he would keep at it till every bone in his hands was broken and probably even after that...

...but I touch his arm.

Squeeze ever so gently.

And he halts.

His head droops. He stares down at his hands.

The knuckles are split open, red raw. Blood is flowing freely.

He stares down wonderingly, as if his hands don't belong to him, are not part of him.

Then, after about a minute, he turns his gaze on me.

He seems lost, confused. A small boy in a giant's body.

But little by little, the confusion clears. Certainty enters his eyes. His face relaxes, the redness suffusing away.

We look at each other.

"Moira," he says.

He sounds grim, but also cool and clear-headed. For the first time in—what is it, a fortnight?—he sounds something close to his old self.

"Hi."

Tentatively, like he's recognising me after a lengthy absence.

"We have work to do, don't we?"

And I nod.

"All right then," he says.

And I smile.

And he says, "What's the plan?"

THE HUE AND cry of men in combat drifted across the rooftops and resounded along the empty streets. Sometimes it was far away, sometimes dangerously close. It almost seemed to be searching for Fen, like some rapacious, amoeboid monster, roving around, feeling blindly for him, but in the event he reached the Bulldog compound without finding himself in the thick of battle again and, indeed, without encountering another living soul along the way.

The compound gate cut across the end of a road, just as indicated on the publican's map. On either side there was a jumble of junk, piled high, every piece of it seemingly locked in place, a wall it would be difficult to scale or dismantle. Looming high over the gate there was a lookout post, with two Bulldogs stationed in it. Fen squared his shoulders and strode towards them with all the self-possession and erectness of bearing he could muster, hoping to convince them, even before he spoke to them, that he meant business.

It didn't work. The two Bulldogs watched him approach, and when he was close enough, one of them made a turning-around gesture in the air.

"Not today, mate."

"Back indoors," the other added. "It's not safe."

"I'm here," Fen said simply, "for my wife."

The two Bulldogs exchanged frowns.

"You what?"

"My wife. She was taken a couple of months back by you lot. I want her back."

The reasonableness of this seemed to confuse them.

"Are you mad?"

"You're having a laugh."

"I've come a long way for her," Fen said, "and I'm not leaving without her."

One of the Bulldogs puffed out his cheeks, then shook his head in a world-weary fashion. "I don't know if you've noticed, pal, but—not to put too fine a point on it—there's a war on."

"Anyway," said the other, "you can't come wandering up like a big twat and think we're going to open up for you and let you in just because you ask us to."

With, of course, the exception of the "like a big twat" part, this was a pretty accurate summation of Fen's plan of action.

Well, the publican had said it was unlikely to work.

What now?

"Then I'll wait," he said.

"Beg pardon?"

"I'll stand here and wait."

"You've got to be fucking kidding."

"I've come fifty miles. I've been through hell and high water to get here. I'll wait."

The two Bulldogs had not heard anything so preposterous in a long time, a fact they conveyed to Fen in no uncertain terms. Beyond that, however, there was little they could say or do. The moron down below wanted to wait, fine, he could wait. For all the good it would do him.

For a while Fen stood at the gate. The two Bulldogs stood in the lookout post. They taunted him sporadically. *Bored yet? Didn't you bring a book to read? Oh, all right then, you can come in—oops, no, sorry, you can't.* He shrugged it off.

Gradually, though, the needling took a nastier turn. The Bulldogs found it irksome that they couldn't get a rise out of him. His refusal to be annoyed, annoyed.

"This wife of yours," said one. "What she look like? I mean, she must be a bit of all right if you've come fifty miles for her."

Fen stuck to his policy of silence.

"See, the reason I'm asking is, I've probably had her."

"Me, too," the other Bulldog chimed in.

"So I thought we can maybe compare notes. She like it missionary?"

"Doggy-fashion?"

"Up the arse?"

"Bet she loves it up the arse."

"All the girls do."

"Not the first time, but once you've broken 'em in..."

"Can't get enough of it, once they've been broken in."

Finally: a reaction.

"She's medium build." Fen kept his face as impassive, his voice as steady, as he could. "About so high. Attractive. She has auburn hair. Her name is Moira Morris."

The two Bulldogs went quiet, as though slapped, and then broke into disbelieving laughter.

"You're *Moira's* husband?"

"Fucking hell."

"The ginge minge."

"King Cunt's private totty."

Fen wasn't sure whether to be encouraged by these remarks or not. "She's with him, then? Your leader? This King Cunt person?"

"In a manner of speaking."

"She isn't with him?"

"The 'our leader' bit, is what I meant. Yeah, she's with him all right."

"But he's not here any more," Fen said, recalling what the publican had told him.

And just like that, he understood that it had all been for nothing. His journey. His sufferings. Moira had left. King Cunt had gone and had dragged her with him, God knows where. He was never going to find her now.

"Who told you that?" one of the Bulldogs wanted to know.

"That's what I heard," Fen replied. "King Cunt has left London."

"Well, whoever said that, they're wrong. He's still here. He just—"

There, the Bulldog broke off and turned to his companion. Fen was too far below them to hear the brief, whispered discussion that followed. All he knew was that, a moment later, both men were looking down at him with a very much altered demeanour.

"Listen," one said. "We've decided to bend the rules a bit. Make a special case for you."

"Seeing as you look an OK sort of bloke," said the other. "And you have come a long way."

"And we're not total wankers."

"We're not wankers at all."

"So this is what we're going to do." The Bulldog pointed to his companion. "Trevor here is going to come down and open the gate and take you to King Cunt's house to see your missus. How about that, eh? Can't say fairer than that."

Fen made the appropriate appreciative noises, but remained sceptical. Even as he watched the Bulldog called Trevor climb out of the lookout post and disappear from view, he was prepared for the possibility that it was all a pretence. Any moment, Trevor would pop back up and both Bulldogs would start laughing and jeering at him again. What was it about men who guarded entry-points, he wondered, that made them so prone to sarcasm, scorn and silly little games? The dullness of the job, he supposed, combined with the absolute power it gave them over people's futures.

Then from behind the gate he heard a loud *clunk*—the sound of something heavy being drawn back. A moment later, the gate was open and there was Trevor, beckoning him inside.

Fen entered the compound on a small but heartening high of gratification. Clearly something about him—his words, his plight, his abundant sincerity—had struck a chord with the two Bulldogs and had won him access through the final obstacle on his long journey. It was a victory of decency over thuggishness. Or perhaps tenacity over thuggishness. A victory over thuggishness, at any rate.

He followed Trevor across the compound, struggling to match the forthright pace set by the Bulldog. There was, as far as he could see, not a great deal of difference between what lay inside the compound wall and what lay outside. Here was the same shabbiness, the same cracked window panes and paving slabs, the same treeless spaces, the same level of disrepair, the same intensity of decline. The wall, it seemed to him, had been thrown arbitrarily around a section of the city. The compound was a fortified piece of anywhere.

He wondered what effect ten weeks in this place would have had on Moira. It was hardly likely that it had not left its mark on her in some way or other. He was, after all, under no illusion as to the purpose for which she and the other Downbourne women had been kidnapped. It wasn't a matter to which he had so far devoted a great deal of thought, by deliberate choice. Only now, with their reunion imminent, did he permit himself to begin to contemplate what would have been done to Moira while she'd been here—what she would have had no choice but to allow to be done. The thought stirred up an angry nausea, which he forced back down. Pointless wasting energy on rage. He was better off waiting to see how Moira herself had been affected by her ordeal. If she could cope with it, so could he.

"Tell me," he said, in the hope that conversation would oblige Trevor to reduce his speed. "This King Cunt—is he a reasonable sort of person? Do you think he can be bargained with?"

"Can't say, really. You catch him on a good day, then maybe."

"And today's a good day?"

"Oh no."

Fen was startled by the offhand malice of the reply. "But you're still taking me to see him."

"It's *why* I'm taking you to see him. We thought it would be amusing."

"You thought it would be amusing. Your and your friend on lookout detail."

"Yeah, me and Larry." Trevor grinned. "See, the King's kind of not the King any more. He doesn't have much to do with the rest of us any more.

He's all shacked up with his redhead, your missus, and this kid, this girl. Playing happy families. Or *un*happy families, it could be, possibly, who knows. Who cares? Anyhow, me and Larry, we thought it'd be funny to drag you along and throw you into the mix. Just for a laugh, as it were."

"Ah. I see."

"Sort of, I don't know, a spanner in the works, along those lines."

Fen laced his voice with as much sarcasm as he dared. "How very ingenious of you."

Trevor simply shrugged. "Yeah, well, look at it this way. I'm not the one who's come fifty miles to try and get his wife back from a bloke twice his size and ten times tougher. Who's ingenious *now*, eh?"

There was, Fen realised, no good answer to that.

I CAN TREMBLE now. Now that it's over. Now that it worked.

I can berate myself for not doing it sooner.

I can say to myself, *well, that was easier than you thought it was going to be,* and feel a wry inward smile forming.

Easy? Well, maybe not.

But I judged him exactly right. I gauged which buttons to press and I pressed them.

I *knew* him.

I don't think I've ever felt this exhilarated.

In the living room, I apply bandages to Craig's hands, binding them tight. Meanwhile, Craig apologises to Zoë. He doesn't have to do this but he wants to. He tells her he's sorry for the way he's been acting this past couple of weeks, although it's clear (to me, at least) that he's saying sorry for a great deal more. Zoë hears him out graciously. She doesn't go so far as to say she forgives him, and I don't think that's what he's looking for anyway, but she lets him know she appreciates the gesture. She asks him if his hands hurt. He tells her they do but it's a pain he can cope with, a pain he thinks is useful.

That out of the way, Craig gets me to bring him up to speed on what's been going on lately in the compound and outside. When I tell him that Neville has gone to war against the Frantik Posse, he nods gravely. Absolutely the right thing to do, of course, but he wonders what sort of battle strategy Neville has adopted.

"On the evidence I've seen," I say, "none at all. Just hit them hard and hope for the best."

"They're tough, the Frantiks. They're no cowards." Craig winces slightly over that last word, as though it's a thorn that's snagged in his brain. "It'll take more than sheer brute force to beat them. If Neville doesn't win today..."

"That'll be bad, yes. Very bad. But, as far as the three of us are concerned, there is a worse possibility."

"What's that?"

"If Neville *does* win. Then he'll no longer be just leader, he'll be a hero.

And consequently, anyone who goes up against him will automatically be the villain."

"Even me."

"Even you."

"So where does that leave us?"

Before we have a chance to explore this vexed question, there's a knock at the door.

Zoë goes to answer it.

I can scarcely believe the words I hear her say next.

"Mr Morris? What—what are *you* doing here?"

Fen had to smile. When was the last time anyone had been quite so pleased and astonished to see him? Apart from Beam, that is.

"Hello, Zoë. I'm not surprised you're surprised. As a matter of fact, I'm pretty surprised to be here myself."

"But— But—" Zoë spun round and called excitedly into the house, "Moira! Come and see who it is! You'll never guess!" She turned back to Fen. "This is terrific. You've come to take us back to Downbourne, haven't you? That's why you're here."

Fen bit his lip. "I hope so, Zoë. If I'm allowed." He threw a glance at Trevor, who answered him with a remorseless grin.

"Fen?"

Moira appeared in the doorway beside Zoë. Behind her was one of the biggest human beings Fen had ever seen, a Bulldog whose hulking massiveness made the hallway of the house, indeed the house itself, seem ridiculously tiny, as though it had been built for dwarves. Fen saw the man's face, didn't like the look of it; noticed his bandaged hands, didn't like the look of those either. He concentrated his attention exclusively on Moira.

She had changed, no question about it. She was not the woman he had said a curt thank-you to in their kitchen all those weeks ago, shortly before he walked out of 12 Crane Street. No longer was there that air of wounded exhaustion about her. Gone, too, was the tightness around her mouth which he had become so used to seeing and which had given the impression that she was forever restraining herself, that even harsher comments than the ones she let out were queuing up on her tongue, effortfully withheld. She seemed taller and she seemed younger, more like the Moira he had known when they were first going out. The light was there in her grey eyes again, the intelligence, the willingness to engage with the world.

She had, in a word, flourished.

And that was wrong. That was not supposed to be.

The weeks of mistreatment at the hands of the Bulldogs should have left her a wreck. She should have been haggard, empty, bewildered. She should have taken one look at him and thrown herself into his arms. That was the reception he had been expecting. The reception he deserved, damn it. An outpouring of relief. Exclamations of joy and gratitude. Tears.

She should have been glad to see him. As glad as Zoë was. Gladder.

And she was not.

Instead, she was looking at him with her eyebrows knotted slightly, her head canted to one side. Something in her face said *irritation*. Something else said *unease*.

He wanted to believe that it was simply that his turning up like this, out of the blue, had startled her. Moira was so taken aback, she didn't know how to react.

But as the seconds ticked by, her expression did not soften into delight. If anything, the opposite.

At first it's like seeing a ghost. How can he be here? He's in Downbourne. Fifty miles south. He has no place being here. He does not fit. His presence jars.

Slowly, though, I accept that it's really him. No ghost. No illusion. No doppelgänger. Fen. Here. Looking a little dusty, a little grubby. His hair needs cutting. He could do with a shave. But Fen. Same old Fen. Stalwart, dependable Fen. Essentially unchanged since I last saw him. As though, as soon as he walked out of our house, he was snatched up by some magical whirlwind, whisked across space and time, and deposited here only slightly the worse for wear. From doorstep to doorstep in a twinkling.

What can I say to him? What does he expect from me?

I don't know.

But then I become aware of Craig standing behind me, and all of a sudden it's as if there are two of me inside me, two Moiras, the Moira I was and the Moira I am, and neither seems real. Each is a part I've played, a costume I've worn. One lived with the man in front of me in a small country town and fell into despair and thought she would never come out. The other lives with the man behind me in this cordoned-off pocket of a South London housing estate and has just pulled off one of the most courageous feats she has ever attempted. In the midst of her triumph, the partner from her old life appears. Past gatecrashes present. Doors burst. Clocks spin out of true. The world warps.

And then comes guilt.

Beside Fen, Trevor shuffled his feet. Of all the possible outcomes of the husband-and-wife reunion that he and Larry had anticipated, dumbstruck staring was, quite clearly, not one. In a way Fen was glad to disappoint, but he himself, of course, had also been hoping for something a little more positive, a little less underwhelming, than this. He groped for words to say to end the deadlock.

"I broke my leg," was what he came up with. To him it had been a crucial moment, the point at which his journey had gone from straightforward to wayward. But stated baldly, out of context, it seemed unimpressive. Banal.

"Oh dear." Somehow Moira managed to sound both intrigued and indifferent, as if one part of her brain was registering the fact that he had suffered a serious injury and supplying the correct sympathetic response while another part was concentrating on a different matter altogether.

"It's what kept me."

"I see."

"I did set out the day after you were kidnapped. Well, the day after the day after."

"Ah."

"But what with one thing and another... You wouldn't believe some of the stuff that's happened to me. Not extraordinary, but still... Stuff."

How eloquent he was being. He felt like one of his own pupils, fumbling out excuses for tardiness.

"There was this stately home..."

He thought a character sketch of Beam might bring a smile to her face, but then remembered that it was at Fairfield that he had abandoned his quest to find her. *Temporarily* abandoned, as it turned out, but the decision had been made in the full and firm belief that it was a permanent one. It was at Fairfield, too, that he had fallen for Jessica, and even though in the end nothing had come of the mutual attraction between her and him, nevertheless he had been prepared to start up a relationship with another woman. Were it not for Beam's death, doubtless he would still be at the Hall right now (perhaps living in adulterous bliss with Jessica, perhaps not, depending on whether his desire for her remained strong enough to blind him to her personality flaws). He would never have embarked at all on his final push to London.

It wasn't that he had come close to giving up on Moira. He *had* given up on her.

Suddenly, he could no longer look her in the eye.

He starts gibbering about breaking a leg, my being kidnapped, things that have happened to him, and I'm sure I'm replying to what he says but all I can think about is that I feel like someone who's been caught red-handed. I tell myself not to turn round. It's what I want to do, more than anything. I force myself to focus on Fen and continue to look as if I'm paying attention. Don't turn round. He mentions something about a stately home. A stately home? Then he goes quiet. His gaze flicks around. Don't turn, I tell myself.

Because I've realised at last, in these past few moments, a truth I've been hiding from myself. Not denying, just not acknowledging.

Don't turn.

Because if I do turn and look at Craig, I will know for sure.

And so, I fear, will Fen.

"YOUR HUSBAND," SAID the massive Bulldog, who it seemed sensible to assume was none other than King Cunt.

Moira, not taking her eyes off Fen, nodded.

King Cunt turned to Trevor. "Well done. Thanks. Nice one."

The sarcasm would have amused Trevor, were it not for the steely glare that went with it. All at once, he was not quite as cocky as he had been. His shoulders rounded. If he had been a dog, his tail would have curled under his balls to protect them.

King Cunt continued to glare at him until the point was well and truly made. Then he looked back at Moira.

"You never said you were married."

"You never asked," Moira replied, thinly.

"You don't have a wedding ring."

"Perhaps I wouldn't wear one in a place like this. Perhaps one of your men stole it off me."

"I assumed..."

"But you never asked. Would it have made a difference? Does it?"

King Cunt frowned. "I don't know."

Now she turned to him. She had been waiting, Fen understood, till she was sure she had the moral high ground. That was like her. That was Moira all over.

He thinks it isn't obvious. Hard man. So hard, nothing soft ever shows.

But the eyes. The eyes are always the giveaway.

His are hurt. As though, somehow, I've deceived him.

I never deceived him.

His discomfort, though, tells me all I need to know.

And my indignation tells him all *he* needs to know.

Moments pass in which nothing is said and nothing has to be.

I look at him and see the image of me, reflected twice in his corneas. Or the image of someone who closely resembles me.

Then the hurt melts from his eyes, and in its place there's a sudden, certain fire.

And in that instant, the reflection shifts, flickers, changes, and now *is* me. Definitely, undeniably me. The other person, the lookalike, is gone.

Behind me, I hear a click in Fen's throat, a stifled gasp.

Then, from far off, comes a shout.

A DOZEN DISPARATE thoughts crashed into Fen's brain, all jostling for attention, like a mob of irate shareholders storming the bankruptcy hearings, demanding to know why their investments are now worthless, why the bubble has burst. He was unable to give one precedence over another. All was tumult. All was incoherence.

Moira...

King Cunt...

He had a vague conception of the enormity of the joke that fate had played on him. He could perceive the folly of his journey, how monstrously misbegotten an undertaking it had been, perhaps from the very outset.

But to frame these impressions into words? To give voice to his outrage, his sense of betrayal, his mortification?

Beyond him. His throat was stopped. Nothing would emerge.

He did not hear the shout that came from the direction of the gate. All he knew was that King Cunt and Trevor were all of a sudden talking to each other in urgent tones. He grasped that it was something to do with the fighting, the "war" he had inadvertently strayed into earlier that morning.

It didn't seem important. Nothing seemed important.

"THE APPROACH ROAD," says Trevor, wide-eyed, disbelieving. "Frantiks on the approach road."

"I heard," says Craig. "Who's on lookout?"

"Me and Larry at the gate. Dave and Carl, I think, at the back."

"That's it?"

"Everyone else went with Neville to Brockley."

"All right. Go get Dave and Carl, then meet me at the gate. Hurry!"

Off Trevor runs. No hesitation, no pause to question who it is who's giving him his orders, not a trace of the insolence he was so full of a moment ago.

"Moira."

"Yes."

"You and Zoë—indoors. Take hubby here with you."

He doesn't wait for an answer, just spins round and sets off toward the gate at a sprint.

I turn to Fen. He looks crushed, dazed, a million miles away. We ought to talk about what's happened, but is there actually anything to talk about? Besides, now is not the time.

I say his name. Twice. Three times.

"Come on, Fen. Best do as we're told."

I reach for his arm. He snatches it back, as though my hand is a snake's head, my fingers fangs. He scans my face, and I get the impression that for the first time in ages he's seeing me, not as he thinks I am, but as I am.

Though it couldn't have come at a worse moment, it is, all the same, a breakthrough. For so long he's been content with the idea of me, denying the unpalatable reality. And it's obvious that that's what he has pursued to London: the idea of me. Me as I used to be. Me as he hoped I could be again. He can't accept that some changes are permanent. For all those months he was holding out, waiting for me to recover, just as we're all waiting for England to recover. Our private country of two, our broken little kingdom, was, he was sure, going to rise again.

He was wrong, and now he knows it, and I'm sorry he had to find out this way. I'm sorry for him. But that's all. That's all I feel for him. Pity.

"Come *on*, Fen."

"Come *on*, Fen."

No point. Indoors? With her? Why?

He didn't want to spend even another minute in her company.

The world whirled around him, as if it, not he, was doing the about-turn. The world began to travel, flowing in reverse on either side of him, hauling him back along the route he had taken from the gate to the house. It was like being on one of those pedestrian conveyor belts in airports, motion without volition. He retraced his steps across the compound, scarcely aware that he himself was supplying the impetus, his legs fulfilling their nature-intended role.

In no time at all, or so it seemed, he was nearing the gate. From the other side of it he could hear the noise-creature that had hunted him after he left the pub. The shouting. The clamouring. The howls and yells.

He wasn't frightened. He was too numbed, too shrivelled inside, to be frightened.

Someone was opening the gate. The big man. Moira's new lover. King Cunt. Trevor's lookout partner, Larry, was with him.

Good, thought Fen. Convenient. The gate being opened. Now all I have to do is walk through.

And that was all he wanted to do. To walk through, walk out of the compound, walk away, leave. There was nothing for him here. And he was well practised at the art of leaving places. Fairfield. Netherholm. The *Jagannatha*. He was a tried-and-tested leaver. Master of the timely departure.

"Fen! Don't!"

Moira's voice—she had followed him?—but there was his exit a few yards away, a widening and welcoming gap between gate and wall, and the street visible through it.

"Craig! Stop him!"

King Cunt, also on the point of leaving the compound, paused. Scowled at Fen, as you would at any hopeless nuisance. Seemed all set on ignoring Moira's plea and letting him pass. Changed his mind at the last moment.

"Fucking hell," King Cunt sighed, and swung his fist.

Thereafter all Fen could see was sky. The cloud cover, riven by low-altitude winds, was beginning to break up. Sunshine was piercing through. It was one of the most awe-inspiring sights he had ever beheld. The slow, soft tearing apart, the glowing-edged holes created, the white fibrous wracks that bridged the fissures, the glimpses of stratospheric blue—a mighty work. He knew that he was in pain. That was how he had come to be lying on the ground, gazing up. His skull rang dully. A bruise was tightening the side of his jaw, just below the ear. There was all sorts of commotion nearby, he knew that too. But above it all, literally above it all, the clouds were parting and it was his privilege to be in a position to watch the whole sublime process unfold, and so he did watch, transfixed, transported, as the nebulous awning over London gradually and inexorably disintegrated, exposing the city once more to the gaze of God.

At first it's hard to make out what's going on. Everything's maul and mêlée out there. Swift, darting attacks, a lot of shirt-grabbing and savage punching, taunts, battle cries, yelps of pain, the flail of weapons, men running. It appears it's not just Frantiks on the approach road, it's Bulldogs too. And then the penny drops: the Bulldogs are losing. The Frantiks have driven them back. It's a rout.

I can't believe it. I don't want to believe it. But the couple of dozen Bulldogs I can see are quite plainly in retreat. They're still fighting, but the Frantiks outnumber them and the battle is moving inexorably in the direction of the gate. The Bulldogs keep giving ground, perhaps because they're aware that they're close to the compound. Inside its walls there will, they hope, be refuge and respite. The Frantiks press home the advantage.

I see Mushroom. He flings himself at a Frantik twice his size. With a sweep of his arm the Frantik repels him. Mushroom scrambles to his feet. The Frantik takes him by the collar, thumps him twice, then tosses him aside like a sack of rubbish. Mushroom picks himself up and, undeterred, staggers once again towards the man.

I see Gary, the Bulldog that Zoë bit. I recognise him only by the wad of dressing on his cheek. One of his eyes is swollen to the size and colour of a plum. His nose is bent out of true and gushing blood. He's limping along, being harried by a pair of Frantiks. He lashes out at them, but for every one of his blows that usefully connects, several of theirs strike home.

I see Neville, bloodied, bug-eyed, yelling. He's ordering the Bulldogs to stand firm, not give way, keep at them. But even as he yells this, he's getting nearer the gate himself. Repeatedly he takes one step towards the advancing Frantiks then two towards the compound.

On they come, the implacable Frantiks, the battered, bedraggled Bulldogs.

Craig, at the gate, hasn't moved. It's almost as if the scene before him is too much for him to take in. Larry likewise.

Then Trevor comes charging past me, with another two Bulldogs—

Dave and Carl, it must be—in tow. The three of them pull up alongside Craig, and Craig gives them the once-over, then gestures grimly at the fighting.

"We can win this," he says.

The three new arrivals, Larry also, nod. They believe him. It's as simple as that. They hear Craig utter four little words, and such is the conviction in his voice that all their misgivings are dispelled. They stiffen. Their hands bunch into fists. Their jaws jut. Craig has told them they can win. Any doubts they may have had about that fact, and about him, are washed clean away. They don't even think to question him.

As if I didn't know already, now it's well and truly confirmed.

King Cunt is back.

Craig launches himself out from the gateway, the other four following close behind. Up the road they go, into the midst of the conflict, to collide head-on with the oncoming Frantiks. I go over to where Fen is lying and crouch down beside him. Sprawled on his back, concussed, he gazes up at the sky. His face is strangely, unblinkingly serene. Knocking him cold is not exactly what I had in mind when I told Craig to stop him, but then under the circumstances it's the only thing Craig could have done, and probably the best thing. I reach down and stroke his hair, for the comfort of human contact, the reassurance, as I watch the battle continue to unfurl.

For a while it seems as though Craig's involvement isn't going to make any difference. The Bulldogs are still outnumbered, still on the defensive. They're in worse shape, too, than the Frantiks, many more of them sporting injuries (although it does cross my mind that blood and bruises don't show up as obviously on dark skin). Skirmishes are taking place close to the gate now, just a few feet away from where I am. The Frantiks are almost inside the compound, and I realise that the moment one of them sets foot across the entrance, that will be it. A vital psychological line will have been crossed. It occurs to me to shut the gate, but I reject the idea. And leave the Bulldogs trapped, with nowhere to fall back to? It also occurs to me to take refuge somewhere indoors, just as Craig advised. But I can't leave Fen here, and I can't carry him with me. Nor can I abandon Craig.

No, all I can do is wait here and watch. And hope.

The light brightens and keeps brightening, shafts of sunshine stabbing down onto the battle scene, haloing the heads of the men fighting. I can't make out where Craig is, then I can. I lose him amid the chaos and find him again. Now he's slamming a Frantik's head against a lamp-post. Now he's delivering a volley of punches to an opponent's ribs. Now Frantiks are swarming over him, and they bring him down through sheer weight of numbers, but then, with a great grimacing grunt of fury, he rises up and throws them off one by one.

And around him the Bulldogs are fighting hard. Not just the four who were on lookout and have come fresh to the fray. All of them. Fighting harder. Fighting back. They have seen Craig in the thick of things. They have seen their King knocking down, swatting aside, pulverising the foe. They take heart from his example. Inspired, they turn on the Frantiks with renewed ferocity.

The chant starts with Craig:

> British Bulldogs!
> We're tough, we're brave, we're class...

Almost straight away, every other Bulldog is singing it. It ripples rapidly outwards from Craig, a chorus of defiance and aggression, gaining volume as it spreads:

> British Bulldogs!
> We're tough, we're brave, we're class...

Louder and louder it gets, until the Bulldogs are all but howling the words.

And that's when the Frantiks know. They look around at one another in consternation. That's when they know that everything has changed, the conflict isn't going their way any more. The chant is a force, a weapon. It gives the Bulldogs strength, unity, identity. Roaring the same seven words over and over at the top of their lungs, they are fearless. Imperious. Impervious to pain.

The Frantiks have no adequate response. They struggle on, but slowly, ineluctably, remorselessly, the tide of battle turns. With King Cunt in the vanguard dishing out punishment left, right and centre, the Bulldogs start pressing the Frantiks back, away from the compound. Stragglers are given short shrift: floored, hammered into submission, bludgeoned senseless, or hurled forwards to join their retreating comrades.

I stop stroking Fen's hair and stand up, barely able to contain my elation. The Frantiks are now at the far end of the approach road. They start to scatter and run.

And then the sky falls to earth, with a sound like a million doors slamming shut.

THE GROUND BUCKED. Fen felt himself being tossed up and caught like a palmful of loose change. Once, twice, three times, and by the third time he was aware of detonations and screaming. A white needle streaked overhead, there and gone in a split second, and then came a flash, an instantaneous bloom of smoke and fire, a *boom*, another mini-earthquake. Debris came scattering down like sown seed.

Fen rolled his head to the side. On the approach road, men were dancing. They moved jerkily, without rhythm, dancing to no tune, no waltz or song, just a series of slow, huge thunderclap drumbeats that arrived at irregular intervals, anything from five to fifteen seconds apart. Now another white needle, now another thumping explosion, and the men staggered in response, sidestepped, twisted into balletic postures, and some clutched each other in a masculine *pas de deux* and some sagged to the ground like dying swans. Black man pirouetted with white man. Pale shaven scalp and dark blue bandanna capered side by side. And the drumbeats continued, slugging, repetitive, deafening, until Fen's ears were overloaded and all he could hear was a continuous tintinnabulation that fluctuated briefly with the pressure wave from each successive impact, dull muddy thud after dull muddy thud amid a general rumbling. Beside him Moira was either screaming or laughing, he couldn't tell which, and then a nearby section of the compound wall disintegrated into its component parts—an office chair, a TV set, a microwave oven, a door, a night-storage radiator, a car tyre, a bathtub, a whole slew of domestic jetsam hurled in all directions, discarded once again, the Bulldogs' hard work undone in the blink of an eye. Then a house on the approach road emptied itself out, voiding dust and glass fragments and shreds of curtain through its windows, then slumping in on itself, depleted. A man on the road did likewise, sinking to his knees, blood blurting from his mouth, nose and ears, his belly burst like a pierced egg sac, his guts unspooling.

Fen was beyond horror. Beyond fear, too. It didn't once cross his mind that one of the missiles—that was what the white needles were, missiles—might have the spot where he was lying as its final destination. At some primal, animal level he understood that death was present, death was imminent, but in the dazed upper levels of consciousness his brain was working with a dreamlike detachment, calmly assessing and assimilating. He was able to marvel at the wondrous strangeness of it all. The changes that destruction wrought. The ungainly dancing of the men on the road. The way his hearing had capitulated to the stunning percussive immensity of the missile hits. Above all how utterly alike everyone here had become—himself, Moira, King Cunt, the British Bulldogs, the Bulldogs' opponents, the people of Lewisham, all of them equally blameless in the face of this awesome, relentless assault from above, their sins and foibles as nothing compared with the grotesque overkill of the International Community, which had granted itself the right to bomb where and when it wished and to decide who deserved to live and who to die. Down here, there were no guilty parties. Down here, in the teeth of this minor apocalypse, there were only innocents.

At what point the bombardment ceased, Fen had no idea. It resounded in his eardrums long after the last missile landed. He realised things were not as they had been only when Moira was suddenly no longer next to him. She was off along the approach road, walking delicately, precariously, her arms outstretched for balance, as though the ground underfoot were made of chunks of chopped rubber. Smoke poured around her, thinning, thickening, thinning again. She skirted bodies, heaps of rubble, bodies half buried in heaps of rubble, bodies that looked like heaps of rubble. She was searching for something. Someone. Fen thought he knew who. Finally she found him, or so he gathered. She halted halfway along the road and, silhouetted by the smoke, became a statue of grief, head lowered, shoulders sunk. It was impossible to tell for sure, but he thought that she was weeping. If so, he sympathised. He knew what it was like to lose love. And he knew, too, that in feeling sorry for her he was, in effect, accepting that he did not hate her for falling in love with another man. He couldn't for the life of him understand what she had seen in King Cunt. *His* Moira would have had nothing but contempt for someone who looked like that, dressed that way, thought a name like King Cunt was impressive and clever. But then she was not *his* Moira any more. It was that simple. She was somebody else now, and it didn't matter why. Why should it matter why, when everyone was blameless, when there were no guilty parties, when there were only innocents?

Slowly, totteringly, Fen got to his feet. On the approach road other survivors were doing the same, rising like ghosts from among the damaged and the dead. Their faces were blank with shock, but in their eyes there was the gradually dawning awareness: *I'm alive*. No triumph in the realisation, just a sweet intake of reprieve. The worst had happened. The worst was over. Ignoring the distinction between friend and foe, the uninjured began tending to the injured. Helping hands were extended. Fen looked for Moira again, but the smoke where she was standing was denser than ever. She was hidden from him. He could not see her at all. She was gone. And he was surprised how little difference this made to him. Surprised, and relieved, and—this was the true revelation, this was what really counted—pleased.

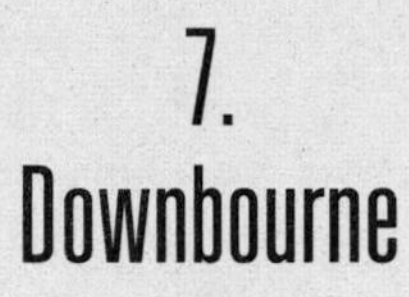

7.
Downbourne

He only narrowly avoided treading on the dead cat.

It lay amid the waste ground's thickets of weed, hind legs protruding onto the pathway. A slender little tabby, flat on its side, eyes half-shut, as though it were merely napping. Not long lifeless, and no marks of violence on its body. Dead of natural causes, then. For what *that* diagnosis was worth. Causes of death, for an animal living wild, were seldom anything other than natural.

Gently Fen bent and touched it, running his fingers across its cold fur, feeling the solid stillness of the flesh beneath. He uttered a few words, an informal requiem, expressing a wish that the cat had had a relatively contented life, then drew his hand away. Immediately, as if on cue, a fly homed in. It alighted at the corner of the cat's mouth and began exploring, prospecting across the pink rim of exposed gum. There would be more flies soon, and in a day or so the cat's body would be writhing with maggots. Life in death. It was how things were supposed be, but Fen pitied the corpse its coming defilement. He stood up, closing his eyes, then turned, opened his eyes, and resumed walking, with the cat preserved in his memory just as it was, deceased but undecayed.

Winter was coming.

Summer was gone, its blaze of heat barely remembered except occasionally, on days like today, when the sun was out and a south wind blew, and the air held an echo of aestival warmth. On days like today, you were reminded that the best of the year was not quite over and done with. But yes, all the same, irrefutably, winter was coming. The ember months had begun, and all over Downbourne faces had taken on that vaguely resigned look, that shadow of weary apprehension. Winter was a miserable season. It was long, it was rainy and grey, it was, perhaps most heinously, boring. You slept a lot in winter. That was about the best that could be said for it. Short days and little to do to fill them: there wasn't much to get out of bed for. Keep the wood fire in the grate burning, keep the kerosene reservoirs in your lanterns topped up... And people died in winter. Old people, and the not-so-old as well.

But today, specifically today, there was no reason to think about any of that. Or rather, there was a reason to avoid thinking about any of that for a while.

Fen could hear the voices coming from the river's edge—an excited hubbub, now and then a shout, a laugh, a cheer, the odd *ooh* and *ahh*. Donald Bailey had brought him the news. "Go and see for yourself, Fen," he had said. "It's not much but it's *something*." And so Fen was going to see for himself, and he was not alone. Word had spread swiftly through town. He emerged from the waste ground to find at least a hundred people gathered on the riverbank near the footbridge, and dozens more converging on the spot. One man was the focal point of the crowd, and he was holding an object aloft for all to examine. It was not a large object. People at the periphery of the crowd had to crane their necks and squint in order to get a glimpse of it. But for all its lack of size, it generated an immense amount of amazement and joy.

Fen held back. Something stayed him, a brief flash of thought.

If only Moira were here.

He didn't often miss her, and when he did it was usually at the most unexpected of moments and for the most unlikely of reasons. He could be performing some quite mundane task—digging in the garden, tidying up at the school, quietly reading a book—and all at once she would stray into his thoughts. Any tangential association could summon her, any chance alignment of situation and memory, or, as now, she could appear in his mind simply because he would have liked her to be where he was, to see what he was seeing.

And then, invariably, he would start to wonder how she was keeping, what she was up to, how her new life was panning out...

I DON'T OFTEN think about him. Days go by and he'll not have entered my mind even once. And then, for no reason at all, I'll find myself saying to myself, *I wonder how he's getting on down there in Downbourne*.

You don't spend a dozen years of your life with someone and then just forget about them in an instant, do you? And you can't help but continue to remember fondly someone who did what Fen did, coming after me like that, an act both so misguided and so heroic that I'm still not sure whether to laugh about it or cry.

There again, he's in the past, he's a part of my life that's gone, and I'm determinedly living in the present now. There's plenty to keep me occupied here in the present. (And, as it happens, there's the future to bear in mind as well now.) So I'm glad that I remember Fen every so often, and glad, also, that I don't remember him *too* often.

The rebuilding work in the compound and on the approach road is almost finished. We've been able to repair more of the damage than I would have thought possible. There's nothing we can do about the houses the bombs totally flattened, of course. We don't have the equipment or the raw materials. But where we can we've mended broken windows, we've retiled caved-in roofs, we've resurrected collapsed ceilings, we've shored up sagging walls, often using bits and pieces salvaged from rubble nearby, so that the destroyed houses have played their part in restoring the undamaged. And the boys, under my foremanship, have worked hard and worked well. A great number of them used to be in the construction trade before the Unlucky Gamble. Putting their old skills to use like this has made them unusually happy. Irrepressibly happy at times, but I don't really mind too much the wolf-whistling and the single entendres. Boys will be boys.

The rebuilding work outside the compound—the job of re-establishing trust and faith among the people of Lewisham—remains very much an ongoing process. It's going to take time. But Craig is out in the borough almost every day, trying his hardest, doing all he can, playing the diplomat, mending fences while I, here in the compound, mend walls.

He tires easily, but that's only to be expected. For a man who was blown out of his shoes by the blast from an International Community missile, he's bearing up remarkably well, all things considered. From time to time he complains about his ribs hurting, but that doesn't get him much sympathy from me. It's his own fault. He refused to stay in bed and allow them time to mend like I told him he should. He was the worst kind of invalid, up and about all the time, finding any excuse not to rest. He wouldn't listen to my advice, so if his bones haven't knitted properly, he has no one but himself to blame.

It was his burns that really worried me, but fortunately they've healed pretty well. The scarring's permanent, but I'm used to it and in certain lights it doesn't even show. A few patches of his skin are a little raised, a little shinier and smoother than the rest—that's all. It's unsightly but it's not gruesome.

Others weren't as lucky as him.

Lauren, for one. Neville's house took a direct hit. They found some of her later. Not much.

Neville himself.

I remember coming across his body. The immediate aftermath of the International Community attack is all a bit hazy for me, but I remember wandering along the approach road, stepping around Bulldogs, around Frantiks, some alive, some not, while smoke billowed up from the burning buildings on either side. I remember I was looking for Craig, although I don't know quite why because I was convinced he was dead, that the missile impacts had obliterated him. But I wandered anyway, through a muffled, ringing world, and everything was in black and white. That's my visual recollection of those minutes, everything for some reason in monochrome, as though, in shock, my eyesight had reverted to a more primitive mode of seeing. And I remember coming across Neville's body and thinking, *oh, there's Neville*, without surprise, as if it was just a matter of course that I should find him there in the roadway, curled in a foetal clench, with a huge gaping hole in his torso. His white skin, his grey innards, his black, black blood. His hopeless, staring eyes.

I want to feel that he got no more than he deserved. I want to feel that nemesis visited him in the form of a piece of shrapnel, that he received due comeuppance for all he did. And sometimes I do think that, although I remember that at the time I felt little about him one way or another. I felt little about any of the dead and the wounded and the unharmed around me. They were just things. Not people any more. Just objects that looked like they might once have been people, some of them moving, some lying still.

Then Craig came tottering towards me through the smoke pall, shoeless, one arm clamped around his chest, charred shreds of clothing and skin hanging off him, a great, shambling, sock-footed mess of a man. I spoke to him but he couldn't hear me properly; I couldn't even hear myself properly. I tried to find out from him how badly he was hurt, using signs and signals. He didn't understand. Then he caught sight of Neville, and for a long while he just stood there, swaying slightly, gazing down at his friend and betrayer. I couldn't make out what was going on in his face. Contempt and pity can often appear the same. Then, stiffly, keeping his upper body as rigid as he could, he knelt, and I thought he might be about to pray for Neville's soul—no reason why he should, no reason why he shouldn't—but instead he reached into Neville's mouth, and took hold of his gold tooth, and began twisting and tugging. The effort caused him agony, I could see, but he persevered. The muscles in his arm bunched and coiled. Still he pulled. He may well have screamed. Abruptly the tooth came free. He held it up between thumb and forefinger, studying it. Then he clasped it in his fist and, with a great deal of wincing and grimacing, got to his feet. And then together, with me supporting much of his weight, we made our way towards the compound entrance.

Days later, I asked him why. What did he want with the tooth?

His reply was simple. "Just taking back what's mine, Moira."

And he continues to take back what's his, reclaiming the borough, resecuring his territory and his right to run it. Peace has been brokered with the Frantik Posse. They've been no less devastated by the missile attack than we Bulldogs have. We're all a little shell-shocked still. It's been a time for taking stock, for reassessment, for rapprochement.

Maybe the International Community has done us a good turn, who knows?

The thing about surviving something like that, having a close encounter with death, being offered a brief glimpse into hell—it gives you a renewed love of life. You want to hold on to it all. You don't want a single minute to slip by unused, uncherished. You live in the moment. You live *for* the moment.

Old clichés, but my God, I understand now how true they are.

So I exist in the present. I don't dwell on the past, not any more. And if I think of the future, it's only because nowadays I have to. I have no choice in the matter.

Because the last three mornings in a row, I've woken up feeling distinctly and familiarly unwell. I haven't thrown up, but only just. Some dry-heaving over the toilet bowl, the nausea slowly abating. I don't think Craig's heard. I don't think he's noticed anything yet.

But I'm going to have to tell him soon.

And it's his child, and so, like him, it'll be strong.

It will be born.

It will survive.

...AND HIS THOUGHTS would turn to the last time he saw her, as the van pulled out of the Bulldog compound, with him and Zoë squashed hip to hip in the passenger seat and that little fellow, Mushroom, driving. The van was the foremost in a convoy of three. Each had a cargo of Downbourne women, who sat wan and tired and silent but with relief evident in their faces nonetheless. There would be much for them to deal with when they got home, many difficult weeks and months ahead. But for now, simple happiness at being free. He remembered the van reaching the compound gate, and Moira being there to watch it on its way. Not a wave from her as the van passed. His eyes met hers, and had she raised her hand he would have reciprocated, but she did not. She stood unmoving and unmoved, and there was nothing in her gaze but solemn acknowledgement. This parting was necessary and hence should not be memorialised or sentimentalised. Here was where she belonged and where Fen did not. The van rolled on, and he watched her reflection recede in the wing-mirror, and he knew—and somehow he had always known—that this was how it would turn out. How it *had to* turn out. All that was taking place now was a confirmation, an affirmation. The mental distance which had manifested between them needed to be reinforced by a geographical distance. It was right and fitting. It was the only way.

It was the only way, and that was why he had subsequently done what he had done at the M25 checkpoint, when the guard cavilled over the bribe Mushroom presented to him.

"Just this?" the guard said, peering at the packets of disposable razors, before gesturing at the three vans. "For all you lot?" He shook his head and sucked on his teeth. "I don't know."

"I forgot," Fen said, reaching across in front of Mushroom. "There's this as well."

The guard took the item Fen was proffering him. He held it up, squinted at it, bit it with the side of his mouth, twirled it around, scrutinised it from every angle, and finally said, "Yeah, all right," and slipped it into a pocket. "On your way then."

"Was that what I think it was?" Mushroom said as they drew away from the checkpoint.

Fen nodded.

"Yours?"

"Moira's."

"Oh," said Mushroom. Then, "Yeah."

It was no great loss. The wedding band had served one purpose, years ago; now it had served another. You might even say that its existence had come full circle (and where better for that to happen than on an orbital motorway?). Fen surrendered it without regret, with just a feeling of satisfying aptness. All was concluded and done. Life could begin afresh.

"Mayor?"

Someone was talking to him. Fen snapped to, realising he had been lost in reverie.

"Hello there, Alan."

Alan Greeley grinned at him, not a little quizzically. Holly-Anne was balanced on his shoulders, and Andrea was standing a short way off, cradling baby Nathan, who, with his stocky body and cuboid head, was a little homunculus replica of his father.

"Away with the fairies, eh?"

Fen gave a sheepish smile. "Afraid so."

"*Real* fairies?" asked Holly-Anne.

"Well, some of them were," Fen said.

She looked behind him, on the off chance that he was telling the truth and some of the little elven folk were still in view, hovering nearby. Seeing none, she frowned, then giggled. "You're silly."

Fen stuck his tongue out. "Exceptionally."

"Have you seen it yet?" Greeley enquired. "Reg's little miracle?"

"Not yet. You?"

"Not yet. There's so many people now, I'm not sure how we're going to get a decent look."

"Well, perhaps I can help you there," Fen said. "Stick close."

He set off towards the crowd, making sure the Greeleys were following. It was nice that he could be confident that the crowd would part for him if requested. He didn't expect it, any more than he expected to be addressed the way Greeley had addressed him, as mayor. If people wished to extend him that courtesy, then fine, but he didn't automatically think it his due. They could call him mayor if they liked or Fen if they liked. They could treat him with deference or as an equal. That was their prerogative. They, after all, had elected him.

But the crowd did part. He was permitted through, and the Greeley family also, to the epicentre of the attention.

A hush fell as he and Reginald Bailey greeted each other. Reginald was looking about as pleased as it was possible for a human being to look. With the kind of pride that comes only from utter vindication, he held out his prize for Fen to inspect.

Fen inspected.

Fen nodded.

Fen pronounced it a marvellous thing indeed.

"Perch," Reginald said, in case Fen had not been able to identify the species (he hadn't).

Fen admired the green stripes, the bright red fins.

"Only a little 'un," Reginald added. "But still..."

But still, it was a fish. Not much bigger than the palm of a man's hand, but it was life from a river that was believed to contain none. Dead now, of course, thanks to Reginald plucking it from its native environment—but where there was one fish, there had to be others. All of a sudden the river was no longer a flow of dilute poison. All of a sudden, in its slow brown turbidity, all manner of possibility lurked.

"Tonight," Fen said, raising his voice so that everyone could hear, "we should have a celebration of some sort, I feel. To mark the occasion."

There was no disagreement from the assembled Downbournians, and consequently that evening, the last truly clement evening of that year, an impromptu festival took place on the riverbank. Tables and chairs were set out. Cooking fires were lit. Food was roasted, alcohol imbibed.

And because it was a special occasion, Fen turned up dressed in what he would come to think of, from there on after, as his ceremonial garb.

It was the first time he had worn it, and he was expecting strange looks as he passed among the revellers, but received none. People simply glanced at him and smiled, as if it came as no surprise to them to see him in this guise. There was the odd double-take, but only because a few individuals didn't immediately recognise who it was they were looking at, all got up in those monochrome clothes (most of which Fen had had to borrow), skin and hair stained with vegetable dye (which, to his surprise, reeked vilely). For a brief, perturbing moment, before the truth dawned, they thought that Michael Hollingbury was among them again.

It wasn't Michael Hollingbury, of course. It was only their mayor, the head of the town council, a man lost and found, who had left without fuss and returned in triumph, bringing back with him wives and mothers and daughters and sisters whom the townsfolk had given up for dead. It was only Fen Morris, decked out in the manner befitting the incarnate spirit of Downbourne, top to toe in a myriad shades of green.

ACKNOWLEDGEMENTS

I'd like to thank Simon Spanton for providing me with research material and for performing yet another bang-up editing job; Jan Bailey for occupational therapy advice; Piers R. Connor at trainweb.org for information relating to railways (I have taken huge liberties with what is technically feasible, for which I beg his indulgence and that of all rail enthusiasts); Eric Brown for his help with the Indian stuff; Guy Stredwick for the M25 traffic jam; Michael Rowley for his continued championing of my work; Ariel for his sterling efforts with the website and for his music recommendations; Pete Crowther for the usual bouncy banter and badinage; Beak for our Filth Sessions; David Mathew and Anne Gay for asking intelligent questions; Andy Cox at *The Third Alternative* for his support and eclecticism; Oisin Murphy-Lawless for being "deadly"; and Nicola Sinclair for being professionally lippy.

During the writing of *Untied Kingdom*, three people in particular helped keep me inspired and (mostly) sane:

Ian Miller—with pearls of Zen wisdom such as "Bend like the young bamboo and hope there's enough spring left for a good fart";

Antony Harwood—unstinting in his encouragement right from the very start;

and of course Lou.

Love on ya!

JAMES LOVEGROVE'S *PANTHEON* SERIES

THE AGE OF RA

UK ISBN: 978 1 844167 46 3 • US ISBN: 978 1 844167 47 0 • £7.99/$7.99

The Ancient Egyptian gods have defeated all the other pantheons and divided the Earth into warring factions. Lt. David Westwynter, a British soldier, stumbles into Freegypt, the only place to have remained independent of the gods, and encounters the followers of a humanist freedom-fighter known as the Lightbringer. As the world heads towards an apocalyptic battle, there is far more to this leader than it seems...

THE AGE OF ZEUS

UK ISBN: 978 1 906735 68 5 • US ISBN: 978 1 906735 69 2 • £7.99/$7.99

The Olympians appeared a decade ago, living incarnations of the Ancient Greek gods, offering order and stability at the cost of placing humanity under the jackboot of divine oppression. Until former London police officer Sam Akehurst receives an invitation to join the Titans, the small band of battlesuited high-tech guerillas squaring off against the Olympians and their mythological monsters in a war they cannot all survive...

THE AGE OF ODIN

UK ISBN: 978 1 907519 40 6 • US ISBN: 978 1 907519 41 3 • £7.99/$7.99

Gideon Coxall was a good soldier but bad at everything else, until a roadside explosive device leaves him with one deaf ear and a British Army half-pension. The Valhalla Project, recruiting useless soldiers like himself, no questions asked, seems like a dream, but the last thing Gid expects is to find himself fighting alongside ancient Viking gods. It seems *Ragnarök* – the fabled final conflict of the Sagas – is looming.

UK ISBN: 978 1 907992 04 9 • US ISBN: 978 1 907992 05 6 • £7.99/$7.99

POLICING THE DAMNED

They live among us, abhorred, marginalised, despised. They are vampires, known politely as the Sunless. The job of policing their community falls to the men and women of SHADE: the Sunless Housing and Disclosure Executive. Captain John Redlaw is London's most feared and respected SHADE officer, a living legend.

But when the vampires start rioting in their ghettos, and angry humans respond with violence of their own, even Redlaw may not be able to keep the peace. Especially when political forces are aligning to introduce a radical answer to the Sunless problem, one that will resolve the situation once and for all...

WWW.SOLARISBOOKS.COM

Follow us on Twitter! www.twitter.com/solarisbooks